THE KEITH LAUMER
MEGAPACK®

THE KEITH LAUMER MEGAPACK®

KEITH LAUMER

WILDSIDE PRESS

Published by Wildside Press LLC.
wildsidepress.com | bcmystery.com

CONTENTS

INTRODUCTION: KEITH LAUMER

John Keith Laumer (1925–1993) was an American science fiction author. Prior to becoming a full-time writer, he was an officer in the United States Air Force (which provided background for his Bolo series) and a diplomat in the United States Foreign Service (which provided ample source material for his Retief series). His older brother March Laumer was also a writer, known for his adult reinterpretations of the Land of Oz (also mentioned in Laumer's *The Other Side of Time*). Frank Laumer, their youngest brother, is a historian and writer.

Keith Laumer was born in Syracuse, New York. He attended Indiana University, 1943-44, and then served in the United States Army in the Second World War in Europe. He later attended Stockholm University, 1948-49, and then received a bachelor's degree in architecture in 1950 from the University of Illinois. He served twice in the US Air Force, 1953-56 and 1960-65, attaining the rank of Captain in the latter tour. In between the two terms in the military, Laumer was a member of the US Foreign Service in South Asia.

In the late 1950s, Laumer returned to Florida and purchased a small two-acre island on a lake in Hernando County near Weeki Wachee. He resided there the rest of his life.

Around this time he turned his attention to writing science fiction. His first work, a short story, was published in April 1959.

Today Laumer is remembered for the Bolo and Retief stories. Stories from the former chronicle the evolution of super tanks that eventually become self-aware through the constant improvement resulting from centuries of intermittent warfare against various alien races. The latter deals with the adventures of a cynical spacefaring diplomat who constantly has to overcome the red-tape-infused failures of people with names like Ambassador Grossblunder. In an interview with Paul Walker of Luna Monthly, Laumer states "I had no shortage of iniquitous memories of the Foreign Service."

In addition to his Bolo and Retief stories, Laumer's more serious adventures included the subjects of time travel and alternate-world adventures such as found in his *The Other Side of Time*, *A Trace of Memory*, and *Dinosaur Beach*.

Four of his shorter works received Hugo or Nebula Award nominations ("In the Queue" was nominated for both) and his novel *A Plague of Demons* (1965) received a nomination for the Nebula Award for Best Novel in 1966.

—Karl Wurf
Rockville, Maryland

THE FROZEN PLANET

Originally published in **Worlds of If Science Fiction,** *September 1961.*

I

"It is rather unusual," Magnan said, "to assign an officer of your rank to courier duty, but this is an unusual mission."

Retief sat relaxed and said nothing. Just before the silence grew awkward, Magnan went on.

"There are four planets in the group," he said. "Two double planets, all rather close to an unimportant star listed as DRI-G 33987. They're called Jorgensen's Worlds, and in themselves are of no importance whatever. However, they lie deep in the sector into which the Soetti have been penetrating.

"Now—" Magnan leaned forward and lowered his voice—"we have learned that the Soetti plan a bold step forward. Since they've met no opposition so far in their infiltration of Terrestrial space, they intend to seize Jorgensen's Worlds by force."

Magnan leaned back, waiting for Retief's reaction. Retief drew carefully on his cigar and looked at Magnan. Magnan frowned.

"This is open aggression, Retief," he said, "in case I haven't made myself clear. Aggression on Terrestrial-occupied territory by an alien species. Obviously, we can't allow it."

Magnan drew a large folder from his desk.

"A show of resistance at this point is necessary. Unfortunately, Jorgensen's Worlds are technologically undeveloped areas. They're farmers or traders. Their industry is limited to a minor role in their economy—enough to support the merchant fleet, no more. The war potential, by conventional standards, is nil."

Magnan tapped the folder before him.

"I have here," he said solemnly, "information which will change that picture completely." He leaned back and blinked at Retief.

* * * *

"All right, Mr. Councillor," Retief said. "I'll play along; what's in the folder?"

Magnan spread his fingers, folded one down.

"First," he said. "The Soetti War Plan—in detail. We were fortunate enough to make contact with a defector from a party of renegade Terrestrials who've been advising the Soetti." He folded another finger. "Next, a battle plan for the Jorgensen's people, worked out by the Theory group." He wrestled a third finger down. "Lastly; an Utter Top Secret schematic for conversion of a standard anti-acceleration field into a potent weapon—a development our systems people have been holding in reserve for just such a situation."

"Is that all?" Retief said. "You've still got two fingers sticking up."

Magnan looked at the fingers and put them away.

"This is no occasion for flippancy, Retief. In the wrong hands, this information could be catastrophic. You'll memorize it before you leave this building."

"I'll carry it, sealed," Retief said. "That way nobody can sweat it out of me."

Magnan started to shake his head.

"Well," he said. "If it's trapped for destruction, I suppose—"

"I've heard of these Jorgensen's Worlds," Retief said. "I remember an agent, a big blond fellow, very quick on the uptake. A wizard with cards and dice. Never played for money, though."

"Umm," Magnan said. "Don't make the error of personalizing this situation, Retief. Overall policy calls for a defense of these backwater worlds. Otherwise the Corps would allow history to follow its natural course, as always."

"When does this attack happen?"

"Less than four weeks."

"That doesn't leave me much time."

"I have your itinerary here. Your accommodations are clear as far as Aldo Cerise. You'll have to rely on your ingenuity to get you the rest of the way."

"That's a pretty rough trip, Mr. Councillor. Suppose I don't make it?"

Magnan looked sour. "Someone at a policy-making level has chosen to put all our eggs in one basket, Retief. I hope their confidence in you is not misplaced."

"This antiac conversion; how long does it take?"

"A skilled electronics crew can do the job in a matter of minutes. The Jorgensens can handle it very nicely; every other man is a mechanic of some sort."

Retief opened the envelope Magnan handed him and looked at the tickets inside.

"Less than four hours to departure time," he said. "I'd better not start any long books."

"You'd better waste no time getting over to Indoctrination," Magnan said.

Retief stood up. "If I hurry, maybe I can catch the cartoon."

"The allusion escapes me," Magnan said coldly. "And one last word. The Soetti are patrolling the trade lanes into Jorgensen's Worlds; don't get yourself interned."

"I'll tell you what," Retief said soberly. "In a pinch, I'll mention your name."

"You'll be traveling with Class X credentials," Magnan snapped. "There must be nothing to connect you with the Corps."

"They'll never guess," Retief said. "I'll pose as a gentleman."

"You'd better be getting started," Magnan said, shuffling papers.

"You're right," Retief said. "If I work at it, I might manage a snootful by takeoff." He went to the door. "No objection to my checking out a needler, is there?"

Magnan looked up. "I suppose not. What do you want with it?"

"Just a feeling I've got."

"Please yourself."

"Some day," Retief said, "I may take you up on that."

II

Retief put down the heavy travel-battered suitcase and leaned on the counter, studying the schedules chalked on the board under the legend "ALDO CERISE—INTERPLANETARY." A thin clerk in a faded sequined blouse and a plastic snakeskin cummerbund groomed his fingernails, watching Retief from the corner of his eye.

Retief glanced at him.

The clerk nipped off a ragged corner with rabbitlike front teeth and spat it on the floor.

"Was there something?" he said.

"Two twenty-eight, due out today for the Jorgensen group," Retief said. "Is it on schedule?"

The clerk sampled the inside of his right cheek, eyed Retief. "Filled up. Try again in a couple of weeks."

"What time does it leave?"

"I don't think—"

"Let's stick to facts," Retief said. "Don't try to think. What time is it due out?"

The clerk smiled pityingly. "It's my lunch hour," he said. "I'll be open in an hour." He held up a thumb nail, frowned at it.

"If I have to come around this counter," Retief said, "I'll feed that thumb to you the hard way."

The clerk looked up and opened his mouth. Then he caught Retief's eye, closed his mouth and swallowed.

"Like it says there," he said, jerking a thumb at the board. "Lifts in an hour. But you won't be on it," he added.

Retief looked at him.

"Some…ah…VIP's required accommodation," he said. He hooked a finger inside the sequined collar. "All tourist reservations were canceled. You'll have to try to get space on the Four-Planet Line ship next—"

"Which gate?" Retief said.

"For…ah…?"

"For the two twenty-eight for Jorgensen's Worlds," Retief said.

"Well," the clerk said. "Gate 19," he added quickly. "But—"

Retief picked up his suitcase and walked away toward the glare sign reading *To Gates 16-30*.

"Another smart alec," the clerk said behind him.

* * * *

Retief followed the signs, threaded his way through crowds, found a covered ramp with the number 228 posted over it. A heavy-shouldered man with a scarred jawline and small eyes was slouching there in a rumpled gray uniform. He put out a hand as Retief started past him.

"Lessee your boarding pass," he muttered.

Retief pulled a paper from an inside pocket, handed it over.

The guard blinked at it.

"Whassat?"

"A gram confirming my space," Retief said. "Your boy on the counter says he's out to lunch."

The guard crumpled the gram, dropped it on the floor and lounged back against the handrail.

"On your way, bub," he said.

Retief put his suitcase carefully on the floor, took a step and drove a right into the guard's midriff. He stepped aside as the man doubled and went to his knees.

"You were wide open, ugly. I couldn't resist. Tell your boss I sneaked past while you were resting your eyes." He picked up his bag, stepped over the man and went up the gangway into the ship.

A cabin boy in stained whites came along the corridor.

"Which way to cabin fifty-seven, son?" Retief asked.

"Up there." The boy jerked his head and hurried on. Retief made his way along the narrow hall, found signs, followed them to cabin fifty-seven.

The door was open. Inside, baggage was piled in the center of the floor. It was expensive looking baggage.

Retief put his bag down. He turned at a sound behind him. A tall, florid man with an expensive coat belted over a massive paunch stood in the open door, looking at Retief. Retief looked back. The florid man clamped his jaws together, turned to speak over his shoulder.

"Somebody in the cabin. Get 'em out." He rolled a cold eye at Retief as he backed out of the room. A short, thick-necked man appeared.

"What are you doing in Mr. Tony's room?" he barked. "Never mind! Clear out of here, fellow! You're keeping Mr. Tony waiting."

"Too bad," Retief said. "Finders keepers."

"You nuts?" The thick-necked man stared at Retief. "I said it's Mr. Tony's room."

"I don't know Mr. Tony. He'll have to bull his way into other quarters."

"We'll see about you, mister." The man turned and went out. Retief sat on the bunk and lit a cigar. There was a sound of voices in the corridor. Two burly baggage-smashers appeared, straining at an oversized trunk. They maneuvered it through the door, lowered it, glanced at Retief and went out. The thick-necked man returned.

"All right, you. Out," he growled. "Or have I got to have you thrown out?"

Retief rose and clamped the cigar between his teeth. He gripped a handle of the brass-bound trunk in each hand, bent his knees and heaved the trunk up to chest level, then raised it overhead. He turned to the door.

"Catch," he said between clenched teeth. The trunk slammed against the far wall of the corridor and burst.

Retief turned to the baggage on the floor, tossed it into the hall. The face of the thick-necked man appeared cautiously around the door jamb.

"Mister, you must be—"

"If you'll excuse me," Retief said, "I want to catch a nap." He flipped the door shut, pulled off his shoes and stretched out on the bed.

* * * *

Five minutes passed before the door rattled and burst open.

Retief looked up. A gaunt leathery-skinned man wearing white ducks, a blue turtleneck sweater and a peaked cap tilted raffishly over one eye stared at Retief.

"Is this the joker?" he grated.

The thick-necked man edged past him, looked at Retief and snorted, "That's him, sure."

"I'm captain of this vessel," the first man said. "You've got two minutes to haul your freight out of here, buster."

"When you can spare the time from your other duties," Retief said, "take a look at Section Three, Paragraph One, of the Uniform Code. That spells out the law on confirmed space on vessels engaged in interplanetary commerce."

"A space lawyer." The captain turned. "Throw him out, boys."

Two big men edged into the cabin, looking at Retief.

"Go on, pitch him out," the captain snapped.

Retief put his cigar in an ashtray, and swung his feet off the bunk.

"Don't try it," he said softly.

One of the two wiped his nose on a sleeve, spat on his right palm, and stepped forward, then hesitated.

"Hey," he said. "This the guy tossed the trunk off the wall?"

"That's him," the thick-necked man called. "Spilled Mr. Tony's possessions right on the deck."

"Deal me out," the bouncer said. "He can stay put as long as he wants to. I signed on to move cargo. Let's go, Moe."

"You'd better be getting back to the bridge, Captain," Retief said. "We're due to lift in twenty minutes."

The thick-necked man and the Captain both shouted at once. The Captain's voice prevailed.

"—twenty minutes…uniform Code…gonna do?"

"Close the door as you leave," Retief said.

The thick-necked man paused at the door. "We'll see you when you come out."

III

Four waiters passed Retief's table without stopping. A fifth leaned against the wall nearby, a menu under his arm.

At a table across the room, the Captain, now wearing a dress uniform and with his thin red hair neatly parted, sat with a table of male passengers. He talked loudly and laughed frequently, casting occasional glances Retief's way.

A panel opened in the wall behind Retief's chair. Bright blue eyes peered out from under a white chef's cap.

"Givin' you the cold shoulder, heh, Mister?"

"Looks like it, old-timer," Retief said. "Maybe I'd better go join the skipper. His party seems to be having all the fun."

"Feller has to be mighty careless who he eats with to set over there."

"I see your point."

"You set right where you're at, Mister. I'll rustle you up a plate."

Five minutes later, Retief cut into a thirty-two ounce Delmonico backed up with mushrooms and garlic butter.

"I'm Chip," the chef said. "I don't like the Cap'n. You can tell him I said so. Don't like his friends, either. Don't like them dern Sweaties, look at a man like he was a worm."

"You've got the right idea on frying a steak, Chip. And you've got the right idea on the Soetti, too," Retief said. He poured red wine into a glass. "Here's to you."

"Dern right," Chip said. "Dunno who ever thought up broiling 'em. Steaks, that is. I got a Baked Alaska coming up in here for dessert. You like brandy in yer coffee?"

"Chip, you're a genius."

"Like to see a feller eat," Chip said. "I gotta go now. If you need anything, holler."

Retief ate slowly. Time always dragged on shipboard. Four days to Jorgensen's Worlds. Then, if Magnan's information was correct, there would be four days to prepare for the Soetti attack. It was a temptation to scan the tapes built into the handle of his suitcase. It would be good to know what Jorgensen's Worlds would be up against.

Retief finished the steak, and the chef passed out the baked Alaska and coffee. Most of the other passengers had left the dining room. Mr. Tony and his retainers still sat at the Captain's table.

As Retief watched, four men arose from the table and sauntered across the room. The first in line, a stony-faced thug with a broken ear, took a cigar from his mouth as he reached the table. He dipped the lighted end in Retief's coffee, looked at it, and dropped it on the tablecloth.

The others came up, Mr. Tony trailing.

"You must want to get to Jorgensen's pretty bad," the thug said in a grating voice. "What's your game, hick?"

Retief looked at the coffee cup, picked it up.

"I don't think I want my coffee," he said. He looked at the thug. "You drink it."

The thug squinted at Retief. "A wise hick," he began.

With a flick of the wrist, Retief tossed the coffee into the thug's face, then stood and slammed a straight right to the chin. The thug went down.

Retief looked at Mr. Tony, still standing open-mouthed.

"You can take your playmates away now, Tony," he said. "And don't bother to come around yourself. You're not funny enough."

Mr. Tony found his voice.

"Take him, Marbles!" he growled.

The thick-necked man slipped a hand inside his tunic and brought out a long-bladed knife. He licked his lips and moved in.

Retief heard the panel open beside him.

"Here you go, Mister," Chip said. Retief darted a glance; a well-honed french knife lay on the sill.

"Thanks, Chip," Retief said. "I won't need it for these punks."

Thick-neck lunged and Retief hit him square in the face, knocking him under the table. The other man stepped back, fumbling a power pistol from his shoulder holster.

"Aim that at me, and I'll kill you," Retief said.

"Go on, burn him!" Mr. Tony shouted. Behind him, the captain appeared, white-faced.

"Put that away, you!" he yelled. "What kind of—"

"Shut up," Mr. Tony said. "Put it away, Hoany. We'll fix this bum later."

"Not on this vessel, you won't," the captain said shakily. "I got my charter to consider."

"Ram your charter," Hoany said harshly. "You won't be needing it long."

"Button your floppy mouth, damn you!" Mr. Tony snapped. He looked at the man on the floor. "Get Marbles out of here. I ought to dump the slob."

He turned and walked away. The captain signaled and two waiters came up. Retief watched as they carted the casualty from the dining room.

The panel opened.

"I usta be about your size, when I was your age," Chip said. "You handled them pansies right. I wouldn't give 'em the time o' day."

"How about a fresh cup of coffee, Chip?" Retief said.

"Sure, Mister. Anything else?"

"I'll think of something," Retief said. "This is shaping up into one of those long days."

* * * *

"They don't like me bringing yer meals to you in yer cabin," Chip said. "But the cap'n knows I'm the best cook in the Merchant Service. They won't mess with me."

"What has Mr. Tony got on the captain, Chip?" Retief asked.

"They're in some kind o' crooked business together. You want some more smoked turkey?"

"Sure. What have they got against my going to Jorgensen's Worlds?"

"Dunno. Hasn't been no tourists got in there fer six or eight months. I sure like a feller that can put it away. I was a big eater when I was yer age."

"I'll bet you can still handle it, Old Timer. What are Jorgensen's Worlds like?"

"One of 'em.s cold as hell and three of 'em.s colder. Most o' the Jorgies live on Svea; that's the least froze up. Man don't enjoy eatin' his own cookin' like he does somebody else's."

"That's where I'm lucky, Chip. What kind of cargo's the captain got aboard for Jorgensen's?"

"Derned if I know. In and out o' there like a grasshopper, ever few weeks. Don't never pick up no cargo. No tourists any more, like I says. Don't know what we even run in there for."

"Where are the passengers we have aboard headed?"

"To Alabaster. That's nine days' run in-sector from Jorgensen's. You ain't got another one of them cigars, have you?"

"Have one, Chip. I guess I was lucky to get space on this ship."

"Plenty o' space, Mister. We got a dozen empty cabins." Chip puffed the cigar alight, then cleared away the dishes, poured out coffee and brandy.

"Them Sweaties is what I don't like," he said.

Retief looked at him questioningly.

"You never seen a Sweaty? Ugly lookin' devils. Skinny legs, like a lobster; big chest, shaped like the top of a turnip; rubbery lookin' head. You can see the pulse beatin' when they get riled."

"I've never had the pleasure," Retief said.

"You prob'ly have it perty soon. Them devils board us nigh ever trip out. Act like they was the Customs Patrol or somethin'."

There was a distant clang, and a faint tremor ran through the floor.

"I ain't superstitious ner nothin'," Chip said. "But I'll be triple-damned if that ain't them boarding us now."

Ten minutes passed before bootsteps sounded outside the door, accompanied by a clicking patter. The doorknob rattled, then a heavy knock shook the door.

"They got to look you over," Chip whispered. "Nosy damn Sweaties."

"Unlock it, Chip." The chef opened the door.

"Come in, damn you," he said.

A tall and grotesque creature minced into the room, tiny hoof-like feet tapping on the floor. A flaring metal helmet shaded the deep-set compound eyes, and a loose mantle flapped around the knobbed knees. Behind the alien, the captain hovered nervously.

"Yo' papiss," the alien rasped.

"Who's your friend, Captain?" Retief said.

"Never mind; just do like he tells you."

"Yo' papiss," the alien said again.

"Okay," Retief said. "I've seen it. You can take it away now."

"Don't horse around," the captain said. "This fellow can get mean."

The alien brought two tiny arms out from the concealment of the mantle, clicked toothed pincers under Retief's nose.

"Quick, soft one."

"Captain, tell your friend to keep its distance. It looks brittle, and I'm tempted to test it."

"Don't start anything with Skaw; he can clip through steel with those snappers."

"Last chance," Retief said. Skaw stood poised, open pincers an inch from Retief's eyes.

"Show him your papers, you damned fool," the captain said hoarsely. "I got no control over Skaw."

* * * *

The alien clicked both pincers with a sharp report, and in the same instant Retief half-turned to the left, leaned away from the alien and drove his right foot against the slender leg above the bulbous knee-joint. Skaw screeched and floundered, greenish fluid spattering from the burst joint.

"I told you he was brittle," Retief said. "Next time you invite pirates aboard, don't bother to call."

"Jesus, what did you do! They'll kill us!" the captain gasped, staring at the figure flopping on the floor.

"Cart poor old Skaw back to his boat," Retief said. "Tell him to pass the word. No more illegal entry and search of Terrestrial vessels in Terrestrial space."

"Hey," Chip said. "He's quit kicking."

The captain bent over Skaw, gingerly rolled him over. He leaned close and sniffed.

"He's dead." The captain stared at Retief. "We're all dead men," he said. "These Soetti got no mercy."

"They won't need it. Tell 'em to sheer off; their fun is over."

"They got no more emotions than a blue crab—"

"You bluff easily, Captain. Show a few guns as you hand the body back. We know their secret now."

"What secret? I—"

"Don't be no dumber than you got to, Cap'n," Chip said. "Sweaties die easy; that's the secret."

"Maybe you got a point," the captain said, looking at Retief. "All they got's a three-man scout. It could work."

He went out, came back with two crewmen. They hauled the dead alien gingerly into the hall.

"Maybe I can run a bluff on the Soetti," the captain said, looking back from the door. "But I'll be back to see you later."

"You don't scare us, Cap'n," Chip said. "Him and Mr. Tony and all his goons. You hit 'em where they live, that time. They're pals o' these Sweaties. Runnin' some kind o' crooked racket."

"You'd better take the captain's advice, Chip. There's no point in your getting involved in my problems."

"They'd of killed you before now, Mister, if they had any guts. That's where we got it over these monkeys. They got no guts."

"They act scared, Chip. Scared men are killers."

"They don't scare me none." Chip picked up the tray. "I'll scout around a little and see what's goin' on. If the Sweaties figure to do anything about that Skaw feller they'll have to move fast; they won't try nothin' close to port."

"Don't worry, Chip. I have reason to be pretty sure they won't do anything to attract a lot of attention in this sector just now."

Chip looked at Retief. "You ain't no tourist, Mister. I know that much. You didn't come out here for fun, did you?"

"That," Retief said, "would be a hard one to answer."

IV

Retief awoke at a tap on his door.

"It's me, Mister. Chip."

"Come on in."

The chef entered the room, locking the door.

"You shoulda had that door locked." He stood by the door, listening, then turned to Retief.

"You want to get to Jorgensen's perty bad, don't you, Mister?"

"That's right, Chip."

"Mr. Tony give the captain a real hard time about old Skaw. The Sweaties didn't say nothin'. Didn't even act surprised, just took the remains and pushed off. But Mr. Tony and that other crook they call Marbles, they was fit to be tied. Took the cap'n in his cabin and talked loud at him fer half a hour. Then the cap'n come out and give some orders to the Mate."

Retief sat up and reached for a cigar.

"Mr. Tony and Skaw were pals, eh?"

"He hated Skaw's guts. But with him it was business. Mister, you got a gun?"

"A 2mm needler. Why?"

"The orders cap'n give was to change course fer Alabaster. We're bypassin' Jorgensen's Worlds. We'll feel the course change any minute."

Retief lit the cigar, reached under the mattress and took out a short-barreled pistol. He dropped it in his pocket, looked at Chip.

"Maybe it was a good thought, at that. Which way to the Captain's cabin?"

* * * *

"This is it," Chip said softly. "You want me to keep an eye on who comes down the passage?"

Retief nodded, opened the door and stepped into the cabin. The captain looked up from his desk, then jumped up.

"What do you think you're doing, busting in here?"

"I hear you're planning a course change, Captain."

"You've got damn big ears."

"I think we'd better call in at Jorgensen's."

"You do, huh?" the captain sat down. "I'm in command of this vessel," he said. "I'm changing course for Alabaster."

"I wouldn't find it convenient to go to Alabaster," Retief said. "So just hold your course for Jorgensen's."

"Not bloody likely."

"Your use of the word 'bloody' is interesting, Captain. Don't try to change course."

The captain reached for the mike on his desk, pressed the key.

"Power Section, this is the captain," he said. Retief reached across the desk, gripped the captain's wrist.

"Tell the mate to hold his present course," he said softly.

"Let go my hand, buster," the captain snarled. Eyes on Retief's, he eased a drawer open with his left hand, reached in. Retief kneed the drawer. The captain yelped and dropped the mike.

"You busted it, you—"

"And one to go," Retief said. "Tell him."

"I'm an officer of the Merchant Service!"

"You're a cheapjack who's sold his bridge to a pack of back-alley hoods."

"You can't put it over, hick."

"Tell him."

The captain groaned and picked up the mike. "Captain to Power Section," he said. "Hold your present course until you hear from me." He dropped the mike and looked up at Retief.

"It's eighteen hours yet before we pick up Jorgensen Control. You going to sit here and bend my arm the whole time?"

Retief released the captain's wrist and turned to the door.

"Chip, I'm locking the door. You circulate around, let me know what's going on. Bring me a pot of coffee every so often. I'm sitting up with a sick friend."

"Right, Mister. Keep an eye on that jasper; he's slippery."

"What are you going to do?" the captain demanded.

Retief settled himself in a chair.

"Instead of strangling you, as you deserve," he said, "I'm going to stay here and help you hold your course for Jorgensen's Worlds."

The captain looked at Retief. He laughed, a short bark.

"Then I'll just stretch out and have a little nap, farmer. If you feel like dozing off sometime during the next eighteen hours, don't mind me."

Retief took out the needler and put it on the desk before him.

"If anything happens that I don't like," he said, "I'll wake you up. With this."

* * * *

"Why don't you let me spell you, Mister?" Chip said. "Four hours to go yet. You're gonna hafta be on yer toes to handle the landing."

"I'll be all right, Chip. You get some sleep."

"Nope. Many's the time I stood four, five watches runnin', back when I was yer age. I'll make another round."

Retief stood up, stretched his legs, paced the floor, stared at the repeater instruments on the wall. Things had gone quietly so far, but the landing would be another matter. The captain's absence from the bridge during the highly complex maneuvering would be difficult to explain....

The desk speaker crackled.

"Captain, Officer of the Watch here. Ain't it about time you was getting up here with the orbit figures?"

Retief nudged the captain. He awoke with a start, sat up.

"Whazzat?" He looked wild-eyed at Retief.

"Watch officer wants orbit figures," Retief said, nodding toward the speaker.

The captain rubbed his eyes, shook his head, picked up the mike. Retief released the safety on the needler with an audible click.

"Watch Officer, I'll...ah...get some figures for you right away. I'm... ah...busy right now."

"What the hell you talking about, busy?" the speaker blared. "You ain't got them figures ready, you'll have a hell of a hot time getting 'em up in the next three minutes. You forgot your approach pattern or something?"

"I guess I overlooked it," the Captain said, looking sideways at Retief. "I've been busy."

"One for your side," Retief said. He reached for the captain.

"I'll make a deal," the captain squalled. "Your life for—"

Retief took aim and slammed a hard right to the captain's jaw. He slumped to the floor.

Retief glanced around the room, yanked wires loose from a motile lamp, trussed the man's hands and feet, stuffed his mouth with paper and taped it.

Chip tapped at the door. Retief opened it and the chef stepped inside, looking at the man on the floor.

"The jasper tried somethin', huh? Figured he would. What we goin' to do now?"

"The captain forgot to set up an approach, Chip. He outfoxed me."

"If we overrun our approach pattern," Chip said, "we can't make orbit at Jorgensen's on automatic. And a manual approach—"

"That's out. But there's another possibility."

Chip blinked. "Only one thing you could mean, Mister. But cuttin' out in a lifeboat in deep space is no picnic."

"They're on the port side, aft, right?"

Chip nodded. "Hot damn," he said. "Who's got the 'tater salad?"

"We'd better tuck the skipper away out of sight."

"In the locker."

The two men carried the limp body to a deep storage chest, dumped it in, closed the lid.

"He won't suffercate. Lid's a lousy fit."

Retief opened the door went into the corridor, Chip behind him.

"Shouldn't oughta be nobody around now," the chef said. "Everybody's mannin' approach stations."

* * * *

At the D deck companionway, Retief stopped suddenly.

"Listen."

Chip cocked his head. "I don't hear nothin'," he whispered.

"Sounds like a sentry posted on the lifeboat deck," Retief said softly.

"Let's take him, Mister."

"I'll go down. Stand by, Chip."

Retief started down the narrow steps, half stair, half ladder. Halfway, he paused to listen. There was a sound of slow footsteps, then silence. Retief palmed the needler, went down the last steps quickly, emerged in the dim light of a low ceilinged room. The stern of a five-man lifeboat bulked before him.

"Freeze, you!" a cold voice snapped.

Retief dropped, rolled behind the shelter of the lifeboat as the whine of a power pistol echoed off metal walls. A lunge, and he was under the boat, on his feet. He jumped, caught the quick-access handle, hauled it down. The outer port cycled open.

Feet scrambled at the bow of the boat. Retief whirled and fired. The guard rounded into sight and fell headlong. Above, an alarm bell jangled. Retief stepped on a stanchion, hauled himself into the open port. A yell rang, then the clatter of feet on the stair.

"Don't shoot, Mister!" Chip shouted.

"All clear, Chip," Retief called.

"Hang on. I'm comin' with ya!"

Retief reached down, lifted the chef bodily through the port, slammed the lever home. The outer door whooshed, clanged shut.

"Take number two, tie in! I'll blast her off," Chip said. "Been through a hundred 'bandon ship drills...."

Retief watched as the chef flipped levers, pressed a fat red button. The deck trembled under the lifeboat.

"Blew the bay doors," Chip said, smiling happily. "That'll cool them jaspers down." He punched a green button.

"Look out, Jorgensen's!" With an ear-splitting blast, the stern rockets fired, a sustained agony of pressure....

Abruptly, there was silence. Weightlessness. Contracting metal pinged loudly. Chip's breathing rasped in the stillness.

"Pulled nine G's there for ten seconds," he gasped. "I gave her full emergency kick-off."

"Any armament aboard our late host?"

"A popgun. Time they get their wind, we'll be clear. Now all we got to do is set tight till we pick up a R and D from Svea Tower. Maybe four, five hours."

"Chip, you're a wonder," Retief said. "This looks like a good time to catch that nap."

"Me too," Chip said. "Mighty peaceful here, ain't it?"

There was a moment's silence.

"Durn!" Chip said softly.

Retief opened one eye. "Sorry you came, Chip?"

"Left my best carvin' knife jammed up 'tween Marbles' ribs," the chef said. "Comes o' doin' things in a hurry."

V

The blonde girl brushed her hair from her eyes and smiled at Retief.

"I'm the only one on duty," she said. "I'm Anne-Marie."

"It's important that I talk to someone in your government, Miss," Retief said.

The girl looked at Retief. "The men you want to see are Tove and Bo Bergman. They will be at the lodge by night-fall."

"Then it looks like we go to the lodge," Retief said. "Lead on, Anne-Marie."

"What about the boat?" Chip asked.

"I'll send someone to see to it tomorrow," the girl said.

"You're some gal," Chip said admiringly. "Dern near six feet, ain't ye? And built, too, what I mean."

They stepped out of the door into a whipping wind.

"Let's go across to the equipment shed and get parkas for you," Anne-Marie said. "It will be cold on the slopes."

"Yeah," Chip said, shivering. "I've heard you folks don't believe in ridin' ever time you want to go a few miles uphill in a blizzard."

"It will make us hungry," Anne-Marie said. "Then Chip will cook a wonderful meal for us all."

Chip blinked. "Been cookin' too long," he muttered. "Didn't know it showed on me that way."

Behind the sheds across the wind-scoured ramp abrupt peaks rose, snow-blanketed. A faint trail led across white slopes, disappearing into low clouds.

"The lodge is above the cloud layer," Anne-Marie said. "Up there the sky is always clear."

It was three hours later, and the sun was burning the peaks red, when Anne-Marie stopped, pulled off her woolen cap and waved at the vista below.

"There you see it," she said. "Our valley."

"It's a mighty perty sight," Chip gasped. "Anything this tough to get a look at ought to be."

Anne-Marie pointed. "There," she said. "The little red house by itself. Do you see it, Retief? It is my father's home-acre."

Retief looked across the valley. Gaily painted houses nestled together, a puddle of color in the bowl of the valley.

"I think you've led a good life there," he said.

Anne-Marie smiled brilliantly. "And this day, too, is good."

Relief smiled back. "Yes," he said. "This day is good."

"It'll be a durn sight better when I got my feet up to that big fire you was talking about, Annie," Chip said.

They climbed on, crossed a shoulder of broken rock, reached the final slope. Above, the lodge sprawled, a long low structure of heavy logs, outlined against the deep-blue twilight sky. Smoke billowed from stone chimneys at either end, and yellow light gleamed from the narrow windows, reflected on the snow. Men and women stood in groups of three or four, skis over their shoulders. Their voices and laughter rang in the icy air.

Anne-Marie whistled shrilly. Someone waved.

"Come," she said. "Meet all my friends."

A man separated himself from the group, walked down the slope to meet them.

"Anne-Marie," he called. "Welcome. It was a long day without you." He came up to them, hugged Anne-Marie, smiled at Retief.

"Welcome," he said. "Come inside and be warm."

They crossed the trampled snow to the lodge and pushed through a heavy door into a vast low-beamed hall, crowded with people, talking, singing, some sitting at long plank tables, others ringed around an eight-foot fireplace at the far side of the room. Anne-Marie led the way to a bench near the fire. She made introductions and found a stool to prop Chip's feet near the blaze.

Chip looked around.

"I never seen so many perty gals before," he said delightedly.

"Poor Chip," one girl said. "His feet are cold." She knelt to pull off his boots. "Let me rub them," she said.

A brunette with blue eyes raked a chestnut from the fire, cracked it and offered it to Retief. A tall man with arms like oak roots passed heavy beer tankards to the two guests.

"Tell us about the places you've seen," someone called. Chip emerged from a long pull at the mug, heaving a sigh.

"Well," he said. "I tell you I been in some places...."

Music started up, rising above the clamor.

"Come, Retief," Anne-Marie said. "Dance with me."

Retief looked at her. "My thought exactly," he said.

* * * *

Chip put down his mug and sighed. "Derned if I ever felt right at home so quick before," he said. "Just seems like these folks know all about me." He scratched behind his right ear. "Annie must o' called 'em up and told 'em our names an' all." He lowered his voice.

"They's some kind o' trouble in the air, though. Some o' the remarks they passed sounds like they're lookin' to have some trouble with the Sweaties. Don't seem to worry 'em none, though."

"Chip," Retief said, "how much do these people know about the Soetti?"

"Dunno," Chip said. "We useta touch down here, regler. But I always jist set in my galley and worked on ship models or somethin'. I hear the Sweaties been nosin' around here some, though."

Two girls came up to Chip. "Hey, I gotta go now, Mister," he said. "These gals got a idea I oughta take a hand in the kitchen."

"Smart girls," Retief said. He turned as Anne-Marie came up.

"Bo Bergman and Tove are not back yet," she said. "They stayed to ski after moonrise."

"That moon is something," Retief said. "Almost like day-light."

"They will come soon, now. Shall we go out to see the moonlight on the snow?"

Outside, long black shadows fell like ink on silver. The top of the cloud layer below glared white under the immense moon.

"Our sister world, Gota," Anne-Marie said. "Nearly as big as Svea. I would like to visit it someday, although they say it's all stone and ice."

"Anne-Marie," Retief said, "how many people live on Jorgensen's Worlds?"

"About fifteen million, most of us here on Svea. There are mining camps and ice-fisheries on Gota. No one lives on Vasa and Skone, but there are always a few hunters there."

"Have you ever fought a war?"

Anne-Marie turned to look at Retief.

"You are afraid for us, Retief," she said. "The Soetti will attack our worlds, and we will fight them. We have fought before. These planets were not friendly ones."

"I thought the Soetti attack would be a surprise to you," Retief said. "Have you made any preparation for it?"

"We have ten thousand merchant ships. When the enemy comes, we will meet them."

Retief frowned. "Are there any guns on this planet? Any missiles?"

Anne-Marie shook her head. "Bo Bergman and Tove have a plan of deployment—"

"Deployment, hell! Against a modern assault force you need modern armament."

"Look!" Anne-Marie touched Retief's arm. "They're coming now."

Two tall grizzled men came up the slope, skis over their shoulders. Anne-Marie went forward to meet them, Retief at her side.

The two came up, embraced the girl, shook hands with Retief, put down their skis.

"Welcome to Svea," Tove said. "Let's find a warm corner where we can talk."

* * * *

Retief shook his head, smiling, as a tall girl with coppery hair offered a vast slab of venison.

"I've caught up," he said, "for every hungry day I ever lived."

Bo Bergman poured Retief's beer mug full.

"Our captains are the best in space," he said. "Our population is concentrated in half a hundred small cities all across the planet. We know where the Soetti must strike us. We will ram their major vessels with unmanned ships. On the ground, we will hunt them down with small-arms."

"An assembly line turning out penetration missiles would have been more to the point."

"Yes," Bo Bergman said. "If we had known."

"How long have you known the Soetti were planning to hit you?"

Tove raised his eyebrows.

"Since this afternoon," he said.

"How did you find out about it? That information is supposed in some quarters to be a well-guarded secret."

"Secret?" Tove said.

Chip pulled at Retief's arm.

"Mister," he said in Retief's ear. "Come here a minute."

Retief looked at Anne-Marie, across at Tove and Bo Bergman. He rubbed the side of his face with his hand.

"Excuse me," he said. He followed Chip to one side of the room.

"Listen!" Chip said. "Maybe I'm goin' bats, but I'll swear there's somethin' funny here. I'm back there mixin' a sauce knowed only to me and the devil and I be dog if them gals don't pass me ever dang spice I need, without me sayin' a word. Come to put my souffle in the oven—she's already set, right on the button at 350. An' just now I'm settin' lookin' at one of 'em bendin' over a tub o' apples—snazzy little brunette name of Leila—derned if she don't turn around and say—" Chip gulped. "Never mind. Point is...." His voice nearly faltered. "It's almost like these folks was readin' my mind!"

Retief patted Chip on the shoulder.

"Don't worry about your sanity, Old Timer," he said. "That's exactly what they're doing."

VI

"We've never tried to make a secret of it," Tove said. "But we haven't advertised it, either."

"It really isn't much," Bo Bergman said. "Not a mutant ability, our scholars say. Rather, it's a skill we've stumbled on, a closer empathy. We are few, and far from the old home world. We've had to learn to break down the walls we had built around our minds."

"Can you read the Soetti?" Retief asked.

Tove shook his head. "They're very different from us. It's painful to touch their minds. We can only sense the sub-vocalized thoughts of a human mind."

"We've seen very few of the Soetti," Bo Bergman said. "Their ships have landed and taken on stores. They say little to us, but we've felt their contempt. They envy us our worlds. They come from a cold land."

"Anne-Marie says you have a plan of defense," Retief said. "A sort of suicide squadron idea, followed by guerrilla warfare."

"It's the best we can devise, Retief. If there aren't too many of them, it might work."

Retief shook his head. "It might delay matters—but not much."

"Perhaps. But our remote control equipment is excellent. And we have plenty of ships, albeit unarmed. And our people know how to live on the slopes—and how to shoot."

"There are too many of them, Tove," Retief said. "They breed like flies and, according to some sources, they mature in a matter of months.

They've been feeling their way into the sector for years now. Set up out-posts on a thousand or so minor planets—cold ones, the kind they like. They want your worlds because they need living space."

"At least, your warning makes it possible for us to muster some show of force, Retief," Bo Bergman said. "That is better than death by ambush."

"Retief must not be trapped here," Anne-Marie said. "His small boat is useless now. He must have a ship."

"Of course," Tove said. "And—"

"My mission here—" Retief said.

"Retief," a voice called. "A message for you. The operator has phoned up a gram."

Retief unfolded the slip of paper. It was short, in verbal code, and signed by Magnan.

"You are recalled herewith," he read. "Assignment canceled. Agreement concluded with Soetti relinquishing all claims so-called Jorgensen system. Utmost importance that under no repeat no circumstances classified intelligence regarding Soetti be divulged to locals. Advise you depart instanter. Soetti occupation imminent."

Retief looked thoughtfully at the scrap of paper, then crumpled it and dropped it on the floor. He turned to Bo Bergman, took a tiny reel of tape from his pocket.

"This contains information," he said. "The Soetti attack plan, a defensive plan instructions for the conversion of a standard anti-acceleration unit into a potent weapon. If you have a screen handy, we'd better get started. We have about seventy-two hours."

* * * *

In the Briefing Room at Svea Tower, Tove snapped off the projector.

"Our plan would have been worthless against that," he said. "We assumed they'd make their strike from a standard in-line formation. This scheme of hitting all our settlements simultaneously, in a random order from all points—we'd have been helpless."

"It's perfect for this defensive plan," Bo Bergman said. "Assuming this antiac trick works."

"It works," Retief said. "I hope you've got plenty of heavy power lead available."

"We export copper," Tove said.

"We'll assign about two hundred vessels to each settlement. Linked up, they should throw up quite a field."

"It ought to be effective up to about fifteen miles, I'd estimate," Tove said. "If it works as it's supposed to."

A red light flashed on the communications panel. Tove went to it, flipped a key.

"Tower, Tove here," he said.

"I've got a ship on the scope, Tove," a voice said. "There's nothing scheduled. ACI 228 by-passed at 1600...."

"Just one?"

"A lone ship, coming in on a bearing of 291/456/653. On manual, I'd say."

"How does this track key in with the idea of ACI 228 making a manual correction for a missed automatic approach?" Retief asked.

Tove talked to the tower, got a reply.

"That's it," he said.

"How long before he touches down?"

Tove glanced at a lighted chart. "Perhaps eight minutes."

"Any guns here?"

Tove shook his head.

"If that's old 228, she ain't got but the one 50mm rifle," Chip said. "She cain't figure on jumpin' the whole planet."

"Hard to say what she figures on," Retief said. "Mr. Tony will be in a mood for drastic measures."

"I wonder what kind o' deal the skunks got with the Sweaties," Chip said. "Prob'ly he gits to scavenge, after the Sweaties kill off the Jorgensens."

"He's upset about our leaving him without saying good-bye, Chip," Retief said. "And you left the door hanging open, too."

Chip cackled. "Old Mr. Tony don't look so good to the Sweaties now, hey, Mister?"

Retief turned to Bo Bergman.

"Chip's right," he said. "A Soetti died on the ship, and a tourist got through the cordon. Tony's out to redeem himself."

"He's on final now," the tower operator said. "Still no contact."

"We'll know soon enough what he has in mind," Tove said.

"Let's take a look."

Outside, the four men watched the point of fire grow, evolve into a ship ponderously settling to rest. The drive faded and cut; silence fell.

* * * *

Inside the Briefing Room, the speaker called out. Bo Bergman went inside, talked to the tower, motioned to the others.

"—over to you," the speaker was saying. There was a crackling moment of silence; then another voice.

"—illegal entry. Send the two of them out. I'll see to it they're dealt with."

Tove flipped a key. "Switch me direct to the ship," he said.

"Right."

"You on ACI 228," Tove said. "Who are you?"

"What's that to you?"

"You weren't cleared to berth here. Do you have an emergency aboard?"

"Never mind that, you," the speaker rumbled. "I tracked the bird in. I got the lifeboat on the screen now. They haven't gone far in nine hours. Let's have 'em."

"You're wasting your time," Tove said.

There was a momentary silence.

"You think so, hah?" the speaker blared. "I'll put it to you straight. I see two guys on their way out in one minute, or I open up."

"He's bluffin'," Chip said. "The popgun won't bear on us."

"Take a look out the window," Retief said.

In the white glare of the moonlight, a loading cover swung open at the stern of the ship, dropped down and formed a sloping ramp. A squat and massive shape appeared in the opening, trundled down onto the snow-swept tarmac.

Chip whistled. "I told you the Captain was slippery," he muttered. "Where the devil'd he git that at?"

"What is it?" Tove asked.

"A tank," Retief said. "A museum piece, by the look of it."

"I'll say," Chip said. "That's a Bolo *Resartus*, Model M. Built mebbe two hunderd years ago in Concordiat times. Packs a wallop, too, I'll tell ye."

The tank wheeled, brought a gun muzzle to bear in the base of the tower.

"Send 'em out," the speaker growled. "Or I blast 'em out."

"One round in here, and I've had a wasted trip," Retief said. "I'd better go out."

"Wait a minute, Mister," Chip said. "I got the glimmerin's of a idear."

"I'll stall them," Tove said. He keyed the mike.

"ACI 228, what's your authority for this demand?"

"I know that machine," Chip said. "My hobby, old-time fightin' machines. Built a model of a *Resartus* once, inch to the foot. A beauty. Now, lessee...."

VII

The icy wind blew snow crystals stingingly against Retief's face.

"Keep your hands in your pockets, Chip," he said. "Numb hands won't hack the program."

"Yeah." Chip looked across at the tank. "Useta think that was a perty thing, that *Resartus*," he said. "Looks mean, now."

"You're getting the target's-eye view," Retief said. "Sorry you had to get mixed up in this, Old Timer."

"Mixed myself in. Durn good thing, too." Chip sighed. "I like these folks," he said. "Them boys didn't like lettin' us come out here, but I'll give 'em credit. They seen it had to be this way, and they didn't set to moanin' about it."

"They're tough people, Chip."

"Funny how it sneaks up on you, ain't it, Mister? Few minutes ago we was eatin' high on the hog. Now we're right close to bein' dead men."

"They want us alive, Chip."

"It'll be a hairy deal, Mister," Chip said. "But t'hell with it. If it works, it works."

"That's the spirit."

"I hope I got them fields o' fire right—"

"Don't worry. I'll bet a barrel of beer we make it."

"We'll find out in about ten seconds," Chip said.

As they reached the tank, the two men broke stride and jumped. Retief leaped for the gun barrel, swung up astride it, ripped off the fur-lined leather cap he wore and, leaning forward, jammed it into the bore of the cannon. The chef sprang for a perch above the fore scanner antenna. With an angry *whuff!* anti-personnel charges slammed from apertures low on the sides of the vehicle. Retief swung around, pulled himself up on the hull.

"Okay, Mister," Chip called. "I'm going under." He slipped down the front of the tank, disappeared between the treads. Retief clambered up, took a position behind the turret, lay flat as it whirled angrily, sonar eyes searching for its tormentors. The vehicle shuddered, backed, stopped, moved forward, pivoted.

Chip reappeared at the front of the tank.

"It's stuck," he called. He stopped to breathe hard, clung as the machine lurched forward, spun to the right, stopped, rocking slightly.

"Take over here," Retief said. He crawled forward, watched as the chef pulled himself up, slipped down past him, feeling for the footholds between the treads. He reached the ground, dropped on his back, hitched himself under the dark belly of the tank. He groped, found the handholds, probed with a foot for the tread-jack lever.

The tank rumbled, backed quickly, turned left and right in a dizzying sine curve. Retief clung grimly, inches from the clashing treads.

The machine ground to a halt. Retief found the lever, braced his back, pushed. The lever seemed to give minutely. He set himself again, put both feet against the frozen bar and heaved.

With a dry rasp, it slid back. Immediately two heavy rods extended themselves, moved down to touch the pavement, grated. The left track creaked as the weight went off it. Suddenly the tank's drive raced, and Retief grabbed for a hold as the right tread clashed, heaved the fifty-ton machine forward. The jacks screeched as they scored the tarmac, then bit in.

The tank pivoted, chips of pavement flying. The jacks extended, lifted the clattering left track clear of the surface as the tank spun like a hamstrung buffalo.

The tank stopped, sat silent, canted now on the extended jacks. Retief emerged from under the machine, jumped, pulled himself above the anti-personnel apertures as another charge rocked the tank. He clambered to the turret, crouched beside Chip. They waited, watching the entry hatch.

Five minutes passed.

"I'll bet Old Tony's givin' the chauffeur hell," Chip said.

The hatch cycled open. A head came cautiously into view in time to see the needler in Retief's hand.

"Come on out," Retief said.

The head dropped. Chip snaked forward to ram a short section of steel rod under the hatch near the hinge. The hatch began to cycle shut, groaned, stopped. There was a sound of metal failing, and the hatch popped open.

Retief half rose, aimed the needler. The walls of the tank rang as the metal splinters ricocheted inside.

"That's one keg o' beer I owe you, Mister," Chip said. "Now let's git outa here before the ship lifts and fries us."

* * * *

"The biggest problem the Jorgensen's people will have is decontaminating the wreckage," Retief said.

Magnan leaned forward. "Amazing," he said. "They just keep coming, did they? Had they no inter-ship communication?"

"They had their orders," Retief said. "And their attack plan. They followed it."

"What a spectacle," Magnan said. "Over a thousand ships, plunging out of control one by one as they entered the stress-field."

"Not much of a spectacle," Retief said. "You couldn't see them. Too far away. They all crashed back in the mountains."

"Oh." Magnan's face fell. "But it's as well they did. The bacterial bombs—"

"Too cold for bacteria. They won't spread."

"Nor will the Soetti," Magnan said smugly, "thanks to the promptness with which I acted in dispatching you with the requisite data." He looked narrowly at Retief. "By the way, you're sure no...ah...message reached you after your arrival?"

"I got something," Retief said, looking Magnan in the eye. "It must have been a garbled transmission. It didn't make sense."

Magnan coughed, shuffled papers. "This information you've report-ed," he said hurriedly. "This rather fantastic story that the Soetti originated in the Cloud, that they're seeking a foothold in the main Galaxy because they've literally eaten themselves out of subsistence—how did you get it? The one or two Soetti we attempted to question, ah...." Magnan coughed again. "There was an accident," he finished. "We got nothing from them."

"The Jorgensens have a rather special method of interrogating prisoners," Retief said. "They took one from a wreck, still alive but unconscious. They managed to get the story from him. He died of it."

"It's immaterial, actually," Magnan said. "Since the Soetti violated their treaty with us the day after it was signed. Had no intention of fair play. Far from evacuating the agreed areas, they had actually occupied half a dozen additional minor bodies in the Whate system."

Retief clucked sympathetically.

"You don't know who to trust, these days," he said.

Magnan looked at him coldly.

"Spare me your sarcasm, Mr. Retief," he said. He picked up a folder from his desk, opened it. "By the way, I have another little task for you, Retief. We haven't had a comprehensive wild-life census report from Brimstone lately—"

"Sorry," Retief said. "I'll be tied up. I'm taking a month off. Maybe more."

"What's that?" Magnan's head came up. "You seem to forget—"

"I'm trying, Mr. Councillor," Retief said. "Good-by now." He reached out and flipped the key. Magnan's face faded from the screen. Retief stood up.

"Chip," he said, "we'll crack that keg when I get back." He turned to Anne-Marie.

"How long," he said, "do you think it will take you to teach me to ski by moonlight?"

GAMBLER'S WORLD

Originally published in **Worlds of If, *November 1961.***

I

Retief paused before a tall mirror to check the overlap of the four sets of lapels that ornamented the vermilion cutaway of a First Secretary and Consul.

"Come along, Retief," Magnan said. "The Ambassador has a word to say to the staff before we go in."

"I hope he isn't going to change the spontaneous speech he plans to make when the Potentate impulsively suggests a trade agreement along the lines they've been discussing for the last two months."

"Your derisive attitude is uncalled for, Retief," Magnan said sharply. "I think you realize it's delayed your promotion in the Corps."

Retief took a last glance in the mirror. "I'm not sure I want a promotion," he said. "It would mean more lapels."

Ambassador Crodfoller pursed his lips, waiting until Retief and Magnan took places in the ring of Terrestrial diplomats around him.

"A word of caution only, gentlemen," he said. "Keep always foremost in your minds the necessity for our identification with the Nenni Caste. Even a hint of familiarity with lower echelons could mean the failure of the mission. Let us remember that the Nenni represent authority here on Petreac. Their traditions must be observed, whatever our personal preferences. Let's go along now. The Potentate will be making his entrance any moment."

Magnan came to Retief's side as they moved toward the salon.

"The Ambassador's remarks were addressed chiefly to you, Retief," he said. "Your laxness in these matters is notorious. Naturally, I believe firmly in democratic principles myself—"

"Have you ever had a feeling, Mr. Magnan, that there's a lot going on here that we don't know about?"

Magnan nodded. "Quite so. Ambassador Crodfoller's point exactly. Matters which are not of concern to the Nenni are of no concern to us."

"Another feeling I get is that the Nenni aren't very bright. Now suppose—"

"I'm not given to suppositions, Retief. We're here to implement the policies of the Chief of Mission. And I should dislike to be in the shoes of a member of the staff whose conduct jeopardized the agreement that will be concluded here tonight."

* * * *

A bearer with a tray of drinks rounded a fluted column, shied as he confronted the diplomats, fumbled the tray, grabbed and sent a glass crashing to the floor.

Magnan leaped back, slapping at the purple cloth of his pants leg. Retief's hand shot out to steady the tray. The servant rolled terrified eyes.

"I'll take one of these, now that you're here," Retief said. He took a glass from the tray, winking at the servant.

"No harm done," he said. "Mr. Magnan's just warming up for the big dance."

A Nenni major-domo bustled up, rubbing his hands politely.

"Some trouble here?" he said. "What happened, Honorables, what, what...."

"The blundering idiot," Magnan spluttered. "How dare—"

"You're quite an actor, Mr. Magnan," Retief said. "If I didn't know about your democratic principles, I'd think you were really mad."

The servant ducked his head and scuttled away.

"Has this fellow...." The major-domo eyed the retreating bearer.

"I dropped my glass," Retief said. "Mr. Magnan's upset because he hates to see liquor wasted."

Retief turned to find himself face-to-face with Ambassador Crodfoller.

"I witnessed that," The Ambassador hissed. "By the goodness of Providence, the Potentate and his retinue haven't appeared yet. But I can assure you the servants saw it. A more un-Nenni-like display I would find it difficult to imagine!"

Retief arranged his features in an expression of deep interest.

"More un-Nenni-like, sir?" he said. "I'm not sure I—"

"Bah!" The Ambassador glared at Retief, "Your reputation has preceded you, sir. Your name is associated with a number of the most bizarre incidents in Corps history. I'm warning you; I'll tolerate nothing." He turned and stalked away.

"Ambassador-baiting is a dangerous sport, Retief," Magnan said.

Retief took a swallow of his drink. "Still," he said, "it's better than no sport at all."

"Your time would be better spent observing the Nenni mannerisms. Frankly, Retief, you're not fitting into the group at all well."

"I'll be candid with you, Mr. Magnan. The group gives me the willies."

"Oh, the Nenni are a trifle frivolous, I'll concede," Magnan said. "But it's with them that we must deal. And you'd be making a contribution to the overall mission if you merely abandoned that rather arrogant manner of yours." Magnan looked at Retief critically. "You can't help your height, of course. But couldn't you curve your back just a bit—and possibly assume a more placating expression? Just act a little more…."

"Girlish?"

"Exactly." Magnan nodded, then looked sharply at Retief.

Retief drained his glass and put it on a passing tray.

"I'm better at acting girlish when I'm well juiced," he said. "But I can't face another sorghum-and-soda. I suppose it would be un-Nenni-like to slip the bearer a credit and ask for a Scotch and water."

"Decidedly." Magnan glanced toward a sound across the room. "Ah, here's the Potentate now!" He hurried off.

Retief watched the bearers coming and going, bringing trays laden with drinks, carrying off empties. There was a lull in the drinking now, as the diplomats gathered around the periwigged Chief of State and his courtiers. Bearers loitered near the service door, eyeing the notables. Retief strolled over to the service door, pushed through it into a narrow white-tiled hall filled with the odors of the kitchen. Silent servants gaped as he passed, watching as he moved along to the kitchen door and stepped inside.

II

A dozen or more low-caste Petreacans, gathered around a long table in the center of the room looked up, startled. A heap of long-bladed bread knives, French knives, carving knives and cleavers lay in the center of the table. Other knives were thrust into belts or held in the hands of the men. A fat man in the yellow sarong of a cook stood frozen in the act of handing a knife to a tall one-eyed sweeper.

Retief took one glance, then let his eyes wander to a far corner of the room. Humming a careless little tune, he sauntered across to the open liquor shelves, selected a garish green bottle and turned unhurriedly back toward the door. The group of servants watched him, transfixed.

As Retief reached the door, it swung inward. Magnan, lips pursed, stood in the doorway.

"I had a premonition," he said.

"I'll bet it was a dandy," Retief said. "You must tell me all about it—in the salon."

"We'll have this out right here," Magnan snapped. "I've warned you!" Magnan's voice trailed off as he took in the scene around the table.

"After you," Retief said, nudging Magnan toward the door.

"What's going on here?" Magnan barked. He stared at the men, started around Retief. A hand stopped him.

"Let's be going," Retief said, propelling Magnan toward the hall.

"Those knives!" Magnan yelped. "Take your hands off me, Retief! What are you men—?"

Retief glanced back. The fat cook gestured suddenly, and the men faded back. The cook stood, arm cocked, a knife across his palm.

"Close the door and make no sound," he said softly.

Magnan pressed back against Retief. "Let's…r-run…." he faltered.

Retief turned slowly, put his hands up.

"I don't run very well with a knife in my back," he said. "Stand very still, Magnan, and do just what he tells you."

"Take them out through the back," the cook said.

"What does he mean?" Magnan spluttered. "Here, you—"

"Silence," the cook said, almost casually. Magnan gaped at him, closed his mouth.

Two of the men with knives came to Retief's side and gestured, grinning broadly.

"Let's go, peacocks," one said.

Retief and Magnan silently crossed the kitchen, went out the back door, stopped on command and stood waiting. The sky was brilliant with stars. A gentle breeze stirred the tree-tops beyond the garden. Behind them the servants talked in low voices.

"You go too, Illy," the cook was saying.

"Do it here," another said.

"And carry their damn dead bodies down?"

"Pitch 'em behind the hedge."

"I said the river. Three of you is plenty for a couple of Nenni. We don't know if we want to—"

"They're foreigners, not Nenni. We don't know—"

"So they're foreign Nenni. Makes no difference. I've seen them. I need every man here; now get going."

"What about the big guy? He looks tough."

"Him? He waltzed into the room and didn't notice a thing. But watch the other one."

At a prod from a knife point, Retief moved off down the walk, two of the escort behind him and Magnan, another going ahead to scout the way.

Magnan moved closer to Retief.

"Say," he said in a whisper. "That fellow in the lead; isn't he the one who spilled the drink? The one you took the blame for?"

"That's him, all right. He doesn't seem nervous any more, I notice."

"You saved him from serious punishment," Magnan said. "He'll be grateful; he'll let us go."

"Better check with the fellows with the knives before you act on that."

"Say something to him," Magnan hissed, "Remind him."

* * * *

The lead man fell back in line with Retief and Magnan.

"These two are scared of you," he said, grinning and jerking a thumb toward the knife-handlers. "They haven't worked around the Nenni like me; they don't know you."

"Don't you recognize this gentleman?" Magnan said.

"He did me a favor," the man said. "I remember."

"What's it all about?" Retief asked.

"The revolution. We're taking over now."

"Who's 'we'?"

"The People's Anti-Fascist Freedom League."

"What are all the knives for?"

"For the Nenni; and for all you foreigners."

"What do you mean?" Magnan gasped.

"We'll slit all the throats at one time. Saves a lot of running around."

"What time will that be?"

"Just at dawn; and dawn comes early, this time of year. By full daylight the PAFFL will be in charge."

"You'll never succeed," Magnan said. "A few servants with knives! You'll all be caught and killed."

"By who, the Nenni?" the man laughed. "You Nenni are a caution."

"But we're not Nenni—"

"We've watched you; you're the same. You're part of the same blood-sucking class."

"There are better ways to, uh, adjust differences," Magnan said. "This killing won't help you, I'll personally see to it that your grievances are heard in the Corps Courts. I can assure you that the plight of the downtrodden workers will be alleviated. Equal rights for all—"

"These threats won't work," the man said. "You don't scare me."

"Threats? I'm promising *relief* to the exploited classes of Petreac!"

"You must be nuts," the man said. "You trying to upset the system or something?"

"Isn't that the purpose of your revolution?"

"Look, Nenni, we're tired of you Nenni getting all the graft. We want our turn. What good would it do us to run Petreac if there's no loot?"

"You mean you intend to oppress the people? But they're your own group."

"Group, schmoop. We're taking all the chances; we're doing the work. We deserve the payoff. You think we're throwing up good jobs for the fun of it?"

"You're basing a revolt on these cynical premises?"

"Wise up, Nenni. There's never been a revolution for any other reason."

"Who's in charge of this?" Retief said.

"Shoke, the head chef."

"I mean the big boss. Who tells Shoke what all to do?"

"Oh, that's Zorn. Look out, here's where we start down the slope. It's slippery."

"Look," Magnan said. "You."

"My name's Illy."

"Mr. Illy, this man showed you mercy when he could have had you beaten."

"Keep moving. Yeah, I said I was grateful."

"Yes," Magnan said, swallowing hard. "A noble emotion, gratitude. You won't regret it."

"I always try to pay back a good turn," Illy said. "Watch your step now on this sea-wall."

"You'll never regret it," Magnan said.

"This is far enough," Illy motioned to one of the knife men. "Give me your knife, Vug."

The man passed his knife to Illy. There was an odor of sea-mud and kelp. Small waves slapped against the stones of the sea-wall. The wind was stronger here.

"I know a neat stroke," Illy said. "Practically painless. Who's first?"

"What do you mean?" Magnan quavered.

"I *said* I was grateful. I'll do it myself, give you a nice clean job. You know these amateurs; botch it up and have a guy floppin' around, yellin' and spatterin' everybody up."

"I'm first," Retief said. He pushed past Magnan, stopped suddenly, drove a straight punch at Illy's mouth.

* * * *

The long blade flicked harmlessly over Retief's shoulder as Illy fell. Retief whirled, leaped past Magnan, took the unarmed servant by the throat and belt, lifted him and slammed him against the third man. Both scrambled, yelped and fell from the sea-wall into the water.

Retief turned back to Illy. He pulled off the man's belt and strapped his hands together.

Magnan found his voice.

"You.... we.... they...."

"I know," Retief said.

"We've got to get back," Magnan said, "Warn them!"

"We'd never get through the rebel cordon around the palace. And if we did, trying to give an alarm would only set the assassinations off early."

"We can't just...."

"We've got to go to the source; this fellow Zorn. Get him to call it off."

"We'd be killed! At least we're safe here."

Illy groaned and opened his eyes. He sat up.

"On your feet, Illy," Retief said.

Illy looked around. "I'm sick," he said.

"The damp air is bad for you. Let's be going." Retief pulled the man to his feet. "Where does Zorn stay when he's in town?" he demanded.

"What happened? Where's Vug and...."

"They had an accident. Fell in the pond."

Illy gazed down at the restless black water.

"I guess I had you Nenni figured wrong."

"Us Nenni have hidden qualities. Let's get moving before Vug and Slug make it to shore and start it all over again."

"No hurry," Illy said. "They can't swim." He spat into the water. "So long, Vug. So long, Toscin. Take a pull, at the Hell Horn for me." He started off along the sea wall toward the sound of the surf.

"You want to see Zorn, I'll take you to see Zorn," he said. "I can't swim either."

III

"I take it," Retief said, "that the casino is a front for his political activities."

"He makes plenty off it. This PAFFL is a new kick. I never heard about it until maybe a couple months ago."

Retief motioned toward a dark shed with an open door.

"We'll stop here," he said, "long enough to strip the gadgets off these uniforms."

Illy, hands strapped behind his back, stood by and watched as Retief and Magnan removed medals, ribbons, orders and insignia from the formal diplomatic garments.

"This may help some," Retief said, "if the word is out that two diplomats are loose."

"It's a breeze," Illy said. "We see cats in purple and orange tailcoats all the time."

"I hope you're right," Retief said. "But if we're called, you'll be the first to go, Illy."

"You're a funny kind of Nenni," Illy said, eyeing Retief, "Toscin and Vug must be wonderin' what happened to 'em."

"If you think I'm good at drowning people, you ought to see me with a knife. Let's get going."

"It's only a little way now," Illy said. "But you better untie me. Somebody's liable to stick their nose in and get me killed."

"I'll take the chance. How do we get to the casino?"

"We follow this street. It twists around and goes under a couple tunnels. When we get to the Drunkard's Stairs we go up and it's right in front of us. A pink front with a sign like a big Luck Wheel."

"Give me your belt, Magnan," Retief said.

Magnan handed it over.

"Lie down, Illy," Retief said.

The servant looked at Retief.

"Vug and Toscin will be glad to see me," he said. "But they'll never believe me." He lay down. Retief strapped his feet together and stuffed a handkerchief in his mouth.

"Why are you doing that?" Magnan asked. "We need him."

"We know the way. And we don't need anyone to announce our arrival. It's only on three-dee that you can march a man through a gang of his pals with a finger in his back."

Magnan looked at the man. "Maybe you'd better, uh, cut his throat," he said.

Illy rolled his eyes.

"That's a very un-Nenni-like suggestion, Mr. Magnan," Retief said. "If we have any trouble finding the casino, I'll give it serious thought."

There were few people in the narrow street. Shops were shuttered, windows dark.

"Maybe they heard about the coup," Magnan said. "They're lying low."

"More likely, they're at the palace picking up their knives."

They rounded a corner, stepped over a man curled in the gutter snoring heavily and found themselves at the foot of a long flight of littered stone steps.

"The Drunkard's Stairs are plainly marked," Magnan sniffed.

"I hear sounds up there," Retief said. "Sounds of merrymaking."

"Maybe we'd better go back."

"Merrymaking doesn't scare me," Retief said. "Come to think of it, I don't know what the word means." He started up, Magnan behind him.

* * * *

At the top of the long stair a dense throng milled in the alley-like street.

A giant illuminated roulette wheel revolved slowly above them. A loudspeaker blared the chant of the croupiers from the tables inside. Magnan and Retief moved through the crowd toward the wide-open doors.

Magnan plucked at Retief's sleeve. "Are you sure we ought to push right in like this? Maybe we ought to wait a bit, look around...."

"When you're where you have no business being," Retief said, "always stride along purposefully. If you loiter, people begin to get curious."

Inside, a mob packed the wide, low-ceilinged room, clustered around gambling devices in the form of towers, tables and basins.

"What do we do now?" Magnan asked.

"We gamble. How much money do you have in your pockets?"

"Why…a few credits." Magnan handed the money to Retief. "But what about the man Zorn?"

"A purple cutaway is conspicuous enough, without ignoring the tables," Retief said. "We've got a hundred credits between us. We'll get to Zorn in due course, I hope."

"Your pleasure, gents," a bullet-headed man said, eyeing the colorful evening clothes of the diplomats. "You'll be wantin' to try your luck at the Zoop tower, I'd guess. A game for real sporting gents."

"Why…ah…" Magnan said.

"What's a zoop tower?" Retief asked.

"Out-of-towners, hey?" The bullet-headed man shifted his dope-stick to the other corner of his mouth. "Zoop is a great little game. Two teams of players buy into the pot. Each player takes a lever; the object is to make the ball drop from the top of the tower into your net. Okay?"

"What's the ante?"

"I got a hundred-credit pot workin' now, gents."

Retief nodded. "We'll try it."

The shill led the way to an eight-foot tower mounted on gimbals. Two perspiring men in trade-class pullovers gripped two of the levers that controlled the tilt of the tower. A white ball lay in a hollow in the thick glass platform at the top. From the center, an intricate pattern of grooves led out to the edge of the glass. Retief and Magnan took chairs before the two free levers.

"When the light goes on, gents, work the lever to jack the tower. You got three gears. Takes a good arm to work top gear. That's this button here. The little knob controls what way you're goin'. May the best team win. I'll take the hundred credits now."

Retief handed over the money. A red light flashed on, and Retief tried the lever.

It moved easily, with a ratcheting sound. The tower trembled, slowly tilted toward the two perspiring workmen pumping frantically at their levers. Magnan started slowly, accelerated as he saw the direction the tower was taking.

"Faster, Retief," he said. "They're winning."

"This is against the clock, gents," the bullet-headed man said. "If nobody wins when the light goes off, the house takes all."

"Crank it over to the left," Retief said.

"I'm getting tired."

"Shift to a lower gear."

The tower leaned. The ball stirred, rolled into a concentric channel. Retief shifted to middle gear, worked the lever. The tower creaked to a stop, started back upright.

"There isn't any lower gear," Magnan gasped. One of the two on the other side of the tower shifted to middle gear; the other followed suit. They worked harder now, heaving against the stiff levers. The tower quivered, moved slowly toward their side.

"I'm exhausted," Magnan gasped. He dropped the lever, lolled back in the chair, gulping air. Retief shifted position, took Magnan's lever with his left hand.

"Shift it to middle gear," Retief said. Magnan gulped, punched the button and slumped back, panting.

"My arm," he said. "I've injured myself."

The two men in pullovers conferred hurriedly as they cranked their levers; then one punched a button and the other reached across, using his left arm to help.

"They've shifted to high," Magnan said. "Give up, it's hopeless."

"Shift me to high," Retief said. "Both buttons!"

Magnan complied. Retief's shoulders bulged. He brought one lever down, then the other, alternately, slowly at first, then faster. The tower jerked, tilted toward him, farther.... The ball rolled in the channel, found an outlet—

Abruptly, both Retief's levers froze.

The tower trembled, wavered and moved back. Retief heaved. One lever folded at the base, bent down and snapped off short. Retief braced his feet, took the other lever with both hands and pulled.

There was a rasp of metal friction, and a loud twang. The lever came free, a length of broken cable flopping into view. The tower fell over as the two on the other side scrambled aside.

"Hey!" Bullet-head yelled. "You wrecked my equipment!"

Retief got up and faced him.

"Does Zorn know you've got your tower rigged for suckers?"

"You tryin' to call me a cheat or something?"

The crowd had fallen back, ringing the two men. Bullet-head glanced around. With a lightning motion, he plucked a knife from somewhere.

"That'll be five hundred credits for the equipment," he said. "Nobody calls Kippy a cheat."

* * * *

Retief picked up the broken lever.

"Don't make me hit you with this, you cheap chiseler."

Kippy looked at the bar.

"Comin' in here," he said indignantly, looking to the crowd for support. "Bustin' up my rig, callin' names...."

"I want a hundred credits," Retief said. "Now."

"Highway robbery!" Kippy yelled.

"Better pay up," somebody called.

"Hit him, mister," someone else said.

A broad-shouldered man with graying hair pushed through the crowd and looked around. "You heard 'em, Kippy. Give," he said.

The shill growled but tucked his knife away. Reluctantly he peeled a bill from a fat roll and handed it over.

The newcomer looked from Retief to Magnan.

"Pick another game, strangers," he said. "Kippy made a little mistake."

"This is small-time stuff," Retief said. "I'm interested in something big."

The broad-shouldered man lit a perfumed dope stick. "What would you call big?" he said softly.

"What's the biggest you've got?"

The man narrowed his eyes, smiling. "Maybe you'd like to try Slam."

"Tell me about it."

"Over here." The crowd opened up, made a path. Retief and Magnan followed across the room to a brightly-lit glass-walled box.

There was an arm-sized opening at waist height. Inside was a hand grip. A two-foot plastic globe a quarter full of chips hung in the center. Apparatus was mounted at the top of the box.

"Slam pays good odds," the man said. "You can go as high as you like. Chips cost you a hundred credits. You start it up by dropping a chip in here." He indicated a slot.

"You take the hand grip. When you squeeze, it unlocks. The globe starts to turn. You can see, it's full of chips. There's a hole at the top. As long as you hold the grip, the bowl turns. The harder you squeeze, the faster it turns. Eventually it'll turn over to where the hole is down, and chips fall out.

"On the other hand, there's contact plates spotted around the bowl. When one of 'em lines up with a live contact, you get quite a little jolt—guaranteed nonlethal. All you've got to do is hold on long enough, and you'll get the payoff."

"How often does this random pattern put the hole down?"

"Anywhere from three minutes to fifteen, with the average run of players. Oh, by the way, one more thing. That lead block up there—" The man motioned with his head toward a one-foot cube suspended by a thick cable. "It's rigged to drop every now and again. Averages five minutes. A warning light flashes first. You can take a chance; sometimes the light's a bluff.

You can set the clock back on it by dropping another chip—or you can let go the grip."

Retief looked at the massive block of metal.

"That would mess up a man's dealing hand, wouldn't it?"

"The last two jokers who were too cheap to feed the machine had to have 'em off. Their arms, I mean. That lead's heavy stuff."

"I don't suppose your machine has a habit of getting stuck, like Kippy's?"

The broad-shouldered man frowned.

"You're a stranger," he said, "You don't know any better."

"It's a fair game, Mister," someone called.

"Where do I buy the chips?"

The man smiled. "I'll fix you up. How many?"

"One."

"A big spender, eh?" The man snickered, but handed over a large plastic chip.

IV

Retief stepped to the machine, dropped the coin.

"If you want to change your mind," the man said, "you can back out now. All it'll cost you is the chip you dropped."

Retief reached through the hole, took the grip. It was leather padded hand-filling. He squeezed it. There was a click and bright lights sprang up. The crowd ah!-ed. The globe began to twirl lazily. The four-inch hole at its top was plainly visible.

"If ever the hole gets in position it will empty very quickly," Magnan said, hopefully.

Suddenly, a brilliant white light flooded the glass cage. A sound went up from the spectators.

"Quick, drop a chip," someone called.

"You've only got ten seconds…."

"Let go!" Magnan yelped.

Retief sat silent, holding the grip, frowning up at the weight. The globe twirled faster now. Then the bright white light winked off.

"A bluff!" Magnan gasped.

"That's risky, stranger," the gray-templed man said.

The globe was turning rapidly now, oscillating from side to side. The hole seemed to travel in a wavering loop, dipping lower, swinging up high, then down again.

"It has to move to the bottom soon," Magnan said. "Slow it down."

"The slower it goes, the longer it takes to get to the bottom," someone said.

There was a crackle and Retief stiffened. Magnan heard a sharp intake of breath. The globe slowed, and Retief shook his head, blinking.

The broad-shouldered man glanced at a meter.

"You took pretty near a full jolt, that time," he said.

The hole in the globe was tracing an oblique course now, swinging to the center, then below.

"A little longer," Magnan said.

"That's the best speed I ever seen on the Slam ball," someone said. "How much longer can he hold it?"

Magnan looked at Retief's knuckles. They showed white against the grip. The globe tilted farther, swung around, then down; two chips fell out, clattered down a chute and into a box.

"We're ahead," Magnan said. "Let's quit."

Retief shook his head. The globe rotated, dipped again; three chips fell.

"She's ready," someone called.

"It's bound to hit soon," another voice added excitedly. "Come on, Mister!"

"Slow down," Magnan said. "So it won't move past too quickly."

"Speed it up, before that lead block gets you," someone called.

The hole swung high, over the top, then down the side. Chips rained out of the hole, six, eight....

"Next pass," a voice called.

The white light flooded the cage. The globe whirled; the hole slid over the top, down, down.... A chip fell, two more....

Retief half rose, clamped his jaw and crushed the grip. Sparks flew. The globe slowed, chips spewing. It stopped, swung back, weighted by the mass of chips at the bottom, and stopped again with the hole centered.

Chips cascaded down the chute, filled the box before Retief, spilled on the floor. The crowd yelled.

Retief released the grip and withdrew his arm at the same instant that the lead block slammed down.

"Good lord," Magnan said. "I felt that through the floor."

Retief turned to the broad-shouldered man.

"This game's all right for beginners," he said. "But I'd like to talk a really big gamble. Why don't we go to your office, Mr. Zorn?"

* * * *

"Your proposition interests me," Zorn said, grinding out the stump of his dope stick in a brass ashtray. "But there's some angles to this I haven't mentioned yet."

"You're a gambler, Zorn, not a suicide," Retief said. "Take what I've offered. The other idea was fancier, I agree, but it won't work."

"How do I know you birds aren't lying?" Zorn snarled. He stood up, strode up and down the room. "You walk in here and tell me I'll have a task force on my neck, that the Corps won't recognize my regime. Maybe you're right. But I've got other contacts. They say different." He whirled, stared at Retief.

"I have pretty good assurance that once I put it over, the Corps will have to recognize me as the legal government of Petreac. They won't meddle in internal affairs."

"Nonsense," Magnan spoke up. "The Corps will never deal with a pack of criminals calling themselves—"

"Watch your language, you!" Zorn rasped.

"I'll admit Mr. Magnan's point is a little weak," Retief said. "But you're overlooking something. You plan to murder a dozen or so officers of the Corps Diplomatique Terrestrienne along with the local wheels. The corps won't overlook that. It can't."

"Their tough luck they're in the middle," Zorn muttered.

"Our offer is extremely generous, Mr. Zorn," Magnan said. "The post you'll get will pay you very well indeed. As against the certain failure of your planned coup, the choice should be simple."

Zorn eyed Magnan. "Offering me a job—it sounds phony as hell. I thought you birds were goody-goody diplomats."

"It's time you knew," Retief said. "There's no phonier business in the Galaxy than diplomacy."

"You'd better take it, Mr. Zorn," Magnan said.

"Don't push me, Junior!" Zorn said. "You two walk into my headquarters empty-handed and big-mouthed. I don't know what I'm talking to you for. The answer is no. N-I-X, no!"

"Who are you afraid of?" Retief said softly.

Zorn glared at him.

"Where do you get that 'afraid' routine? I'm top man here!"

"Don't kid around, Zorn. Somebody's got you under their thumb. I can see you squirming from here."

"What if I let your boys alone?" Zorn said suddenly. "The Corps won't have anything to say then, huh?"

"The Corps has plans for Petreac, Zorn. You aren't part of them. A revolution right now isn't part of them. Having the Potentate and the whole Nenni caste slaughtered isn't part of them. Do I make myself clear?"

"Listen," Zorn said urgently, pulling a chair around. "I'll tell you guys a few things. You ever heard of a world they call Rotune?"

"Certainly," Magnan said. "It's a near neighbor of yours. Another backward—that is, emergent—"

"Okay," Zorn said. "You guys think I'm a piker, do you? Well, let me wise you up. The Federal Junta on Rotune is backing my play. I'll be recognized by Rotune, and the Rotune fleet will stand by in case I need any help. I'll present the CDT with what you call a *fait accompli*."

"What does Rotune get out of this? I thought they were your traditional enemies."

"Don't get me wrong. I've got no use for Rotune; but our interests happen to coincide right now."

"Do they?" Retief smiled grimly. "You can spot a sucker as soon as he comes through that door out there—but you go for a deal like this!"

"What do you mean?" Zorn looked angrily at Retief. "It's fool-proof."

"After you get in power, you'll be fast friends with Rotune, is that it?"

"Friends, hell! Just give me time to get set, and I'll square a few things with that—"

"Exactly. And what do you suppose they have in mind for you?"

"What are you getting at?"

"Why is Rotune interested in your take-over?"

Zorn studied Retief's face. "I'll tell you why," he said. "It's you birds. You and your trade agreement. You're here to tie Petreac into some kind of trade combine. That cuts Rotune out. Well, we're doing all right out here. We don't need any commitments to a lot of fancy-pants on the other side of the Galaxy."

"That's what Rotune has sold you, eh?" Retief said, smiling.

"Sold, nothing!"

Zorn ground out his dope-stick, lit another. He snorted angrily.

"Okay; what's your idea?" he asked after a moment.

"You know what Petreac is getting in the way of imports as a result of the agreement?"

"Sure. A lot of junk."

"To be specific," Retief said, "there'll be 50,000 Tatone B-3 dry washers; 100,000 Glo-float motile lamps; 100,000 Earthworm Minor garden cultivators; 25,000 Veco space heaters; and 75,000 replacement elements for Ford Monomeg drives."

"Like I said. A lot of junk."

Retief leaned back, looking sardonically at Zorn, "Here's the gimmick, Zorn," he said. "The Corps is getting a little tired of Petreac and Rotune carrying on their two-penny war out here. Your privateers have a nasty habit of picking on innocent bystanders. After studying both sides, the Corps has decided Petreac would be a little easier to do business with. So this trade agreement was worked out. The Corps can't openly sponsor an arms shipment to a belligerent. But personal appliances are another story."

"So what do we do—plow 'em under with back-yard cultivators?" Zorn looked at Retief, puzzled. "What's the point?"

"You take the sealed monitor unit from the washer, the repeller field generator from the lamp, the converter control from the cultivator, et cetera, et cetera. You fit these together according to some very simple instructions. Presto! You have one hundred thousand Standard-class Y hand blasters. Just the thing to turn the tide in a stalemated war fought with obsolete arms."

"Good lord!" Magnan said. "Retief, are you—"

"I have to tell him," Retief said. "He has to know what he's putting his neck into."

"Weapons, hey?" Zorn said. "And Rotune knows about it?"

"Sure they know about it. It's not too hard to figure out. And there's more. They want the CDT delegation included in the massacre for a reason. It will put Petreac out of the picture; the trade agreement will go to Rotune; and you and your new regime will find yourselves looking down the muzzles of your own blasters."

Zorn threw his dope-stick to the floor with a snarl.

"I should have smelled something when that Rotune smoothie made his pitch." Zorn looked at his watch.

"I've got two hundred armed men in the palace. We've got about forty minutes to get over there before the rocket goes up."

V

"You'd better stay here on this terrace out of the way until I've spread the word," Zorn said. "Just in case."

"Let me caution you against any…ah…slip-ups, Mr. Zorn," Magnan said. "The Nenni are not to be molested—"

Zorn looked at Retief.

"Your friend talks too much," he said. "I'll keep my end of it. He'd better keep his."

"Nothing's happened yet, you're sure?" Magnan said.

"I'm sure," Zorn said. "Ten minutes to go. Plenty of time."

"I'll just step into the salon to assure myself that all is well," Magnan said.

"Suit yourself," Zorn said. "Just stay clear of the kitchen, or you'll get your throat cut." He sniffed at his dope-stick. "What's keeping Shoke?" he muttered.

Magnan stepped to a tall glass door, eased it open and poked his head through the heavy draperies. As he moved to draw back, a voice was faintly audible. Magnan paused, head still through the drapes.

"What's going on there?" Zorn rasped. He and Retief stepped up behind Magnan.

"—breath of air, ha-ha," Magnan was saying.

"Well, come along, Magnan!" Ambassador Crodfoller's voice snapped.

Magnan shifted from one foot to the other then pushed through the drapes.

"Where've you been, Mr. Magnan?" The Ambassador's voice was sharp.

"Oh…ah…a slight accident, Mr. Ambassador."

"What's happened to your shoes? Where are your insignia and decorations?"

"I—ah—spilled a drink on them. Sir. Ah—listen…."

The sound of an orchestra came up suddenly, blaring a fanfare.

Zorn shifted restlessly, ear against the glass.

"What's your friend pulling?" he rasped. "I don't like this."

"Keep cool, Zorn," Retief said. "Mr. Magnan is doing a little emergency salvage on his career."

The music died away with a clatter.

"—My God," Ambassador Crodfoller's voice was faint. "Magnan, you'll be knighted for this. Thank God you reached me. Thank God it's not too late. I'll find some excuse. I'll get a gram off at once."

"But you—"

"It's all right, Magnan. You were in time. Another ten minutes and the agreement would have been signed and transmitted. The wheels would have been put in motion. My career ruined…."

Retief felt a prod at his back. He turned.

"Doublecrossed," Zorn said softly. "So much for the word of a diplomat."

Retief looked at the short-barreled needler in Zorn's hand.

"I see you hedge your bets, Zorn," he said.

"We'll wait here," Zorn said, "until the excitement's over inside. I wouldn't want to attract any attention right now."

"Your politics are still lousy, Zorn. The picture hasn't changed. Your coup hasn't got a chance."

"Skip it. I'll take up one problem at a time."

"Magnan's mouth has a habit of falling open at the wrong time—"

"That's my good luck that I heard it. So there'll be no agreement, no guns, no fat job for Tammany Zorn, hey? Well, I can still play it the other way, What have I got to lose?"

With a movement too quick to follow, Retief's hand chopped down across Zorn's wrist. The needler clattered as Zorn reeled, and then Retief's hand clamped Zorn's arm and whirled him around.

"In answer to your last question," Retief said, "your neck."

"You haven't got a chance, doublecrosser," Zorn gasped.

"Shoke will be here in a minute," Retief said. "Tell him it's all off."

"Twist harder, Mister," Zorn said. "Break it off at the shoulder. I'm telling him nothing!"

"The kidding's over, Zorn," Retief said. "Call it off or I'll kill you."

"I believe you," Zorn said. "But you won't have long to remember it."

"All the killing will be for nothing," Retief said. "You'll be dead and the Rotunes will step into the power vacuum."

"So what? When I die, the world ends."

"Suppose I make you another offer, Zorn?"

"Why would it be any better than the last one, chiseler?"

Retief released Zorn's arm, pushed him away, stooped and picked up the needler.

"I could kill you, Zorn. You know that."

"Go ahead!"

Retief reversed the needler, held it out.

"I'm a gambler too, Zorn. I'm gambling you'll listen to what I have to say."

Zorn snatched the gun, stepped back. He looked at Retief.

"That wasn't the smartest bet you ever made, Mister; but go ahead. You've got maybe ten seconds."

"Nobody doublecrossed you, Zorn. Magnan put his foot in it. Too bad. Is that a reason to kill yourself and a lot of other people who've bet their lives on you?"

"They gambled and lost. Tough."

"Maybe you haven't lost yet—if you don't quit."

"Get to the point!"

Retief spoke earnestly for a minute and a half. Zorn stood, gun aimed, listening. Then both men turned as footsteps approached along the terrace. A fat man in a yellow sarong padded up to Zorn.

Zorn tucked the needler in his waistband.

"Hold everything, Shoke," he said. "Tell the boys to put the knives away. Spread the word fast. It's all off."

* * * *

"I want to commend you, Retief," Ambassador Crodfoller said expansively. "You mixed very well at last night's affair. Actually, I was hardly aware of your presence."

"I've been studying Mr. Magnan's work," Retief said.

"A good man, Magnan. In a crowd, he's virtually invisible."

"He knows when to disappear all right."

"This has been in many ways a model operation, Retief." The Ambassador patted his paunch contentedly. "By observing local social customs and blending harmoniously with the court, I've succeeded in establishing a fine, friendly, working relationship with the Potentate."

"I understand the agreement has been postponed."

The Ambassador chuckled. "The Potentate's a crafty one. Through... ah...a special study I have been conducting, I learned last night that he had hoped to, shall I say, 'put one over' on the Corps."

"Great heavens," Retief said.

"Naturally, this placed me in a difficult position. It was my task to quash this gambit, without giving any indication that I was aware of its existence."

"A hairy position indeed," Retief said.

"Quite casually, I informed the Potentate that certain items which had been included in the terms of the agreement had been deleted and others substituted. I admired him at that moment, Retief. He took it coolly—appearing completely indifferent—perfectly dissembling his very serious disappointment."

"I noticed him dancing with three girls wearing a bunch of grapes apiece. He's very agile for a man of his bulk."

"You mustn't discount the Potentate! Remember, beneath that mask of frivolity, he had absorbed a bitter blow."

"He had me fooled," Retief said.

"Don't feel badly; I confess at first I failed to sense his shrewdness." The Ambassador nodded and moved off along the corridor.

Retief turned and went into an office. Magnan looked up from his desk.

"Ah," he said. "Retief. I've been meaning to ask you. About the...ah... blasters. Are you—?"

Retief leaned on Magnan's desk, looked at him.

"I thought that was to be our little secret."

"Well, naturally I—" Magnan closed his mouth, swallowed. "How is it, Retief," he said sharply, "that you were aware of this blaster business, when the Ambassador himself wasn't?"

"Easy," Retief said. "I made it up."

"You what!" Magnan looked wild. "But the agreement—it's been revised! Ambassador Crodfoller has gone on record...."

"Too bad. Glad *I* didn't tell him about it."

Magnan leaned back and closed his eyes.

"It was big of you to take all the...blame," Retief said, "when the Ambassador was talking about knighting people."

Magnan opened his eyes.

"What about that gambler, Zorn? Won't he be upset?"

"It's all right," Retief said, "I made another arrangement. The business about making blasters out of common components wasn't completely imaginary. You can actually do it, using parts from an old-fashioned disposal unit."

"What good will that do him?" Magnan whispered, looking nervous. "We're not shipping in any old-fashioned disposal units."

"We don't need to," Retief said. "They're already installed in the palace kitchen—and in a few thousand other places, Zorn tells me."

"If this ever leaks...." Magnan put a hand to his forehead.

"I have his word on it that the Nenni slaughter is out. This place is ripe for a change. Maybe Zorn is what it needs."

"But how can we *know?*" Magnan yelped. "How can we be sure?"

"We can't," Retief said. "But it's not up to the Corps to meddle in Petreacs' internal affairs." He leaned over, picked up Magnan's desk lighter and lit a cigar. He blew a cloud of smoke toward the ceiling. "Right?"

Magnan looked at him, nodded weakly. "Right."

"I'd better be getting along to my desk," Retief said. "Now that the Ambassador feels that I'm settling down at last—"

"Retief," Magnan said, "tonight, I implore you. Stay out of the kitchen—no matter what."

Retief raised his eyebrows.

"I know," Magnan said. "If you hadn't interfered, we'd all have had our throats cut. But at least," he added, "we'd have died in accordance with regulations!"

THE YILLIAN WAY

Originally published in If, *January 1962.*

I

Jame Retief, vice-consul and third secretary in the Diplomatic Corps, followed the senior members of the terrestrial mission across the tarmac and into the gloom of the reception building. The gray-skinned Yill guide who had met the arriving embassy at the foot of the ramp hurried away. The councillor, two first secretaries and the senior attaches gathered around the ambassador, their ornate uniforms bright in the vast dun-colored room.

Ten minutes passed. Retief strolled across to the nearest door and looked through the glass panel at the room beyond. Several dozen Yill lounged in deep couches, sipping lavender drinks from slender glass tubes. Black-tunicked servants moved about inconspicuously, offering trays. A party of brightly-dressed Yill moved toward the entrance doors. One of the party, a tall male, made to step before another, who raised a hand languidly, fist clenched. The first Yill stepped back and placed his hands on top of his head. Both Yill were smiling and chatting as they passed through the doors.

Retief turned away to rejoin the Terrestrial delegation waiting beside a mound of crates made of rough greenish wood stacked on the bare concrete floor.

As Retief came up, Ambassador Spradley glanced at his finger watch and spoke to the man beside him.

"Ben, are you quite certain our arrival time was made clear?"

Second Secretary Magnan nodded emphatically. "I stressed the point, Mr. Ambassador. I communicated with Mr. T'Cai-Cai just before the light-er broke orbit, and I specifically——"

"I hope you didn't appear truculent, Mr. Magnan," the ambassador said sharply.

"No indeed, Mr. Ambassador. I merely——"

"You're sure there's no VIP room here?" The ambassador glanced around the cavernous room. "Curious that not even chairs have been provided."

"If you'd care to sit on one of these crates——"

"Certainly not." The ambassador looked at his watch again and cleared his throat.

"I may as well make use of these few moments to outline our approach for the more junior members of the staff; it's vital that the entire mission work in harmony in the presentation of the image. We Terrestrials are a kindly, peace-loving race." The ambassador smiled in a kindly, peace-loving way.

"We seek only a reasonable division of spheres of influence with the Yill." He spread his hands, looking reasonable.

"We are a people of high culture, ethical, sincere." The smile was replaced abruptly by pursed lips.

"We'll start by asking for the entire Sirenian System, and settle for half. We'll establish a foothold on all the choicer worlds. And, with shrewd handling, in a century we'll be in a position to assert a wider claim."

The ambassador glanced around. "If there are no questions——"

* * * *

Retief stepped forward. "It's my understanding, Mr. Ambassador, that we hold the prior claim to the Sirenian System. Did I understand your Excellency to say that we're ready to concede half of it to the Yill without a struggle?"

Ambassador Spradley looked up at Retief, blinking. The younger man loomed over him. Beside him, Magnan cleared his throat in the silence.

"Vice-Consul Retief merely means——"

"I can interpret Mr. Retief's remark," the ambassador snapped. He assumed a fatherly expression.

"Young man, you're new to the Service. You haven't yet learned the team play, the give-and-take of diplomacy. I shall expect you to observe closely the work of the experienced negotiators of the mission. You must learn the importance of subtlety."

"Mr. Ambassador," Magnan said, "I think the reception committee is arriving." He pointed. Half a dozen tall, short-necked Yill were entering through a side door. The leading Yill hesitated as another stepped in his path. He raised a fist, and the other moved aside, touching the top of his head perfunctorily with both hands. The group started across the room toward the Terrestrials. Retief watched as a slender alien came forward and spoke passable Terran in a reedy voice.

"I am P'Toi. Come this way...." He turned, and the group moved toward the door, the ambassador leading. As he reached for the door, the interpreter darted ahead and shouldered him aside. The other Yill stopped, waiting.

The ambassador almost glared, then remembered the image. He smiled and beckoned the Yill ahead. They milled uncertainly, muttering in the native tongue, then passed through the door.

The Terran party followed.

"—— give a great deal to know what they're saying," Retief overheard as he came up.

"Our interpreter has forged to the van," the ambassador said. "I can only assume he'll appear when needed."

"A pity we have to rely on a native interpreter," someone said.

"Had I known we'd meet this rather uncouth reception," the ambassador said stiffly, "I would have audited the language personally, of course, during the voyage out."

"Oh, no criticism intended, of course, Mr. Ambassador."

"Heavens," Magnan put in. "Who would have thought——"

Retief moved up behind the ambassador.

"Mr. Ambassador," he said, "I——"

"Later, young man," the ambassador snapped. He beckoned to the first councillor, and the two moved off, heads together.

Outside, a bluish sun gleamed in a dark sky. Retief watched his breath form a frosty cloud in the chill air. A broad doughnut-wheeled vehicle was drawn up to the platform. The Yill gestured the Terran party to the gaping door at the rear, then stood back, waiting.

Retief looked curiously at the gray-painted van. The legend written on its side in alien symbols seemed to read "egg nog."

* * * *

The ambassador entered the vehicle, the other Terrestrials following. It was as bare of seats as the Terminal building. What appeared to be a defunct electronic chassis lay in the center of the floor.

Retief glanced back. The Yill were talking excitedly. None of them entered the car. The door was closed, and the Terrans braced themselves under the low roof as the engine started up with a whine of worn turbos.

The van moved off.

It was an uncomfortable ride. Retief put out an arm as the vehicle rounded a corner, just catching the ambassador as he staggered, off-balance. The ambassador glared at him, settled his heavy tri-corner hat and stood stiffly until the car lurched again.

Retief stooped, attempting to see out through the single dusty window. They seemed to be in a wide street lined with low buildings.

They passed through a massive gate, up a ramp, and stopped. The door opened. Retief looked out at a blank gray facade, broken by tiny windows at irregular intervals. A scarlet vehicle was drawn up ahead, the Yill reception committee emerging from it. Through its wide windows Retief saw rich upholstery and caught a glimpse of glasses clamped to a tiny bar.

P'Toi, the Yill interpreter, came forward, gestured to a small door. Magnan opened it, waiting for the ambassador.

As he stepped to it, a Yill thrust himself ahead and hesitated. Ambassador Spradley drew himself up, glaring. Then he twisted his mouth into a frozen smile and stepped aside.

The Yill looked at each other then filed through the door.

Retief was the last to enter. As he stepped inside, a black-clad servant slipped past him, pulled the lid from a large box by the door and dropped in a paper tray heaped with refuse. There were alien symbols in flaking paint on the box. They seemed, Retief noticed, to spell "egg nog."

II

The shrill pipes and whining reeds had been warming up for an hour when Retief emerged from his cubicle and descended the stairs to the banquet hall.

Standing by the open doors, he lit a slender cigar and watched through narrowed eyes as obsequious servants in black flitted along the low wide corridor, carrying laden trays into the broad room, arranging settings on a great four-sided table forming a hollow square that almost filled the room. Rich brocades were spread across the center of the side nearest the door, flanked by heavily decorated white cloths. Beyond, plain white extended to the far side, where metal dishes were arranged on the bare table top.

A richly dressed Yill approached, stepped aside to allow a servant to pass and entered the room.

Retief turned at the sound of Terran voices behind him. The ambassador came up, trailed by two diplomats. He glanced at Retief, adjusted his ruff and looked into the banquet hall.

"Apparently we're to be kept waiting again," he muttered. "After having been informed at the outset that the Yill have no intention of yielding an inch, one almost wonders...."

"Mr. Ambassador," Retief said. "Have you noticed———"

"However," Ambassador Spradley said, eyeing Retief, "a seasoned diplomatist must take these little snubs in stride. In the end—— Ah, there, Magnan." He turned away, talking.

Somewhere a gong clanged.

In a moment, the corridor was filled with chattering Yill who moved past the group of Terrestrials into the banquet hall. P'Toi, the Yill interpreter, came up and raised a hand.

"Waitt heere...."

More Yill filed into the dining room to take their places. A pair of helmeted guards approached, waving the Terrestrials back. An immense gray-jowled Yill waddled to the doors and passed through, followed by more guards.

"The Chief of State," Retief heard Magnan say. "The Admirable F'Kau-Kau-Kau."

"I have yet to present my credentials," Ambassador Spradley said. "One expects some latitude in the observances of protocol, but I confess...." He wagged his head.

The Yill interpreter spoke up.

"You now whill lhie on yourr intesstinss, and creep to fesstive board there." He pointed across the room.

"Intestines?" Ambassador Spradley looked about wildly.

"Mr. P'Toi means our stomachs, I wouldn't wonder," Magnan said. "He just wants us to lie down and crawl to our seats, Mr. Ambassador."

"What the devil are you grinning at, you idiot?" the ambassador snapped.

* * * *

Magnan's face fell.

Spradley glanced down at the medals across his paunch.

"This is.... I've never...."

"Homage to godss," the interpreter said.

"Oh. Oh, religion," someone said.

"Well, if it's a matter of religious beliefs...." The ambassador looked dubiously around.

"Golly, it's only a couple of hundred feet," Magnan offered.

Retief stepped up to P'Toi.

"His Excellency the Terrestrial Ambassador will not crawl," he said clearly.

"Here, young man! I said nothing——"

"Not to crawl?" The interpreter wore an unreadable Yill expression.

"It is against our religion," Retief said.

"Againsst?"

"We are votaries of the Snake Goddess," Retief said. "It is a sacrilege to crawl." He brushed past the interpreter and marched toward the distant table.

The others followed.

Puffing, the ambassador came to Retief's side as they approached the dozen empty stools on the far side of the square opposite the brocaded position of the Admirable F'Kau-Kau-Kau.

"Mr. Retief, kindly see me after this affair," he hissed. "In the meantime, I hope you will restrain any further rash impulses. Let me remind you *I* am chief of mission here."

Magnan came up from behind.

"Let me add my congratulations, Retief," he said. "That was fast thinking——"

"Are you out of your mind, Magnan?" the ambassador barked. "I am extremely displeased!"

"Why," Magnan stuttered, "I was speaking sarcastically, of course, Mr. Ambassador. Didn't you notice the kind of shocked little gasp I gave when he did it?"

The Terrestrials took their places, Retief at the end. The table before them was of bare green wood, with an array of shallow pewter dishes.

Some of the Yill at the table were in plain gray, others in black. All eyed them silently. There was a constant stir among them as one or another rose and disappeared and others sat down. The pipes and reeds were shrilling furiously, and the susurration of Yillian conversation from the other tables rose ever higher in competition.

A tall Yill in black was at the ambassador's side now. The nearby Yill fell silent as he began ladling a whitish soup into the largest of the bowls before the Terrestrial envoy. The interpreter hovered, watching.

"That's quite enough," Ambassador Spradley said, as the bowl overflowed. The Yill servant rolled his eyes, dribbled more of the soup into the bowl.

"Kindly serve the other members of my staff," the ambassador said. The interpreter said something in a low voice. The servant moved hesitantly to the next stool and ladled more soup.

* * * *

Retief watched, listening to the whispers around him. The Yill at the table were craning now to watch. The soup ladler was ladling rapidly, rolling his eyes sideways. He came to Retief, reached out with the full ladle for the bowl.

"No," Retief said.

The ladler hesitated.

"None for me," Retief said.

The interpreter came up and motioned to the servant, who reached again, ladle brimming.

"I…DON'T…LIKE…IT!" Retief said, his voice distinct in the sudden hush. He stared at the interpreter, who stared back, then waved the servant away.

"Mr. Retief!" a voice hissed.

Retief looked down at the table. The ambassador was leaning forward, glaring at him, his face a mottled crimson.

"I'm warning you, Mr. Retief," he said hoarsely. "I've eaten sheep's eyes in the Sudan, ka swe in Burma, hundred-year *cug* on Mars and everything else that has been placed before me in the course of my diplomatic career. And, by the holy relics of Saint Ignatz, you'll do the same!" He snatched up a spoon-like utensil and dipped it into his bowl.

"Don't eat that, Mr. Ambassador," Retief said.

The ambassador stared, eyes wide. He opened his mouth, guided the spoon toward it——

Retief stood, gripped the table under its edge and heaved. The immense wooden slab rose and tilted, dishes sliding. It crashed to the floor with a ponderous slam.

Whitish soup splattered across the terrazzo. A couple of odd bowls rolled across the room. Cries rang out from the Yill, mingling with a strangled yell from Ambassador Spradley.

Retief walked past the wild-eyed members of the mission to the sputtering chief. "Mr. Ambassador," he said. "I'd like——"

"You'd like! I'll break you, you young hoodlum! Do you realize——"

"Pleass...." The interpreter stood at Retief's side.

"My apologies," Ambassador Spradley said, mopping his forehead. "My profound apologies."

"Be quiet," Retief said.

"Wha—what?"

"Don't apologize," Retief said. P'Toi was beckoning.

"Pleasse, arll come."

Retief turned and followed him.

The portion of the table they were ushered to was covered with an embroidered white cloth, set with thin porcelain dishes. The Yill already seated there rose, amid babbling, and moved down the table. The black-clad Yill at the end table closed ranks to fill the vacant seats. Retief sat down and found Magnan at his side.

"What's going on here?" the second secretary said angrily.

"They were giving us dog food," Retief said. "I overheard a Yill. They seated us at the bottom of the servants' table——"

"You mean you know their language?"

"I learned it on the way out. Enough, at least."

The music burst out with a clangorous fanfare, and a throng of jugglers, dancers and acrobats poured into the center of the hollow square, frantically juggling, dancing and back-flipping. Black-clad servants swarmed suddenly, heaping mounds of fragrant food on the plates of Yill and Terrestrials alike, pouring a pale purple liquor into slender glasses. Retief sampled the Yill food. It was delicious.

Conversation was impossible in the din. He watched the gaudy display and ate heartily.

III

Retief leaned back, grateful for the lull in the music. The last of the dishes were whisked away, and more glasses filled. The exhausted entertainers stopped to pick up the thick square coins the diners threw.

Retief sighed. It had been a rare feast.

"Retief," Magnan said in the comparative quiet, "what were you saying about dog food as the music came up?"

Retief looked at him. "Haven't you noticed the pattern, Mr. Magnan? The series of deliberate affronts?"

"Deliberate affronts! Just a minute, Retief. They're uncouth, yes, crowding into doorways and that sort of thing...." He looked at Retief uncertainly.

"They herded us into a baggage warehouse at the terminal. Then they hauled us here in a garbage truck——"

"Garbage truck!"

"Only symbolic, of course. They ushered us in the tradesman's entrance, and assigned us cubicles in the servants' wing. Then we were seated with the coolie class sweepers at the bottom of the table."

"You must be.... I mean, we're the Terrestrial delegation! Surely these Yill must realize our power."

"Precisely, Mr. Magnan. But——"

With a clang of cymbals the musicians launched a renewed assault. Six tall, helmeted Yill sprang into the center of the floor and paired off in a wild performance, half dance, half combat. Magnan pulled at Retief's arm, his mouth moving.

Retief shook his head. No one could talk against a Yill orchestra in full cry. He sampled a bright red wine and watched the show.

There was a flurry of action, and two of the dancers stumbled and collapsed, their partner-opponents whirling away to pair off again, describe the elaborate pre-combat ritual, and abruptly set to, dulled sabres clashing—and two more Yill were down, stunned. It was a violent dance.

Retief watched, the drink forgotten.

The last two Yill approached and retreated, whirled, bobbed and spun, feinted and postured—and on the instant, clashed, straining chest-to-chest—then broke apart, heavy weapons chopping, parrying, as the music mounted to a frenzy.

Evenly matched, the two hacked, thrust, blow for blow, across the floor, then back, defense forgotten, slugging it out.

And then one was slipping, going down, helmet awry. The other, a giant, muscular Yill, spun away, whirled in a mad skirl of pipes as coins showered—then froze before a gaudy table, raised the sabre and slammed it down in a resounding blow across the gay cloth before a lace and bow-bedecked Yill in the same instant that the music stopped.

In utter silence the dancer-fighter stared across the table at the seated Yill.

With a shout, the Yill leaped up, raised a clenched fist. The dancer bowed his head, spread his hands on his helmet.

Retief took a deep gulp of a pale yellow liqueur and leaned forward to watch. The beribboned Yill waved a hand negligently, spilled a handful of coins across the table and sat down.

The challenger spun away in a screeching shrill of music. Retief caught his eye for an instant as he passed.

And then the dancer stood rigid before the brocaded table—and the music stopped off short as the sabre slammed down before a heavy Yill in ornate metallic coils. The challenged Yill rose and raised a fist. The other ducked his head, put his hands on his helmet. Coins rolled. The dancer moved on.

Twice more the dancer struck the table in ritualistic challenge, exchanged gestures, bent his neck and passed on. He circled the broad floor, sabre twirling, arms darting in an intricate symbolism. The orchestra blared shrilly, unmuffled now by the surf-roar of conversation. The Yill, Retief noticed suddenly, were sitting silent, watching. The dancer was closer now, and then he was before Retief, poised, towering, sabre above his head.

The music cut, and in the startling instantaneous silence, the heavy sabre whipped over and down with an explosive concussion that set dishes dancing on the table-top.

The Yill's eyes held on Retief's. In the silence, Magnan tittered drunkenly. Retief pushed back his stool.

"Steady, my boy," Ambassador Spradley called. Retief stood, the Yill topping his six foot three by an inch. In a motion almost too quick to follow, Retief reached for the sabre, twitched it from the Yill's grip, swung it in a whistling cut. The Yill ducked, sprang back, snatched up a sabre dropped by another dancer.

"Someone stop the madman!" Spradley howled.

Retief leaped across the table, sending fragile dishes spinning.

The other danced back, and only then did the orchestra spring to life with a screech and a mad tattoo of high-pitched drums.

Making no attempt to following the weaving pattern of the Yill bolero, Retief pressed the other, fending off vicious cuts with the blunt weapon, chopping back relentlessly. Left hand on hip, Retief matched blow for blow, driving the other back.

Abruptly, the Yill abandoned the double role. Dancing forgotten, he settled down in earnest, cutting, thrusting, parrying; and now the two stood toe to toe, sabres clashing in a lightning exchange. The Yill gave a step, two, then rallied, drove Retief back, back——

And the Yill stumbled. His sabre clattered, and Retief dropped his point as the other wavered past him and crashed to the floor.

The orchestra fell silent in a descending wail of reeds. Retief drew a deep breath and wiped his forehead.

"Come back here, you young fool!" Spradley called hoarsely.

Retief hefted the sabre, turned, eyed the brocade-draped table. He started across the floor. The Yill sat as if paralyzed.

"Retief, no!" Spradley yelped.

Retief walked directly to the Admirable F'Kau-Kau-Kau, stopped, raised the sabre.

"Not the chief of state," someone in the Terrestrial mission groaned.

Retief whipped the sabre down. The dull blade split the cloth and clove the hardwood table. There was utter silence.

The Admirable F'Kau-Kau-Kau rose, seven feet of obese gray Yill. Broad face expressionless to any Terran eyes, he raised a fist like a jewel-studded ham.

Retief stood rigid for a long moment. Then, gracefully, he inclined his head, placed his finger tips on his temples.

Behind him, there was a clatter as Ambassador Spradley collapsed. Then the Admirable F'Kau-Kau-Kau cried out and reached across the table to embrace the Terrestrial, and the orchestra went mad.

Gray hands helped Retief across the table, stools were pushed aside to make room at F'Kau-Kau-Kau's side. Retief sat, took a tall flagon of coal-black brandy pressed on him by his neighbor, clashed glasses with The Admirable and drank.

IV

Retief turned at the touch on his shoulder.

"The Ambassador wants to speak to you, Retief," Magnan said.

Retief looked across to where Ambassador Spradley sat glowering behind the plain tablecloth.

"Under the circumstances," Retief said, "you'd better ask him to come over here."

"The ambassador?" Magnan's voice cracked.

"Never mind the protocol," Retief said. "The situation is still delicate." Magnan went away.

"The feast ends," F'Kau-Kau-Kau said. "Now you and I, Retief, must straddle the Council Stool."

"I'll be honored, Admirable," Retief said. "I must inform my colleagues."

"Colleagues?" F'Kau-Kau-Kau said. "It is for chiefs to parley. Who shall speak for a king while he yet has tongue for talk?"

"The Yill way is wise," Retief said.

F'Kau-Kau-Kau emptied a squat tumbler of pink beer. "I will treat with you, Retief, as viceroy, since as you say your king is old and the space between worlds is far. But there shall be no scheming underlings privy to our dealings." He grinned a Yill grin. "Afterwards we shall carouse, Retief. The Council Stool is hard and the waiting handmaidens delectable. This makes for quick agreement."

Retief smiled. "The king is wise."

"Of course, a being prefers wenches of his own kind," F'Kau-Kau-Kau said. He belched. "The Ministry of Culture has imported several Terry—excuse me, Retief—Terrestrial joy-girls, said to be top-notch specimens. At least they have very fat watchamacallits."

"The king is most considerate," Retief said.

"Let us to it then, Retief. I may hazard a fling with one of your Terries, myself. I fancy an occasional perversion." F'Kau-Kau-Kau dug an elbow into Retief's side and bellowed with laughter.

Ambassador Spradley hurried to intercept Retief as he crossed to the door at F'Kau-Kau-Kau's side.

"Retief, kindly excuse yourself, I wish a word with you." His voice was icy. Magnan stood behind him, goggling.

"Mr. Ambassador, forgive my apparent rudeness," Retief said. "I don't have time to explain now——"

"Rudeness!" Spradley barked. "Don't have time, eh? Let me tell you———"

"Lower your voice, Mr. Ambassador," Retief said.

Spradley quivered, mouth open, speechless.

"If you'll sit down and wait quietly," Retief said, "I think——"

"*You* think!" Spradley spluttered.

* * * *

"Silence!" Retief said. Spradley looked up at Retief's face. He stared for a moment into Retief's gray eyes, closed his mouth and swallowed.

"The Yill seem to have gotten the impression I'm in charge," Retief said, "We'll have to keep it up."

"But—but—" Spradley stuttered. Then he straightened. "That is the last straw," he whispered hoarsely. "*I* am the Terrestrial Ambassador Extraordinary and Minister Plenipotentiary. Magnan has told me that we've been studiedly insulted, repeatedly, since the moment of our arrival. Kept waiting in baggage rooms, transported in refuse lorries, herded about with servants, offered swill at table. Now I and my senior staff, are left cooling our heels, without so much as an audience while this—this multiple Kau person hobnobs with—with—"

Spradley's voice broke. "I may have been a trifle hasty, Retief, in attempting to restrain you. Blaspheming the native gods and dumping the banquet table are rather extreme measures, but your resentment was perhaps partially justified. I am prepared to be lenient with you." He fixed a choleric eye on Retief.

"I am walking out of this meeting, Mr. Retief. I'll take no more of these deliberate personal——"

"That's enough," Retief snapped. "You're keeping the king waiting. Get back to your chair and sit there until I come back."

Magnan found his voice. "What are you going to do, Retief?"

"I'm going to handle the negotiation," Retief said. He handed Magnan his empty glass. "Now go sit down and work on the Image."

* * * *

At his desk in the VIP suite aboard the orbiting Corps vessel, Ambassador Spradley pursed his lips and looked severely at Vice-Consul Retief.

"Further," he said, "you have displayed a complete lack of understanding of Corps discipline, the respect due a senior agent, even the basic courtesies. Your aggravated displays of temper, ill-timed outbursts of violence and almost incredible arrogance in the assumption of authority make your further retention as an officer-agent of the Diplomatic Corps impossible. It will therefore be my unhappy duty to recommend your immediate——"

There was a muted buzz from the communicator. The ambassador cleared his throat.

"Well?"

"A signal from Sector HQ, Mr. Ambassador," a voice said.

"Well, read it," Spradley snapped. "Skip the preliminaries."

"Congratulations on the unprecedented success of your mission. The articles of agreement transmitted by you embody a most favorable resolution of the difficult Sirenian situation, and will form the basis of continued amicable relations between the Terrestrial States and the Yill Empire. To you and your staff, full credit is due for a job well done. Signed, Deputy Assistant Secretary——"

Spradley cut off the voice impatiently.

He shuffled papers, eyed Retief sharply.

"Superficially, of course, an uninitiated observer might leap to the conclusion that the—ah—results that were produced in spite of these...ah... irregularities justify the latter." The Ambassador smiled a sad, wise smile. "This is far from the case," he said. "I——"

The communicator burped softly.

"Confound it!" Spradley muttered. "Yes?"

"Mr. T'Cai-Cai has arrived," the voice said. "Shall I——"

"Send him in at once." Spradley glanced at Retief. "Only a two-syllable man, but I shall attempt to correct these false impressions, make some amends...."

The two Terrestrials waited silently until the Yill Protocol chief tapped at the door.

"I hope," the ambassador said, "that you will resist the impulse to take advantage of your unusual position." He looked at the door. "Come in."

T'Cai-Cai stepped into the room, glanced at Spradley, turned to greet Retief in voluble Yill. He rounded the desk to the ambassador's chair, motioned him from it and sat down.

* * * *

"I have a surprise for you, Retief," he said, in Terran. "I myself have made use of the teaching machine you so kindly lent us."

"That's fine. T'Cai-Cai," Retief said. "I'm sure Mr. Spradley will be interested in hearing what we have to say."

"Never mind," the Yill said. "I am here only socially." He looked around the room.

"So plainly you decorate your chamber. But it has a certain austere charm." He laughed a Yill laugh.

"Oh, you are a strange breed, you Terrestrials. You surprised us all. You know, one hears such outlandish stories. I tell you in confidence, we had expected you to be overpushes."

"Pushovers," Spradley said, tonelessly.

"Such restraint! What pleasure you gave to those of us, like myself of course, who appreciated your grasp of protocol. Such finesse! How subtly you appeared to ignore each overture, while neatly avoiding actual contamination. I can tell you, there were those who thought—poor fools—that you had no grasp of etiquette. How gratified we were, we professionals, who could appreciate your virtuosity—when you placed matters on a comfortable basis by spurning the cats'-meat. It was sheer pleasure then, waiting, to see what form your compliment would take."

The Yill offered orange cigars, stuffed one in his nostril.

"I confess even I had not hoped that you would honor our Admirable so signally. Oh, it is a pleasure to deal with fellow professionals, who understand the meaning of protocol!"

Ambassador Spradley made a choking sound.

"This fellow has caught a chill," T'Cai-Cai said. He eyed Spradley dubiously. "Step back, my man. I am highly susceptible.

"There is one bit of business I shall take pleasure in attending to, my dear Retief," T'Cai-Cai went on. He drew a large paper from his reticule.

"The Admirable is determined than none other than yourself shall be accredited here. I have here my government's exequatur confirming you as Terrestrial consul-general to Yill. We shall look forward to your prompt return."

Retief looked at Spradley.

"I'm sure the Corps will agree," he said.

"Then I shall be going," T'Cai-Cai said. He stood up. "Hurry back to us, Retief. There is much that I would show you of Yill."

"I'll hurry," Retief said and, with a Yill wink: "Together we shall see many high and splendid things!"

THE MADMAN FROM EARTH

Originally published in **Worlds of If Science Fiction,** *March 1962.*

I

"The Consul for the Terrestrial States," Retief said, "presents his compliments, et cetera, to the Ministry of Culture of the Groacian Autonomy, and with reference to the Ministry's invitation to attend a recital of interpretive grimacing, has the honor to express regret that he will be unable—"

"You can't turn this invitation down," Administrative Assistant Meuhl said flatly. "I'll make that 'accepts with pleasure'."

Retief exhaled a plume of cigar smoke.

"Miss Meuhl," he said, "in the past couple of weeks I've sat through six light-concerts, four attempts at chamber music, and god knows how many assorted folk-art festivals. I've been tied up every off-duty hour since I got here—"

"You can't offend the Groaci," Miss Meuhl said sharply. "Consul Whaffle would never have been so rude."

"Whaffle left here three months ago," Retief said, "leaving me in charge."

"Well," Miss Meuhl said, snapping off the dictyper. "I'm sure I don't know what excuse I can give the Minister."

"Never mind the excuses," Retief said. "Just tell him I won't be there." He stood up.

"Are you leaving the office?" Miss Meuhl adjusted her glasses. "I have some important letters here for your signature."

"I don't recall dictating any letters today, Miss Meuhl," Retief said, pulling on a light cape.

* * * *

"I wrote them for you. They're just as Consul Whaffle would have wanted them."

"Did you write all Whaffle's letters for him, Miss Meuhl?"

"Consul Whaffle was an extremely busy man," Miss Meuhl said stiffly. "He had complete confidence in me."

"Since I'm cutting out the culture from now on," Retief said, "I won't be so busy."

"Well!" Miss Meuhl said. "May I ask where you'll be if something comes up?"

"I'm going over to the Foreign Office Archives."

Miss Meuhl blinked behind thick lenses. "Whatever for?"

Retief looked thoughtfully at Miss Meuhl. "You've been here on Groac for four years, Miss Meuhl. What was behind the coup d'etat that put the present government in power?"

"I'm sure I haven't pried into—"

"What about that Terrestrial cruiser? The one that disappeared out this way about ten years back?"

"Mr. Retief, those are just the sort of questions we *avoid* with the Groaci. I certainly hope you're not thinking of openly intruding—"

"Why?"

"The Groaci are a very sensitive race. They don't welcome outworlders raking up things. They've been gracious enough to let us live down the fact that Terrestrials subjected them to deep humiliation on one occasion."

"You mean when they came looking for the cruiser?"

"I, for one, am ashamed of the high-handed tactics that were employed, grilling these innocent people as though they were criminals. We try never to reopen that wound, Mr. Retief."

"They never found the cruiser, did they?"

"Certainly not on Groac."

Retief nodded. "Thanks, Miss Meuhl," he said. "I'll be back before you close the office." Miss Meuhl's face was set in lines of grim disapproval as he closed the door.

* * * *

The pale-featured Groacian vibrated his throat-bladder in a distressed bleat.

"Not to enter the Archives," he said in his faint voice. "The denial of permission. The deep regret of the Archivist."

"The importance of my task here," Retief said, enunciating the glottal dialect with difficulty. "My interest in local history."

"The impossibility of access to outworlders. To depart quietly."

"The necessity that I enter."

"The specific instructions of the Archivist." The Groacian's voice rose to a whisper. "To insist no longer. To give up this idea!"

"OK, Skinny, I know when I'm licked," Retief said in Terran. "To keep your nose clean."

Outside, Retief stood for a moment looking across at the deeply carved windowless stucco facades lining the street, then started off in the direction of the Terrestrial Consulate General. The few Groacians on the street eyed him furtively, veered to avoid him as he passed. Flimsy high-wheeled ground cars puffed silently along the resilient pavement. The air was clean and cool.

At the office, Miss Meuhl would be waiting with another list of complaints.

Retief studied the carving over the open doorways along the street. An elaborate one picked out in pinkish paint seemed to indicate the Groacian equivalent of a bar. Retief went in.

A Groacian bartender was dispensing clay pots of alcoholic drink from the bar-pit at the center of the room. He looked at Retief and froze in mid-motion, a metal tube poised over a waiting pot.

"To enjoy a cooling drink," Retief said in Groacian, squatting down at the edge of the pit. "To sample a true Groacian beverage."

"To not enjoy my poor offerings," the Groacian mumbled. "A pain in the digestive sacs; to express regret."

"To not worry," Retief said, irritated. "To pour it out and let me decide whether I like it."

"To be grappled in by peace-keepers for poisoning of—foreigners." The barkeep looked around for support, found none. The Groaci customers, eyes elsewhere, were drifting away.

"To get the lead out," Retief said, placing a thick gold-piece in the dish provided. "To shake a tentacle."

"The procuring of a cage," a thin voice called from the sidelines. "The displaying of a freak."

* * * *

Retief turned. A tall Groacian vibrated his mandibles in a gesture of contempt. From his bluish throat coloration, it was apparent the creature was drunk.

"To choke in your upper sac," the bartender hissed, extending his eyes toward the drunk. "To keep silent, litter-mate of drones."

"To swallow your own poison, dispenser of vileness," the drunk whispered. "To find a proper cage for this zoo-piece." He wavered toward Retief. "To show this one in the streets, like all freaks."

"Seen a lot of freaks like me, have you?" Retief asked, interestedly.

"To speak intelligibly, malodorous outworlder," the drunk said. The barkeep whispered something, and two customers came up to the drunk, took his arms and helped him to the door.

"To get a cage!" the drunk shrilled. "To keep the animals in their own stinking place."

"I've changed my mind," Retief said to the bartender. "To be grateful as hell, but to have to hurry off now." He followed the drunk out the door.

The other Groaci released him, hurried back inside. Retief looked at the weaving alien.

"To begone, freak," the Groacian whispered.

"To be pals," Retief said. "To be kind to dumb animals."

"To have you hauled away to a stockyard, ill-odored foreign livestock."

"To not be angry, fragrant native," Retief said. "To permit me to chum with you."

"To flee before I take a cane to you!"

"To have a drink together—"

"To not endure such insolence!" The Groacian advanced toward Retief. Retief backed away.

"To hold hands," Retief said. "To be palsy-walsy—"

The Groacian reached for him, missed. A passer-by stepped around him, head down, scuttled away. Retief backed into the opening to a narrow crossway and offered further verbal familiarities to the drunken local, who followed, furious. Retief backed, rounded a corner into a narrow alley-like passage, deserted, silent…except for the following Groacian.

Retief stepped around him, seized his collar and yanked. The Groacian fell on his back. Retief stood over him. The downed native half-rose; Retief put a foot against his chest and pushed.

"To not be going anywhere for a few minutes," Retief said. "To stay right here and have a nice long talk."

* * * *

II

"There you are!" Miss Meuhl said, eyeing Retief over her lenses. "There are two gentlemen waiting to see you. Groacian gentlemen."

"Government men, I imagine. Word travels fast." Retief pulled off his cape. "This saves me the trouble of paying another call at the Foreign Ministry."

"What have you been doing? They seem very upset, I don't mind telling you."

"I'm sure you don't. Come along. And bring an official recorder."

Two Groaci wearing heavy eye-shields and elaborate crest ornaments indicative of rank rose as Retief entered the room. Neither offered a courteous snap of the mandibles, Retief noted. They were mad, all right.

"I am Fith, of the Terrestrial Desk, Ministry of Foreign Affairs, Mr. Consul," the taller Groacian said, in lisping Terran. "May I present Shluh, of the Internal Police?"

"Sit down, gentlemen," Retief said. They resumed their seats. Miss Meuhl hovered nervously, then sat on the edge of a comfortless chair.

"Oh, it's such a pleasure—" she began.

"Never mind that," Retief said. "These gentlemen didn't come here to sip tea today."

"So true," Fith said. "Frankly, I have had a most disturbing report, Mr. Consul. I shall ask Shluh to recount it." He nodded to the police chief.

"One hour ago," The Groacian said, "a Groacian national was brought to hospital suffering from serious contusions. Questioning of this individual revealed that he had been set upon and beaten by a foreigner. A Terrestrial, to be precise. Investigation by my department indicates that the description of the culprit closely matches that of the Terrestrial Consul."

Miss Meuhl gasped audibly.

"Have you ever heard," Retief said, looking steadily at Fith, "of a Terrestrial cruiser, the *ISV Terrific*, which dropped from sight in this sector nine years ago?"

"Really!" Miss Meuhl exclaimed, rising. "I wash my hands—"

"Just keep that recorder going," Retief snapped.

"I'll not be a party—"

"You'll do as you're told, Miss Meuhl," Retief said quietly. "I'm telling you to make an official sealed record of this conversation."

Miss Meuhl sat down.

Fith puffed out his throat indignantly. "You reopen an old wound, Mr. Consul. It reminds us of certain illegal treatment at Terrestrial hands—"

"Hogwash," Retief said. "That tune went over with my predecessors, but it hits a sour note with me."

"All our efforts," Miss Meuhl said, "to live down that terrible episode! And you—"

"Terrible? I understand that a Terrestrial task force stood off Groac and sent a delegation down to ask questions. They got some funny answers, and stayed on to dig around a little. After a week they left. Somewhat annoying to the Groaci, maybe—at the most. If they were innocent."

"IF!" Miss Meuhl burst out.

"If, indeed!" Fith said, his weak voice trembling. "I must protest your—"

* * * *

"Save the protests, Fith. You have some explaining to do. And I don't think your story will be good enough."

"It is for you to explain! This person who was beaten—"

"Not beaten. Just rapped a few times to loosen his memory."

"Then you admit—"

"It worked, too. He remembered lots of things, once he put his mind to it."

Fith rose; Shluh followed suit.

"I shall ask for your immediate recall, Mr. Consul. Were it not for your diplomatic immunity, I should do more—"

"Why did the government fall, Fith? It was just after the task force paid its visit, and before the arrival of the first Terrestrial diplomatic mission."

"This is an internal matter!" Fith cried, in his faint Groacian voice. "The new regime has shown itself most amiable to you Terrestrials. It has outdone itself—"

"—to keep the Terrestrial consul and his staff in the dark," Retief said. "And the same goes for the few terrestrial businessmen you've visaed. This continual round of culture; no social contacts outside the diplomatic circle; no travel permits to visit out-lying districts, or your satellite—"

"Enough!" Fith's mandibles quivered in distress. "I can talk no more of this matter—"

"You'll talk to me, or there'll be a task force here in five days to do the talking," Retief said.

"You can't!" Miss Meuhl gasped.

Retief turned a steady look on Miss Meuhl. She closed her mouth. The Groaci sat down.

"Answer me this one," Retief said, looking at Shluh. "A few years back—about nine, I think—there was a little parade held here. Some curious looking creatures were captured. After being securely caged, they were exhibited to the gentle Groaci public. Hauled through the streets. Very educational, no doubt. A highly cultural show.

"Funny thing about these animals. They wore clothes. They seemed to communicate with each other. Altogether it was a very amusing exhibit.

"Tell me, Shluh, what happened to those six Terrestrials after the parade was over?"

* * * *

Fith made a choked noise and spoke rapidly to Shluh in Groacian. Shluh retracted his eyes, shrank down in his chair. Miss Meuhl opened her mouth, closed it and blinked rapidly.

"How did they die?" Retief snapped. "Did you murder them, cut their throats, shoot them or bury them alive? What amusing end did you figure out for them? Research, maybe? Cut them open to see what made them yell...."

"No!" Fith gasped. "I must correct this terrible false impression at once."

"False impression, hell," Retief said. "They were Terrans! A simple narco-interrogation would get that out of any Groacian who saw the parade."

"Yes," Fith said weakly. "It is true, they were Terrestrials. But there was no killing."

"They're alive?"

"Alas, no. They…died."

Miss Meuhl yelped faintly.

"I see," Retief said. "They died."

"We tried to keep them alive, of course. But we did not know what foods—"

"Didn't take the trouble to find out, either, did you?"

"They fell ill," Fith said. "One by one…."

"We'll deal with that question later," Retief said. "Right now, I want more information. Where did you get them? Where did you hide the ship? What happened to the rest of the crew? Did they 'fall ill' before the big parade?"

"There were no more! Absolutely, I assure you!"

"Killed in the crash landing?"

"No crash landing. The ship descended intact, east of the city. The… terrestrials…were unharmed. Naturally, we feared them. They were strange to us. We had never before seen such beings."

"Stepped off the ship with guns blazing, did they?"

"Guns? No, no guns—"

"They raised their hands, didn't they? Asked for help. You helped them; helped them to death."

"How could we know?" Fith moaned.

"How could you know a flotilla would show up in a few months looking for them, you mean? That was a shock, wasn't it? I'll bet you had a brisk time of it hiding the ship, and shutting everybody up. A close call, eh?"

"We were afraid," Shluh said. "We are a simple people. We feared the strange creatures from the alien craft. We did not kill them, but we felt it was as well they…did not survive. Then, when the warships came, we realized our error. But we feared to speak. We purged our guilty leaders, concealed what had happened, and…offered our friendship. We invited the opening of diplomatic relations. We made a blunder, it is true, a great blunder. But we have tried to make amends…."

"Where is the ship?"

"The ship?"

"What did you do with it? It was too big to just walk off and forget. Where is it?"

The two Groacians exchanged looks.

"We wish to show our contrition," Fith said. "We will show you the ship."

"Miss Meuhl," Retief said. "If I don't come back in a reasonable length of time, transmit that recording to Regional Headquarters, sealed." He stood, looked at the Groaci.

"Let's go," he said.

* * * *

Retief stooped under the heavy timbers shoring the entry to the cavern. He peered into the gloom at the curving flank of the space-burned hull.

"Any lights in here?" he asked.

A Groacian threw a switch. A weak bluish glow sprang up.

Retief walked along the raised wooden catwalk, studying the ship. Empty emplacements gaped below lensless scanner eyes. Littered decking was visible within the half-open entry port. Near the bow the words 'IVS Terrific B7 New Terra' were lettered in bright chrome duralloy.

"How did you get it in here?" Retief asked.

"It was hauled here from the landing point, some nine miles distant," Fith said, his voice thinner than ever. "This is a natural crevasse. The vessel was lowered into it and roofed over."

"How did you shield it so the detectors didn't pick it up?"

"All here is high-grade iron ore," Fith said, waving a member. "Great veins of almost pure metal."

Retief grunted. "Let's go inside."

Shluh came forward with a hand-lamp. The party entered the ship.

Retief clambered up a narrow companionway, glanced around the interior of the control compartment. Dust was thick on the deck, the stanchions where acceleration couches had been mounted, the empty instrument panels, the litter of sheared bolts, scraps of wire and paper. A thin frosting of rust dulled the exposed metal where cutting torches had sliced away heavy shielding. There was a faint odor of stale bedding.

"The cargo compartment—" Shluh began.

"I've seen enough," Retief said.

Silently, the Groacians led the way back out through the tunnel and into the late afternoon sunshine. As they climbed the slope to the steam car, Fith came to Retief's side.

"Indeed, I hope that this will be the end of this unfortunate affair," he said. "Now that all has been fully and honestly shown—"

"You can skip all that," Retief said. "You're nine years late. The crew was still alive when the task force called, I imagine. You killed them—or let them die—rather than take the chance of admitting what you'd done."

"We were at fault," Fith said abjectly. "Now we wish only friendship."

"The *Terrific* was a heavy cruiser, about twenty thousand tons." Retief looked grimly at the slender Foreign Office official. "Where is she, Fith? I won't settle for a hundred-ton lifeboat."

* * * *

Fith erected his eye stalks so violently that one eye-shield fell off.

"I know nothing of…of…." He stopped. His throat vibrated rapidly as he struggled for calm.

"My government can entertain no further accusations, Mr. Consul," he said at last. "I have been completely candid with you, I have overlooked your probing into matters not properly within your sphere of responsibility. My patience is at an end."

"Where is that ship?" Retief rapped out. "You never learn, do you? You're still convinced you can hide the whole thing and forget it. I'm telling you you can't."

"We return to the city now," Fith said. "I can do no more."

"You can and you will, Fith," Retief said. "I intend to get to the truth of this matter."

Fith spoke to Shluh in rapid Groacian. The police chief gestured to his four armed constables. They moved to ring Retief in.

Retief eyed Fith. "Don't try it," he said. "You'll just get yourself in deeper."

Fith clacked his mandibles angrily, eye stalks canted aggressively toward the Terrestrial.

"Out of deference to your diplomatic status, Terrestrial, I shall ignore your insulting remarks," Fith said in his reedy voice. "Let us now return to the city."

Retief looked at the four policemen. "I see your point," he said.

Fith followed him into the car, sat rigidly at the far end of the seat.

"I advise you to remain very close to your consulate," Fith said. "I advise you to dismiss these fancies from your mind, and to enjoy the cultural aspects of life at Groac. Especially, I should not venture out of the city, or appear overly curious about matters of concern only to the Groacian government."

In the front seat, Shluh looked straight ahead. The loosely-sprung vehicle bobbed and swayed along the narrow highway. Retief listened to the rhythmic puffing of the motor and said nothing.

* * * *

III

"Miss Meuhl," Retief said, "I want you to listen carefully to what I'm going to tell you. I have to move rapidly now, to catch the Groaci off guard."

"I'm sure I don't know what you're talking about," Miss Meuhl snapped, her eyes sharp behind the heavy lenses.

"If you'll listen, you may find out," Retief said. "I have no time to waste, Miss Meuhl. They won't be expecting an immediate move—I hope—and that may give me the latitude I need."

"You're still determined to make an issue of that incident!" Miss Meuhl snorted. "I really can hardly blame the Groaci. They are not a sophisticated race; they had never before met aliens."

"You're ready to forgive a great deal, Miss Meuhl. But it's not what happened nine years ago I'm concerned with. It's what's happening now. I've told you that it was only a lifeboat the Groaci have hidden out. Don't you understand the implication? That vessel couldn't have come far. The cruiser itself must be somewhere near by. I want to know where!"

"The Groaci don't know. They're a very cultured, gentle people. You can do irreparable harm to the reputation of Terrestrials if you insist—"

"That's my decision," Retief said. "I have a job to do and we're wasting time." He crossed the room to his desk, opened a drawer and took out a slim-barreled needler.

"This office is being watched. Not very efficiently, if I know the Groaci. I think I can get past them all right."

"Where are you going with…that?" Miss Meuhl stared at the needler. "What in the world—"

"The Groaci won't waste any time destroying every piece of paper in their files relating to this thing. I have to get what I need before it's too late. If I wait for an official Inquiry Commission, they'll find nothing but blank smiles."

"You're out of your mind!" Miss Meuhl stood up, quivering with indignation. "You're like a…a…."

"You and I are in a tight spot, Miss Meuhl. The logical next move for the Groaci is to dispose of both of us. We're the only ones who know what happened. Fith almost did the job this afternoon, but I bluffed him out—for the moment."

Miss Meuhl emitted a shrill laugh. "Your fantasies are getting the better of you," she gasped. "In danger, indeed! Disposing of me! I've never heard anything so ridiculous."

"Stay in this office. Close and safe-lock the door. You've got food and water in the dispenser. I suggest you stock up, before they shut the supply down. Don't let anyone in, on any pretext whatever. I'll keep in touch with you via hand-phone."

"What are you planning to do?"

"If I don't make it back here, transmit the sealed record of this afternoon's conversation, along with the information I've given you. Beam it through on a mayday priority. Then tell the Groaci what you've done and sit tight. I think you'll be all right. It won't be easy to blast in here and anyway, they won't make things worse by killing you. A force can be here in a week."

"I'll do nothing of the sort! The Groaci are very fond of me! You… Johnny-come-lately! Roughneck! Setting out to destroy—"

"Blame it on me if it will make you feel any better," Retief said, "but don't be fool enough to trust them." He pulled on a cape, opened the door.

"I'll be back in a couple of hours," he said. Miss Meuhl stared after him silently as he closed the door.

* * * *

It was an hour before dawn when Retief keyed the combination to the safe-lock and stepped into the darkened consular office. He looked tired.

Miss Meuhl, dozing in a chair, awoke with a start. She looked at Retief, rose and snapped on a light, turned to stare.

"What in the world—Where have you been? What's happened to your clothing?"

"I got a little dirty. Don't worry about it." Retief went to his desk, opened a drawer and replaced the needler.

"Where have you been?" Miss Meuhl demanded. "I stayed here—"

"I'm glad you did," Retief said. "I hope you piled up a supply of food and water from the dispenser, too. We'll be holed up here for a week, at least." He jotted figures on a pad. "Warm up the official sender. I have a long transmission for Regional Headquarters."

"Are you going to tell me where you've been?"

"I have a message to get off first, Miss Meuhl," Retief said sharply. "I've been to the Foreign Ministry," he added. "I'll tell you all about it later."

"At this hour? There's no one there…."

"Exactly."

Miss Meuhl gasped. "You mean you broke in? You burgled the Foreign Office?"

"That's right," Retief said calmly. "Now—"

"This is absolutely the end!" Miss Meuhl said. "Thank heaven I've already—"

"Get that sender going, woman!" Retief snapped. "This is important."

"I've already done so, Mr. Retief!" Miss Meuhl said harshly. "I've been waiting for you to come back here…." She turned to the communicator, flipped levers. The screen snapped aglow, and a wavering long-distance image appeared.

"He's here now," Miss Meuhl said to the screen. She looked at Retief triumphantly.

"That's good," Retief said. "I don't think the Groaci can knock us off the air, but—"

"I have done my duty, Mr. Retief," Miss Meuhl said. "I made a full report to Regional Headquarters last night, as soon as you left this office. Any doubts I may have had as to the rightness of that decision have been completely dispelled by what you've just told me."

Retief looked at her levelly. "You've been a busy girl, Miss Meuhl. Did you mention the six Terrestrials who were killed here?"

"That had no bearing on the matter of your wild behavior! I must say, in all my years in the Corps, I've never encountered a personality less suited to diplomatic work."

* * * *

The screen crackled, the ten-second transmission lag having elapsed. "Mr. Retief," the face on the screen said, "I am Counsellor Pardy, DSO-1, Deputy Under-secretary for the region. I have received a report on your conduct which makes it mandatory for me to relieve you administratively, vice Miss Yolanda Meuhl, DAO-9. Pending the findings of a Board of Inquiry, you will—"

Retief reached out and snapped off the communicator. The triumphant look faded from Miss Meuhl's face.

"Why, what is the meaning—"

"If I'd listened any longer, I might have heard something I couldn't ignore. I can't afford that, at this moment. Listen, Miss Meuhl," Retief went on earnestly, "I've found the missing cruiser."

"You heard him relieve you!"

"I heard him say he was *going* to, Miss Meuhl. But until I've heard and acknowledged a verbal order, it has no force. If I'm wrong, he'll get my resignation. If I'm right, that suspension would be embarrassing all around."

"You're defying lawful authority! I'm in charge here now." Miss Meuhl stepped to the local communicator.

"I'm going to report this terrible thing to the Groaci at once, and offer my profound—"

"Don't touch that screen," Retief said. "You go sit in that corner where I can keep an eye on you. I'm going to make a sealed tape for transmission to Headquarters, along with a call for an armed task force. Then we'll settle down to wait."

Retief ignored Miss Meuhl's fury as he spoke into the recorder.

The local communicator chimed. Miss Meuhl jumped up, staring at it.

"Go ahead," Retief said. "Answer it."

A Groacian official appeared on the screen.

"Yolanda Meuhl," he said without preamble, "for the Foreign Minister of the Groacian Autonomy, I herewith accredit you as Terrestrial Consul to Groac, in accordance with the advices transmitted to my government direct from the Terrestrial Headquarters. As consul, you are requested to make available for questioning Mr. J. Retief, former consul, in connection with the assault on two peace keepers and illegal entry into the offices of the Ministry for Foreign Affairs."

"Why, why," Miss Meuhl stammered. "Yes, of course. And I do want to express my deepest regrets—"

* * * *

Retief rose, went to the communicator, assisted Miss Meuhl aside.

"Listen carefully, Fith," he said. "Your bluff has been called. You don't come in and we don't come out. Your camouflage worked for nine years, but it's all over now. I suggest you keep your heads and resist the temptation to make matters worse than they are."

"Miss Meuhl," Fith said, "a peace squad waits outside your consulate. It is clear you are in the hands of a dangerous lunatic. As always, the Groaci wish only friendship with the Terrestrials, but—"

"Don't bother," Retief said. "You know what was in those files I looked over this morning."

Retief turned at a sound behind him. Miss Meuhl was at the door, reaching for the safe-lock release....

"Don't!" Retief jumped—too late.

The door burst inward. A crowd of crested Groaci pressed into the room, pushed Miss Meuhl back, aimed scatter guns at Retief. Police Chief Shluh pushed forward.

"Attempt no violence, Terrestrial," he said. "I cannot promise to restrain my men."

"You're violating Terrestrial territory, Shluh," Retief said steadily. "I suggest you move back out the same way you came in."

"I invited them here," Miss Meuhl spoke up. "They are here at my express wish."

"Are they? Are you sure you meant to go this far, Miss Meuhl? A squad of armed Groaci in the consulate?"

"You are the consul, Miss Yolanda Meuhl," Shluh said. "Would it not be best if we removed this deranged person to a place of safety?"

"You're making a serious mistake, Shluh," Retief said.

"Yes," Miss Meuhl said. "You're quite right, Mr. Shluh. Please escort Mr. Retief to his quarters in this building—"

"I don't advise you to violate my diplomatic immunity, Fith," Retief said.

"As chief of mission," Miss Meuhl said quickly, "I hereby waive immunity in the case of Mr. Retief."

Shluh produced a hand recorder. "Kindly repeat your statement, Madam, officially," he said. "I wish no question to arise later."

"Don't be a fool, woman," Retief said. "Don't you see what you're letting yourself in for? This would be a hell of a good time for you to figure out whose side you're on."

"I'm on the side of common decency!"

"You've been taken in. These people are concealing—"

"You think all women are fools, don't you, Mr. Retief?" She turned to the police chief and spoke into the microphone he held up.

"That's an illegal waiver," Retief said. "I'm consul here, whatever rumors you've heard. This thing's coming out into the open, whatever you do. Don't add violation of the Consulate to the list of Groacian atrocities."

"Take the man," Shluh said.

* * * *

Two tall Groaci came to Retief's side, guns aimed at his chest.

"Determined to hang yourselves, aren't you?" Retief said. "I hope you have sense enough not to lay a hand on this poor fool here." He jerked a thumb at Miss Meuhl. "She doesn't know anything. I hadn't had time to tell her yet. She thinks you're a band of angels."

The cop at Retief's side swung the butt of his scatter-gun, connected solidly with Retief's jaw. Retief staggered against a Groacian, was caught and thrust upright, blood running down onto his shirt. Miss Meuhl yelped. Shluh barked at the guard in shrill Groacian, then turned to stare at Miss Meuhl.

"What has this man told you?"

"I—nothing. I refused to listen to his ravings."

"He said nothing to you of some…alleged…involvement?"

"I've told you!" Miss Meuhl said sharply. She looked at the blood on Retief's shirt.

"He told me nothing," she whispered. "I swear it."

"Let it lie, boys," Retief said. "Before you spoil that good impression."

Shluh looked at Miss Meuhl for a long moment. Then he turned.

"Let us go," he said. He turned back to Miss Meuhl. "Do not leave this building until further advice," he said.

"But…I am the Terrestrial consul!"

"For your safety, madam. The people are aroused at the beating of Groacian nationals by an…alien."

"So long, Meuhlsie," Retief said. "You played it real foxy."

"You'll…lock him in his quarters?" Miss Meuhl said.

"What is done with him is now a Groacian affair, Miss Meuhl. You yourself have withdrawn the protection of your government."

"I didn't mean—"

"Don't start having second thoughts," Retief said. "They can make you miserable."

"I had no choice," Miss Meuhl said. "I had to consider the best interest of the Service."

"My mistake, I guess," Retief said. "I was thinking of the best interests of a Terrestrial cruiser with three hundred men aboard."

"Enough," Shluh said. "Remove this criminal." He gestured to the peace keepers.

"Move along," he said to Retief. He turned to Miss Meuhl.

"A pleasure to deal with you, Madam."

IV

Retief stood quietly in the lift, stepped out at the ground floor and followed docilely down the corridor and across the pavement to a waiting steam car.

One of the peace keepers rounded the vehicle to enter on the other side. Two stooped to climb into the front seat. Shluh gestured Retief into the back seat and got in behind him. The others moved off on foot.

The car started up and pulled away. The cop in the front seat turned to look at Retief.

"To have some sport with it, and then to kill it," he said.

"To have a fair trial first," Shluh said. The car rocked and jounced, rounded a corner, puffed along between ornamented pastel facades.

"To have a trial and then to have a bit of sport," the cop said.

"To suck the eggs in your own hill," Retief said. "To make another stupid mistake."

Shluh raised his short ceremonial club and cracked Retief across the temple. Retief shook his head, tensed—

The cop in the front seat beside the driver turned and rammed the barrel of his scatter-gun against Retief's ribs.

"To make no move, outworlder," he said. Shluh raised his club and carefully struck Retief again. He slumped.

The car swayed, rounded another corner. Retief slid over against the police chief.

"To fend this animal—" Shluh began. His weak voice was cut off short as Retief's hand shot out, took him by the throat and snapped him down onto the floor. As the guard on Retief's left lunged, Retief uppercut him, slamming his head against the door post. He grabbed the scatter-gun as it fell, pushed into the mandibles of the Groacian in the front seat.

"To put your popgun over the seat—carefully—and drop it," he said.

The driver slammed on his brakes, whirled to raise his gun. Retief cracked the gun barrel against the head of the Groacian before him, then swiveled to aim it at the driver.

"To keep your eyestalks on the road," he said. The driver grabbed at the tiller and shrank against the window, watching Retief with one eye, driving with the other.

"To gun this thing," Retief said. "To keep moving."

Shluh stirred on the floor. Retief put a foot on him, pressed him back. The cop beside Retief moved. Retief pushed him off the seat onto the floor.

He held the scatter-gun with one hand and mopped at the blood on his face with the other. The car bounded over the irregular surface of the road, puffing furiously.

"Your death will not be an easy one, Terrestrial," Shluh said in Terran.

"No easier than I can help," Retief said. "Shut up for now, I want to think."

* * * *

The car passed the last of the relief-crusted mounds, sped along between tilled fields.

"Slow down," Retief said. The driver obeyed.

"Turn down this side road."

The car bumped off onto an unpaved surface, threaded its way back among tall stalks.

"Stop here." The car stopped. It blew off steam and sat trembling as the hot engine idled roughly.

Retief opened the door, took his foot off Shluh.

"Sit up," he ordered. "You two in front listen carefully." Shluh sat up, rubbing his throat.

"Three of you are getting out here," Retief said. "Good old Shluh is going to stick around to drive for me. If I get that nervous feeling that the cops are after me, I'll toss him out to confuse them. That will be pretty messy, at high speed. Shluh, tell them to sit tight until dark and forget about sounding any alarms. I'd hate to see your carapace split and spill loveable you all over the pavement."

"To burst your throat sac, evil-smelling beast!" Shluh hissed.

"Sorry, I haven't got one." Retief put the gun under Shluh's ear. "Tell them, Shluh. I can drive myself, in a pinch."

"To do as the foreign one says; to stay hidden until dark," Shluh said.

"Everybody out," Retief said. "And take this with you." He nudged the unconscious Groacian. "Shluh, you get in the driver's seat. You others stay where I can see you."

Retief watched as the Groaci silently followed instructions.

"All right, Shluh," Retief said softly. "Let's go. Take me to Groac Spaceport by the shortest route that doesn't go through the city. And be very careful about making any sudden movements."

* * * *

Forty minutes later, Shluh steered the car up to the sentry-guarded gate in the security fence surrounding the military enclosure at Groac Spaceport.

"Don't yield to any rash impulses," Retief whispered as a crested Groacian soldier came up. Shluh grated his mandibles in helpless fury.

"Drone-master Shluh, Internal Security," he croaked. The guard tilted his eyes toward Retief.

"The guest of the Autonomy," Shluh added. "To let me pass or to rot in this spot, fool?"

"To pass, Drone-master," the sentry mumbled. He was still staring at Retief as the car moved jerkily away.

"You are as good as pegged out on the hill in the pleasure pits now, Terrestrial," Shluh said in Terran. "Why do you venture here?"

"Pull over there in the shadow of the tower and stop," Retief said.

Shluh complied. Retief studied the row of four slender ships parked on the ramp, navigation lights picked out against the early dawn colors of the sky.

"Which of those boats are ready to lift?" Retief demanded.

Shluh swiveled a choleric eye.

"All of them are shuttles; they have no range. They will not help you."

"To answer the question, Shluh, or to get another crack on the head."

"You are not like other Terrestrials! You are a mad dog!"

"We'll rough out a character sketch of me later. Are they all fueled up? You know the procedures here. Did those shuttles just get in, or is that the ready line?"

"Yes. All are fueled and ready for take-off."

"I hope you're right, Shluh. You and I are going to drive over and get in one; if it doesn't lift, I'll kill you and try the next. Let's go."

"You are mad! I have told you—these boats have not more than ten thousand ton-seconds capacity. They are useful only for satellite runs."

"Never mind the details. Let's try the first in line."

Shluh let in the clutch and the steam car clanked and heaved, rolled off toward the line of boats.

"Not the first in line," Shluh said suddenly. "The last is the more likely to be fueled. But—"

"Smart grasshopper," Retief said. "Pull up to the entry port, hop out and go right up. I'll be right behind you."

"The gangway guard. The challenging of—"

"More details. Just give him a dirty look and say what's necessary. You know the technique."

* * * *

The car passed under the stern of the first boat, then the second. There was no alarm. It rounded the third and shuddered to a stop by the open port of the last vessel.

"Out," Retief said. "To make it snappy."

Shluh stepped from the car, hesitated as the guard came to attention, then hissed at him and mounted the steps. The guard looked wonderingly at Retief, mandibles slack.

"An outworlder!" he said. He unlimbered his scatter-gun. "To stop here, meat-faced one."

Shluh froze, turned.

"To snap to attention, litter-mate of drones!" Retief rasped in Groacian. The guard jumped, waved his eye stalks and came to attention.

"About face!" Retief hissed. "Hell out of here—to march!"

The guard tramped off across the ramp. Retief took the steps two at a time, slammed the port shut behind himself.

"I'm glad your boys have a little discipline, Shluh," Retief said. "What did you say to him?"

"I but—"

"Never mind. We're in. Get up to the control compartment."

"What do you know of Groacian naval vessels?"

"Plenty. This is a straight copy from the lifeboat you lads hijacked. I can run it. Get going."

Retief followed Shluh up the companionway into the cramped control room.

"Tie in, Shluh," Retief ordered.

"This is insane!" Shluh said. "We have only fuel enough for a one-way transit to the satellite. We cannot enter orbit, nor can we land again! To lift this boat is death—unless your destination is our moon."

"The moon is down, Shluh," Retief said. "And so are we. But not for long. Tie in."

"Release me," Shluh gasped. "I promise you immunity."

"If I have to tie you in myself, I might bend your head in the process."

Shluh crawled onto the couch, strapped in.

"Give it up," he said. "I will see that you are reinstated—with honor! I will guarantee a safe conduct."

"Countdown," Retief said. He threw in the autopilot.

"It is death!" Shluh screeched.

The gyros hummed; timers ticked; relays closed. Retief lay relaxed on the acceleration pad. Shluh breathed noisily, his mandibles clicking rapidly.

"That I had fled in time," Shluh said in a hoarse whisper. "This is not a good death...."

"No death is a good death," Retief said. "Not for a while yet." The red light flashed on in the center of the panel, and abruptly sound filled the universe. The ship trembled, lifted.

Retief could hear Shluh's whimpering even through the roar of the drive.

"Perihelion," Shluh said dully. "To begin now the long fall back."

"Not quite," Retief said. "I figure eighty-five seconds to go." He scanned the instruments, frowning.

"We will not reach the surface, of course," Shluh said in Terran. "The pips on the screen are missiles. We have a rendezvous in space, Retief. In your madness, may you be content."

"They're fifteen minutes behind us, Shluh. Your defenses are sluggish."

"Nevermore to burrow in the gray sands of Groac," Shluh said.

Retief's eyes were fixed on a dial face.

"Any time now," he said softly. Shluh counted his eye stalks.

"What do you seek?"

Retief stiffened.

"Look at the screen," he said. Shluh looked. A glowing point, off-center, moving rapidly across the grid....

"What—"

"Later!"

Shluh watched as Retief's eyes darted from one needle to another.

"How...."

"For your own neck's sake, Shluh," Retief said, "you'd better hope this works." He flipped the sending key.

"2396 TR-42 G, this is the Terrestrial Consul at Groac, aboard Groac 902, vectoring on you at an MP fix of 91/54/94. Can you read me? Over."

"What forlorn gesture is this?" Shluh whispered. "You cry in the night to emptiness!"

"Button your mandibles," Retief snapped, listening. There was a faint hum of stellar background noise. Retief repeated his call, waited.

"Maybe they hear but can't answer," he muttered. He flipped the key.

"2396, you've got twenty seconds to lock a tractor beam on me, or I'll be past you like a shot of rum past a sailor's bridgework...."

"To call into the void!" Shluh said. "To—"

"Look at the DV screen."

* * * *

Shluh twisted his head, looked. Against the background mist of stars, a shape loomed, dark and inert.

"It is...a ship!" Shluh said. "A monster ship!"

"That's her," Retief said. "Nine years and a few months out of New Terra on a routine mapping mission. The missing cruiser—the IVS *Terrific*."

"Impossible!" Shluh hissed. "The hulk swings in a deep cometary orbit."

"Right. And now it's making its close swing past Groac."

"You think to match orbits with the derelict? Without power? Our meeting will be a violent one, if that is your intent."

"We won't hit; we'll make our pass at about five thousand yards."

"To what end, Terrestrial? You have found your lost ship. Then what? Is this glimpse worth the death we die?"

"Maybe they're not dead," Retief said.

"Not dead?" Shluh lapsed into Groacian. "To have died in the burrow of one's youth. To have burst my throat sac ere I embarked with a mad alien to call up the dead."

"2396, make it snappy," Retief called. The speaker crackled heedlessly. The dark image on the screen drifted past, dwindling now.

"Nine years, and the mad one speaking as to friends," Shluh raved. "Nine years dead, and still to seek them."

"Another twenty seconds," Retief said softly, "and we're out of range. Look alive, boys."

"Was this your plan, Retief?" Shluh asked in Terran. "Did you flee Groac and risk all on this slender thread?"

"How long would I have lasted in one of your Groaci prisons?"

"Long and long, my Retief," Shluh hissed, "under the blade of an artist."

Abruptly, the ship trembled, seemed to drag, rolling the two passengers in their couches. Shluh hissed as the restraining harness cut into him. The shuttle boat was pivoting heavily, upending. Crushing acceleration forces built. Shluh gasped and cried out shrilly.

"What…is…it?"

"It looks," Retief said, "like we've had a little bit of luck."

V

"On our second pass," the gaunt-faced officer said, "they let fly with something. I don't know how it got past our screens. It socked home in the stern and put the main pipe off the air. I threw full power to the emergency shields, and broadcast our identification on a scatter that should have hit every receiver within a parsec. Nothing. Then the transmitter blew. I was a fool to send the boat down but I couldn't believe, somehow…."

"In a way it's lucky you did, Captain. That was my only lead."

"They tried to finish us after that. But with full power to the screens, nothing they had could get through. Then they called on us to surrender."

Retief nodded. "I take it you weren't tempted?"

"More than you know. It was a long swing out on our first circuit. Then, coming back in, we figured we'd hit. As a last resort I would have pulled back power from the screens and tried to adjust the orbit with the steering jets. But the bombardment was pretty heavy; I don't think we'd have made it. Then we swung past and headed out again. We've got a three year period. Don't think I didn't consider giving up."

"Why didn't you?"

"The information we have is important. We've got plenty of stores aboard. Enough for another ten years, if necessary. Sooner or later, I knew Search Command would find us."

Retief cleared his throat. "I'm glad you stuck with it, Captain. Even a backwater world like Groac can kill a lot of people when it runs amok."

"What I didn't know," the captain went on, "was that we're not in a stable orbit. We're going to graze atmosphere pretty deeply this pass, and in another sixty days we'd be back to stay. I guess the Groaci would be ready for us."

"No wonder they were sitting on this so tight," Retief said. "They were almost in the clear."

"And you're here now," the captain said. "Nine years, and we weren't forgotten. I knew we could count on—"

"It's over now, Captain," Retief said. "That's what counts."

"Home," the captain said. "After nine years...."

* * * *

"I'd like to take a look at the films you mentioned," Retief said. "The ones showing the installations on the satellite."

The captain complied. Retief watched as the scene unrolled, showing the bleak surface of the tiny moon as the *Terrific* had seen it nine years before.

In harsh black and white, row on row of identical hulls cast long shadows across the pitted metallic surface of the satellite. Retief whistled.

"They had quite a little surprise in store. Your visit must have panicked them."

"They should be about ready to go, by now. Nine years...."

"Hold the picture," Retief said suddenly. "What's that ragged black line across the plain there?"

"I think it's a fissure. The crystalline structure—"

"I've got what may be an idea," Retief said. "I had a look at some classified files last night, at the foreign office. One was a progress report on a fissionable stockpile. It didn't make much sense at the time. Now I get the picture. Which is the 'north' end of that crevasse?"

"At the top of the picture."

"Unless I'm badly mistaken, that's the bomb dump. The Groaci like to tuck things underground. I wonder what a direct hit with a fifty mega-ton missile would do to it?"

"If that's an ordnance storage dump," the captain said, "it's an experiment I'd like to try."

"Can you hit it?"

"I've got fifty heavy missiles aboard. If I fire them in direct sequence, it should saturate the defenses. Yes, I can hit it."

"The range isn't too great?"

"These are the de luxe models," the captain smiled balefully. "Video guidance. We could steer them into a bar and park 'em on a stool."

"What do you say we try it?"

"I've been wanting a solid target for a long time," the captain said.

* * * *

Retief waved a hand toward the screen.

"That expanding dust cloud used to be the satellite of Groac, Shluh," he said. "Looks like something happened to it."

The police chief stared at the picture.

"Too bad," Retief said. "But then it wasn't of any importance, was it, Shluh?"

Shluh muttered incomprehensibly.

"Just a bare hunk of iron, Shluh. That's what the foreign office told me when I asked for information."

"I wish you'd keep your prisoner out of sight," the captain said. "I have a hard time keeping my hands off him."

"Shluh wants to help, Captain. He's been a bad boy and I have a feeling he'd like to cooperate with us now. Especially in view of the imminent arrival of a Terrestrial ship, and the dust cloud out there."

"What do you mean?"

"Captain, you can ride it out for another week, contact the ship when it arrives, get a tow in and your troubles are over. When your films are shown in the proper quarter, a task force will come out here. They'll reduce Groac to a sub-technical cultural level, and set up a monitor system to insure she doesn't get any more expansionist ideas. Not that she can do much now, with her handy iron mine in the sky gone."

"That's right; and—"

"On the other hand," Retief said, "there's what I might call the diplomatic approach...."

He explained at length. The captain looked at him thoughtfully.

"I'll go along," he said. "What about this fellow?"

Retief turned to Shluh. The Groacian shuddered, eye stalks retracted.

"I will do it," he said faintly.

"Right," Retief said. "Captain, if you'll have your men bring in the transmitter from the shuttle, I'll place a call to a fellow named Fith at the foreign office." He turned to Shluh. "And when I get him, Shluh, you'll do everything exactly as I've told you—or have terrestrial monitors dictating in Groac City."

* * * *

"Quite candidly, Retief," Counsellor Pardy said, "I'm rather non-plussed. Mr. Fith of the foreign office seemed almost painfully lavish in your praise. He seems most eager to please you. In the light of some of the evidence I've turned up of highly irregular behavior on your part, it's difficult to understand."

"Fith and I have been through a lot together," Retief said. "We understand each other."

"You have no cause for complacency, Retief," Pardy said. "Miss Meuhl was quite justified in reporting your case. Of course, had she known that you were assisting Mr. Fith in his marvelous work, she would have modified her report somewhat, no doubt. You should have confided in her."

"Fith wanted to keep it secret, in case it didn't work out," Retief said. "You know how it is."

"Of course. And as soon as Miss Meuhl recovers from her nervous breakdown, there'll be a nice promotion awaiting her. The girl more than deserves it for her years of unswerving devotion to Corps policy."

"Unswerving," Retief said. "I'll sure go along with that."

"As well you may, Retief. You've not acquitted yourself well in this assignment. I'm arranging for a transfer. You've alienated too many of the local people...."

"But as you said, Fith speaks highly of me...."

"Oh, true. It's the cultural intelligentsia I'm referring to. Miss Meuhl's records show that you deliberately affronted a number of influential groups by boycotting—"

"Tone deaf," Retief said. "To me a Groacian blowing a nose-whistle sounds like a Groacian blowing a nose-whistle."

"You have to come to terms with local aesthetic values," Pardy explained. "Learn to know the people as they really are. It's apparent from some of the remarks Miss Meuhl quoted in her report that you held the Groaci in rather low esteem. But how wrong you were! All the while, they were working unceasingly to rescue those brave lads marooned aboard our cruiser. They pressed on even after we ourselves had abandoned the search. And when they discovered that it had been a collision with their satellite which disabled the craft, they made that magnificent gesture—unprecedented. One hundred thousand credits in gold to each crew member, as a token of Groacian sympathy."

"A handsome gesture," Retief murmured.

* * * *

"I hope, Retief, that you've learned from this incident. In view of the helpful part you played in advising Mr. Fith in matters of procedure to assist in his search, I'm not recommending a reduction in grade. We'll overlook the affair, give you a clean slate. But in future, I'll be watching you closely."

"You can't win 'em all," Retief said.

"You'd better pack up. You'll be coming along with us in the morning." Pardy shuffled his papers together.

"I'm sorry," he said, "that I can't file a more flattering report on you. I would have liked to recommend your promotion, along with Miss Meuhl's."

"That's okay," Retief said. "I have my memories."

RETIEF OF THE RED-TAPE MOUNTAIN

Originally published in **Worlds of If Science Fiction,** *May 1962.*

"It's true," Consul Passwyn said, "I requested assignment as principal officer at a small post. But I had in mind one of those charming resort worlds, with only an occasional visa problem, or perhaps a distressed spaceman or two a year. Instead, I'm zoo-keeper to these confounded settlers. And not for one world, mind you, but eight!" He stared glumly at Vice-Consul Retief.

"Still," Retief said, "it gives an opportunity to travel—"

"Travel!" the consul barked. "I hate travel. Here in this backwater system particularly—" He paused, blinked at Retief and cleared his throat. "Not that a bit of travel isn't an excellent thing for a junior officer. Marvelous experience."

He turned to the wall-screen and pressed a button. A system triagram appeared: eight luminous green dots arranged around a larger disk representing the primary. He picked up a pointer, indicating the innermost planet.

"The situation on Adobe is nearing crisis. The confounded settlers—a mere handful of them—have managed, as usual, to stir up trouble with an intelligent indigenous life form, the Jaq. I can't think why they bother, merely for a few oases among the endless deserts. However I have, at last, received authorization from Sector Headquarters to take certain action." He swung back to face Retief. "I'm sending you in to handle the situation, Retief—under sealed orders." He picked up a fat buff envelope. "A pity they didn't see fit to order the Terrestrial settlers out weeks ago, as I suggested. Now it is too late. I'm expected to produce a miracle—a rapprochement between Terrestrial and Adoban and a division of territory. It's idiotic. However, failure would look very bad in my record, so I shall expect results."

He passed the buff envelope across to Retief.

"I understood that Adobe was uninhabited," Retief said, "until the Terrestrial settlers arrived."

"Apparently, that was an erroneous impression." Passwyn fixed Retief with a watery eye. "You'll follow your instructions to the letter. In a delicate situation such as this, there must be no impulsive, impromptu element introduced. This approach has been worked out in detail at Sector. You need merely implement it. Is that entirely clear?"

"Has anyone at Headquarters ever visited Adobe?"

"Of course not. They all hate travel. If there are no other questions, you'd best be on your way. The mail run departs the dome in less than an hour."

"What's this native life form like?" Retief asked, getting to his feet.

"When you get back," said Passwyn, "you tell me."

* * * *

The mail pilot, a leathery veteran with quarter-inch whiskers, spat toward a stained corner of the compartment, leaned close to the screen.

"They's shootin' goin' on down there," he said. "See them white puffs over the edge of the desert?"

"I'm supposed to be preventing the war," said Retief. "It looks like I'm a little late."

The pilot's head snapped around. "War?" he yelped. "Nobody told me they was a war goin' on on 'Dobe. If that's what that is, I'm gettin' out of here."

"Hold on," said Retief. "I've got to get down. They won't shoot at you."

"They shore won't, sonny. I ain't givin' 'em the chance." He started punching keys on the console. Retief reached out, caught his wrist.

"Maybe you didn't hear me. I said I've got to get down."

The pilot plunged against the restraint, swung a punch that Retief blocked casually. "Are you nuts?" the pilot screeched. "They's plenty shootin' goin' on fer me to see it fifty miles out."

"The mail must go through, you know."

"Okay! You're so dead set on gettin' killed, you take the skiff. I'll tell 'em to pick up the remains next trip."

"You're a pal. I'll take your offer."

The pilot jumped to the lifeboat hatch and cycled it open. "Get in. We're closin' fast. Them birds might take it into their heads to lob one this way...."

Retief crawled into the narrow cockpit of the skiff, glanced over the controls. The pilot ducked out of sight, came back, handed Retief a heavy old-fashioned power pistol. "Long as you're goin' in, might as well take this."

"Thanks." Retief shoved the pistol in his belt. "I hope you're wrong."

"I'll see they pick you up when the shootin's over—one way or another."

The hatch clanked shut. A moment later there was a jar as the skiff dropped away, followed by heavy buffeting in the backwash from the departing mail boat. Retief watched the tiny screen, hands on the manual controls. He was dropping rapidly: forty miles, thirty-nine....

A crimson blip showed on the screen, moving out.

Retief felt sweat pop out on his forehead. The red blip meant heavy radiation from a warhead. Somebody was playing around with an outlawed but by no means unheard of fission weapon. But maybe it was just on a high trajectory and had no connection with the skiff....

Retief altered course to the south. The blip followed.

He checked instrument readings, gripped the controls, watching. This was going to be tricky. The missile bored closer. At five miles Retief threw the light skiff into maximum acceleration, straight toward the oncoming bomb. Crushed back in the padded seat, he watched the screen, correcting course minutely. The proximity fuse should be set for no more than 1000 yards.

At a combined speed of two miles per second, the skiff flashed past the missile, and Retief was slammed violently against the restraining harness in the concussion of the explosion...a mile astern, and harmless.

Then the planetary surface was rushing up with frightening speed. Retief shook his head, kicked in the emergency retro-drive. Points of light arced up from the planet face below. If they were ordinary chemical warheads the skiff's meteor screens should handle them. The screen flashed brilliant white, then went dark. The skiff flipped on its back. Smoke filled the tiny compartment. There was a series of shocks, a final bone-shaking concussion, then stillness, broken by the ping of hot metal contracting.

* * * *

Coughing, Retief disengaged himself from the shock-webbing. He beat out sparks in his lap, groped underfoot for the hatch and wrenched it open. A wave of hot jungle air struck him. He lowered himself to a bed of shattered foliage, got to his feet...and dropped flat as a bullet whined past his ear.

He lay listening. Stealthy movements were audible from the left.

He inched his way to the shelter of a broad-boled dwarf tree. Somewhere a song lizard burbled. Whining insects circled, scented alien life, buzzed off. There was another rustle of foliage from the underbrush five yards away. A bush quivered, then a low bough dipped.

Retief edged back around the trunk, eased down behind a fallen log. A stocky man in grimy leather shirt and shorts appeared, moving cautiously, a pistol in his hand.

As he passed, Retief rose, leaped the log and tackled him.

They went down together. The stranger gave one short yell, then struggled in silence. Retief flipped him onto his back, raised a fist—

"Hey!" the settler yelled. "You're as human as I am!"

"Maybe I'll look better after a shave," said Retief. "What's the idea of shooting at me?"

"Lemme up. My name's Potter. Sorry 'bout that. I figured it was a Flap-jack boat; looks just like 'em. I took a shot when I saw something move. Didn't know it was a Terrestrial. Who are you? What you doin' here? We're pretty close to the edge of the oases. That's Flap-jack country over there." He waved a hand toward the north, where the desert lay.

"I'm glad you're a poor shot. That missile was too close for comfort."

"Missile, eh? Must be Flap-jack artillery. We got nothing like that."

"I heard there was a full-fledged war brewing," said Retief. "I didn't expect—"

"Good!" Potter said. "We figured a few of you boys from Ivory would be joining up when you heard. You are from Ivory?"

"Yes. I'm—"

"Hey, you must be Lemuel's cousin. Good night! I pretty near made a bad mistake. Lemuel's a tough man to explain something to."

"I'm—"

"Keep your head down. These damn Flap-jacks have got some wicked hand weapons. Come on...." He moved off silently on all fours. Retief followed. They crossed two hundred yards of rough country before Potter got to his feet, took out a soggy bandana and mopped his face.

"You move good for a city man. I thought you folks on Ivory just sat under those domes and read dials. But I guess bein' Lemuel's cousin you was raised different."

"As a matter of fact—"

"Have to get you some real clothes, though. Those city duds don't stand up on 'Dobe."

Retief looked down at the charred, torn and sweat-soaked powder-blue blazer and slacks.

"This outfit seemed pretty rough-and-ready back home," he said. "But I guess leather has its points."

"Let's get on back to camp. We'll just about make it by sundown. And, look. Don't say anything to Lemuel about me thinking you were a Flap-jack."

"I won't, but—"

Potter was on his way, loping off up a gentle slope. Retief pulled off the sodden blazer, dropped it over a bush, added his string tie and followed Potter.

II

"We're damn glad you're here, mister," said a fat man with two revolvers belted across his paunch. "We can use every hand. We're in bad shape.

We ran into the Flap-jacks three months ago and we haven't made a smart move since. First, we thought they were a native form we hadn't run into before. Fact is, one of the boys shot one, thinkin' it was fair game. I guess that was the start of it." He stirred the fire, added a stick.

"And then a bunch of 'em hit Swazey's farm here," Potter said. "Killed two of his cattle, and pulled back."

"I figure they thought the cows were people," said Swazey. "They were out for revenge."

"How could anybody think a cow was folks?" another man put in. "They don't look nothin' like—"

"Don't be so dumb, Bert," said Swazey. "They'd never seen Terries before. They know better now."

Bert chuckled. "Sure do. We showed 'em the next time, didn't we, Potter? Got four."

"They walked right up to my place a couple days after the first time," Swazey said. "We were ready for 'em. Peppered 'em good. They cut and run."

"Flopped, you mean. Ugliest lookin' critters you ever saw. Look just like a old piece of dirty blanket humpin' around."

"It's been goin' on this way ever since. They raid and then we raid. But lately they've been bringing some big stuff into it. They've got some kind of pint-sized airships and automatic rifles. We've lost four men now and a dozen more in the freezer, waiting for the med ship. We can't afford it. The colony's got less than three hundred able-bodied men."

"But we're hanging onto our farms," said Potter. "All these oases are old sea-beds—a mile deep, solid topsoil. And there's a couple of hundred others we haven't touched yet. The Flap-jacks won't get 'em while there's a man alive."

"The whole system needs the food we can raise," Bert said. "These farms we're trying to start won't be enough but they'll help."

"We been yellin' for help to the CDT, over on Ivory," said Potter. "But you know these Embassy stooges."

"We heard they were sending some kind of bureaucrat in here to tell us to get out and give the oases to the Flap-jacks," said Swazey. He tightened his mouth. "We're waitin' for him...."

"Meanwhile we got reinforcements comin' up, eh, boys?" Bert winked at Retief. "We put out the word back home. We all got relatives on Ivory and Verde."

"Shut up, you damn fool!" a deep voice grated.

"Lemuel!" Potter said. "Nobody else could sneak up on us like that."

"If I'd a been a Flap-jack; I'd of et you alive," the newcomer said, moving into the ring of fire, a tall, broad-faced man in grimy leather. He eyed Retief.

"Who's that?"

"What do ya mean?" Potter spoke in the silence. "He's your cousin...."

"He ain't no cousin of mine," Lemuel said slowly. He stepped to Retief.

"Who you spyin' for, stranger?" he rasped.

Retief got to his feet. "I think I should explain—"

A short-nosed automatic appeared in Lemuel's hand, a clashing note against his fringed buckskins.

"Skip the talk. I know a fink when I see one."

"Just for a change, I'd like to finish a sentence," said Retief. "And I suggest you put your courage back in your pocket before it bites you."

"You talk too damned fancy to suit me."

"Maybe. But I'm talking to suit me. Now, for the last time, put it away."

Lemuel stared at Retief. "You givin' me orders...?"

Retief's left fist shot out, smacked Lemuel's face dead center. He stumbled back, blood starting from his nose; the pistol fired into the dirt as he dropped it. He caught himself, jumped for Retief...and met a straight right that snapped him onto his back: out cold.

"Wow!" said Potter. "The stranger took Lem...in two punches!"

"One," said Swazey. "That first one was just a love tap."

Bert froze. "Hark, boys," he whispered. In the sudden silence a night lizard called. Retief strained, heard nothing. He narrowed his eyes, peered past the fire—

With a swift lunge he seized up the bucket of drinking water, dashed it over the fire, threw himself flat. He heard the others hit the dirt a split second behind him.

"You move fast for a city man," breathed Swazey beside him. "You see pretty good too. We'll split and take 'em from two sides. You and Bert from the left, me and Potter from the right."

"No," said Retief. "You wait here. I'm going out alone."

"What's the idea...?"

"Later. Sit tight and keep your eyes open." Retief took a bearing on a treetop faintly visible against the sky and started forward.

* * * *

Five minutes' stealthy progress brought him to a slight rise of ground. With infinite caution he raised himself, risking a glance over an out-cropping of rock.

The stunted trees ended just ahead. Beyond, he could make out the dim contour of rolling desert. Flap-jack country. He got to his feet, clambered over the stone—still hot after a day of tropical heat—and moved forward twenty yards. Around him he saw nothing but drifted sand, palely visible in the starlight, and the occasional shadow of jutting shale slabs. Behind him the jungle was still.

He sat down on the ground to wait.

It was ten minutes before a movement caught his eye. Something had separated itself from a dark mass of stone, glided across a few yards of open ground to another shelter. Retief watched. Minutes passed. The shape moved again, slipped into a shadow ten feet distant. Retief felt the butt of the power pistol with his elbow. His guess had better be right this time....

There was a sudden rasp, like leather against concrete, and a flurry of sand as the Flap-jack charged.

Retief rolled aside, then lunged, threw his weight on the flopping Flap-jack—a yard square, three inches thick at the center and all muscle. The ray-like creature heaved up, curled backward, its edge rippling, to stand on the flattened rim of its encircling sphincter. It scrabbled with prehensile fringe-tentacles for a grip on Retief's shoulders. He wrapped his arms around the alien and struggled to his feet. The thing was heavy. A hundred pounds at least. Fighting as it was, it seemed more like five hundred.

The Flap-jack reversed its tactics, went limp. Retief grabbed, felt a thumb slip into an orifice—

The alien went wild. Retief hung on, dug the thumb in deeper.

"Sorry, fellow," he muttered between clenched teeth. "Eye-gouging isn't gentlemanly, but it's effective...."

The Flap-jack fell still, only its fringes rippling slowly. Retief relaxed the pressure of his thumb; the alien gave a tentative jerk; the thumb dug in.

The alien went limp again, waiting.

"Now we understand each other," said Retief. "Take me to your leader."

* * * *

Twenty minutes' walk into the desert brought Retief to a low rampart of thorn branches: the Flap-jacks' outer defensive line against Terry forays. It would be as good a place as any to wait for the move by the Flap-jacks. He sat down and eased the weight of his captive off his back, but kept a firm thumb in place. If his analysis of the situation was correct, a Flap-jack picket should be along before too long....

A penetrating beam of red light struck Retief in the face, blinked off. He got to his feet. The captive Flap-jack rippled its fringe in an agitated way. Retief tensed his thumb in the eye-socket.

"Sit tight," he said. "Don't try to do anything hasty...." His remarks were falling on deaf ears—or no ears at all—but the thumb spoke as loudly as words.

There was a slither of sand. Another. He became aware of a ring of presences drawing closer.

Retief tightened his grip on the alien. He could see a dark shape now, looming up almost to his own six-three. It looked like the Flap-jacks came in all sizes.

A low rumble sounded, like a deep-throated growl. It strummed on, faded out. Retief cocked his head, frowning.

"Try it two octaves higher," he said.

"Awwrrp! Sorry. Is that better?" a clear voice came from the darkness.

"That's fine," Retief said. "I'm here to arrange a prisoner exchange."

"Prisoners? But we have no prisoners."

"Sure you have. Me. Is it a deal?"

"Ah, yes, of course. Quite equitable. What guarantees do you require?"

"The word of a gentleman is sufficient." Retief released the alien. It flopped once, disappeared into the darkness.

"If you'd care to accompany me to our headquarters," the voice said, "we can discuss our mutual concerns in comfort."

"Delighted."

Red lights blinked briefly. Retief glimpsed a gap in the thorny barrier, stepped through it. He followed dim shapes across warm sand to a low cave-like entry, faintly lit with a reddish glow.

"I must apologize for the awkward design of our comfort-dome," said the voice. "Had we known we would be honored by a visit—"

"Think nothing of it," Retief said. "We diplomats are trained to crawl."

Inside, with knees bent and head ducked under the five-foot ceiling, Retief looked around at the walls of pink-toned nacre, a floor like burgundy-colored glass spread with silken rugs and a low table of polished red granite that stretched down the center of the spacious room, set out with silver dishes and rose-crystal drinking-tubes.

III

"Let me congratulate you," the voice said.

Retief turned. An immense Flap-jack, hung with crimson trappings, rippled at his side. The voice issued from a disk strapped to its back. "You fight well. I think we will find in each other worthy adversaries."

"Thanks. I'm sure the test would be interesting, but I'm hoping we can avoid it."

"Avoid it?" Retief heard a low humming coming from the speaker in the silence. "Well, let us dine," the mighty Flap-jack said at last. "We can resolve these matters later. I am called Hoshick of the Mosaic of the Two Dawns."

"I'm Retief." Hoshick waited expectantly, "... of the Mountain of Red Tape," Retief added.

"Take place, Retief," said Hoshick. "I hope you won't find our rude couches uncomfortable." Two other large Flap-jacks came into the room, communed silently with Hoshick. "Pray forgive our lack of translating devices," he said to Retief. "Permit me to introduce my colleagues...."

A small Flap-jack rippled the chamber bearing on its back a silver tray laden with aromatic food. The waiter served the four diners, filled the drinking tubes with yellow wine. It smelled good.

"I trust you'll find these dishes palatable," said Hoshick. "Our metabolisms are much alike, I believe." Retief tried the food. It had a delicious nut-like flavor. The wine was indistinguishable from Chateau d'Yquem.

"It was an unexpected pleasure to encounter your party here," said Hoshick. "I confess at first we took you for an indigenous earth-grubbing form, but we were soon disabused of that notion." He raised a tube, manipulating it deftly with his fringe tentacles. Retief returned the salute and drank.

"Of course," Hoshick continued, "as soon as we realized that you were sportsmen like ourselves, we attempted to make amends by providing a bit of activity for you. We've ordered out our heavier equipment and a few trained skirmishers and soon we'll be able to give you an adequate show. Or so I hope."

"Additional skirmishers?" said Retief. "How many, if you don't mind my asking?"

"For the moment, perhaps only a few hundred. There-after...well, I'm sure we can arrange that between us. Personally I would prefer a contest of limited scope. No nuclear or radiation-effect weapons. Such a bore, screening the spawn for deviations. Though I confess we've come upon some remarkably useful sports. The rangerform such as you made captive, for example. Simple-minded, of course, but a fantastically keen tracker."

"Oh, by all means," Retief said. "No atomics. As you pointed out, spawn-sorting is a nuisance, and then too, it's wasteful of troops."

"Ah, well, they are after all expendable. But we agree: no atomics. Have you tried the ground-gwack eggs? Rather a specialty of my Mosaic...."

"Delicious," said Retief. "I wonder. Have you considered eliminating weapons altogether?"

* * * *

A scratchy sound issued from the disk. "Pardon my laughter," Hoshick said, "but surely you jest?"

"As a matter of fact," said Retief, "we ourselves seldom use weapons."

"I seem to recall that our first contact of skirmishforms involved the use of a weapon by one of your units."

"My apologies," said Retief. "The—ah—the skirmishform failed to recognize that he was dealing with a sportsman."

"Still, now that we have commenced so merrily with weapons...." Hoshick signaled and the servant refilled tubes.

"There is an aspect I haven't yet mentioned," Retief went on. "I hope you won't take this personally, but the fact is, our skirmishforms think of weapons as something one employs only in dealing with certain specific life-forms."

"Oh? Curious. What forms are those?"

"Vermin. Or 'varmints' as some call them. Deadly antagonists, but lacking in caste. I don't want our skirmishforms thinking of such worthy adversaries as yourself as varmints."

"Dear me! I hadn't realized, of course. Most considerate of you to point it out." Hoshick clucked in dismay. "I see that skirmishforms are much the same among you as with us: lacking in perception." He laughed scratchily. "Imagine considering us as—what was the word?—varmints."

"Which brings us to the crux of the matter. You see, we're up against a serious problem with regard to skirmishforms. A low birth rate. Therefore we've reluctantly taken to substitutes for the mass actions so dear to the heart of the sportsman. We've attempted to put an end to these contests altogether...."

Hoshick coughed explosively, sending a spray of wine into the air. "What are you saying?" he gasped. "Are you proposing that Hoshick of the Mosaic of the Two Dawns abandon honor....?"

"Sir!" said Retief sternly. "You forget yourself. I, Retief of the Red Tape Mountain, make an alternate proposal more in keeping with the newest sporting principles."

"New?" cried Hoshick. "My dear Retief, what a pleasant surprise! I'm enthralled with novel modes. One gets so out of touch. Do elaborate."

"It's quite simple, really. Each side selects a representative and the two individuals settle the issue between them."

"I...um...fear I don't understand. What possible significance could one attach to the activities of a couple of random skirmishforms?"

"I haven't made myself clear," said Retief. He took a sip of wine. "We don't involve the skirmishforms at all. That's quite passe."

"You don't mean...?"

"That's right. You and me."

* * * *

Outside on the starlit sand Retief tossed aside the power pistol, followed it with the leather shirt Swazey had lent him. By the faint light he could just make out the towering figure of the Flap-jack rearing up before him, his trappings gone. A silent rank of Flap-jack retainers were grouped behind him.

"I fear I must lay aside the translator now, Retief," said Hoshick. He sighed and rippled his fringe tentacles. "My spawn-fellows will never credit this. Such a curious turn fashion has taken. How much more pleasant it is to observe the action of the skirmishforms from a distance."

"I suggest we use Tennessee rules," said Retief. "They're very liberal. Biting, gouging, stomping, kneeing and of course choking, as well as the usual punching, shoving and kicking."

"Hmmm. These gambits seem geared to forms employing rigid endo-skeletons; I fear I shall be at a disadvantage."

"Of course," Retief said, "if you'd prefer a more plebeian type of contest...."

"By no means. But perhaps we could rule out tentacle-twisting, just to even it."

"Very well. Shall we begin?"

With a rush Hoshick threw himself at Retief, who ducked, whirled, and leaped on the Flap-jack's back...and felt himself flipped clear by a mighty ripple of the alien's slab-like body. Retief rolled aside as Hoshick turned on him; he jumped to his feet and threw a right hay-maker to Hoshick's mid-section. The alien whipped his left fringe around in an arc that connected with Retief's jaw, sent him spinning onto his back...and Hoshick's weight struck him.

Retief twisted, tried to roll. The flat body of the alien blanketed him. He worked an arm free, drumming blows on the leathery back. Hoshick nestled closer.

Retief's air was running out. He heaved up against the smothering weight. Nothing budged.

It was like burial under a dump-truck-load of concrete.

He remembered the rangerform he had captured. The sensitive orifice had been placed ventrally, in what would be the thoracic area....

He groped, felt tough hide set with horny granules. He would be missing skin tomorrow...if there was a tomorrow. His thumb found the orifice and probed.

The Flap-jack recoiled. Retief held fast, probed deeper, groping with the other hand. If the alien were bilaterally symmetrical there would be a set of ready made hand-holds....

* * * *

There were.

Retief dug in and the Flap-jack writhed, pulled away. Retief held on, scrambled to his feet, threw his weight against the alien and fell on top of him, still gouging. Hoshick rippled his fringe wildly, flopped in terror, then went limp.

Retief relaxed, released his hold and got to his feet, breathing hard. Hoshick humped himself over onto his ventral side, lifted and moved gingerly over to the sidelines. His retainers came forward, assisted him into his trappings, strapped on the translator. He sighed heavily, adjusted the volume.

"There is much to be said for the old system," he said. "What a burden one's sportsmanship places on one at times."

"Great sport, wasn't it?" said Retief. "Now, I know you'll be eager to continue. If you'll just wait while I run back and fetch some of our gougerforms—"

"May hide-ticks devour the gougerforms!" Hoshick bellowed. "You've given me such a sprong-ache as I'll remember each spawning-time for a year."

"Speaking of hide-ticks," said Retief, "we've developed a biterform—"

"Enough!" Hoshick roared, so loudly that the translator bounced on his hide. "Suddenly I yearn for the crowded yellow sands of Jaq. I had hoped...." He broke off, drew a rasping breath. "I had hoped, Retief," he said, speaking sadly now, "to find a new land here where I might plan my own Mosaic, till these alien sands and bring forth such a crop of paradise-lichen as should glut the markets of a hundred worlds. But my spirit is not equal to the prospect of biterforms and gougerforms without end. I am shamed before you...."

"To tell you the truth, I'm old-fashioned myself. I'd rather watch the action from a distance too."

"But surely your spawn-fellows would never condone such an attitude."

"My spawn-fellows aren't here. And besides, didn't I mention it? No one who's really in the know would think of engaging in competition by mere combat if there were any other way. Now, you mentioned tilling the sand, raising lichens—things like that—"

"That on which we dined but now," said Hoshick, "and from which the wine is made."

"The big news in fashionable diplomacy today is farming competition. Now, if you'd like to take these deserts and raise lichen, we'll promise to stick to the oases and vegetables."

Hoshick curled his back in attention. "Retief, you're quite serious? You would leave all the fair sand hills to us?"

"The whole works, Hoshick. I'll take the oases."

Hoshick rippled his fringes ecstatically. "Once again you have outdone me, Retief," he cried. "This time, in generosity."

"We'll talk over the details later. I'm sure we can establish a set of rules that will satisfy all parties. Now I've got to get back. I think some of the gougerforms are waiting to see me."

IV

It was nearly dawn when Retief gave the whistled signal he had agreed on with Potter, then rose and walked into the camp circle. Swazey stood up.

"There you are," he said. "We been wonderin' whether to go out after you."

Lemuel came forward, one eye black to the cheekbone. He held out a raw-boned hand. "Sorry I jumped you, stranger. Tell you the truth, I thought you was some kind of stool-pigeon from the CDT."

Bert came up behind Lemuel. "How do you know he ain't, Lemuel?" he said. "Maybe he—"

Lemuel floored Bert with a backward sweep of his arm. "Next cotton-picker says some embassy Johnny can cool me gets worse'n that."

"Tell me," said Retief. "How are you boys fixed for wine?"

"Wine? Mister, we been livin' on stump water for a year now. 'Dobe's fatal to the kind of bacteria it takes to ferment likker."

"Try this." Retief handed over a sqat jug. Swazey drew the cork, sniffed, drank and passed it to Lemuel.

"Mister, where'd you get that?"

"The Flap-jacks make it. Here's another question for you: Would you concede a share in this planet to the Flap-jacks in return for a peace guarantee?"

At the end of a half hour of heated debate Lemuel turned to Retief. "We'll make any reasonable deal," he said. "I guess they got as much right here as we have. I think we'd agree to a fifty-fifty split. That'd give about a hundred and fifty oases to each side."

"What would you say to keeping all the oases and giving them the desert?"

Lemuel reached for the wine jug, eyes on Retief. "Keep talkin', mister," he said. "I think you got yourself a deal."

* * * *

Consul Passwyn glanced up at Retief, went on perusing a paper.

"Sit down, Retief," he said absently. "I thought you were over on Pueblo, or Mud-flat, or whatever they call that desert."

"I'm back."

Passwyn eyed him sharply. "Well, well, what is it you need, man? Speak up. Don't expect me to request any military assistance, no matter how things are...."

Retief passed a bundle of documents across the desk. "Here's the Treaty. And a Mutual Assistance Pact declaration and a trade agreement."

"Eh?" Passwyn picked up the papers, riffled through them. He leaned back in his chair, beamed.

"Well, Retief. Expeditiously handled." He stopped, blinked at Retief. "You seem to have a bruise on your jaw. I hope you've been conducting yourself as befits a member of the Embassy staff."

"I attended a sporting event," Retief said. "One of the players got a little excited."

"Well…it's one of the hazards of the profession. One must pretend an interest in such matters." Passwyn rose, extended a hand. "You've done well, my boy. Let this teach you the value of following instructions to the letter."

Outside, by the hall incinerator drop, Retief paused long enough to take from his briefcase a large buff envelope, still sealed, and drop it in the slot.

AIDE MEMOIRE

Originally published in **Worlds of If Science Fiction,** *July 1962.*

I

Across the table from Retief, Ambassador Magnan rustled a stiff sheet of parchment and looked grave.

"This aide memoire," he said, "was just handed to me by the Cultural Attache. It's the third on the subject this week. It refers to the matter of sponsorship of Youth groups—"

"Some youths," Retief said. "Average age, seventy-five."

"The Fustians are a long-lived people," Magnan snapped. "These matters are relative. At seventy-five, a male Fustian is at a trying age—"

"That's right. He'll try anything—in the hope it will maim somebody."

"Precisely the problem," Magnan said. "But the Youth Movement is the important news in today's political situation here on Fust. And sponsorship of Youth groups is a shrewd stroke on the part of the Terrestrial Embassy. At my suggestion, well nigh every member of the mission has leaped at the opportunity to score a few p—that is, cement relations with this emergent power group—the leaders of the future. You, Retief, as Councillor, are the outstanding exception."

"I'm not convinced these hoodlums need my help in organizing their rumbles," Retief said. "Now, if you have a proposal for a pest control group—"

"To the Fustians this is no jesting matter," Magnan cut in. "This group—" he glanced at the paper—"known as the Sexual, Cultural, and Athletic Recreational Society, or SCARS for short, has been awaiting sponsorship for a matter of weeks now."

"Meaning they want someone to buy them a clubhouse, uniforms, equipment and anything else they need to complete their sexual, cultural and athletic development," Retief said.

"If we don't act promptly," Magnan said, "the Groaci Embassy may well anticipate us. They're very active here."

"That's an idea," said Retief. "Let 'em. After awhile they'll go broke instead of us."

"Nonsense. The group requires a sponsor. I can't actually order you to step forward. However...." Magnan let the sentence hang in the air. Retief raised one eyebrow.

"For a minute there," he said, "I thought you were going to make a positive statement."

Magnan leaned back, lacing his fingers over his stomach. "I don't think you'll find a diplomat of my experience doing anything so naive," he said.

"I like the adult Fustians," said Retief. "Too bad they have to lug half a ton of horn around on their backs. I wonder if surgery would help."

"Great heavens, Retief," Magnan sputtered. "I'm amazed that even you would bring up a matter of such delicacy. A race's unfortunate physical characteristics are hardly a fit matter for Terrestrial curiosity."

"Well, of course your experience of the Fustian mentality is greater than mine. I've only been here a month. But it's been my experience, Mr. Ambassador, that few races are above improving on nature. Otherwise you, for example, would be tripping over your beard."

Magnan shuddered. "Please—never mention the idea to a Fustian."

Retief stood. "My own program for the day includes going over to the dockyards. There are some features of this new passenger liner the Fustians are putting together that I want to look into. With your permission, Mr. Ambassador...?"

Magnan snorted. "Your pre-occupation with the trivial disturbs me, Retief. More interest in substantive matters—such as working with Youth groups—would create a far better impression."

"Before getting too involved with these groups, it might be a good idea to find out a little more about them," said Retief. "Who organizes them? There are three strong political parties here on Fust. What's the alignment of this SCARS organization?"

"You forget, these are merely teenagers, so to speak," Magnan said. "Politics mean nothing to them...yet."

"Then there are the Groaci. Why their passionate interest in a two-horse world like Fust? Normally they're concerned with nothing but business. But what has Fust got that they could use?"

"You may rule out the commercial aspect in this instance," said Magnan. "Fust possesses a vigorous steel-age manufacturing economy. The Groaci are barely ahead of them."

"Barely," said Retief. "Just over the line into crude atomics...like fission bombs."

Magnan shook his head, turned back to his papers. "What market exists for such devices on a world at peace? I suggest you address your attention to the less spectacular but more rewarding work of studying the social patterns of the local youth."

"I've studied them," said Retief. "And before I meet any of the local youth socially I want to get myself a good blackjack."

II

Retief left the sprawling bungalow-type building that housed the chancery of the Terrestrial Embassy, swung aboard a passing flat-car and leaned back against the wooden guard rail as the heavy vehicle trundled through the city toward the looming gantries of the shipyards.

It was a cool morning. A light breeze carried the fishy odor of Fusty dwellings across the broad cobbled avenue. A few mature Fustians lumbered heavily along in the shade of the low buildings, audibly wheezing under the burden of their immense carapaces. Among them, shell-less youths trotted briskly on scaly stub legs. The driver of the flat-car, a labor-caste Fustian with his guild colors emblazoned on his back, heaved at the tiller, swung the unwieldy conveyance through the shipyard gates, creaked to a halt.

"Thus I come to the shipyard with frightful speed," he said in Fustian. "Well I know the way of the naked-backs, who move always in haste."

Retief climbed down, handed him a coin. "You should take up professional racing," he said. "Daredevil."

He crossed the littered yard and tapped at the door of a rambling shed. Boards creaked inside. Then the door swung back.

A gnarled ancient with tarnished facial scales and a weathered carapace peered out at Retief.

"Long-may-you-sleep," said Retief. "I'd like to take a look around, if you don't mind. I understand you're laying the bedplate for your new liner today."

"May-you-dream-of-the-deeps," the old fellow mumbled. He waved a stumpy arm toward a group of shell-less Fustians standing by a massive hoist. "The youths know more of bedplates than do I, who but tend the place of papers."

"I know how you feel, old-timer," said Retief. "That sounds like the story of my life. Among your papers do you have a set of plans for the vessel? I understand it's to be a passenger liner."

The oldster nodded. He shuffled to a drawing file, rummaged, pulled out a sheaf of curled prints and spread them on the table. Retief stood silently, running a finger over the uppermost drawing, tracing lines....

"What does the naked-back here?" barked a deep voice behind Retief. He turned. A heavy-faced Fustian youth, wrapped in a mantle, stood at the open door. Beady yellow eyes set among fine scales bored into Retief.

"I came to take a look at your new liner," said Retief.

"We need no prying foreigners here," the youth snapped. His eye fell on the drawings. He hissed in sudden anger.

"Doddering hulk!" he snapped at the ancient. "May you toss in nightmares! Put by the plans!"

"My mistake," Retief said. "I didn't know this was a secret project."

The youth hesitated. "It is not a secret project," he muttered. "Why should it be secret?"

"You tell me."

The youth worked his jaws and rocked his head from side to side in the Fusty gesture of uncertainty. "There is nothing to conceal," he said. "We merely construct a passenger liner."

"Then you don't mind if I look over the drawings," said Retief. "Who knows? Maybe some day I'll want to reserve a suite for the trip out."

The youth turned and disappeared. Retief grinned at the oldster. "Went for his big brother, I guess," he said. "I have a feeling I won't get to study these in peace here. Mind if I copy them?"

"Willingly, light-footed one," said the old Fustian. "And mine is the shame for the discourtesy of youth."

Retief took out a tiny camera, flipped a copying lens in place, leafed through the drawings, clicking the shutter.

"A plague on these youths," said the oldster, "who grow more virulent day by day."

"Why don't you elders clamp down?"

"Agile are they and we are slow of foot. And this unrest is new. Unknown in my youth was such insolence."

"The police—"

"Bah!" the ancient rumbled. "None have we worthy of the name, nor have we needed ought ere now."

"What's behind it?"

"They have found leaders. The spiv, Slock, is one. And I fear they plot mischief." He pointed to the window. "They come, and a Soft One with them."

Retief pocketed the camera, glanced out the window. A pale-featured Groaci with an ornately decorated crest stood with the youths, who eyed the hut, then started toward it.

"That's the military attache of the Groaci Embassy," Retief said. "I wonder what he and the boys are cooking up together?"

"Naught that augurs well for the dignity of Fust," the oldster rumbled. "Flee, agile one, while I engage their attentions."

"I was just leaving," Retief said. "Which way out?"

"The rear door," the Fustian gestured with a stubby member. "Rest well, stranger on these shores." He moved to the entrance.

"Same to you, pop," said Retief. "And thanks."

He eased through the narrow back entrance, waited until voices were raised at the front of the shed, then strolled off toward the gate.

* * * *

The second dark of the third cycle was lightening when Retief left the Embassy technical library and crossed the corridor to his office. He flipped on a light. A note was tucked under a paperweight:

"Retief—I shall expect your attendance at the IAS dinner at first dark of the fourth cycle. There will be a brief but, I hope, impressive Sponsorship ceremony for the SCARS group, with full press coverage, arrangements for which I have managed to complete in spite of your intransigence."

Retief snorted and glanced at his watch. Less than three hours. Just time to creep home by flat-car, dress in ceremonial uniform and creep back.

Outside he flagged a lumbering bus. He stationed himself in a corner and watched the yellow sun, Beta, rise rapidly above the low skyline. The nearby sea was at high tide now, under the pull of the major sun and the three moons, and the stiff breeze carried a mist of salt spray.

Retief turned up his collar against the dampness. In half an hour he would be perspiring under the vertical rays of a third-noon sun, but the thought failed to keep the chill off.

Two Youths clambered up on the platform, moving purposefully toward Retief. He moved off the rail, watching them, weight balanced.

"That's close enough, kids," he said. "Plenty of room on this scow. No need to crowd up."

"There are certain films," the lead Fustian muttered. His voice was unusually deep for a Youth. He was wrapped in a heavy cloak and moved awkwardly. His adolescence was nearly at an end, Retief guessed.

"I told you once," said Retief. "Don't crowd me."

The two stepped close, slit mouths snapping in anger. Retief put out a foot, hooked it behind the scaly leg of the overaged juvenile and threw his weight against the cloaked chest. The clumsy Fustian tottered, fell heavily. Retief was past him and off the flat-car before the other Youth had completed his vain lunge toward the spot Retief had occupied. The Terrestrial waved cheerfully at the pair, hopped aboard another vehicle, watched his would-be assailants lumber down from their car, tiny heads twisted to follow his retreating figure.

So they wanted the film? Retief reflected, thumbing a cigar alight. They were a little late. He had already filed it in the Embassy vault, after running a copy for the reference files.

And a comparison of the drawings with those of the obsolete Mark XXXV battle cruiser used two hundred years earlier by the Concordiat Naval Arm showed them to be almost identical, gun emplacements and all. The term "obsolete" was a relative one. A ship which had been outmoded in the armories of the Galactic Powers could still be king of the walk in the Eastern Arm.

But how had these two known of the film? There had been no one present but himself and the old-timer—and he was willing to bet the elderly Fustian hadn't told them anything.

At least not willingly....

Retief frowned, dropped the cigar over the side, waited until the flat-car negotiated a mud-wallow, then swung down and headed for the shipyard.

* * * *

The door, hinges torn loose, had been propped loosely back in position. Retief looked around at the battered interior of the shed. The old fellow had put up a struggle.

There were deep drag-marks in the dust behind the building. Retief followed them across the yard. They disappeared under the steel door of a warehouse.

Retief glanced around. Now, at the mid-hour of the fourth cycle, the workmen were heaped along the edge of the refreshment pond, deep in their siesta. He took a multi-bladed tool from a pocket, tried various fittings in the lock. It snicked open.

He eased the door aside far enough to enter.

Heaped bales loomed before him. Snapping on the tiny lamp in the handle of the combination tool, Retief looked over the pile. One stack seemed out of alignment...and the dust had been scraped from the floor before it. He pocketed the light, climbed up on the bales, looked over into a nest made by stacking the bundles around a clear spot. The aged Fustian lay in it, on his back, a heavy sack tied over his head.

Retief dropped down inside the ring of bales, sawed at the tough twine and pulled the sack free.

"It's me, old fellow," Retief said. "The nosy stranger. Sorry I got you into this."

The oldster threshed his gnarled legs. He rocked slightly and fell back. "A curse on the cradle that rocked their infant slumbers," he rumbled. "But place me back on my feet and I hunt down the youth, Slock, though he flee to the bottommost muck of the Sea of Torments."

"How am I going to get you out of here? Maybe I'd better get some help."

"Nay. The perfidious Youths abound here," said the old Fustian. "It would be your life."

"I doubt if they'd go that far."

"Would they not?" The Fustian stretched his neck. "Cast your light here. But for the toughness of my hide...."

Retief put the beam of the light on the leathery neck. A great smear of thick purplish blood welled from a ragged cut. The oldster chuckled, a sound like a seal coughing.

"Traitor, they called me. For long they sawed at me—in vain. Then they trussed me and dumped me here. They think to return with weapons to complete the task."

"Weapons? I thought it was illegal!"

"Their evil genius, the Soft One," said the Fustian. "He would provide fuel to the Devil himself."

"The Groaci again," said Retief. "I wonder what their angle is."

"And I must confess, I told them of you, ere I knew their full intentions. Much can I tell you of their doings. But first, I pray, the block and tackle."

Retief found the hoist where the Fustian directed him, maneuvered it into position, hooked onto the edge of the carapace and hauled away. The immense Fustian rose slowly, teetered…then flopped on his chest.

Slowly he got to his feet.

"My name is Whonk, fleet one," he said. "My cows are yours."

"Thanks. I'm Retief. I'd like to meet the girls some time. But right now, let's get out of here."

Whonk leaned his bulk against the ponderous stacks of baled kelp, bulldozed them aside. "Slow am I to anger," he said, "but implacable in my wrath. Slock, beware!"

"Hold it," said Retief suddenly. He sniffed. "What's that odor?" He flashed the light around, played it over a dry stain on the floor. He knelt, sniffed at the spot.

"What kind of cargo was stacked here, Whonk? And where is it now?"

Whonk considered. "There were drums," he said. "Four of them, quite small, painted an evil green, the property of the Soft Ones, the Groaci. They lay here a day and a night. At full dark of the first period they came with stevedores and loaded them aboard the barge *Moss Rock*."

"The VIP boat. Who's scheduled to use it?"

"I know not. But what matters this? Let us discuss cargo movements after I have settled a score with certain Youths."

"We'd better follow this up first, Whonk. There's only one substance I know of that's transported in drums and smells like that blot on the floor. That's titanite: the hottest explosive this side of a uranium pile."

III

Beta was setting as Retief, Whonk puffing at his heels, came up to the sentry box beside the gangway leading to the plush interior of the official luxury space barge *Moss Rock*.

"A sign of the times," said Whonk, glancing inside the empty shelter. "A guard should stand here, but I see him not. Doubtless he crept away to sleep."

"Let's go aboard and take a look around."

They entered the ship. Soft lights glowed in utter silence. A rough box stood on the floor, rollers and pry-bars beside it—a discordant note in the muted luxury of the setting. Whonk rummaged in it.

"Curious," he said. "What means this?" He held up a stained cloak of orange and green, a metal bracelet, papers.

"Orange and green," mused Relief. "Whose colors are those?"

"I know not." Whonk glanced at the arm-band. "But this is lettered." He passed the metal band to Retief.

"SCARS," Retief read. He looked at Whonk. "It seems to me I've heard the name before," he murmured. "Let's get back to the Embassy—fast."

Back on the ramp Retief heard a sound...and turned in time to duck the charge of a hulking Fustian youth who thundered past him and fetched up against the broad chest of Whonk, who locked him in a warm embrace.

"Nice catch, Whonk. Where'd he sneak out of?"

"The lout hid there by the storage bin," rumbled Whonk. The captive youth thumped fists and toes fruitlessly against the oldster's carapace.

"Hang onto him," said Retief. "He looks like the biting kind."

"No fear. Clumsy I am, yet not without strength."

"Ask him where the titanite is tucked away."

"Speak, witless grub," growled Whonk, "lest I tweak you in twain."

The youth gurgled.

"Better let up before you make a mess of him," said Retief. Whonk lifted the Youth clear of the floor, then flung him down with a thump that made the ground quiver. The younger Fustian glared up at the elder, mouth snapping.

"This one was among those who trussed me and hid me away for the killing," said Whonk. "In his repentance he will tell all to his elder."

"That's the same young squirt that tried to strike up an acquaintance with me on the bus," Retief said. "He gets around."

The youth scrambled to hands and knees, scuttled for freedom. Retief planted a foot on his dragging cloak; it ripped free. He stared at the bare back of the Fustian—

"By the Great Egg!" Whonk exclaimed, tripping the refugee as he tried to rise. "This is no Youth! His carapace has been taken from him!"

Retief looked at the scarred back. "I thought he looked a little old. But I thought—"

"This is not possible," Whonk said wonderingly. "The great nerve trunks are deeply involved. Not even the cleverest surgeon could excise the carapace and leave the patient living."

"It looks like somebody did the trick. But let's take this boy with us and get out of here. His folks may come home."

"Too late," said Whonk. Retief turned.

Three youths came from behind the sheds.

"Well," Retief said. "It looks like the SCARS are out in force tonight. Where's your pal?" he said to the advancing trio. "The sticky little bird with the eye-stalks? Back at his Embassy, leaving you suckers holding the bag, I'll bet."

"Shelter behind me, Retief," said Whonk.

"Go get 'em, old-timer." Retief stooped, picked up one of the pry-bars. "I'll jump around and distract them."

Whonk let out a whistling roar and charged for the immature Fustians. They fanned out...and one tripped, sprawled on his face. Retief whirled the metal bar he had thrust between the Fustian's legs, slammed it against the skull of another, who shook his head, turned on Retief...and bounced off the steel hull of the *Moss Rock* as Whonk took him in full charge.

Retief used the bar on another head. His third blow laid the Fustian on the pavement, oozing purple. The other two club members departed hastily, seriously dented but still mobile.

Retief leaned on his club, breathing hard. "Tough heads these kids have got. I'm tempted to chase those two lads down, but I've got another errand to run. I don't know who the Groaci intended to blast, but I have a sneaking suspicion somebody of importance was scheduled for a boat ride in the next few hours. And three drums of titanite is enough to vaporize this tub and everyone aboard her."

"The plot is foiled," said Whonk. "But what reason did they have?"

"The Groaci are behind it. I have an idea the SCARS didn't know about this gambit."

"Which of these is the leader?" asked Whonk. He prodded a fallen Youth with a horny toe. "Arise, dreaming one."

"Never mind him, Whonk. We'll tie these two up and leave them here. I know where to find the boss."

* * * *

A stolid crowd filled the low-ceilinged banquet hall. Retief scanned the tables for the pale blobs of Terrestrial faces, dwarfed by the giant armored bodies of the Fustians. Across the room Magnan fluttered a hand. Retief headed toward him. A low-pitched vibration filled the air: the rumble of subsonic Fustian music.

Retief slid into his place beside Magnan. "Sorry to be late, Mr. Ambassador."

"I'm honored that you chose to appear at all," said Magnan coldly. He turned back to the Fustian on his left.

"Ah, yes, Mr. Minister," he said. "Charming, most charming. So joyous."

The Fustian looked at him, beady-eyed. "It is the *Lament of Hatching*," he said; "our National Dirge."

"Oh," said Magnan. "How interesting. Such a pleasing balance of instruments—"

"It is a droon solo," said the Fustian, eyeing the Terrestrial Ambassador suspiciously.

"Why don't you just admit you can't hear it," Retief whispered loudly. "And if I may interrupt a moment—"

Magnan cleared his throat. "Now that our Mr. Retief has arrived, perhaps we could rush right along to the Sponsorship ceremonies."

"This group," said Retief, leaning across Magnan, "the SCARS. How much do you know about them, Mr. Minister?"

"Nothing at all," the huge Fustian elder rumbled. "For my taste, all Youths should be kept penned with the livestock until they grow a carapace to tame their irresponsibility."

"We mustn't lose sight of the importance of channeling youthful energies," said Magnan.

"Labor gangs," said the minister. "In my youth we were indentured to the dredge-masters. I myself drew a muck sledge."

"But in these modern times," put in Magnan, "surely it's incumbent on us to make happy these golden hours."

The minister snorted. "Last week I had a golden hour. They set upon me and pelted me with overripe stench-fruit."

"But this was merely a manifestation of normal youthful frustrations," cried Magnan. "Their essential tenderness—"

"You'd not find a tender spot on that lout yonder," the minister said, pointing with a fork at a newly arrived Youth, "if you drilled boreholes and blasted."

"Why, that's our guest of honor," said Magnan, "a fine young fellow! Slop I believe his name is."

"Slock," said Retief. "Eight feet of armor-plated orneriness. And—"

Magnan rose and tapped on his glass. The Fustians winced at the, to them, supersonic vibrations. They looked at each other muttering. Magnan tapped louder. The Minister drew in his head, eyes closed. Some of the Fustians rose, tottered for the doors; the noise level rose. Magnan redoubled his efforts. The glass broke with a clatter and green wine gushed on the tablecloth.

"What in the name of the Great Egg!" the Minister muttered. He blinked, breathing deeply.

"Oh, forgive me," blurted Magnan, dabbing at the wine.

"Too bad the glass gave out," said Retief. "In another minute you'd have cleared the hall. And then maybe I could have gotten a word in sideways. There's a matter you should know about—"

"Your attention, please," Magnan said, rising. "I see that our fine young guest has arrived, and I hope that the remainder of his committee will be along in a moment. It is my pleasure to announce that our Mr. Retief has had the good fortune to win out in the keen bidding for the pleasure of sponsoring this lovely group."

Retief tugged at Magnan's sleeve. "Don't introduce me yet," he said. "I want to appear suddenly. More dramatic, you know."

"Well," murmured Magnan, glancing down at Retief, "I'm gratified to see you entering into the spirit of the event at last." He turned his attention back to the assembled guests. "If our honored guest will join me on the rostrum...?" he said. "The gentlemen of the press may want to catch a few shots of the presentation."

Magnan stepped up on the low platform at the center of the wide room, took his place beside the robed Fustian youth and beamed at the cameras.

"How gratifying it is to take this opportunity to express once more the great pleasure we have in sponsoring SCARS," he said, talking slowly for the benefit of the scribbling reporters. "We'd like to think that in our modest way we're to be a part of all that the SCARS achieve during the years ahead."

Magnan paused as a huge Fustian elder heaved his bulk up the two low steps to the rostrum, approached the guest of honor. He watched as the newcomer paused behind Slock, who did not see the new arrival.

Retief pushed through the crowd, stepped up to face the Fustian youth. Slock stared at him, drew back.

"You know me, Slock," said Retief loudly. "An old fellow named Whonk told you about me, just before you tried to saw his head off, remember? It was when I came out to take a look at that battle cruiser you're building."

IV

With a bellow Slock reached for Retief—and choked off in mid-cry as the Fustian elder, Whonk, pinioned him from behind, lifting him clear of the floor.

"Glad you reporters happened along," said Retief to the gaping newsmen. "Slock here had a deal with a sharp operator from the Groaci Embassy. The Groaci were to supply the necessary hardware and Slock, as foreman at the shipyards, was to see that everything was properly installed. The next step, I assume, would have been a local take-over, followed by a little interplanetary war on Flamenco or one of the other nearby worlds… for which the Groaci would be glad to supply plenty of ammo."

Magnan found his tongue. "Are you mad, Retief?" he screeched. "This group was vouched for by the Ministry of Youth!"

"The Ministry's overdue for a purge," snapped Retief. He turned back to Slock. "I wonder if you were in on the little diversion that was planned for today. When the *Moss Rock* blew, a variety of clues were to be planted where they'd be easy to find…with SCARS written all over them. The Groaci would thus have neatly laid the whole affair squarely at the door of the Terrestrial Embassy…whose sponsorship of the SCARS had received plenty of publicity."

"The *Moss Rock*?" said Magnan. "But that was—Retief! This is idiotic. Slock himself was scheduled to go on a cruise tomorrow!"

Slock roared suddenly, twisting violently. Whonk teetered, his grip loosened…and Slock pulled free and was off the platform, butting his way through the milling oldsters on the dining room floor. Magnan watched, open-mouthed.

"The Groaci were playing a double game, as usual," Retief said. "They intended to dispose of this fellow Slock, once he'd served their purpose."

"Well, don't stand there," yelped Magnan over the uproar. "If Slock is the ring-leader of a delinquent gang…!" He moved to give chase.

Retief grabbed his arm. "Don't jump down there! You'd have as much chance of getting through as a jack-rabbit through a threshing contest."

Ten minutes later the crowd had thinned slightly. "We can get through now," Whonk called. "This way." He lowered himself to the floor, bulled through to the exit. Flashbulbs popped. Retief and Magnan followed in Whonk's wake.

In the lounge Retief grabbed the phone, waited for the operator, gave a code letter. No reply. He tried another.

"No good," he said after a full minute had passed. "Wonder what's loose?" He slammed the phone back in its niche. "Let's grab a cab."

* * * *

In the street the blue sun, Alpha, peered like an arc light under a low cloud layer, casting flat shadows across the mud of the avenue. The three mounted a passing flat-car. Whonk squatted, resting the weight of his immense shell on the heavy plank flooring.

"Would that I too could lose this burden, as has the false youth we bludgeoned aboard the *Moss Rock*," he sighed. "Soon will I be forced into retirement. Then a mere keeper of a place of papers such as I will rate no more than a slab on the public strand, with once-daily feedings. And even for a man of high position, retirement is no pleasure. A slab in the Park of Monuments is little better. A dismal outlook for one's next thousand years!"

"You two carry on to the police station," said Retief. "I want to play a hunch. But don't take too long. I may be painfully right."

"What—?" Magnan started.

"As you wish, Retief," said Whonk.

The flat-car trundled past the gate to the shipyard and Retief jumped down, headed at a run for the VIP boat. The guard post still stood vacant. The two Youths whom he and Whonk had left trussed were gone.

"That's the trouble with a peaceful world," Retief muttered. "No police protection." He stepped down from the lighted entry and took up a position behind the sentry box. Alpha rose higher, shedding a glaring blue-white light without heat. Retief shivered. Maybe he'd guessed wrong....

There was a sound in the near distance, like two elephants colliding.

Retief looked toward the gate. His giant acquaintance, Whonk, had re-appeared and was grappling with a hardly less massive opponent. A small figure became visible in the melee, scuttled for the gate. Headed off by the battling titans, he turned and made for the opposite side of the shipyard. Retief waited, jumped out and gathered in the fleeing Groaci.

"Well, Yith," he said, "how's tricks? You should pardon the expression."

"Release me, Retief!" the pale-featured alien lisped, his throat bladder pulsating in agitation. "The behemoths vie for the privilege of dismembering me out of hand!"

"I know how they feel. I'll see what I can do...for a price."

"I appeal to you," Yith whispered hoarsely. "As a fellow diplomat, a fellow alien, a fellow soft-back—"

"Why don't you appeal to Slock, as a fellow skunk?" said Retief. "Now keep quiet...and you may get out of this alive."

The heavier of the two struggling Fustians threw the other to the ground. There was another brief flurry, and then the smaller figure was on its back, helpless.

"That's Whonk, still on his feet," said Retief. "I wonder who he's caught—and why."

Whonk came toward the *Moss Rock* dragging the supine Fustian, who kicked vainly. Retief thrust Yith down well out of sight behind the sentry box. "Better sit tight, Yith. Don't try to sneak off; I can outrun you. Stay here and I'll see what I can do." He stepped out and hailed Whonk.

Puffing like a steam engine Whonk pulled up before him. "Sleep, Retief!" He panted. "You followed a hunch; I did the same. I saw something strange in this one when we passed him on the avenue. I watched, followed him here. Look! It is Slock, strapped into a dead carapace! Now many things become clear."

* * * *

Retief whistled. "So the Youths aren't all as young as they look. Somebody's been holding out on the rest of you Fustians!"

"The Soft One," Whonk said. "You laid him by the heels, Retief. I saw. Produce him now."

"Hold on a minute, Whonk. It won't do you any good—"

Whonk winked broadly. "I must take my revenge!" he roared. "I shall test the texture of the Soft One! His pulped remains will be scoured up by the ramp-washers and mailed home in bottles!"

Retief whirled at a sound, caught up with the scuttling Yith fifty feet away, hauled him back to Whonk.

"It's up to you, Whonk," he said. "I know how important ceremonial revenge is to you Fustians. I will not interfere."

"Mercy!" Yith hissed, eye-stalks whipping in distress. "I claim diplomatic immunity!"

"No diplomat am I," rumbled Whonk. "Let me see; suppose I start with one of those obscenely active eyes—" He reached....

"I have an idea," said Retief brightly. "Do you suppose—just this once—you could forego the ceremonial revenge if Yith promised to arrange for a Groaci Surgical Mission to de-carapace you elders?"

"But," Whonk protested, "those eyes! What a pleasure to pluck them, one by one!"

"Yess," hissed Yith, "I swear it! Our most expert surgeons...platoons of them, with the finest of equipment."

"I have dreamed of how it would be to sit on this one, to feel him squash beneath my bulk...."

"Light as a whissle feather shall you dance," Yith whispered. "Shell-less shall you spring in the joy of renewed youth—"

"Maybe just one eye," said Whonk grudgingly. "That would leave him four."

"Be a sport," said Retief.

"Well."

"It's a deal then," said Retief. "Yith, on your word as a diplomat, an alien, a soft-back and a skunk, you'll set up the mission. Groaci surgical skill is an export that will net you more than armaments. It will be a whissle feather in your cap—if you bring it off. And in return, Whonk won't sit on you. And I won't prefer charges of interference in the internal affairs of a free world."

Behind Whonk there was a movement. Slock, wriggling free of the borrowed carapace, struggled to his feet...in time for Whonk to seize him, lift him high and head for the entry to the *Moss Rock*.

"Hey," Retief called. "Where are you going?"

"I would not deny this one his reward," called Whonk. "He hoped to cruise in luxury. So be it."

"Hold on," said Retief. "That tub is loaded with titanite!"

"Stand not in my way, Retief. For this one in truth owes me a vengeance."

Retief watched as the immense Fustian bore his giant burden up the ramp and disappeared within the ship.

"I guess Whonk means business," he said to Yith, who hung in his grasp, all five eyes goggling. "And he's a little too big for me to stop."

Whonk reappeared, alone, climbed down.

"What did you do with him?" said Retief. "Tell him you were going to—"

"We had best withdraw," said Whonk. "The killing radius of the drive is fifty yards."

"You mean—"

"The controls are set for Groaci. Long-may-he-sleep."

* * * *

"It was quite a bang," said Retief. "But I guess you saw it, too."

"No, confound it," Magnan said. "When I remonstrated with Hulk, or Whelk—"

"Whonk."

"—the ruffian thrust me into an alley bound in my own cloak. I'll most certainly complain to the Minister."

"How about the surgical mission?"

"A most generous offer," said Magnan. "Frankly, I was astonished. I think perhaps we've judged the Groaci too harshly."

"I hear the Ministry of Youth has had a rough morning of it," said Retief. "And a lot of rumors are flying to the effect that Youth Groups are on the way out."

Magnan cleared his throat, shuffled papers. "I—ah—have explained to the press that last night's—ah—"

"Fiasco."

"—affair was necessary in order to place the culprits in an untenable position. Of course, as to the destruction of the VIP vessel and the presumed death of, uh, Slop."

"The Fustians understand," said Retief. "Whonk wasn't kidding about ceremonial vengeance."

"The Groaci had been guilty of gross misuse of diplomatic privilege," said Magnan. "I think that a note—or perhaps an Aide Memoire: less formal...."

"The *Moss Rock* was bound for Groaci," said Retief. "She was already in her transit orbit when she blew. The major fragments will arrive on schedule in a month or so. It should provide quite a meteorite display.

I think that should be all the *aide* the Groaci's *memoires* will need to keep their tentacles off Fust."

"But diplomatic usage—"

"Then, too, the less that's put in writing, the less they can blame you for, if anything goes wrong."

"That's true," said Magnan, lips pursed. "Now you're thinking constructively, Retief. We may make a diplomat of you yet." He smiled expansively.

"Maybe. But I refuse to let it depress me." Retief stood up. "I'm taking a few weeks off…if you have no objection, Mr. Ambassador. My pal Whonk wants to show me an island down south where the fishing is good."

"But there are some extremely important matters coming up," said Magnan. "We're planning to sponsor Senior Citizen Groups—"

"Count me out. All groups give me an itch."

"Why, what an astonishing remark, Retief! After all, we diplomats are ourselves a group."

"Uh-huh," Retief said.

Magnan sat quietly, mouth open, and watched as Retief stepped into the hall and closed the door gently behind him.

CULTURAL EXCHANGE

Originally published in **Worlds of If Science Fiction***, September 1962.*

I

Second Secretary Magnan took his green-lined cape and orange-feathered beret from the clothes tree. "I'm off now, Retief," he said. "I hope you'll manage the administrative routine during my absence without any unfortunate incidents."

"That seems a modest enough hope," Retief said. "I'll try to live up to it."

"I don't appreciate frivolity with reference to this Division," Magnan said testily. "When I first came here, the Manpower Utilization Directorate, Division of Libraries and Education was a shambles. I fancy I've made MUDDLE what it is today. Frankly, I question the wisdom of placing you in charge of such a sensitive desk, even for two weeks. But remember. Yours is purely a rubber-stamp function."

"In that case, let's leave it to Miss Furkle. I'll take a couple of weeks off myself. With her poundage, she could bring plenty of pressure to bear."

"I assume you jest, Retief," Magnan said sadly. "I should expect even you to appreciate that Bogan participation in the Exchange Program may be the first step toward sublimation of their aggressions into more cultivated channels."

"I see they're sending two thousand students to d'Land," Retief said, glancing at the Memo for Record. "That's a sizable sublimation."

Magnan nodded. "The Bogans have launched no less than four military campaigns in the last two decades. They're known as the Hoodlums of the Nicodemean Cluster. Now, perhaps, we shall see them breaking that precedent and entering into the cultural life of the Galaxy."

"Breaking and entering," Retief said. "You may have something there. But I'm wondering what they'll study on d'Land. That's an industrial world of the poor but honest variety."

"Academic details are the affair of the students and their professors," Magnan said. "Our function is merely to bring them together. See that you don't antagonize the Bogan representative. This will be an excellent opportunity for you to practice your diplomatic restraint—not your strong point, I'm sure you'll agree."

A buzzer sounded. Retief punched a button. "What is it, Miss Furkle?"

"That—bucolic person from Lovenbroy is here again." On the small desk screen, Miss Furkle's meaty features were compressed in disapproval.

"This fellow's a confounded pest. I'll leave him to you, Retief," Magnan said. "Tell him something. Get rid of him. And remember: here at Corps HQ, all eyes are upon you."

"If I'd thought of that, I'd have worn my other suit," Retief said.

Magnan snorted and passed from view. Retief punched Miss Furkle's button.

"Send the bucolic person in."

* * * *

A tall broad man with bronze skin and gray hair, wearing tight trousers of heavy cloth, a loose shirt open at the neck and a short jacket, stepped into the room. He had a bundle under his arm. He paused at sight of Retief, looked him over momentarily, then advanced and held out his hand. Retief took it. For a moment the two big men stood, face to face. The newcomer's jaw muscles knotted. Then he winced.

Retief dropped his hand and motioned to a chair.

"That's nice knuckle work, mister," the stranger said, massaging his hand. "First time anybody ever did that to me. My fault though. I started it, I guess." He grinned and sat down.

"What can I do for you?" Retief said.

"You work for this Culture bunch, do you? Funny. I thought they were all ribbon-counter boys. Never mind. I'm Hank Arapoulous. I'm a farmer. What I wanted to see you about was—" He shifted in his chair. "Well, out on Lovenbroy we've got a serious problem. The wine crop is just about ready. We start picking in another two, three months. Now I don't know if you're familiar with the Bacchus vines we grow…?"

"No," Retief said. "Have a cigar?" He pushed a box across the desk. Arapoulous took one. "Bacchus vines are an unusual crop," he said, puffing the cigar alight. "Only mature every twelve years. In between, the vines don't need a lot of attention, so our time's mostly our own. We like to farm, though. Spend a lot of time developing new forms. Apples the size of a melon—and sweet—"

"Sounds very pleasant," Retief said. "Where does the Libraries and Education Division come in?"

Arapoulous leaned forward. "We go in pretty heavy for the arts. Folks can't spend all their time hybridizing plants. We've turned all the land area we've got into parks and farms. Course, we left some sizable forest areas for hunting and such. Lovenbroy's a nice place, Mr. Retief."

"It sounds like it, Mr. Arapoulous. Just what—"

"Call me Hank. We've got long seasons back home. Five of 'em. Our year's about eighteen Terry months. Cold as hell in winter; eccentric orbit, you know. Blue-black sky, stars visible all day. We do mostly painting and sculpture in the winter. Then Spring; still plenty cold. Lots of skiing, bob-sledding, ice skating; and it's the season for woodworkers. Our furniture—"

"I've seen some of your furniture," Retief said. "Beautiful work."

Arapoulous nodded. "All local timbers too. Lots of metals in our soil and those sulphates give the woods some color, I'll tell you. Then comes the Monsoon. Rain—it comes down in sheets. But the sun's getting closer. Shines all the time. Ever seen it pouring rain in the sunshine? That's the music-writing season. Then summer. Summer's hot. We stay inside in the daytime and have beach parties all night. Lots of beach on Lovenbroy; we're mostly islands. That's the drama and symphony time. The theatres are set up on the sand, or anchored off-shore. You have the music and the surf and the bonfires and stars—we're close to the center of a globular cluster, you know...."

"You say it's time now for the wine crop?"

"That's right. Autumn's our harvest season. Most years we have just the ordinary crops. Fruit, grain, that kind of thing; getting it in doesn't take long. We spend most of the time on architecture, getting new places ready for the winter or remodeling the older ones. We spend a lot of time in our houses. We like to have them comfortable. But this year's different. This is Wine Year."

Arapoulous puffed on his cigar, looked worriedly at Retief. "Our wine crop is our big money crop," he said. "We make enough to keep us going. But this year...."

"The crop isn't panning out?"

"Oh, the crop's fine. One of the best I can remember. Course, I'm only twenty-eight; I can't remember but two other harvests. The problem's not the crop."

"Have you lost your markets? That sounds like a matter for the Commercial—"

"Lost our markets? Mister, nobody that ever tasted our wines ever settled for anything else!"

"It sounds like I've been missing something," said Retief. "I'll have to try them some time."

Arapoulous put his bundle on the desk, pulled off the wrappings. "No time like the present," he said.

Retief looked at the two squat bottles, one green, one amber, both dusty, with faded labels, and blackened corks secured by wire.

"Drinking on duty is frowned on in the Corps, Mr. Arapoulous," he said.

"This isn't *drinking*. It's just wine." Arapoulous pulled the wire retainer loose, thumbed the cork. It rose slowly, then popped in the air. Arapoulous caught it. Aromatic fumes wafted from the bottle. "Besides, my feelings would be hurt if you didn't join me." He winked.

Retief took two thin-walled glasses from a table beside the desk. "Come to think of it, we also have to be careful about violating quaint native customs."

Arapoulous filled the glasses. Retief picked one up, sniffed the deep rust-colored fluid, tasted it, then took a healthy swallow. He looked at Arapoulous thoughtfully.

"Hmmm. It tastes like salted pecans, with an undercurrent of crusted port."

"Don't try to describe it, Mr. Retief," Arapoulous said. He took a mouthful of wine, swished it around his teeth, swallowed. "It's Bacchus wine, that's all. Nothing like it in the Galaxy." He pushed the second bottle toward Retief. "The custom back home is to alternate red wine and black."

* * * *

Retief put aside his cigar, pulled the wires loose, nudged the cork, caught it as it popped up.

"Bad luck if you miss the cork," Arapoulous said, nodding. "You probably never heard about the trouble we had on Lovenbroy a few years back?"

"Can't say that I did, Hank." Retief poured the black wine into two fresh glasses. "Here's to the harvest."

"We've got plenty of minerals on Lovenbroy," Arapoulous said, swallowing wine. "But we don't plan to wreck the landscape mining 'em. We like to farm. About ten years back some neighbors of ours landed a force. They figured they knew better what to do with our minerals than we did. Wanted to strip-mine, smelt ore. We convinced 'em otherwise. But it took a year, and we lost a lot of men."

"That's too bad," Retief said. "I'd say this one tastes more like roast beef and popcorn over a Riesling base."

"It put us in a bad spot," Arapoulous went on. "We had to borrow money from a world called Croanie. Mortgaged our crops. Had to start exporting art work too. Plenty of buyers, but it's not the same when you're doing it for strangers."

"Say, this business of alternating drinks is the real McCoy," Retief said. "What's the problem? Croanie about to foreclose?"

"Well, the loan's due. The wine crop would put us in the clear. But we need harvest hands. Picking Bacchus grapes isn't a job you can turn over to machinery—and anyway we wouldn't if we could. Vintage season is the high point of living on Lovenbroy. Everybody joins in. First, there's the picking in the fields. Miles and miles of vineyards covering the mountain sides, and crowding the river banks, with gardens here and there. Big vines, eight feet high, loaded with fruit, and deep grass growing between. The wine-carriers keep on the run, bringing wine to the pickers. There's prizes for the biggest day's output, bets on who can fill the most baskets in an hour…. The sun's high and bright, and it's just cool enough to give you plenty of energy. Come nightfall, the tables are set up in the garden plots, and the feast is laid on: roast turkeys, beef, hams, all kinds of fowl. Big salads. Plenty of fruit. Fresh-baked bread…and wine, plenty of wine. The cooking's done by a different crew each night in each garden, and there's prizes for the best crews.

"Then the wine-making. We still tramp out the vintage. That's mostly for the young folks but anybody's welcome. That's when things start to get loosened up. Matter of fact, pretty near half our young-uns are born after a vintage. All bets are off then. It keeps a fellow on his toes though. Ever tried to hold onto a gal wearing nothing but a layer of grape juice?"

* * * *

"Never did," Retief said. "You say most of the children are born after a vintage. That would make them only twelve years old by the time—"

"Oh, that's Lovenbroy years; they'd be eighteen, Terry reckoning."

"I was thinking you looked a little mature for twenty-eight," Retief said.

"Forty-two, Terry years," Arapoulous said. "But this year it looks bad. We've got a bumper crop—and we're short-handed. If we don't get a big vintage, Croanie steps in. Lord knows what they'll do to the land. Then next vintage time, with them holding half our grape acreage—"

"You hocked the vineyards?"

"Yep. Pretty dumb, huh? But we figured twelve years was a long time."

"On the whole," Retief said, "I think I prefer the black. But the red is hard to beat.…"

"What we figured was, maybe you Culture boys could help us out. A loan to see us through the vintage, enough to hire extra hands. Then we'd repay it in sculpture, painting, furniture—"

"Sorry, Hank. All we do here is work out itineraries for traveling side-shows, that kind of thing. Now, if you needed a troop of Groaci nose-flute players—"

"Can they pick grapes?"

"Nope. Anyway, they can't stand the daylight. Have you talked this over with the Labor Office?"

"Sure did. They said they'd fix us up with all the electronics specialists and computer programmers we wanted—but no field hands. Said it was what they classified as menial drudgery; you'd have thought I was trying to buy slaves."

The buzzer sounded. Miss Furkle's features appeared on the desk screen.

"You're due at the Intergroup Council in five minutes," she said. "Then afterwards, there are the Bogan students to meet."

"Thanks." Retief finished his glass, stood. "I have to run, Hank," he said. "Let me think this over. Maybe I can come up with something. Check with me day after tomorrow. And you'd better leave the bottles here. Cultural exhibits, you know."

* * * *

II

As the council meeting broke up, Retief caught the eye of a colleague across the table.

"Mr. Whaffle, you mentioned a shipment going to a place called Croanie. What are they getting?"

Whaffle blinked. "You're the fellow who's filling in for Magnan, over at MUDDLE," he said. "Properly speaking, equipment grants are the sole concern of the Motorized Equipment Depot, Division of Loans and Exchanges." He pursed his lips. "However, I suppose there's no harm in telling you. They'll be receiving heavy mining equipment."

"Drill rigs, that sort of thing?"

"Strip mining gear." Whaffle took a slip of paper from a breast pocket, blinked at it. "Bolo Model WV/1 tractors, to be specific. Why is MUDDLE interested in MEDDLE's activities?"

"Forgive my curiosity, Mr. Whaffle. It's just that Croanie cropped up earlier today. It seems she holds a mortgage on some vineyards over on—"

"That's not MEDDLE's affair, sir," Whaffle cut in. "I have sufficient problems as Chief of MEDDLE without probing into MUDDLE'S business."

"Speaking of tractors," another man put in, "we over at the Special Committee for Rehabilitation and Overhaul of Under-developed Nations' General Economies have been trying for months to get a request for mining equipment for d'Land through MEDDLE—"

"SCROUNGE was late on the scene," Whaffle said. "First come, first served. That's our policy at MEDDLE. Good day, gentlemen." He strode off, briefcase under his arm.

"That's the trouble with peaceful worlds," the SCROUNGE committeeman said. "Boge is a troublemaker, so every agency in the Corps is out to pacify her. While my chance to make a record—that is, assist peace-loving d'Land—comes to naught." He shook his head.

"What kind of university do they have on d'Land?" asked Retief. "We're sending them two thousand exchange students. It must be quite an institution."

"University? D'Land has one under-endowed technical college."

"Will all the exchange students be studying at the Technical College?"

"Two thousand students? Hah! Two *hundred* students would overtax the facilities of the college."

"I wonder if the Bogans know that?"

"The Bogans? Why, most of d'Land's difficulties are due to the unwise trade agreement she entered into with Boge. Two thousand students indeed!" He snorted and walked away.

* * * *

Retief stopped by the office to pick up a short cape, then rode the elevator to the roof of the 230-story Corps HQ building and hailed a cab to the port. The Bogan students had arrived early. Retief saw them lined up on the ramp waiting to go through customs. It would be half an hour before they were cleared through. He turned into the bar and ordered a beer.

A tall young fellow on the next stool raised his glass.

"Happy days," he said.

"And nights to match."

"You said it." He gulped half his beer. "My name's Karsh. Mr. Karsh. Yep, Mr. Karsh. Boy, this is a drag, sitting around this place waiting…."

"You meeting somebody?"

"Yeah. Bunch of babies. Kids. How they expect—Never mind. Have one on me."

"Thanks. You a Scoutmaster?"

"I'll tell you what I am. I'm a cradle-robber. You know—" he turned to Retief—"not one of those kids is over eighteen." He hiccupped. "Students, you know. Never saw a student with a beard, did you?"

"Lots of times. You're meeting the students, are you?"

The young fellow blinked at Retief. "Oh, you know about it, huh?"

"I represent MUDDLE."

Karsh finished his beer, ordered another. "I came on ahead. Sort of an advance guard for the kids. I trained 'em myself. Treated it like a game, but they can handle a CSU. Don't know how they'll act under pressure. If I had my old platoon—"

He looked at his beer glass, pushed it back. "Had enough," he said. "So long, friend. Or are you coming along?"

Retief nodded. "Might as well."

* * * *

At the exit to the Customs enclosure, Retief watched as the first of the Bogan students came through, caught sight of Karsh and snapped to attention, his chest out.

"Drop that, mister," Karsh snapped. "Is that any way for a student to act?"

The youth, a round-faced lad with broad shoulders, grinned.

"Heck, no," he said. "Say, uh, Mr. Karsh, are we gonna get to go to town? We fellas were thinking—"

"You were, hah? You act like a bunch of school kids! I mean…no! Now line up!"

"We have quarters ready for the students," Retief said. "If you'd like to bring them around to the west side, I have a couple of copters laid on."

"Thanks," said Karsh. "They'll stay here until take-off time. Can't have the little dears wandering around loose. Might get ideas about going over the hill." He hiccupped. "I mean they might play hookey."

"We've scheduled your re-embarkation for noon tomorrow. That's a long wait. MUDDLE's arranged theater tickets and a dinner."

"Sorry," Karsh said. "As soon as the baggage gets here, we're off." He hiccupped again. "Can't travel without our baggage, y'know."

"Suit yourself," Retief said. "Where's the baggage now?"

"Coming in aboard a Croanie lighter."

"Maybe you'd like to arrange for a meal for the students here."

"Sure," Karsh said. "That's a good idea. Why don't you join us?" Karsh winked. "And bring a few beers."

"Not this time," Retief said. He watched the students, still emerging from Customs. "They seem to be all boys," he commented. "No female students?"

"Maybe later," Karsh said. "You know, after we see how the first bunch is received."

Back at the MUDDLE office, Retief buzzed Miss Furkle.

"Do you know the name of the institution these Bogan students are bound for?"

"Why, the University at d'Land, of course."

"Would that be the Technical College?"

Miss Furkle's mouth puckered. "I'm sure I've never pried into these details."

"Where does doing your job stop and prying begin, Miss Furkle?" Retief said. "Personally, I'm curious as to just what it is these students are travelling so far to study—at Corps expense."

"Mr. Magnan never—"

"For the present. Miss Furkle, Mr. Magnan is vacationing. That leaves me with the question of two thousand young male students headed for a world with no classrooms for them…a world in need of tractors. But the tractors are on their way to Croanie, a world under obligation to Boge. And Croanie holds a mortgage on the best grape acreage on Lovenbroy."

"Well!" Miss Furkle snapped, small eyes glaring under unplucked brows. "I hope you're not questioning Mr. Magnan's wisdom!"

"About Mr. Magnan's wisdom there can be no question," Retief said. "But never mind. I'd like you to look up an item for me. How many tractors will Croanie be getting under the MEDDLE program?"

"Why, that's entirely MEDDLE business," Miss Furkle said. "Mr. Magnan always—"

"I'm sure he did. Let me know about the tractors as soon as you can."

* * * *

Miss Furkle sniffed and disappeared from the screen. Retief left the office, descended forty-one stories, followed a corridor to the Corps Library. In the stacks he thumbed through catalogues, pored over indices.

"Can I help you?" someone chirped. A tiny librarian stood at his elbow.

"Thank you, ma'am," Retief said. "I'm looking for information on a mining rig. A Bolo model WV tractor."

"You won't find it in the industrial section," the librarian said. "Come along." Retief followed her along the stacks to a well-lit section lettered ARMAMENTS. She took a tape from the shelf, plugged it into the viewer, flipped through and stopped at a squat armored vehicle.

"That's the model WV," she said. "It's what is known as a continental siege unit. It carries four men, with a half-megaton/second firepower."

"There must be an error somewhere," Retief said. "The Bolo model I want is a tractor. Model WV M-1—"

"Oh, the modification was the addition of a bulldozer blade for demolition work. That must be what confused you."

"Probably—among other things. Thank you."

Miss Furkle was waiting at the office. "I have the information you wanted," she said. "I've had it for over ten minutes. I was under the impression you needed it urgently, and I went to great lengths—"

"Sure," Retief said. "Shoot. How many tractors?"

"Five hundred."

"Are you sure?"

Miss Furkle's chins quivered. "Well! If you feel I'm incompetent—"

"Just questioning the possibility of a mistake, Miss Furkle. Five hundred tractors is a lot of equipment."

"Was there anything further?" Miss Furkle inquired frigidly.

"I sincerely hope not," Retief said.

III

Leaning back in Magnan's padded chair with power swivel and hip-u-matic concontour, Retief leafed through a folder labelled "CERP 7-602-Ba; CROANIE (general)." He paused at a page headed Industry.

Still reading, he opened the desk drawer, took out the two bottles of Bacchus wine and two glasses. He poured an inch of wine into each and sipped the black wine meditatively.

It would be a pity, he reflected, if anything should interfere with the production of such vintages....

Half an hour later he laid the folder aside, keyed the phone and put through a call to the Croanie Legation. He asked for the Commercial Attache.

"Retief here, Corps HQ," he said airily. "About the MEDDLE shipment, the tractors. I'm wondering if there's been a slip up. My records show we're shipping five hundred units...."

"That's correct. Five hundred."

Retief waited.

"Ah...are you there, Retief?"

"I'm still here. And I'm still wondering about the five hundred tractors."

"It's perfectly in order. I thought it was all settled. Mr. Whaffle—"

"One unit would require a good-sized plant to handle its output," Retief said. "Now Croanie subsists on her fisheries. She has perhaps half a dozen pint-sized processing plants. Maybe, in a bind, they could handle the ore ten WV's could scrape up...if Croanie had any ore. It doesn't. By the way, isn't a WV a poor choice as a mining outfit? I should think—"

"See here, Retief! Why all this interest in a few surplus tractors? And in any event, what business is it of yours how we plan to use the equipment? That's an internal affair of my government. Mr. Whaffle—"

"I'm not Mr. Whaffle. What are you going to do with the other four hundred and ninety tractors?"

"I understood the grant was to be with no strings attached!"

"I know it's bad manners to ask questions. It's an old diplomatic tradition that any time you can get anybody to accept anything as a gift, you've scored points in the game. But if Croanie has some scheme cooking—"

"Nothing like that, Retief. It's a mere business transaction."

"What kind of business do you do with a Bolo WV? With or without a blade attached, it's what's known as a continental siege unit."

"Great Heavens, Retief! Don't jump to conclusions! Would you have us branded as warmongers? Frankly—is this a closed line?"

"Certainly. You may speak freely."

"The tractors are for transshipment. We've gotten ourselves into a difficult situation, balance-of-payments-wise. This is an accommodation to a group with which we have rather strong business ties."

"I understand you hold a mortgage on the best land on Lovenbroy," Retief said. "Any connection?"

"Why…ah…no. Of course not, ha ha."

"Who gets the tractors eventually?"

"Retief, this is unwarranted interference!"

"Who gets them?"

"They happen to be going to Lovenbroy. But I scarcely see—"

"And who's the friend you're helping out with an unauthorized transshipment of grant material?"

"Why…ah…I've been working with a Mr. Gulver, a Bogan representative."

"And when will they be shipped?"

"Why, they went out a week ago. They'll be half way there by now. But look here, Retief, this isn't what you're thinking!"

"How do you know what I'm thinking? I don't know myself." Retief rang off, buzzed the secretary.

"Miss Furkle, I'd like to be notified immediately of any new applications that might come in from the Bogan Consulate for placement of students."

"Well, it happens, by coincidence, that I have an application here now. Mr. Gulver of the Consulate brought it in."

"Is Mr. Gulver in the office? I'd like to see him."

"I'll ask him if he has time."

"Great. Thanks." It was half a minute before a thick-necked red-faced man in a tight hat walked in. He wore an old-fashioned suit, a drab shirt, shiny shoes with round toes and an ill-tempered expression.

"What is it you wish?" he barked. "I understood in my discussions with the other…ah…civilian there'd be no further need for these irritating conferences."

"I've just learned you're placing more students abroad, Mr. Gulver. How many this time?"

"Two thousand."

"And where will they be going?"

"Croanie. It's all in the application form I've handed in. Your job is to provide transportation."

"Will there be any other students embarking this season?"

"Why…perhaps. That's Boge's business." Gulver looked at Retief with pursed lips. "As a matter of fact, we had in mind dispatching another two thousand to Featherweight."

"Another under-populated world—and in the same cluster, I believe," Retief said. "Your people must be unusually interested in that region of space."

"If that's all you wanted to know, I'll be on my way. I have matters of importance to see to."

After Gulver left, Retief called Miss Furkle in. "I'd like to have a break-out of all the student movements that have been planned under the present program," he said. "And see if you can get a summary of what MEDDLE has been shipping lately."

Miss Furkle compressed her lips. "If Mr. Magnan were here, I'm sure he wouldn't dream of interfering in the work of other departments. I… overheard your conversation with the gentleman from the Croanie Legation—"

"The lists, Miss Furkle."

"I'm not accustomed," Miss Furkle said, "to intruding in matters outside our interest cluster."

"That's worse than listening in on phone conversations, eh? But never mind. I need the information, Miss Furkle."

"Loyalty to my Chief—"

"Loyalty to your pay-check should send you scuttling for the material I've asked for," Retief said. "I'm taking full responsibility. Now scat."

The buzzer sounded. Retief flipped a key. "MUDDLE, Retief speaking…."

Arapoulous's brown face appeared on the desk screen.

"How-do, Retief. Okay if I come up?"

"Sure, Hank. I want to talk to you."

In the office, Arapoulous took a chair. "Sorry if I'm rushing you, Retief," he said. "But have you got anything for me?"

Retief waved at the wine bottles. "What do you know about Croanie?"

"Croanie? Not much of a place. Mostly ocean. All right if you like fish, I guess. We import our seafood from there. Nice prawns in monsoon time. Over a foot long."

"You on good terms with them?"

"Sure, I guess so. Course, they're pretty thick with Boge."

"So?"

"Didn't I tell you? Boge was the bunch that tried to take us over here a dozen years back. They'd've made it too, if they hadn't had a lot of bad luck. Their armor went in the drink, and without armor they're easy game."

Miss Furkle buzzed. "I have your lists," she said shortly.

"Bring them in, please."

* * * *

The secretary placed the papers on the desk. Arapoulous caught her eye and grinned. She sniffed and marched from the room.

"What that gal needs is a slippery time in the grape mash," Arapoulous observed. Retief thumbed through the papers, pausing to read from time to time. He finished and looked at Arapoulous.

"How many men do you need for the harvest, Hank?" Retief inquired.

Arapoulous sniffed his wine glass and looked thoughtful.

"A hundred would help," he said. "A thousand would be better. Cheers."

"What would you say to two thousand?"

"Two thousand? Retief, you're not fooling?"

"I hope not." He picked up the phone, called the Port Authority, asked for the dispatch clerk.

"Hello, Jim. Say, I have a favor to ask of you. You know that contingent of Bogan students. They're traveling aboard the two CDT transports. I'm interested in the baggage that goes with the students. Has it arrived yet? Okay, I'll wait."

Jim came back to the phone. "Yeah, Retief, it's here. Just arrived. But there's a funny thing. It's not consigned to d'Land. It's ticketed clear through to Lovenbroy."

"Listen, Jim," Retief said. "I want you to go over to the warehouse and take a look at that baggage for me."

Retief waited while the dispatch clerk carried out the errand. The level in the two bottles had gone down an inch when Jim returned to the phone.

"Hey, I took a look at that baggage, Retief. Something funny going on. Guns. 2mm needlers, Mark XII hand blasters, power pistols—"

"It's okay, Jim. Nothing to worry about. Just a mix-up. Now, Jim, I'm going to ask you to do something more for me. I'm covering for a friend. It seems he slipped up. I wouldn't want word to get out, you understand. I'll send along a written change order in the morning that will cover you officially. Meanwhile, here's what I want you to do...."

Retief gave instructions, then rang off and turned to Arapoulous.

"As soon as I get off a couple of TWX's, I think we'd better get down to the port, Hank. I think I'd like to see the students off personally."

IV

Karsh met Retief as he entered the Departures enclosure at the port.

"What's going on here?" he demanded. "There's some funny business with my baggage consignment. They won't let me see it! I've got a feeling it's not being loaded."

"You'd better hurry, Mr. Karsh," Retief said. "You're scheduled to blast off in less than an hour. Are the students all loaded?"

"Yes, blast you! What about my baggage? Those vessels aren't moving without it!"

"No need to get so upset about a few toothbrushes, is there, Mr. Karsh?" Retief said blandly. "Still, if you're worried—" He turned to Arapoulous.

"Hank, why don't you walk Mr. Karsh over to the warehouse and… ah…take care of him?"

"I know just how to handle it," Arapoulous said.

The dispatch clerk came up to Retief. "I caught the tractor equipment," he said. "Funny kind of mistake, but it's okay now. They're being off-loaded at d'Land. I talked to the traffic controller there. He said they weren't looking for any students."

"The labels got switched, Jim. The students go where the baggage was consigned. Too bad about the mistake, but the Armaments Office will have a man along in a little while to dispose of the guns. Keep an eye out for the luggage. No telling where it's gotten to."

"Here!" a hoarse voice yelled. Retief turned. A disheveled figure in a tight hat was crossing the enclosure, arms waving.

"Hi there, Mr. Gulver," Retief called. "How's Boge's business coming along?"

"Piracy!" Gulver blurted as he came up to Retief, puffing hard. "You've got a hand in this, I don't doubt! Where's that Magnan fellow?"

"What seems to be the problem?" Retief said.

"Hold those transports! I've just been notified that the baggage shipment has been impounded. I'll remind you, that shipment enjoys diplomatic free entry!"

"Who told you it was impounded?"

"Never mind! I have my sources!"

Two tall men buttoned into gray tunics came up. "Are you Mr. Retief of CDT?" one said.

"That's right."

"What about my baggage!" Gulver cut in. "And I'm warning you, if those ships lift without—"

"These gentlemen are from the Armaments Control Commission," Retief said. "Would you like to come along and claim your baggage, Mr. Gulver?"

"From where? I—" Gulver turned two shades redder about the ears. "Armaments?"

"The only shipment I've held up seems to be somebody's arsenal," Retief said. "Now if you claim this is your baggage…."

"Why, impossible," Gulver said in a strained voice. "Armaments? Ridiculous. There's been an error…."

* * * *

At the baggage warehouse Gulver looked glumly at the opened cases of guns. "No, of course not," he said dully. "Not my baggage. Not my baggage at all."

Arapoulous appeared, supporting the stumbling figure of Mr. Karsh.

"What—what's this?" Gulver spluttered. "Karsh? What's happened?"

"He had a little fall. He'll be okay," Arapoulous said.

"You'd better help him to the ship," Retief said. "It's ready to lift. We wouldn't want him to miss it."

"Leave him to me!" Gulver snapped, his eyes slashing at Karsh. "I'll see he's dealt with."

"I couldn't think of it," Retief said. "He's a guest of the Corps, you know. We'll see him safely aboard."

Gulver turned, signaled frantically. Three heavy-set men in identical drab suits detached themselves from the wall, crossed to the group.

"Take this man," Gulver snapped, indicating Karsh, who looked at him dazedly, reached up to rub his head.

"We take our hospitality seriously," Retief said. "We'll see him aboard the vessel."

Gulver opened his mouth.

"I know you feel bad about finding guns instead of school books in your luggage," Retief said, looking Gulver in the eye. "You'll be busy straightening out the details of the mix-up. You'll want to avoid further complications."

"Ah. Ulp. Yes," Gulver said. He appeared unhappy.

Arapoulous went on to the passenger conveyor, turned to wave.

"Your man—he's going too?" Gulver blurted.

"He's not our man, properly speaking," Retief said. "He lives on Lovenbroy."

"Lovenbroy?" Gulver choked. "But...the...I...."

"I know you said the students were bound for d'Land," Retief said. "But I guess that was just another aspect of the general confusion. The course plugged into the navigators was to Lovenbroy. You'll be glad to know they're still headed there—even without the baggage."

"Perhaps," Gulver said grimly, "perhaps they'll manage without it."

"By the way," Retief said. "There was another funny mix-up. There were some tractors—for industrial use, you'll recall. I believe you co-operated with Croanie in arranging the grant through MEDDLE. They were erroneously consigned to Lovenbroy, a purely agricultural world. I saved you some embarrassment, I trust, Mr. Gulver, by arranging to have them off-loaded at d'Land."

"D'Land! You've put the CSU's in the hands of Boge's bitterest enemies!"

"But they're only tractors, Mr. Gulver. Peaceful devices. Isn't that correct?"

"That's…correct." Gulver sagged. Then he snapped erect. "Hold the ships!" he yelled. "I'm canceling the student exchange—"

His voice was drowned by the rumble as the first of the monster transports rose from the launch pit, followed a moment later by the second, Retief watched them out of sight, then turned to Gulver.

"They're off," he said. "Let's hope they get a liberal education."

* * * *

V

Retief lay on his back in deep grass by a stream, eating grapes. A tall figure appeared on the knoll above him and waved.

"Retief!" Hank Arapoulous bounded down the slope and embraced Retief, slapping him on the back. "I heard you were here—and I've got news for you. You won the final day's picking competition. Over two hundred bushels! That's a record!"

"Let's get on over to the garden. Sounds like the celebration's about to start."

In the flower-crowded park among the stripped vines, Retief and Arapoulous made their way to a laden table under the lanterns. A tall girl dressed in loose white, and with long golden hair, came up to Arapoulous.

"Delinda, this is Retief—today's winner. And he's also the fellow that got those workers for us."

Delinda smiled at Retief. "I've heard about you, Mr. Retief. We weren't sure about the boys at first. Two thousand Bogans, and all confused about their baggage that went astray. But they seemed to like the picking." She smiled again.

"That's not all. Our gals liked the boys," Hank said. "Even Bogans aren't so bad, minus their irons. A lot of 'em will be staying on. But how come you didn't tell me you were coming, Retief? I'd have laid on some kind of big welcome."

"I liked the welcome I got. And I didn't have much notice. Mr. Magnan was a little upset when he got back. It seems I exceeded my authority."

Arapoulous laughed. "I had a feeling you were wheeling pretty free, Retief. I hope you didn't get into any trouble over it."

"No trouble," Retief said. "A few people were a little unhappy with me. It seems I'm not ready for important assignments at Departmental level. I was shipped off here to the boondocks to get a little more experience."

"Delinda, look after Retief," said Arapoulous. "I'll see you later. I've got to see to the wine judging." He disappeared in the crowd.

"Congratulations on winning the day," said Delinda. "I noticed you at work. You were wonderful. I'm glad you're going to have the prize."

"Thanks. I noticed you too, flitting around in that white nightie of yours. But why weren't you picking grapes with the rest of us?"

"I had a special assignment."

"Too bad. You should have had a chance at the prize."

Delinda took Retief's hand. "I wouldn't have anyway," she said. "I'm the prize."

THE DESERT AND THE STARS

Originally published in **Worlds of If Science Fiction***, November 1962.*

"I'm not at all sure," Under-Secretary Sternwheeler said, "that I fully understand the necessity for your…ah…absenting yourself from your post of duty, Mr. Retief. Surely this matter could have been dealt with in the usual way—assuming any action is necessary."

"I had a sharp attack of writer's cramp, Mr. Secretary," Retief said. "So I thought I'd better come along in person—just to be sure I was positive of making my point."

"Eh?"

"Why, ah, there were a number of dispatches," Deputy Under-Secretary Magnan put in. "Unfortunately, this being end-of-the-fiscal-year time, we found ourselves quite inundated with reports. Reports, reports, reports—"

"Not criticizing the reporting system, are you, Mr. Magnan?" the Under-Secretary barked.

"Gracious, no," Magnan said. "I love reports."

"It seems nobody's told the Aga Kagans about fiscal years," Retief said. "They're going right ahead with their program of land-grabbing on Flamme. So far, I've persuaded the Boyars that this is a matter for the Corps, and not to take matters into their own hands."

The Under-Secretary nodded. "Quite right. Carry on along the same lines. Now, if there's nothing further—"

"Thank you, Mr. Secretary," Magnan said, rising. "We certainly appreciate your guidance."

"There is a little something further," said Retief, sitting solidly in his chair. "What's the Corps going to do about the Aga Kagans?"

The Under-Secretary turned a liverish eye on Retief. "As Minister to Flamme, you should know that the function of a diplomatic representative is merely to…what shall I say…?"

"String them along?" Magnan suggested.

"An unfortunate choice of phrase," the Under-Secretary said. "However, it embodies certain realities of Galactic politics. The Corps must concern itself with matters of broad policy."

"Sixty years ago the Corps was encouraging the Boyars to settle Flamme," Retief said. "They were assured of Corps support."

"I don't believe you'll find that in writing," said the Under-Secretary blandly. "In any event, that was sixty years ago. At that time a foothold against Neo-Concordiatist elements was deemed desirable. Now the situation has changed."

"The Boyars have spent sixty years terraforming Flamme," Retief said. "They've cleared jungle, descummed the seas, irrigated deserts, set out forests. They've just about reached the point where they can begin to enjoy it. The Aga Kagans have picked this as a good time to move in. They've landed thirty detachments of 'fishermen'—complete with armored trawlers mounting 40 mm infinite repeaters—and another two dozen parties of 'homesteaders'—all male and toting rocket launchers."

"Surely there's land enough on the world to afford space to both groups," the Under-Secretary said. "A spirit of co-operation—"

* * * *

"The Boyars needed some co-operation sixty years ago," Retief said. "They tried to get the Aga Kagans to join in and help them beat back some of the saurian wild life that liked to graze on people. The Corps didn't like the idea. They wanted to see an undisputed anti-Concordiatist enclave. The Aga Kagans didn't want to play, either. But now that the world is tamed, they're moving in."

"The exigencies of diplomacy require a flexible policy—"

"I want a firm assurance of Corps support to take back to Flamme," Retief said. "The Boyars are a little naive. They don't understand diplomatic triple-speak. They just want to hold onto the homes they've made out of a wasteland."

"I'm warning you, Retief!" the Under-Secretary snapped, leaning forward, wattles quivering. "Corps policy with regard to Flamme includes no inflammatory actions based on outmoded concepts. The Boyars will have to accommodate themselves to the situation!"

"That's what I'm afraid of," Retief said. "They're not going to sit still and watch it happen. If I don't take back concrete evidence of Corps backing, we're going to have a nice hot little shooting war on our hands."

The Under-Secretary pushed out his lips and drummed his fingers on the desk.

"Confounded hot-heads," he muttered. "Very well, Retief. I'll go along to the extent of a Note; but positively no further."

"A Note? I was thinking of something more like a squadron of Corps Peace Enforcers running through a few routine maneuvers off Flamme."

"Out of the question. A stiffly worded Protest Note is the best I can do. That's final."

Back in the corridor, Magnan turned to Retief. "When will you learn not to argue with Under-Secretaries? One would think you actively disliked the idea of ever receiving a promotion. I was astonished at the Under-Secretary's restraint. Frankly, I was stunned when he actually agreed to a Note. I, of course, will have to draft it." Magnan pulled at his lower lip thoughtfully. "Now, I wonder, should I view with deep concern an act of open aggression, or merely point out an apparent violation of technicalities...."

"Don't bother," Retief said. "I have a draft all ready to go."

"But how—?"

"I had a feeling I'd get paper instead of action," Retief said. "I thought I'd save a little time all around."

"At times, your cynicism borders on impudence."

"At other times, it borders on disgust. Now, if you'll run the Note through for signature, I'll try to catch the six o'clock shuttle."

"Leaving so soon? There's an important reception tonight. Some of our biggest names will be there. An excellent opportunity for you to join in the diplomatic give-and-take."

"No, thanks. I want to get back to Flamme and join in something mild, like a dinosaur hunt."

"When you get there," said Magnan, "I hope you'll make it quite clear that this matter is to be settled without violence."

"Don't worry. I'll keep the peace, if I have to start a war to do it."

* * * *

On the broad verandah at Government House, Retief settled himself comfortably in a lounge chair. He accepted a tall glass from a white-jacketed waiter and regarded the flamboyant Flamme sunset, a gorgeous blaze of vermillion and purple that reflected from a still lake, tinged the broad lawn with color, silhouetted tall poplars among flower beds.

"You've done great things here in sixty years, Georges," said Retief. "Not that natural geological processes wouldn't have produced the same results, given a couple of hundred million years."

"Don't belabor the point," the Boyar Chef d'Regime said. "Since we seem to be on the verge of losing it."

"You're forgetting the Note."

"A Note," Georges said, waving his cigar. "What the purple polluted hell is a Note supposed to do? I've got Aga Kagan claim-jumpers camped in the middle of what used to be a fine stand of barley, cooking sheep's brains over dung fires not ten miles from Government House—and upwind at that."

"Say, if that's the same barley you distill your whiskey from, I'd call that a first-class atrocity."

"Retief, on your say-so, I've kept my boys on a short leash. They've put up with plenty. Last week, while you were away, these barbarians sailed that flotilla of armor-plated junks right through the middle of one of our best oyster breeding beds. It was all I could do to keep a bunch of our men from going out in private helis and blasting 'em out of the water."

"That wouldn't have been good for the oysters, either."

"That's what I told 'em. I also said you'd be back here in a few days with something from Corps HQ. When I tell 'em all we've got is a piece of paper, that'll be the end. There's a strong vigilante organization here that's been outfitting for the last four weeks. If I hadn't held them back with assurances that the CDT would step in and take care of this invasion, they would have hit them before now."

* * * *

"That would have been a mistake," said Retief. "The Aga Kagans are tough customers. They're active on half a dozen worlds at the moment. They've been building up for this push for the last five years. A show of resistance by you Boyars without Corps backing would be an invitation to slaughter—with the excuse that you started it."

"So what are we going to do? Sit here and watch these goat-herders take over our farms and fisheries?"

"Those goat-herders aren't all they seem. They've got a first-class modern navy."

"I've seen 'em. They camp in goat-skin tents, gallop around on animal-back, wear dresses down to their ankles—"

"The 'goat-skin' tents are a high-polymer plastic, made in the same factory that turns out those long flowing bullet-proof robes you mention. The animals are just for show. Back home they use helis and ground cars of the most modern design."

The Chef d'Regime chewed his cigar.

"Why the masquerade?"

"Something to do with internal policies, I suppose."

"So we sit tight and watch 'em take our world away from us. That's what I get for playing along with you, Retief. We should have clobbered these monkeys as soon as they set foot on our world."

"Slow down, I haven't finished yet. There's still the Note."

"I've got plenty of paper already. Rolls and rolls of it."

"Give diplomatic processes a chance," said Retief. "The Note hasn't even been delivered yet. Who knows? We may get surprising results."

"If you expect me to supply a runner for the purpose, you're out of luck. From what I hear, he's likely to come back with his ears stuffed in his hip pocket."

"I'll deliver the Note personally," Retief said. "I could use a couple of escorts—preferably strong-arm lads."

The Chef d'Regime frowned, blew out a cloud of smoke. "I wasn't kidding about these Aga Kagans," he said. "I hear they have some nasty habits. I don't want to see you operated on with the same knives they use to skin out the goats."

"I'd be against that myself. Still, the mail must go through."

"Strong-arm lads, eh? What have you got in mind, Retief?"

"A little muscle in the background is an old diplomatic custom," Retief said.

The Chef d'Regime stubbed out his cigar thoughtfully. "I used to be a pretty fair elbow-wrestler myself," he said. "Suppose I go along…?"

"That," said Retief, "should lend just the right note of solidarity to our little delegation." He hitched his chair closer. "Now, depending on what we run into, here's how we'll play it…."

* * * *

II

Eight miles into the rolling granite hills west of the capital, a black-painted official air-car flying the twin flags of Chief of State and Terrestrial Minister skimmed along a foot above a pot-holed road. Slumped in the padded seat, the Boyar Chef d'Regime waved his cigar glumly at the surrounding hills.

"Fifty years ago this was bare rock," he said. "We've bred special strains of bacteria here to break down the formations into soil, and we followed up with a program of broad-spectrum fertilization. We planned to put the whole area into crops by next year. Now it looks like the goats will get it."

"Will that scrubland support a crop?" Retief said, eyeing the lichen-covered knolls.

"Sure. We start with legumes and follow up with cereals. Wait until you see this next section. It's an old flood plain, came into production thirty years ago. One of our finest—"

The air-car topped a rise. The Chef dropped his cigar and half rose, with a hoarse yell. A herd of scraggly goats tossed their heads among a stand of ripe grain. The car pulled to a stop. Retief held the Boyar's arm.

"Keep calm, Georges," he said. "Remember, we're on a diplomatic mission. It wouldn't do to come to the conference table smelling of goats."

"Let me at 'em." Georges roared. "I'll throttle 'em with my bare hands!"

A bearded goat eyed the Boyar Chef sardonically, jaw working. "Look at that long-nosed son!" The goat gave a derisive bleat and took another mouthful of ripe grain.

"Did you see that?" Georges yelled. "They've trained the son of a—"

"Chin up, Georges," Retief said. "We'll take up the goat problem along with the rest."

"I'll murder 'em."

"Hold it, Georges. Look over there."

A hundred yards away, a trio of brown-cloaked horsemen topped a rise, paused dramatically against the cloudless pale sky, then galloped down the slope toward the car, rifles bobbing at their backs, cloaks billowing out behind. Side by side they rode, through the brown-golden grain, cutting three narrow swaths that ran in a straight sweep from the ridge to the air-car where Retief and the Chef d'Regime hovered, waiting.

Georges scrambled for the side of the car. "Just wait 'til I get my hands on him!"

Retief pulled him back. "Sit tight and look pleased, Georges. Never give the opposition a hint of your true feelings. Pretend you're a goat lover—and hand me one of your cigars."

The three horsemen pulled up in a churn of chaff and a clatter of pebbles. Georges coughed, batting a hand at the settling dust. Retief peeled the cigar unhurriedly, sniffed, at it and thumbed it alight. He drew at it, puffed out a cloud of smoke and glanced casually at the trio of Aga Kagan cavaliers.

"Peace be with you," he intoned in accent-free Kagan. "May your shadows never grow less."

* * * *

The leader of the three, a hawk-faced man with a heavy beard, unlimbered his rifle. He fingered it, frowning ferociously.

"Have no fear," Retief said, smiling graciously. "He who comes as a guest enjoys perfect safety."

A smooth-faced member of the threesome barked an oath and leveled his rifle at Retief.

"Youth is the steed of folly," Retief said. "Take care that the beardless one does not disgrace his house."

The leader whirled on the youth and snarled an order. He lowered the rifle, muttering. Blackbeard turned back to Retief.

"Begone, interlopers," he said. "You disturb the goats."

"Provision is not taken to the houses of the generous," Retief said. "May the creatures dine well ere they move on."

"Hah! The goats of the Aga Kaga graze on the lands of the Aga Kaga." The leader edged his horse close, eyed Retief fiercely. "We welcome no intruders on our lands."

"To praise a man for what he does not possess is to make him appear foolish," Retief said. "These are the lands of the Boyars. But enough of these pleasantries. We seek audience with your ruler."

"You may address me as 'Exalted One'," the leader said. "Now dismount from that steed of Shaitan."

"It is written, if you need anything from a dog, call him 'sir'," Retief said. "I must decline to impute canine ancestry to a guest. Now you may conduct us to your headquarters."

"Enough of your insolence!" The bearded man cocked his rifle. "I could blow your heads off!"

"The hen has feathers, but it does not fly," Retief said. "We have asked for escort. A slave must be beaten with a stick; for a free man, a hint is enough."

"You mock me, pale one. I warn you—"

"Only love makes me weep," Retief said. "I laugh at hatred."

"Get out of the car!"

Retief puffed at his cigar, eyeing the Aga Kagan cheerfully. The youth in the rear moved forward, teeth bared.

"Never give in to the fool, lest he say, 'He fears me,'" Retief said.

"I cannot restrain my men in the face of your insults," the bearded Aga Kagan roared. "These hens of mine have feathers—and talons as well!"

"When God would destroy an ant, he gives him wings," Retief said. "Distress in misfortune is another misfortune."

The bearded man's face grew purple.

Retief dribbled the ash from his cigar over the side of the car.

"Now I think we'd better be getting on," he said briskly. "I've enjoyed our chat, but we do have business to attend to."

The bearded leader laughed shortly. "Does the condemned man beg for the axe?" he enquired rhetorically. "You shall visit the Aga Kaga, then. Move on! And make no attempt to escape, else my gun will speak you a brief farewell."

The horsemen glowered, then, at a word from the leader, took positions around the car. Georges started the vehicle forward, following the leading rider. Retief leaned back and let out a long sigh.

"That was close," he said. "I was about out of proverbs."

"You sound as though you'd brought off a coup," Georges said. "From the expression on the whiskery one's face, we're in for trouble. What was he saying?"

"Just a routine exchange of bluffs," Retief said. "Now when we get there, remember to make your flattery sound like insults and your insults sound like flattery, and you'll be all right."

"These birds are armed. And they don't like strangers," Georges said. "Maybe I should have boned up on their habits before I joined this expedition."

"Just stick to the plan," Retief said. "And remember: a handful of luck is better than a camel-load of learning."

* * * *

The air car followed the escort down a long slope to a dry river bed and across it, through a barren stretch of shifting sand to a green oasis set with canopies.

The armed escort motioned the car to a halt before an immense tent of glistening black. Before the tent armed men lounged under a pennant bearing a lion *couchant* in crimson on a field verte.

"Get out," Blackbeard ordered. The guards eyed the visitors, their drawn sabers catching sunlight. Retief and Georges stepped from the car onto rich rugs spread on the grass. They followed the ferocious gesture of the bearded man through the opening into a perfumed interior of luminous shadows. A heavy odor of incense hung in the air, and the strumming of stringed instruments laid a muted pattern of sound behind the decorations of gold and blue, silver and green. At the far end of the room, among a bevy of female slaves, a large and resplendently clad man with blue-black hair and a clean-shaven chin popped a grape into his mouth. He wiped his fingers negligently on a wisp of silk offered by a handmaiden, belched loudly and looked the callers over.

Blackbeard cleared his throat. "Down on your faces in the presence of the Exalted One, the Aga Kaga, ruler of East and West."

"Sorry," Retief said firmly. "My hay-fever, you know."

The reclining giant waved a hand languidly.

"Never mind the formalities," he said. "Approach."

Retief and Georges crossed the thick rugs. A cold draft blew toward them. The reclining man sneezed violently, wiped his nose on another silken scarf and held up a hand.

"Night and the horses and the desert know me," he said in resonant tones. "Also the sword and the guest and paper and pen—" He paused, wrinkled his nose and sneezed again. "Turn off that damned air-conditioner," he snapped.

He settled himself and motioned the bearded man to him. The two exchanged muted remarks. Then the bearded man stepped back, ducked his head and withdrew to the rear.

"Excellency," Retief said, "I have the honor to present M. Georges Duror, Chef d'Regime of the Planetary government."

"Planetary government?" The Aga Kaga spat grape seeds on the rug. "My men have observed a few squatters along the shore. If they're in distress, I'll see about a distribution of goat-meat."

"It is the punishment of the envious to grieve at anothers' plenty," Retief said. "No goat-meat will be required."

"Ralph told me you talk like a page out of Mustapha ben Abdallah Katib Jelebi," the Aga Kaga said. "I know a few old sayings myself. For example, 'A Bedouin is only cheated once.'"

"We have no such intentions, Excellency," Retief said. "Is it not written, 'Have no faith in the Prince whose minister cheats you'?"

"I've had some unhappy experiences with strangers," the Aga Kaga said. "It is written in the sands that all strangers are kin. Still, he who visits rarely is a welcome guest. Be seated."

III

Handmaidens brought cushions, giggled and fled. Retief and Georges settled themselves comfortably. The Aga Kaga eyed them in silence.

"We have come to bear tidings from the Corps Diplomatique Terrestrienne," Retief said solemnly. A perfumed slave girl offered grapes.

"Modest ignorance is better than boastful knowledge," the Aga Kaga said. "What brings the CDT into the picture?"

"The essay of the drunkard will be read in the tavern," Retief said. "Whereas the words of kings...."

"Very well, I concede the point." The Aga Kaga waved a hand at the serving maids. "Depart, my dears. Attend me later. You too, Ralph. These are mere diplomats. They are men of words, not deeds."

The bearded man glared and departed. The girls hurried after him.

"Now," the Aga Kaga said. "Let's drop the wisdom of the ages and get down to the issues. Not that I don't admire your repertoire of platitudes. How do you remember them all?"

"Diplomats and other liars require good memories," said Retief. "But as you point out, small wisdom to small minds. I'm here to effect a settlement of certain differences between yourself and the planetary authorities. I have here a Note, which I'm conveying on behalf of the Sector Under-Secretary. With your permission, I'll read it."

"Go ahead." The Aga Kaga kicked a couple of cushions onto the floor, eased a bottle from under the couch and reached for glasses.

"The Under-Secretary for Sector Affairs presents his compliments to his Excellency, the Aga Kaga of the Aga Kaga, Primary Potentate, Hereditary Sheik, Emir of the—"

"Yes, yes. Skip the titles."

Retief flipped over two pages.

"...and with reference to the recent relocation of persons under the jurisdiction of his Excellency, has the honor to point out that the territories now under settlement comprise a portion of that area, hereinafter designated as Sub-sector Alpha, which, under terms of the Agreement entered into by his Excellency's predecessor, and as referenced in Sector Ministry's Notes numbers G-175846573957-b and X-7584736 c-1, with particular pertinence to that body designated in the Revised Galactic Catalogue,

Tenth Edition, as amended, Volume Nine, reel 43, as 54 Cygni Alpha, otherwise referred to hereinafter as Flamme—"

"Come to the point," the Aga Kaga cut in. "You're here to lodge a complaint that I'm invading territories to which someone else lays claim, is that it?" He smiled broadly, offered dope-sticks and lit one. "Well, I've been expecting a call. After all, it's what you gentlemen are paid for. Cheers."

"Your Excellency has a lucid way of putting things," Retief said.

"Call me Stanley," the Aga Kaga said. "The other routine is just to please some of the old fools—I mean the more conservative members of my government. They're still gnawing their beards and kicking themselves because their ancestors dropped science in favor of alchemy and got themselves stranded in a cultural dead end. This charade is supposed to prove they were right all along. However, I've no time to waste in neurotic compensations. I have places to go and deeds to accomplish."

"At first glance," Retief said, "it looks as though the places are already occupied, and the deeds are illegal."

* * * *

The Aga Kaga guffawed. "For a diplomat, you speak plainly, Retief. Have another drink." He poured, eyeing Georges. "What of M. Duror? How does he feel about it?"

Georges took a thoughtful swallow of whiskey. "Not bad," he said. "But not quite good enough to cover the odor of goats."

The Aga Kaga snorted. "I thought the goats were overdoing it a bit myself," he said. "Still, the graybeards insisted. And I need their support."

"Also," Georges said distinctly, "I think you're soft. You lie around letting women wait on you, while your betters are out doing an honest day's work."

The Aga Kaga looked startled. "Soft? I can tie a knot in an iron bar as big as your thumb." He popped a grape into his mouth. "As for the rest, your pious views about the virtues of hard labor are as childish as my advisors' faith in the advantages of primitive plumbing. As for myself, I am a realist. If two monkeys want the same banana, in the end one will have it, and the other will cry morality. The days of my years are numbered, praise be to God. While they last, I hope to eat well, hunt well, fight well and take my share of pleasure. I leave to others the arid satisfactions of self-denial and other perversions."

"You admit you're here to grab our land, then," Georges said. "That's the damnedest piece of bare-faced aggression—"

"Ah, ah!" The Aga Kaga held up a hand. "Watch your vocabulary, my dear sir. I'm sure that 'justifiable yearnings for territorial self-realization' would be more appropriate to the situation. Or possibly 'legitimate aspirations, for self-determination of formerly exploited peoples' might fit the case. Aggression is, by definition, an activity carried on only by those who have inherited the mantle of Colonial Imperialism."

"Imperialism! Why, you Aga Kagans have been the most notorious planet-grabbers in Sector history, you—you—"

"Call me Stanley." The Aga Kaga munched a grape. "I merely face the realities of popular folk-lore. Let's be pragmatic; it's a matter of historical association. Some people can grab land and pass it off lightly as a moral duty; others are dubbed imperialist merely for holding onto their own. Unfair, you say. But that's life, my friends. And I shall continue to take every advantage of it."

"We'll fight you!" Georges bellowed. He took another gulp of whiskey and slammed the glass down. "You won't take this world without a struggle!"

"Another?" the Aga Kaga said, offering the bottle. Georges glowered as his glass was filled. The Aga Kaga held the glass up to the light.

"Excellent color, don't you agree?" He turned his eyes on Georges.

"It's pointless to resist," he said. "We have you outgunned and outmanned. Your small nation has no chance against us. But we're prepared to be generous. You may continue to occupy such areas as we do not immediately require until such time as you're able to make other arrangements."

"And by the time we've got a crop growing out of what was bare rock, you'll be ready to move in," the Boyar Chef d'Regime snapped. "But you'll find that we aren't alone!"

* * * *

"Quite alone," the Aga said. He nodded sagely. "Yes, one need but read the lesson of history. The Corps Diplomatique will make expostulatory noises, but it will accept the *fait accompli*. You, my dear sir, are but a very small nibble. We won't make the mistake of excessive greed. We shall inch our way to empire—and those who stand in our way shall be dubbed warmongers."

"I see you're quite a student of history, Stanley," Retief said. "I wonder if you recall the eventual fate of most of the would-be empire nibblers of the past?"

"Ah, but they grew incautious. They went too far, too fast."

"The confounded impudence," Georges rasped. "Tells us to our face what he has in mind!"

"An ancient and honorable custom, from the time of *Mein Kampf* and the *Communist Manifesto* through the *Porcelain Wall* of Leung. Such declarations have a legendary quality. It's traditional that they're never taken at face value."

"But always," Retief said, "there was a critical point at which the man on horseback could have been pulled from the saddle."

"*Could* have been," the Aga Kaga chuckled. He finished the grapes and began peeling an orange. "But they never were. Hitler could have been stopped by the Czech Air Force in 1938; Stalin was at the mercy of the primitive atomics of the west in 1946; Leung was grossly over-extended at Rangoon. But the onus of that historic role could not be overcome. It has been the fate of your spiritual forebears to carve civilization from the wilderness and then, amid tearing of garments and the heaping of ashes of self-accusation on your own confused heads, to withdraw, leaving the spoils for local political opportunists and mob leaders, clothed in the mystical virtue of native birth. Have a banana."

"You're stretching your analogy a little too far," Retief said. "You're banking on the inaction of the Corps. You could be wrong."

"I shall know when to stop," the Aga Kaga said.

"Tell me, Stanley," Retief said, rising. "Are we quite private here?"

"Yes, perfectly so," the Aga Kaga said. "None would dare to intrude in my council." He cocked an eyebrow at Retief. "You have a proposal to make in confidence? But what of our dear friend Georges? One would not like to see him disillusioned."

"Don't worry about Georges. He's a realist, like you. He's prepared to deal in facts. Hard facts, in this case."

The Aga Kaga nodded thoughtfully. "What are you getting at?"

"You're basing your plan of action on the certainty that the Corps will sit by, wringing its hands, while you embark on a career of planetary piracy."

"Isn't it the custom?" the Aga Kaga smiled complacently.

"I have news for you, Stanley. In this instance, neck-wringing seems more in order than hand-wringing."

The Aga Kaga frowned. "Your manner—"

"Never mind our manners!" Georges blurted, standing. "We don't need any lessons from goat-herding land-thieves!"

The Aga Kaga's face darkened. "You dare to speak thus to me, pig of a muck-grubber!"

* * * *

With a muffled curse Georges launched himself at the potentate. The giant rolled aside. He grunted as the Boyar's fist thumped in his short ribs; then he chopped down on Georges' neck. The Chef d'Regime slid off onto the floor as the Aga Kaga bounded to his feet, sending fruit and silken cushions flying.

"I see it now!" he hissed. "An assassination attempt!" He stretched his arms, thick as tree-roots—a grizzly in satin robes. "Your heads will ring together like gongs before I have done with you!" He lunged for Retief. Retief came to his feet, feinted with his left and planted a short right against the Aga Kaga's jaw with a solid smack. The potentate stumbled, grabbed; Retief slipped aside. The Aga Kaga whirled to face Retief.

"A slippery diplomat, by all the houris in Paradise!" he grated, breathing hard. "But a fool. True to your medieval code of chivalry, you attacked singly, a blunder I would never have made. And you shall die for your idiocy!" He opened his mouth to bellow—

"You sure look foolish, with your fancy hair-do down in your eyes," Retief said. "The servants will get a big laugh out of it."

With a choked yell, the Aga Kaga dived for Retief, missed as he leaped aside. The two went to the mat together and rolled, sending a stool skittering. Grunts and curses echoed as the two big men strained, muscles popping. Retief groped for a scissors hold; the Aga Kaga seized his foot, bit hard. Retief bent nearly double, braced himself and slammed the potentate against the rug. Dust flew. Then the two were on their feet, circling.

"Many times have I longed to broil a diplomat over a slow fire," the Aga Kaga snarled. "Tonight will see it come to pass!"

"I've seen it done often at staff meetings," said Retief. "It seems to have no permanent effect."

The Aga Kaga reached for Retief, who feinted left, hammered a right to the chin. The Aga Kaga tottered. Retief measured him, brought up a haymaker. The potentate slammed to the rug—out cold.

* * * *

Georges rolled over, sat up. "Let me at the son of a—" he muttered.

"Take over, Georges," Retief said, panting. "Since he's in a mood to negotiate now, we may as well get something accomplished."

Georges eyed the fallen ruler, who stirred, groaned lugubriously. "I hope you know what you're doing," Georges said. "But I'm with you in any case." He straddled the prone body, plucked a curved knife from the low table and prodded the Aga Kaga's Adam's apple. The monarch opened his eyes.

"Make one little peep and your windbag will spring a leak," Georges said. "Very few historical figures have accomplished anything important after their throats were cut."

"Stanley won't yell," Retief said. "We're not the only ones who're guilty of cultural idiocy. He'd lose face something awful if he let his followers see him like this." Retief settled himself on a tufted ottoman. "Right, Stanley?"

The Aga Kaga snarled.

Retief selected a grape and ate it thoughtfully. "These aren't bad, Georges. You might consider taking on a few Aga Kagan vine-growers—purely on a yearly contract basis, of course."

The Aga Kaga groaned, rolling his eyes.

"Well, I believe we're ready to get down to diplomatic proceedings now," Retief said. "Nothing like dealing in an atmosphere of realistic good fellowship. First, of course, there's the matter of the presence of aliens lacking visas." He opened his briefcase, withdrew a heavy sheet of parchment. "I have the document here, drawn up and ready for signature. It provides for the prompt deportation of such persons, by Corps Transport, all expenses to be borne by the Aga Kagan government. That's agreeable, I assume?" Retief looked expectantly at the purple face of the prone potentate. The Aga Kaga grunted a strangled grunt.

"Speak up, Stanley," Retief said. "Give him plenty of air, Georges."

"Shall I let some in through the side?"

"Not yet. I'm sure Stanley wants to be agreeable."

The Aga Kaga snarled.

"Maybe just a little then, Georges," Retief said judiciously. Georges jabbed the knife in far enough to draw a bead of blood. The Aga Kaga grunted.

"Agreed!" he snorted. "By the beard of the prophet, when I get my hands on you...."

"Second item: certain fields, fishing grounds, et cetera, have suffered damage due to the presence of the aforementioned illegal immigrants. Full compensation will be made by the Aga Kagan government. Agreed?"

* * * *

The Aga Kaga drew a breath, tensed himself; Georges jabbed with the knife point. His prisoner relaxed with a groan. "Agreed!" he grated. "A vile tactic! You enter my tent under the guise of guests, protected by diplomatic immunity—"

"I had the impression we were herded in here at sword point," said Retief. "Shall we go on? Now there's the little matter of restitution for violation of sovereignty, reparations for mental anguish, payment for damaged fences, roads, drainage canals, communications, et cetera, et cetera. Shall I read them all?"

"Wait until the news of this outrage is spread abroad!"

"They'd never believe it," Retief said. "History would prove it impossible. And on mature consideration, I'm sure you won't want it noised about that you entertained visiting dignitaries flat on your back."

"What about the pollution of the atmosphere by goats?" Georges put in. "And don't overlook the muddying of streams, the destruction of timber for camp fires and—"

"I've covered all that sort of thing under a miscellaneous heading," Retief said. "We can fill it in at leisure when we get back."

"Bandits!" the Aga Kaga hissed. "Thieves! Dogs of unreliable imperialists!"

"It is disillusioning, I know," Retief said. "Still, of such little surprises is history made. Sign here." He held the parchment out and offered a pen. "A nice clear signature, please. We wouldn't want any quibbling about the legality of the treaty, after conducting the negotiation with such scrupulous regard for the niceties."

"Niceties! Never in history has such an abomination been perpetrated!"

"Oh, treaties are always worked out this way, when it comes right down to it. We've just accelerated the process a little. Now, if you'll just sign like a good fellow, we'll be on our way. Georges will have his work cut out for him, planning how to use all this reparations money."

The Aga Kaga gnashed his teeth: Georges prodded. The Aga Kaga seized the pen and scrawled his name. Retief signed with a flourish. He tucked the treaty away in his briefcase, took out another.

"This is just a safe-conduct, to get us out of the door and into the car," he said. "Probably unnecessary, but it won't hurt to have it, in case you figure out some way to avoid your obligations as a host."

The Aga Kaga signed the document after another prod from Georges.

"One more paper, and I'll be into the jugular," he said.

* * * *

"We're all through now," said Retief. "Stanley, we're going to have to run now. I'm going to strap up your hands and feet a trifle; it shouldn't take you more than ten minutes or so to get loose, stick a band-aid on your neck and—"

"My men will cut you down for the rascals you are!"

"By that time, we'll be over the hill," Retief continued. "At full throttle; we'll be at Government House in an hour, and of course I won't waste any time transmitting the treaty to Sector HQ. And the same concern for face that keeps you from yelling for help will insure that the details of the negotiation remain our secret."

"Treaty! That scrap of paper!"

"I confess the Corps is a little sluggish about taking action at times," Retief said, whipping a turn of silken cord around the Aga Kaga's ankles. "But once it's got signatures on a legal treaty, it's extremely stubborn about all parties adhering to the letter. It can't afford to be otherwise, as I'm sure you'll understand." He cinched up the cord, went to work on the hands. The Aga Kaga glared at him balefully.

"To the Pit with the Corps! The ferocity of my revenge—"

"Don't talk nonsense, Stanley. There are several squadrons of Peace Enforcers cruising in the Sector just now. I'm sure you're not ready to make any historical errors by taking them on." Retief finished and stood.

"Georges, just stuff a scarf in Stanley's mouth. I think he'd prefer to work quietly until he recovers his dignity." Retief buckled his briefcase, selected a large grape and looked down at the Aga Kaga.

"Actually, you'll be glad you saw things our way, Stanley," he said. "You'll get all the credit for the generous settlement. Of course, it will be a striking precedent for any other negotiations that may become necessary if you get grabby on other worlds in this region. And if your advisors want to know why the sudden change of heart, just tell them you've decided to start from scratch on an unoccupied world. Mention the virtues of thrift and hard work. I'm confident you can find plenty of historical examples to support you."

"Thanks for the drink," said Georges. "Drop in on me at Government House some time and we'll crack another bottle."

"And don't feel bad about your project's going awry," Retief said. "In the words of the prophet, 'Stolen goods are never sold at a loss.'"

* * * *

"A remarkable about-face, Retief," Magnan said. "Let this be a lesson to you. A stern Note of Protest can work wonders."

"A lot depends on the method of delivery," Retief said.

"Nonsense. I knew all along the Aga Kagans were a reasonable and peace-loving people. One of the advantages of senior rank, of course, is the opportunity to see the big picture. Why, I was saying only this morning—"

The desk screen broke into life. The mottled jowls of Under-Secretary Sternwheeler appeared.

"Magnan! I've just learned of the Flamme affair. Who's responsible?"

"Why, ah…I suppose that I might be said—"

"This is your work, is it?"

"Well…Mr. Retief did play the role of messenger."

"Don't pass the buck, Magnan!" the Under-Secretary barked. "What the devil went on out there?"

"Just a routine Protest Note. Everything is quite in order."

"Bah! Your over-zealousness has cost me dear. I was feeding Flamme to the Aga Kagans to consolidate our position of moral superiority for use as a lever in a number of important negotiations. Now they've backed out! Aga Kaga emerges from the affair wreathed in virtue. You've destroyed a very pretty finesse in power politics, Mr. Magnan! A year's work down the drain!"

"But I thought—"

"I doubt that, Mr. Magnan, I doubt that very much!" The Under-Secretary rang off.

"This is a fine turn of events," Magnan groaned. "Retief, you know very well Protest Notes are merely intended for the historical record! No one ever takes them seriously."

"You and the Aga Kaga ought to get together," said Retief. "He's a great one for citing historical parallels. He's not a bad fellow, as a matter of fact. I have an invitation from him to visit Kaga and go mud-pig hunting. He was so impressed by Corps methods that he wants to be sure we're on his side next time. Why don't you come along?"

"Hmmm. Perhaps I should cultivate him. A few high-level contacts never do any harm. On the other hand, I understand he lives in a very loose way, feasting and merrymaking. Frivolous in the extreme. No wife, you understand, but hordes of lightly clad women about. And in that connection, the Aga Kagans have some very curious notions as to what constitutes proper hospitality to a guest."

Retief rose, pulled on the powder blue cloak and black velvet gauntlets of a Career Minister.

"Don't let it worry you," he said. "You'll have a great time. And as the Aga Kaga would say, 'Ugliness is the best safeguard of virginity.'"

SALINE SOLUTION

Originally published in **Worlds of If Science Fiction,** *March 1963.*

I

Consul-General Magnan gingerly fingered the heavily rubber-banded sheaf of dog-eared documents. "I haven't rushed into precipitate action on this claim, Retief," he said. "The Consulate has grave responsibilities here in the Belt. One must weigh all aspects of the situation, consider the ramifications. What consequences would arise from a grant of minerals rights on the planetoid to this claimant?"

"The claim looked all right to me," Retief said. "Seventeen copies with attachments. Why not process it? You've had it on your desk for a week."

Magnan's eyebrows went up. "You've a personal interest in this claim, Retief?"

"Every day you wait is costing them money. That hulk they use for an ore-carrier is in a parking orbit piling up demurrage."

"I see you've become emotionally involved in the affairs of a group of obscure miners. You haven't yet learned the true diplomat's happy faculty of non-identification with specifics—or should I say identification with non-specifics?"

"They're not a wealthy outfit, you know. In fact, I understand this claim is their sole asset—unless you want to count the ore-carrier."

"The Consulate is not concerned with the internal financial problems of the Sam's Last Chance Number Nine Mining Company."

"Careful," Retief said. "You almost identified yourself with a specific that time."

"Hardly, my dear Retief," Magnan said blandly. "The implication is mightier than the affidavit. You should study the records of the giants of galactic diplomacy: Crodfoller, Passwyn, Spradley, Nitworth, Sternwheeler, Rumpwhistle. The roll-call of those names rings like the majestic tread of...of...."

"Dinosaurs?" Retief suggested.

"An apt simile," Magnan nodded. "Those mighty figures, those armored hides—"

"Those tiny brains—"

Magnan smiled sadly. "I see you're indulging your penchant for distorted facetiae. Perhaps one day you'll learn their true worth."

"I already have my suspicions."

The intercom chimed. Miss Gumble's features appeared on the desk screen.

"Mr. Leatherwell to see you, Mr. Magnan. He has no appointment—"

Magnan's eyebrows went up. "Send Mr. Leatherwell right in." He looked at Retief. "I had no idea Leatherwell was planning a call. I wonder what he's after?" Magnan looked anxious. "He's an important figure in Belt minerals circles. It's important to avoid arousing antagonism, while maintaining non-commitment. You may as well stay. You might pick up some valuable pointers technique-wise."

* * * *

The door swung wide. Leatherwell strode into the room, his massive paunch buckled into fashionable vests of turquoise velvet and hung with the latest in fluorescent watch charms. He extended a large palm and pumped Magnan's flaccid arm vigorously.

"Ah, there, Mr. Consul-General. Good of you to receive me." He wiped his hand absently on his thigh, eyeing Retief questioningly.

"Mr. Retief, my Vice-Consul and Minerals Officer," Magnan said. "Do take a chair, Mr. Leatherwell. In what capacity can I serve today?"

"I am here, gentlemen," Leatherwell said, putting an immense yellow briefcase on Magnan's desk and settling himself in a power rocker, "on behalf of my company, General Minerals. General Minerals has long been aware, gentlemen, of the austere conditions obtaining here in the Belt, to which public servants like yourselves are subjected." Leatherwell bobbed with the pitch of the rocker, smiling complacently at Magnan. "General Minerals is more than a great industrial combine. It is an organization with a heart." Leatherwell reached for his breast pocket, missed, tried again. "How do you turn this damned thing off?" he growled.

Magnan half-rose, peering over Leatherwell's briefcase. "The switch just there—on the arm."

The executive fumbled. There was a *click*, and the chair subsided with a sigh of compressed air.

"That's better." Leatherwell drew out a long slip of blue paper.

"To alleviate the boredom and brighten the lives of that hardy group of Terrestrials laboring here on Ceres to bring free enterprise to the Belt, General Minerals is presenting to the Consulate—on their behalf—one hundred thousand credits for the construction of a Joy Center, to be equipped with the latest and finest in recreational equipment, including a Gourmet Model C banquet synthesizer, a forty-foot sublimation chamber, a five thousand tape library—with a number of choice items unobtainable in Boston—a twenty-foot Tri-D tank and other amenities too numerous to mention." Leatherwell leaned back, beaming expectantly.

"Why, Mr. Leatherwell. We're overwhelmed, of course." Magnan smiled dazedly past the briefcase. "But I wonder if it's quite proper...."

"The gift is to the people, Mr. Consul. You merely accept on their behalf."

"I wonder if General Minerals realizes that the hardy Terrestrials laboring on Ceres are limited to the Consular staff?" Retief said. "And the staff consists of Mr. Magnan, Miss Gumble and myself."

"Mr. Leatherwell is hardly interested in these details, Retief," Magnan cut in. "A public-spirited offer indeed, sir. As Terrestrial Consul—and on behalf of all Terrestrials here in the Belt—I accept with a humble awareness of—"

"Now, there was one other little matter." Leatherwell leaned forward to open the briefcase, glancing over Magnan's littered desktop. He extracted a bundle of papers, dropped them on the desk, then drew out a heavy document and passed it across to Magnan.

"Just a routine claim. I'd like to see it rushed through, as we have in mind some loading operations in the vicinity next week."

"Certainly Mr. Leatherwell."

Magnan glanced at the papers, paused to read. He looked up. "Ah—"

"Something the matter, Mr. Consul?" Leatherwell demanded.

"It's just that—ah—I seem to recall—as a matter of fact...." Magnan looked at Retief. Retief took the papers, looked over the top sheet.

"95739-A. Sorry, Mr. Leatherwell. General Minerals has been anticipated. We're processing a prior claim."

"Prior claim?" Leatherwell barked. "You've issued the grant?"

"Oh, no indeed, Mr. Leatherwell," Magnan replied quickly. "The claim hasn't yet been processed."

"Then there's no difficulty," Leatherwell boomed. He glanced at his finger watch. "If you don't mind, I'll wait and take the grant along with me. I assume it will only take a minute or two to sign it and affix seals and so on?"

"The other claim was filed a full week ago—" Retief started.

"Bah!" Leatherwell waved a hand impatiently. "These details can be arranged." He fixed an eye on Magnan. "I'm sure all of us here understand that it's in the public interest that minerals properties go to responsible firms, with adequate capital for proper development."

"Why, ah," Magnan said.

"The Sam's Last Chance Number Nine Mining Company is a duly chartered firm. Their claim is valid."

"I know that hole-in-corner concern," Leatherwell snapped. "Mere irresponsible opportunists. General Minerals has spent millions—millions, I say—of the stockholders' funds in minerals explorations. Are they to be balked in realizing a fair return on their investment because these…these… adventures have stumbled on a deposit? Not that the property is of any real value, of course," he added. "Quite an ordinary bit of rock. But General Minerals would find it convenient to consolidate its holdings."

"There are plenty of other rocks floating around in the Belt. Why not—"

"One moment, Retief," Magnan cut in. He looked across the desk at his junior with a severe expression. "As Consul-General, I'm quite capable of determining the relative merits of claims. As Mr. Leatherwell has pointed out, it's in the public interest to consider the question in depth."

Leatherwell cleared his throat. "I might state at this time that General Minerals is prepared to be generous in dealing with these interlopers. I believe we would be prepared to go so far as to offer them free title to certain GM holdings in exchange for their release of any alleged rights to the property in question—merely to simplify matters, of course."

"That seems more than fair to me," Magnan glowed.

"The Sam's people have a clear priority," Retief said. "I logged the claim in last Friday."

"They have far from a clear title." Leatherwell snapped. "And I can assure you GM will contest their claim, if need be, to the Supreme Court!"

"Just what holdings did you have in mind offering them, Mr. Leatherwell?" Magnan asked nervously.

Leatherwell reached into his briefcase and drew out a paper.

"2645-P," he read. "A quite massive body. Crustal material, I imagine. It should satisfy these squatters' desire to own real estate in the Belt."

"I'll make a note of that," Magnan said, reaching for a pad.

"That's a Bona Fide offer, Mr. Leatherwell?" Retief asked.

"Certainly!"

"I'll record it as such," Magnan said, scribbling.

"And who knows?" Leatherwell said. "It may turn out to contain some surprisingly rich finds."

"And if they won't accept it?" Retief asked.

"Then I daresay General Minerals will find a remedy in the courts, sir!"

"Oh, I hardly think that will be necessary," Magnan said.

"Then there's another routine matter," Leatherwell said. He passed a second document across to Magnan. "GM is requesting an injunction to restrain these same parties from aggravated trespass. I'd appreciate it if you'd push it through at once. There's a matter of a load of illegally obtained ore involved, as well."

"Certainly Mr. Leatherwell. I'll see to it myself."

"No need for that. The papers are all drawn up. Our legal department will vouch for their correctness. Just sign here." Leatherwell spread out the paper and handed Magnan a pen.

"Wouldn't it be a good idea to read that over first?" Retief said.

* * * *

Leatherwell frowned impatiently. "You'll have adequate time to familiarize yourself with the details later, Retief," Magnan snapped, taking the pen. "No need to waste Mr. Leatherwell's valuable time." He scratched a signature on the paper.

Leatherwell rose, gathered up his papers from Magnan's desk, dumped them into the briefcase. "Riff-raff, of course. Their kind has no business in the Belt."

Retief rose, crossed to the desk, and held out a hand. "I believe you gathered in an official document along with your own, Mr. Leatherwell. By error, of course."

"What's that?" Leatherwell bridled. Retief smiled, waiting. Magnan opened his mouth.

"It was under your papers, Mr. Leatherwell," Retief said. "It's the thick one, with the rubber bands."

Leatherwell dug in his briefcase, produced the document. "Well, fancy finding this here," he growled. He shoved the papers into Retief's hand.

"You're a very observant young fellow." He closed the briefcase with a snap. "I trust you'll have a bright future with the CDT."

"Really, Retief," Magnan said reprovingly. "There was no need to trouble Mr. Leatherwell."

Leatherwell directed a sharp look at Retief and a bland one at Magnan. "I trust you'll communicate the proposal to the interested parties. Inasmuch as time is of the essence of the GM position, our offer can only be held open until 0900 Greenwich, tomorrow. I'll call again at that time to finalize matters. I trust there'll be no impediment to a satisfactory settlement at that time. I should dislike to embark on lengthy litigation."

Magnan hurried around his desk to open the door. He turned back to fix Retief with an exasperated frown.

"A crass display of boorishness, Retief," he snapped. "You've embarrassed a most influential member of the business community—and for nothing more than a few miserable forms."

"Those forms represent somebody's stake in what might be a valuable property."

"They're mere paper until they've been processed!"

"Still—"

"My responsibility is to the Public interest—not to a fly-by-night group of prospectors."

"They found it first."

"Bah! A worthless rock. After Mr. Leatherwell's munificent gesture—"

"Better rush his check through before he thinks it over and changes his mind."

"Good heavens!" Magnan clutched the check, buzzed for Miss Gumble. She swept in, took Magnan's instructions and left. Retief waited while Magnan glanced over the injunction, then nodded.

"Quite in order. A person called Sam Mancziewicz appears to be the principal. The address given is the Jolly Barge Hotel; that would be that converted derelict ship in orbit 6942, I assume?"

Retief nodded. "That's what they call it."

"As for the ore-carrier, I'd best impound it, pending the settlement of the matter." Magnan drew a form from a drawer, filled in blanks, shoved the paper across the desk. He turned and consulted a wall chart. "The hotel is nearby at the moment, as it happens. Take the Consulate dinghy. If you get out there right away, you'll catch them before the evening binge has developed fully."

"I take it that's your diplomatic way of telling me that I'm now a process server." Retief took the papers and tucked them into an inside pocket.

"One of the many functions a diplomat is called on to perform in a small consular post. Excellent experience. I needn't warn you to be circumspect. These miners are an unruly lot—especially when receiving bad news."

"Aren't we all." Retief rose. "I don't suppose there's any prospect of your signing off that claim so that I can take a little good news along, too?"

"None whatever," Magnan snapped. "They've been made a most generous offer. If that fails to satisfy them, they have recourse through the courts."

"Fighting a suit like that costs money. The Sam's Last Chance Mining Company hasn't got any."

"Need I remind you—"

"I know. That's none of our concern."

"On your way out," Magnan said as Retief turned to the door, "ask Miss Gumble to bring in the Gourmet catalog from the Commercial Library. I want to check on the specifications of the Model C Banquet synthesizer."

An hour later, nine hundred miles from Ceres and fast approaching the Jolly Barge Hotel, Retief keyed the skiff's transmitter.

"CDT 347-89 calling Navy FP-VO-6."

"Navy VO-6 here, CDT," a prompt voice came back. A flickering image appeared on the small screen. "Oh, hi there, Mr. Retief. What brings you out in the cold night air?"

"Hello, Henry. I'm estimating the Jolly Barge in ten minutes. It looks like a busy night ahead. I may be moving around a little. How about keeping an eye on me? I'll be carrying a personnel beacon. Monitor it, and if I switch it into high, come in fast. I can't afford to be held up. I've got a big meeting in the morning."

"Sure thing, Mr. Retief. We'll keep an eye open."

* * * *

Retief dropped a ten-credit note on the bar, accepted a glass and a squat bottle of black Marsberry brandy and turned to survey the low-ceilinged room, a former hydroponics deck now known as the Jungle Bar. Under the low ceiling, unpruned *Ipomoea batatas* and *Lathyrus odoratus* vines sprawled in a tangle that filtered the light of the S-spectrum glare panels to a muted green. A six-foot trideo screen, salvaged from the wreck of a Concordiat transport, blared taped music in the style of two centuries past. At the tables, heavy-shouldered men in bright-dyed suit liners played cards, clanked bottles and shouted.

Carrying the bottle and glass, Retief moved across to an empty chair at one of the tables.

"You gentlemen mind if I join you?"

Five unshaven faces turned to study Retief's six foot three, his close cut black hair, his non-commital gray coverall, the scars on his knuckles. A redhead with a broken nose nodded. "Pull up a chair, stranger."

"You workin' a claim, pardner?"

"Just looking around."

"Try a shot of this rock juice."

"Don't do it, Mister. He makes it himself."

"Best rock juice this side of Luna."

"Say, feller—"

"The name's Retief."

"Retief, you ever play Drift?"

"Can't say that I did."

"Don't gamble with Sam, pardner. He's the local champ."

"How do you play it?"

The black-browed miner who had suggested the game rolled back his sleeve to reveal a sinewy forearm, put his elbow on the table.

"You hook forefingers, and put a glass right up on top. The man that takes a swallow wins. If the drink spills, it's drinks for the house."

"A man don't often win out-right," the redhead said cheerfully. "But it makes for plenty of drinkin'."

Retief put his elbow on the table. "I'll give it a try."

The two men hooked forefingers. The redhead poured a tumbler half full of rock juice, placed it atop the two fists. "Okay, boys. Go!"

The man named Sam gritted his teeth; his biceps tensed, knuckles grew white. The glass trembled. Then it moved—toward Retief. Sam hunched his shoulders, straining.

"That's the stuff, Mister!"

"What's the matter, Sam? You tired?"

The glass moved steadily closer to Retief's face.

"A hundred the new man makes it!"

"Watch Sam! Any minute now…."

The glass slowed, paused. Retief's wrist twitched and the glass crashed to the table top. A shout went up. Sam leaned back with a sigh, massaging his hand.

"That's some arm you got, Mister," he said. "If you hadn't jumped just then…."

"I guess the drinks are on me," Retief said.

* * * *

Two hours later Retief's Marsberry bottle stood empty on the table beside half a dozen others.

"We were lucky," Sam Mancziewicz was saying. "You figure the original volume of the planet; say 245,000,000,000 cubic miles. The deBerry theory calls for a collapsed-crystal core no more than a mile in diameter. There's your odds."

"And you believe you've found a fragment of this core?"

"Damn right we have. Couple of million tons if it's an ounce. And at three credits a ton delivered at Port Syrtis, we're set for life. About time, too. Twenty years I've been in the Belt. Got two kids I haven't seen for five years. Things are going to be different now."

"Hey, Sam; tone it down. You don't have to broadcast to every claim jumper in the Belt."

"Our claim's on file at the Consulate," Sam said. "As soon as we get the grant—"

"When's that gonna be? We been waitin' a week now."

"I've never seen any collapsed-crystal metal," Retief said. "I'd like to take a look at it."

"Sure. Come on, I'll run you over. It's about an hour's run. We'll take our skiff. You want to go along, Willy?"

"I got a bottle to go," Willy said. "See you in the morning."

The two men descended in the lift to the boat bay, suited up and strapped into the cramped boat. A bored attendant cycled the launch doors, levered the release that propelled the skiff out and clear of the Jolly Barge Hotel. Retief caught a glimpse of a tower of lights spinning majestically against the black of space as the drive hurled the tiny boat away.

* * * *

III

Retief's feet sank ankle deep into the powdery surface that glinted like snow in the glare of the distant sun.

"It's funny stuff," Sam's voice sounded in his ear. "Under a gee of gravity, you'd sink out of sight. The stuff cuts diamond like butter—but temperature changes break it down into a powder. A lot of it's used just like this, as an industrial abrasive. Easy to load, too. Just drop a suction line, put on ambient pressure and start pumping."

"And this whole rock is made of the same material?"

"Sure is. We ran plenty of test bores and a full schedule of soundings. I've got the reports back aboard *Gertie*—that's our lighter."

"And you've already loaded a cargo here?"

"Yep. We're running out of capital fast. I need to get that cargo to port in a hurry—before the outfit goes into involuntary bankruptcy. With this, that'd be a crime."

"What do you know about General Minerals, Sam?"

"You thinking of hiring on with them? Better read the fine print in your contract before you sign. Sneakiest bunch this side of a burglar's convention."

"They own a chunk of rock known as 2645-P. Do you suppose we could find it?"

"Oh, you're buying it, hey? Sure, we can find it. You damn sure want to look it over good if General Minerals is selling."

Back aboard the skiff, Mancziewicz flipped the pages of the chart book, consulted a table. "Yep, she's not too far off. Let's go see what GM's trying to unload."

* * * *

The skiff hovered two miles from the giant boulder known as 2645-P. Retief and Mancziewicz looked it over at high magnification. "It don't look like much, Retief," Sam said. "Let's go down and take a closer look."

The boat dropped rapidly toward the scarred surface of the tiny world, a floating mountain, glaring black and white in the spotlight of the sun. Sam frowned at his instrument panel.

"That's funny. My ion counter is revving up. Looks like a drive trail, not more than an hour or two old. Somebody's been here."

The boat grounded. Retief and Sam got out. The stony surface was littered with rock fragments varying in size from pebbles to great slabs twenty feet long, tumbled in a loose bed of dust and sand. Retief pushed off gently, drifted up to a vantage point atop an upended wedge of rock. Sam joined him.

"This is all igneous stuff," he said. "Not likely we'll find much here that would pay the freight to Syrtis—unless maybe you lucked onto some Bodean artifacts. They bring plenty."

He flipped a binocular in place as he talked, scanned the riven landscape. "Hey!" he said. "Over there!"

Retief followed Sam's pointing glove. He studied the dark patch against a smooth expanse of eroded rock.

"A friend of mine came across a chunk of the old planetary surface two years ago," Sam said thoughtfully. "Had a tunnel in it that'd been used as a storage depot by the Bodeans. Took out over two ton of hardware. Course, nobody's discovered how the stuff works yet, but it brings top prices."

"Looks like water erosion," Retief said.

"Yep. This could be another piece of surface, all right. Could be a cave over there. The Bodeans liked caves, too. Must have been some war—but then, if it hadn't been, they wouldn't have tucked so much stuff away underground where it could weather the planetary breakup."

They descended, crossed the jumbled rocks with light, thirty-foot leaps.

"It's a cave, all right," Sam said, stooping to peer into the five-foot bore. Retief followed him inside.

"Let's get some light in here." Mancziewicz flipped on a beam. It glinted back from dull polished surfaces of Bodean synthetic. Sam's low whistle sounded in Retief's headset.

"That's funny," Retief said.

"Funny, hell! It's hilarious. General Minerals trying to sell off a worthless rock to a tenderfoot—and it's loaded with Bodean artifacts. No telling how much is here; the tunnel seems to go quite a ways back."

"That's not what I mean. Do you notice your suit warming up?"

"Huh? Yeah, now that you mention it."

Retief rapped with a gauntleted hand on the satiny black curve of the nearest Bodean artifact. It clunked dully through the suit "That's not metal," he said. "It's plastic."

"There's something fishy here," Sam said. "This erosion; it looks more like a heat beam."

"Sam," Retief said, turning, "it appears to me somebody has gone to a great deal of trouble to give a false impression here."

Sam snorted. "I told you they were a crafty bunch." He started out of the cave, then paused, went to one knee to study the floor. "But maybe they outsmarted themselves. Look here!"

Retief looked. Sam's beam reflected from a fused surface of milky white, shot through with dirty yellow. He snapped a pointed instrument in place on his gauntlet, dug at one of the yellow streaks. It furrowed under the gouge, a particle adhering to the instrument. With his left hand, Mancziewicz opened a pouch clipped to his belt, carefully deposited the sample in a small orifice on the device in the pouch. He flipped a key, squinted at a dial.

"Atomic weight 197.2," he said. Retief turned down the audio volume on his headset as Sam's laughter rang in his helmet.

"Those clowns were out to stick you, Retief," he gasped, still chuckling. "They salted the rock with a cave full of Bodean artifacts—"

"Fake Bodean artifacts," Retief put in.

"They planed off the rock so it would look like an old beach, and then cut this cave with beamers. And they were boring through practically solid gold!"

"As good as that?"

Mancziewicz flashed the light around. "This stuff will assay out at a thousand credits a ton, easy. If the vein doesn't run to five thousand tons, the beers are on me." He snapped off the light. "Let's get moving, Retief. You want to sew this deal up before they get around to taking another look at it."

Back in the boat, Retief and Mancziewicz opened their helmets. "This calls for a drink," Sam said, extracting a pressure flask from the map case. "This rock's worth as much as mine, maybe more. You hit it lucky, Retief. Congratulations." He thrust out a hand.

"I'm afraid you've jumped to a couple of conclusions, Sam," Retief said. "I'm not out here to buy mining properties."

"You're not—then why—but man! Even if you didn't figure on buying…." He trailed off as Retief shook his head, unzipped his suit to reach to an inside pocket, take out a packet of folded papers.

"In my capacity as Terrestrial Vice-Consul, I'm serving you with an injunction restraining you from further exploitation of the body known as 95739-A." He handed a paper across to Sam. "I also have here an Order impounding the vessel *Gravel Gertie II*."

Sam took the papers silently, sat looking at them. He looked up at Retief. "Funny. When you beat me at Drift and then threw the game so you wouldn't show me up in front of the boys, I figured you for a right guy. I've been spilling my heart out to you like you were my old grandma. An old-timer in the game like me." He dropped a hand, brought it up with a Browning 2mm pointed at Retief's chest.

"I could shoot you and dump you here with a slab over you, toss these papers in the John and hightail it with the load…."

"That wouldn't do you much good in the long run, Sam. Besides you're not a criminal or an idiot."

Sam chewed his lip. "My claim is on file in the Consulate, legal and proper. Maybe by now the grant's gone through."

"Other people have their eye on your rock, Sam. Ever meet a fellow called Leatherwell?"

"General Minerals, huh? They haven't got a leg to stand on."

"The last time I saw your claim, it was still lying in the pending file. Just a bundle of paper until it's validated by the Consul. If Leatherwell contests it…well, his lawyers are on annual retainer. How long could you keep the suit going, Sam?"

Mancziewicz closed his helmet with a decisive snap, motioned to Retief to do the same. He opened the hatch, sat with the gun on Retief.

"Get out, paper-pusher." His voice sounded thin in the headphones. "You'll get lonesome, maybe, but your suit will keep you alive a few days. I'll tip somebody off before you lose too much weight. I'm going back and see if I can't stir up a little action at the Consulate."

Retief climbed out, walked off fifty yards. He watched as the skiff kicked off in a quickly dispersed cloud of dust, dwindled rapidly away to a bright speck that was lost against the stars. Then he extracted the locator beacon from the pocket of his suit and thumbed the control.

Twenty minutes later, aboard Navy FP-VO-6, Retief pulled off his helmet. "Fast work, Henry. I've got a couple of calls to make. Put me through to your HQ, will you? I want a word with Commander Hayle."

The young naval officer raised the HQ, handed the mike to Retief.

"Vice-Consul Retief here, Commander. I'd like you to intercept a skiff, bound from my present position toward Ceres. There's a Mr. Mancziewicz aboard. He's armed, but not dangerous. Collect him and see that he's delivered to the Consulate at 0900 Greenwich tomorrow.

"Next item: The Consulate has impounded an ore-carrier, *Gravel Gertie II*. It's in a parking orbit ten miles off Ceres. I want it taken in tow." Retief gave detailed instruction. Then he asked for a connection through the Navy switchboard to the Consulate. Magnan's voice answered.

"Retief speaking, Mr. Consul. I have some news that I think will interest you—"

"Where are you, Retief? What's wrong with the screen? Have you served the injunction?"

"I'm aboard the Navy patrol vessel. I've been out looking over the situation, and I've made a surprising discovery. I don't think we're going to have any trouble with the Sam's people; they've looked over the body— 2645-P—and it seems General Minerals has slipped up. There appears to be a highly valuable deposit there."

"Oh? What sort of deposit?"

"Mr. Mancziewicz mentioned collapsed crystal metal," Retief said.

"Well, most interesting." Magnan's voice sounded thoughtful.

"Just thought you'd like to know. This should simplify the meeting in the morning.

"Yes," Magnan said. "Yes, indeed. I think this makes everything very simple...."

* * * *

At 0845 Greenwich, Retief stepped into the outer office of the Consular suite.

"...fantastic configuration," Leatherwell's bass voice rumbled, "covering literally acres. My xenogeologists are somewhat confused by the formations. They had only a few hours to examine the site; but it's clear from the extent of the surface indications that we have a very rich find here. Very rich indeed. Beside it, 95739-A dwindles into insignificance. Very fast thinking on your part, Mr. Consul, to bring the matter to my attention."

"Not at all, Mr. Leatherwell. After all—"

"Our tentative theory is that the basic crystal fragment encountered the core material at some time, and gathered it in. Since we had been working on—that is, had landed to take samples on the other side of the body, this anomalous deposit escaped our attention completely."

Retief stepped into the room.

"Good morning, gentlemen. Has Mr. Mancziewicz arrived?"

"Mr. Mancziewicz is under restraint by the Navy. I've had a call that he'd be escorted here."

"Arrested, eh?" Leatherwell nodded. "I told you these people were an irresponsible group. In a way it seems a pity to waste a piece of property like 95739-A on them."

"I understood General Minerals was claiming that rock," Retief said, looking surprised.

Leatherwell and Magnan exchanged glances. "Ah, GM has decided to drop all claim to the body," Leatherwell said. "As always, we wish to encourage enterprise on the part of the small operators. Let them keep the property. After all GM has other deposits well worth exploiting." He smiled complacently.

"What about 2645-P? You've offered it to the Sam's group."

"That offer is naturally withdrawn!" Leatherwell snapped.

"I don't see how you can withdraw the offer," Retief said. "It's been officially recorded. It's a Bona Fide contract, binding on General Minerals, subject to—"

"Out of the goodness of our corporate heart," Leatherwell roared, "we've offered to relinquish our legitimate, rightful claim to asteroid 2645-P. And you have the infernal gall to spout legal technicalities! I have half a mind to withdraw my offer to withdraw!"

"Actually," Magnan put in, eyeing a corner of the room, "I'm not at all sure I could turn up the record of the offer of 2645-P. I noted it down on a bit of scratch paper—"

"That's all right," Retief said, "I had my pocket recorder going. I sealed the record and deposited it in the Consular archives."

There was a clatter of feet outside. Miss Gumble appeared on the desk screen. "There are a number of persons here—" she began.

* * * *

The door banged open. Sam Mancziewicz stepped into the room, a sailor tugging at each arm. He shook them loose, stared around the room. His eyes lighted on Retief. "How did you get here...?"

"Look here, Monkeywits or whatever your name is," Leatherwell began, popping out of his chair.

Mancziewicz whirled, seized the stout executive by the shirt front and lifted him onto his tiptoes. "You double-barreled copper-bottomed oak-lined son-of-a—"

"Don't spoil him, Sam," Retief said casually. "He's here to sign off all rights—if any—to 95739-A. It's all yours—if you want it."

Sam glared into Leatherwell's eyes. "That right?" he grated. Leatherwell bobbed his head, his chins compressed into bulging folds.

"However," Retief went on, "I wasn't at all sure you'd still be agreeable, since he's made your company a binding offer of 2645-P in return for clear title to 95739-A."

Mancziewicz looked across at Retief with narrowed eyes. He released Leatherwell, who slumped into his chair. Magnan darted around his desk to minister to the magnate. Behind them, Retief closed one eye in a broad wink at Mancziewicz.

"...still, if Mr. Leatherwell will agree, in addition to guaranteeing your title to 95739-A, to purchase your output at four credits a ton, FOB his collection station—"

Mancziewicz looked at Leatherwell. Leatherwell hesitated, then nodded. "Agreed," he croaked.

"...and to open his commissary and postal facilities to all prospectors operating in the belt...."

Leatherwell swallowed, eyes bulging, glanced at Mancziewicz's face. He nodded. "Agreed."

"...then I think I'd sign an agreement releasing him from his offer."

Mancziewicz looked at Magnan.

"You're the Terrestrial Consul-General," he said. "Is that the straight goods?"

Magnan nodded. "If Mr. Leatherwell agrees—"

"He's already agreed," Retief said. "My pocket recorder, you know."

"Put it in writing," Mancziewicz said.

Magnan called in Miss Gumble. The others waited silently while Magnan dictated. He signed the paper with a flourish, passed it across to Mancziewicz. He read it, re-read it, then picked up the pen and signed. Magnan impressed the Consular seal on the paper.

"Now the grant," Retief said. Magnan signed the claim, added a seal. Mancziewicz tucked the papers away in an inner pocket. He rose.

"Well, gents, I guess maybe I had you figured wrong," he said. He looked at Retief. "Uh…got time for a drink?"

"I shouldn't drink during office hours," Retief said. He rose. "So I'll take the rest of the day off."

* * * *

"I don't get it," Sam said signalling for refills. "What was the routine with the injunction—and impounding *Gertie*? You could have got hurt."

"I don't think so," Retief said. "If you'd meant business with that Browning, you'd have flipped the safety off. As for the injunction—orders are orders."

"I've been thinking," Sam said. "That gold deposit. It was a plant, too, wasn't it?"

"I'm just a bureaucrat, Sam. What would I know about gold?"

"A double-salting job," Sam said. "I was supposed to spot the phoney hardware—and then fall for the gold plant. When Leatherwell put his proposition to me, I'd grab it. The gold was worth plenty, I'd figure, and I couldn't afford a legal tangle with General Minerals. The lousy skunk! And you must have spotted it and put it up to him."

The bar-tender leaned across to Retief. "Wanted on the phone."

In the booth, Magnan's agitated face stared a Retief.

"Retief, Mr. Leatherwell's in a towering rage! The deposit on 2645-P; it was merely a surface film, barely a few inches thick! The entire deposit wouldn't fill an ore-boat." A horrified expression dawned on Magnan's face. "Retief," he gasped, "what did you do with the impounded ore-carrier?"

"Well, let me see," Retief said. "According to the Space Navigation Code, a body in orbit within twenty miles of any inhabited airless body constitutes a navigational hazard. Accordingly, I had it towed away."

"And the cargo?"

"Well, accelerating all that mass was an expensive business, so to save the taxpayer's credits, I had it dumped."

"Where?" Magnan croaked.

"On some unimportant asteroid—as specified by Regulations." He smiled blandly at Magnan. Magnan looked back numbly.

"But you said—"

"All I said was that there was what looked like a valuable deposit on 2645-P. It turned out to be a bogus gold mine that somebody had rigged up in a hurry. Curious, eh?"

"But you told me—"

"And you told Mr. Leatherwell. Indiscreet of you, Mr. Consul. That was a privileged communication; classified information, official use only."

"You led me to believe there was collapsed crystal!"

"I said Sam had mentioned it. He told me his asteroid was made of the stuff."

Magnan swallowed hard, twice. "By the way," he said dully. "You were right about the check. Half an hour ago Mr. Leatherwell tried to stop payment. He was too late."

"All in all, it's been a big day for Leatherwell," Retief said. "Anything else?"

"I hope not," Magnan said. "I sincerely hope not." He leaned close to the screen. "You'll consider the entire affair as...confidential? There's no point in unduly complicating relationships."

"Have no fear, Mr. Consul," Retief said cheerfully. "You won't find me identifying with anything as specific as triple-salting an asteroid."

Back at the table, Sam called for another bottle of rock juice.

"That Drift's a pretty good game," Retief said. "But let me show you one I learned out on Yill...."

[Transcriber's Note: No Section II heading in original text.]

MIGHTIEST QORN

Originally published in **Worlds of If Science Fiction,** *July 1963.*

I

Ambassador Nitworth glowered across his mirror-polished, nine-foot platinum desk at his assembled staff.

"Gentlemen, are any of you familiar with a race known as the Qornt?"

There was a moment of profound silence. Nitworth leaned forward, looking solemn.

"They were a warlike race known in this sector back in Concordiat times, perhaps two hundred years ago. They vanished as suddenly as they had appeared. There was no record of where they went." He paused for effect.

"They have now reappeared—occupying the inner planet of this system!"

"But, sir," Second Secretary Magnan offered. "That's uninhabited Terrestrial territory...."

"Indeed, Mr. Magnan?" Nitworth smiled icily. "It appears the Qornt do not share that opinion." He plucked a heavy parchment from a folder before him, harrumphed and read aloud:

His Supreme Excellency The Qorn, Regent of Qornt, Over-Lord of the Galactic Destiny, Greets the Terrestrials and, with reference to the presence in mandated territory of Terrestrial squatters, has the honor to advise that he will require the use of his outer world on the thirtieth day. Then will the Qornt come with steel and fire. Receive, Terrestrials, renewed assurances of my awareness of your existence, and let Those who dare gird for the contest.

"Frankly, I wouldn't call it conciliatory," Magnan said.

Nitworth tapped the paper with a finger.

"We have been served, gentlemen, with nothing less than an Ultimatum!"

"Well, we'll soon straighten these fellows out—" the Military Attache began.

"There happens to be more to this piece of truculence than appears on the surface," the Ambassador cut in. He paused, waiting for interested frowns to settle into place.

"Note, gentlemen, that these invaders have appeared on terrestrial controlled soil—and without so much as a flicker from the instruments of the Navigational Monitor Service!"

The Military Attache blinked. "That's absurd," he said flatly. Nitworth slapped the table.

"We're up against something new, gentlemen! I've considered every hypothesis from cloaks of invisibility to time travel! The fact is—the Qornt fleets are indetectible!"

* * * *

The Military Attache pulled at his lower lip. "In that case, we can't try conclusions with these fellows until we have an indetectible drive of our own. I recommend a crash project. In the meantime—"

"I'll have my boys start in to crack this thing," the Chief of the Confidential Terrestrial Source Section spoke up. "I'll fit out a couple of volunteers with plastic beaks—"

"No cloak and dagger work, gentlemen! Long range policy will be worked out by Deep-Think teams back at the Department. Our role will be a holding action. Now I want suggestions for a comprehensive, well rounded and decisive course for meeting this threat. Any recommendation?"

The Political Officer placed his fingertips together. "What about a stiff Note demanding an extra week's time?"

"No! No begging," the Economic Officer objected. "I'd say a calm, dignified, aggressive withdrawal—as soon as possible."

"We don't want to give them the idea we spook easily," the Military Attache said. "Let's delay the withdrawal—say, until tomorrow."

"Early tomorrow," Magnan said. "Or maybe later today."

"Well, I see you're of a mind with me," Nitworth nodded. "Our plan of action is clear, but it remains to be implemented. We have a population of over fifteen million individuals to relocate." He eyed the Political Officer. "I want five proposals for resettlement on my desk by oh-eight-hundred hours tomorrow." Nitworth rapped out instructions. Harried-looking staff members arose and hurried from the room. Magnan eased toward the door.

"Where are you going, Magnan?" Nitworth snapped.

"Since you're so busy, I thought I'd just slip back down to Com Inq. It was a most interesting orientation lecture, Mr. Ambassador. Be sure to let us know how it works out."

"Kindly return to your chair," Nitworth said coldly. "A number of chores remain to be assigned. I think you, Magnan, need a little field experience. I want you to get over to Roolit I and take a look at these Qornt personally."

Magnan's mouth opened and closed soundlessly.

"Not afraid of a few Qornt, are you, Magnan?"

"Afraid? Good lord, no, ha ha. It's just that I'm afraid I may lose my head and do something rash if I go."

"Nonsense! A diplomat is immune to heroic impulses. Take Retief along. No dawdling, now! I want you on the way in two hours. Notify the transport pool at once. Now get going!"

Magnan nodded unhappily and went into the hall.

"Oh, Retief," Nitworth said. Retief turned.

"Try to restrain Mr. Magnan from any impulsive moves—in any direction."

* * * *

II

Retief and Magnan topped a ridge and looked down across a slope of towering tree-shrubs and glossy violet-stemmed palms set among flamboyant blossoms of yellow and red, reaching down to a strip of white beach with the blue sea beyond.

"A delightful vista," Magnan said, mopping at his face. "A pity we couldn't locate the Qornt. We'll go back now and report—"

"I'm pretty sure the settlement is off to the right," Retief said. "Why don't you head back for the boat, while I ease over and see what I can observe."

"Retief, we're engaged in a serious mission. This is not a time to think of sightseeing."

"I'd like to take a good look at what we're giving away."

"See here, Retief! One might almost receive the impression that you're questioning Corps policy!"

"One might, at that. The Qornt have made their play, but I think it might be valuable to take a look at their cards before we fold. If I'm not back at the boat in an hour, lift without me."

"You expect me to make my way back alone?"

"It's directly down-slope—" Retief broke off, listening. Magnan clutched at his arm.

There was a sound of crackling foliage. Twenty feet ahead, a leafy branch swung aside. An eight-foot biped stepped into view, long, thin, green-clad legs with back-bending knees moving in quick, bird-like steps. A pair of immense black-lensed goggles covered staring eyes set among bushy green hair above a great bone-white beak. The crest bobbed as the creature cocked its head, listening.

Magnan gulped audibly. The Qornt froze, head tilted, beak aimed directly at the spot where the Terrestrials stood in the deep shade of a giant trunk.

"I'll go for help," Magnan squeaked. He whirled and took three leaps into the brush.

A second great green-clad figure rose up to block his way. He spun, darted to the left. The first Qornt pounced, grappled Magnan to its narrow chest. Magnan yelled, threshing and kicking, broke free, turned—and collided with the eight-foot alien, coming in fast from the right. All three went down in a tangle of limbs.

Retief jumped forward, hauled Magnan free, thrust him aside and stopped, right fist cocked. The two Qornt lay groaning feebly.

"Nice piece of work, Mr. Magnan," Retief said. "You nailed both of them."

* * * *

"Those undoubtedly are the most bloodthirsty, aggressive, merciless countenances it has ever been my misfortune to encounter," Magnan said. "It hardly seems fair. Eight feet tall *and* faces like that!"

The smaller of the two captive Qornt ran long, slender fingers over a bony shin, from which he had turned back the tight-fitting green trousers.

"It's not broken," he whistled nasally in passable Terrestrial, eyeing Magnan through the heavy goggles, now badly cracked. "Small thanks to you."

Magnan smiled loftily. "I daresay you'll think twice before interfering with peaceable diplomats in future."

"Diplomats? Surely you jest."

"Never mind us," Retief said. "It's you fellows we'd like to talk about. How many of you are there?"

"Only Zubb and myself."

"I mean altogether. How many Qornt?"

The alien whistled shrilly.

"Here, no signalling!" Magnan snapped, looking around.

"That was merely an expression of amusement."

"You find the situation amusing? I assure you, sir, you are in perilous straits at the moment. I *may* fly into another rage, you know."

"Please, restrain yourself. I was merely somewhat astonished—" a small whistle escaped—"at being taken for a Qornt."

"Aren't you a Qornt?"

"I? Great snail trails, no!" More stifled whistles of amusement escaped the beaked face. "Both Zubb and I are Verpp. Naturalists, as it happens."

"You certainly *look* like Qornt."

"Oh, not at all—except perhaps to a Terrestrial. The Qornt are sturdily built rascals, all over ten feet in height. And, of course, they do nothing but quarrel. A drone caste, actually."

"A caste? You mean they're biologically the same as you?"

"Not at all! A Verpp wouldn't think of fertilizing a Qornt."

"I mean to say, you are of the same basic stock—descended from a common ancestor, perhaps."

"We are all Pud's creatures."

"What are the differences between you, then?"

"Why, the Qornt are argumentive, boastful, lacking in appreciation for the finer things of life. One dreads to contemplate descending to *their* level."

"Do you know anything about a Note passed to the Terrestrial Ambassador at Smorbrod?" Retief asked.

* * * *

The beak twitched. "Smorbrod? I know of no place called Smorbrod."

"The outer planet of this system."

"Oh, yes. We call it Guzzum. I had heard that some sort of creatures had established a settlement there, but I confess I pay little note to such matters."

"We're wasting time, Retief," Magnan said. "We must truss these chaps up, hurry back to the boat and make our escape. You heard what they said."

"Are there any Qornt down there at the harbor, where the boats are?" Retief asked.

"At Tarroon, you mean? Oh, yes. Planning some adventure."

"That would be the invasion of Smorbrod," Magnan said. "And unless we hurry, Retief, we're likely to be caught there with the last of the evacuees!"

"How many Qornt would you say there are at Tarroon?"

"Oh, a very large number. Perhaps fifteen or twenty."

"Fifteen or twenty what?" Magnan looked perplexed.

"Fifteen or twenty Qornt."

"You mean that there are only fifteen or twenty individual Qornt in all?"

Another whistle. "Not at all. I was referring to the local Qornt only. There are more at the other Centers, of course."

"And the Qornt are responsible for the ultimatum—unilaterally?"

"I suppose so; it sounds like them. A truculent group, you know. And interplanetary relations *are* rather a hobby of theirs."

Zubb moaned and stirred. He sat up slowly, rubbing his head. He spoke to his companion in a shrill alien clatter of consonants.

"What did he say?"

"Poor Zubb. He blames me for his bruises, since it was my idea to gather you as specimens."

"You should have known better than to tackle that fierce-looking creature," Zubb said, pointing his beak at Magnan.

"How does it happen that you speak Terrestrial?" Retief asked.

"Oh, one picks up all sorts of dialects."

"It's quite charming, really," Magnan said. "Such a quaint, archaic accent."

"Suppose we went down to Tarroon," Retief asked. "What kind of reception would we get?"

"That depends. I wouldn't recommend interfering with the Gwil or the Rheuk; it's their nest-mending time, you know. The Boog will be busy mating—such a tedious business—and of course the Qornt are tied up with their ceremonial feasting. I'm afraid no one will take any notice of you."

"Do you mean to say," Magnan demanded, "that these ferocious Qornt, who have issued an ultimatum to the Corps Diplomatique Terrestrienne—who openly avow their occupied world—would ignore Terrestrials in their midst?"

"If at all possible."

Retief got to his feet.

"I think our course is clear, Mr. Magnan. It's up to us to go down and attract a little attention."

* * * *

III

"I'm not at all sure we're going about this in the right way," Magnan puffed, trotting at Retief's side. "These fellows Zubb and Slun—Oh, they seem affable enough, but how can we be sure we're not being led into a trap?"

"We can't."

Magnan stopped short. "Let's go back."

"All right," Retief said. "Of course there may be an ambush—"

Magnan moved off. "Let's keep going."

The party emerged from the undergrowth at the edge of a great brush-grown mound. Slun took the lead, rounded the flank of the hillock, halted at a rectangular opening cut into the slope.

"You can find your way easily enough from here," he said. "You'll excuse us, I hope—"

"Nonsense, Slun!" Zubb pushed forward. "I'll escort our guests to Qornt Hall." He twittered briefly to his fellow Verpp. Slun twittered back.

"I don't like it, Retief," Magnan whispered. "Those fellows are plotting mischief."

"Threaten them with violence, Mr Magnan. They're scared of you."

"That's true. And the drubbing they received was well-deserved. I'm a patient man, but there are occasions—"

"Come along, please," Zubb called. "Another ten minutes' walk—"

"See here, we have no interest in investigating this barrow," Magnan announced. "We wish you to take us direct to Tarroon to interview your military leaders regarding the ultimatum!"

"Yes, yes, of course. Qornt Hall lies here inside the village."

"This is Tarroon?"

"A modest civic center, sir, but there are those who love it."

"No wonder we didn't observe their works from the air," Magnan muttered. "Camouflaged." He moved hesitantly through the opening.

The party moved along a wide, deserted tunnel which sloped down steeply, then leveled off and branched. Zubb took the center branch, ducking slightly under the nine-foot ceiling lit at intervals with what appeared to be primitive incandescent panels.

"Few signs of an advanced technology here," Magnan whispered. "These creatures must devote all their talents to warlike enterprise."

Ahead, Zubb slowed. A distant susurration was audible, a sustained high-pitched screeching. "Softly, now. We approach Qornt Hall. They can be an irascible lot when disturbed at their feasting."

"When will the feast be over?" Magnan called hoarsely.

"In another few weeks, I should imagine, if, as you say, they've scheduled an invasion for next month."

"Look here, Zubb." Magnan shook a finger at the tall alien. "How is it that these Qornt are allowed to embark on piratical ventures of this sort without reference to the wishes of the majority?"

"Oh, the majority of the Qornt favor the move, I imagine."

"These few hotheads are permitted to embroil the planet in war?"

"Oh, they don't embroil the planet in war. They merely—"

"Retief, this is fantastic! I've heard of iron-fisted military cliques before, but this is madness!"

"Come softly, now." Zubb beckoned, moving toward a bend in the yellow-lit corridor. Retief and Magnan moved forward.

* * * *

The corridor debouched through a high double door into a vast oval chamber, high-domed, gloomy, paneled in dark wood and hung with tattered banners, scarred halberds, pikes, rusted longswords, crossed spears over patinaed hauberks, pitted radiation armor, corroded power rifles, the immense mummified heads of horned and fanged animals. Great guttering torches in wall brackets and in stands along the length of the long table shed a smoky light that reflected from the mirror polish of the red granite floor, gleamed on polished silver bowls and paper-thin glass, shone jewel-red and gold through dark bottles—and cast long flickering shadows behind the fifteen trolls at the board.

Lesser trolls—beaked, bush-haired, great-eyed—trotted briskly, bird-kneed, bearing steaming platters, stood in groups of three strumming slender bottle-shaped lutes, or pranced an intricate-patterned dance, unnoticed in the shrill uproar as each of the magnificently draped, belted, feathered and jeweled Qornt carried on a shouted conversation with an equally noisy fellow.

"A most interesting display of barbaric splendor," Magnan breathed. "Now we'd better be getting back."

"Ah, a moment," Zubb said. "Observe the Qornt—the tallest of the feasters—he with the head-dress of crimson, purple, silver and pink."

"Twelve feet if he's an inch," Magnan estimated. "And now we really must hurry along—"

"That one is chief among these rowdies. I'm sure you'll want a word with him. He controls not only the Tarroonian vessels but those from the other Centers as well."

"What kind of vessels? Warships?"

"Certainly. What other kind would the Qornt bother with?"

"I don't suppose," Magnan said casually, "that you'd know the type, tonnage, armament and manning of these vessels? And how many units comprise the fleet? And where they're based at present?"

"They're fully automated twenty-thousand-ton all-purpose dread-naughts. They mount a variety of weapons. The Qornt are fond of that sort of thing. Each of the Qornt has his own, of course. They're virtually identical, except for the personal touches each individual has given his ship."

"Great heavens, Retief!" Magnan exclaimed in a whisper. "It sounds as though these brutes employ a battle armada as simpler souls might a set of toy sailboats!"

Retief stepped past Magnan and Zubb to study the feasting hall. "I can see that their votes would carry all the necessary weight."

"And now an interview with the Qorn himself," Zubb shrilled. "If you'll kindly step along, gentlemen...."

"That won't be necessary," Magnan said hastily, "I've decided to refer the matter to committee."

"After having come so far," Zubb said, "it would be a pity to miss having a cosy chat."

There was a pause.

"Ah...Retief," Magnan said. "Zubb has just presented a most compelling argument...."

Retief turned. Zubb stood gripping an ornately decorated power pistol in one bony hand, a slim needler in the other. Both were pointed at Magnan's chest.

"I suspected you had hidden qualities, Zubb," Retief commented.

"See here, Zubb! We're diplomats!" Magnan started.

"Careful, Mr. Magnan; you may goad him to a frenzy."

"By no means," Zubb whistled. "I much prefer to observe the frenzy of the Qornt when presented with the news that two peaceful Verpp have been assaulted and kidnapped by bullying interlopers. If there's anything that annoys the Qornt, it's Qornt-like behavior in others. Now step along, please."

"Rest assured, this will be reported!"

"I doubt it."

"You'll face the wrath of Enlightened Galactic Opinion!"

"Oh? How big a navy does Enlightened Galactic Opinion have?"

"Stop scaring him, Mr. Magnan. He may get nervous and shoot." Retief stepped into the banquet hall, headed for the resplendent figure at the head of the table. A trio of flute-players broke off in mid-bleat, staring. An inverted pyramid of tumblers blinked as Retief swung past, followed by Magnan and the tall Verpp. The shrill chatter at the table faded.

Qorn turned as Retief came up, blinking three-inch eyes. Zubb stepped forward, gibbered, waving his arms excitedly. Qorn pushed back his chair—a low, heavily padded stool—and stared unwinking at Retief, moving his head to bring first one great round eye, then the other, to bear. There were small blue veins in the immense fleshy beak. The bushy hair, springing out in a giant halo around the grayish, porous-skinned face, was wiry, stiff, moss-green, with tufts of chartreuse fuzz surrounding what appeared to be tympanic membranes. The tall head-dress of scarlet silk and purple feathers was slightly askew, and a loop of pink pearls had slipped down above one eye.

Zubb finished his speech and fell silent, breathing hard.

Qorn looked Retief over in silence, then belched.

"Not bad," Retief said admiringly. "Maybe we could get up a match between you and Ambassador Sternwheeler. You've got the volume on him, but he's got timbre."

"So," Qorn hooted in a resonant tenor. "You come from Guzzum, eh? Or Smorbrod, as I think you call it. What is it you're after? More time? A compromise? Negotiations? Peace?" He slammed a bony hand against the table. "The answer is *no*!"

Zubb twittered. Qorn cocked an eye, motioned to a servant. "Chain that one." He indicated Magnan. His eyes went to Retief. "This one's bigger; you'd best chain him, too."

"Why, your Excellency—" Magnan started, stepping forward.

"Stay back!" Qorn hooted. "Stand over there where I can keep an eye on you."

"Your Excellency, I'm empowered—"

"Not here, you're not!" Qorn trumpeted. "Want peace, do you? Well, I don't want peace! I've had a surfeit of peace these last two centuries! I want action! Loot! Adventure! Glory!" He turned to look down the table. "How about it, fellows? It's war to the knife, eh?"

* * * *

There was a momentary silence from all sides.

"I guess so," grunted a giant Qornt in iridescent blue with flame-colored plumes.

Qorn's eyes bulged. He half rose. "We've been all over this," he bassooned. He clamped bony fingers on the hilt of a light rapier. "I thought I'd made my point!"

"Oh, sure, Qorn."

"You bet."

"I'm convinced."

Qorn rumbled and resumed his seat. "All for one and one for all, that's us."

"And you're the one, eh, Qorn?" Retief commented.

Magnan cleared his throat. "I sense that some of you gentlemen are not convinced of the wisdom of this move," he piped, looking along the table at the silks, jewels, beaks, feather-decked crests and staring eyes.

"Silence!" Qorn hooted. "No use your talking to my loyal lieutenants anyway," he added. "They do whatever I convince them they ought to do."

"But I'm sure that on more mature consideration—"

"I can lick any Qornt in the house." Qorn said. "That's why I'm Qorn." He belched again.

A servant came up staggering under a weight of chain, dropped it with a crash at Magnan's feet. Zubb aimed the guns while the servant wrapped three loops around Magnan's wrists, snapped a lock in place.

"You next!" The guns pointed at Retief's chest. He held out his arms. Four loops of silvery-gray chain in half-inch links dropped around them. The servant cinched them up tight, squeezed a lock through the ends and closed it.

"Now," Qorn said, lolling back in his chair, glass in hand. "There's a bit of sport to be had here, lads. What shall we do with them?"

"Let them go," the blue and flame Qornt said glumly.

"You can do better than that," Qorn hooted. "Now here's a suggestion: we carve them up a little—lop off the external labiae and pinnae, say—and ship them back."

"Good lord! Retief, he's talking about cutting off our ears and sending us home mutilated! What a barbaric proposal!"

"It wouldn't be the first time a Terrestrial diplomat got a trimming," Retief commented.

"It should have the effect of stimulating the Terries to put up a reasonable scrap," Qorn said judiciously. "I have a feeling that they're thinking of giving up without a struggle."

"Oh, I doubt that," the blue-and-flame Qornt said. "Why should they?"

Qorn rolled an eye at Retief and another at Magnan. "Take these two," he hooted. "I'll wager they came here to negotiate a surrender!"

"Well," Magnan started.

"Hold it, Mr. Magnan," Retief said. "I'll tell him."

"What's your proposal?" Qorn whistled, taking a gulp from his goblet. "A fifty-fifty split? Monetary reparations? Alternate territory? I can assure you, it's useless. We Qornt *like* to fight."

"I'm afraid you've gotten the wrong impression, your Excellency," Retief said blandly. "We didn't come to negotiate. We came to deliver an Ultimatum."

"What?" Qorn trumpeted. Behind Retief, Magnan spluttered.

"We plan to use this planet for target practice," Retief said. "A new type hell bomb we've worked out. Have all your people off of it in seventy-two hours, or suffer the consequences."

IV

"You have the gall," Qorn stormed, "to stand here in the center of Qornt Hall—uninvited, at that—and in chains—"

"Oh, these," Retief said. He tensed his arms. The soft aluminum links stretched and broke. He shook the light metal free. "We diplomats like to go along with colorful local customs, but I wouldn't want to mislead you. Now, as to the evacuation of Roolit I—"

Zubb screeched, waved the guns. The Qornt were jabbering.

"I told you they were brutes," Zubb shrilled.

Qorn slammed his fist down on the table. "I don't care what they are!" he honked. "Evacuate, hell! I can field eighty-five combat-ready ships!"

"And we can englobe every one of them with a thousand Peace Enforcers with a hundred megatons/second firepower each."

"Retief." Magnan tugged at his sleeve. "Don't forget their superdrive."

"That's all right. They don't have one."

"But—"

"We'll take you on!" Qorn French-horned. "We're the Qorn! We glory in battle! We live in fame or go down in—"

"Hogwash," the flame-and-blue Qorn cut in. "If it wasn't for you, Qorn, we could sit around and feast and brag and enjoy life without having to prove anything."

"Qorn, you seem to be the fire-brand here," Retief said. "I think the rest of the boys would listen to reason—"

"Over my dead body!"

"My idea exactly," Retief said. "You claim you can lick any man in the house. Unwind yourself from your ribbons and step out here on the floor, and we'll see how good you are at backing up your conversation."

* * * *

Magnan hovered at Retief's side. "Twelve feet tall," he moaned. "And did you notice the size of those hands?"

Retief watched as Qorn's aides helped him out of his formal trappings. "I wouldn't worry too much, Mr. Magnan. This is a light-Gee world. I doubt if old Qorn would weigh up at more than two-fifty standard pounds here."

"But that phenomenal reach—"

"I'll peck away at him at knee level. When he bends over to swat me, I'll get a crack at him."

Across the cleared floor, Qorn shook off his helpers with a snort.

"Enough! Let me at the upstart!"

Retief moved out to meet him, watching the upraised backward-jointed arms. Qorn stalked forward, long lean legs bent, long horny feet clacking against the polished floor. The other aliens—both servitors and bejeweled Qornt—formed a wide circle, all eyes unwaveringly on the combatants.

Qorn struck suddenly, a long arm flashing down in a vicious cut at Retief, who leaned aside, caught one lean shank below the knee. Qorn bent to haul Retief from his leg—and staggered back as a haymaker took him just below the beak. A screech went up from the crowd as Retief leaped clear.

Qorn hissed and charged. Retief whirled aside, then struck the alien's off-leg in a flying tackle. Qorn leaned, arms windmilling, crashed to the floor. Retief whirled, dived for the left arm, whipped it behind the narrow back, seized Qorn's neck in a stranglehold and threw his weight backward. Qorn fell on his back, his legs squatted out at an awkward angle. He squawked and beat his free arm on the floor, reaching in vain for Retief.

Zubb stepped forward, pistols ready. Magnan stepped before him.

"Need I remind you, sir," he said icily, "that this is an official diplomatic function? I can brook no interference from disinterested parties."

Zubb hesitated. Magnan held out a hand. "I must ask you to hand me your weapons, Zubb."

"Look here," Zubb began.

"I *may* lose my temper," Magnan hinted. Zubb lowered the guns, passed them to Magnan. He thrust them into his belt with a sour smile, turned back to watch the encounter.

Retief had thrown a turn of violet silk around Qorn's left wrist, bound it to the alien's neck. Another wisp of stuff floated from Qorn's shoulder. Retief, still holding Qorn in an awkward sprawl, wrapped it around one out-flung leg, trussed ankle and thigh together. Qorn flopped, hooting. At each movement, the constricting loop around his neck, jerked his head back, the green crest tossing wildly.

"If I were you, I'd relax," Retief said, rising and releasing his grip. Qorn got a leg under him; Retief kicked it. Qorn's chin hit the floor with a hollow clack. He wilted, an ungainly tangle of over-long limbs and gay silks.

Retief turned to the watching crowd. "Next?" he called.

The blue and flame Qornt stepped forward. "Maybe this would be a good time to elect a new leader," he said. "Now, my qualifications—"

"Sit down," Retief said loudly. He stepped to the head of the table, seated himself in Qorn's vacated chair. "A couple of you finish trussing Qorn up for me."

"But we must select a leader!"

"That won't be necessary, boys. I'm your new leader."

* * * *

"As I see it," Retief said, dribbling cigar ashes into an empty wine glass, "you Qornt like to be warriors, but you don't particularly like to fight."

"We don't mind a little fighting—within reason. And, of course, as Qornt, we're expected to die in battle. But what I say is, why rush things?"

"I have a suggestion," Magnan said. "Why not turn the reins of government over to the Verpp? They seem a level-headed group."

"What good would that do? Qornt are Qornt. It seems there's always one among us who's a slave to instinct—and, naturally, we have to follow him."

"Why?"

"Because that's the way it's done."

"Why not do it another way?" Magnan offered. "Now, I'd like to suggest community singing—"

"If we gave up fighting, we might live too long. Then what would happen?"

"Live too long?" Magnan looked puzzled.

"When estivating time comes there'd be no burrows for us. Anyway, with the new Qornt stepping on our heels—"

"I've lost the thread," Magnan said. "Who are the new Qornt?"

"After estivating, the Verpp moult, and then they're Qornt, of course. The Gwil become Boog, the Boog become Rheuk, the Rheuk metamorphosize into Verpp—"

"You mean Slun and Zubb—the mild-natured naturalists—will become warmongers like Qorn?"

"Very likely. 'The milder the Verpp, the wilder the Qorn,' as the old saying goes."

"What do Qornt turn into?" Retief asked.

"Hmmmm. That's a good question. So far, none have survived Qornthood."

"Have you thought of forsaking your warlike ways?" Magnan asked. "What about taking up sheepherding and regular church attendance?"

"Don't mistake me. We Qornt like a military life. It's great sport to sit around roaring fires and drink and tell lies and then go dashing off to enjoy a brisk affray and some leisurely looting afterward. But we prefer a nice numerical advantage. Not this business of tackling you Terrestrials over on Guzzum—that was a mad notion. We had no idea what your strength was."

"But now that's all off, of course," Magnan chirped. "Now that we've had diplomatic relations and all—"

"Oh, by no means. The fleet lifts in thirty days. After all, we're Qornt; we have to satisfy our drive to action."

"But Mr. Retief is your leader now. He won't let you!"

"Only a dead Qornt stays home when Attack day comes. And even if he orders us all to cut our own throats, there are still the other Centers—all with their own leaders. No, gentlemen, the Invasion is definitely on."

"Why don't you go invade somebody else?" Magnan suggested. "I could name some very attractive prospects—outside my sector, of course."

"Hold everything," Retief said. "I think we've got the basis of a deal here...."

V

At the head of a double column of gaudily caparisoned Qornt, Retief and Magnan strolled across the ramp toward the bright tower of the CDT Sector HQ. Ahead, gates opened, and a black Corps limousine emerged, flying an Ambassadorial flag under a plain square of white.

"Curious," Magnan commented. "I wonder what the significance of the white ensign might be?"

Retief raised a hand. The column halted with a clash of accoutrements and a rasp of Qornt boots. Retief looked back along the line. The high white sun flashed on bright silks, polished buckles, deep-dyed plumes, butts of pistols, the soft gleam of leather.

"A brave show indeed," Magnan commented approvingly. "I confess the idea has merit."

The limousine pulled up with a squeal of brakes, stood on two fat-tired wheels, gyros humming softly. The hatch popped up. A portly diplomat stepped out.

"Why, Ambassador Nitworth," Magnan glowed. "This is very kind of you."

"Keep cool, Magnan," Nitworth said in a strained voice. "We'll attempt to get you out of this."

He stepped past Magnan's out-stretched hand and looked hesitantly at the ramrod-straight line of Qornt, eighty-five strong—and beyond, at the eighty-five tall Qornt dreadnaughts.

"Good afternoon, sir...ah, Your Excellency," Nitworth said, blinking up at the leading Qornt. "You are Commander of the Strike Force, I assume?"

"Nope," the Qornt said shortly.

"I...ah...wish to request seventy-two hours in which to evacuate Headquarters," Nitworth plowed on.

"Mr. Ambassador." Retief said. "This—"

"Don't panic, Retief. I'll attempt to secure your release," Nitworth hissed over his shoulder. "Now—"

"You will address our leader with more respect!" the tall Qornt hooted, eyeing Nitworth ominously from eleven feet up.

"Oh, yes indeed, sir...your Excellency...Commander. Now, about the invasion—"

"Mr. Secretary," Magnan tugged at Nitworth's sleeve.

"In heaven's name, permit me to negotiate in peace!" Nitworth snapped. He rearranged his features. "Now your Excellency, we've arranged to evacuate Smorbrod, of course, just as you requested—"

"Requested?" the Qornt honked.

"Ah...demanded, that is. Quite rightly of course. Ordered. Instructed. And, of course, we'll be only too pleased to follow any other instructions you might have."

"You don't quite get the big picture, Mr. Secretary," Retief said. "This isn't—"

"Silence, confound you!" Nitworth barked. The leading Qornt looked at Retief. He nodded. Two bony hands shot out, seized Nitworth and stuffed a length of bright pink silk into his mouth, then spun him around and held him facing Retief.

"If you don't mind my taking this opportunity to brief you, Mr. Ambassador," Retief said blandly. "I think I should mention that this isn't an invasion fleet. These are the new recruits for the Peace Enforcement Corps."

Magnan stepped forward, glanced at the gag in Ambassador Nitworth's mouth, hesitated, then cleared his throat. "We felt," he said, "that the establishment of a Foreign Brigade within the P. E. Corps structure would provide the element of novelty the Department has requested in our recruiting, and at the same time would remove the stigma of Terrestrial chauvinism from future punitive operations."

Nitworth stared, eyes bulging. He grunted, reaching for the gag, caught the Qornt's eye on him, dropped his hands to his sides.

"I suggest we get the troops in out of the hot sun," Retief said. Magnan edged close. "What about the gag?" he whispered.

"Let's leave it where it is for a while," Retief murmured. "It may save us a few concessions."

* * * *

An hour later, Nitworth, breathing freely again, glowered across his desk at Retief and Magnan.

"This entire affair," he rumbled, "has made me appear to be a fool!"

"But we who are privileged to serve on your staff already know just how clever you are," Magnan burbled.

Nitworth purpled. "You're skirting insolence, Magnan," he roared. "Why was I not informed of the arrangements? What was I to assume at the sight of eighty-five war vessels over my headquarters, unannounced?"

"We tried to get through, but our wavelengths—"

"Bah! Sterner souls than I would have quailed at the spectacle!"

"Oh, you were perfectly justified in panicking—"

"I did *not* panic!" Nitworth bellowed. "I merely adjusted to the apparent circumstances. Now, I'm of two minds as to the advisability of this foreign legion idea of yours. Still, it may have merit. I believe the wisest course would be to dispatch them on a long training cruise in an uninhabited sector of space—"

The office windows rattled. "What the devil!" Nitworth turned, stared out at the ramp where a Qornt ship rose slowly on a column of pale blue light. The vibration increased as a second ship lifted, then a third.

Nitworth whirled on Magnan. "What's this! Who ordered these recruits to embark without my permission?"

"I took the liberty of giving them an errand to run, Mr. Secretary," Retief said. "There was that little matter of the Groaci infiltrating the Sirenian System. I sent the boys off to handle it."

"Call them back at once!"

"I'm afraid that won't be possible. They're under orders to maintain total communications silence until completion of the mission."

Nitworth drummed his fingers on the desk top. Slowly, a thoughtful expression dawned. He nodded.

"This may work out," he said. "I *should* call them back, but since the fleet is out of contact, I'm unable to do so, correct? Thus I can hardly be held responsible for any over-enthusiasm in chastising the Groaci."

He closed one eye in a broad wink at Magnan. "Very well, gentlemen, I'll overlook the irregularity this time. Magnan, see to it the Smorbrodian public are notified they can remain where they are. And by the way, did you by any chance discover the technique of the indetectable drive the Qornt use?"

"No, sir. That is, yes, sir."

"Well? Well?"

"There isn't any. The Qornt were there all the while. Underground."

"Underground? Doing what?"

"Hibernating—for two hundred years at a stretch."

* * * *

Outside in the corridor, Magnan came up to Retief, who stood talking to a tall man in a pilot's coverall.

"I'll be tied up, sending through full details on my—our—your recruiting theme, Retief," Magnan said. "Suppose you run into the city to assist the new Verpp Consul in settling in."

"I'll do that, Mr. Magnan. Anything else?"

Magnan raised his eyebrows. "You're remarkably compliant today, Retief. I'll arrange transportation."

"Don't bother, Mr. Magnan. Cy here will run me over. He was the pilot who ferried us over to Roolit I, you recall."

"I'll be with you as soon as I pack a few phone numbers, Retief," the pilot said. He moved off. Magnan followed him with a disapproving eye. "An uncouth sort, I fancied. I trust you're not consorting with his kind socially."

"I wouldn't say that, exactly," Retief said. "We just want to go over a few figures together."

THE GOVERNOR OF GLAVE

Originally published in **Worlds of If Science Fiction,** *November 1963.*

I

Retief turned back the gold-encrusted scarlet cuff of the mess jacket of a First Secretary and Consul, gathered in the three eight-sided black dice, shook them by his right ear and sent them rattling across the floor to rebound from the bulk-head.

"Thirteen's the point," the Power Section Chief called. "Ten he makes it!"

"Oh…Mr. Retief," a strained voice called. Retief looked up. A tall thin youth in the black-trimmed gray of a Third Secretary flapped a sheet of paper from the edge of the circle surrounding the game. "The Ambassador's compliments, sir, and will you join him and the staff in the conference room at once?"

Retief rose and dusted his knees. "That's all for now, boys," he said. "I'll take the rest of your money later." He followed the junior diplomat from the ward room, along the bare corridors of the crew level, past the glare panel reading NOTICE—FIRST CLASS ONLY BEYOND THIS POINT, through the chandeliered and draped ballroom and along a stretch of soundless carpet to a heavy door bearing a placard with the legend CONFERENCE IN SESSION.

"Ambassador Sternwheeler seemed quite upset, Mr. Retief," the messenger said.

"He usually is, Pete." Retief took a cigar from his breast pocket. "Got a light?"

The Third Secretary produced a permatch. "I don't know why you smoke those things instead of dope sticks, Mr. Retief," he said. "The Ambassador hates the smell."

Retief nodded. "I only smoke this kind at conferences. It makes for shorter sessions." He stepped into the room. Ambassador Sternwheeler eyed him down the length of the conference table.

"Ah, Mr. Retief honors us with his presence. Do be seated, Retief." He fingered a yellow Departmental despatch. Retief took a chair, puffing out a dense cloud of smoke.

"As I have been explaining to the remainder of my staff for the past quarter-hour," Sternwheeler rumbled, "I've been the recipient of important intelligence." He blinked at Retief expectantly. Retief raised his eyebrows in polite inquiry.

"It seems," Sternwheeler went on, "that there has been a change in regime on Glave. A week ago, the government which invited the dispatch of this mission—and to which we're accredited—was overthrown. The former ruling class has fled into exile. A popular workers' and peasants' junta has taken over."

"Mr. Ambassador," Counsellor Magnan broke in, rising. "I'd like to be the first—" he glanced around the table—"or one of the first, anyway, to welcome the new government of Glave into the family of planetary ruling bodies—"

* * * *

"Sit down, Magnan!" Sternwheeler snapped. "Of course the Corps always recognizes *de facto* sovereignty. The problem is merely one of acquainting ourselves with the policies of this new group—a sort of blue-collar coalition, it seems. In what position that leaves this Embassy I don't yet know."

"I suppose this means we'll spend the next month in a parking orbit," Counsellor Magnan sighed.

"Unfortunately," Sternwheeler went on, "the entire affair has apparently been carried off without recourse to violence, leaving the Corps no excuse to move in—that is, it appears our assistance in restoring order will not be required."

"Glave was one of the old Contract Worlds," Retief said. "What's become of the Planetary Manager General and the technical staff? And how do the peasants and workers plan to operate the atmospheric purification system, the Weather Control station, the tide regulation complexes?"

"I'm more concerned at present with the status of the Mission! Will we be welcomed by these peasants or peppered with buckshot?"

"You say that this is a popular junta, and that the former leaders have fled into exile," Retief said. "May I ask the source?"

"The despatch cites a 'reliable Glavian source'."

"That's officialese for something cribbed from a broadcast news tape. Presumably the Glavian news services are in the hands of the revolution. In that case—"

"Yes, yes, there is the possibility that the issue is yet in doubt. Of course we'll have to exercise caution in making our approach. It wouldn't do to make overtures to the wrong side."

"Oh, I think we need have no fear on that score," the Chief of the Political Section spoke up. "I know these entrenched cliques. Once challenged by an aroused populace, they scuttle for safety—with large balances safely tucked away in neutral banks."

"I'd like to go on record," Magnan piped, "as registering my deep gratification at this fulfillment of popular aspirations—"

"The most popular aspiration I know of is to live high off someone else's effort," Retief said. "I don't know of anyone outside the Corps who's managed it."

* * * *

"Gentlemen!" Sternwheeler bellowed. "I'm awaiting your constructive suggestions—not an exchange of political views. We'll arrive off Glave in less than six hours. I should like before that time to have developed some notion regarding to whom I shall expect to offer my credentials!"

There was a discreet tap at the door; it opened and the young Third Secretary poked his head in.

"Mr. Ambassador, I have a reply to your message—just received from Glave. It's signed by the Steward of the GFE, and I thought you'd want to see it at once...."

"Yes, of course; let me have it."

"What's the GFE?" someone asked.

"It's the revolutionary group," the messenger said, passing the message over.

"GFE? GFE? What do the letters SIGNIFY?"

"Glorious Fun Eternally," Retief suggested. "Or possibly Goodies For Everybody."

"I believe that's 'Glavian Free Electorate'," the Third Secretary said.

Sternwheeler stared at the paper, lips pursed. His face grew pink. He slammed the paper on the table.

"Well, gentlemen! It appears our worst fears have been realized! This is nothing less than a warning! A threat! We're advised to divert course and bypass Glave entirely. It seems the GFE wants no interference from meddling foreign exploiters, as they put it!"

Magnan rose. "If you'll excuse me Mr. Ambassador, I want to get off a message to Sector HQ to hold my old job for me—"

"Sit down, you idiot!" Sternwheeler roared. "If you think I'm consenting to have my career blighted—my first Ambassadorial post whisked out from under me—the Corps made a fool of—"

"I'd like to take a look at that message," Retief said. It was passed along to him. He read it.

"I don't believe this applies to us, Mr. Ambassador."

* * * *

"What are you talking about? It's addressed to me by name!"

"It merely states that 'meddling foreign exploiters' are unwelcome. Meddling foreigners we are, but we don't qualify as exploiters unless we show a profit—and this appears to be shaping up as a particularly profitless venture."

"What are you proposing, Mr. Retief?"

"That we proceed to make planetfall as scheduled, greet our welcoming committee with wide diplomatic smiles, hint at largesse in the offing and settle down to observe the lie of the land."

"Just what I was about to suggest," Magnan said.

"That might be dangerous," Sternwheeler said.

"That's why I didn't suggest it," Magnan said.

"Still it's essential that we learn more of the situation than can be gleaned from official broadcasts," Sternwheeler mused. "Now, while I can't justify risking the entire Mission, it might be advisable to dispatch a delegation to sound out the new regime."

"I'd like to volunteer," Magnan said, rising.

"Of course, the delegates may be murdered—"

"—but unfortunately, I'm under treatment at the moment." Magnan sat down.

"—which will place us in an excellent position, propaganda-wise."

"What a pity I can't go," the Military Attache said. "But my place is with my troops."

"The only troops you've got are the Assistant Attache and your secretary," Magnan pointed out.

"Say, I'd like to be down there in the thick of things," the Political Officer said. He assumed a grave expression. "But of course I'll be needed here, to interpret results."

"I appreciate your attitude, gentlemen," Sternwheeler said, studying the ceiling. "But I'm afraid I must limit the privilege of volunteering for this hazardous duty to those officers of more robust physique, under forty years of age—"

"Tsk. I'm forty-one," Magnan said.

"—and with a reputation for adaptability." His glance moved along the table.

"Do you mind if I run along now, Mr. Ambassador?" Retief said. "It's time for my insulin shot."

Sternwheeler's mouth dropped open.

"Just kidding," Retief said. "I'll go. But I have one request, Mr. Ambassador: no further communication with the ground until I give the all-clear."

* * * *

II

Retief grounded the lighter, in-cycled the lock and stepped out. The hot yellow Glavian sun beat down on a broad expanse of concrete, an abandoned service cart and a row of tall ships casting black shadows toward the silent control tower. A wisp of smoke curled up from the shed area at the rim of the field. There was no other sign of life.

Retief walked over to the cart, tossed his valise aboard, climbed into the driver's seat and headed for the operations building. Beyond the port, hills rose, white buildings gleaming against the deep green slopes. Near the ridge, a vehicle moved ant-like along a winding road, a dust trail rising behind it. Faintly a distant shot sounded.

Papers littered the ground before the Operations Building. Retief pushed open the tall glass door, stood listening. Slanting sunlight reflected from a wide polished floor, at the far side of which illuminated lettering over empty counters read IMMIGRATION, HEALTH and CUSTOMS. He crossed to the desk, put the valise down, then leaned across the counter. A worried face under an oversized white cap looked up at him.

"You can come out now," Retief said. "They've gone."

The man rose, dusting himself off. He looked over Retief's shoulder. "Who's gone?"

"Whoever it was that scared you."

"Whatta ya mean? I was looking for my pencil."

"Here it is." Retief plucked a worn stub from the pocket of the soiled shirt sagging under the weight of braided shoulderboards. "You can sign me in as a Diplomatic Representative. A break for you—no formalities necessary. Where can I catch a cab for the city?"

The man eyed Retief's bag. "What's in that?"

"Personal belongings under duty-free entry."

"Guns?"

"No, thanks, just a cab."

"You got no gun?" The man raised his voice.

"That's right, fellows," Retief called out. "No gun; no knife, not even a small fission bomb. Just a few pairs of socks and some reading matter."

A brown-uniformed man ran from behind the Customs Counter, holding a long-barreled blast-rifle centered on the Corps insignia stitched to the pocket of Retief's powder-blue blazer.

"Don't try nothing," he said. "You're under arrest."

"It can't be overtime parking. I've only been here five minutes."

"Hah!" The gun-handler moved out from the counter, came up to Retief. "Empty out your pockets!" he barked. "Hands overhead!"

"I'm just a diplomat, not a contortionist," Retief said, not moving. "Do you mind pointing that thing in some other direction?"

"Looky here, Mister, I'll give the orders. We don't need anybody telling us how to run our business."

"I'm telling you to shift that blaster before I take it away from you and wrap it around your neck," Retief said conversationally. The cop stepped back uncertainly, lowering the gun.

"Jake! Horny! Pud! come on out!"

Three more brown uniforms emerged from concealment.

"Who are you fellows hiding from, the top sergeant?" Retief glanced over the ill-fitting uniforms, the unshaved faces, the scuffed boots. "Tell you what. When he shows up, I'll engage him in conversation. You beat it back to the barracks and grab a quick bath—"

"That's enough smart talk." The biggest of the three newcomers moved up to Retief. "You stuck your nose in at the wrong time. We just had a change of management around here."

"I heard about it," Retief said. "Who do I complain to?"

"Complain? What about?"

"The port's a mess," Retief barked. "Nobody on duty to receive official visitors! No passenger service facilities! Why, do you know I had to carry my own bag—"

"All right, all right, that's outside my department. You better see the boss."

"The boss? I thought you got rid of the bosses."

"We did, but now we got new ones."

"They any better than the old ones?"

"This guy asks too many questions," the man with the gun said. "Let's let Sozier answer 'em."

"Who's he?"

"He's the Military Governor of the City."

"Now we're getting somewhere," Retief said. "Lead the way, Jake—and don't forget my bag."

* * * *

Sozier was a small man with thin hair oiled across a shiny scalp, prominent ears and eyes like coal chips set in rolls of fat. He glowered at Retief from behind a polished desk occupying the center of a spacious office.

"I warned you off," he snapped. "You came anyway." He leaned forward and slammed a fist down on the desk. "You're used to throwing your weight around, but you won't throw it around here! There'll be no spies pussyfooting around Glave!"

"Looking for what, Mr. Sozier?"

"Call me General!"

"Mind if I sit down?" Retief pulled out a chair, seated himself and took out a cigar. "Curiously enough," he said, lighting up, "the Corps has no intention of making any embarrassing investigations. We deal with the existing government, no questions asked." His eyes held the other's. "Unless, of course, there are evidences of atrocities or other illegal measures."

The coal-chip eyes narrowed. "I don't have to make explanations to you or anybody else."

"Except, presumably, the Glavian Free Electorate," Retief said blandly. "But tell me, General—who's actually running the show?"

A speaker on the desk buzzed. "Hey, Corporal Sozier! Wes's got them two hellions cornered. They're holed up in the Birthday Cake—"

"General Sozier, damn you! and plaster your big mouth shut!" He gestured to one of the uniformed men standing by.

"You! Get Trundy and Little Moe up here—pronto!" He swiveled back to Retief. "You're in luck. I'm too busy right now to bother with you. You get back over to the port and leave the same way you came—and tell your blood-sucking friends the easy pickings are over as far as Glave's concerned. You won't lounge around here living high and throwing big parties and cooking up your dirty deals to get fat on at the expense of the working man."

Retief dribbled ash on Sozier's desk and glanced at the green uniform front bulging between silver buttons.

"Who paid for your potbelly, Sozier?" he inquired carelessly.

Sozier's eyes narrowed to slits. "I could have you shot!"

"Stop playing games with me, Sozier," Retief rapped. "There's a squadron of Peace Enforcers standing by just in case any apprentice statesmen forget the niceties of diplomatic usage. I suggest you start showing a little intelligence about now, or even Horny and Pud are likely to notice."

* * * *

Sozier's fingers squeaked on the arms of his chair. He swallowed.

"You might start by assigning me an escort for a conducted tour of the capital," Retief went on. "I want to be in a position to confirm that order has been re-established, and that normal services have been restored. Otherwise it may be necessary to send in a Monitor Unit to straighten things out."

"You know you can't meddle with the internal affairs of a sovereign world!"

Retief sighed. "The trouble with taking over your boss's job is discovering its drawbacks. It's disillusioning, I know, Sozier, but—"

"All right! Take your tour! You'll find everything running as smooth as silk! Utilities, police, transport, environmental control—"

"What about Space Control? Glave Tower seems to be off the air."

"I shut it down. We don't need anything and we don't want anything from the outside."

"Where's the new Premier keeping himself? Does he share your passion for privacy?"

The general got to his feet. "I'm letting you take your look, Mr. Big Nose. I'm giving you four hours. Then out! And the next meddling bureaucrat that tries to cut atmosphere on Glave without a clearance gets burned!"

"I'll need a car."

"Jake! You stick close to this bird. Take him to the main power plant, the water works and the dispatch center. Ride him around town and show him we're doing okay without a bunch of leeches bossing us. Then dump him at the port—and see that he leaves."

"I'll plan my own itinerary, thanks. I can't promise I'll be finished in four hours—but I'll keep you advised."

"I warned you—"

"I heard you. Five times. And I only warned you once. You're getting ahead of me." Retief rose, motioned to the hulking guard. "Come on, Jake. We've got a lot of ground to cover before we come back for our dinner."

* * * *

III

At the curb, Retief held out his hand. "Give me the power cylinder out of your rifle, Jake."

"Huh?"

"Come on, Jake. You've got a nervous habit of playing with the firing stud. We don't want any accidents."

"How do you get it out? They only give me this thing yesterday."

Retief pocketed the cylinder. "You sit in back. I'll drive." He wheeled the car off along a broad avenue crowded with vehicles and lined with flowering palms, behind which stately white buildings reared up into the pale sky.

"Nice looking city, Jake," Retief said conversationally. "What's the population?"

"I dunno. I only been here a year."

"What about Horny and Pud? Are they natives?"

"Whatta ya mean, natives? They're just as civilized as me."

"My boner, Jake. Known Sozier long?"

"Sure. He useta come around to the club."

"I take it he was in the army under the old regime?"

"Yeah—but he didn't like the way they run it. Nothing but band playing and fancy marching. There wasn't nobody to fight."

"Just between us, Jake—where did the former Planetary Manager General go?" Retief watched Jake's heavy face in the mirror. Jake jumped, clamped his mouth shut.

"I don't know nothing."

Half an hour later, after a tour of the commercial center, Retief headed towards the city's outskirts. The avenue curved, leading up along the flank of a low hill.

"I must admit I'm surprised, Jake," Retief said. "Everything seems orderly. No signs of riots or panic. Power, water, communications normal—just as the general said. Remarkable, isn't it, considering that the entire managerial class has packed up and left?"

"You wanta see the Power Plant?" Retief could see perspiration beaded on the man's forehead under the uniform cap.

"Sure. Which way?" With Jake directing, Retief ascended to the ridge top, cruised past the blank white facade of the station.

"Quiet, isn't it?" Retief pulled the car in to the curb. "Let's go inside."

"Huh? Corporal Sozier didn't say nothing—"

"You're right, Jake. That leaves it to our discretion."

"He won't like it."

"The corporal's a busy man, Jake. We won't worry him by telling him about it."

Jake followed Retief up the walk. The broad double doors were locked. "Let's try the back."

The narrow door set in the high blank wall opened as Retief approached. A gun barrel poked out, followed by a small man with bushy red hair. He looked Retief over.

"Who's this party, Jake?" he barked.

"Sozier said show him the plant," Jake said.

"What we need is more guys to pull duty, not tourists. Anyway, *I'm* Chief Engineer here. Nobody comes in here 'less I like their looks." Retief moved forward, stood looking down at the redhead. The little man hesitated, then waved him past. "Lucky for you I like your looks." Inside, Retief surveyed the long room, the giant converter units, the massive busbars. Armed men—some in uniform, some in work clothes or loud sport shirts—stood here and there. Other men read meters, adjusted controls or inspected dials.

"You've got more guards than workers," Retief said. "Expecting trouble?"

The redhead bit the corner from a plug of spearmint. He glanced around the plant. "Things is quiet now; but you never know."

"Rather old-fashioned equipment isn't it? When was it installed?"

"Huh? I dunno. What's wrong with it?"

"What's your basic power source, a core sink? Lithospheric friction? Sub-crustal hydraulics?"

"Beats me, Mister. I'm the boss here, not a dern mechanic."

* * * *

A gray-haired man carrying a clipboard walked past, studied a panel, made notes, glanced up to catch Retief's eye, moved on.

"Everything seems to be running normally," Retief remarked.

"Sure. Why not?"

"Records being kept up properly?"

"Sure. Some of these guys, all they do is walk around looking at dials and writing stuff on paper. If it was me, I'd put 'em to work."

Retief strolled over to the gray-haired man, now scribbling before a bank of meters. He glanced at the clipboard.

Power off at sunset. Tell Corasol was scrawled in block letters across the record sheet. Retief nodded, rejoined his guard.

"All right, Jake. Let's have a look at the communications center."

Back in the car, headed west, Retief studied the blank windows of office buildings, the milling throngs in beer bars, shooting galleries, tattoo parlors, billiard halls, pinball arcades, bordellos and half-credit casinos.

"Everybody seems to be having fun," he remarked.

Jake stared out the window.

"Yeah."

"Too bad you're on duty, Jake. You could be out there joining in."

"Soon as the corporal gets things organized, I'm opening me up a place to show dirty tri-di's. I'll get my share."

"Meanwhile, let the rest of 'em have their fun, eh Jake?"

"Look, Mister, I been thinking. Maybe you better gimme back that kick-stick you taken outa my gun...."

"Sorry, Jake; no can do. Tell me, what was the real cause of the revolution? Not enough to eat? Too much regimentation?"

"Naw, we always got plenty to eat. There wasn't none of that regimentation up till I joined up in the corporal's army."

"Rigid class structure, maybe? Educational discrimination?"

Jake nodded. "Yeah, it was them schools done it. All the time trying to make a feller do some kind of class. Big shots. Know it all. Gonna make us sit around and view tapes. Figgered they was better than us."

"And Sozier's idea was you'd take over, and you wouldn't have to be bothered."

"Aw, it wasn't Sozier's idea. He ain't the big leader."

"Where does the big leader keep himself?"

"I dunno. I guess he's pretty busy right now." Jake snickered. "Some of them guys call themselves colonels turned out not to know nothing about how to shoot off the guns."

"Shooting, eh? I thought it was a sort of peaceful revolution. The managerial class were booted out, and that was that."

"I don't know nothing," Jake snapped. "How come you keep trying to get me to say stuff I ain't supposed to talk about? You want to get me in trouble?"

* * * *

"Oh, you're already in trouble, Jake. But if you stick with me, I'll try to get you out of it. Where exactly did the refugees head for? How did they leave? Must have been a lot of them; I'd say in a city of this size alone, they'd run into the thousands."

"I don't know."

"Of course, it depends on your definition of a big shot. Who's included in that category, Jake?"

"You know, the slick-talking ones; the fancy dressers; the guys that walk around and tell other guys what to do. We do all the work and they get all the big pay."

"I suppose that would cover scientists, professional men, executives, technicians of all sorts, engineers, teachers—all that crowd."

"Yeah, them are the ones."

"And once you got them out of the way, the regular fellows would have a chance. Chaps that don't spend all their time taking baths and reading books and using big words; good Joes that don't mind picking their noses in public."

"We got as much right as anybody—"

"Jake, who's Corasol?"

"He's—I don't know."

"I thought I overheard his name somewhere."

"Uh, here's the communication center," Jake cut in.

Retief swung into a parking lot under a high blank facade. He set the brake and stepped out.

"Lead the way, Jake."

"Look, Mister, the corporal only wanted me to show you the outside."

"Anything to hide, Jake?"

Jake shook his head angrily and stamped past Retief. "When I joined up with Sozier, I didn't figger I'd be getting in this kind of mess."

"I know, Jake. It's tough. Sometimes it seems like a fellow works harder after he's thrown out the parasites than he did before."

A cautious guard let Retief and Jake inside, followed them along brightlit aisles among consoles, cables, batteries of instruments. Armed men in careless uniforms lounged, watching. Here and there a silent technician worked quietly.

Retief paused by one, an elderly man in a neat white coverall, with a purple spot under one eye.

"Quite a bruise you've got there," Retief commented heartily. "Power failure at sunset," he added softly. The technician hesitated, nodded and moved on.

Back in the car, Retief gave Jake directions. At the end of three hours, he had seen twelve smooth-running, heavily guarded installations.

"So far, so good, Jake," he said. "Next stop, Sub-station Number Nine." In the mirror, Jake's face stiffened. "Hey, you can't go down there—"

"Something going on there, Jake?"

"That's where—I mean, no. I don't know."

"I don't want to miss anything, Jake. Which way?"

"I ain't going down there," Jake said sullenly.

Retief braked. "In that case, I'm afraid our association is at an end, Jake."

"You mean…you're getting out here?"

"No, you are."

"Huh? Now wait a minute, Mister! The corporal said I was to stay with you."

Retief accelerated. "That's settled, then. Which way?"

* * * *

IV

Retief pulled the car to a halt two hundred yards from the periphery of a loose crowd of brown-uniformed men who stood in groups scattered across a broad plaza, overflowing into a stretch of manicured lawn before the bare, functional facade of sub-station number Nine. In the midst of the besieging mob, Sozier's red face and bald head bobbed as he harangued a cluster of green-uniformed men from his place in the rear of a long open car.

"What's it all about, Jake?" Retief enquired. "Since the parasites have all left peacefully, I'm having a hard time figuring out who'd be holed up in the pumping station—and why. Maybe they haven't gotten the word that it's all going to be fun and games from now on."

"If the corporal sees you over here—"

"Ah, the good corporal. Glad you mentioned him, Jake. He's the man to see." Retief stepped out of the car and started through the crowd. A heavy lorry loaded with an immense tank with the letter H blazoned on its side trundled into the square from a side street, moved up to a position before the building. A smaller car pulled alongside Sozier's limousine. The driver stepped down, handed something to Sozier. A moment later, Sozier's amplified voice boomed across the crowd.

"You in there, Corasol! This is General Sozier, and I'm warning you to come out now or you and your smart friends are in for a big surprise. You think I won't blast you out because I don't want to wreck the planet. You see the tank aboard the lorry that just pulled up? It's full of gas—and I got plenty of hoses out here to pump it inside with. I'll put men on the roof and squirt it in the ventilators."

Sozier's voice echoed and died. The militiamen eyed the station. Nothing happened.

"I know you can hear me, damn you!" Sozier squalled. "You'd better get the doors open and get out here fast!"

Retief stepped to Sozier's side. "Say, Corporal, I didn't know you went in for practical jokes."

Sozier jerked around to gape at Retief.

"What are you doing here!" he burst out. "I told Jake—where is that—"

"Jake didn't like the questions I was asking," Retief said, "so he marched me up here to report to you."

"Jake, you damn fool!" Sozier roared. "I got a good mind—"

* * * *

"I disagree, Sozier," Retief cut in. "I think you're a complete imbecile. Sitting out here in the open yelling at the top of your lungs, for example. Corasol and his party might get annoyed and spray that fancy car you've swiped with something a lot more painful than words."

"Eh?" Sozier's head whipped around to stare at the building.

"Isn't that a gun I see sticking out?"

Sozier dropped. "Where?"

"My mistake. Just a foreign particle on my contact lenses." Retief leaned on the car. "On the other hand, Sozier, most murderers are sneaky about it. I think making a public announcement is a nice gesture on your part. The Monitors won't have any trouble deciding who to hang when they come in to straighten out this mess."

Sozier scrambled back onto his seat. "Monitors?" he snarled. "I don't think so. I don't think you'll be around to do any blabbering to anybody." He raised his voice. "Jake! March this spy over to the sidelines. If he tries anything, shoot him!" He gave Retief a baleful grin. "I'll lay the body out nice and ship it back to your cronies. Accidents will happen, you know. It'll be a week or two before they get around to following up—and by then I'll have this little problem under control."

Jake looked at Retief uncertainly, fingering his empty rifle.

Retief put his hands up. "I guess you got me, Jake," he said. "Careful of that gun, now."

Jake glanced at Sozier, gulped, aimed the rifle at Retief and nodded toward the car. As Retief moved off, a murmur swept across the crowd. Retief glanced back. A turret on the station roof was rotating slowly. A shout rose; men surged away from the building, scuffling for way; Sozier yelled. His car started up, moved forward, horns blaring. As Retief watched, a white stream arced up from the turret, catching the sun as it spanned the lawn, plunged down to strike the massed men in a splatter of spray. It searched across the mob, came to rest on Sozier's car. Uniformed men scrambled for safety as the terrified driver gunned the heavy vehicle. The hose followed the car, dropping a solid stream of water on Sozier, kicking and flailing in the back seat. As the car passed from view, down a side street, water was overflowing the sides.

"The corporal will feel all the better for an invigorating swim in his mobile pool," Retief commented. "By the way, Jake, I have to be going now. It wouldn't be fair to send you back to your boss without something to back up your story that you were outnumbered, so—"

Retief's left fist shot out to connect solidly with Jake's jaw. Jake dropped the gun and sat down hard. Retief turned and headed for the pumping station. The hose had shut down now. A few men were standing, eyeing the building anxiously. Others watched his progress across the square. As Retief passed, he caught scattered comments:

"—seen that bird before."

"—where he's headed."

"—feller Sozier was talking to…."

"Hey, you!"

Retief was on the grass now. Ahead, the blank wall loomed up. He walked on briskly.

"Stop that jasper!" a shout rang out. There was a sharp whine and a black spot appeared on the wall ahead. Near it, a small personnel door abruptly swung inward. Retief sprinted, plunged through the opening as a second shot seared the paint on the doorframe. The door clanged behind him. Retief glanced over the half dozen men confronting him.

"I'm Retief, CDT, acting Charge," he said. "Which of you gentlemen is Manager-General Corasol?"

* * * *

Corasol was a tall, wide-shouldered man of fifty, with shrewd eyes, a ready smile, capable-looking hands and an urbane manner. He and Retief sat at a table at one side of the large room, under a maze of piping, tanks and valves. Corasol poured amber fluid into square glass tumblers.

"We spotted you by the blazer," he said. "Baby blue and gold braid stand out in a crowd."

Retief nodded. "The uniform has its uses," he agreed. He tried the drink. "Say, what is this? It's not bad."

"Sugarweed rum. Made from a marine plant. We have plenty of ocean here on Glave; there's only the one continent, you know, and it's useless for agriculture."

"Weather?"

"That's part of it. Glave is moving into what would be a major glaciation if it weren't for a rather elaborate climatic control installation. Then there are the tides. Half the continent would be inundated twice a year when our satellite is at aphelion; there's a system of baffles, locks and deep-water pumps that maintain the shore-line more or less constant. We still keep our cities well inland. Then there are the oxygen generators, the atmosphere filtration complex, vermin control and so on. Glave in its natural state is a rather hostile world."

"I'm surprised that your mines can support it all."

"Oh, they don't." Corasol shook his head. "Two hundred years ago, when the company first opened up Glave, it was economical enough. Quintite was a precious mineral in those days. Synthetics have long since taken over. Even fully automated, the mines barely support the public services and welfare system."

"I seem to recall a reference in the Post Report to the effect that a company petition to vacate its charter had been denied...."

Corasol nodded, smiling wryly. "The CDT seemed to feel that as long as any of the world's residents desired to remain, the Company was constrained to oblige them. The great majority departed long ago, of course. Relocated to other operational areas. Only the untrainables, living off welfare funds—and a skeleton staff of single men to operate the technical installations—have stayed on."

"That explains the mechanics of the recent uprising," Retief said.

The bottle clinked against glasses for a second round. "What about the good corporal?" Retief asked. "Assuming he's a strong swimmer, you should be hearing from him soon."

Corasol glanced at his finger watch. "I imagine he'll be launching his gas attack any minute."

"The prospect doesn't seem to bother you."

"Sozier is a clever enough chap in his own way," Corasol said. "But he has a bad habit of leaping to conclusions. He's gotten hold of a tank of what someone has told him is gas—as indeed it is. Hydrogen, for industrial use. It seems the poor fellow is under the impression that anything masquerading as gas will have a lethal effect."

"He may be right—if he pumps it in fast enough."

"Oh, he won't be pumping it. Not after approximately five minutes from now."

"Hmmm. I think I'm beginning to see the light. 'Power off at sunset.'"

Corasol nodded. "I don't think he realizes somehow that all his vehicles are operating off broadcast power."

"Still, he has a good-sized crowd of hopefuls with him. How do you plan to get through them?"

"We don't. We go under. There's an extensive system of service ways underlying the city; another detail which I believe has escaped the corporal's notice."

"You'll be heading for the port?"

"Yes—eventually. First, we have a few small chores to see to. Sozier has quite a number of our technical men working at gun point to keep various services going."

Retief nodded. "It won't be easy breaking them out. I made a fast tour of the city this afternoon. Locked doors, armed guards—"

"Oh, the locks are power-operated, too. Our fellows will know what to do when the power fails. I think the sudden darkness will eliminate any problem from the guards."

The lights flickered and died. The whine of the turbines was suddenly noticeable, descending. Faint cries sounded from outside.

Corasol switched on a small portable lantern. "All ready, gentlemen?" he called, rising. "Let's move out. We want to complete this operation before dawn."

* * * *

Four hours later, Retief stood with Corasol in a low-ceilinged tunnel, white-tiled, brilliantly lit by a central glare strip, watching as the last of the column of men released from forced labor in the city's utilities installations filed past. A solidly-built man with pale blond hair came up, breathing hard.

"How did it go, Taine?" Corasol asked.

"They're beginning to catch on, Mr. Corasol. We had a brisk time of it at Station Four. Everybody's clear now. No one killed, but we had a few injuries."

Corasol nodded. "The last few crews in have reported trouble. Ah—what about—"

Taine shook his head. "Sorry, sir. No trace. No one's seen them. But they're probably at the port ahead of us, hiding out. They'd know we'd arrive eventually."

"I suppose so. You sent word to them well in advance...."

"Suppose I stand by here with a few men. We'll patrol the tunnels in case they show up. We have several hours before daylight."

"Yes. I'll go along and see to the preparations at Exit Ten. We'll make our sortie at oh-five-hundred. If you haven't seen anything of them by then...."

"I'm sure they're all right."

"They'd better be." Corasol said grimly "Let's be off, Retief."

"If it's all the same to you, Mr. Manager-General, I'll stay here with Taine. I'll join you later."

"As you wish. I don't imagine there'll be any trouble—but if there is, having a CDT observer along will lend a certain air to the operation." He smiled, shook Retief's hand and moved off along the tunnel. The echo of feet and voices grew faint, faded to silence. Taine turned to the three men detailed to him, conversed briefly, sent them off along branching corridors. He glanced at Retief.

"Mr. Retief, you're a diplomat. This errand is not a diplomatic one."

"I've been on a few like that, too, Mr. Taine."

Taine studied Retief's face. "I can believe that," he said. "However, I think you'd better rejoin the main party."

"I might be of some use here, if your missing men arrive under fire."

"Missing men?" Taine's mouth twisted in a sour smile. "You fail to grasp the picture, Mr. Retief. There'll be no missing men arriving."

"Oh? I understood you were waiting here to meet them."

"Not men, Mr. Retief. It happens that Corasol has twin daughters, aged nineteen. They haven't been seen since the trouble began."

* * * *

V

Half an hour passed. Retief leaned against the tunnel wall, arms folded, smoking a cigar in silence. Taine paced, ten yards up the corridor, ten yards back....

"You seem nervous, Mr. Taine," Retief said.

Taine stopped pacing, eyed Retief coldly. "You'd better go along now," he said decisively. "Just follow the main tunnel. It's about a mile."

"Plenty of time yet, Mr. Taine." Retief smiled and drew on his cigar. "Your three men are still out."

"They won't be back here. We'll rendezvous at Exit Ten."

"Am I keeping you from something, Taine?"

"I can't be responsible for your safety if you stay here."

"Oh? You think I might fall victim to an accident?"

Taine narrowed his eyes. "It could happen," he said harshly.

"Where were the girls last seen?" Retief asked suddenly.

"How would I know?"

"Weren't you the one who got word to them?"

"Maybe you'd better keep out of this."

"You sent your men off; now you're eager to see me retire to a safe position. Why the desire for solitude, Taine? You wouldn't by any chance have plans?"

"That's enough," Taine snapped. "On your way. That's an order!"

"There are some aspects of this situation that puzzle me, Mr. Taine. Mr. Corasol has explained to me how he and his Division Chiefs—including you—were surprised in the executive suite at Planetary Central by a crowd of Sozier's bully-boys. They came in past the entire security system without an alarm. Corasol and the others put up a surprisingly good fight and made it to the service elevators—and from there to the sub-station. There was even time to order an emergency alert to the entire staff—but somehow, they were all caught at their stations and kept on the job at gun point. Now, I should think that you, as Chief of Security as well as Communications, should have some ideas as to how all this came about."

"Are you implying—"

"Let me guess, Taine. You have a deal with Sozier. He takes over, ousts the legal owners, and sets himself up to live off the fat of the land, with you as his technical chief. Then, I imagine, you'd find it easy enough to dispose of Sozier—and you'd be in charge."

* * * *

Without warning Taine put his head down and charged. Retief dropped his cigar, side-stepped and planted a solid right on Taine's jaw. He staggered, went to his hands and knees.

"I suppose you'd like to get word to Sozier that his work force is arriving at the port at oh-five-hundred," Retief said. "Of course, he'll want to have a good-sized reception committee on hand as they come out."

Taine plunged to his feet, threw a vicious left that went past Retief's ear, then abruptly dropped, clamped a lock on Retief's leg, twisted—

The two men rolled, came to rest with Taine on top, Retief face-down, his arm bent back and doubled. Taine, red-faced and puffing, grunted as he applied pressure.

"You know a lot about me," he grated, "but you overlooked the fact that I've been Glavian Judo champion for the past nine years."

"You're a clever man, Taine," Retief said between clenched teeth. "Too clever to think it will work."

"It will work. Glave's never had a CDT mission here before. We're too small. Corasol invited your Embassy in because he had an idea there was something in the wind. That forced my hand. I've had to move hastily. But by the time I invite observers in to see for themselves, everything will be running smoothly. I can even afford to let Corasol and the others go—I'll have hostages for his good behavior."

"You've been wanting to boast about it to someone who could appreciate your cleverness, I see. Sozier must be an unappreciative audience."

"Sozier's a filthy pig—but he had his uses."

"What do you plan to do now?"

"I've been wondering that myself—but I think the best solution is to simply break your arm for now. You should be easy to control then. It's quite simple. I merely apply pressure, thus...."

"Judo is a very useful technique," Retief said. "But in order to make it work, you have to be a pretty good man...." He moved suddenly, shifting his position. Taine grabbed, holding Retief's arm by the wrist and elbow, his own arm levering Retief's back, back.... Retief twisted onto his side, then his back. Taine grunted, following the movement, straining. Slowly, Retief sat up against Taine's weight. Then, with a surge, he straightened his arm. Taine's grip broke. Retief came to his feet. Taine scrambled up in time to meet a clean uppercut that snapped him onto his back—out cold.

* * * *

"Ah, there you are," Retief said as Taine's eyes fluttered and opened. "You've had a nice nap—almost fifteen minutes. Feeling better?"

Taine snarled, straining against the bonds on his wrists.

"Gold braid has its uses," Retief commented. "Now that you're back, perhaps you can answer a question for me. What's the Birthday Cake?"

Taine spat. Retief went to stand over him.

"Time is growing short, Mr. Taine. It will be dawn in another two hours. I can't afford the luxury of coaxing you."

"You won't get away with this."

Retief looked at the glowing end of his cigar. "This won't be subtle, I agree—but it will work."

"You're bluffing."

Retief leaned closer. "In my place—would you hesitate?" he asked softly.

Taine cursed, struggled to break free, eyes on the cigar.

"What kind of diplomat are you?" he snarled.

"The modern variety. Throat-cutting, thumb-screws, poison and stiletto work were popular in Machiavelli's time; nowadays we go in more for the administrative approach—but the cigar-end still has its role."

"Look, we can come to an agreement—"

"What's the Birthday Cake?" Retief snapped.

"I'm in a position to do a lot for you!"

"Last chance—"

"It's the official Residence of the Manager-General!" Taine screeched, writhing away from the cigar.

"Where is it? Talk fast!"

"You'll never get close! There's a seven-foot wall and by this time the grounds are swarming with Sozier's men."

"Nevertheless, I want to know where it is—and the information had better be good. If I don't come back, you'll have a long wait."

Taine groaned. "All right. Put that damned cigar away. I'll tell you what I can…."

* * * *

Retief stood in the shadow of a vine-grown wall, watching the relief of the five-man guard detail at the main gate to the Residence grounds. The bluish light of the Glavian satellite reflected from the rain-pocked street, glinted from the leaves of a massive tree ten yards from the gate. The chill in the air cut through Retief's wet clothes. The men at the gate huddled, hands in pockets, coat collars turned up, backs to the wind—and to Retief. He moved silently forward, caught a low branch of the tree, pulled himself up.

The men at the gate exchanged muttered remarks. One lit a cigarette. Retief waited, then moved higher. The guards talked in low voices, edged closer to the shelter of the gate-house. Retief lowered himself onto the wall, dropped down onto the sodden lawn, crouched, waiting. There was no alarm.

Through the trees the dark shape of the house loomed up, its top storey defiantly ablaze with lights. Retief moved off silently, from the shadow of one tree to the next, swinging in an arc that would bring him to the rear of the great round structure. He froze as the heavy footfalls of one of Sozier's pickets slogged past five yards from him, then moved on. The glow of a campfire flickered near the front of the house. Retief could make out the shapes of men around it—a dozen or two, at least. Probably as many more warmed themselves at each of the other fires visible on the grounds—and most of the rest had doubtless found dryer shelter in the lee of the house itself.

Retief reached the conservatory at the rear of the house, studied the dark path leading to the broad terrace, picked out the squat shape of the utilities manifold behind a screen of shrubbery. So far, Taine's information had been accurate. The next step was to—

There was a faint sound from high above, followed by a whoosh! Then with a sharp crack! a flare appeared overhead, rocking gracefully, floating down gently under a small parachute. Below it, inky shadows rocked in unison.

In the raw white light, Retief counted eighteen men clinging to hand-holds on the side of the house, immobile in the pitiless glare. Above them, a face appeared, then a second, peering over the edge of the fourth-storey gallery. Both figures rose, unlimbering four-foot bows, fitting arrows to strings—

Whok! Whok! Two men lost their holds and fell, yelling, to slam into the heavy shrubbery. A second flight of arrows found marks. Retief watched from the shadows as man after man dropped to flounder in the wet foliage. Several jumped before the deadly bows were turned on them. As the flare faded, the last of the men plunged down to crash among their fellows. Retief stepped out, ran swiftly to the manifold, forcing his way among the close-growing screen, scrambled to its top. His hand fell on a spent arrow. He picked it up.

It was a stout wooden shaft twenty inches long, terminating in a rubber suction cup. Retief snorted, dropped the arrow and started up.

* * * *

VI

Twenty feet above ground level, the wide windows of the third floor sun terrace presented a precarious handhold as Retief swung back a foot and kicked in a panel. Inside, he dimly made out the shape of a broad carpeted room, curving out of sight in both directions. There were wide-leaved tropical plants in boxes, groups of padded chairs, low tables with bowls of fruit. Retief made his way past them, found an inner door, went into a dark hall. At the far end, voices exchanged shouted questions. Feet pounded. A flicker of light from a hand lantern splashed across the wall, disappeared. Retief found a stair, went up it noiselessly. According to Taine, the elevator to the top floor apartment should be to the left—

Retief flattened himself to the wall. Footsteps sounded near at hand. He moved quickly to a doorway. There was a murmur of voices, the wavering light of lanterns. A party of uniformed men tiptoed past a cross corridor, struggling under the weight of a massive log two feet in diameter and twelve feet long.

"…on signal, hit it all together. Then…" someone was saying.

Retief waited, listening. There was the creak of a door, the fumbling of awkwardly laden feet on a stair, hoarse breathing, a muffled curse.

"…got my fingers, you slob!" a voice snarled.

"Shaddup!" another voice hissed.

There was a long moment of silence, then a muffled command—followed an instant later by a thunderous crash, a shout—cut off abruptly by a ponderous *blam!* followed instantly by a roar like a burst dam, mingled with yells, thumps, crashes. A foamy wash of water surged along the cross corridor, followed a moment later by a man sliding on his back, then another, two more, the log, fragments of a door, more men.

In the uproar, Retief moved along to the elevator, felt over the control panel, located a small knurled button. He turned it. The panel came away. He fumbled cautiously, found a toggle switch, flipped it. A light sprang up in the car. Instantly Retief flipped the light switch; the glow faded. He waited. No alarm. Men were picking themselves up, shouting.

"...them broads dropped a hundred-gallon bag of water..." Someone complained.

"...up there fast, men. We got the door okay!"

Feet thumped. Yells sounded.

"No good, Wes! They got a safe or something in the way!"

Retief silently closed the lift door, pressed the button. With a sigh, the car slid upward, came to a gentle stop. He eased the door open, looked out into a dim-lit entrance hall. Footsteps sounded beyond a door. He waited; the clack of high heels crossing a floor. Retief stepped out of the car, went to the door, glanced into a spacious lounge with rich furniture, deep rugs, paintings, a sweep of glass, and in an alcove at the far side, a bar. Retief crossed the room, poured a stiff drink into a paper-thin glass and drained it.

The high-heeled steps were coming back now. A door opened. Two leggy young women in shorts, with red-gold hair bound back by ribbons—one green, one blue—stepped into the room. One girl held a coil of insulated wire; the other, a heavy-looking gray-enameled box eight inches on a side.

"Now, see if you can tinker that generator to get a little more juice, Lyn," the girl with the wire said. "I'll start stringing...."

Her voice died as she caught sight of Retief. He raised his glass. "My compliments, ladies. I see you're keeping yourselves amused."

"Who...who are you?" Lyn faltered.

"My name's Retief. Your father sent me along to carry your bags. It's lucky I arrived when I did, before any of those defenseless chaps outside were seriously injured."

"You're not...one of them?"

"Of course he's not, Lyn," the second girl said. "He's much too good-looking."

"That's good," Lyn said crisply. "I didn't want to have to use this thing." She tossed a bright-plated 2 mm needler onto a chair and sat down. "Dad's all right, isn't he?"

"He's fine, and we've got to be going. Tight schedule, you know. And you'd better get some clothes on. It's cold outside."

Lyn nodded. "Environmental Control went off the air six hours ago. You can already feel snow coming."

"Don't you suppose we have time to just rig up one little old circuit?" the other twin wheedled. "Nothing serious; just enough to tickle."

"We planned to wire all the window frames, the trunk we used to block the stair, the lift shaft—"

"And then we thought we'd try to drop a loop down and pick up the gallery guard rail, and maybe some of that wrought-iron work around the front of the house—"

"Sorry, girls; no time."

Five minutes later, the twins were ready, wrapped in fur robes. Retief had exchanged his soaked blazer for a down-lined weatherproof.

"The lift will take us all the way down, won't it?" he asked.

Lyn nodded. "We can go out through the wine cellar."

Retief picked up the needler and handed it to Lyn. "Hang on to this," he said. "You may need it yet."

* * * *

A cold wind whipped the ramp as dawn lightened the sky.

"It's hard to believe," Corasol said. "What made him do it?"

"He saw a chance to own it all."

"He can have it," Corasol's communicator beeped. He put it to his ear. "Everything's ship-shape and ready to lift," a tiny voice said.

Corasol turned to Retief. "Let's go aboard."

"Hold it," Retief said. "There's someone coming."

Corasol spoke into the communicator. "Keep him covered."

The man slogging across the concrete was short, wrapped in heavy garments. Over his head a white cloth fluttered from a stick.

"From the set of those bat-ears, I'd say it was the good corporal."

"I wonder what he wants."

Sozier stopped twenty feet from Retief and Corasol.

"I want to…ah…talk to you, Corasol," he said.

"Certainly, General. Go right ahead."

"Look here, Corasol. You can't do this. My men will freeze. We'll starve. I've been thinking it over, and I've decided that we can reach an understanding."

Corasol waited.

"I mean, we can get together on this thing. Compromise. Maybe I acted a little hasty." Sozier looked from Corasol to Retief. "You're from the CDT. You tell him. I'll guarantee his people full rights…."

Retief puffed at his cigar in silence. Sozier started again.

"Look, I'll give you a full voice in running things. A fifty-fifty split. Whatta you say?"

"I'm afraid the proposal doesn't interest me, General," Corasol said.

"Never mind the General stuff," Sozier said desperately. "Listen, you can run it. Just give me and my boys a little say-so."

"Sorry." Corasol shook his head. "Not interested, General."

"Okay, okay! You win! Just come on back and get things straightened out! I got a belly full of running things!"

"I'm afraid I have other plans, General. For some time I've wanted to transfer operations to a world called Las Palmas on which we hold a charter. It has a naturally delightful climate, and I'm told the fishing is good. I leave Glave to the Free Electorate with my blessing. Good-by, General." He turned to the ship.

"You got to stay here!" Sozier howled. "We'll complain to the CDT! And don't call me General! I'm a Corporal—"

"You're a General now—whether you like it or not." Corasol said bluntly. He shivered. There was a hint of ice in the air. "If you or any of your men ever decide to go to work, General, I daresay we can train you for employment on Las Palmas. In the meantime—Long Live the Revolution!"

"You can't do this! I'll sue!"

"Calm down, Sozier," Retief said. "Go back to town and see if you can get your radio working. Put in a call for Mr. Magnan aboard the CDT vessel. Tell him your troubles. It will make his day. And a word of advice: Mr. Magnan hates a piker—so ask for plenty."

* * * *

"My boy, I'm delighted," Ambassador Sternwheeler boomed. "A highly professional piece of work. A stirring testimonial to the value of the skilled negotiator!"

"You're too kind, Mr. Ambassador." Retief said, glancing at his watch.

"And Magnan tells me that not only will the Mission be welcomed, and my job secure for another year—that is, I shall have an opportunity to serve—but a technical mission has been requested as well. I shall look forward to meeting General Sozier. He sounds a most reasonable chap."

"Oh, you'll like him, Mr. Ambassador. A true democrat, willing to share all you have."

Counsellor of Embassy Magnan tapped and entered the office.

"Forgive the intrusion, Mr. Ambassador," he said breathlessly, "but I must—"

"Well, what is it, man? The deal hasn't gone sour?"

"Oh, far from it! I've been exploring General Sozier's economic situation with him via scope, and it seems he'll require a loan."

"Yes, yes? How much?"

Magnan inhaled proudly. "Twenty. Million. Credits."

"No!"

"Yes!"

"Magnificent! Good lord, Magnan, you're a genius! This will mean promotions all around. Why, the administrative load alone—"

"I can't wait to make planetfall, Mr. Ambassador. I'm all a-bubble with plans. I hope they manage to get the docking facilities back in operation soon."

"Help is on the way, my dear Magnan. I'm assured the Environmental Control installations will be coming back in operation again within a year or two."

"My, didn't those ice-caps form quickly. And in the open sea."

"Mere scum ice. As my Counsellor for Technical Affairs, you'll be in charge of the ice-breaking operation once we're settled in. I imagine you'll want to spend considerable time in the field. I'll be expecting a record of how every credit is spent."

"I'm more the executive type," Magnan said. "Possibly Retief—"

A desk speaker hummed. "Mr. Corasol's lighter has arrived to ferry Mr. Retief across to the Company ship…."

"Sorry you won't be with us, Retief," Sternwheeler said heartily. He turned to Magnan. "Manager-General Corasol has extended Retief an ex-equatur as Consul General to Las Palmas."

* * * *

Retief nodded. "Much as I'd like to be out in that open boat with you, breaking ice, I'm afraid duty calls elsewhere."

"Your own post? I'm not sure he's experienced enough, Mr. Ambassador. Now, I—"

"He was requested by name, Magnan. It seems the Manager-General's children took a fancy to him."

"Eh? How curious. I never thought you were particularly interested in infant care, Retief."

"Perhaps I haven't been, Mr. Magnan." Retief draped his short blue cape over his left arm and turned to the door. "But remember the diplomat's motto: be adaptable…."

THE KING OF THE CITY

Originally published in **Galaxy Magazine,** *August 1961.*

I stood in the shadows and looked across at the rundown lot with the windblown trash packed against the wire mesh barrier fence and the yellow glare panel that said HAUG ESCORT. There was a row of city-scarred hacks parked on the cracked ramp. They hadn't suffered the indignity of a wash-job for a long time. And the two-story frame building behind them— that had once been somebody's country house—now showed no paint except the foot-high yellow letters over the office door.

Inside the office a short broad man with small eyes and yesterday's beard gnawed a cigar and looked at me.

"Portal-to-portal escort cost you two thousand C's," he said. "Guaranteed."

"Guaranteed how?" I asked.

He waved the cigar. "Guaranteed you get into the city and back out again in one piece." He studied his cigar. "If somebody don't plug you first," he added.

"How about a one-way trip?"

"My boy got to come back out, ain't he?"

I had spent my last brass ten-dollar piece on a cup of coffee eight hours before, but I had to get into the city. This was the only idea I had left.

"You've got me wrong," I said. "I'm not a customer. I want a job."

"Yeah?" He looked at me again, with a different expression, like a guy whose new-found girl friend has just mentioned a price.

"You know Gra'nyauk?"

"Sure," I said. "I grew up here."

He asked me a few more questions, then thumbed a button centered in a ring of grime on the wall behind him. A chair scraped beyond the door; it opened and a tall bony fellow with thick wrists and an adams apple set among heavy neck tendons came in.

The man behind the desk pointed at me with his chin.

"Throw him out, Lefty."

Lefty gave me a resentful look, came around the desk and reached for my collar. I leaned to the right and threw a hard left jab to the chin. He rocked back and sat down.

"I get the idea," I said. "I can make it out under my own power." I turned to the door.

"Stick around, mister. Lefty's just kind of a like a test for separating the men from the boys."

"You mean I'm hired?"

He sighed. "You come at a good time. I'm short of good boys."

I helped Lefty up, then dusted off a chair and listened to a half-hour briefing on conditions in the city. They weren't good. Then I went upstairs to the chart room to wait for a call.

* * * *

It was almost ten o'clock when Lefty came into the room where I was looking over the maps of the city. He jerked his head.

"Hey, you."

A weasel-faced man who had been blowing smoke in my face slid off his stool, dropped his cigarette and smeared it under his shoe.

"You," Lefty said. "The new guy."

I belted my coat and followed him down the dark stairway, and out across the littered tarmac, glistening wet under the polyarcs, to where Haug stood talking to another man I hadn't seen before.

Haug flicked a beady glance my way, then turned to the stranger. He was a short man of about fifty with a mild expressionless face and expensive clothes.

"Mr. Stenn, this is Smith. He's your escort. You do like he tells you and he'll get you into the city and see your party and back out again in one piece."

The customer looked at me. "Considering the fee I'm paying, I sincerely hope so," he murmured.

"Smith, you and Mr. Stenn take number 16 here." Haug patted a hinge-sprung hood, painted a bilious yellow and scabbed with license medallions issued by half a dozen competing city governments.

Haug must have noticed something in Stenn's expression.

"It ain't a fancy-looking hack, but she's got full armor, heavy-duty gyros, crash-shocks, two-way music and panic gear. I ain't got a better hack in the place."

Stenn nodded, popped the hatch and got in. I climbed in the front and adjusted the seat and controls to give me a little room. When I kicked over the turbos they sounded good.

"Better tie in, Mr. Stenn," I said. "We'll take the Canada turnpike in. You can brief me on the way."

I wheeled 16 around and out under the glare-sign that read "HAUG ESCORT." In the eastbound linkway I boosted her up to 90. From the way the old bus stepped off, she had at least a megahorse under the hood. Maybe

Haug wasn't lying, I thought. I pressed an elbow against the power pistol strapped to my side.

I liked the feel of it there. Maybe between it and old 16 I could get there and back after all.

* * * *

"My destination," Stenn said, "is the Manhattan section."

That suited me perfectly. In fact, it was the first luck I'd had since I burned the uniform. I looked in the rear viewer at Stenn's face. He still wore no expression. He seemed like a mild little man to be wanting into the cage with the tigers.

"That's pretty rough territory, Mr. Stenn," I said. He didn't answer.

"Not many tourists go there," I went on. I wanted to pry a little information from him.

"I'm a businessman," Stenn said.

I let it go at that. Maybe he knew what he was doing. For me, there was no choice. I had one slim lead, and I had to play it out to the end. I swung through the banked curves of the intermix and onto the turnpike and opened up to full throttle.

It was fifteen minutes before I saw the warning red lights ahead. Haug had told me about this. I slowed.

"Here's our first roadblock, Mr. Stenn," I said. "This is an operator named Joe Naples. All he's after is his toll. I'll handle him; you sit tight in the hack. Don't say anything, don't do anything, no matter what happens. Understand?"

"I understand," Stenn said mildly.

I pulled up. My lights splashed on the spikes of a Mark IX tank trap. I set the parking jacks and got out.

"Remember what I told you," I said. "No matter what." I walked up into the beam of the lights.

A voice spoke from off to the side.

"Douse 'em, Rube."

I went back and cut the lights. Three men sauntered out onto the highway.

"Keep the hands away from the sides, Rube."

One of the men was a head taller than the others. I couldn't see his face in the faint red light from the beacon, but I knew who he was.

"Hello, Naples," I said.

He came up to me. "You know me, Rube?"

"Sure," I said. "The first thing Haug told me was pay my respects to Mr. Naples."

Naples laughed. "You hear that, boys? They know me pretty good on the outside, ha?"

He looked at me, not laughing any more. "I don't see you before."

"My first trip."

He jerked a thumb at the hack. "Who's your trick?"

"A businessman. Name is Stenn."

"Yeah? What kind business?"

I shook my head. "We don't quiz the cash customers, Joe."

"Let's take a look." Naples moved off toward the hack, the boys at his side. I followed. Naples looked in at Stenn. Stenn sat relaxed and looked straight ahead. Naples turned away, nodded to one of his helpers. The two moved off a few yards.

The other man, a short bullet-headed thug in a grease-spatted overcoat, stood by the hack, staring in at Stenn. He took a heavy old-style automatic from his coat pocket, pulled open the door. He aimed the gun at Stenn's head and carefully squeezed the trigger.

The hammer clicked emptily.

"Ping," he said. He thrust the gun back in his pocket, kicked the door shut and went over to join Naples.

"Okay, Rube," Naples called.

I went over to him.

"I guess maybe you on the level," he said. "Standard fee. Five hundred, Old Federal notes."

I had to be careful now. I held a bland expression, reached in—slowly—took out my wallet. I extracted two hundred-C notes and held them out.

Naples looked at them, unmoving. The thug in the dirty overcoat moved up close, and suddenly swung the edge of his palm at my wrist. I was ready; I flicked my hand aside and chopped him hard at the base of the neck. He dropped.

I was still holding out the money.

"That clown isn't worthy of a place in the Naples organization," I said.

Naples looked down at the man, stirred him with his foot.

"A clown," he said. He took the money and tucked it in his shirt pocket. "Okay, Rube," he said. "My regards to Haug."

I got in the hack and moved up to the barrier. It started up, trundled aside. Naples was bending over the man I had downed. He took the pistol from the pocket of the overcoat, jacked the action and aimed. There was a sharp crack. The overcoat flopped once. Naples smiled over at me.

"He ain't worthy a place in the Naples organization," he said.

I waved a hand vaguely and gunned off down the road.

II

The speaker in my ear hummed.

I grunted an acknowledgement and a blurred voice said, "Smith, listen. When you cross the South Radial, pick up the Midwest Feed-off. Take it easy and watch for Number Nine Station. Pull off there. Got it?"

I recognized the voice. It was Lefty, Haug's Number One boy. I didn't answer.

"What was the call?" Stenn asked.

"I don't know," I said. "Nothing."

The lights of the South Radial Intermix were in sight ahead now.

I slowed to a hundred and thought about it. My personal motives told me to keep going, my job as a paid Escort was to get my man where he wanted to go. That was tough enough, without detours. I eased back up to one-fifty, took the Intermix with gyros screaming, and curved out onto the thruway.

The speaker hummed. "What are you trying to pull, wise guy?" He sounded mad. "That was the South Radial you just passed up—"

"Yeah," I said. "That's right. Smitty takes 'em there and he brings 'em back. Don't call us, we'll call you."

There was a long hum from the speaker. "Oh, a wiseacre," it said finally. "Listen, rookie, you got a lot to learn. This guy is bankrolled. I seen the wad when he paid Haug off. So all right, we cut you in. Now, get this…."

He gave me detailed instructions. When he was finished, I said, "Don't wait up for me."

I took the speaker out of my ear and dropped it into the disposal slot. We drove along quietly for quite a while.

I was beginning to recognize my surroundings. This section of the turnpike had been opened the year before I left home. Except for the lack of traffic and the dark windows along the way it hadn't changed.

I was wondering just what Lefty's next move would be when a pair of powerful beams came on from the left, then pulled onto the highway, speeding up to pace me. I rocketed past before he had made full speed. I heard a loud spang, and glass chips scattered on my shoulder. I twisted and looked. A starred hole showed in the bubble, above the rear seat.

* * * *

"Duck!" I yelled. Stenn leaned over, put his head down.

The beams were gaining on me. I twisted the rear viewer, hit the I/R switch. A three-ton combat car, stripped, but still mounting twin infinite repeaters. Against that, old 16 was a kiddie car. I held my speed and tried to generate an idea. What I came up with wasn't good, but it was all I had.

A half a mile ahead there should be a level-split, one of those awkward ones that caused more than one pile-up in the first few months the turnpike was open. Maybe my playmates didn't know about it.

They were about to overtake me now. I slowed just a little, and started fading to the right. They followed me, crowding my rear wheel. I heard the spang again, twice, but nothing hit me. I was on the paved shoulder now, and could barely see the faded yellow cross-hatching that warned of the abutment that divided the pavement ahead.

I held the hack in the yellow until the last instant, then veered right and cleared the concrete barrier by a foot, hit the down-curve at a hundred and eighty in a howl of gyros and brakes—and the thunderous impact of the combat car.

Then I was off the pavement, fighting the wheel, slamming through underbrush, then miraculously back on the hard surface and coasting to a stop in the clear.

I took a deep breath and looked back. The burning remains of the car were scattered for a quarter of a mile along the turnpike. That would have been me if I had gauged it wrong.

I looked at the canopy of the hack. Three holes, not a foot apart, right where a passenger's head would be if he were sitting upright. Stenn was unconcernedly brushing glass dust from his jacket.

"Very neat, Mr. Smith," he said. "Now shall we resume our journey?"

"Maybe it's time you leveled with me, Stenn," I said.

He raised his eyebrows at me slightly.

"When Joe Naples' boy Friday pointed the gun at your head you didn't bat an eyelash," I said.

"I believe those were your instructions," Stenn said mildly.

"Pretty good for a simple businessman. I don't see you showing any signs of the shakes now, either, after what some might call a harrowing experience."

"I have every confidence in your handling—"

"Nuts, Stenn. Those three holes are pretty well grouped, wouldn't you say? The man that put them there was hitting where he was aiming. And he was aiming for you."

"Why me?" Stenn looked almost amused.

"I thought it was a little shakedown crew, out to teach me a lesson," I said. "Until I saw where the shots were going."

Stenn looked at me thoughtfully. He reached up and took a micro-speaker from his ear.

"The twin to the one you rashly disposed of," he said. "Mr. Haug was kind enough to supply it—for a fee. I must tell you that I had a gun in my hand as we approached the South Radial Intermix. Had you accepted the invitation to turn off, I would have halted the car, shot you and gone on alone. Happily, you chose to resist the temptation, for reasons of your own...." He looked at me inquiringly.

"Maybe I'm sap enough to take the job seriously," I said.

"That may possibly be true," Stenn said.

"What's your real errand here, Stenn? Frankly, I don't have time to get involved."

"Really? One wonders if you have irons in the fire, Smith. But never mind. I shan't pry. Are we going on?"

I gave him my stern penetrating look.

"Yeah," I said. "We're going on."

* * * *

In twenty minutes, we were on the Inner Concourse and the polyarcs were close together, lighting the empty sweep of banked pavement. The lights of the city sparkled across the sky ahead, and gave me a ghostly touch of the old thrill of coming home.

I doused that feeling fast. After eight years there was nothing left there for me to come home to. The city had a lethal welcome for intruders; it wouldn't be smart to forget that.

I didn't see the T-Bird until his spot hit my eyes and he was beside me, crowding.

I veered and hit the brakes, with a half-baked idea of dropping back and cutting behind him, but he stayed with me. I had a fast impression of squealing metal and rubber, and then I was skidding to a stop up against the deflector rails with the T-Bird slanted across my prow. Its lid popped almost before the screech died away, and I was looking down the muzzles of two power pistols. I kept both hands on the wheel, where they could see them, and sat tight.

I wondered whose friends we had met this time.

Two men climbed out, the pistols in sight, and came up to the hack. The first one was a heavy-set Slavic type zipped into a tight G. I. weather suit. He motioned. I opened up and got out, not making any sudden movements. Stenn followed. A cold wind was whipping along the concourse, blowing a fine misty rain hard against my cheek. The polyarcs cast black shadows on gray faces.

The smaller man moved over to Stenn and crowded him back against the hack. The Slav motioned again, and I moved over by the T-Bird. He fished my wallet out and put it in his pocket without looking at it. I heard the other man say something to Stenn, and then the sound of a blow. I turned my head slowly, so as not to excite my watchdog. Stenn was picking himself up. He started going through his pockets, showing everything to the man with the gun, then dropping it on the ground. The wind blew cards and papers along until they soaked up enough water to stick. Stenn carried a lot of paper.

* * * *

The gunny said something and Stenn started pulling off his coat. He turned it inside out, and held it out. The gunny shook his head, and motioned to my Slav. He looked at me, and I tried to read his mind. I moved across toward the hack. I must have guessed right because he didn't shoot me. The Slav pocketed his gun and took the coat. Methodically, he tore the lining out, found nothing, dropped the ripped garment and kicked it aside. I shifted position, and the Slav turned and backhanded me up against the hack.

"Lay off him, Heavy," the other hood said. "Maxy didn't say nothing about this mug. He's just a Escort."

Heavy started to get his gun out again. I had an idea he was thinking about using it. Maybe that's why I did what I did. As his hand dipped into his pocket, I lunged, wrapped an arm around him and yanked out my own artillery. I held onto a handful of the weather suit and dug the pistol in hard. He stood frozen. Heavy wasn't as dumb as he looked.

His partner had backed a step, the pistol in his hand covering all of us.

"Drop it, Slim," I said. "No hard feelings, and we'll be on our way."

Stenn stood absolutely motionless. He was still wearing his mild expression.

"Not a chance, mug," the gunny said softly. No one moved.

"Even if you're ready to gun your way through your pal, I can't miss. Better settle for a draw."

"Maxy don't like draws, mister."

"Stenn," I said. "Get in the T-Bird. Head back the way we came, and don't slow down to read any billboards."

Stenn didn't move.

* * * *

"Get going," I said. "Slim won't shoot."

"I employed you," Stenn said, "to take care of the heroics."

"If you've got any better ideas it's time to speak up, Stenn. This is your only out, the way I see it."

Stenn looked at the man with the gun.

"You referred to someone named 'Maxy.' Would that by any chance be Mr. Max Arena?"

Slim looked at him and thought about it.

"Could be," he said.

Stenn came slowly over to the Slav. Standing well out of the line of fire, he carefully put a hand in the loose pocket of the weather suit and brought out the pistol. I saw Slim's eyes tighten. He was having to make some tough decisions in a hurry.

Stenn moved offside, pistol in hand.

"Move away from him, Smith," he said.

I didn't know what he had in mind, but it didn't seem like the time to argue. I moved back.

"Drop your gun," he said.

I risked a glance at his mild expression.

"Are you nuts?"

"I came here to see Mr. Arena," he said. "This seems an excellent opportancy."

"Does it? I—"

"Drop it now, Smith. I won't warn you again."

I dropped it.

Slim swiveled on Stenn. He was still in an awkward spot.

"I want you to take me to Mr. Arena," Stenn said. "I have a proposition to put before him." He lowered the gun and handed it to Heavy.

It seemed like a long time until Slim lowered his gun.

"Heavy, put him in the back seat." He motioned me ahead, watched me as he climbed in the T-Bird.

"Nice friends you got, mug," he said. The T-Bird started up, backed, and roared off toward the city. I stood under the polyarcs and watched the tail glare out of sight.

Max Arena was the man I had come to the city to find.

III

Old number 16 was canted against the deflector rail, one side shredded into curled strips of crumpled metal. I looked closer. Under the flimsy fairings, gray armor showed. Maybe there was more to Haug's best hack than met the eye. I climbed in and kicked over the starter. The turbos sounded as good as ever. I eased the gyros in; she backed off the rail with a screech of ripped metal.

I had lost my customer, but I still had wheels.

The smart thing to do now would be to head back out the turnpike to Haug's lot, turn in my badge and keep moving, south. I could give up while I was still alive. All I had to do was accept the situation.

I had a wide choice. I could sign on with the New Confeds, or the Free Texans, or any one of the other splinter republics trying to set up shop in the power vacuum. I might try to get in to one of the Enclaves and convince its Baron he needed another trained bodyguard. Or I could take a post with one of the king-pins in the city.

As a last resort I could go back and find a spot in the Naples organization. I happened to know they had a vacancy.

I was just running through mental exercises to hear myself think. I couldn't settle for the kind of world I had found when I touched planet three months back, after eight years in deep space with Hayle's squadron. When the Interim Administration shot him for treason, I burned my uniform and disappeared. My years in the Service had given me a tough hide and a knack for staying alive; my worldly assets consisted of the clothes I stood in, my service pistol and a few souvenirs of my travels. For two months I had been scraping along on the cash I had in my pocket, buying drinks for drifters in cheap bars, looking for a hint, any lead at all, that would give me a chance to do what had to be done. Max Arena was the lead. Maybe a dud lead—but I had to find out.

The city lights loomed just a few miles away. I was wasting time sitting here; I steered the hack out into the highway and headed for them.

* * * *

Apparently Lefty's influence didn't extend far beyond the South Radial. The two roadblocks I passed in the next five miles took my money, accepted my story that I was on my way to pick up a fare, said to say hello to Haug and passed me on my way.

Haug's sour yellow color scheme seemed to carry some weight with the town Organizations, too. I was well into the city, cruising along the third level Crossover, before I had any trouble. I was doing about fifty, watching where I was going and looking for the Manhattan Intermix, when a battered Gyrob four-seater trundled out across the fairway and stopped. I swerved and jumped lanes; the Gyrob backed, blocking me. I kicked my safety frame down and floor-boarded the hack, steering straight for him. At the last instant he tried to pull out of the way.

He was too late.

I clipped him across his aft quarter, and caught a glimpse of the underside of the car as it stood on its nose, slammed through the deflector and over the side. Old 16 bucked and I got a good crack across the jaw from the ill-fitting frame, and then I was screeching through the Intermix and out onto the Manhattan Third level.

Up ahead, the glare panels at the top of the Blue Tower reared up half a mile into the wet night sky. It wasn't a hard address to find. Getting inside would be another matter.

I pulled up a hundred yards from the dark cave they used to call the limousine entrance and looked the situation over. The level was deserted—like the whole city seemed, from the street. But there were lights in the windows, level after level of them stretching up and away as far as you could see. There were plenty of people in the city—about ten million, even after the riots and the Food Scare and the collapse of legal government. The automated city supply system had gone on working, and the Kingpins, the big time criminals, had stepped in and set things up to suit their tastes. Life went on—but not out in the open. Not after dark.

I knew almost nothing about Arena. Judging from his employees, he was Kingpin of a prosperous outfit. The T-Bird was an expensive late model, and the two thugs handled themselves like high-priced talent. I couldn't expect to walk into his HQ without jumping a few hurdles. Maybe I should have invited myself along with Stenn and his new friends. On the other hand, there were advantages to arriving unannounced.

It was a temptation to drive in, with the hack's armor between me and any little surprises that might be waiting, but I liked the idea of staging a surprise of my own. I eased into drive and moved along to a parking ramp, swung around and down and stopped in the shadow of the retaining wall.

I set the brake and took a good look around. There was nothing in sight. Arena might have a power cannon trained on me from his bedroom window, for all I knew, but I had to get a toe into the water sometime. I shut down the turbo, and in the silence popped the lid and stepped out. The rain had stopped, and the moon showed as a bright spot on the high mist. I felt hungry and a little bit unreal, as though this were happening to somebody else.

* * * *

I moved over to the side of the parking slab, clambered over the deflector rail and studied the shadows under the third level roadway. I could barely make out the catwalks and service ways. I was wondering whether to pull off my hard-soled shoes for the climb when I heard footsteps, close. I gauged the distance to the hack, and saw I couldn't make it. I got back over the rail and waited.

He came into sight, rangy, shock-haired and preternaturally thin in tight traditional dress.

When he got close I saw that he was young, in his early twenties at most. He would be carrying a knife.

"Hey, Mister," he whined. "Got a cigarette?"

"Sure, young fellow," I said, sounding a little nervous. I threw in a shaky laugh to help build the picture. I took a cigarette from a pack, put the pack back in my pocket, held the weed out. He strutted up to me, reached out and flipped the cigarette from my fingers. I edged back and used the laugh again.

"Hey, he liked that," the punk whined. "He thinks that's funny. He got a sense of humor."

"Heh, heh," I said. "Just out getting a little air."

"Gimme another cigarette, funny man."

I took the pack out, watching. I got out a cigarette and held it gingerly, arm bent. As he reached for it, I drew back. He snatched for it. That put him in position.

I dropped the pack, clenched my two hands together, ducked down and brought them up hard under his chin. He backflipped, rolled over and started crawling.

I let him go.

I went over the rail without stopping to think it over and crossed the girder to the catwalk that ran under the boulevard above. I groped my way along to where the service way branched off for the Blue Tower, then stopped and looked up. A strip of luminous sky showed between the third level and the facade of the building. Anybody watching from the right spot would see me cross, walking on the narrow footway. It was a chance I'd have to take. I started to move out, and heard running feet. I froze.

The feet slid to a stop on the level above, a few yards away.

"What's up, Crackers?" somebody growled.

"The mark sapped me down."

* * * *

That was interesting. I had been spotted and the punk had been sent to welcome me. Now I knew where I stood. The opposition had made their first mistake.

"He was starting to cross under when I spot him," Crackers went on, breathing heavily. "He saps me and I see I can't handle him and I go for help."

Someone answered in a guttural whisper. Crackers lowered his voice. It wouldn't take long now for reinforcements to arrive and flush me out. I edged farther and chanced a look. I saw two heads outlined above. They didn't seem to be looking my way, so I started across, walking silently toward a narrow loading platform with a wide door opening from it.

Below me, a lone light reflected from the wet pavement of the second level, fifty feet down; the blank wall of the Blue Tower dropped past it sheer to the glistening gutters at ground level. Then I was on the platform and trying the door.

It didn't open.

It was what I should have expected. Standing in the full light from the glare panel above the entry, I felt as exposed as a fan-dancer's navel. There was no time to consider alternatives. I grabbed my power pistol, flipped it to beam fire and stood aside with an arm across my face. I gave the latch a blast, then kicked the door hard. It was solid as a rock. Behind and above me, I heard Crackers yell.

I beamed the lock again, tiny droplets of molten metal spattering like needles against my face and hand. The door held.

"Drop it and lift 'em, mug," a deep voice yelled. I twisted to look up at the silhouettes against the deflector rail. I recognized the Slavic face of the man called Heavy. So he could talk after all.

"You're under my iron, mug," he called. "Freeze or I'll burn you."

I believed him, but I had set something in motion that couldn't stop now. There was nothing to go back to; the only direction for me was on the way I was headed—deeper into trouble. I was tired of being the mouse in a cat's game. I had taken the initiative and I was keeping it.

I turned, set the power pistol at full aperture, and poured it to the armored door. Searing heat reflected from the barrier, smoke boiled, metal melted and ran. Through the stink of burning steel, I smelled scorched hair—and felt heat rake the back of my neck and hands. Heavy was beaming me at wide aperture, but the range was just too far for a fast kill. The door sagged and fell in. I jumped through the glowing opening, hit the floor and rolled to damp out my smouldering coat.

* * * *

I got to my feet. There was no time now to stop and feel the pain of my burns. They would expect me to go up—so I would go down. The Blue Tower covered four city blocks and was four hundred stories high. There was plenty of room in it for a man to lose himself.

I ran along the corridor, found a continuous service belt and hopped on, lay flat, rode it through the slot. I came out into the light of the service corridor below, my gun ready, then down and around again. I saw no one.

It took ten minutes to cover the eighteen floors down to the sub-basement. I rolled off the belt and looked around.

The whole space was packed with automatics; the Blue Tower was a self-sufficient city in itself. I recognized generators, heat pumps, air plants. None of them were operating. The city services were all still functioning, apparently. What it would be like in another ten or twenty years of anarchy was anybody's guess. But when the city systems failed the Blue Tower could go on on its own.

Glare panels lit the aisles dimly. I prowled along looking for an elevator bank. The first one I found indicated the car at the hundred-eightieth floor. I went on, found another indicating the twentieth. While I watched, the indicator moved, started down. I was getting ready to duck when it stopped at the fifth. I waited; it didn't move.

I went around to the side of the bank, found the master switch. I went back, punched for the car. When the door whooshed open, I threw the switch.

I had to work fast now. I stepped into the dark car, reached up and slid open the access panel in the top, then jumped, caught the edge and pulled myself up. The glare panels inside the shaft showed me the pony power pack on top of the car, used by repairmen and inspectors when the main power was off. I lit a per-match to read the fine print on the panel. I was in luck. It was a through car to the four-hundredth. I pushed a couple of buttons, and the car started up. I lay flat behind the machinery.

As the car passed the third floor feet came into view; two men stood beyond the transparent door, guns in their hands, watching the car come up. They didn't see me. One of them thumbed the button frantically. The car kept going.

There were men at almost every floor now. I went on up, passed the hundredth floor, the one-fiftieth, and kept going. I began to feel almost safe—for the moment.

I was gambling now on what little I knew of the Blue Tower from the old days when all the biggest names congregated there. The top floor was a lavish apartment that had been occupied by a retired fleet admiral, a Vice-President and a uranium millionaire, in turn. If I knew anything about Kingpins, that's where Max Arena would hang his hat.

The elevator was slow. Lying there I had time to start thinking about my burned hide. My scalp was hit worst, and then my hands; and my shoulders were sticking to the charred coat. I had been travelling on adrenalin since Heavy had beamed me, and now the reaction was starting to hit.

It would have to wait; I had work to do.

Just below the three hundred and ninety-eighth floor I punched the button and the car stopped. I stood up, feeling dizzy. I grabbed for the rungs on the wall, hung on. The wall of the shaft seemed to sway…back….

Sure, I told myself. The top of the building sways fifteen feet in a high wind. Why shouldn't I feel it? I dismissed the thought that it was dead calm outside now, and started up the ladder.

It was a hard climb. I hung on tight, and concentrated on moving one hand at a time. The collar of my coat rasped my raw neck. I passed up the 398th and 9th—and rammed my head smack against a dead end. No service entry to the penthouse. I backed down to the 399th.

I found the lever and eased the door open, then waited, gun in hand. Nothing happened. I couldn't wait any longer. I pushed the door wide, stepped off into the hall. Still nobody in sight, but I could hear voices. To my left a discreet stair carpeted in violet velvet eased up in a gentle curve. I didn't hesitate; I went up.

The door at the top was an austere slab of bleached teak. I tried the polished brass lever; the door swung open silently, and I stepped across the threshold and was looking across a plain of honey-colored down at a man sitting relaxed in a soft chair of pale leather.

He waved a hand cheerfully. "Come on in," he said.

IV

Max Arena was a broad-shouldered six-footer, with clean-shaven blue jaws, coarse gray-flecked black hair brushed back from a high forehead, a deeper tan than was natural for the city in November, and very white teeth. He was showing them now in a smile. He waved a hand toward a chair, not even glancing at the gun in my hand. I admired the twinkle of light on the polished barrel of a Norge stunner at his elbow and decided to ignore it too.

"I been following your progress with considerable interest," Arena said genially. "The boys had orders not to shoot. I guess Luvitch sort of lost his head."

"It's nothing," I said, "that a little skin graft won't clear up in a year or so."

"Don't feel bad. You're the first guy ever made it in here under his own steam without an invitation."

"And with a gun in his hand," I said.

"We won't need guns," he said. "Not right away."

I went over to one of the big soft chairs and sat down, put the gun in my lap.

"Why didn't you shoot as I came in?"

Arena jiggled his foot. "I like your style," he said. "You handled Heavy real good. He's supposed to be my toughest boy."

"What about the combat car? More friends of yours?"

"Nah," he said, chuckling easily. "Some Jersey boys heard I had a caller. They figured to knock him off on general principles. A nifty." He stopped laughing. "The Gyrob was mine; a remoted job. Nice piece of equipment. You cost me real dough tonight."

"Gee," I said. "That's tough."

"And besides," he said, "I know who you are."

I waited. He leaned over and picked something off the table. It was my wallet.

"I used to be in the Navy myself. Academy man, believe it or not. Almost, anyway. Kicked out three weeks before graduation. A frame. Well, practically a frame; there was plenty of guys doing what I was doing."

"That where you learned to talk like a hood?"

For a second Arena almost didn't smile.

"I am perfectly capable of expressing myself like a little gentleman, when I feel so inclined," he said, "but I say to hell with it."

"You must have been before my time," I said.

"A year or two. And I was using a different name then. But that wasn't my only hitch with the Service. When the Trouble started, I enlisted. I wanted some action. When the Navy found out they had a qualified Power

Section man on their hands, I went up fast. Within fourteen months I was a J. G. How about that?"

"Very commendable."

"So that's how I knew about the trick I. D. under the emulsion on the snapshot. You should have ditched it, Maclamore. Or should I say Captain Maclamore?"

* * * *

My mouth opened, but I couldn't think of a snappy answer to that one. I was in trouble. I had meant to play it by ear once I reached Arena to get the information I needed. That was out now. He knew me. He had topped my aces before I played them.

Suddenly Arena was serious. "You came to the right man, Maclamore. You heard I had one of your buddies here, right? I let the word leak; I thought it might bring more of you in. I was lucky to get Admiral Hayle's deputy."

"What do you want with me?"

Arena leaned forward. "There were eight of you. Hayle and his aide, Wolfgang, were shot when they wouldn't spill to the Provisional Government—or whatever that mob calls itself. Margan got himself killed in some kind of tangle near Denver. The other four boys pulled a fast one and ducked out with the scout you guys came back in. They were riding dry tanks—the scout had maybe thirty ton/hours fuel aboard—so they haven't left the planet. That leaves you stranded. With six sets of Federal law looking for you. Right?"

"I can't argue with what's in the newspapers," I said.

"Well, I don't know. I got a couple newspapers. But here's where I smell a deal, Maclamore. You want to know where that scout boat is. Played right, you figure you got a good chance of a raid on an arsenal or a power plant to pick up a few slugs of the heavy stuff; then you high-tail out, join up with the rest of the squadron and, with the ordnance you pack, you can sit off and dictate the next move." Arena leaned back and took a deep breath. His eyes didn't leave me.

"Okay. I got one of you here. I found out something from him. He gave me enough I know you boys got something up your sleeve. But he don't have the whole picture. I need more info. You can give it to me. If I like what I hear, I'm in a position to help—like, for example, with the fuel problem. And you cut me in for half. Fair enough?"

"Who is it you've got?"

He shook his head. "Uh-uh."

"What did he tell you?"

"Not enough. What was Hayle holding out? You birds found something out there. What was it?"

"We found a few artifacts on Mars," I said. "Not Martian in origin; visitors. We surveyed—"

"Don't string me, Maclamore. I'm willing to give you a fair deal, but if you make it tough for me—"

"How do you know I haven't got a detonator buried under my left ear," I said. "You can't pry information out of me, Arena."

"I think you want to live, Maclamore. I think you got something you want to live for. I want a piece of it."

"I can make a deal with you, Arena," I said. "Return me and my ship-mate to our scout boat. Fuel us up. You might throw in two qualified men to help handle the ship—minus their black-jacks, preferably—then clear out. We'll handle the rest. And I'll remember, with gratitude."

Arena was silent for a long moment.

* * * *

"Yeah, I could do that, Maclamore," he said finally. "But I won't. Max Arena is not a guy to pick up the crumbs—or wait around for handouts. I want in. All the way in."

"This time you'll have to settle for what you can get, Arena." I put the gun away and stood up.

I had a feeling I would have to put it over now or not at all.

"The rest of the squadron is still out there. If we don't show, they'll carry on alone. They're supplied for a century's operation. They don't need us."

That was true up to a point. The squadron had everything—except fuel.

"You figure you got it made if you can get your hands on that scout-boat," Arena said. "You figure to pick up fuel pretty easy by knocking off say the Lackawanna Pile."

"It shouldn't be too tough; a fleet boat of the Navy packs a wallop."

Arena tapped his teeth with a slim paper-cutter.

"You're worried your outfit will wind up Max Arena's private Navy, right? I'll tell you something. You think I'm sitting on top of the world, huh? I own this town, and everybody in it. All the luxury and fancy dinners and women I can use. And you know what? I'm bored."

"And you think running the Navy might be diverting?"

"Call it whatever you want to. There's something big going on out there, and I don't plan to be left out."

"Arena, when I clear atmosphere, we'll talk. Take it or leave it."

The smile was gone now. Arena looked at me, rubbing a finger along his blue cheek.

"Suppose I was to tell you I know where your other three boys are, Maclamore?"

"Do you?" I said.

"And the boat," Arena said. "The works."

"If you've got them here, I want to see them, Arena. If not, don't waste my time."

"I haven't exactly got 'em here, Maclamore. But I know a guy that knows where they are."

"Yeah." I said.

Arena looked mad. "Okay, I'll give it to you, Maclamore. I got a partner in this deal. Between us we got plenty. But we need what you got, too."

"I've made my offer, Arena. It stands."

"Have I got your word on that, Maclamore?" He stood up and came over to stand before me. "The old Academy word. You wouldn't break that, would you Maclamore?"

"I'll do what I said."

Arena walked to his desk, a massive boulder of Jadeite, cleaved and polished to a mirror surface. He thumbed a key.

"Send him in here," he said.

I waited. Arena sat down and looked across at me.

Thirty seconds passed and then the door opened and Stenn walked in.

Stenn glanced at me. "Well," he said. "Mr. Smith."

"The Smith routine is just a gag," Arena said. "His name is—Maclamore."

For an instant, I thought I saw a flash of expression on Stenn's face. He crossed the room and sat down.

"Well," he said. "A very rational move, your coming here. I trust you struck a profitable bargain?" He looked hard at me, and this time there was expression. Hate, I would call it, offhand.

"Not much of a deal at that, Stenn," Arena said. "The captain is a tough nut to crack. He wants my help with no strings attached. I think I'm going to buy it."

"How much information has he given you?"

Arena laughed. "Nothing," he said. "Max Arena going for a deal like that. Funny, huh? But that's the way the fall-out fogs 'em."

"And what have you arranged?"

"I turn him loose, him and Williams. I figure you'll go along, Stenn, and let him have the three guys you got. Williams will tell him where the Scout boat is, so there's no percentage in your holding out."

"What else?"

"What else is there?" Arena spread his hands. "They pick up the boat, fuel up—someplace—and they're off. And the captain here gives me the old Academy word he cuts me in, once he's clear."

There was a long silence. Arena smiled comfortably; Stenn sat calmly, looking at each of us in turn. I crossed my fingers and tried to look bored.

"Very well," Stenn said. "I seem to be presented with a *fait accompli....*"

I let a long breath out. I was going to make it....

"...But I would suggest that before committing yourself, you take the precaution of searching Mr. Maclamore's person. One never knows."

I could feel the look on my face. So could Arena.

"So," he said. "Another nifty." He didn't seem to move, but the stunner was in his hand. He wasn't smiling now, and the stunner caught me easily.

V

The lights came on, and I blinked, looking around the room.

My mementos didn't look like much, resting in the center of Arena's polished half-acre of desk top. The information was stored in the five tiny rods, less than an inch long, and the projector was a flat polyhedron the size of a pill-box. But the information they contained was worth more than all the treasure sunk in all the seas.

"This is merely a small sample," Stenn said. "The star surveys are said to be unbelievably complete. They represent a mapping task which would require a thousand years."

"The angles," Arena said. "Just figuring the angles will take plenty time."

"And this is what you almost let him walk out with," Stenn said.

Arena gave me a slashing look.

"Don't let your indignation run away with you, Arena," Stenn said. "I don't think you remembered to mention the fuel situation to Mr. Maclamore, did you?"

Arena turned to Stenn, looming over the smaller man. "Maybe you better button your lip," he said quietly. "I don't like the way you use it."

"Afraid I'll lower you in the gentleman's esteem?" Stenn said. He looked Arena in the eye.

"Nuts to the gentleman's esteem," Arena said.

"You thought you'd squeeze me out, Arena," Stenn said. "You didn't need me any more. You intended to let Maclamore and Williams go and have them followed. There was no danger of an escape, since you knew they'd find no fuel."

He turned to me. "During your years in space, Mr. Maclamore, technology moved on. And politics as well. Power fuels could be used to construct bombs. Ergo, all stations were converted for short half-life secondaries, and the primary materials stored at Fort Knox. You would have found yourself fuelless and therefore helpless. Mr. Arena would have arrived soon thereafter to seize the scout-boat."

"What would he want with the boat without fuel?" I asked.

"Mr. Arena was foresighted enough to stock up some years ago," Stenn said. "I understand he has enough metal hoarded to power your entire squadron for an indefinite time."

"Why tell this guy that?" Arena asked. "Kick him to hell out of here and let's get busy. You gab too much."

"I see that I'm tacitly reinstated as a partner," Stenn said. "Most gratifying."

"Max Arena is no welcher," Arena said. "You tipped me to the tapes, so you're in."

"Besides which you perhaps sense that I have other valuable contributions to make."

"I figure you to pull your weight."

"What are your plans for Mr. Maclamore?"

"I told you. Kick him out. He'll never wise up and cooperate with us."

"First, you'd better ask him a few more questions."

"Why? So he'll blow his head off and mess up my rug, like…." Arena stopped. "You won't get anything out of him."

"A man of his type has a strong aversion to suicide. He won't die to protect trivial information. And if he does—we'll know there's something important being held out."

"I don't like messy stuff," Arena said.

"I'll be most careful," Stenn said. "Get me some men in here to secure him to a chair, and we'll have a nice long chat with him."

"No messy stuff," Arena repeated. He crossed to his desk, thumbed a lever and spoke to someone outside.

Stenn was standing in front of me.

"Let him think he's pumping you," he hissed.

"Find out where his fuel is stored. I'm on your side." Then Arena was coming back, and Stenn was looking at me indifferently.

* * * *

Arena had overcome his aversion to messy stuff sufficiently to hit me in the mouth now and then during the past few hours. It made talking painful, but I kept at it.

"How do I know you have Williams?" I said.

Arena crossed to his desk, took out a defaced snapshot.

"Here's his I.D.," he said. "Take a look." He tossed it over. Stenn held it up.

"Let me talk to him."

"For what?"

"See how he feels about it," I mumbled. I was having trouble staying awake. I hadn't seen a bed for three days. It was hard to remember what information I was supposed to get from Arena.

"He'll join in if you do," Arena said. "Give up. Don't fight. Let it happen."

"You say you've got fuel. You're a liar. You've got no fuel."

"I got plenty fuel, wise guy," Arena yelled. He was tired too.

"Lousy crook," I said. "Can't even cheat a little without getting caught at it."

"Who's caught now, swabbie?" Arena was getting mad. That suited me.

"You're a lousy liar, Arena. You can't hide hot metal. Even Stenn ought to know that."

"What else was in the cache, Maclamore?" Stenn asked—for the hundredth time. He slapped me—also for the hundredth time. It jarred me and stung. It was the last straw. If Stenn was acting, I'd help him along. I lunged against the wires, swung a foot and caught him under the ribs. He oofed and fell off his chair.

"Don't push me any farther, you small-time chiselers," I yelled. "You've got nothing but a cast brass gall to offer. There's no hole deep enough to hide out power metal, even if a dumb slob like you thought of it."

"Dumb slob?" Arena barked. "You think a dumb slob could have built the organization I did, put this town in his hip pocket? I started stock-piling metal five years ago—a year before the ban. No hole deep enough, huh? It don't need to be so deep when it's got two feet of lead shielding over it."

"So you smuggled a few tons of lead into the Public Library and filed it under Little Bo Peep."

"The two feet was there ahead of me, wisenheimer. Remember the Polaris sub that used to be drydocked at Norfolk for the tourists to rubberneck?"

"Decommissioned and sold for scrap," I said. "Years ago."

"But not scrapped. Rusted in a scrapyard for five years. Then I bought her—beefed up her shielding—loaded her and sank her in ten fathoms of water in Cartwright Bay."

"That," Stenn said, "is the information we need."

Arena whirled. Stenn was still sitting on the floor. He had a palm gun in his hand, and it was pointed at the monogram on Arena's silk shirt.

"A cross," Arena said. "A lousy cross...."

* * * *

"Move back, Arena." Stenn got to his feet, eyes on Arena.

"Where'd you have the stinger stashed?"

"In my hand. Stop there."

Stenn moved over to me. Eyes on Arena, he reached for the twisted ends of wire, started loosening them.

"I don't want to be nosey," I said. "But just where the hell do you fit into this, Stenn?"

"Naval Intelligence," Stenn said.

Arena cursed. "I knew that name should have rung a bell. Vice Admiral Stenn. The papers said you got yours when the Navy was purged."

"A few of us eluded the net."

Arena heaved a sigh.

"Well, fellows," he said—and jumped.

Stenn's shot went wild, and Arena left-hooked him down behind the chair. As he followed, Stenn came up fast, landed a hard left, followed up, drove Arena back. I yanked at my wires. Almost—

Then Arena, a foot taller, hammered a brutal left-right, and Stenn sagged. Carefully Arena aimed a right cross to the jaw. Stenn dropped.

Arena wiped an arm across his face.

"The little man tried, Mister. Let's give him that."

He walked past my chair, stooped for Stenn's gun. I heaved, slammed against him, and the light chair collapsed as we went over. Arena landed a kick, then I was on my feet, shaking a slat loose from the dangling wire. Arena stepped in, threw a whistling right. I ducked it, landed a hard punch to the midriff, another on the jaw. Arena backed, bent over but still strong. I couldn't let him rest. I was after him, took two in the face, ducked a hay-maker that left him wide open just long enough for me to put everything I had in an uppercut that sent him back across his fancy desk. He sprawled, then slid onto the floor.

I went to him, kicked him lightly in the ribs.

"Where's Williams," I said. I kept kicking and asking. After five tries, Arena shook his head and tried to sit up. I put a foot in his face and he re-laxed. I asked him again.

"You didn't learn this kind of tactics at the Academy," Arena whined.

"It's the times," I said. "They have a coarsening effect."

"Williams was a fancy-pants," Arena said. "No guts. He pulled the stopper."

"Talk plainer," I said, and kicked him again, hard—but I knew what he meant.

"Blew his lousy head off," Arena yelled. "I gassed him and tried scop on him. He blew. He was out cold, and he blew."

"Yeah," I said. "Hypnotics will trigger it."

"Fancy goddam wiring job," Arena muttered, wiping blood from his face.

* * * *

I got the wire and trussed Arena up. I had to clip him twice before I finished. I went through his pockets, looked at things, recovered my souvenirs. I went over to Stenn. He was breathing.

Arena was watching. "He's okay, for crissake," he said. "What kind of punch you think I got?"

I hoisted Stenn onto my shoulder.

"So long, Arena," I said. "I don't know why I don't blow your brains out. Maybe it's that Navy Cross citation in your wallet."

"Listen," Arena said. "Take me with you."

"A swell idea," I said. "I'll pick up a couple of tarantulas, too."

"You're trying for the hack, right?"

"Sure. What else?"

"The roof," he said. "I got six, eight rotos on the roof. One high-speed job. You'll never make the hack."

"Why tell me?"

"I got eight hundred gun boys in this building alone. They know you're here. The hack is watched, the whole route. You can't get through."

"What do you care?"

"If the boys bust in here after a while and find me like this…. They'll bury me with the wires still on, Maclamore."

"How do I get to the roof?"

He told me. I went to the right corner, pushed the right spot, and a panel slid aside. I looked back at Arena.

"I'll make a good sailor, Maclamore," he said.

"Don't crawl, Arena," I said. I went up the short stair, came out onto a block-square pad.

Arena was right about the rotos. Eight of them. I picked the four-place Cad, and got Stenn tied in. He was coming to, muttering. He was still fighting Arena, he thought.

"…I'll hold…you…get out…."

"Take it easy, Stenn," I said. "Nothing can touch this bus. Where's the boat?" I shook him. "Where's the boat, Stenn?"

He came around long enough to tell me. It wasn't far—less than an hour's run.

"Stand by, Admiral," I said. "I'll be right back."

"Where…you…."

"We need every good man we can get," I said. "And I think I know a guy that wants to join the Navy."

EPILOGUE

Admiral Stenn turned away from the communicator screen.

"I think we'd be justified in announcing victory now, Commodore." As usual, he sounded like a professor of diction, but he was wearing a big grin.

"Whatever you say, chief," I said, with an even sappier smile.

I made the official announcement that a provisional Congress had accepted the resignations of all claims by former office holders, and that new elections would be underway in a week.

I switched over to Power Section. The NCO in charge threw me a snappy highball. Damned if he wasn't grinning too.

"I guess we showed 'em who's got the muscle, Commodore," he said.

"Your firepower demonstration was potent, Max," I said. "You must have stayed up nights studying the tapes."

"We've hardly scratched the surface yet," he said.

"I'll be crossing back to *Alaska* now, Mac," Stenn said.

I watched him move across the half-mile void to the flagship. Five minutes later the patrol detail broke away to take up surveillance orbits. They would be getting all the shore leave for the next few years, but I was glad my squadron had been detailed to go with the flagship on the Deep Space patrol. I wanted to be there when we followed those star surveys back to where their makers came from. Stenn wasn't the man to waste time, either. He'd be getting under way any minute. It was time to give my orders. I flipped the communicator key to the squadron link-up.

"Escort Commander to Escort," I said. "Now hear this...."

THE LONG REMEMBERED THUNDER

Originally published in Worlds of Tomorrow, *April 1963.*

I

In his room at the Elsby Commercial Hotel, Tremaine opened his luggage and took out a small tool kit, used a screwdriver to remove the bottom cover plate from the telephone. He inserted a tiny aluminum cylinder, crimped wires and replaced the cover. Then he dialed a long-distance Washington number and waited half a minute for the connection.

"Fred, Tremaine here. Put the buzzer on." A thin hum sounded on the wire as the scrambler went into operation.

"Okay, can you read me all right? I'm set up in Elsby. Grammond's boys are supposed to keep me informed. Meantime, I'm not sitting in this damned room crouched over a dial. I'll be out and around for the rest of the afternoon."

"I want to see results," the thin voice came back over the filtered hum of the jamming device. "You spent a week with Grammond—I can't wait another. I don't mind telling you certain quarters are pressing me."

"Fred, when will you learn to sit on your news breaks until you've got some answers to go with the questions?"

"I'm an appointive official," Fred said sharply. "But never mind that. This fellow Margrave—General Margrave. Project Officer for the hyperwave program—he's been on my neck day and night. I can't say I blame him. An unauthorized transmitter interfering with a Top Secret project, progress slowing to a halt, and this Bureau—"

"Look, Fred. I was happy in the lab. Headaches, nightmares and all. Hyperwave is my baby, remember? You elected me to be a leg-man: now let me do it my way."

"I felt a technical man might succeed where a trained investigator could be misled. And since it seems to be pinpointed in your home area—"

"You don't have to justify yourself. Just don't hold out on me. I sometimes wonder if I've seen the complete files on this—"

"You've seen all the files! Now I want answers, not questions! I'm warning you, Tremaine. Get that transmitter. I need someone to hang!"

* * * *

Tremaine left the hotel, walked two blocks west along Commerce Street and turned in at a yellow brick building with the words ELSBY MUNICIPAL POLICE cut in the stone lintel above the door. Inside, a heavy man with a creased face and thick gray hair looked up from behind an ancient Underwood. He studied Tremaine, shifted a toothpick to the opposite corner of his mouth.

"Don't I know you, mister?" he said. His soft voice carried a note of authority.

Tremaine took off his hat. "Sure you do, Jess. It's been a while, though."

The policeman got to his feet. "Jimmy," he said, "Jimmy Tremaine." He came to the counter and put out his hand. "How are you, Jimmy? What brings you back to the boondocks?"

"Let's go somewhere and sit down, Jess."

In a back room Tremaine said, "To everybody but you this is just a visit to the old home town. Between us, there's more."

Jess nodded. "I heard you were with the guv'ment."

"It won't take long to tell; we don't know much yet." Tremaine covered the discovery of the powerful unidentified interference on the high-security hyperwave band, the discovery that each transmission produced not one but a pattern of "fixes" on the point of origin. He passed a sheet of paper across the table. It showed a set of concentric circles, overlapped by a similar group of rings.

"I think what we're getting is an echo effect from each of these points of intersection. The rings themselves represent the diffraction pattern—"

"Hold it, Jimmy. To me it just looks like a beer ad. I'll take your word for it."

"The point is this, Jess: we think we've got it narrowed down to this section. I'm not sure of a damn thing, but I think that transmitter's near here. Now, have you got any ideas?"

"That's a tough one, Jimmy. This is where I should come up with the news that Old Man Whatchamacallit's got an attic full of gear he says is a time machine. Trouble is, folks around here haven't even taken to TV. They figure we should be content with radio, like the Lord intended."

"I didn't expect any easy answers, Jess. But I was hoping maybe you had something…"

"Course," said Jess, "there's always Mr. Bram…"

"Mr. Bram," repeated Tremaine. "Is he still around? I remember him as a hundred years old when I was kid."

"Still just the same, Jimmy. Comes in town maybe once a week, buys his groceries and hikes back out to his place by the river."

"Well, what about him?"

"Nothing. But he's the town's mystery man. You know that. A little touched in the head."

"There were a lot of funny stories about him, I remember," Tremaine said. "I always liked him. One time he tried to teach me something I've forgotten. Wanted me to come out to his place and he'd teach me. I never did go. We kids used to play in the caves near his place, and sometimes he gave us apples."

* * * *

"I've never seen any harm in Bram," said Jess. "But you know how this town is about foreigners, especially when they're a mite addled. Bram has blue eyes and blond hair—or did before it turned white—and he talks just like everybody else. From a distance he seems just like an ordinary American. But up close, you feel it. He's foreign, all right. But we never did know where he came from."

"How long's he lived here in Elsby?"

"Beats me, Jimmy. You remember old Aunt Tress, used to know all about ancestors and such as that? She couldn't remember about Mr. Bram. She was kind of senile, I guess. She used to say he'd lived in that same old place out on the Concord road when she was a girl. Well, she died five years ago…in her seventies. He still walks in town every Wednesday…or he did up till yesterday anyway."

"Oh?" Tremaine stubbed out his cigarette, lit another. "What happened then?"

"You remember Soup Gaskin? He's got a boy, name of Hull. He's Soup all over again."

"I remember Soup," Tremaine said. "He and his bunch used to come in the drug store where I worked and perch on the stools and kid around with me, and Mr. Hempleman would watch them from over back of the prescription counter and look nervous. They used to raise cain in the other drug store…."

"Soup's been in the pen since then. His boy Hull's the same kind. Him and a bunch of his pals went out to Bram's place one night and set it on fire."

"What was the idea of that?"

"Dunno. Just meanness, I reckon. Not much damage done. A car was passing by and called it in. I had the whole caboodle locked up here for six hours. Then the sob sisters went to work: poor little tyke routine, high spirits, you know the line. All of 'em but Hull are back in the streets playin' with matches by now. I'm waiting for the day they'll make jail age."

"Why Bram?" Tremaine persisted. "As far as I know, he never had any dealings to speak of with anybody here in town."

"Oh hoh, you're a little young, Jimmy," Jess chuckled. "You never knew about Mr. Bram—the young Mr. Bram—and Linda Carroll."

Tremaine shook his head.

"Old Miss Carroll. School teacher here for years; guess she was retired by the time you were playing hookey. But her dad had money, and in her day she was a beauty. Too good for the fellers in these parts. I remember her ridin by in a high-wheeled shay, when I was just a nipper. Sitting up proud and tall, with that red hair piled up high. I used to think she was some kind of princess...."

"What about her and Bram? A romance?"

Jess rocked his chair back on two legs, looked at the ceiling, frowning. "This would ha' been about nineteen-oh-one. I was no more'n eight years old. Miss Linda was maybe in her twenties—and that made her an old maid, in those times. The word got out she was setting her cap for Bram. He was a good-looking young feller then, over six foot, of course, broad backed, curly yellow hair—and a stranger to boot. Like I said, Linda Carroll wanted nothin to do with the local bucks. There was a big shindy planned. Now, you know Bram was funny about any kind of socializing; never would go any place at night. But this was a Sunday afternoon and someways or other they got Bram down there; and Miss Linda made her play, right there in front of the town, practically. Just before sundown they went off together in that fancy shay. And the next day, she was home again—alone. That finished off her reputation, as far as the biddies in Elsby was concerned. It was ten years 'fore she even landed the teaching job. By that time, she was already old. And nobody was ever fool enough to mention the name Bram in front of her."

Tremaine got to his feet. "I'd appreciate it if you'd keep your ears and eyes open for anything that might build into a lead on this, Jess. Meantime, I'm just a tourist, seeing the sights."

"What about that gear of yours? Didn't you say you had some kind of detector you were going to set up?"

"I've got an oversized suitcase," Tremaine said. "I'll be setting it up in my room over at the hotel."

"When's this bootleg station supposed to broadcast again?"

"After dark. I'm working on a few ideas. It might be an infinitely repeating logarithmic sequence, based on—"

"Hold it, Jimmy. You're over my head." Jess got to his feet. "Let me know if you want anything. And by the way—" he winked broadly—"I always did know who busted Soup Gaskin's nose and took out his front teeth."

II

Back in the street, Tremaine headed south toward the Elsby Town Hall, a squat structure of brownish-red brick, crouched under yellow autumn trees at the end of Sheridan Street. Tremaine went up the steps and past heavy double doors. Ten yards along the dim corridor, a hand-lettered cardboard sign over a black-varnished door said "MUNICIPAL OFFICE OF RECORD." Tremaine opened the door and went in.

A thin man with garters above the elbow looked over his shoulder at Tremaine.

"We're closed," he said.

"I won't be a minute," Tremaine said. "Just want to check on when the Bram property changed hands last."

The man turned to Tremaine, pushing a drawer shut with his hip. "Bram? He dead?"

"Nothing like that. I just want to know when he bought the place."

The man came over to the counter, eyeing Tremaine. "He ain't going to sell, mister, if that's what you want to know."

"I want to know when he bought."

The man hesitated, closed his jaw hard. "Come back tomorrow," he said.

Tremaine put a hand on the counter, looked thoughtful. "I was hoping to save a trip." He lifted his hand and scratched the side of his jaw. A folded bill opened on the counter. The thin man's eyes darted toward it. His hand eased out, covered the bill. He grinned quickly.

"See what I can do," he said.

It was ten minutes before he beckoned Tremaine over to the table where a two-foot-square book lay open. An untrimmed fingernail indicated a line written in faded ink:

"May 19. Acreage sold, One Dollar and other G&V consid. NW Quarter Section 24, Township Elsby. Bram. (see Vol. 9 & cet.)"

"Translated, what does that mean?" said Tremaine.

"That's the ledger for 1901; means Bram bought a quarter section on the nineteenth of May. You want me to look up the deed?"

"No, thanks," Tremaine said. "That's all I needed." He turned back to the door.

"What's up, mister?" the clerk called after him. "Bram in some kind of trouble?"

"No. No trouble."

The man was looking at the book with pursed lips. "Nineteen-oh-one," he said. "I never thought of it before, but you know, old Bram must be dern near to ninety years old. Spry for that age."

"I guess you're right."

The clerk looked sideways at Tremaine. "Lots of funny stories about old Bram. Useta say his place was haunted. You know; funny noises and lights. And they used to say there was money buried out at his place."

"I've heard those stories. Just superstition, wouldn't you say?"

"Maybe so." The clerk leaned on the counter, assumed a knowing look. "There's one story that's not superstition…."

Tremaine waited.

"You—uh—paying anything for information?"

"Now why would I do that?" Tremaine reached for the door knob.

The clerk shrugged. "Thought I'd ask. Anyway—I can swear to this. Nobody in this town's ever seen Bram between sundown and sunup."

* * * *

Untrimmed sumacs threw late-afternoon shadows on the discolored stucco facade of the Elsby Public Library. Inside, Tremaine followed a paper-dry woman of indeterminate age to a rack of yellowed newsprint.

"You'll find back to nineteen-forty here," the librarian said. "The older are there in the shelves."

"I want nineteen-oh-one, if they go back that far."

The woman darted a suspicious look at Tremaine. "You have to handle these old papers carefully."

"I'll be extremely careful." The woman sniffed, opened a drawer, leafed through it, muttering.

"What date was it you wanted?"

"Nineteen-oh-one; the week of May nineteenth."

The librarian pulled out a folded paper, placed it on the table, adjusted her glasses, squinted at the front page. "That's it," she said. "These papers keep pretty well, provided they're stored in the dark. But they're still flimsy, mind you."

"I'll remember." The woman stood by as Tremaine looked over the front page. The lead article concerned the opening of the Pan-American Exposition at Buffalo. Vice-President Roosevelt had made a speech. Tremaine leafed over, reading slowly.

On page four, under a column headed *County Notes* he saw the name Bram:

Mr. Bram has purchased a quarter section of fine grazing land, north of town, together with a sturdy house, from J. P. Spivey of Elsby. Mr. Bram will occupy the home and will continue to graze a few head of stock. Mr. Bram, who is a newcomer to the county, has been a resident of Mrs. Stoate's Guest Home in Elsby for the past months.

"May I see some earlier issues; from about the first of the year?"

The librarian produced the papers. Tremaine turned the pages, read the heads, skimmed an article here and there. The librarian went back to her desk. An hour later, in the issue for July 7, 1900, an item caught his eye:

A Severe Thunderstorm. Citizens of Elsby and the country were much alarmed by a violent cloudburst, accompanied by lightning and thunder, during the night of the fifth. A fire set in the pine woods north of Spivey's farm destroyed a considerable amount of timber and threatened the house before burning itself out along the river.

The librarian was at Tremaine's side. "I have to close the library now. You'll have to come back tomorrow."

Outside, the sky was sallow in the west: lights were coming on in windows along the side streets. Tremaine turned up his collar against a cold wind that had risen, started along the street toward the hotel.

A block away a black late-model sedan rounded a corner with a faint squeal of tires and gunned past him, a heavy antenna mounted forward of the left rear tail fin whipping in the slipstream. Tremaine stopped short, stared after the car.

"Damn!" he said aloud. An elderly man veered, eyeing him sharply. Tremaine set off at a run, covered the two blocks to the hotel, yanked open the door to his car, slid into the seat, made a U-turn, and headed north after the police car.

* * * *

Two miles into the dark hills north of the Elsby city limits, Tremaine rounded a curve. The police car was parked on the shoulder beside the highway just ahead. He pulled off the road ahead of it and walked back. The door opened. A tall figure stepped out.

"What's your problem, mister?" a harsh voice drawled.

"What's the matter? Run out of signal?"

"What's it to you, mister?"

"Are you boys in touch with Grammond on the car set?"

"We could be."

"Mind if I have a word with him? My name's Tremaine."

"Oh," said the cop, "you're the big shot from Washington." He shifted chewing tobacco to the other side of his jaw. "Sure, you can talk to him." He turned and spoke to the other cop, who muttered into the mike before handing it to Tremaine.

The heavy voice of the State Police chief crackled. "What's your beef, Tremaine?"

"I thought you were going to keep your men away from Elsby until I gave the word, Grammond."

"That was before I knew your Washington stuffed shirts were holding out on me."

"It's nothing we can go to court with, Grammond. And the job you were doing might have been influenced if I'd told you about the Elsby angle."

Grammond cursed. "I could have put my men in the town and taken it apart brick by brick in the time—"

"That's just what I don't want. If our bird sees cops cruising, he'll go underground."

"You've got it all figured, I see. I'm just the dumb hick you boys use for the spade work, that it?"

"Pull your lip back in. You've given me the confirmation I needed."

"Confirmation, hell! All I know is that somebody somewhere is punching out a signal. For all I know, it's forty midgets on bicycles, pedalling all over the damned state. I've got fixes in every county—"

"The smallest hyperwave transmitter Uncle Sam knows how to build weighs three tons," said Tremaine. "Bicycles are out."

Grammond snorted. "Okay, Tremaine," he said. "You're the boy with all the answers. But if you get in trouble, don't call me; call Washington."

* * * *

Back in his room, Tremaine put through a call.

"It looks like Grammond's not willing to be left out in the cold, Fred. Tell him if he queers this—"

"I don't know but what he might have something," the voice came back over the filtered hum. "Suppose he smokes them out—"

"Don't go dumb on me, Fred. We're not dealing with West Virginia moonshiners."

"Don't tell me my job, Tremaine!" the voice snapped. "And don't try out your famous temper on me. I'm still in charge of this investigation."

"Sure. Just don't get stuck in some senator's hip pocket." Tremaine hung up the telephone, went to the dresser and poured two fingers of Scotch into a water glass. He tossed it down, then pulled on his coat and left the hotel.

He walked south two blocks, turned left down a twilit side street. He walked slowly, looking at the weathered frame houses. Number 89 was a once-stately three-storied mansion overgrown with untrimmed vines, its windows squares of sad yellow light. He pushed through the gate in the ancient picket fence, mounted the porch steps and pushed the button beside the door, a dark panel of cracked varnish. It was a long minute before the door opened. A tall woman with white hair and a fine-boned face looked at him coolly.

"Miss Carroll," Tremaine said. "You won't remember me, but I—"

"There is nothing whatever wrong with my faculties, James," Miss Carroll said calmly. Her voice was still resonant, a deep contralto. Only a faint quaver reflected her age—close to eighty, Tremaine thought, startled.

"I'm flattered you remember me, Miss Carroll," he said.

"Come in." She led the way to a pleasant parlor set out with the furnishings of another era. She motioned Tremaine to a seat and took a straight chair across the room from him.

"You look very well, James," she said, nodding. "I'm pleased to see that you've amounted to something."

"Just another bureaucrat, I'm afraid."

"You were wise to leave Elsby. There is no future here for a young man."

"I often wondered why you didn't leave, Miss Carroll. I thought, even as a boy, that you were a woman of great ability."

"Why did you come today, James?" asked Miss Carroll.

"I…." Tremaine started. He looked at the old lady. "I want some information. This is an important matter. May I rely on your discretion?"

"Of course."

"How long has Mr. Bram lived in Elsby?"

Miss Carroll looked at him for a long moment. "Will what I tell you be used against him?"

"There'll be nothing done against him, Miss Carroll…unless it needs to be in the national interest."

"I'm not at all sure I know what the term 'national interest' means, James. I distrust these glib phrases."

"I always liked Mr. Bram," said Tremaine. "I'm not out to hurt him."

"Mr. Bram came here when I was a young woman. I'm not certain of the year."

"What does he do for a living?"

"I have no idea."

"Why did a healthy young fellow like Bram settle out in that isolated piece of country? What's his story?"

"I'm…not sure that anyone truly knows Bram's story."

"You called him 'Bram', Miss Carroll. Is that his first name…or his last?"

"That is his only name. Just…Bram."

"You knew him well once, Miss Carroll. Is there anything—"

A tear rolled down Miss Carroll's faded cheek. She wiped it away impatiently.

"I'm an unfulfilled old maid, James," she said. "You must forgive me."

Tremaine stood up. "I'm sorry. Really sorry. I didn't mean to grill you. Miss Carroll. You've been very kind. I had no right…."

Miss Carroll shook her head. "I knew you as a boy, James. I have complete confidence in you. If anything I can tell you about Bram will be helpful to you, it is my duty to oblige you; and it may help him." She paused. Tremaine waited.

"Many years ago I was courted by Bram. One day he asked me to go with him to his house. On the way he told me a terrible and pathetic tale. He said that each night he fought a battle with evil beings, alone, in a cave beneath his house."

Miss Carroll drew a deep breath and went on. "I was torn between pity and horror. I begged him to take me back. He refused." Miss Carroll twisted her fingers together, her eyes fixed on the long past. "When we reached the house, he ran to the kitchen. He lit a lamp and threw open a concealed panel. There were stairs. He went down…and left me there alone.

"I waited all that night in the carriage. At dawn he emerged. He tried to speak to me but I would not listen.

"He took a locket from his neck and put it into my hand. He told me to keep it and, if ever I should need him, to press it between my fingers in a secret way…and he would come. I told him that until he would consent to see a doctor, I did not wish him to call. He drove me home. He never called again."

"This locket," said Tremaine, "do you still have it?"

Miss Carroll hesitated, then put her hand to her throat, lifted a silver disc on a fine golden chain. "You see what a foolish old woman I am, James."

"May I see it?"

She handed the locket to him. It was heavy, smooth. "I'd like to examine this more closely," he said. "May I take it with me?"

Miss Carroll nodded.

"There is one other thing," she said, "perhaps quite meaningless…."

"I'd be grateful for any lead."

"Bram fears the thunder."

III

As Tremaine walked slowly toward the lighted main street of Elsby a car pulled to a stop beside him. Jess leaned out, peered at Tremaine and asked:

"Any luck, Jimmy?"

Tremaine shook his head. "I'm getting nowhere fast. The Bram idea's a dud, I'm afraid."

"Funny thing about Bram. You know, he hasn't showed up yet. I'm getting a little worried. Want to run out there with me and take a look around?"

"Sure. Just so I'm back by full dark."

As they pulled away from the curb Jess said, "Jimmy, what's this about State Police nosing around here? I thought you were playing a lone hand from what you were saying to me."

"I thought so too, Jess. But it looks like Grammond's a jump ahead of me. He smells headlines in this; he doesn't want to be left out."

"Well, the State cops could be mighty handy to have around. I'm wondering why you don't want 'em in. If there's some kind of spy ring working—"

"We're up against an unknown quantity. I don't know what's behind this and neither does anybody else. Maybe it's a ring of Bolsheviks…and maybe it's something bigger. I have the feeling we've made enough mistakes in the last few years; I don't want to see this botched."

The last pink light of sunset was fading from the clouds to the west as Jess swung the car through the open gate, pulled up under the old trees before the square-built house. The windows were dark. The two men got out, circled the house once, then mounted the steps and rapped on the door. There was a black patch of charred flooring under the window, and the paint on the wall above it was bubbled. Somewhere a cricket set up a strident chirrup, suddenly cut off. Jess leaned down, picked up an empty shotgun shell. He looked at Tremaine. "This don't look good," he said. "You suppose those fool boys…?"

He tried the door. It opened. A broken hasp dangled. He turned to Tremaine. "Maybe this is more than kid stuff," he said. "You carry a gun?"

"In the car."

"Better get it."

Tremaine went to the car, dropped the pistol in his coat pocket, rejoined Jess inside the house. It was silent, deserted. In the kitchen Jess flicked the beam of his flashlight around the room. An empty plate lay on the oilcloth-covered table.

"This place is empty," he said. "Anybody'd think he'd been gone a week."

"Not a very cozy—" Tremaine broke off. A thin yelp sounded in the distance.

"I'm getting jumpy," said Jess. "Dern hounddog, I guess."

A low growl seemed to rumble distantly. "What the devil's that?" Tremaine said.

Jess shone the light on the floor. "Look here," he said. The ring of light showed a spatter of dark droplets all across the plank floor.

"That's blood, Jess.…" Tremaine scanned the floor. It was of broad slabs, closely laid, scrubbed clean but for the dark stains.

"Maybe he cleaned a chicken. This is the kitchen."

"It's a trail." Tremaine followed the line of drops across the floor. It ended suddenly near the wall.

"What do you make of it. Jimmy?"

A wail sounded, a thin forlorn cry, trailing off into silence. Jess stared at Tremaine. "I'm too damned old to start believing in spooks," he said. "You suppose those damn-fool boys are hiding here, playing tricks?"

"I think." Tremaine said, "that we'd better go ask Hull Gaskin a few questions."

* * * *

At the station Jess led Tremaine to a cell where a lanky teen-age boy lounged on a steel-framed cot, blinking up at the visitor under a mop of greased hair.

"Hull, this is Mr. Tremaine," said Jess. He took out a heavy key, swung the cell door open. "He wants to talk to you."

"I ain't done nothin," Hull said sullenly. "There ain't nothin wrong with burnin out a Commie, is there?"

"Bram's a Commie, is he?" Tremaine said softly. "How'd you find that out, Hull?"

"He's a foreigner, ain't he?" the youth shot back. "Besides, we heard...."

"What did you hear?"

"They're lookin for the spies."

"Who's looking for spies?"

"Cops."

"Who says so?"

The boy looked directly at Tremaine for an instant, flicked his eyes to the corner of the cell. "Cops was talkin about 'em," he said.

"Spill it, Hull," the policeman said. "Mr. Tremaine hasn't got all night."

"They parked out east of town, on 302, back of the woodlot. They called me over and asked me a bunch of questions. Said I could help 'em get them spies. Wanted to know all about any funny-actin people around hers."

"And you mentioned Bram?"

The boy darted another look at Tremaine. "They said they figured the spies was out north of town. Well, Bram's a foreigner, and he's out that way, ain't he?"

"Anything else?"

The boy looked at his feet.

"What did you shoot at, Hull?" Tremaine said.

The boy looked at him sullenly.

"You know anything about the blood on the kitchen floor?"

"I don't know what you're talkin about," Hull said. "We was out squirrel-huntin."

"Hull, is Mr. Bram dead?"

"What you mean?" Hull blurted. "He was—"

"He was what?"

"Nothin."

"The Chief won't like it if you hold out on him, Hull," Tremaine said. "He's bound to find out."

Jess looked at the boy. "Hull's a pretty dumb boy," he said. "But he's not that dumb. Let's have it, Hull."

The boy licked his lips. "I had Pa's 30-30, and Bovey Lay had a twelve-gauge...."

"What time was this?"

"Just after sunset."

"About seven-thirty, that'd be," said Jess. "That was half an hour before the fire was spotted."

"I didn't do no shootin. It was Bovey. Old Bram jumped out at him, and he just fired off the hip. But he didn't kill him. He seen him run off...."

"You were on the porch when this happened. Which way did Bram go?"

"He...run inside."

"So then you set fire to the place. Whose bright idea was that?"

Hull sat silent. After a moment Tremaine and Jess left the cell.

"He must have gotten clear, Jimmy," said Jess. "Maybe he got scared and left town."

"Bram doesn't strike me as the kind to panic." Tremaine looked at his watch. "I've got to get on my way, Jess. I'll check with you in the morning."

Tremaine crossed the street to the Paradise Bar and Grill, pushed into the jukebox-lit interior, took a stool and ordered a Scotch and water. He sipped the drink, then sat staring into the dark reflection in the glass. The idea of a careful reconnoitre of the Elsby area was gone, now, with police swarming everywhere. It was too bad about Bram. It would be interesting to know where the old man was...and if he was still alive. He'd always seemed normal enough in the old days: a big solid-looking man, middle-aged, always pleasant enough, though he didn't say much. He'd tried hard, that time, to interest Tremaine in learning whatever it was....

Tremaine put a hand in his jacket pocket, took out Miss Carroll's locket. It was smooth, the size and shape of a wrist-watch chassis. He was fingering it meditatively when a rough hand slammed against his shoulder, half knocking him from the stool. Tremaine caught his balance, turned, looked into the scarred face of a heavy-shouldered man in a leather jacket.

"I heard you was back in town, Tremaine," the man said.

The bartender moved up. "Looky here, Gaskin, I don't want no trouble—"

"Shove it!" Gaskin squinted at Tremaine, his upper lip curled back to expose the gap in his teeth. "You tryin to make more trouble for my boy, I hear. Been over to the jail, stickin your nose in."

Tremaine dropped the locket in his pocket and stood up. Gaskin hitched up his pants, glanced around the room. Half a dozen early drinkers stared, wide-eyed. Gaskin squinted at Tremaine. He smelled of unwashed flannel.

"Sicked the cops onto him. The boy was out with his friends, havin a little fun. Now there he sets in jail."

Tremaine moved aside from the stool, started past the man. Soup Gaskin grabbed his arm.

"Not so fast! I figger you owe me damages. I—"

"Damage is what you'll get," said Tremaine. He slammed a stiff left to Gaskin's ribs, drove a hard right to the jaw. Gaskin jack-knifed backwards, tripped over a bar stool, fell on his back. He rolled over, got to hands and knees, shook his head.

"Git up, Soup!" someone called. "Hot dog!" offered another.

"I'm calling the police!" the bartender yelled.

"Never mind," a voice said from the door. A blue-jacketed State Trooper strolled into the room, fingers hooked into his pistol belt, the steel caps on his boot heels clicking with each step. He faced Tremaine, feet apart.

"Looks like you're disturbin the peace, Mr. Tremaine," he said.

"You wouldn't know who put him up to it, would you?" Tremaine said.

"That's a dirty allegation," the cop grinned. "I'll have to get off a hot letter to my congressman."

Gaskin got to his feet, wiped a smear of blood across his cheek, then lunged past the cop and swung a wild right. Tremaine stepped aside, landed a solid punch on Gaskin's ear. The cop stepped back against the bar. Soup whirled, slammed out with lefts and rights. Tremaine lashed back with a straight left; Gaskin slammed against the bar, rebounded, threw a knockout right…aand Tremaine ducked, landed a right upper-cut that sent Gaskin reeling back, bowled over a table, sent glasses flying. Tremaine stood over him.

"On your feet, jailbird," he said. "A workout is exactly what I needed."

"Okay, you've had your fun," the State cop said. "I'm taking you in, Tremaine."

Tremaine looked at him. "Sorry, copper," he said. "I don't have time right now." The cop looked startled, reached for his revolver.

"What's going on here, Jimmy?" Jess stood in the door, a huge .44 in his hand. He turned his eyes on the trooper.

"You're a little out of your jurisdiction," he said. "I think you better move on 'fore somebody steals your bicycle."

The cop eyed Jess for a long moment, then holstered his pistol and stalked out of the bar. Jess tucked his revolver into his belt, looked at Gaskin sitting on the floor, dabbing at his bleeding mouth. "What got into you, Soup?"

"I think the State boys put him up to it," Tremaine said. "They're looking for an excuse to take me out of the picture."

Jess motioned to Gaskin. "Get up, Soup. I'm lockin you up alongside that boy of yours."

Outside, Jess said, "You got some bad enemies there, Jimmy. That's a tough break. You ought to hold onto your temper with those boys. I think maybe you ought to think about getting over the state line. I can run you to the bus station, and send your car along...."

"I can't leave now, Jess. I haven't even started."

IV

In his room, Tremaine doctored the cut on his jaw, then opened his trunk, checked over the detector gear. The telephone rang.

"Tremaine? I've been on the telephone with Grammond. Are you out of your mind? I'm—"

"Fred," Tremaine cut in, "I thought you were going to get those state cops off my neck."

"Listen to me, Tremaine. You're called off this job as of now. Don't touch anything! You'd better stay right there in that room. In fact, that's an order!"

"Don't pick now to come apart at the seams, Fred," Tremaine snapped.

"I've ordered you off! That's all!" The phone clicked and the dial tone sounded. Tremaine dropped the receiver in its cradle, then walked to the window absently, his hand in his pocket.

He felt broken pieces and pulled out Miss Carroll's locket. It was smashed, split down the center. It must have gotten it in the tussle with Soup, Tremaine thought. It looked—

He squinted at the shattered ornament. A maze of fine wires was exposed, tiny condensers, bits of glass.

In the street below, tires screeched. Tremaine looked down. A black car was at the curb, doors sprung. Four uniformed men jumped out, headed for the door. Tremaine whirled to the phone. The desk clerk came on.

"Get me Jess—fast!"

The police chief answered.

"Jess, the word's out I'm poison. An earful of State law is at the front door. I'm going out the back. Get in their way all you can." Tremaine dropped the phone, grabbed up the suitcase and let himself out into the hall. The back stairs were dark. He stumbled, cursed, made it to the service entry. Outside, the alley was deserted.

He went to the corner, crossed the street, thrust the suitcase into the back seat of his car and slid into the driver's seat. He started up and eased away from the curb. He glanced in the mirror. There was no alarm.

It was a four-block drive to Miss Carroll's house. The housekeeper let Tremaine in.

"Oh, yes, Miss Carroll is still up," she said. "She never retires until nine. I'll tell her you're here, Mr. Tremaine."

* * * *

Tremaine paced the room. On his third circuit Miss Carroll came in.

"I wouldn't have bothered you if it wasn't important," Tremaine said. "I can't explain it all now. You said once you had confidence in me. Will you come with me now? It concerns Bram…and maybe a lot more than just Bram."

Miss Carroll looked at him steadily. "I'll get my wrap."

On the highway Tremaine said, "Miss Carroll, we're headed for Bram's house. I take it you've heard of what happened out there?"

"No, James. I haven't stirred out of the house. What is it?"

"A gang of teen-age toughs went out last night. They had guns. One of them took a shot at Bram. And Bram's disappeared. But I don't think he's dead."

Miss Carroll gasped. "Why? Why did they do it?"

"I don't think they know themselves."

"You say…you believe he still lives…."

"He must be alive. It dawned on me a little while ago…a little late, I'll admit. The locket he gave you. Did you ever try it?"

"Try it? Why…no. I don't believe in magic, James."

"Not magic. Electronics. Years ago Bram talked to me about radio. He wanted to teach me. Now I'm here looking for a transmitter. That transmitter was busy last night. I think Bram was operating it."

There was a long silence.

"James," Miss Carroll said at last, "I don't understand."

"Neither do I, Miss Carroll. I'm still working on finding the pieces. But let me ask you: that night that Bram brought you out to his place. You say he ran to the kitchen and opened a trapdoor in the floor—"

"Did I say floor? That was an error: the panel was in the wall."

"I guess I jumped to the conclusion. Which wall?"

"He crossed the room. There was a table, with a candlestick. He went around it and pressed his hand against the wall, beside the wood-box. The panel slid aside. It was very dark within. He ducked his head, because the opening was not large, and stepped inside…."

"That would be the east wall…to the left of the back door?"

"Yes."

"Now, Miss Carroll, can you remember exactly what Bram said to you that night? Something about fighting something, wasn't it?"

"I've tried for sixty years to put it out of my mind, James. But I remember every word, I think." She was silent for a moment.

* * * *

"I was beside him on the buggy seat. It was a warm evening, late in spring. I had told him that I loved him, and...he had responded. He said that he would have spoken long before, but that he had not dared. Now there was that which I must know.

"His life was not his own, he said. He was not...native to this world. He was an agent of a mighty power, and he had trailed a band of criminals...." She broke off. "I could not truly understand that part, James. I fear it was too incoherent. He raved of evil beings who lurked in the shadows of a cave. It was his duty to wage each night an unceasing battle with occult forces."

"What kind of battle? Were these ghosts, or demons, or what?"

"I don't know. Evil powers which would be unloosed on the world, unless he met them at the portal as the darkness fell and opposed them."

"Why didn't he get help?"

"Only he could stand against them. I knew little of abnormal psychology, but I understood the classic evidence of paranoia. I shrank from him. He sat, leaning forward, his eyes intent. I wept and begged him to take me back. He turned his face to me, and I saw the pain and anguish in his eyes. I loved him...and feared him. And he would not turn back. Night was falling, and the enemy awaited him."

"Then, when you got to the house...?"

"He had whipped up the horses, and I remember how I clung to the top braces, weeping. Then we were at the house. Without a word he jumped down and ran to the door. I followed. He lit a lamp and turned to me. From somewhere there was a wailing call, like an injured animal. He shouted something—an unintelligible cry—and ran toward the back of the house. I took up the lamp and followed. In the kitchen he went to the wall, pressed against it. The panel opened. He looked at me. His face was white.

"'In the name of the High God. Linda Carroll, I entreat you....'

"I screamed. And he hardened his face, and went down...and I screamed and screamed again...." Miss Carroll closed her eyes, drew a shuddering breath.

"I'm sorry to have put you through this, Miss Carroll," Tremaine said. "But I had to know."

Faintly in the distance a siren sounded. In the mirror, headlights twinkled half a mile behind. Tremaine stepped on the gas. The powerful car leaped ahead.

"Are you expecting trouble on the road, James?"

"The State police are unhappy with me, Miss Carroll. And I imagine they're not too pleased with Jess. Now they're out for blood. But I think I can outrun them."

"James." Miss Carroll said, sitting up and looking behind. "If those are police officers, shouldn't you stop?"

"I can't, Miss Carroll. I don't have time for them now. If my idea means anything, we've got to get there fast...."

* * * *

Bram's house loomed gaunt and dark as the car whirled through the gate, ground to a stop before the porch. Tremaine jumped out, went around the car and helped Miss Carroll out. He was surprised at the firmness of her step. For a moment, in the fading light of dusk, he glimpsed her profile. *How beautiful she must have been....*

He reached into the glove compartment for a flashlight.

"We haven't got a second to waste," he said. "That other car's not more than a minute behind us." He reached into the back of the car, hauled out the heavy suitcase. "I hope you remember how Bram worked that panel."

On the porch Tremaine's flashlight illuminated the broken hasp. Inside, he led the way along a dark hall, pushed into the kitchen.

"It was there," Miss Carroll said, pointing. Outside, an engine sounded on the highway, slowing, turning in. Headlights pushed a square of cold light across the kitchen wall. Tremaine jumped to the spot Miss Carroll had indicated, put the suitcase down, felt over the wall.

"Give me the light, James," Miss Carroll said calmly. "Press there." She put the spot on the wall. Tremaine leaned against it. Nothing happened. Outside, there was the thump of car doors; a muffled voice barked orders.

"Are you sure...?"

"Yes. Try again, James."

Tremaine threw himself against the wall, slapped at it, searching for a hidden latch.

"A bit higher; Bram was a tall man. The panel opened below...."

Tremaine reached higher, pounded, pushed up, sideways—

With a click a three by four foot section of wall rolled silently aside. Tremaine saw greased metal slides and, beyond, steps leading down.

"They are on the porch now, James," said Miss Carroll.

"The light!" Tremaine reached for it, threw a leg over the sill. He reached back, pulled the suitcase after him. "Tell them I kidnapped you, Miss Carroll. And thanks."

Miss Carroll held out her hand. "Help me, James. I hung back once before. I'll not repeat my folly."

Tremaine hesitated for an instant, then reached out, handed Miss Carroll in. Footsteps sounded in the hall. The flashlight showed Tremaine a black pushbutton bolted to a two by four stud. He pressed it. The panel slid back in place.

Tremaine flashed the light on the stairs.

"Okay, Miss Carroll," he said softly. "Let's go down."

* * * *

There were fifteen steps, and at the bottom, a corridor, with curved walls of black glass, and a floor of rough boards. It went straight for twenty feet and ended at an old-fashioned five-panel wooden door. Tremaine tried the brass knob. The door opened on a room shaped from a natural cave, with waterworn walls of yellow stone, a low uneven ceiling, and a packed-earth floor. On a squat tripod in the center of the chamber rested an apparatus of black metal and glass, vaguely gunlike, aimed at the blank wall. Beside it, in an ancient wooden rocker, a man lay slumped, his shirt blood-caked, a black puddle on the floor beneath him.

"Bram!" Miss Carroll gasped. She went to him, took his hand, staring into his face.

"Is he dead?" Tremaine said tightly.

"His hands are cold…but there is a pulse."

A kerosene lantern stood by the door. Tremaine lit it, brought it to the chair. He took out a pocket knife, cut the coat and shirt back from Bram's wound. A shotgun blast had struck him in the side; there was a lacerated area as big as Tremaine's hand.

"It's stopped bleeding," he said. "It was just a graze at close range, I'd say." He explored further. "It got his arm too, but not as deep. And I think there are a couple of ribs broken. If he hasn't lost too much blood…." Tremaine pulled off his coat, spread it on the floor.

"Let's lay him out here and try to bring him around."

Lying on his back on the floor, Bram looked bigger than his six-foot-four, younger than his near-century, Tremaine thought. Miss Carroll knelt at the old man's side, chafing his hands, murmuring to him.

Abruptly a thin cry cut the air.

Tremaine whirled, startled. Miss Carroll stared, eyes wide. A low rumble sounded, swelled louder, broke into a screech, cut off.

"Those are the sounds I heard that night," Miss Carroll breathed. "I thought afterwards I had imagined them, but I remember…. James, what does it mean?"

"Maybe it means Bram wasn't as crazy as you thought," Tremaine said.

Miss Carroll gasped sharply. "James! Look at the wall—"

Tremaine turned. Vague shadows moved across the stone, flickering, wavering.

"What the devil…!"

Bram moaned, stirred. Tremaine went to him. "Bram!" he said. "Wake up!"

Bram's eyes opened. For a moment he looked dazedly at Tremaine, then at Miss Carroll. Awkwardly he pushed himself to a sitting position.

"Bram…you must lie down," Miss Carroll said.

"Linda Carroll," Bram said. His voice was deep, husky.

"Bram, you're hurt…"

A mewling wail started up. Bram went rigid "What hour is this?" he grated.

"The sun has just gone down; it's after seven—"

Bram tried to get to his feet. "Help me up," he ordered. "Curse the weakness…."

Tremaine got a hand under the old man's arm. "Careful, Bram," he said. "Don't start your wound bleeding again."

"To the Repellor," Bram muttered. Tremaine guided him to the rocking chair, eased him down. Bram seized the two black pistol-grips, squeezed them.

"You, young man," Bram said. "Take the circlet there; place it about my neck."

* * * *

The flat-metal ring hung from a wire loop. Tremaine fitted it over Bram's head. It settled snugly over his shoulders, a flange at the back against his neck.

"Bram," Tremaine said. "What's this all about?"

"Watch the wall there. My sight grows dim. Tell me what you see."

"It looks like shadows: but what's casting them?"

"Can you discern details?"

"No. It's like somebody waggling their fingers in front of a slide projector."

"The radiation from the star is yet too harsh," Bram muttered. "But now the node draws close. May the High Gods guide my hand!"

A howl rang out, a raw blast of sound. Bram tensed. "What do you see?" he demanded.

"The outlines are sharper. There seem to be other shapes behind the moving ones. It's like looking through a steamy window…." Beyond the misty surface Tremaine seemed to see a high narrow chamber, bathed in white light. In the foreground creatures like shadowy caricatures of men paced to and fro. "They're like something stamped out of alligator hide," Tremaine whispered. "When they turn and I see them edge-on, they're thin…."

"An effect of dimensional attenuation. They strive now to match matrices with this plane. If they succeed, this earth you know will lie at their feet."

"What are they? Where are they? That's solid rock—"

"What you see is the Niss Command Center. It lies in another world than this, but here is the multihedron of intersection. They bring their harmonic generators to bear here in the hope of establishing an aperture of focus."

"I don't understand half of what you're saying, Bram. And the rest I don't believe. But with this staring me in the face, I'll have to act as though I did."

* * * *

Suddenly the wall cleared. Like a surface of moulded glass the stone threw back ghostly highlights. Beyond it, the Niss technicians, seen now in sharp detail, worked busily, silently, their faces like masks of ridged red-brown leather. Directly opposite Bram's Repellor, an apparatus like an immense camera with a foot-wide silvered lens stood aimed, a black-clad Niss perched in a saddle atop it. The white light flooded the cave, threw black shadows across the floor. Bram hunched over the Repellor, face tensed in strain. A glow built in the air around the Niss machine. The alien technicians stood now, staring with tiny bright-red eyes. Long seconds passed. The black-clad Niss gestured suddenly. Another turned to a red-marked knife-switch, pulled. As suddenly as it had cleared, the wall went milky, then dulled to opacity. Bram slumped back, eyes shut, breathing hoarsely.

"Near were they then," he muttered, "I grow weak...."

"Let me take over," Tremaine said. "Tell me how."

"How can I tell you? You will not understand."

"Maybe I'll understand enough to get us through the night."

Bram seemed to gather himself. "Very well. This must you know...."

"I am an agent in the service of the Great World. For centuries we have waged war against the Niss, evil beings who loot the continua. They established an Aperture here, on your Earth. We detected it, and found that a Portal could be set up here briefly. I was dispatched with a crew to counter their move—"

"You're talking gibberish," Tremaine said. "I'll pass the Great World and the continua...but what's an Aperture?"

"A point of material contact between the Niss world and this plane of space-time. Through it they can pump this rich planet dry of oxygen, killing it—then emerge to feed on the corpse."

"What's a Portal?"

"The Great World lies in a different harmonic series than do Earth and the Niss World. Only at vast intervals can we set up a Portal of temporary identity as the cycles mesh. We monitor the Niss emanations, and forestall them when we can, now in this plane, now in that."

"I see: denial to the enemy."

"But we were late. Already the multihedron was far advanced. A blinding squall lashed outside the river cave where the Niss had focused the Aperture, and the thunder rolled as the ionization effect was propagated in the atmosphere. I threw my force against the Niss Aperture, but could not destroy it…but neither could they force their entry."

"And this was sixty years ago? And they're still at it?"

* * * *

"You must throw off the illusion of time! To the Niss only a few days have passed. But here—where I spend only minutes from each night in the engagement, as the patterns coincide—it has been long years."

"Why don't you bring in help? Why do you have to work alone?"

"The power required to hold the Portal in focus against the stresses of space-time is tremendous. Even then the cycle is brief. It gave us first a fleeting contact of a few seconds; it was through that that we detected the Niss activity here. The next contact was four days later, and lasted twenty-four minutes—long enough to set up the Repellor. I fought them then…and saw that victory was in doubt. Still, it was a fair world; I could not let it go without a struggle. A third identity was possible twenty days later; I elected to remain here until then, attempt to repel the Niss, then return home at the next contact. The Portal closed, and my crew and I settled down to the engagement.

"The next night showed us in full the hopelessness of the contest. By day, we emerged from where the Niss had focussed the Aperture, and explored this land, and came to love its small warm sun, its strange blue sky, its mantle of green…and the small humble grass-blades. To us of an ancient world it seemed a paradise of young life. And then I ventured into the town…and there I saw such a maiden as the Cosmos has forgotten, such was her beauty….

"The twenty days passed. The Niss held their foothold—yet I had kept them back.

"The Portal reopened. I ordered my crew back. It closed. Since then, have I been alone…."

"Bram," Miss Carroll said. "Bram…you stayed when you could have escaped—and I—"

"I would that I could give you back those lost years, Linda Carroll," Bram said. "I would that we could have been together under a brighter sun than this."

"You gave up your world, to give this one a little time," Tremaine said. "And we rewarded you with a shotgun blast."

"Bram…when will the Portal open again?"

"Not in my life, Linda Carroll. Not for ten thousand years."

"Why didn't you recruit help?" Tremaine said. "You could have trained someone…."

"I tried, at first. But what can one do with frightened rustics? They spoke of witchcraft, and fled."

"But you can't hold out forever. Tell me how this thing works. It's time somebody gave you a break!"

V

Bram talked for half an hour, while Tremaine listened. "If I should fail," he concluded, "take my place at the Repellor. Place the circlet on your neck. When the wall clears, grip the handles and pit your mind against the Niss. Will that they do not come through. When the thunder rolls, you will know that you have failed."

"All right. I'll be ready. But let me get one thing straight: this Repellor of yours responds to thoughts, is that right? It amplifies them—"

"It serves to focus the power of the mind. But now let us make haste. Soon, I fear, will they renew the attack."

"It will be twenty minutes or so, I think," said Tremaine. "Stay where you are and get some rest."

Bram looked at him, his blue eyes grim under white brows. "What do you know of this matter, young man?"

"I think I've doped out the pattern; I've been monitoring these transmissions for weeks. My ideas seemed to prove out okay the last few nights."

"No one but I in all this world knew of the Niss attack. How could you have analyzed that which you knew not of?"

"Maybe you don't know it, Bram, but this Repellor of yours has been playing hell with our communications. Recently we developed what we thought was a Top Secret project—and you're blasting us off the air."

"This is only a small portable unit, poorly screened," Bram said. "The resonance effects are unpredictable. When one seeks to channel the power of thought—"

"Wait a minute!" Tremaine burst out.

"What is it?" Miss Carroll said, alarmed.

"Hyperwave," Tremaine said. "Instantaneous transmission. And thought. No wonder people had headaches—and nightmares! We've been broadcasting on the same band as the human mind!"

"This 'hyperwave'," Bram said. "You say it is instantaneous?"

"That's supposed to be classified information."

"Such a device is new in the cosmos," Bram said. "Only a protoplasmic brain is known to produce a null-lag excitation state."

Tremaine frowned. "Bram, this Repellor focuses what I'll call thought waves for want of a better term. It uses an interference effect to damp out the Niss harmonic generator. What if we poured more power to the Repellor?"

"No. The power of the mind cannot be amplified—"

"I don't mean amplification; I mean an additional source. I have a hyperwave receiver here. With a little rewiring, it'll act as a transmitter. Can we tie it in?"

Bram shook his head. "Would that I were a technician," he said. "I know only what is required to operate the device."

"Let me take a look," Tremaine said. "Maybe I can figure it out."

"Take care. Without it, we fall before the Niss."

"I'll be careful." Tremaine went to the machine, examined it, tracing leads, identifying components.

"This seems clear enough," he said. "These would be powerful magnets here; they give a sort of pinch effect. And these are refracting-field coils. Simple, and brilliant. With this idea, we could beam hyperwave—"

"First let us deal with the Niss!"

"Sure." Tremaine looked at Bram. "I think I can link my apparatus to this," he said. "Okay if I try?"

"How long?"

"It shouldn't take more than fifteen minutes."

"That leaves little time."

"The cycle is tightening," Tremaine said. "I figure the next transmissions…or attacks…will come at intervals of under five minutes for several hours now; this may be the last chance."

"Then try," said Bram.

Tremaine nodded, went to the suitcase, took out tools and a heavy black box, set to work. Linda Carroll sat by Bram's side, speaking softly to him. The minutes passed.

"Okay," Tremaine said. "This unit is ready." He went to the Repellor, hesitated a moment, then turned two nuts and removed a cover.

"We're off the air," he said. "I hope my formula holds."

* * * *

Bram and Miss Carroll watched silently as Tremaine worked. He strung wires, taped junctions, then flipped a switch on the hyperwave set and tuned it, his eyes on the dials of a smaller unit.

"Nineteen minutes have passed since the last attack," Bram said. "Make haste."

"I'm almost done," Tremaine said.

A sharp cry came from the wall. Tremaine jumped. "What the hell makes those sounds?"

"They are nothing—mere static. But they warn that the harmonic generators are warming." Bram struggled to his feet. "Now comes the assault."

"The shadows!" Miss Carroll cried.

Bram sank into the chair, leaned back, his face pale as wax in the faint glow from the wall. The glow grew brighter; the shadows swam into focus.

"Hurry, James," Miss Carroll said. "It comes quickly."

Bram watched through half-closed eyes. "I must man the Repellor. I...." He fell back in the chair, his head lolling.

"Bram!" Miss Carroll cried. Tremaine snapped the cover in place, whirled to the chair, dragged it and its occupant away from the machine, then turned, seized the grips. On the wall the Niss moved in silence, readying the attack. The black-clad figure was visible, climbing to his place. The wall cleared. Tremaine stared across at the narrow room, the gray-clad Niss. They stood now, eyes on him. One pointed. Others erected leathery crests.

Stay out, you ugly devils, Tremaine thought. *Go back, retreat, give up....*

Now the blue glow built in a flickering arc across the Niss machine. The technicians stood, staring across the narrow gap, tiny red eyes glittering in the narrow alien faces. Tremaine squinted against the brilliant white light from the high-vaulted Niss Command Center. The last suggestion of the sloping surface of the limestone wall was gone. Tremaine felt a draft stir; dust whirled up, clouded the air. There was an odor of iodine.

Back, Tremaine thought. *Stay back....*

There was a restless stir among the waiting rank of Niss. Tremaine heard the dry shuffle of horny feet against the floor, the whine of the harmonic generator. His eyes burned. As a hot gust swept around him he choked and coughed.

NO! he thought, hurling negation like a weightless bomb. *FAIL! RETREAT!*

* * * *

Now the Niss moved, readying a wheeled machine, rolling it into place. Tremaine coughed rackingly, fought to draw a breath, blinking back blindness. A deep thrumming started up; grit particles stung his cheek, the backs of his hands. The Niss worked rapidly, their throat gills visibly dilated now in the unaccustomed flood of oxygen....

Our oxygen, Tremaine thought. *The looting has started already, and I've failed, and the people of Earth will choke and die....*

From what seemed an immense distance, a roll of thunder trembled at the brink of audibility, swelling.

The black-clad Niss on the alien machine half rose, erecting a black-scaled crest, exulting. Then, shockingly, his eyes fixed on Tremaine's, his trap-like mouth gaped, exposing a tongue like a scarlet snake, a cavernous pink throat set with a row of needle-like snow-white teeth. The tongue flicked out, a gesture of utter contempt.

And suddenly Tremaine was cold with deadly rage. *We have a treatment for snakes in this world,* he thought with savage intensity. *We crush 'em under our heels....* He pictured a writhing rattler, broken-backed, a club descending; a darting red coral snake, its venom ready, slashed in the blades of a power mower; a cottonmouth, smashed into red ruin by a shotgun blast....

BACK, SNAKE, he thought. *DIE! DIE!*

The thunder faded.

And atop the Niss Generator, the black-clad Niss snapped his mouth shut, crouched.

"DIE!" Tremaine shouted. "Die!"

The Niss seemed to shrink in on himself, shivering. His crest went flaccid, twitched twice. The red eyes winked out and the Niss toppled from the machine. Tremaine coughed, gripped the handles, turned his eyes to a gray-uniformed Niss who scrambled up to replace the operator.

I SAID DIE, SNAKE!

The Niss faltered, tumbled back among his fellows, who darted about now like ants in a broached anthill. One turned red eyes on Tremaine, then scrambled for the red cut-out switch.

NO, YOU DON'T, Tremaine thought. *IT'S NOT THAT EASY, SNAKE. DIE!*

The Niss collapsed. Tremaine drew a rasping breath, blinked back tears of pain, took in a group of Niss in a glance.

Die!

* * * *

They fell. The others turned to flee then, but like a scythe Tremaine's mind cut them down, left them in windrows. Hate walked naked among the Niss and left none living.

Now the machines. Tremaine thought. He fixed his eyes on the harmonic generator. It melted into slag. Behind it, the high panels set with jewel-like lights blackened, crumpled into wreckage. Suddenly the air was clean again. Tremaine breathed deep. Before him the surface of the rock swam into view.

NO! Tremaine thought thunderously. *HOLD THAT APERTURE OPEN!*

The rock-face shimmered, faded. Tremaine looked into the white-lit room, at the blackened walls, the huddled dead. *No pity,* he thought. *You would have sunk those white teeth into soft human throats, sleeping in the dark...as you've done on a hundred worlds. You're a cancer in the cosmos. And I have the cure.*

WALLS, he thought, *COLLAPSE!*

The roof before him sagged, fell in. Debris rained down from above, the walls tottered, went down. A cloud of roiled dust swirled, cleared to show a sky blazing with stars.

Dust, stay clear, Tremaine thought. *I want good air to breathe for the work ahead.* He looked out across a landscape of rock, ghostly white in the starlight.

LET THE ROCKS MELT AND FLOW LIKE WATER!

An upreared slab glowed, slumped, ran off in yellow rivulets that were lost in the radiance of the crust as it bubbled, belching released gasses. A wave of heat struck Tremaine. *Let it be cool here*, he thought. *Now, Niss world....*

"No!" Bram's voice shouted. "Stop, stop!"

Tremaine hesitated. He stared at the vista of volcanic fury before him. *I could destroy it all*, he thought. *And the stars in the Niss sky....*

"Great is the power of your hate, man of Earth," Bram cried. "But curb it now, before you destroy us all!"

"Why?" Tremaine shouted. "I can wipe out the Niss and their whole diseased universe with them, with a thought!"

"Master yourself," Bram said hoarsely. "Your rage destroys you! One of the suns you see in the Niss sky is your Sol!"

"Sol?" Tremaine said. "Then it's the Sol of a thousand years ago. Light takes time to cross a galaxy. And the earth is still here...so it wasn't destroyed!"

"Wise are you," Bram said. "Your race is a wonder in the Cosmos, and deadly is your hate. But you know nothing of the forces you unloose now. Past time is as mutable as the steel and rock you melted but now."

"Listen to him, James," Miss Carroll pleaded. "Please listen."

Tremaine twisted to look at her, still holding the twin grips. She looked back steadily, her head held high. Beside her, Bram's eyes were sunken deep in his lined face.

"Jess said you looked like a princess once, Miss Carroll," Tremaine said, "when you drove past with your red hair piled up high. And Bram: you were young, and you loved her. The Niss took your youth from you. You've spent your life here, fighting them, alone. And Linda Carroll waited through the years, because she loved you...and feared you. The Niss did that. And you want me to spare them?"

"You have mastered them," said Bram. "And you are drunk with the power in you. But the power of love is greater than the power of hate. Our love sustained us; your hate can only destroy."

Tremaine locked eyes with the old man. He drew a deep breath at last, let it out shudderingly. "All right," he said "I guess the God complex got me." He looked back once more at the devastated landscape. "The Niss will remember this encounter, I think. They won't try Earth again."

"You've fought valiantly, James, and won," Miss Carroll said. "Now let the power go."

Tremaine turned again to look at her. "You deserve better than this, Miss Carroll," he said. "Bram, you said time is mutable. Suppose—"

"Let well enough alone," Bram said. "Let it go!"

"Once, long ago, you tried to explain this to Linda Carroll. But there was too much against it; she couldn't understand. She was afraid. And you've suffered for sixty years. Suppose those years had never been. Suppose I had come that night...instead of now—"

"It could never be!"

"It can if I will it!" Tremaine gripped the handles tighter. *Let this be THAT night*, he thought fiercely. *The night in 1901, when Bram's last contact failed. Let it be that night, five minutes before the portal closed. Only this machine and I remain as we are now; outside there are gas lights in the farm houses along the dirt road to Elsby, and in the town horses stand in the stables along the cinder alleys behind the houses; and President McKinley is having dinner in the White House....*

* * * *

There was a sound behind Tremaine. He whirled. The ravaged scene was gone. A great disc mirror stood across the cave, intersecting the limestone wall. A man stepped through it, froze at the sight of Tremaine. He was tall, with curly blond hair, fine-chiseled features, broad shoulders.

"Fdazh ha?" he said. Then his eyes slid past Tremaine, opened still wider in astonishment. Tremaine followed the stranger's glance. A young woman, dressed in a negligee of pale silk, stood in the door, a hair-brush in her hand, her red hair flowing free to her waist. She stood rigid in shock.

Then....

"Mr. Bram...!" she gasped. "What—"

Tremaine found his voice. "Miss Carroll, don't be afraid," he said. "I'm your friend, you must believe me."

Linda Carroll turned wide eyes to him. "Who are you?" she breathed. "I was in my bedroom—"

"I can't explain. A miracle has been worked here tonight...on your behalf." Tremaine turned to Bram. "Look—" he started.

"What man are you?" Bram cut in in heavily accented English. "How do you come to this place?"

"Listen to me, Bram!" Tremaine snapped. "Time is mutable. You stayed here, to protect Linda Carroll—and Linda Carroll's world. You've just made that decision, right?" Tremaine went on, not waiting for a reply. "You were stuck here...for sixty years. Earth technology developed fast.

One day a man stumbled in here, tracing down the signal from your Repellor; that was me. You showed me how to use the device…and with it I wiped out the Niss. And then I set the clock back for you and Linda Carroll. The Portal closes in two minutes. Don't waste time…."

"Mutable time?" Bram said. He went past Tremaine to Linda. "Fair lady of Earth," he said. "Do not fear…."

"Sir, I hardly know you," Miss Carroll said. "How did I come here, hardly clothed—"

"Take her, Bram!" Tremaine shouted. "Take her and get back through that Portal—fast." He looked at Linda Carroll. "Don't be afraid," he said. "You know you love him; go with him now, or regret it all your days."

"Will you come?" asked Bram. He held out his hand to her. Linda hesitated, then put her hand in his. Bram went with her to the mirror surface, handed her through. He looked back at Tremaine.

"I do not understand, man of Earth," he said "But I thank you." Then he was gone.

* * * *

Alone in the dim-lit grotto Tremaine let his hands fall from the grips, staggered to the rocker and sank down. He felt weak, drained of strength. His hands ached from the strain of the ordeal. How long had it lasted? Five minutes? An hour? Or had it happened at all…?

But Bram and Linda Carroll were gone. He hadn't imagined that. And the Niss were defeated.

But there was still his own world to contend with. The police would be waiting, combing through the house. They would want to know what he had done with Miss Carroll. Maybe there would be a murder charge. There'd be no support from Fred and the Bureau. As for Jess, he was probably in a cell now, looking a stiff sentence in the face for obstructing justice….

Tremaine got to his feet, cast a last glimpse at the empty room, the outlandish shape of the Repellor, the mirrored portal. It was a temptation to step through it. But this was his world, with all its faults. Perhaps later, when his strength returned, he could try the machine again….

The thought appalled him. *The ashes of hate are worse than the ashes of love*, he thought. He went to the stairs, climbed them, pressed the button. Nothing happened. He pushed the panel aside by hand and stepped into the kitchen. He circled the heavy table with the candlestick, went along the hall and out onto the porch. It was almost the dawn of a fresh spring day. There was no sign of the police. He looked at the grassy lawn, the row of new-set saplings.

Strange, he thought. *I don't remember any saplings. I thought I drove in under a row of trees….* He squinted into the misty early morning gloom. His car was gone. That wasn't too surprising; the cops had impounded it, no doubt. He stepped down, glanced at the ground ahead. It was smooth, with a faint footpath cut through the grass. There was no mud, no sign of tire tracks—

The horizon seemed to spin suddenly. *My God!!* Tremaine thought *I've left myself in the year 1901...!*

* * * *

He whirled, leaped up on the porch, slammed through the door and along the hall, scrambled through the still-open panel, bounded down the stairs and into the cave—

The Repellor was gone. Tremaine leaped forward with a cry—and under his eyes, the great mirror twinkled, winked out. The black box of the hyperwave receiver lay alone on the floor, beside the empty rocker. The light of the kerosene lamp reflected from the featureless wall.

Tremaine turned, stumbled up the steps, out into the air. The sun showed a crimson edge just peeping above distant hills.

1901, Tremaine thought. *The century has just turned. Somewhere a young fellow named Ford is getting ready to put the nation on wheels, and two boys named Wright are about to give it wings. No one ever heard of a World War, or the roaring Twenties, or Prohibition, or FDR, or the Dust Bowl, or Pearl Harbor. And Hiroshima and Nagasaki are just two cities in distant floral Japan....*

He walked down the path, stood by the rutted dirt road. Placid cows nuzzled damp grass in the meadow beyond it. In the distance a train hooted.

There are railroads, Tremaine thought. *But no jet planes, no radio, no movies, no automatic dish-washers. But then there's no TV, either. That makes up for a lot. And there are no police waiting to grill me, and no murder charge, and no neurotic nest of bureaucrats waiting to welcome me back....*

He drew a deep breath. The air was sweet. *I'm here*, he thought. *I feel the breeze on my face and the firm sod underfoot. It's real, and it's all there is now, so I might as well take it calmly. After all, a man with my education ought to be able to do well in this day and age!*

Whistling, Tremaine started the ten-mile walk into town.

THE NIGHT OF THE TROLLS

Originally published in Worlds of Tomorrow, *October 1963.*

I

It was different this time. There was a dry pain in my lungs, and a deep ache in my bones, and a fire in my stomach that made me want to curl into a ball and mew like a kitten. My mouth tasted as though mice had nested in it, and when I took a deep breath wooden knives twisted in my chest.

I made a mental note to tell Mackenzie a few things about his pet controlled-environment tank—just as soon as I got out of it. I squinted at the over-face panel: air pressure, temperature, humidity, O-level, blood sugar, pulse and respiration—all okay. That was something. I flipped the intercom key and said, "Okay, Mackenzie, let's have the story. You've got problems...."

I had to stop to cough. The exertion made my temples pound.

"How long have you birds run this damned exercise?" I called. "I feel lousy. What's going on around here?"

No answer.

This was supposed to be the terminal test series. They couldn't all be out having coffee. The equipment had more bugs than a two-dollar hotel room. I slapped the emergency release lever. Mackenzie wouldn't like it, but to hell with it! From the way I felt, I'd been in the tank for a good long stretch this time—maybe a week or two. And I'd told Ginny it would be a three-dayer at the most. Mackenzie was a great technician, but he had no more human emotions than a used-car salesman. This time I'd tell him.

Relays were clicking, equipment was reacting, the tank cover sliding back. I sat up and swung my legs aside, shivering suddenly.

It was cold in the test chamber. I looked around at the dull gray walls, the data recording cabinets, the wooden desk where Mac sat by the hour re-running test profiles—

That was funny. The tape reels were empty and the red equipment light was off. I stood, feeling dizzy. Where was Mac? Where were Bonner and Day, and Mallon?

"Hey!" I called. I didn't even get a good echo.

Someone must have pushed the button to start my recovery cycle; where were they hiding now? I took a step, tripped over the cables trailing behind me. I unstrapped and pulled the harness off. The effort left me breathing hard. I opened one of the wall lockers; Banner's pressure suit hung limply from the rack beside a rag-festooned coat hanger. I looked in three more lockers. My clothes were missing—even my bathrobe. I also missed the usual bowl of hot soup, the happy faces of the techs, even Mac's sour puss. It was cold and silent and empty here—more like a morgue than a top priority research center.

I didn't like it. What the hell was going on?

There was a weather suit in the last locker. I put it on, set the temperature control, palmed the door open and stepped out into the corridor. There were no lights, except for the dim glow of the emergency route indicators. There was a faint, foul odor in the air.

I heard a dry scuttling, saw a flick of movement. A rat the size of a red squirrel sat up on his haunches and looked at me as if I were something to eat. I made a kicking motion and he ran off, but not very far.

My heart was starting to thump a little harder now. The way it does when you begin to realize that something's wrong—bad wrong.

* * * *

Upstairs in the Admin Section, I called again. The echo was a little better here. I went along the corridor strewn with papers, past the open doors of silent rooms. In the Director's office, a blackened wastebasket stood in the center of the rug. The air-conditioner intake above the desk was felted over with matted dust nearly an inch thick. There was no use shouting again.

The place was as empty as a robbed grave—except for the rats.

At the end of the corridor, the inner security door stood open. I went through it and stumbled over something. In the faint light, it took me a moment to realize what it was.

He had been an M. P., in steel helmet and boots. There was nothing left but crumbled bone and a few scraps of leather and metal. A .38 revolver lay nearby. I picked it up, checked the cylinder and tucked it in the thigh pocket of the weather suit. For some reason, it made me feel a little better.

I went on along B corridor and found the lift door sealed. The emergency stairs were nearby. I went to them and started the two hundred foot climb to the surface.

The heavy steel doors at the tunnel had been blown clear.

I stepped past the charred opening, looked out at a low gray sky burning red in the west. Fifty yards away, the 5000-gallon water tank lay in a tangle of rusty steel. What had it been? Sabotage, war, revolution—an accident? And where was everybody?

I rested for a while, then went across the innocent-looking fields to the west, dotted with the dummy buildings that were supposed to make the site look from the air like another stretch of farm land complete with barns, sheds and fences. Beyond the site, the town seemed intact: there were lights twinkling here and there, a few smudges of smoke rising.

Whatever had happened at the site, at least Ginny would be all right—Ginny and Tim. Ginny would be worried sick, after—how long? A month? Maybe more. There hadn't been much left of that soldier....

* * * *

I twisted to get a view to the south, and felt a hollow sensation in my chest. Four silo doors stood open; the Colossus missiles had hit back—at something. I pulled myself up a foot or two higher for a look at the Primary Site. In the twilight, the ground rolled smooth and unbroken across the spot where *Prometheus* lay ready in her underground berth. Down below, she'd be safe and sound maybe. She had been built to stand up to the stresses of a direct extra-solar orbital launch; with any luck, a few near-misses wouldn't have damaged her.

My arms were aching from the strain of holding on. I climbed down and sat on the ground to get my breath, watching the cold wind worry the dry stalks of dead brush around the fallen tank.

At home, Ginny would be alone, scared, maybe even in serious difficulty. There was no telling how far municipal services had broken down. But before I headed that way, I had to make a quick check on the ship. *Prometheus* was a dream that I—and a lot of others—had lived with for three years. I had to be sure.

I headed toward the pillbox that housed the tunnel head on the off-chance that the car might be there.

It was almost dark and the going was tough; the concrete slabs under the sod were tilted and dislocated. Something had sent a ripple across the ground like a stone tossed into a pond.

I heard a sound and stopped dead. There was a clank and rumble from beyond the discolored walls of the blockhouse a hundred yards away. Rusted metal howled; then something as big as a beached freighter moved into view.

Two dull red beams glowing near the top of the high silhouette swung, flashed crimson and held on me. A siren went off—an ear-splitting whoop! *whoop!* WHOOP!

It was an unmanned Bolo Mark II Combat Unit on automated sentry duty—and its intruder-sensing circuits were tracking me.

The Bolo pivoted heavily; the whoop! whoop! sounded again; the robot watchdog was bellowing the alarm.

I felt sweat pop out on my forehead. Standing up to a Mark II Bolo without an electropass was the rough equivalent of being penned in with an ill-tempered dinosaur. I looked toward the Primary blockhouse: too far. The same went for the perimeter fence. My best bet was back to the tunnel mouth. I turned to sprint for it, hooked a foot on a slab and went down hard....

I got up, my head ringing, tasting blood in my mouth. The chipped pavement seemed to rock under me. The Bolo was coming up fast. Running was no good, I had to have a better idea.

I dropped flat and switched my suit control to maximum insulation.

The silvery surface faded to dull black. A two-foot square of tattered paper fluttered against a projecting edge of concrete; I reached for it, peeled it free, then fumbled with a pocket flap, brought out a permatch, flicked it alight. When the paper was burning well, I tossed it clear. It whirled away a few feet, then caught in a clump of grass.

"Keep moving, damn you!" I whispered. The swearing worked. The gusty wind pushed the paper on. I crawled a few feet and pressed myself into a shallow depression behind the slab. The Bolo churned closer; a loose treadplate was slapping the earth with a rhythmic thud. The burning paper was fifty feet away now, a twinkle of orange light in the deep twilight.

At twenty yards, looming up like a pagoda, the Bolo halted, sat rumbling and swiveling its rust-streaked turret, looking for the radiating source its IR had first picked up. The flare of the paper caught its electronic attention. The turret swung, then back. It was puzzled. It whooped again, then reached a decision.

Ports snapped open. A volley of anti-personnel slugs whoofed into the target; the scrap of paper disappeared in a gout of tossed dirt.

I hugged the ground like gold lame hugs a torch singer's hip and waited; nothing happened. The Bolo sat, rumbling softly to itself. Then I heard another sound over the murmur of the idling engine, a distant roaring, like a flight of low-level bombers. I raised my head half an inch and took a look. There were lights moving beyond the field—the paired beams of a convoy approaching from the town.

* * * *

The Bolo stirred, moved heavily forward until it towered over me no more than twenty feet away. I saw gun ports open high on the armored facade—the ones that housed the heavy infinite repeaters. Slim black muzzles slid into view, hunted for an instant, then depressed and locked.

They were bearing on the oncoming vehicles that were spreading out now in a loose skirmish line under a roiling layer of dust. The watchdog was getting ready to defend its territory—and I was caught in the middle. A blue-white floodlight lanced out from across the field, glared against the scaled plating of the Bolo. I heard relays click inside the monster fighting machine, and braced myself for the thunder of her battery....

There was a dry rattle.

The guns traversed, clattering emptily. Beyond the fence the floodlight played for a moment longer against the Bolo, then moved on across the ramp, back, across and back, searching....

Once more the Bolo fired its empty guns. Its red IR beams swept the scene again; then relays snicked, the impotent guns retracted, the port covers closed.

Satisfied, the Bolo heaved itself around and moved off, trailing a stink of ozone and ether, the broken tread thumping like a cripple on a stair.

I waited until it disappeared in the gloom two hundred yards away, then cautiously turned my suit control to vent off the heat. Full insulation could boil a man in his own gravy in less than half an hour.

The floodlight had blinked off now. I got to my hands and knees and started toward the perimeter fence. The Bolo's circuits weren't tuned as fine as they should have been; it let me go.

* * * *

There were men moving in the glare and dust, beyond the rusty lacework that had once been a chain-link fence. They carried guns and stood in tight little groups, staring across toward the blockhouse.

I moved closer, keeping flat and avoiding the avenues of yellowish light thrown by the headlamps of the parked vehicles—halftracks, armored cars, a few light manned tanks.

There was nothing about the look of this crowd that impelled me to leap up and be welcomed. They wore green uniforms, and half of them sported beards. What the hell: had Castro landed in force?

I angled off to the right, away from the big main gate that had been manned day and night by guards with tommyguns. It hung now by one hinge from a scarred concrete post, under a cluster of dead polyarcs in corroded brackets. The big sign that had read GLENN AEROSPACE CENTER—AUTHORIZED PERSONNEL ONLY lay face down in hip-high underbrush.

More cars were coming up. There was a lot of talk and shouting; a squad of men formed and headed my way, keeping to the outside of the fallen fence.

I was outside the glare of the lights now. I chanced a run for it, got over the sagged wire and across a potholed blacktop road before they reached me. I crouched in the ditch and watched as the detail dropped men in pairs at fifty-yard intervals.

Another five minutes and they would have intercepted me—along with whatever else they were after.

I worked my way back across an empty lot and found a strip of lesser underbrush lined with shaggy trees, beneath which a patch of cracked sidewalk showed here and there.

Several things were beginning to be a little clearer now: The person who had pushed the button to bring me out of stasis hadn't been around to greet me, because no one pushed it. The automatics, triggered by some malfunction, had initiated the recovery cycle.

The system's self-contained power unit had been designed to maintain a star-ship crewman's minimal vital functions indefinitely, at reduced body temperature and metabolic rate. There was no way to tell exactly how long I had been in the tank. From the condition of the fence and the roads, it had been more than a matter of weeks—or even months.

Had it been a year…or more? I thought of Ginny and the boy, waiting at home—thinking the old man was dead, probably. I'd neglected them before for my work, but not like this….

Our house was six miles from the base, in the foothills on the other side of town. It was a long walk, the way I felt—but I had to get there.

II

Two hours later, I was clear of the town, following the river bank west.

I kept having the idea that someone was following me. But when I stopped to listen, there was never anything there; just the still, cold night, and the frogs, singing away patiently in the low ground to the south.

When the ground began to rise, I left the road and struck off across the open field. I reached a wide street, followed it in a curve that would bring me out at the foot of Ridge Avenue—my street. I could make out the shapes of low, rambling houses now.

It had been the kind of residential section the local Junior Chamber members had hoped to move into some day. Now the starlight that filtered through the cloud cover showed me broken windows, doors that sagged open, automobiles that squatted on flat, dead tires under collapsing car shelters—and here and there a blackened, weed-grown foundation, like a gap in a row of rotting teeth.

The neighborhood wasn't what it had been. How long had I been away? How long…?

I fell down again, hard this time. It wasn't easy getting up. I seemed to weigh a hell of a lot for a guy who hadn't been eating regularly. My breathing was very fast and shallow now, and my skull was getting ready to split and give birth to a live alligator—the ill-tempered kind. It was only a few hundred yards more; but why the hell had I picked a place halfway up a hill?

I heard the sound again—a crackle of dry grass. I got the pistol out and stood flatfooted in the middle of the street, listening hard.

All I heard was my stomach growling. I took the pistol off cock and started off again, stopped suddenly a couple of times to catch him off-guard; nothing. I reached the corner of Ridge Avenue, started up the slope. Behind me, a stick popped loudly.

I picked that moment to fall down again. Heaped leaves saved me from another skinned knee. I rolled over against a low fieldstone wall and propped myself against it. I had to use both hands to cock the pistol. I stared into the dark, but all I could see were the little lights whirling again. The pistol got heavy; I put it down, concentrated on taking deep breaths and blinking away the fireflies.

I heard footsteps plainly, close by. I shook my head, accidentally banged it against the stone behind me. That helped. I saw him, not over twenty feet away, coming up the hill toward me, a black-haired man with a full beard, dressed in odds and ends of rags and furs, gripping a polished club with a leather thong.

I reached for the pistol, found only leaves, tried again, touched the gun and knocked it away. I was still groping when I heard a scuffle of feet. I swung around, saw a tall, wide figure with a mane of untrimmed hair.

He hit the bearded man like a pro tackle taking out the practice dummy. They went down together hard and rolled over in a flurry of dry leaves. The cats were fighting over the mouse; that was my signal to leave quietly.

I made one last grab for the gun, found it, got to my feet and staggered off up the grade that seemed as steep now as penthouse rent. And from down slope, I heard an engine gunned, the clash of a heavy transmission that needed adjustment. A spotlight flickered, made shadows dance.

I recognized a fancy wrought-iron fence fronting a vacant lot; that had been the Adams house. Only half a block to go—but I was losing my grip fast. I went down twice more, then gave up and started crawling. The lights were all around now, brighter than ever. My head split open, dropped off and rolled downhill.

A few more yards and I could let it all go. Ginny would put me in a warm bed, patch up my scratches, and feed me soup. Ginny would… Ginny….

* * * *

I was lying with my mouth full of dead leaves. I heard running feet, yells. An engine idled noisily down the block.

I got my head up and found myself looking at chipped brickwork and the heavy brass hinges from which my front gate had hung. The gate was gone and there was a large chunk of brick missing. Some delivery truck had missed his approach.

I got to my feet, took a couple of steps into deep shadow with feet that felt as though they'd been amputated and welded back on at the ankle. I stumbled, fetched up against something scaled over with rust. I held on, blinked and made out the seeping flank of my brand new '79 Pontiac. There was a crumbled crust of whitish glass lining the bright-work strip that had framed the rear window.

A fire…?

A footstep sounded behind me, and I suddenly remembered several things, none of them pleasant. I felt for my gun; it was gone. I moved back along the side of the car, tried to hold on.

No use. My arms were like unsuccessful pie crust. I slid down among dead leaves, sat listening to the steps coming closer. They stopped, and through a dense fog that had sprung up suddenly I caught a glimpse of a tall white-haired figure standing over me.

Then the fog closed in and swept everything away.

* * * *

I lay on my back this time, looking across at the smoky yellow light of a thick brown candle guttering in the draft from a glassless window. In the center of the room, a few sticks of damp-looking wood heaped on the cracked asphalt tiles burned with a grayish flame. A thin curl of acrid smoke rose up to stir cobwebs festooned under ceiling beams from which wood veneer had peeled away. Light alloy truss-work showed beneath.

It was a strange scene, but not so strange that I didn't recognize it: it was my own living room—looking a little different than when I had seen it last. The odors were different, too; I picked out mildew, badly-cured leather, damp wool, tobacco.…

I turned my head. A yard from the rags I lay on, the white-haired man, looking older than pharaoh, sat sleeping with his back against the wall.

The shotgun was gripped in one big, gnarled hand. His head was tilted back, blue-veined eyelids shut. I sat up, and at my movement his eyes opened.

He lay relaxed for a moment, as though life had to return from some place far away. Then he raised his head. His face was hollow and lined. His white hair was thin. A coarse-woven shirt hung loose across wide shoulders that had been Herculean once. But now Hercules was old, old. He looked at me expectantly.

"Who are you?" I said. "Why did you follow me? What happened to the house? Where's my family? Who owns the bully-boys in green?" My jaw hurt when I spoke. I put my hand up and felt it gingerly.

"You fell," the old man said, in a voice that rumbled like a subterranean volcano.

"The understatement of the year, Pop." I tried to get up. Nausea knotted my stomach.

"You have to rest," the old man said, looking concerned. "Before the Baron's men come...." He paused, looking at me as though he expected me to say something profound.

"I want to know where the people are that live here!" My yell came out as weak as church-social punch. "A woman and a boy...."

He was shaking his head. "You have to do something quick. The soldiers will come back, search every house—"

I sat up, ignoring the little men driving spikes into my skull. "I don't give a damn about soldiers! Where's my family? What's happened?" I reached out and gripped his arm. "How long was I down there? What year is this?"

* * * *

He only shook his head. "Come, eat some food. Then I can help you with your plan."

It was no use talking to the old man; he was senile.

I got off the cot. Except for the dizziness and a feeling that my knees were made of papier-mache, I was all right. I picked up the hand-formed candle, stumbled into the hall.

It was a jumble of rubbish. I climbed through, pushed open the door to my study. There was my desk, the tall bookcase with the glass doors, the gray rug, the easy chair. Aside from a layer of dust and some peeling wall paper, it looked normal. I flipped the switch. Nothing happened.

"What is that charm?" the old man said behind me. He pointed to the light switch.

"The power's off," I said. "Just habit."

He reached out and flipped the switch up, then down again. "It makes a pleasing sound."

"Yeah." I picked up a book from the desk; it fell apart in my hands.

I went back into the hall, tried the bedroom door, looked in at heaped leaves, the remains of broken furniture, an empty window frame. I went on to the end of the hall and opened the door to the bedroom.

Cold night wind blew through a barricade of broken timbers. The roof had fallen in, and a sixteen-inch tree trunk slanted through the wreckage. The old man stood behind me, watching.

"Where is she, damn you?" I leaned against the door frame to swear and fight off the faintness. "Where's my wife?"

The old man looked troubled. "Come, eat now...."

"Where is she? Where's the woman who lived here?"

He frowned, shook his head dumbly. I picked my way through the wreckage, stepped out into knee-high brush. A gust blew my candle out. In the dark I stared at my back yard, the crumbled pit that had been the barbecue grill, the tangled thickets that had been rose beds—and a weathered length of boards upended in the earth.

"What the hell's this...?" I fumbled out a permatch, lit my candle, leaned close and read the crude letters cut into the crumbling wood: VIRGINIA ANNE JACKSON. BORN JAN. 8 1957. KILL BY THE DOGS WINTER 1992.

III

The Baron's men came twice in the next three days. Each time the old man carried me, swearing but too weak to argue, out to a lean-to of branches and canvas in the woods behind the house. Then he disappeared, to come back an hour or two later and haul me back to my rag bed by the fire.

Three times a day he gave me a tin pan of stew, and I ate it mechanically. My mind went over and over the picture of Ginny, living on for twelve years in the slowly decaying house, and then—

It was too much. There are some shocks the mind refuses.

I thought of the tree that had fallen and crushed the east wing. An elm that size was at least fifty to sixty years old—maybe older. And the only elm on the place had been a two-year sapling. I knew it well; I had planted it.

The date carved on the headboard was 1992. As nearly as I could judge another thirty-five years had passed since then at least. My shipmates—Banner, Day, Mallon—they were all dead, long ago. How had they died? The old man was too far gone to tell me anything useful. Most of my questions produced a shake of the head and a few rumbled words about charms, demons, spells, and the Baron.

"I don't believe in spells," I said. "And I'm not too sure I believe in this Baron. Who is he?"

"The Baron Trollmaster of Filly. He holds all this country—" the old man made a sweeping gesture with his arm—"all the way to Jersey."

"Why was he looking for me? What makes me important?"

"You came from the Forbidden Place. Everyone heard the cries of the Lesser Troll that stands guard over the treasure there. If the Baron can learn your secrets of power—"

"Troll, hell! That's nothing but a Bolo on automatic!"

"By any name every man dreads the monster. A man who walks in its shadow has much *mana*. But the others—the ones that run in a pack like dogs—would tear you to pieces for a demon if they could lay hands on you."

"You saw me back there. Why didn't you give me away? And why are you taking care of me now?"

He shook his head—the all-purpose answer to any question.

I tried another tack: "Who was the rag man you tackled just outside? Why was he laying for me?"

The old man snorted. "Tonight the dogs will eat him. But forget that. Now we have to talk about your plan—"

"I've got about as many plans as the senior boarder in Death Row. I don't know if you know it, Old Timer, but somebody slid the world out from under me while I wasn't looking."

The old man frowned. I had the thought that I wouldn't like to have him mad at me, for all his white hair....

* * * *

He shook his head. "You must understand what I tell you. The soldiers of the Baron will find you some day. If you are to break the spell—"

"Break the spell, eh?" I snorted. "I think I get the idea, Pop. You've got it in your head that I'm a valuable property of some kind. You figure I can use my supernatural powers to take over this menagerie—and you'll be in on the ground floor. Well, listen, you old idiot! I spent sixty years—maybe more—in a stasis tank two hundred feet underground. My world died while I was down there. This Baron of yours seems to own everything now. If you think I'm going to get myself shot bucking him, forget it!"

The old man didn't say anything.

"Things don't seem to be broken up much," I went on. "It must have been gas, or germ warfare—or fallout. Damn few people around. You're still able to live on what you can loot from stores; automobiles are still sitting where they were the day the world ended. How old were you when it happened, Pop? The war, I mean. Do you remember it?"

He shook his head. "The world has always been as it is now."

"What year were you born?"

He scratched at his white hair. "I knew the number once. But I've forgotten."

"I guess the only way I'll find out how long I was gone is to saw that damned elm in two and count the rings—but even that wouldn't help much; I don't know when it blew over. Never mind. The important thing now is to talk to this Baron of yours. Where does he stay?"

The old man shook his head violently. "If the Baron lays his hands on you, he'll wring the secrets from you on the rack! I know his ways. For five years I was a slave in the Palace Stables."

"If you think I'm going to spend the rest of my days in this rat nest, you got another guess on the house! This Baron has tanks, an army. He's kept a little technology alive. That's the outfit for me—not this garbage detail! Now, where's this place of his located?"

"The guards will shoot you on sight like a pack-dog!"

"There has to be a way to get to him, old man! Think!"

The old head was shaking again. "He fears assassination. You can never approach him…." He brightened. "Unless you know a spell of power?"

I chewed my lip. "Maybe I do at that. You wanted me to have a plan. I think I feel one coming on. Have you got a map?"

He pointed to the desk beside me. I tried the drawers, found mice, roaches, moldy money—and a stack of folded maps. I opened one carefully; faded ink on yellowed paper, falling apart at the creases. The legend in the corner read: "PENNSYLVANIA 40M:1. Copyright 1970 by ESSO Corporation."

"This will do, Pop," I said. "Now, tell me all you can about this Baron of yours."

"You'll destroy him?"

"I haven't even met the man."

"He is evil."

"I don't know; he owns an army. That makes up for a lot…."

* * * *

After three more days of rest and the old man's stew, I was back to normal—or near enough. I had the old man boil me a tub of water for a bath and a shave. I found a serviceable pair of synthetic fiber long-johns in a chest of drawers, pulled them on and zipped the weather suit over them, then buckled on the holster I had made from a tough plastic.

"That completes my preparations, Pop," I said. "It'll be dark in another half hour. Thanks for everything."

He got to his feet, a worried look on his lined face, like a father the first time Junior asks for the car.

"The Baron's men are everywhere."

"If you want to help, come along and back me up with that shotgun of yours." I picked it up. "Have you got any shells for this thing?"

He smiled, pleased now. "There are shells—but the magic is gone from many."

"That's the way magic is, Pop. It goes out of things before you notice."

"Will you destroy the Great Troll now?"

"My motto is let sleeping trolls lie. I'm just paying a social call on the Baron."

The joy ran out of his face like booze from a dropped jug.

"Don't take it so hard, Old Timer. I'm not the fairy prince you were expecting. But I'll take care of you—if I make it."

I waited while he pulled on a moth-eaten mackinaw. He took the shotgun and checked the breech, then looked at me.

"I'm ready," he said.

"Yeah," I said. "Let's go…."

* * * *

The Baronial palace was a forty-story slab of concrete and glass that had been known in my days as the Hilton Garden East. We made it in three hours of groping across country in the dark, at the end of which I was puffing but still on my feet. We moved out from the cover of the trees and looked across a dip in the ground at the lights, incongruously cheerful in the ravaged valley.

"The gates are there—" the old man pointed—"guarded by the Great Troll."

"Wait a minute. I thought the Troll was the Bolo back at the Site."

"That's the Lesser Troll. This is the Great One."

I selected a few choice words and muttered them to myself. "It would have saved us some effort if you'd mentioned this Troll a little sooner, Old Timer. I'm afraid I don't have any spells that will knock out a Mark II, once it's got its dander up."

He shook his head. "It lies under enchantment. I remember the day when it came, throwing thunderbolts. Many men were killed. Then the Baron commanded it to stand at his gates to guard him."

"How long ago was this, Old Timer?"

He worked his lips over the question. "Long ago," he said finally. "Many winters."

"Let's go take a look."

We picked our way down the slope, came up along a rutted dirt road to the dark line of trees that rimmed the palace grounds. The old man touched my arm.

"Softly here. Maybe the Troll sleeps lightly...."

I went the last few yards, eased around a brick column with a dead lantern on top, stared across fifty yards of waist-high brush at a dark silhouette outlined against the palace lights.

Cables, stretched from trees outside the circle of weeds, supported a weathered tarp which drooped over the Bolo. The wreckage of a helicopter lay like a crumpled dragonfly at the far side of the ring. Nearer, fragments of a heavy car chassis lay scattered. The old man hovered at my shoulder.

"It looks as though the gate is off limits," I hissed. "Let's try farther along."

He nodded. "No one passes here. There is a second gate, there." He pointed. "But there are guards."

"Let's climb the wall between gates."

"There are sharp spikes on top the wall. But I know a place, farther on, where the spikes have been blunted."

"Lead on, Pop."

Half an hour of creeping through wet brush brought us to the spot we were looking for. It looked to me like any other stretch of eight-foot masonry wall overhung with wet poplar trees.

"I'll go first," the old man said, "to draw the attention of the guard."

"Then who's going to boost me up? I'll go first."

He nodded, cupped his hands and lifted me as easily as a sailor lifting a beer glass. Pop was old—but he was nobody's softie.

I looked around, then crawled up, worked my way over the corroded spikes, dropped down on the lawn.

Immediately I heard a crackle of brush. A man stood up not ten feet away. I lay flat in the dark trying to look like something that had been there a long time....

I heard another sound, a thump and a crashing of brush. The man before me turned, disappeared in the darkness. I heard him beating his way through shrubbery; then he called out, got an answering shout from the distance.

I didn't loiter. I got to my feet and made a sprint for the cover of the trees along the drive.

IV

Flat on the wet ground, under the wind-whipped branches of an ornamental cedar, I blinked the fine misty rain from my eyes, waiting for the half-hearted alarm behind me to die down.

There were a few shouts, some sounds of searching among the shrubbery. It was a bad night to be chasing imaginary intruders in the Baronial grounds. In five minutes, all was quiet again.

I studied the view before me. The tree under which I lay was one of a row lining a drive. It swung in a graceful curve, across a smooth half-mile of dark lawn, to the tower of light that was the Palace of the Baron of Filly. The silhouetted figures of guards and late-arriving guests moved against the gleam from the collonaded entrance. On a terrace high above, dancers twirled under colored lights. The faint glow of the repellor field kept the cold rain at a distance. In a lull in the wind, I heard music, faintly. The Baron's weekly Grand Ball was in full swing.

I saw shadows move across the wet gravel before me, then heard the purr of an engine. I hugged the ground and watched a long svelte Mercedes—about a '68 model, I estimated—barrel past.

The mob in the city ran in packs like dogs, but the Baron's friends did a little better for themselves.

I got to my feet and moved off toward the palace, keeping well in the shadows. When the drive swung to the right to curve across in front of the building, I left it, went to hands and knees and followed a trimmed privet hedge, past dark rectangles of formal garden to the edge of a secondary pond of light from the garages. I let myself down on my belly and watched the shadows that moved on the graveled drive.

There seemed to be two men on duty—no more. Waiting around wouldn't improve my chances. I got to my feet, stepped out into the drive and walked openly around the corner of the gray fieldstone building into the light.

A short, thickset man in greasy Baronial green looked at me incuriously. My weather suit looked enough like ordinary coveralls to get me by—at least for a few minutes. A second man, tilted back against the wall in a wooden chair, didn't even turn his head.

"Hey!" I called. "You birds got a three-ton jack I can borrow?"

Shorty looked me over sourly. "Who you drive for, Mac?"

"The High Duke of Jersey. Flat. Left rear. On a night like this. Some luck."

"The Jersey can't afford a jack?"

* * * *

I stepped over the short man, prodded him with a forefinger. "He could buy you and gut you on the altar any Saturday night of the week, low-pockets. And he'd get a kick out of doing it. He's like that."

"Can't a guy crack a harmless joke without somebody talks about altar-bait? You wanna jack, take a jack."

The man in the chair opened one eye and looked me over. "How long you on the Jersey payroll?" he growled.

"Long enough to know who handles the rank between Jersey and Filly." I yawned, looked around the wide, cement floored garage, glanced over the four heavy cars with the Filly crest on their sides.

"Where's the kitchen? I'm putting a couple of hot coffees under my belt before I go back out into that."

"Over there. A flight up and to your left. Tell the cook Pintsy invited you."

"I tell him Jersey sent me, low-pockets." I moved off in a dead silence, opened the door and stepped up into spicy-scented warmth.

A deep carpet—even here—muffled my footsteps. I could hear the clash of pots and crockery from the kitchen a hundred feet distant along the hallway. I went along to a deep-set doorway ten feet from the kitchen, tried the knob and looked into a dark room. I pushed the door shut and leaned against it, watching the kitchen. Through the woodwork I could feel the thump of the bass notes from the orchestra blasting away three flights up. The odors of food—roast fowl, baked ham, grilled horsemeat—curled under the kitchen door and wafted under my nose. I pulled my belt up a notch and tried to swallow the dryness in my throat. The old man had fed me a half a gallon of stew, before we left home, but I was already working up a fresh appetite.

Five slow minutes passed. Then the kitchen door swung open and a tall round-shouldered fellow with a shiny bald scalp stepped into view, a tray balanced on the spread fingers of one hand. He turned, the black tails of his cutaway swirling, called something behind him and started past me. I stepped out, clearing my throat. He shied, whirled to face me. He was good at his job: The two dozen tiny glasses on the tray stood fast. He blinked, got an indignant remark ready—

I showed him the knife the old man had lent me—a bone-handled job with a six-inch switch-blade. "Make a sound and I'll cut your throat," I said softly. "Put the tray on the floor."

He started to back. I brought the knife up. He took a good look, licked his lips, crouched quickly and put the tray down.

"Turn around."

I stepped in and chopped him at the base of the neck with the edge of my hand. He folded like a two-dollar umbrella.

I wrestled the door open and dumped him inside, paused a moment to listen. All quiet. I worked his black coat and trousers off, unhooked the stiff white dickey and tie. He snored softly. I pulled the clothes on over the weather suit. They were a fair fit. By the light of my pencil flash, I cut down a heavy braided cord hanging by a high window, used it to truss the waiter's hands and feet together behind him. There was a small closet opening off the room. I put him in it, closed the door and stepped back into the hall. Still quiet. I tried one of the drinks. It wasn't bad.

I took another, then picked up the tray and followed the sounds of music.

* * * *

The grand ballroom was a hundred yards long, fifty wide, with walls of rose, gold and white, banks of high windows hung with crimson velvet, a vaulted ceiling decorated with cherubs and a polished acre of floor on which gaudily gowned and uniformed couples moved in time to the heavy beat of the traditional fox-trot. I moved slowly along the edge of the crowd, looking for the Baron.

A hand caught my arm and hauled me around. A glass fell off my tray, smashed on the floor.

A dapper little man in black and white headwaiter's uniform glared up at me.

"What do you think you're doing, cretin?" he hissed. "That's the genuine ancient stock you're slopping on the floor." I looked around quickly; no one else seemed to be paying any attention.

"Where are you from?" he snapped. I opened my mouth—

"Never mind, you're all the same." He waggled his hands disgustedly. "The field-hands they send me—a disgrace to the Black. Now, you! Stand up! Hold your tray proudly, gracefully! Step along daintily, not like a knight taking the field! And pause occasionally—just on the chance that some noble guest might wish to drink."

"You bet, pal," I said. I moved on, paying a little more attention to my waiting. I saw plenty of green uniforms; pea green, forest green, emerald green—but they were all hung with braid and medals. According to Pop, the Baron affected a spartan simplicity. The diffidence of absolute power.

There were high white and gold doors every few yards along the side of the ballroom. I spotted one standing open and sidled toward it. It wouldn't hurt to reconnoiter the area.

Just beyond the door, a very large sentry in a bottle-green uniform almost buried under gold braid moved in front of me. He was dressed like a toy soldier, but there was nothing playful about the way he snapped his power gun to the ready. I winked at him.

"Thought you boys might want a drink," I hissed. "Good stuff."

He looked at the tray, licked his lips. "Get back in there, you fool," he growled. "You'll get us both hung."

"Suit yourself, pal." I backed out. Just before the door closed between us, he lifted a glass off the tray.

* * * *

I turned, almost collided with a long lean cookie in a powder-blue outfit complete with dress sabre, gold frogs, leopard-skin facings, a pair of knee-length white gloves looped under an epaulette, a pistol in a fancy holster and an eighteen-inch swagger stick. He gave me the kind of look old maids give sin.

"Look where you're going, swine," he said in a voice like a pine board splitting.

"Have a drink, Admiral," I suggested.

He lifted his upper lip to show me a row of teeth that hadn't had their annual trip to the dentist lately. The ridges along each side of his mouth turned greenish white. He snatched for the gloves on his shoulder, fumbled them; they slapped the floor beside me.

"I'd pick those up for you, Boss," I said, "But I've got my tray...."

He drew a breath between his teeth, chewed it into strips and snorted it back at me, then snapped his fingers and pointed with his stick toward the door behind me.

"Through there, instantly!" It didn't seem like the time to argue; I pulled it open and stepped through.

The guard in green ducked his glass and snapped to attention when he saw the baby-blue outfit. My new friend ignored him, made a curt gesture to me. I got the idea, trailed along the wide, high, gloomy corridor to a small door, pushed through it into a well-lit tile-walled latrine. A big-eyed slave in white ducks stared.

Blue-boy jerked his head. "Get out!" The slave scuttled away. Blue-boy turned to me.

"Strip off your jacket, slave! Your owner has neglected to teach you discipline."

I looked around quickly, saw that we were alone.

"Wait a minute while I put the tray down, corporal," I said. "We don't want to waste any of the good stuff." I turned to put the tray on a soiled linen bin, caught a glimpse of motion in the mirror.

I ducked, and the nasty-looking little leather quirt whistled past my ear, slammed against the edge of a marble-topped lavatory with a crack like a pistol shot. I dropped the tray, stepped in fast and threw a left to Blue-boy's jaw that bounced his head against the tiled wall. I followed up with a right to the belt buckle, then held him up as he bent over, gagging, and hit him hard under the ear.

I hauled him into a booth, propped him up and started shedding the waiter's blacks.

V

I left him on the floor wearing my old suit, and stepped out into the hall.

I liked the feel of his pistol at my hip. It was an old fashioned .38, the same model I favored. The blue uniform was a good fit, what with the weight I'd lost. Blue-boy and I had something in common after all.

The latrine attendant goggled at me. I grimaced like a quadruple amputee trying to scratch his nose and jerked my head toward the door I had come out of. I hoped the gesture would look familiar.

"Truss that mad dog and throw him outside the gates," I snarled. I stamped off down the corridor, trying to look mad enough to discourage curiosity.

Apparently it worked. Nobody yelled for the cops.

I reentered the ballroom by another door, snagged a drink off a passing tray, checked over the crowd. I saw two more powder-blue get-ups, so I wasn't unique enough to draw special attention. I made a mental note to stay well away from my comrades in blue. I blended with the landscape, chatting and nodding and not neglecting my drinking, working my way toward a big arched doorway on the other side of the room that looked like the kind of entrance the head man might use. I didn't want to meet him. Not yet. I just wanted to get him located before I went any further.

A passing wine slave poured a full inch of the genuine ancient stock into my glass, ducked his head and moved on. I gulped it like sour bar whiskey. My attention was elsewhere.

A flurry of activity near the big door indicated that maybe my guess had been accurate. Potbellied officials were forming up in a sort of reception line near the big double door. I started to drift back into the rear rank, bumped against a fat man in medals and a sash who glared, fingered a monocle with a plump ring-studded hand and said, "Suggest you take your place, Colonel," in a suety voice.

I must have looked doubtful, because he bumped me with his paunch, and growled, "Foot of the line! Next to the Equerry, you idiot." He elbowed me aside and waddled past.

I took a step after him, reached out with my left foot and hooked his shiny black boot. He leaped forward, off balance, medals jangling. I did a fast fade while he was still groping for his monocle, eased into a spot at the end of the line.

The conversation died away to a nervous murmur. The doors swung back and a pair of guards with more trimmings than a phoney stock certificate stamped into view, wheeled to face each other and presented arms— chrome-plated automatic rifles, in this case. A dark-faced man with thinning gray hair, a pug nose and a trimmed gray van Dyke came into view, limping slightly from a stiffish knee.

His unornamented gray outfit made him as conspicuous in this gathering as a crane among peacocks. He nodded perfunctorily to left and right, coming along between the waiting rows of flunkeys, who snapped-to as he came abreast, wilted and let out sighs behind him. I studied him closely. He was fifty, give or take the age of a bottle of second-rate bourbon, with the weather-beaten complexion of a former outdoor man and the same look of alertness grown bored that a rattlesnake farmer develops—just before the fatal bite.

He looked up and caught my eye on him, and for a moment I thought he was about to speak. Then he went on past.

At the end of the line, he turned abruptly and spoke to a man who hurried away. Then he engaged in conversation with a cluster of head-bobbing guests.

I spent the next fifteen minutes casually getting closer to the door nearest the one the Baron had entered by. I looked around; nobody was paying any attention to me. I stepped past a guard who presented arms. The door closed softly, cutting off the buzz of talk and the worst of the music.

I went along to the end of the corridor. From the transverse hall, a grand staircase rose in a sweep of bright chrome and pale wood. I didn't know where it led, but it looked right. I headed for it, moving along briskly like a man with important business in mind and no time for light chit-chat.

* * * *

Two flights up, in a wide corridor of muted lights, deep carpets, brocaded wall hangings, mirrors, urns, and an odor of expensive tobacco and *coeur de Russe* a small man in black bustled from a side corridor. He saw me. He opened his mouth, closed it, half turned away, then swung back to face me. I recognized him; he was the head-waiter who had pointed out the flaws in my waiting style half an hour earlier.

"Here," he started—

I chopped him short with a roar of what I hoped was authentic upper-crust rage.

"Direct me to his Excellency's apartments, scum! And thank your guardian imp I'm in too great haste to cane you for the insolent look about you!"

He went pale, gulped hard and pointed. I snorted and stamped past him down the turning he had indicated.

This was Baronial country, all right. A pair of guards stood at the far end of the corridor.

I'd passed half a dozen with no more than a click of heels to indicate they saw me. These two shouldn't be any different—and it wouldn't look good if I turned and started back at sight of them. The first rule of the gate-crasher is to look as if you belong where you are.

I headed in their direction.

When I was fifty feet from them, they both shifted rifles—not to present-arms position, but at the ready. The nickle-plated bayonets were aimed right at me. It was no time for me to look doubtful; I kept on coming. At twenty feet, I heard their rifle bolts snick home. I could see the expressions on their faces now; they looked as nervous as a couple of teen-age sailors on their first visit to a joy-house.

"Point those butter knives into the corner, you banana-fingered cotton choppers!" I said, looking bored and didn't waver. I unlimbered my swagger stick and slapped my gloved hand with it, letting them think it over. The gun muzzles dropped—just slightly. I followed up fast.

"Which is the anteroom to the Baron's apartments?" I demanded.

"Uh...this here is his Excellency's apartments, sir, but—"

"Never mind the lecture, you milk-faced fool," I cut in. "Do you think I'd be here if it weren't? Which is the anteroom, damn you!"

"We got orders, sir. Nobody's to come closer than that last door back there."

"We got orders to shoot," the other interrupted. He was a little older—maybe twenty-two. I turned on him.

"I'm waiting for an answer to a question!"

"Sir, the Articles—"

I narrowed my eyes. "I think you'll find paragraph Two B covers Special Cosmic Top Secret Couriers. When you go off duty, report yourselves on punishment. Now, the anteroom! And be quick about it!"

The bayonets were sagging now. The younger of the two licked his lips. "Sir, we never been inside. We don't know how it's laid out in there. If the colonel wants to just take a look...."

The other guard opened his mouth to say something. I didn't wait to find out what it was. I stepped between them, muttering something about bloody recruits and important messages, and worked the fancy handle on the big gold and white door. I paused to give the two sentries a hard look.

"I hope I don't have to remind you that any mention of the movements of a Cosmic Courier is punishable by slow death. Just forget you ever saw me." I went on in and closed the door without waiting to catch the reaction to that one.

The Baron had done well by himself in the matter of decor. The room I was in—a sort of lounge-cum-bar—was paved in two-inch-deep nylon fuzz, the color of a fog at sea, that foamed up at the edges against walls of pale blue brocade with tiny yellow flowers. The bar was a teak log split down the middle and—polished. The glasses sitting on it were like tissue paper engraved with patterns of nymphs and satyrs. Subdued light came from somewhere, along with a faint melody that seemed to speak of youth, long ago.

I went on into the next room. I found more soft light, the glow of hand-rubbed rare woods, rich fabrics and wide windows with a view of dark night sky. The music was coming from a long, low, built-in speaker with a lamp, a heavy crystal ashtray and a display of hothouse roses. There was a scent in the air. Not the *coeur de Russe* and Havana leaf I'd smelled in the hall, but a subtler perfume.

I turned and looked into the eyes of a girl with long black lashes. Smooth black hair came down to bare shoulders. An arm as smooth and white as whipped cream was draped over a chair back, the hand holding an eight-inch cigarette holder and sporting a diamond as inconspicuous as a chrome-plated hub-cap.

"You must want something pretty badly," she murmured, batting her eyelashes at me. I could feel the breeze at ten feet. I nodded. Under the circumstances, that was about the best I could do.

"What could it be," she mused, "that's worth being shot for?" Her voice was like the rest of her: smooth, polished and relaxed—and with plenty of moxie held in reserve. She smiled casually, drew on her cigarette, tapped ashes onto the rug.

"Something bothering you, Colonel?" she inquired. "You don't seem talkative."

"I'll do my talking when the Baron arrives," I said.

"In that case, Jackson," said a husky voice behind me, "you can start any time you like."

* * * *

I held my hands clear of my body and turned around slowly—just in case there was a nervous gun aimed at my spine. The Baron was standing near the door, unarmed, relaxed. There were no guards in sight. The girl looked mildly amused. I put my hand on the pistol butt.

"How do you know my name?" I asked.

The Baron waved toward a chair. "Sit down, Jackson," he said, almost gently. "You've had a tough time of it—but you're all right now." He walked past me to the bar, poured out two glasses, turned and offered me one. I felt a little silly standing there fingering the gun; I went over and took the drink.

"To the old days." The Baron raised his glass.

I drank. It was the genuine ancient stock, all right. "I asked you how you knew my name," I said.

"That's easy. I used to know you."

He smiled faintly. There was something about his face....

"You look well in the uniform of the Penn-dragoons," he said. "Better than you ever did in Aerospace blue."

"Good God!" I said. "Toby Mallon!"

He ran a hand over his bald head. "A little less hair on top, plus a beard as compensation, a few wrinkles, a slight pot. Oh, I've changed, Jackson."

"I had it figured as close to eighty years," I said. "The trees, the condition of the buildings—"

"Not far off the mark. Seventy-eight years this spring."

"You're a well-preserved hundred and ten, Toby."

He shook his head. "You weren't the only one in the tanks. But you had a better unit than I did. Mine gave out twenty years ago."

"You mean—you walked into this cold—just like I did?"

He nodded. "I know how you feel. Rip Van Winkle had nothing on us."

"Just one question, Toby. The men you sent out to pick me up seemed more interested in shooting than talking. I'm wondering why."

Mallon threw out his hands, "A little misunderstanding, Jackson. You made it; that's all that counts. Now that you're here, we've got some planning to do together. I've had it tough these last twenty years. I started off with nothing: a few hundred scavengers living in the ruins, hiding out every time Jersey or Dee-Cee raided for supplies. I built an organization, started a systematic salvage operation. I saved everything the rats and the weather hadn't gotten to, spruced up my palace here and stocked it. It's a rich province, Jackson—"

"And now you own it all. Not bad, Toby."

"They say knowledge is power. I had the knowledge."

I finished my drink and put the glass on the bar.

"What's this planning you say we have to do?"

Mallon leaned back on one elbow.

"Jackson, it's been a long haul—alone. It's good to see an old ship-mate. But we'll dine first."

"I might manage to nibble a little something. Say a horse, roasted whole. Don't bother to remove the saddle."

He laughed. "First we eat," he said. "Then we conquer the world."

VI

I squeezed the last drop from the Beaujolais bottle and watched the girl whose name was Renada, hold a light for the cigar Mallon had taken from a silver box. My blue mess jacket and holster hung over the back of the chair. Everything was cosy now.

"Time for business, Jackson," Mallon said. He blew out smoke and looked at me through it. "How did things look—inside."

"Dusty. But intact, below ground level. Upstairs, there's blast damage and weathering. I don't suppose it's changed much since you came out twenty years ago. As far as I could tell, the Primary Site is okay."

Mallon leaned forward. "Now, you made it out past the Bolo. How did it handle itself? Still fully functional?"

I sipped my wine, thinking over my answer, remembering the Bolo's empty guns....

"It damn near gunned me down. It's getting a little old and it can't see as well as it used to, but it's still a tough baby."

Mallon swore suddenly. "It was Mackenzie's idea. A last-minute move when the tech crews had to evacuate. It was a dusting job, you know."

"I hadn't heard. How did you find out all this?"

Mallon shot me a sharp look. "There were still a few people around who'd been in it. But never mind that. What about the Supply Site? That's what we're interested in. Fuel, guns, even some nuclear stuff. Heavy equipment; there's a couple more Bolos, moth-balled, I understand. Maybe we'll even find one or two of the Colossus missiles still in their silos. I made an air recon a few years back before my chopper broke down—"

"I think two silo doors are still in place. But why the interest in armament?"

Mallon snorted. "You've got a few things to learn about the setup, Jackson. I need that stuff. If I hadn't lucked into a stock of weapons and ammo in the armory cellar, Jersey would be wearing the spurs in my palace right now!"

I drew on my cigar and let the silence stretch out.

"You said something about conquering the world, Toby. I don't suppose by any chance you meant that literally?"

Mallon stood up, his closed fists working like a man crumpling unpaid bills. "They all want what I've got! They're all waiting." He walked across the room, back. "I'm ready to move against them now! I can put four thousand trained men in the field—"

"Let's get a couple of things straight, Mallon," I cut in. "You've got the natives fooled with this Baron routine. But don't try it on me. Maybe it was even necessary once; maybe there's an excuse for some of the stories I've heard. That's over now. I'm not interested in tribal warfare or gang rumbles. I need—"

"Better remember who's running things here, Jackson!" Mallon snapped. "It's not what you need that counts." He took another turn up and down the room, then stopped, facing me.

* * * *

"Look, Jackson. I know how to get around in this jungle; you don't. If I hadn't spotted you and given some orders, you'd have been gunned down before you'd gone ten feet past the ballroom door."

"Why'd you let me in? I might've been gunning for you."

"You wanted to see the Baron alone. That suited me, too. If word got out—" He broke off, cleared his throat. "Let's stop wrangling, Jackson. We can't move until the Bolo guarding the site has been neutralized. There's only one way to do that: knock it out! And the only thing that can knock out a Bolo is another Bolo."

"So?"

"I've got another Bolo, Jackson. It's been covered, maintained. It can go up against the Troll—" he broke off, laughed shortly. "That's what the mob called it."

"You could have done that years ago. Where do I come in?"

"You're checked out on a Bolo, Jackson. You know something about this kind of equipment."

"Sure. So do you."

"I never learned," he said shortly.

"Who's kidding who, Mallon? We all took the same orientation course less than a month ago—"

"For me it's been a long month. Let's just say I've forgotten."

"You parked that Bolo at your front gate and then forgot how you did it, eh?"

"Nonsense. It's always been there."

I shook my head. "I know different."

Mallon looked wary. "Where'd you get that idea?"

"Somebody told me."

Mallon ground his cigar out savagely on the damask cloth. "You'll point the scum out to me!"

"I don't give a damn whether you moved it or not. Anybody with your training can figure out the controls of a Bolo in half an hour—"

"Not well enough to take on the Tr—another Bolo."

I took a cigar from the silver box, picked up the lighter from the table, turned the cigar in the flame. Suddenly it was very quiet in the room.

I looked across at Mallon. He held out his hand.

"I'll take that," he said shortly.

I blew out smoke, squinted through it at Mallon. He sat with his hand out, waiting. I looked down at the lighter.

It was a heavy windproof model, with embossed Aerospace wings. I turned it over. Engraved letters read: *Lieut. Commander Don G. Banner, USAF*. I looked up. Renada sat quietly, holding my pistol trained dead on my belt buckle.

* * * *

"I'm sorry you saw that," Mallon said. "It could cause misunderstandings."

"Where's Banner?"

"He…died. I told you—"

"You told me a lot of things, Toby. Some of them might even be true. Did you make him the same offer you've made me?"

Mallon darted a look at Renada. She sat holding the pistol, looking at me distantly, without expression.

"You've got the wrong idea, Jackson—" Mallon started.

"You and he came out about the same time," I said. "Or maybe you got the jump on him by a few days. It must have been close; otherwise you'd never have taken him. Don was a sharp boy."

"You're out of your mind!" Mallon snapped. "Why, Banner was my friend!"

"Then why do you get nervous when I find his lighter on your table? There could be ten perfectly harmless explanations."

"I don't make explanations," Mallon said flatly.

"That attitude is hardly the basis for a lasting partnership, Toby. I have an unhappy feeling there's something you're not telling me."

Mallon pulled himself up in the chair. "Look here, Jackson. We've no reason to fall out. There's plenty for both of us—and one day I'll be needing a successor. It was too bad about Banner, but that's ancient history now. Forget it. I want you with me, Jackson! Together we can rule the Atlantic seaboard—or even more!"

I drew on my cigar, looking at the gun in Renada's hand. "You hold the aces, Toby. Shooting me would be no trick at all."

"There's no trick involved, Jackson!" Mallon snapped. "After all," he went on, almost wheedling now, "we're old friends. I want to give you a break, share with you—"

"I don't think I'd trust him if I were you, Mr. Jackson," Renada's quiet voice cut in. I looked at her. She looked back calmly. "You're more important to him than you think."

"That's enough, Renada," Mallon barked. "Go to your room at once."

"Not just yet, Toby," she said. "I'm also curious about how Commander Banner died." I looked at the gun in her hand.

It wasn't pointed at me now. It was aimed at Mallon's chest.

* * * *

Mallon sat sunk deep in his chair, looking at me with eyes like a python with a bellyache. "You're fools, both of you," he grated. "I gave you everything, Renada. I raised you like my own daughter. And you, Jackson. You could have shared with me—all of it."

"I don't need a share of your delusions, Toby. I've got a set of my own. But before we go any farther, let's clear up a few points. Why haven't you been getting any mileage out of your tame Bolo? And what makes me important in the picture?"

"He's afraid of the Bolo machine," Renada said. "There's a spell on it which prevents men from approaching—even the Baron."

"Shut your mouth, you fool!" Mallon choked on his fury. I tossed the lighter in my hand and felt a smile twitching at my mouth.

"So Don was too smart for you after all. He must have been the one who had control of the Bolo. I suppose you called for a truce, and then shot him out from under the white flag. But he fooled you. He plugged a command into the Bolo's circuits to fire on anyone who came close—unless he was Banner."

"You're crazy!"

"It's close enough. You can't get near the Bolo. Right? And after twenty years, the bluff you've been running on the other Barons with your private troll must be getting a little thin. Any day now, one of them may decide to try you."

Mallon twisted his face in what may have been an attempt at a placating smile. "I won't argue with you, Jackson. You're right about the command circuit. Banner set it up to fire an anti-personnel blast at anyone coming within fifty yards. He did it to keep the mob from tampering with the machine. But there's a loophole. It wasn't only Banner who could get close. He set it up to accept any of the *Prometheus* crew—except me. He hated me. It was a trick to try to get me killed."

"So you're figuring I'll step in and de-fuse her for you, eh, Toby? Well, I'm sorry as hell to disappoint you, but somehow in the confusion I left my electro pass behind."

Mallon leaned toward me. "I told you we need each other, Jackson: I've got your pass. Yours and all the others. Renada, hand me my black box." She rose and moved across to the desk, holding the gun on Mallon—and on me, too, for that matter.

"Where'd you get my pass, Mallon?"

"Where do you think? They're the duplicates from the vault in the old command block. I knew one day one of you would come out. I'll tell you, Jackson, it's been hell, waiting all these years—and hoping. I gave orders that any time the Great Troll bellowed, the mob was to form up and stop anybody who came out. I don't know how you got through them...."

"I was too slippery for them. Besides," I added, "I met a friend."

"A friend? Who's that?"

"An old man who thought I was Prince Charming, come to wake everybody up. He was nuts. But he got me through."

Renada came back, handed me a square steel box. "Let's have the key, Mallon," I said. He handed it over. I opened the box, sorted through half a dozen silver-dollar-sized ovals of clear plastic, lifted one out.

"Is it a magical charm?" Renada asked, sounding awed. She didn't seem so sophisticated now—but I liked her better human.

"Just a synthetic crystalline plastic, designed to resonate to a pattern peculiar to my E.E.G." I said. "It amplifies the signal and gives off a characteristic emission that the Psychotronic circuit in the Bolo picks up."

"That's what I thought. Magic."

"Call it magic, then, kid." I dropped the electropass in my pocket, stood and looked at Renada. "I don't doubt that you know how to use that gun, honey, but I'm leaving now. Try not to shoot me."

* * * *

"You're a fool if you try it," Mallon barked. "If Renada doesn't shoot you, my guards will. And even if you made it, you'd still need me!"

"I'm touched by your concern, Toby. Just why do I need you?"

"You wouldn't get past the first sentry post without help, Jackson. These people know me as the Trollmaster. They're in awe of me—of my *Mana*. But together—we can get to the controls of the Bolo, then use it to knock out the sentry machine at the Site—"

"Then what? With an operating Bolo I don't need anything else. Better improve the picture, Toby. I'm not impressed."

He wet his lips.

"It's *Prometheus*, do you understand? She's stocked with everything from Browning needlers to Norge stunners. Tools, weapons, instruments. And the power plants alone."

"I don't need needlers if I own a Bolo, Toby."

Mallon used some profanity. "You'll leave your liver and lights on the palace altar, Jackson. I promise you that!"

"Tell him what he wants to know, Toby." Renada said. Mallon narrowed his eyes at her. "You'll live to regret this, Renada."

"Maybe I will, Toby. But you taught me how to handle a gun—and to play cards for keeps."

The flush faded out of his face and left it pale. "All right, Jackson," he said, almost in a whisper. "It's not only the equipment. It's…the men."

I heard a clock ticking somewhere.

"What men, Toby?" I said softly.

"The crew. Day, Macy, the others. They're still in there, Jackson—aboard the ship, in stasis. We were trying to get the ship off when the attack came. There was forty minutes' warning. Everything was ready to go. You were on a test run; there wasn't time to cycle you out.…"

"Keep talking," I rapped.

* * * *

"You know how the system was set up; it was to be a ten-year run out, with an automatic turn-around at the end of that time if Alpha Centauri wasn't within a milli-parsec." He snorted. "It wasn't. After twenty years, the instruments checked. They were satisfied. There was a planetary mass within the acceptable range. So they brought me out." He snorted again. "The longest dry run in history. I unstrapped and came out to see what was going on. It took me a little while to realize what had happened. I went back in and cycled Banner and Mackenzie out. We went into the town; you know what we found. I saw what we had to do, but Banner and Mac argued. The fools wanted to reseal *Prometheus* and proceed with the launch. For what? So we could spend the rest of our lives squatting in the ruins, when by stripping the ship we could make ourselves kings?"

"So there was an argument?" I prompted.

"I had a gun. I hit Mackenzie in the leg, I think—but they got clear, found a car and beat me to the Site. There were two Bolos. What chance did I have against them?" Mallon grinned craftily. "But Banner was a fool. He died for it." The grin dropped like a stripper's bra. "But when I went to claim my spoils, I discovered how the jackals had set the trap for me."

"That was downright unfriendly of them, Mallon. Oddly enough, it doesn't make me want to stay and hold your hand."

"Don't you understand yet!" Mallon's voice was a dry screech. "Even if you got clear of the Palace, used the Bolo to set yourself up as Baron—

you'd never be safe! Not as long as one man was still alive aboard the ship. You'd never have a night's rest, wondering when one of them would walk out to challenge your rule…."

"Uneasy lies the head, eh, Toby? You remind me of a queen bee. The first one out of the chrysalis dismembers all her rivals."

"I don't mean to kill them. That would be a waste. I mean to give them useful work to do."

"I don't think they'd like being your slaves, Toby. And neither would I." I looked at Renada. "I'll be leaving you now," I said. "Whichever way you decide, good luck."

"Wait." She stood. "I'm going with you."

I looked at her. "I'll be traveling fast, honey. And that gun in my back may throw off my timing."

She stepped to me, reversed the pistol and laid it in my hand.

"Don't kill him, Mr. Jackson. He was always kind to me."

"Why change sides now? According to Toby, my chances look not too good."

"I never knew before how Commander Banner died," she said. "He was my great-grandfather."

VII

Renada came back bundled in a gray fur as I finished buckling on my holster.

"So long, Toby," I said. "I ought to shoot you in the belly just for Don—but—"

I saw Renada's eyes widen at the same instant that I heard the click.

I dropped flat and rolled behind Mallon's chair—and a gout of blue flame yammered into the spot where I'd been standing. I whipped the gun up and around into the peach-colored upholstery an inch from Toby's ear.

"The next one nails you to the chair," I yelled. "Call 'em off!" There was a moment of dead silence. Toby sat frozen. I couldn't see who'd been doing the shooting. Then I heard a moan. Renada.

"Let the girl alone or I'll kill him," I called.

Toby sat rigid, his eyes rolled toward me.

"You can't kill me, Jackson! I'm all that's keeping you alive."

"You can't kill me either, Toby. You need my magic touch, remember? Maybe you'd better give us a safe-conduct out of here. I'll take the freeze off your Bolo—after I've seen to my business."

Toby licked his lips. I heard Renada again. She was trying not to moan—but moaning anyway.

"You tried, Jackson. It didn't work out," Toby said through gritted teeth. "Throw out your gun and stand up. I won't kill you—you know that. You do as you're told and you may still live to a ripe old age—and the girl, too."

She screamed then—a mindless ululation of pure agony.

"Hurry up, you fool, before they tear her arm off," Mallon grated. "Or shoot. You'll get to watch her for twenty-four hours under the knife. Then you'll have your turn."

I fired again—closer this time. Mallon jerked his head and cursed.

"If they touch her again, you get it, Toby," I said. "Send her over here. Move!"

"Let her go!" Mallon snarled. Renada stumbled into sight, moved around the chair, then crumpled suddenly to the rug beside me.

"Stand up, Toby," I ordered. He rose slowly. Sweat glistened on his face now. "Stand over here." He moved like a sleepwalker. I got to my feet. There were two men standing across the room beside a small open door. A sliding panel. Both of them held power rifles leveled—but aimed offside, away from the Baron.

"Drop 'em." I said. They looked at me, then lowered the guns, tossed them aside.

I opened my mouth to tell Mallon to move ahead, but my tongue felt thick and heavy. The room was suddenly full of smoke. In front of me, Mallon was wavering like a mirage. I started to tell him to stand still, but with my thick tongue, it was too much trouble. I raised the gun, but somehow it was falling to the floor,—slowly, like a leaf—and then I was floating, too, on waves that broke on a dark sea....

* * * *

"Do you think you're the first idiot who thought he could kill me?" Mallon raised a contemptuous lip. "This room's rigged ten different ways."

I shook my head, trying to ignore the film before my eyes and the nausea in my body. "No, I imagine lots of people would like a crack at you, Toby. One day one of them's going to make it."

"Get him on his feet," Mallon snapped. Hard hands clamped on my arms, hauled me off the cot. I worked my legs, but they were like yesterday's celery; I sagged against somebody who smelled like uncured hides.

"You seem drowsy," Mallon said. "We'll see if we can't wake you up."

A thumb dug into my neck. I jerked away, and a jab under the ribs doubled me over.

"I have to keep you alive—for the moment," Mallon said. "But you won't get a lot of pleasure out of it."

I blinked hard. It was dark in the room. One of my handlers had a ring of beard around his mouth—I could see that much. Mallon was standing before me, hands on hips. I aimed a kick at him, just for fun. It didn't work out; my foot seemed to be wearing a lead boat. The unshaven man hit me in the mouth and Toby chuckled.

"Have your fun, Dunger," he said, "but I'll want him alive and on his feet for the night's work. Take him out and walk him in the fresh air. Report to me at the Pavillion of the Troll in an hour." He turned to something and gave orders about lights and gun emplacements, and I heard Renada's name mentioned.

Then he was gone and I was being dragged through the door and along the corridor.

The exercise helped. By the time the hour had passed, I was feeling weak but normal—except for an aching head and a feeling that there was a strand of spiderweb interfering with my vision. Toby had given me a good meal. Maybe before the night was over he'd regret that mistake....

Across the dark grounds, an engine started up, spluttered, then settled down to a steady hum.

"It's time," the one with the whiskers said. He had a voice like soft cheese to match his smell. He took another half-twist in the arm he was holding.

"Don't break it," I grunted. "It belongs to the Baron, remember?"

Whiskers stopped dead. "You talk too much—and too smart." He let my arm go and stepped back. "Hold him, Pig Eye." The other man whipped a forearm across my throat and levered my head back; then Whiskers un-limbered the two-foot club from his belt and hit me hard in the side, just under the ribs. Pig Eye let go and I folded over and waited while the pain swelled up and burst inside me.

Then they hauled me back to my feet. I couldn't feel any bone ends grating, so there probably weren't any broken ribs—if that was any consolation.

* * * *

There were lights glaring now across the lawn. Moving figures cast long shadows against the trees lining the drive—and on the side of the Bolo Combat Unit parked under its canopy by the sealed gate.

A crude breastwork had been thrown up just over fifty yards from it. A wheel-mounted generator putted noisily in the background, laying a layer of bluish exhaust in the air.

Mallon was waiting with a 9 mm power rifle in his hands as we came up, my two guards gripping me with both hands to demonstrate their zeal, and me staggering a little more than was necessary. I saw Renada standing by, wrapped in a gray fur. Her face looked white in the harsh light. She made a move toward me and a greenback caught her arm.

"You know what to do, Jackson," Mallon said speaking loudly against the clatter of the generator. He made a curt gesture and a man stepped up and buckled a stout chain to my left ankle. Mallon held out my electropass. "I want you to walk straight to the Bolo. Go in by the side port. You've got one minute to cancel the instructions punched into the command circuit and climb back outside. If you don't show, I close a switch there—" he pointed to a wooden box mounting an open circuitbreaker, with a tangle of heavy cable leading toward the Bolo—"and you cook in your shoes. The same thing happens if I see the guns start to traverse or the anti-personnel ports open." I followed the coils of armored wire from the chain on my ankle back to the wooden box—and on to the generator.

"Crude, maybe, but it will work. And if you get any idea of letting fly a round or two at random—remember the girl will be right beside me."

I looked across at the giant machine. "Suppose it doesn't recognize me? It's been a while. Or what if Don didn't plug my identity pattern in to the recognition circuit?"

"In that case, you're no good to me anyway," Mallon said flatly.

I caught Renada's eye, gave her a wink and a smile I didn't feel, and climbed up on top of the revetment.

I looked back at Mallon. He was old and shrunken in the garish light, his smooth gray suit rumpled, his thin hair mussed, the gun held in a white-knuckled grip. He looked more like a harrassed shopkeeper than a would-be world-beater.

"You must want the Bolo pretty bad to take the chance, Toby," I said. "I'll think about taking that wild shot. You sweat me out."

I flipped slack into the wire trailing my ankle, jumped down and started across the smooth-trimmed grass, a long black shadow stalking before me. The Bolo sat silent, as big as a bank in the circle of the spotlight. I could see the flecks of rust now around the port covers, the small vines that twined up her sides from the ragged stands of weeds that marked no-man's land.

There was something white in the brush ahead. Broken human bones.

I felt my stomach go rigid again. The last man had gotten this far; I wasn't in the clear yet....

I passed two more scattered skeletons in the next twenty feet. They must have come in on the run, guinea pigs to test the alertness of the Bolo. Or maybe they'd tried creeping up, dead slow, an inch a day; it hadn't worked....

Tiny night creatures scuttled ahead. They would be safe here in the shadow of the troll where no predator bigger than a mouse could move. I stumbled, diverted my course around a ten-foot hollow, the eroded crater of a near miss.

Now I could see the great moss-coated treads, sunk a foot into the earth, the nests of field mice tucked in the spokes of the yard-high bogies. The entry hatch was above, a hairline against the great curved flank. There were rungs set in the flaring tread shield. I reached up, got a grip and hauled myself up. My chain clanked against the metal. I found the door lever, held on and pulled.

It resisted, then turned. There was the hum of a servo motor, a crackling of dead gaskets. The hairline widened and showed me a narrow companionway, green-anodized dural with black polymer treads, a bulkhead with a fire extinguisher, an embossed steel data plate that said BOLO DIVISION OF GENERAL MOTORS CORPORATION and below, in smaller type, UNIT, COMBAT, BOLO MARK III.

I pulled myself inside and went up into the Christmas tree glow of instrument lights.

The control cockpit was small, utilitarian, with two deep-padded seats set among screens, dials, levers. I sniffed the odors of oil, paint, the characteristic ether and ozone of a nuclear generator. There was a faint hum in the air from idling relay servos. The clock showed ten past four. Either it was later than I thought, or the chronometer had lost time in the last eighty years. But I had no time to lose....

I slid into the seat, flipped back the cover of the command control console. The Cancel key was the big white one. I pulled it down and let it snap back, like a clerk ringing up a sale.

A pattern of dots on the status display screen flicked out of existence. Mallon was safe from his pet troll now.

It hadn't taken me long to carry out my orders. I knew what to do next; I'd planned it all during my walk out. Now I had thirty seconds to stack the deck in my favor.

I reached down, hauled the festoon of quarter-inch armored cable up in front of me. I hit a switch, and the inner conning cover—a disk of inch-thick armor—slid back. I shoved a loop of the flexible cable up through the aperture, reversed the switch. The cover slid back—sliced the armored cable like macaroni.

I took a deep breath, and my hands went to the combat alert switch, hovered over it.

It was the smart thing to do—the easy thing. All I had to do was punch a key, and the 9 mm's would open up, scythe Mallon and his crew down like cornstalks.

But the scything would mow Renada down, along with the rest. And if I went—even without firing a shot—Mallon would keep his promise to cut that white throat....

My head was out of the noose now but I would have to put it back—for a while.

I leaned sideways, reached back under the panel, groped for a small fuse box. My fingers were clumsy. I took a breath, tried again. The fuse dropped out in my hand. The Bolo's IR circuit was dead now. With a few more seconds to work, I could have knocked out other circuits—but the time had run out.

I grabbed the cut ends of my lead wire, knotted them around the chain and got out fast.

VIII

Mallon waited, crouched behind the revetment.

"It's safe now, is it?" he grated. I nodded. He stood, gripping his gun. "Now we'll try it together."

I went over the parapet, Mallon following with his gun ready. The lights followed us to the Bolo. Mallon clambered up to the open port, looked around inside, then dropped back down beside me. He looked excited now.

"That does it, Jackson! I've waited a long time for this. Now I've got all the *Mana* there is!"

"Take a look at the cable on my ankle," I said softly. He narrowed his eyes, stepped back, gun aimed, darted a glance at the cable looped to the chain.

"I cut it, Toby. I was alone in the Bolo with the cable cut—and I didn't fire. I could have taken your toy and set up in business for myself, but I didn't."

"What's that supposed to buy you?" Mallon rasped.

"As you said—we need each other. That cut cable proves you can trust me."

Mallon smiled. It wasn't a nice smile. "Safe, were you? Come here." I walked along with him to the back of the Bolo. A heavy copper wire hung across the rear of the machine, trailing off into the grass in both directions.

"I'd have burned you at the first move. Even with the cable cut, the armored cover would have carried the full load right into the cockpit with you. But don't be nervous. I've got other jobs for you." He jabbed the gun muzzle hard into my chest, pushing me back. "Now get moving," he snarled. "And don't ever threaten the Baron again."

"The years have done more than shrivel your face, Toby," I said. "They've cracked your brain."

He laughed, a short bark. "You could be right. What's sane and what isn't? I've got a vision in my mind—and I'll make it come true. If that's insanity, it's better than what the mob has."

Back at the parapet, Mallon turned to me. "I've had this campaign planned in detail for years, Jackson. Everything's ready. We move out in half an hour—before any traitors have time to take word to my enemies. Pig Eye and Dunger will keep you from being lonely while I'm away. When I get back—Well, maybe you're right about working together." He gestured and my whiskery friend and his sidekick loomed up. "Watch him," he said.

"Genghis Khan is on the march, eh?" I said, "With nothing between you and the goodies but a five-hundred ton Bolo...."

"The Lesser Troll...." He raised his hands and made crushing motions, like a man crumbling dry earth. "I'll trample it under my treads."

"You're confused, Toby. The Bolo has treads. You just have a couple of fallen arches."

"It's the same. I am the Great Troll." He showed me his teeth and walked away.

* * * *

I moved along between Dunger and Pig Eye, towards the lights of the garage.

"The back entrance again," I said. "Anyone would think you were ashamed of me."

"You need more training, hah?" Dunger rasped. "Hold him, Pig Eye." He unhooked his club and swung it loosely in his hand, glancing around. We were near the trees by the drive. There was no one in sight except the crews near the Bolo and a group by the front of the palace. Pig Eye gave my arm a twist and shifted his grip to his old favorite strangle hold. I was hoping he would.

Dunger whipped the club up, and I grabbed Pig Eye's arm with both hands and leaned forward like a Japanese admiral reporting to the Emperor. Pig Eye went up and over just in time to catch Dunger's club across the back. They went down together. I went for the club, but Whiskers was faster than he looked. He rolled clear, got to his knees, and laid it across my left arm, just below the shoulder.

I heard the bone go....

* * * *

I was back on my feet, somehow. Pig Eye lay sprawled before me. I heard him whining as though from a great distance. Dunger stood six feet away, the ring of black beard spread in a grin like a hyena smelling dead meat.

"His back's broke," he said. "Hell of a sound he's making. I been waiting for you; I wanted you to hear it."

"I've heard it," I managed. My voice seemed to be coming off a worn sound track. "Surprised...you didn't work me over...while I was busy with the arm."

"Uh-uh. I like a man to know what's going on when I work him over." He stepped in, rapped the broken arm lightly with the club. Fiery agony choked a groan off in my throat. I backed a step, he stalked me.

"Pig Eye wasn't much, but he was my pal. When I'm through with you, I'll have to kill him. A man with a broken back's no use to nobody. His'll be finished pretty soon now, but not with you. You'll be around a long time yet; but I'll get a lot of fun out of you before the Baron gets back."

I was under the trees now. I had some wild thoughts about grabbing up a club of my own, but they were just thoughts. Dunger set himself and his eyes dropped to my belly. I didn't wait for it; I lunged at him. He laughed and stepped back, and the club cracked my head. Not hard; just enough to send me down. I got my legs under me and started to get up—

There was a hint of motion from the shadows behind Dunger. I shook my head to cover any expression that might have showed, let myself drop back.

"Get up," Dunger said. The smile was gone now. He aimed a kick. "Get up—"

He froze suddenly, then whirled. His hearing must have been as keen as a jungle cat's; I hadn't heard a sound.

The old man stepped into view, his white hair plastered wet to his skull, his big hands spread. Dunger snarled, jumped in and whipped the club down; I heard it hit. There was flurry of struggle, then Dunger stumbled back, empty-handed.

I was on my feet again now. I made a lunge for Dunger as he roared and charged. The club in the old man's hand rose and fell. Dunger crashed past and into the brush. The old man sat down suddenly, still holding the club. Then he let it fall and lay back. I went toward him and Dunger rushed me from the side. I went down again.

I was dazed, but not feeling any pain now. Dunger was standing over the old man. I could see the big lean figure lying limply, arms outspread—and a white bone handle, incongruously new and neat against the shabby mackinaw. The club lay on the ground a few feet away. I started crawling for it. It seemed a long way, and it was hard for me to move my legs, but I kept at it. The light rain was falling again now, hardly more than a mist. Far away there were shouts and the sound of engines starting up. Mallon's convoy was moving out. He had won. Dunger had won, too. The old man had tried, but it hadn't been enough. But if I could reach the club, and swing it just once….

Dunger was looking down at the old man. He leaned, withdrew the knife, wiped it on his trouser leg, hitching up his pants to tuck it away in its sheath. The club was smooth and heavy under my hand. I got a good grip on it, got to my feet. I waited until Dunger turned, and then I hit him across the top of the skull with everything I had left….

* * * *

I thought the old man was dead until he blinked suddenly. His features looked relaxed now, peaceful, the skin like parchment stretched over bone. I took his gnarled old hand and rubbed it. It was as cold as a drowned sailor.

"You waited for me, Old-Timer?" I said inanely. He moved his head minutely, and looked at me. Then his mouth moved. I leaned close to catch what he was saying. His voice was fainter than lost lope.

"Mom…told me…wait for you…. She said…you'd…come back some day…."

I felt my jaw muscles knotting.

Inside me something broke and flowed away like molten metal. Suddenly my eyes were blurred—and not only with rain. I looked at the old face before me, and for a moment, I seemed to see a ghostly glimpse of another face, a small round face that looked up.

He was speaking again. I put my head down:

"Was I…good…boy…Dad?" Then the eyes closed.

I sat for a long time, looking at the still face. Then I folded the hands on the chest and stood.

"You were more than a good boy, Timmy," I said. "You were a good man."

IX

My blue suit was soaking wet and splattered with mud, plus a few flecks of what Dunger had used for brains, but it still carried the gold eagles on the shoulders.

The attendant in the garage didn't look at my face. The eagles were enough for him. I stalked to a vast black Bentley—a '70 model, I guessed, from the conservative eighteen-inch tail fins—and jerked the door open. The gauge showed three-quarters full. I opened the glove compartment, rummaged, found nothing. But then it wouldn't be up front with the chauffeur….

I pulled open the back door. There was a crude black leather holster riveted against the smooth pale-gray leather, with the butt of a 4 mm showing. There was another one on the opposite door, and a power rifle slung from straps on the back of the driver's seat.

Whoever owned the Bentley was overcompensating his insecurity. I took a pistol, tossed it onto the front seat and slid in beside it. The attendant gaped at me as I eased my left arm into my lap and twisted to close the door. I started up. There was a bad knock, but she ran all right. I flipped a switch and cold lances of light speared out into the rain.

At the last instant, the attendant started forward with his mouth open to say something, but I didn't wait to hear it. I gunned out into the night, slung into the graveled drive, and headed for the gate. Mallon had had it all his way so far, but maybe it still wasn't too late….

Two sentries, looking miserable in shiny black ponchos, stepped out of the guard hut as I pulled up. One peered in at me, then came to a sloppy position of attention and presented arms. I reached for the gas pedal and the second sentry called something. The first man looked startled, then swung the gun down to cover me. I eased a hand toward my pistol, brought it up fast and fired through the glass. Then the Bentley was roaring off into the dark along the potholed road that led into town. I thought I heard a shot behind me, but I wasn't sure.

I took the river road south of town, pounding at reckless speed over the ruined blacktop, gaining on the lights of Mallon's horde paralleling me a mile to the north. A quarter mile from the perimeter fence, the Bentley broke a spring and skidded into a ditch.

I sat for a moment taking deep breaths to drive back the compulsive drowsiness that was sliding down over my eyes like a visor. My arm throbbed like a cauterized stump. I needed a few minutes rest....

A sound brought me awake like an old maid smelling cigar smoke in the bedroom: the rise and fall of heavy engines in convoy. Mallon was coming up at flank speed.

I got out of the car and headed off along the road at a trot, holding my broken arm with my good one to ease the jarring pain. My chances had been as slim as a gambler's wallet all along, but if Mallon beat me to the objective, they dropped to nothing.

* * * *

The eastern sky had taken on a faint gray tinge, against which I could make out the silhouetted gate posts and the dead floodlights a hundred yards ahead.

The roar of engines was getting louder. There were other sounds, too: a few shouts, the chatter of a 9 mm, the *boom!* of something heavier, and once a long-drawn *whoosh!* of falling masonry. With his new toy, Mallon was dozing his way through the men and buildings that got in his way.

I reached the gate, picked my way over fallen wire mesh, then headed for the Primary Site.

I couldn't run now. The broken slabs tilted crazily, in no pattern. I slipped, stumbled, but kept my feet. Behind me, headlights threw shadows across the slabs. It wouldn't be long now before someone in Mallon's task force spotted me and opened up with the guns—

The whoop! *whoop!* WHOOP! of the guardian Bolo cut across the field.

Across the broken concrete I saw the two red eyes flash, sweeping my way. I looked toward the gate. A massed rank of vehicles stood in a battalion front just beyond the old perimeter fence, engines idling, ranged for a hundred yards on either side of a wide gap at the gate. I looked for the high silhouette of Mallon's Bolo, and saw it far off down the avenue, picked out in red, white and green navigation lights, a jeweled dreadnaught. A glaring cyclopean eye at the top darted a blue-white cone of light ahead, swept over the waiting escort, outlined me like a set-shifter caught onstage by the rising curtain.

The whoop! whoop! sounded again; the automated sentry Bolo was bearing down on me along the dancing lane of light.

I grabbed at the plastic disk in my pocket as though holding it in my hand would somehow heighten its potency. I didn't know if the Lesser Troll was programmed to exempt me from destruction or not; and there was only one way to find out.

It wasn't too late to turn around and run for it. Mallon might shoot—or he might not. I could convince him that he needed me, that together we could grab twice as much loot. And then, when he died—

I wasn't really considering it; it was the kind of thought that flashes through a man's mind like heat lightning when time slows in the instant of crisis. It was hard to be brave with broken bone ends grating, but what I had to do didn't take courage. I was a small, soft, human grub, stepped on but still moving, caught on the harsh plain of broken concrete between the clash of chrome-steel titans. But I knew which direction to take.

The Lesser Troll rushed toward me in a roll of thunder and I went to meet it.

* * * *

It stopped twenty yards from me, loomed massive as a cliff. Its heavy guns were dead. I knew. Without them it was no more dangerous than a farmer with a shotgun—

But against me a shotgun was enough.

The slab under me trembled as if in anticipation. I squinted against the dull red IR beams that pivoted to hold me, waiting while the Troll considered. Then the guns elevated, pointed over my head like a benediction. The Bolo knew me.

The guns traversed fractionally. I looked back toward the enemy line, saw the Great Troll coming up now, closing the gap, towering over its waiting escort like a planet among moons. And the guns of the Lesser Troll tracked it as it came—the empty guns, that for twenty years had held Mallon's scavengers at bay.

The noise of engines was deafening now. The waiting line moved restlessly, pulverizing old concrete under churning treads. I didn't realize I was being fired on until I saw chips fly to my left, and heard the howl of richochets.

It was time to move. I scrambled for the Bolo, snorted at the stink of hot oil and ozone, found the rusted handholds, and pulled myself up—

Bullets spanged off metal above me. Someone was trying for me with a power rifle.

The broken arm hung at my side like a fence-post nailed to my shoulder, but I wasn't aware of the pain now. The hatch stood open half an inch. I grabbed the lever, strained; it swung wide. No lights came up to meet me. With the port cracked, they'd burned out long ago. I dropped down inside, wriggled through the narrow crawl space into the cockpit. It was smaller than the Mark III—and it was occupied.

In the faint green light from the panel, the dead man crouched over the controls, one desiccated hand in a shriveled black glove clutching the control bar. He wore a GI weather suit and a white crash helmet, and one foot was twisted nearly backward, caught behind a jack lever.

The leg had been broken before he died. He must have jammed the foot and twisted it so that the pain would hold off the sleep that had come at last. I leaned forward to see the face. The blackened and mummified features showed only the familiar anonymity of death, but the bushy reddish mustache was enough.

"Hello, Mac," I said. "Sorry to keep you waiting; I got held up."

I wedged myself into the co-pilot's seat, flipped the IR screen switch. The eight-inch panel glowed, showed me the enemy Bolo trampling through the fence three hundred yards away, then moving onto the ramp, dragging a length of rusty chain-link like a bridal train behind it.

I put my hand on the control bar. "I'll take it now, Mac." I moved the bar, and the dead man's hand moved with it.

"Okay, Mac," I said. "We'll do it together."

* * * *

I hit the switches, canceling the pre-set response pattern. It had done its job for eighty years, but now it was time to crank in a little human strategy.

My Bolo rocked slightly under a hit and I heard the tread shields drop down. The chair bucked under me as Mallon moved in, pouring in the fire.

Beside me, Mac nodded patiently. It was old stuff to him. I watched the tracers on the screen. Hosing me down with contact exploders probably gave Mallon a lot of satisfaction, but it couldn't hurt me. It would be a different story when he tired of the game and tried the heavy stuff.

I threw in the drive, backed rapidly. Mallon's tracers followed for a few yards, then cut off abruptly. I pivoted, flipped on my polyarcs, raced for the position I had selected across the field, then swung to face Mallon as he moved toward me. It had been a long time since he had handled the controls of a Bolo; he was rusty, relying on his automatics. I had no heavy rifles, but my pop-guns were okay. I homed my 4 mm solid-slug cannon on Mallon's polyarc, pressed the FIRE button.

There was a scream from the high-velocity-feed magazine. The blue-white light flared and went out. The Bolo's defenses could handle anything short of an H-bomb, pick a missile out of the stratosphere fifty miles away, devastate a county with one round from its mortars—but my BB gun at point-blank range had poked out its eye.

I switched everything off and sat silent, waiting. Mallon had come to a dead stop. I could picture him staring at the dark screens, slapping levers and cursing. He would be confused, wondering what had happened. With his lights gone, he'd be on radar now—not very sensitive at this range, not too conscious of detail....

I watched my panel. An amber warning light winked. Mallon's radar was locked on me.

He moved forward again, then stopped; he was having trouble making up his mind. I flipped a key to drop a padded shock frame in place, and braced myself. Mallon would be getting mad now.

Crimson danger lights flared on the board and I rocked under the recoil as my interceptors flashed out to meet Mallon's C-S C's and detonate them in incandescent rendezvous over the scarred concrete between us. My screens went white, then dropped back to secondary brilliance, flashing stark black-and-white. My ears hummed like trapped hornets.

The sudden silence was like a vault door closing.

I sagged back, feeling like Quasimodo after a wild ride on the bells. The screens blinked bright again, and I watched Mallon, sitting motionless now in his near blindness. On his radar screen I would show as a blurred hill; he would be wondering why I hadn't returned his fire, why I hadn't turned and run, why...why....

He lurched and started toward me. I waited, then eased back, slowly. He accelerated, closing in to come to grips at a range where even the split micro-second response of my defenses would be too slow to hold off his fire. And I backed, letting him gain, but not too fast....

Mallon couldn't wait.

He opened up, throwing a mixed bombardment from his 9 mm's, his infinite repeaters, and his C-S C's. I held on, fighting the battering frame, watching the screens. The gap closed; a hundred yards, ninety, eighty.

The open silo yawned in Mallon's path now, but he didn't see it. The mighty Bolo came on, guns bellowing in the night, closing for the kill. On the brink of the fifty-foot-wide, hundred-yard-deep pit, it hesitated as though sensing danger. Then it moved forward.

I saw it rock, dropping its titanic prow, showing its broad back, gouging the blasted pavement as its guns bore on the ground. Great sheets of sparks flew as the treads reversed, too late. The Bolo hung for a moment longer, then slid down majestically as a sinking liner, its guns still firing into the pit like a challenge to Hell. And then it was gone. A dust cloud boiled for a moment, then whipped away as displaced air tornadoed from the open mouth of the silo.

And the earth trembled under the impact far below.

X

The doors of the Primary Site blockhouse were nine-foot-high, eight-inch-thick panels of solid chromalloy that even a Bolo would have slowed down for, but they slid aside for my electropass like a shower curtain at the YW. I went into a shadowy room where eighty years of silence hung like black crepe on a coffin. The tiled floor was still immaculate, the air fresh. Here at the heart of the Aerospace Center, all systems were still go.

In the Central Control bunker, nine rows of green lights glowed on the high panel over red letters that spelled out STAND BY TO FIRE. A foot to the left, the big white lever stood in the unlocked position, six inches from the outstretched fingertips of the mummified corpse strapped into the controller's chair. To the right, a red glow on the monitor panel indicated the locked doors open.

I rode the lift down to K level, stepped out onto the steel-railed platform that hugged the sweep of the starship's hull and stepped through into the narrow COC.

On my right, three empty stasis tanks stood open, festooned cabling draped in disorder. To the left were the four sealed covers under which Day, Macy, Cruciani and Black waited. I went close, read dials. Slender needles trembled minutely to the beating of sluggish hearts.

They were alive.

I left the ship, sealed the inner and outer ports. Back in the control bunker, the monitor panel showed ALL CLEAR FOR LAUNCH now. I studied the timer, set it, turned back to the master panel. The white lever was smooth and cool under my hand. It seated with a click. The red hand of the launch clock moved off jerkily, the ticking harsh in the silence.

Outside, the Bolo waited. I climbed to a perch in the open conning tower twenty feet above the broken pavement, moved off toward the west where sunrise colors picked out the high towers of the palace.

I rested the weight of my splinted and wrapped arm on the balcony rail, looking out across the valley and the town to the misty plain under which *Prometheus* waited.

"There's something happening now," Renada said. I took the binoculars, watched as the silo doors rolled back.

"There's smoke," Renada said.

"Don't worry, just cooling gases being vented off." I looked at my watch. "Another minute or two and man makes the biggest jump since the first lungfish crawled out on a mud-flat."

"What will they find out there?"

I shook my head. "*Homo Terra Firma* can't even conceive of what *Homo Astra* has ahead of him."

"Twenty years they'll be gone. It's a long time to wait."

"We'll be busy trying to put together a world for them to come back to. I don't think we'll be bored."

"Look!" Renada gripped my good arm. A long silvery shape, huge even at the distance of miles, rose slowly out of the earth, poised on a brilliant ball of white fire. Then the sound came, a thunder that penetrated my bones, shook the railing under my hand. The fireball lengthened into a silver-white column with the ship balanced at its tip. Then the column broke free, rose up, up....

I felt Renada's hand touch mine. I gripped it hard. Together we watched as *Prometheus* took man's gift of fire back to the heavens.

THE STAR-SENT KNAVES

Originally published in Worlds of Tomorrow, *June 1963.*

I

Clyde W. Snithian was a bald eagle of a man, dark-eyed, pot-bellied, with the large, expressive hands of a rug merchant. Round-shouldered in a loose cloak, he blinked small reddish eyes at Dan Slane's travel-stained six foot one.

"Kelly here tells me you've been demanding to see me." He nodded toward the florid man at his side. He had a high, thin voice, like something that needed oiling. "Something about important information regarding safeguarding my paintings."

"That's right, Mr. Snithian," Dan said. "I believe I can be of great help to you."

"Help how? If you've got ideas of bilking me...." The red eyes bored into Dan like hot pokers.

"Nothing like that, sir. Now, I know you have quite a system of guards here—the papers are full of it—"

"Damned busybodies! Sensation-mongers! If it wasn't for the press, I'd have no concern for my paintings today!"

"Yes sir. But my point is, the one really important spot has been left unguarded."

"Now, wait a minute—" Kelly started.

"What's that?" Snithian cut in.

"You have a hundred and fifty men guarding the house and grounds day and night—"

"Two hundred and twenty-five," Kelly snapped.

"—but no one at all in the vault with the paintings," Slane finished.

"Of course not," Snithian shrilled. "Why should I post a man in the vault? It's under constant surveillance from the corridor outside."

"The Harriman paintings were removed from a locked vault," Dan said. "There was a special seal on the door. It wasn't broken."

"By the saints, he's right," Kelly exclaimed. "Maybe we ought to have a man in that vault."

"Another idiotic scheme to waste my money," Snithian snapped. "I've made you responsible for security here, Kelly! Let's have no more nonsense. And throw this nincompoop out!" Snithian turned and stalked away, his cloak flapping at his knees.

"I'll work cheap," Dan called after him as Kelly took his arm. "I'm an art lover."

"Never mind that," Kelly said, escorting Dan along the corridor. He turned in at an office and closed the door.

"Now, as the old buzzard said, I'm responsible for security here. If those pictures go, my job goes with them. Your vault idea's not bad. Just how cheap would you work?"

"A hundred dollars a week," Dan said promptly. "Plus expenses," he added.

Kelly nodded. "I'll fingerprint you and run a fast agency check. If you're clean, I'll put you on, starting tonight. But keep it quiet."

* * * *

Dan looked around at the gray walls, with shelves stacked to the low ceiling with wrapped paintings. Two three-hundred-watt bulbs shed a white glare over the tile floor, a neat white refrigerator, a bunk, an arm-chair, a bookshelf and a small table set with paper plates, plastic utensils and a portable radio—all hastily installed at Kelly's order. Dan opened the refrigerator, looked over the stock of salami, liverwurst, cheese and beer. He opened a loaf of bread, built up a well-filled sandwich, keyed open a can of beer.

It wasn't fancy, but it would do. Phase one of the plan had gone off without a hitch.

Basically, his idea was simple. Art collections had been disappearing from closely guarded galleries and homes all over the world. It was obvious that no one could enter a locked vault, remove a stack of large canvases and leave, unnoticed by watchful guards—and leaving the locks undamaged.

Yet the paintings were gone. Someone had been in those vaults—someone who hadn't entered in the usual way.

Theory failed at that point; that left the experimental method. The Snithian collection was the largest west of the Mississippi. With such a target, the thieves were bound to show up. If Dan sat in the vault—day and night—waiting—he would see for himself how they operated.

He finished his sandwich, went to the shelves and pulled down one of the brown-paper bundles. Loosening the string binding the package, he slid a painting into view. It was a gaily colored view of an open-air cafe, with a group of men and women in gay-ninetyish costumes gathered at a table. He seemed to remember reading something about it in a magazine. It was a cheerful scene; Dan liked it. Still, it hardly seemed worth all the effort....

He went to the wall switch and turned off the lights. The orange glow of the filaments died, leaving only a faint illumination from the night-light over the door. When the thieves arrived, it might give him a momentary advantage if his eyes were adjusted to the dark. He groped his way to the bunk.

So far, so good, he reflected, stretching out. When they showed up, he'd have to handle everything just right. If he scared them off there'd be no second chance. He would have lost his crack at—whatever his discovery might mean to him.

But he was ready. Let them come.

* * * *

Eight hours, three sandwiches and six beers later, Dan roused suddenly from a light doze and sat up on the cot. Between him and the crowded shelving, a palely luminous framework was materializing in mid-air.

The apparition was an open-work cage—about the size and shape of an out-house minus the sheathing, Dan estimated breathlessly. Two figures were visible within the structure, sitting stiffly in contoured chairs. They glowed, if anything, more brightly than the framework.

A faint sound cut into the stillness—a descending whine. The cage moved jerkily, settling toward the floor. Long blue sparks jumped, crackling, to span the closing gap; with a grate of metal, the cage settled against the floor. The spectral men reached for ghostly switches....

The glow died.

Dan was aware of his heart thumping painfully under his ribs. His mouth was dry. This was the moment he'd been planning for, but now that it was here—

Never mind. He took a deep breath, ran over the speeches he had prepared for the occasion:

Greeting, visitors from the Future....

Hopelessly corny. What about: *Welcome to the Twentieth Century....*

No good; it lacked spontaneity. The men were rising, their backs to Dan, stepping out of the skeletal frame. In the dim light it now looked like nothing more than a rough frame built of steel pipe, with a cluster of levers in a console before the two seats. And the thieves looked ordinary enough: Two men in gray coveralls, one slender and balding, the other shorter and round-faced. Neither of them noticed Dan, sitting rigid on the cot. The thin man placed a lantern on the table, twiddled a knob. A warm light sprang up. The visitors looked at the stacked shelves.

"Looks like the old boy's been doing all right," the shorter man said. "Fathead's gonna be pleased."

"A very gratifying consignment," his companion said. "However, we'd best hurry, Manny. How much time have we left on this charge?"

"Plenty. Fifteen minutes anyway."

The thin man opened a package, glanced at a painting.

"Ah, magnificent. Almost the equal of Picasso in his puce period."

Manny shuffled through the other pictures in the stack.

"Like always," he grumbled. "No nood dames. I like nood dames."

"Look at this, Manny! The textures alone—"

Manny looked. "Yeah, nice use of values," he conceded. "But I still prefer nood dames, Fiorello."

"And this!" Fiorello lifted the next painting. "Look at that gay play of rich browns!"

"I seen richer browns on Thirty-third Street," Manny said. "They was popular with the sparrows."

"Manny, sometimes I think your aspirations—"

"Whatta ya talkin? I use a roll-on." Manny, turning to place a painting in the cage, stopped dead as he caught sight of Dan. The painting clattered to the floor. Dan stood, cleared his throat. "Uh...."

"Oh-oh," Manny said. "A double-cross."

"I've—ah—been expecting you gentlemen," Dan said. "I—"

"I told you we couldn't trust no guy with nine fingers on each hand," Manny whispered hoarsely. He moved toward the cage. "Let's blow, Fiorello."

"Wait a minute," Dan said. "Before you do anything hasty—"

"Don't start nothing, Buster," Manny said cautiously. "We're plenty tough guys when aroused."

"I want to talk to you," Dan insisted. "You see, these paintings—"

"Paintings? Look, it was all a mistake. Like, we figured this was the gent's room—"

"Never mind, Manny," Fiorello cut in. "It appears there's been a leak."

Dan shook his head. "No leak. I simply deduced—"

"Look, Fiorello," Manny said. "You chin if you want to; I'm doing a fast fade."

"Don't act hastily, Manny. You know where you'll end."

"Wait a minute!" Dan shouted. "I'd like to make a deal with you fellows."

"Ah-hah!" Kelly's voice blared from somewhere. "I knew it! Slane, you crook!"

* * * *

Dan looked about wildly. The voice seemed to be issuing from a speaker. It appeared Kelly hedged his bets.

"Mr. Kelly, I can explain everything!" Dan called. He turned back to Fiorello. "Listen, I figured out—"

"Pretty clever!" Kelly's voice barked. "Inside job. But it takes more than the likes of you to out-fox an old-timer like Eddie Kelly."

"Perhaps you were right, Manny," Fiorello said. "Complications are arising. We'd best depart with all deliberate haste." He edged toward the cage.

"What about this ginzo?" Manny jerked a thumb toward Dan. "He's on to us."

"Can't be helped."

"Look—I want to go with you!" Dan shouted.

"I'll bet you do!" Kelly's voice roared. "One more minute and I'll have the door open and collar the lot of you! Came up through a tunnel, did you?"

"You can't go, my dear fellow," Fiorello said. "Room for two, no more."

Dan whirled to the cot, grabbed up the pistol Kelly had supplied. He aimed it at Manny. "You stay here, Manny! I'm going with Fiorello in the time machine."

"Are you nuts?" Manny demanded.

"I'm flattered, dear boy," Fiorello said, "but—"

"Let's get moving. Kelly will have that lock open in a minute."

"You can't leave me here!" Manny spluttered, watching Dan crowd into the cage beside Fiorello.

"We'll send for you," Dan said. "Let's go, Fiorello."

The balding man snatched suddenly for the gun. Dan wrestled with him. The pistol fell, bounced on the floor of the cage, skidded into the far corner of the vault. Manny charged, reaching for Dan as he twisted aside; Fiorello's elbow caught him in the mouth. Manny staggered back into the arms of Kelly, bursting red-faced into the vault.

"Manny!" Fiorello released his grip on Dan, lunged to aid his companion. Kelly passed Manny to one of three cops crowding in on his heels. Dan clung to the framework as Fiorello grappled with Kelly. A cop pushed past them, spotted Dan, moved in briskly for the pinch. Dan grabbed a lever at random and pulled.

Sudden silence fell as the walls of the room glowed blue. A spectral Kelly capered before the cage, fluorescing in the blue-violet. Dan swallowed hard and nudged a second lever. The cage sank like an elevator into the floor, vivid blue washing up its sides.

Hastily he reversed the control. Operating a time machine was tricky business. One little slip, and the Slane molecules would be squeezing in among brick and mortar particles....

But this was no time to be cautious. Things hadn't turned out just the way he'd planned, but after all, this was what he'd wanted—in a way. The time machine was his to command. And if he gave up now and crawled back into the vault, Kelly would gather him in and pin every art theft of the past decade on him.

It couldn't be *too* hard. He'd take it slowly, figure out the controls....

* * * *

Dan took a deep breath and tried another lever. The cage rose gently, in eerie silence. It reached the ceiling and kept going. Dan gritted his teeth as an eight-inch band of luminescence passed down the cage. Then he was emerging into a spacious kitchen. A blue-haloed cook waddled to a luminous refrigerator, caught sight of Dan rising slowly from the floor, stumbled back, mouth open. The cage rose, penetrated a second ceiling. Dan looked around at a carpeted hall.

Cautiously he neutralized the control lever. The cage came to rest an inch above the floor. As far as Dan could tell, he hadn't traveled so much as a minute into the past or future.

He looked over the controls. There should be one labeled "Forward" and another labeled "Back", but all the levers were plain, unadorned black. They looked, Dan decided, like ordinary circuit-breaker type knife-switches. In fact, the whole apparatus had the appearance of something thrown together hastily from common materials. Still, it worked. So far he had only found the controls for maneuvering in the usual three dimensions, but the time switch was bound to be here somewhere....

Dan looked up at a movement at the far end of the hall.

A girl's head and shoulders appeared, coming up a spiral staircase. In another second she would see him, and give the alarm—and Dan needed a few moments of peace and quiet in which to figure out the controls. He moved a lever. The cage drifted smoothly sideways, sliced through the wall with a flurry of vivid blue light. Dan pushed the lever back. He was in a bedroom now, a wide chamber with flouncy curtains, a four-poster under a flowered canopy, a dressing table—

The door opened and the girl stepped into the room. She was young. Not over eighteen, Dan thought—as nearly as he could tell with the blue light playing around her face. She had long hair tied with a ribbon, and long legs, neatly curved. She wore shorts and carried a tennis racquet in her left hand and an apple in her right. Her back to Dan and the cage, she tossed the racquet on a table, took a bite of the apple, and began briskly unbuttoning her shirt.

Dan tried moving a lever. The cage edged toward the girl. Another; he rose gently. The girl tossed the shirt onto a chair and undid the zipper down the side of the shorts. Another lever; the cage shot toward the outer wall as the girl reached behind her back....

Dan blinked at the flash of blue and looked down. He was hovering twenty feet above a clipped lawn.

He looked at the levers. Wasn't it the first one in line that moved the cage ahead? He tried it, shot forward ten feet. Below, a man stepped out on the terrace, lit a cigarette, paused, started to turn his face up—

Dan jabbed at a lever. The cage shot back through the wall. He was in a plain room with a depression in the floor, a wide window with a planter filled with glowing blue plants—

The door opened. Even blue, the girl looked graceful as a deer as she took a last bite of the apple and stepped into the ten-foot-square sunken tub. Dan held his breath. The girl tossed the apple core aside, seemed to suddenly become aware of eyes on her, whirled—

With a sudden lurch that threw Dan against the steel bars, the cage shot through the wall into the open air and hurtled off with an acceleration that kept him pinned, helpless. He groped for the controls, hauled at a lever. There was no change. The cage rushed on, rising higher. In the distance, Dan saw the skyline of a town, approaching with frightful speed. A tall office building reared up fifteen stories high. He was headed dead for it—

He covered his ears, braced himself—

With an abruptness that flung him against the opposite side of the cage, the machine braked, shot through the wall and slammed to a stop. Dan sank to the floor of the cage, breathing hard. There was a loud *click!* and the glow faded.

With a lunge, Dan scrambled out of the cage. He stood looking around at a simple brown-painted office, dimly lit by sunlight filtered through elaborate venetian blinds. There were posters on the wall, a potted plant by the door, a heap of framed paintings beside it, and at the far side of the room a desk. And behind the desk—Something.

II

Dan gaped at a head the size of a beachball, mounted on a torso like a hundred-gallon bag of water. Two large brown eyes blinked at him from points eight inches apart. Immense hands with too many fingers unfolded and reached to open a brown paper carton, dip in, then toss three peanuts, deliberately, one by one, into a gaping mouth that opened just above the brown eyes.

"Who're you?" a bass voice demanded from somewhere near the floor.

"I'm…I'm…Dan Slane…your honor."

"What happened to Manny and Fiorello?"

"They—I—There was this cop. Kelly—"

"Oh-oh." The brown eyes blinked deliberately. The many-fingered hands closed the peanut carton and tucked it into a drawer.

"Well, it was a sweet racket while it lasted," the basso voice said. "A pity to terminate so happy an enterprise. Still…." A noise like an amplified Bronx cheer issued from the wide mouth.

"How…what…?"

"The carrier returns here automatically when the charge drops below a critical value," the voice said. "A necessary measure to discourage big ideas on the part of wisenheimers in my employ. May I ask how you happen to be aboard the carrier, by the way?"

"I just wanted—I mean, after I figured out—that is, the police…I went for help," Dan finished lamely.

"Help? Out of the picture, unfortunately. One must maintain one's anonymity, you'll appreciate. My operation here is under wraps at present. Ah, I don't suppose you brought any paintings?"

Dan shook his head. He was staring at the posters. His eyes, accustoming themselves to the gloom of the office, could now make out the vividly drawn outline of a creature resembling an alligator-headed giraffe rearing up above scarlet foliage. The next poster showed a face similar to the beachball behind the desk, with red circles painted around the eyes. The next was a view of a yellow volcano spouting fire into a black sky.

"Too bad." The words seemed to come from under the desk. Dan squinted, caught a glimpse of coiled purplish tentacles. He gulped and looked up to catch a brown eye upon him. Only one. The other seemed to be busily at work studying the ceiling.

"I hope," the voice said, "that you ain't harboring no reactionary racial prejudices."

"Gosh, no," Dan reassured the eye. "I'm crazy about—uh—"

"Vorplischers," the voice said. "From Vorplisch, or Vega, as you call it." The Bronx cheer sounded again. "How I long to glimpse once more my native fens! Wherever one wanders, there's no pad like home."

"That reminds me," Dan said. "I have to be running along now." He sidled toward the door.

"Stick around, Dan," the voice rumbled. "How about a drink? I can offer you Chateau Neuf du Pape, '59, Romance Conte, '32, goat's milk, Pepsi—"

"No, thanks."

"If you don't mind, I believe I'll have a Big Orange." The Vorplischer swiveled to a small refrigerator, removed an immense bottle fitted with a nipple and turned back to Dan. "Now, I got a proposition which may be of some interest to you. The loss of Manny and Fiorello is a serious blow, but we may yet recoup the situation. You made the scene at a most opportune time. What I got in mind is, with those two clowns out of the picture, a vacancy exists on my staff, which you might well fill. How does that grab you?"

"You mean you want me to take over operating the time machine?"

"Time machine?" The brown eyes blinked alternately. "I fear some confusion exists. I don't quite dig the significance of the term."

"That thing," Dan jabbed a thumb toward the cage. "The machine I came here in. You want me—"

"Time machine," the voice repeated. "Some sort of chronometer, perhaps?"

"Huh?"

"I pride myself on my command of the local idiom, yet I confess the implied concept snows me." The nine-fingered hands folded on the desk. The beachball head leaned forward interestedly. "Clue me, Dan. What's a time machine?"

"Well, it's what you use to travel through time."

The brown eyes blinked in agitated alternation. "Apparently I've loused up my investigation of the local cultural background. I had no idea you were capable of that sort of thing." The immense head leaned back, the wide mouth opening and closing rapidly. "And to think I've been spinning my wheels collecting primitive 2-D art!"

"But—don't you have a time machine? I mean, isn't that one?"

"That? That's merely a carrier. Now tell me more about your time machines. A fascinating concept! My superiors will be delighted at this development—and astonished as well. They regard this planet as Endsville."

* * * *

"Your superiors?" Dan eyed the window; much too far to jump. Maybe he could reach the machine and try a getaway—

"I hope you're not thinking of leaving suddenly," the beachball said, following Dan's glance. One of the eighteen fingers touched a six-inch yellow cylinder lying on the desk. "Until the carrier is fueled, I'm afraid it's quite useless. But, to put you in the picture, I'd best introduce myself and explain my mission here. I'm Blote, Trader Fourth Class, in the employ of the Vegan Confederation. My job is to develop new sources of novelty items for the impulse-emporiums of the entire Secondary Quadrant."

"But the way Manny and Fiorello came sailing in through the wall! That *has* to be a time machine they were riding in. Nothing else could just materialize out of thin air like that."

"You seem to have a time-machine fixation, Dan," Blote said. "You shouldn't assume, just because you people have developed time travel, that everyone has. Now—" Blote's voice sank to a bass whisper—"I'll make a deal with you, Dan. You'll secure a small time machine in good condition for me. And in return—"

"*I'm* supposed to supply *you* with a time machine?"

Blote waggled a stubby forefinger at Dan. "I dislike pointing it out, Dan, but you are in a rather awkward position at the moment. Illegal entry, illegal possession of property, trespass—then doubtless some embarrassment exists back at the Snithian residence. I daresay Mr. Kelly would have a warm welcome for you. And, of course, I myself would deal rather harshly with any attempt on your part to take a powder." The Vegan flexed all eighteen fingers, drummed his tentacles under the desk, and rolled one eye, bugging the other at Dan.

"Whereas, on the other hand," Blote's bass voice went on, "you and me got the basis of a sweet deal. You supply the machine, and I fix you up with an abundance of the local medium of exchange. Equitable enough, I should say. What about it, Dan?"

"Ah, let me see," Dan temporized. "Time machine. Time machine—"

"Don't attempt to weasel on me, Dan," Blote rumbled ominously.

"I'd better look in the phone book," Dan suggested.

Silently, Blote produced a dog-eared directory. Dan opened it.

"Time, time. Let's see...." He brightened. "Time, Incorporated; local branch office. Two twenty-one Maple Street."

"A sales center?" Blote inquired. "Or a manufacturing complex?"

"Both," Dan said. "I'll just nip over and—"

"That won't be necessary, Dan," Blote said. "I'll accompany you." He took the directory, studied it.

"Remarkable! A common commodity, openly on sale, and I failed to notice it. Still, a ripe nut can fall from a small tree as well as from a large." He went to his desk, rummaged, came up with a handful of fuel cells. "Now, off to gather in the time machine." He took his place in the carrier, patted the seat beside him with a wide hand. "Come, Dan. Get a wiggle on."

* * * *

Hesitantly, Dan moved to the carrier. The bluff was all right up to a point—but the point had just about been reached. He took his seat. Blote moved a lever. The familiar blue glow sprang up. "Kindly direct me, Dan," Blote demanded. "Two twenty-one Maple Street, I believe you said."

"I don't know the town very well," Dan said, "but Maple's over that way."

Blote worked levers. The carrier shot out into a ghostly afternoon sky. Faint outlines of buildings, like faded negatives, spread below. Dan looked around, spotted lettering on a square five-story structure.

"Over there," he said. Blote directed the machine as it swooped smoothly toward the flat roof Dan indicated.

"Better let me take over now," Dan suggested. "I want to be sure to get us to the right place."

"Very well, Dan."

Dan dropped the carrier through the roof, passed down through a dimly seen office. Blote twiddled a small knob. The scene around the cage grew even fainter. "Best we remain unnoticed," he explained.

The cage descended steadily. Dan peered out, searching for identifying landmarks. He leveled off at the second floor, cruised along a barely visible corridor. Blote's eyes rolled, studying the small chambers along both sides of the passage at once.

"Ah, this must be the assembly area," he exclaimed. "I see the machines employ a bar-type construction, not unlike our carriers."

"That's right," Dan said, staring through the haziness. "This is where they do time...." He tugged at a lever suddenly; the machine veered left, flickered through a barred door, came to a halt. Two nebulous figures loomed beside the cage. Dan cut the switch. If he'd guessed wrong—

The scene fluoresced, sparks crackling, then popped into sharp focus. Blote scrambled out, brown eyes swivelling to take in the concrete walls, the barred door and—

"You!" a hoarse voice bellowed.

"Grab him!" someone yelled.

Blote recoiled, threshing his ambulatory members in a fruitless attempt to regain the carrier as Manny and Fiorello closed in. Dan hauled at a lever. He caught a last glimpse of three struggling, blue-lit figures as the carrier shot away through the cell wall.

III

Dan slumped back against the seat with a sigh. Now that he was in the clear, he would have to decide on his next move—fast. There was no telling what other resources Blote might have. He would have to hide the carrier, then—

A low growling was coming from somewhere, rising in pitch and volume. Dan sat up, alarmed. This was no time for a malfunction.

The sound rose higher, into a penetrating wail. There was no sign of mechanical trouble. The carrier glided on, swooping now over a nebulous landscape of trees and houses. Dan covered his ears against the deafening shriek, like all the police sirens in town blaring at once. If the carrier stopped it would be a long fall from here. Dan worked the controls, dropping toward the distant earth.

The noise seemed to lessen, descending the scale. Dan slowed, brought the carrier in to the corner of a wide park. He dropped the last few inches and cut the switch.

As the glow died, the siren faded into silence.

Dan stepped from the carrier and looked around. Whatever the noise was, it hadn't attracted any attention from the scattered pedestrians in the park. Perhaps it was some sort of burglar alarm. But if so, why hadn't it gone into action earlier? Dan took a deep breath. Sound or no sound, he would have to get back into the carrier and transfer it to a secluded spot where he could study it at leisure. He stepped back in, reached for the controls—

There was a sudden chill in the air. The bright surface of the dials before him frosted over. There was a loud *pop!* like a flashbulb exploding. Dan stared from the seat at an iridescent rectangle which hung suspended near the carrier. Its surface rippled, faded to blankness. In a swirl of frosty air, a tall figure dressed in a tight-fitting white uniform stepped through.

Dan gaped at the small rounded head, the dark-skinned long-nosed face, the long, muscular arms, the hands, their backs tufted with curly red-brown hair, the strange long-heeled feet in soft boots. A neat pillbox cap with a short visor was strapped low over the deep-set yellowish eyes, which turned in his direction. The wide mouth opened in a smile which showed square yellowish teeth.

"*Alors, monsieur,*" the new-comer said, bending his knees and back in a quick bow. "*Vous ete une indigine, n'est ce pas?*"

"No compree," Dan choked out "Uh…juh no parlay Fransay…."

"My error. This is the Anglic colonial sector, isn't it? Stupid of me. Permit me to introduce myself. I'm Dzhackoon, Field Agent of Class five, Inter-dimensional Monitor Service."

"That siren," Dan said. "Was that you?"

Dzhackoon nodded. "For a moment, it appeared you were disinclined to stop. I'm glad you decided to be reasonable."

"What outfit did you say you were with?" Dan asked.

"The Inter-dimensional Monitor Service."

"Inter-what?"

"Dimensional. The word is imprecise, of course, but it's the best our language coder can do, using the Anglic vocabulary."

"What do you want with me?"

* * * *

Dzhackoon smiling reprovingly. "You know the penalty for operation of an unauthorized reversed-phase vehicle in Interdicted territory. I'm afraid you'll have to come along with me to Headquarters."

"Wait a minute! You mean you're arresting me?"

"That's a harsh term, but I suppose it amounts to that."

"Look here, uh—Dzhackoon. I just wandered in off the street. I don't know anything about Interdicts and reversed-whozis vehicles. Just let me out of here."

Dzhackoon shook his head. "I'm afraid you'll have to tell it to the Inspector." He smiled amiably, gestured toward the shimmering rectangle through which he had arrived. From the edge, it was completely invisible. It looked, Dan thought, like a hole snipped in reality. He glanced at Dzhackoon. If he stepped in fast and threw a left to the head and followed up with a right to the short ribs—

"I'm armed, of course," the Agent said apologetically.

"Okay," Dan sighed. "But I'm going under protest."

"Don't be nervous," Dzhackoon said cheerfully. "Just step through quickly."

Dan edged up to the glimmering surface. He gritted his teeth, closed his eyes and took a step. There was a momentary sensation of searing heat….

His eyes flew open. He was in a long, narrow room with walls finished in bright green tile. Hot yellow light flooded down from the high ceiling. Along the wall, a series of cubicles were arranged. Tall, white-uniformed creatures moved briskly about. Nearby stood a group of short, immensely burly individuals in yellow. Lounging against the wall at the far end of the room, Dan glimpsed a round-shouldered figure in red, with great bushes of hair fringing a bright blue face. An arm even longer than Dzhackoon's wielded a toothpick on a row of great white fangs.

"This way," Dzhackoon said. Dan followed him to a cubicle, curious eyes following him. A creature indistinguishable from the Field Agent except for a twist of red braid on each wrist looked up from a desk.

"I've picked up that reversed-phase violator, Ghunt," Dzhackoon said. "Anglic Sector, Locus C 922A4."

Ghunt rose. "Let me see; Anglic Sector…. Oh, yes." He extended a hand. Dan took it gingerly; it was a strange hand—hot, dry and coarse-skinned, like a dog's paw. He pumped it twice and let it go.

"Wonderfully expressive," Ghunt said. "Empty hand, no weapon. The implied savagery…." He eyed Dan curiously.

"Remarkable. I've studied your branch, of course, but I've never had the pleasure of actually seeing one of you chaps before. That skin; amazing. Ah…may I look at your hands?"

Dan extended a hand. The other took it in bony fingers, studied it, turned it over, examined the nails. Stepping closer, he peered at Dan's eyes and hair.

"Would you mind opening your mouth, please?" Dan complied. Ghunt clucked, eyeing the teeth. He walked around Dan, murmuring his wonderment.

"Uh…pardon my asking," Dan said, "but are you what—uh—people are going to look like in the future?"

"Eh?" The round yellowish eyes blinked; the wide mouth curved in a grin. "I doubt that very much, old chap." He chuckled. "Can't undo half a million years of divergent evolution, you know."

* * * *

"You mean you're from the past?" Dan croaked.

"The past? I'm afraid I don't follow you."

"You don't mean—we're all going to die out and monkeys are going to take over?" Dan blurted.

"Monkeys? Let me see. I've heard of them. Some sort of small primate, like a miniature Anthropos. You have them at home, do you? Fascinating!" He shook his head regretfully. "I certainly wish regulations allowed me to pay your sector a visit."

"But you *are* time travelers," Dan insisted.

"Time travelers?" Ghunt laughed aloud.

"An exploded theory," Dzhackoon said. "Superstition."

"Then how did you get to the park from here?"

"A simple focused portal. Merely a matter of elementary stressed-field mechanics."

"That doesn't tell me much," Dan said. "Where am I? Who are you?"

"Explanations are in order, of course," Ghunt said. "Have a chair. Now, if I remember correctly, in your locus, there are only a few species of Anthropos extant—"

"Just the one," Dzhackoon put in. "These fellows look fragile, but oh, brother!"

"Oh, yes; I recall. This was the locus where the hairless variant systematically hunted down other varieties." He clucked at Dan reprovingly. "Don't you find it lonely?"

"Of course, there are a couple of rather curious retarded forms there," Dzhackoon said. "Actual living fossils; sub-intellectual Anthropos. There's one called the gorilla, and the chimpanzee, the orangutan, the gibbon—and, of course, a whole spectrum of the miniature forms."

"I suppose that when the ferocious mutation established its supremacy, the others retreated to the less competitive ecological niches and expanded at that level," Ghunt mused. "Pity. I assume the gorilla and the others are degenerate forms?"

"Possibly."

"Excuse me," Dan said. "But about that explanation…."

"Oh, sorry. Well, to begin with Dzhackoon and I are—ah—Australopithecines, I believe your term is. We're one of the many varieties of Anthropos native to normal loci. The workers in yellow, whom you may have noticed, are akin to your extinct Neanderthals. Then there are the Pekin derivatives—the blue-faced chaps—and the Rhodesians——"

"What are these loci you keep talking about? And how can cave men still be alive?"

Ghunt's eyes wandered past Dan. He jumped to his feet. "Ah, good day, Inspector!" Dan turned. A grizzled Australopithecine with a tangle of red braid at collar and wrists stared at him glumly.

"Harrumph!" the Inspector said. "Albinism and alopecia. Not catching, I hope?"

"A genetic deficiency, excellency," Dzhackoon said. "This is a Homo Sapiens, a naturally bald form from a rather curious locus."

"Sapiens? Sapiens? Now, that seems to ring a bell." The olster blinked at Dan. "You're not—" He waggled fingers in instinctive digital-mnemonic stimulus. Abruptly he stiffened. "Why, this is one of those fratricidal deviants!" He backed off. "He should be under restraint, Ghunt! Constable! Get a strong-arm squad in here! This creature is dangerous!"

* * * *

"Inspector. I'm sure—" Ghunt started.

"That's an order!" the Inspector barked. He switched to an incomprehensible language, bellowed more commands. Several of the thickset Neanderthal types appeared, moving in to seize Dan's arms. He looked around at chinless, wide-mouthed brown faces with incongruous blue eyes and lank blond hair.

"What's this all about?" he demanded. "I want a lawyer!"

"Never mind that!" the Inspector shouted. "I know how to deal with miscreants of your stripe!" He stared distastefully at Dan. "Hairless! Putty-colored! Revolting! Planning more mayhem, are you? Preparing to branch out into the civilized loci to wipe out all competitive life, is that it?"

"I brought him here, Inspector," Dzhackoon put in. "It was a routine traffic violation."

"I'll decide what's routine here! Now, Sapiens! What fiendish scheme have you up your sleeve, eh?"

"Daniel Slane, civilian, social security number 456-7329-988," Dan said.

"Eh?"

"Name, rank and serial number," Dan explained. "I'm not answering any other questions."

"This means penal relocation, Sapiens! Unlawful departure from native locus, willful obstruction of justice—"

"You forgot being born without permission, and unauthorized breathing."

"Insolence!" the Inspector snarled. "I'm warning you, Sapiens, it's in my power to make things miserable for you. Now, how did you induce Agent Dzhackoon to bring you here?"

"Well, a good fairy came and gave me three wishes—"

"Take him away," the Inspector screeched. "Sector 97; an unoccupied locus."

"Unoccupied? That seems pretty extreme, doesn't it?" one of the guards commented, wrinkling his heavily ridged brow.

"Unoccupied! If it bothers you, perhaps I can arrange for you to join him there!"

The Neanderthaloid guard yawned widely, showing white teeth. He nodded to Dan, motioned him ahead. "Don't mind Spoghodo," he said loudly. "He's getting old."

"Sorry about all this," a voice hissed near Dan's ear. Dzhackoon—or Ghunt, he couldn't say which—leaned near. "I'm afraid you'll have to go along to the penal area, but I'll try to straighten things out later."

Back in the concourse, Dan's guard escorted him past cubicles where busy IDMS agents reported to harassed seniors, through an archway into a room lined with narrow gray panels. It looked like a gym locker room.

"Ninety-seven," the guard said. He went to a wall chart, studied the fine print with the aid of a blunt, hairy finger, then set a dial on the wall. "Here we go," he said. He pushed a button beside one of the lockers. Its surface clouded and became iridescent.

"Just step through fast. Happy landings."

"Thanks," Dan ducked his head and pushed through the opening in a puff of frost.

* * * *

He was standing on a steep hillside, looking down across a sweep of meadow to a plain far below. There were clumps of trees, and a river. In the distance a herd of animals grazed among low shrubbery. No road wound along the valley floor; no boats dotted the river; no village nestled at its bend. The far hills were innocent of trails, fences, houses, the rectangles of plowed acres. There were no contrails in the wide blue sky. No vagrant aroma of exhaust fumes, no mutter of internal combustion, no tin cans, no pop bottles—

In short, no people.

Dan turned. The Portal still shimmered faintly in the bright air. He thrust his head through, found himself staring into the locker room. The yellow-clad Neanderthaloid glanced at him.

"Say," Dan said, ignoring the sensation of a hot wire around his neck, "can't we talk this thing over?"

"Better get your head out of there before it shuts down," the guard said cheerfully. "Otherwise—ssskkkttt!"

"What about some reading matter? And look, I get these head colds. Does the temperature drop here at night? Any dangerous animals? What do I eat?"

"Here," the guard reached into a hopper, took out a handful of pamphlets. "These are supposed to be for guys that are relocated without prejudice. You know, poor slobs that just happened to see too much; but I'll let you have one. Let's see…anglic, Anglic…." He selected one, handed it to Dan.

"Thanks."

"Better get clear."

Dan withdrew his head. He sat down on the grass and looked over the booklet. It was handsomely printed in gay colors. WELCOME TO RELOCATION CENTER NO. 23 said the cover. Below the heading was a photo of a group of sullen-looking creatures of varying heights and degrees of hairiness wearing paper hats. The caption read: *New-comers Are Welcomed Into a Gay Round of Social Activity. Hi, New-comer!*

Dan opened the book. A photo showed a scene identical to the one before him, except that in place of the meadow, there was a park-like expanse of lawn, dotted with rambling buildings with long porches lined with rockers. There were picnic tables under spreading trees, and beyond, on the river, a yacht basin crowded with canoes and row-boats.

"Life In a Community Center is Grand Fun!" Dan read. "Activities! Brownies, Cub Scouts, Boy Scouts, Girl Scouts, Sea Scouts, Tree Scouts, Cave Scouts, PTA, Shriners, Bear Cult, Rotary, Daughters of the Eastern Star, Mothers of the Big Banana, Dianetics—you name it! A Group for Everyone, and Everyone in a Group!

Classes in conversational Urdu, Sprotch, Yiddish, Gaelic, Fundu, etc; knot-tying, rug-hooking, leather-work, Greek Dancing, finger-painting and many, many others!

Little Theatre!

Indian Dance Pageants!

Round Table Discussions!

Town Meetings!

Dan thumbed on through the pages of emphatic print, stopped at a double-page spread labeled, *A Few Do's and Don'ts.*

* All of us want to make a GO of relocation. So—let's remember the Uranium Rule: Don't Do It! The Other Guy May Be Bigger!

* Remember the Other Fellow's Taboos!

What to you might be merely a wholesome picnic or mating bee may offend others. What some are used to doing in groups, others consider a solitary activity. Most taboos have to do with eating, sex, elimination or gods; so remember look before you sit down, lie down, squat down or kneel down!

* Ladies With Beards Please Note:

Friend husband may be on the crew clearing clogged drains—so watch that shedding in the lavatories, eh, girls? And you fellas, too! Sure, good grooming pays—but groom each other out in the open, okay?

* * * *

* NOTE: There has been some agitation for separate but equal facilities. Now, honestly, folks; is that in the spirit of Center No. 23? Males and females *will continue to use the same johns* as always. No sexual chauvinism will be tolerated.

* * * *

* A Word To The Kiddies!
No brachiating will be permitted in the Social Center area. After all, a lot of the Dads sleep up there. There are plenty of other trees!

* * * *

* Daintiness Pays!
In these more-active-than-ever days, Personal Effluvium can get away from us almost before we notice. And that hearty scent may not be as satisfying to others as it is to ourselves! So remember, fellas: watch that P. E.! (Lye soap, eau de Cologne, flea powder and other beauty aids available at supply shed!)

Dan tossed the book aside. There were worse things than solitude. It looked like a pretty nice world—and it was all his.

The entire North American continent, all of South America, Europe, Asia, Africa—the works. He could cut down trees, build a hut, furnish it. There'd be hunting—he could make a bow and arrows—and the skins would do to make clothes. He could start a little farming, fish the streams, sun bathe—all the things he'd never had time to do back home. It wouldn't be so bad. And eventually Dzhackoon would arrange for his release. It might be just the kind of vacation—

"Ah Dan, my boy!" a bass voice boomed. Dan jumped and spun around.

Blote's immense face blinked at him from the Portal. There was a large green bruise over one eye. He wagged a finger reproachfully.

"That was a dirty trick, Dan. My former employees were somewhat disgruntled, I'm sorry to say. But we'd best be off now. There's no time to waste."

"How did you get here?" Dan demanded.

"I employed a pocket signaler to recall my carrier—and none too soon." He touched his bruised eye gingerly. "A glance at the instruments showed me that you had visited the park. I followed and observed a TDMS Portal.

Being of an adventurous turn and, of course, concerned for your welfare, I stepped through—"

"Why didn't they arrest you? I was picked up for operating the carrier."

"They had some such notion. A whiff of stun gas served to discourage them. Now let's hurry along before the management revives."

"Wait a minute, Blote. I'm not sure I want to be rescued by you—in spite of your concern for my welfare."

"Rubbish, Dan! Come along." Blote looked around. "Frightful place! No population! No commerce! No deals!"

"It has its compensations. I think I'll stay. You run along."

"Abandon a colleague? Never!"

"If you're still expecting me to deliver a time machine, you're out of luck. I don't have one."

"No? Ah, well, in a way I'm relieved. Such a device would upset accepted physical theory. Now, Dan, you mustn't imagine I harbor ulterior motives—but I believe our association will yet prove fruitful."

Dan rubbed a finger across his lower lip thoughtfully. "Look, Blote. You need my help. Maybe you can help me at the same time. If I come along, I want it understood that we work together. I have an idea—"

"But of course, Dan! Now shake a leg!"

Dan sighed and stepped through the portal. The yellow-clad guard lay on the floor, snoring. Blote led the way back into the great hall. TDMS officials were scattered across the floor, slumped over desks, or lying limp in chairs. Blote stopped before one of a row of shimmering portals.

"After you, Dan."

"Are you sure this is the right one?"

"Quite."

Dan stepped through in the now familiar chill and found himself back in the park. A small dog sniffing at the carrier caught sight of Blote, lowered his leg and fled.

"I want to pay Mr. Snithian a visit," Dan said, climbing into a seat.

"My idea exactly," Blote agreed, lowering his bulk into place.

"Don't get the idea I'm going to help you steal anything."

"Dan! A most unkind remark. I merely wish to look into certain matters."

"Just so you don't start looking into the safe."

Blote tsked, moved a lever. The carrier climbed over a row of blue trees and headed west.

IV

Blote brought the carrier in high over the Snithian Estate, dropped lower and descended gently through the roof. The pale, spectral servants moving about their duties in the upper hall failed to notice the wraith-like cage passing soundlessly among them.

In the dining room, Dan caught sight of the girl—Snithian's daughter, perhaps—arranging shadowy flowers on a sideboard.

"Let me take it," Dan whispered. Blote nodded. Dan steered for the kitchen, guided the carrier to the spot on which he had first emerged from the vault, then edged down through the floor. He brought the carrier to rest and neutralized all switches in a shower of sparks and blue light.

The vault door stood open. There were pictures stacked on the bunk now, against the wall, on the floor. Dan stepped from the carrier, went to the nearest heap of paintings. They had been dumped hastily, it seemed. They weren't even wrapped. He examined the topmost canvas, still in a heavy frame; as though, he reflected, it had just been removed from a gallery wall—

"Let's look around for Snithian," Dan said. "I want to talk to him."

"I suggest we investigate the upper floors, Dan. Doubtless his personal pad is there."

"You use the carrier; I'll go up and look the house over."

"As you wish, Dan." Blote and the carrier flickered and faded from view.

Dan stooped, picked up the pistol he had dropped in the scuffle with Fiorello and stepped out into the hall. All was silent. He climbed stairs, looked into rooms. The house seemed deserted. On the third floor he went along a corridor, checking each room. The last room on the west side was fitted as a study. There was a stack of paintings on a table near the door. Dan went to them, examined the top one.

It looked familiar. Wasn't it one that *Look* said was in the Art Institute at Chicago?

There was a creak as of an un-oiled hinge. Dan spun around. A door stood open at the far side of the room—a connecting door to a bedroom, probably.

"Keep well away from the carrier, Mr. Slane," a high thin voice said from the shadows. The tall, cloaked figure of W. Clyde Snithian stepped into view, a needle-barreled pistol in his hand.

"I thought you'd be back," he piped. "It makes my problem much simpler. If you hadn't appeared soon, it would have been necessary for me to shift the scene of my operations. That would have been a nuisance."

* * * *

Dan eyed the gun. "There are a lot more paintings downstairs than there were when I left," he said. "I don't know much about art, but I recognize a few of them."

"Copies," Snithian snapped.

"This is no copy," Dan tapped the top painting on the stack. "It's an original. You can feel the brush-work."

"Not prints, of course. Copies." Snithian whinnied. "Exact copies."

"These paintings are stolen, Mr. Snithian. Why would a wealthy man like you take to stealing art?"

"I'm not here to answer questions, Mr. Slane!" The weapon in Snithian's hand bugged. A wave of pain swept over Dan. Snithian cackled, lowering the gun. "You'll soon learn better manners."

Dan's hand went to his pocket, came out holding the automatic. He aimed it at Snithian's face. The industrialist froze, eyes on Dan's gun.

"Drop the gun." Snithian's weapon clattered to the floor. "Now let's go and find Kelly."

"Wait!" Snithian shrilled. "I can make you a rich man, Slane."

"Not by stealing paintings."

"You don't understand. This is more than petty larceny!"

"That's right. It's grand larceny. These pictures are worth thousands."

"I can show you things that will completely change your attitude. Actually, I've acted throughout in the best interests of humanity!"

Dan gestured with the gun. "Don't plan anything clever. I'm not used to guns. This thing will go off at the least excuse, and then I'd have a murder to explain."

"That would be an inexcusable blunder on your part!" Snithian keened. "I'm a very important figure, Slane." He crossed the deep-pile rug to a glass-doored cabinet. "This," he said, taking out a flat black box, "contains a fortune in precious stones." He lifted the lid. Dan stepped closer. A row of brilliant red gems nestled in a bed of cotton.

"Rubies?"

"Flawless—and perfectly matched." Snithian whinnied. "*Perfectly* matched. Worth a fortune. They're yours, if you cooperate."

"You said you were going to change my attitude. Better get started."

* * * *

"Listen to me, Slane. I'm not operating independently. I'm employed by the Ivroy, whose power is incalculable. My assignment has been to rescue from destruction irreplaceable works of art fated to be consumed in atomic fire."

"What do you mean—fated?"

"The Ivroy knows these things. These paintings—all your art—are unique in the galaxy. Others admire but they cannot emulate. In the cosmos of the far future, the few surviving treasures of dawn art will be valued beyond all other wealth. They alone will give a renewed glimpse of the universe as it appeared to the eyes of your strange race in its glory."

"My strange race?"

Snithian drew himself up. "I am not of your race." He threw his cloak aside and straightened.

Dan gaped as Snithian's body unfolded, rising up, long, three-jointed arms flexing, stretching out. The bald head ducked now under the beamed ceiling. Snithian chuckled shrilly.

"What about that inflexible attitude of yours, now, Mr. Slane?" he piped. "Have I made my point?"

"Yes, but—" Dan squeaked. He cleared his throat and tried again. "But I've still got the gun."

"Oh, that." An eight-foot arm snaked out, flicked the gun aside. "I've only temporized with you because you can be useful to me, Mr. Slane. I dislike running about, and I therefore employ locals to do my running for me. Accept my offer of employment, and you'll be richly rewarded."

"Why me?"

"You already know of my presence here. If I can enlist your loyalty, there will be no need to dispose of you, with the attendant annoyance from police, relatives and busybodies. I'd like you to act as my agent in the collection of the works."

"Nuts to you!" Dan said. "I'm not helping any bunch of skinheads commit robbery."

"This is for the Ivroy, you fool!" Snithian said. "The mightiest power in the cosmos!"

"This Ivroy doesn't sound so hot to me—robbing art galleries—"

"To be adult is to be disillusioned. Only realities count. But no matter. The question remains: Will you serve me loyally?"

"Hell, no!" Dan snapped.

"Too bad. I see you mean what you say. It's to be expected, I suppose. Even an infant fire-cat has fangs."

"You're damn right I mean it. How did you get Manny and Fiorello on your payroll? I'm surprised even a couple of bums would go to work for a scavenger like you."

"I suppose you refer to the precious pair recruited by Blote. That was a mistake, I fear. It seemed perfectly reasonable at the time. Tell me, how did you overcome the Vegan? They're a very capable race, generally speaking."

"You and he work together, eh?" Dan said. "That makes things a little clearer. This is the collection station and Blote is the fence."

"Enough of your conjectures. You leave me no choice but to dispose of you. It's a nuisance, but it can't be helped. I'm afraid I'll have to ask you to accompany me down to the vault."

Dan eyed the door; if he were going to make a break, now was the time—

* * * *

The whine of the carrier sounded. The ghostly cage glided through the wall and settled gently between Dan and Snithian. The glow died.

Blote waved cheerfully to Dan as he eased his grotesque bulk from the seat.

"Good day to you, Snithian," Blote boomed. "I see you've met Dan. An enterprising fellow."

"What brings you here, Gom Blote?" Snithian shrilled. "I thought you'd be well on your way to Vorplisch by now."

"I was tempted, Snithian. But I don't spook easy. There is the matter of some unfinished business."

"Excellent!" Snithian exclaimed. "I'll have another consignment ready for you by tomorrow."

"Tomorrow! How is it possible, with Manny and Fiorello lodged in the hoosegow?" Blote looked around; his eye fell on the stacked paintings. He moved across to them, lifted one, glanced at the next, then shuffled rapidly through the stack. He turned.

"What duplicity is this, Snithian!" he rumbled. "All identical! Our agreement called for limited editions, not mass production! My principals will be furious! My reputation—"

"Shrivel your reputation!" Snithian keened. "I have more serious problems at the moment! My entire position's been compromised. I'm faced with the necessity for disposing of this blundering fool!"

"Dan? Why, I'm afraid I can't allow that, Snithian." Blote moved to the carrier, dumped an armful of duplicate paintings in the cage. "Evidence," he said. "The confederation has methods for dealing with sharp practice. Come, Dan, if you're ready...."

"You dare to cross me?" Snithian hissed. "I, who act for the Ivroy?"

Blote motioned to the carrier. "Get in, Dan. We'll be going now." He rolled both eyes to bear on Snithian. "And I'll deal with you later," he rumbled. "No one pulls a fast one on Gom Blote, Trader Fourth Class—or on the Vegan Federation."

Snithian moved suddenly, flicking out a spidery arm to seize the weapon he had dropped, aim and trigger. Dan, in a wash of pain, felt his knees fold. He fell slackly to the floor. Beside him, Blote sagged, his tentacles limp.

"I credited you with more intelligence," Snithian cackled. "Now I have an extra ton of protoplasm to dispose of. The carrier will be useful in that connection."

V

Dan felt a familiar chill in the air. A Portal appeared. In a puff of icy mist, a tall figure stepped through.

Gone was the tight uniform. In its place, the lanky Australopithecine wore skin-tight blue-jeans and a loose sweat shirt. An oversized beret clung to the small round head. Immense dark glasses covered the yellowish eyes, and sandals flapped on the bare, long-toed feet. Dzhackoon waved a long cigarette holder at the group.

"Ah, a stroke of luck! How nice to find you standing by. I had expected to have to conduct an intensive search within the locus. Thus the native dress. However—" Dzhackoon's eyes fell on Snithian standing stiffly by, the gun out of sight.

"You're of a race unfamiliar to me," he said. "Still, I assume you're aware of the Interdict on all Anthropoid populated loci?"

"And who might you be?" Snithian inquired loftily.

"I'm a Field Agent of the Inter-dimensional Monitor Service."

"Ah, yes. Well, your Interdict means nothing to me. I'm operating directly under Ivroy auspices." Snithian touched a glittering pin on his drab cloak.

Dzhackoon sighed. "There goes the old arrest record."

"He's a crook!" Dan cut in. "He's been robbing art galleries!"

"Keep calm, Dan," Blote murmured, "no need to be overly explicit."

The Agent turned to look the Trader over.

"Vegan, aren't you? I imagine you're the fellow I've been chasing."

"Who, me?" the bass voice rumbled. "Look, officer, I'm a home-loving family man, just passing through. As a matter of fact—"

The uniformed creature nodded toward the paintings in the carrier. "Gathered a few souvenirs, I see."

"For the wives and kiddy. Just a little something to brighten up the hive."

"The penalty for exploitation of a sub-cultural anthropoid-occupied body is stasis for a period not to exceed one reproductive cycle. If I recall my Vegan biology, that's quite a period."

"Why, officer! Surely you're not putting the arm on a respectable law-abiding being like me? Why, I lost a tentacle fighting in defense of peace—" As he talked, Blote moved toward the carrier.

"—your name, my dear fellow," he went on. "I'll mention it to the Commissioner, a very close friend of mine." Abruptly the Vegan reached for a lever—

The long arms in the tight white jacket reached to haul him back effortlessly. "That was unwise, sir. Now I'll be forced to recommend subliminal reorientation during stasis." He clamped stout handcuffs on Blote's broad wrists.

"You Vegans," he said, dusting his hands briskly. "Will you never learn?"

* * * *

"Now, officer," Blote said, "You're acting hastily. Actually, I'm working in the interest of this little world, as my associate Dan will gladly confirm. I have information which will be of considerable interest to you. Snithian has stated that he is in the employ of the Ivroy—"

"If the Ivroy's so powerful, why was it necessary to hire Snithian to steal pictures?" Dan interrupted.

"Perish the thought, Dan. Snithian's assignment was merely to duplicate works of art and transmit them to the Ivroy."

"Here," Snithian cut in. "Restrain that obscene mouth!"

Dzhackoon raised a hand. "Kindly remain silent, sir. Permit my prisoners their little chat."

"You may release them to my custody," Snithian snapped.

Dzhackoon shook his head. "Hardly, sir. A most improper suggestion— even from an agent of the Ivroy." He nodded at Dan. "You may continue."

"How do you duplicate works of art?" Dan demanded.

"With a matter duplicator. But, as I was saying, Snithian saw an opportunity to make extra profits by retaining the works for repeated duplications and sale to other customers—such as myself."

"You mean there are other—customers—around?"

"I have dozens of competitors, Dan, all busy exporting your artifacts. You are an industrious and talented race, you know."

"What do they buy?"

"A little of everything, Dan. It's had an influence on your designs already, I'm sorry to say. The work is losing its native purity."

Dan nodded. "I have had the feeling some of this modern furniture was designed for Martians."

"Ganymedans, mostly. The Martians are graphic arts fans, while your automobiles are designed for the Plutonian trade. They have a baroque sense of humor."

"What will the Ivroy do when he finds out Snithian's been double-crossing him?"

"He'll think of something, I daresay. I blame myself for his defection, in a way. You see, it was my carrier which made it possible for Snithian to carry out his thefts. Originally, he would simply enter a gallery, inconspicuously scan a picture, return home and process the recording through the duplicator. The carrier gave him the idea of removing works en masse, duplicating them and returning them the next day. Alas, I agreed to join forces with him. He grew greedy. He retained the paintings here and proceeded to produce vast numbers of copies—which he doubtless sold to my competitors, the crook!"

Dzhackoon had whipped out a notebook and was jotting rapidly.

"Now, let's have those names and addresses," he said. "This will be the biggest round-up in TDMS history."

"And the pinch will be yours, dear sir," Blote said. "I foresee early promotion for you." He held out his shackled wrists. "Would you mind?"

"Well…." Dzhackoon unlocked the cuffs. "I think I'm on firm ground. Just don't mention it to Inspector Spoghodo."

"You can't do that!" Snithian snapped. "These persons are dangerous!"

"That is my decision. Now—"

Snithian brought out the pistol with a sudden movement. "I'll brook no interference from meddlers—"

* * * *

There was a sound from the door. All heads turned. The girl Dan had seen in the house stood in the doorway, glancing calmly from Snithian to Blote to Dzhackoon. When her eyes met Dan's she smiled. Dan thought he had never seen such a beautiful face—and the figure matched.

"Get out, you fool!" Snithian snapped. "No; come inside, and shut the door."

"Leave the girl out of this, Snithian," Dan croaked.

"Now I'll have to destroy all of you," Snithian keened. "You first of all, ugly native!" He aimed the gun at Dan.

"Put the gun down, Mr. Snithian," the girl said in a warm, melodious voice. She seemed completely unworried by the grotesque aliens, Dan noted abstractedly.

Snithian swiveled on her. "You dare—!"

"Oh, yes, I dare, Snithian." Her voice had a firm ring now. Snithian stared at her. "Who…are you…?"

"I am the Ivroy."

Snithian wilted. The gun fell to the floor. His fantastically tall figure drooped, his face suddenly gray.

"Return to your home, Snithian," the girl said sadly. "I will deal with you later."

"But…but…." His voice was a thin squeak.

"Did you think you could conceal your betrayal from the Ivroy?" she said softly.

Snithian turned and blundered from the room, ducking under the low door. The Ivroy turned to Dzhackoon.

"You and your Service are to be commended," she said. "I leave the apprehension of the culprits to you." She nodded at Blote. "I will rely on you to assist in the task—and to limit your operations thereafter to non-interdicted areas."

"But of course, your worship. You have my word as a Vegan. Do visit me on Vorplisch some day. I'd love the wives and kiddy to meet you." He blinked rapidly. "So long, Dan. It's been crazy cool."

Dzhackoon and Blote stepped through the Portal. It shimmered and winked out. The Ivroy faced Dan. He swallowed hard, watching the play of light in the shoulder-length hair, golden, fine as spun glass....

"Your name is Dan?"

"Dan Slane," he said. He took a deep breath. "Are you really the Ivroy?"

"I am of the Ivroy, who are many and one."

"But you look like—just a beautiful girl."

The Ivroy smiled. Her teeth were as even as matched pearls, Dan thought, and as white as—

"I *am* a girl, Dan. We are cousins, you and I—separated by the long mystery of time."

"Blote—and Dzhackoon and Snithian, too—seemed to think the Ivroy ran the Universe. But—"

The Ivroy put her hand on Dan's. It was as soft as a flower petal.

"Don't trouble yourself over this just now, Dan. Would you like to become my agent? I need a trustworthy friend to help me in my work here."

"Doing what?" Dan heard himself say.

"Watching over the race which will one day become the Ivroy."

"I don't understand all this—but I'm willing to try."

"There will be much to learn, Dan. The full use of the mind, control of aging and disease.... Our work will require many centuries."

"Centuries? But—"

"I'll teach you, Dan."

"It sounds great," Dan said. "Too good to be true. But how do you know I'm the man for the job? Don't I have to take some kind of test?"

She looked up at him, smiling, her lips slightly parted. On impulse, Dan put a hand under her chin, drew her face close and kissed her on the mouth....

A full minute later, the Ivroy, nestled in Dan's arms, looked up at him again.

"You passed the test," she said.

GREYLORN

Originally published in Amazing Science Fiction Stories, *April 1959.*

PROLOGUE

The murmur of conversation around the conference table died as the World Secretary entered the room and took his place at the head of the table.

"Ladies and Gentlemen," he said. "I'll not detain you with formalities today. The representative of the Navy Department is waiting outside to present the case for his proposal. You all know something of the scheme; it has been heard and passed as feasible by the Advisory Group. It will now be our responsibility to make the decision. I ask that each of you in forming a conclusion remember that our present situation can only be described as desperate, and that desperate measures may be in order."

The Secretary turned and nodded to a braided admiral seated near the door who left the room and returned a moment later with a young gray-haired Naval Officer.

"Members of the Council," said the admiral, "this is Lieutenant Commander Greylorn." All eyes followed the officer as he walked the length of the room to take the empty seat at the end of the table.

"Please proceed, Commander," said the Secretary.

"Thank you, Mr. Secretary." The Commander's voice was unhurried and low, yet it carried clearly and held authority. He began without preliminary.

"When the World Government dispatched the Scouting Forces forty-three years ago, an effort was made to contact each of the twenty-five worlds to which this government had sent Colonization parties during the Colonial Era of the middle Twentieth Centuries. With the return of the last of the scouts early this year, we were forced to realize that no assistance would be forthcoming from that source."

The Commander turned his eyes to the world map covering the wall. With the exception of North America and a narrow strip of coastal waters, the entire map was tinted an unhealthy pink.

"The latest figures compiled by the Department of the Navy indicate that we are losing area at the rate of one square mile every twenty-one hours. The organism's faculty for developing resistance to our chemical and biological measures appears to be evolving rapidly. Analyses of atmospheric samples indicate the level of noxious content rising at a steady rate. In other words, in spite of our best efforts, we are not holding our own against the Red Tide."

A mutter ran around the table, as Members shifted uncomfortably in their seats.

* * * *

"A great deal of thought has been applied to the problem of increasing our offensive ability. This in the end is still a question of manpower and raw resources. We do not have enough. Our small improvements in effectiveness have been progressively offset by increasing casualties and loss of territory. In the end, alone, we must lose."

The Commander paused, as the murmur rose and died again. "There is however, one possibility still unexplored," he said. "And recent work done at the Polar Research Station places the possibility well within the scope of feasibility. At the time the attempt was made to establish contact with the colonies, one was omitted. It alone now remains to be sought out. I refer to the Omega Colony."

A portly Member leaned forward and burst out, "The location of the colony is unknown!"

The Secretary intervened. "Please permit the Commander to complete his remarks. There will be ample opportunity for discussion when he has finished."

"This contact was not attempted for two reasons," the Commander continued. "First, the precise location was not known; second, the distance was at least twice that of the earlier colonies. At the time, there was a feeling of optimism which seemed to make the attempt superfluous. Now the situation has changed. The possibility of contacting Omega Colony now assumes paramount importance.

"The development of which I spoke is a new application of drive principle which has given to us a greatly improved effective velocity for space propulsion. Forty years ago, the minimum elapsed time of return travel to the presumed sector within which the Omega World should lie was about a century. Today we have the techniques to construct a small scouting vessel capable of making the transit in just over five years. We cannot hold out here for a century, perhaps; but we can manage a decade.

"As for location, we know the initial target point toward which Omega was launched. The plan was of course that a precise target should be selected by the crew after approaching the star group closely enough to permit telescopic planetary resolution and study. There is no reason why the crew of a scout could not make the same study and examination of possible targets, and with luck find the colony.

"Omega was the last colonial venture undertaken by our people, two centuries after the others. It was the best equipped and largest expedition of them all. It was not limited to one destination, little known, but had a presumably large selection of potentials from which to choose; and her planetary study facilities were extremely advanced. I have full confidence that Omega made a successful planetfall and has by now established a vigorous new society.

"Honorable Members of the Council, I submit that all the resources of this Government should be at once placed at the disposal of a task force with the assigned duty of constructing a fifty-thousand-ton scouting vessel, and conducting an exhaustive survey of a volume of space of one thousand A.U.'s centered on the so-called Omega Cluster."

The World Secretary interrupted the babble which arose with the completion of the officer's presentation.

"Ladies and gentlemen, time is of the essence of our problem. Let's proceed at once to orderly interrogation. Mr. Klayle, lead off, please."

* * * *

The portly Councillor glared at the Commander. "The undertaking you propose, sir, will require a massive diversion of our capacities from defense. That means losing ground at an increasing rate to the obscenity crawling over our planet. That same potential applied to direct offensive measures may yet turn the balance in our favor. Against this, the possibility of a scouting party stumbling over the remains of a colony the location of which is almost completely problematical, and which by analogy with all of the earlier colonial attempts has at best managed to survive as a marginal foothold, is so fantastically remote as to be inconsiderable."

The Commander listened coolly, seriously. "Mr. Councillor," he replied, "as to our defensive measures, we have passed the point of diminishing returns. We have more knowledge now than we are capable of employing against the plague. Had we not neglected the physical sciences as we have for the last two centuries, we might have developed adequate measures before we had been so far reduced in numbers and area as to be unable to produce and employ the new weapons our laboratories have belatedly developed. Now we must be realistic; there is no hope in that direction.

"As to the location of the Omega World, our plan is based on the fact that the selection was not made at random. Our scout will proceed along the Omega course line as known to us from the observations which were carried on for almost three years after its departure. We propose to continue on that line, carrying out systematic observation of each potential sun in turn. As we detect planets, we will alter course only as necessary to satisfy ourselves as to the possibility of suitability of the planet. We can safely assume that Omega will not have bypassed any likely target. If we should have more than one prospect under consideration at any time, we shall examine them in turn. If the Omega World has developed successfully, ample evidence should be discernible at a distance."

* * * *

Klayle muttered "Madness," and subsided. The angular member on his left spoke gently, "Mr. Greylorn, why, if this colonial venture has met with the success you assume, has its government not reestablished contact with the mother world during the last two centuries?"

"On that score, Mr. Councillor, we can only conjecture," the Commander said. "The outward voyage may have required as much as fifty or sixty years. After that, there must have followed a lengthy period of development and expansion in building the new world. It is not to be expected that the pioneers would be ready to expend resources in expeditionary ventures for some time."

"I do not completely understand your apparent confidence in the ability of the hypothetical Omega culture to supply massive aid to us, even if its people should be so inclined," said a straight-backed woman member. "The time seems very short for the mastery of an alien world."

"The population development plan, Madam, provided for an increase from the original 10,000 colonists to approximately 40,000 within twenty years, after which the rate of increase would of course rapidly grow. Assuming sixty years for planetfall, the population should now number over one hundred sixty millions. Given population, all else follows."

Two hours later, the World Secretary summed up. "Ladies and gentlemen, we have the facts before us. There still exist differences in interpretation, which however will not be resolved by continued repetition. I now call for a vote on the resolution proposed by the Military Member and presented by Commander Greylorn."

There was silence in the Council Chamber as the votes were recorded and tabulated. Then the World Secretary sighed softly.

"Commander," he said, "the Council has approved the resolution. I'm sure that there will be general agreement that you will be placed at the head of the project, since you were director of the team which developed the new drive and are also the author of the plan. I wish you the best of luck." He rose and extended his hand.

The first keel plate of the Armed Courier Vessel *Galahad* was laid thirty-two hours later.

CHAPTER 1

I expected trouble when I left the bridge. The tension that had been building for many weeks was ready for release in violence. The ship was silent as I moved along the passageway. Oddly silent, I thought; something was brewing.

I stopped before the door of my cabin, listening; then I put my ear to the wall. I caught the faintest of sounds from within; a muffled click, voices. Someone was inside, someone attempting to be very quiet. I was not overly surprised. Sooner or later the trouble had had to come into the open. I looked up the passage, dim in the green glow of the nightlights. There was no one in sight.

I listened. There were three voices, too faint to identify. The clever thing for me to do now would be to walk back up to the bridge, and order the Provost Marshall to clear my cabin, but I had an intuitive feeling that that was not the way to handle the situation. It would make things much simpler all around if I could push through this with as little commotion as possible.

There was no point in waiting. I took out my key and placed it soundlessly in the slot. As the door slid back I stepped briskly into the room. Kramer, the Medical Officer, and Joyce, Assistant Communications Officer, stood awkwardly, surprised. Fine, the Supply Officer, was sprawled on my bunk. He sat up quickly.

They were a choice selection. Two of them were wearing sidearms. I wondered if they were ready to use them, or if they knew just how far they were prepared to go. My task would be to keep them from finding out.

I avoided looking surprised. "Good evening, gentlemen," I said cheerfully. I stepped to the liquor cabinet, opened it, poured Scotch into a glass. "Join me in a drink?" I said.

None of them answered. I sat down. I had to move just a little faster than they did, and by holding the initiative, keep them off balance. They had counted on hearing my approach, having a few moments to get set, and using my surprise against me. I had reversed their play and taken the advantage. How long I could keep it depended on how well I played my few cards. I plunged ahead, as I saw Kramer take a breath and wrinkle his brow, about to make his pitch.

"The men need a change, a break in the monotony," I said. "I've been considering a number of possibilities." I fixed my eyes on Fine as I talked. He sat stiffly on the edge of my bunk. Already he was regretting his boldness in presuming to rumple the Captain's bed.

"It might be a good bit of drill to set up a few live missile runs on random targets," I said. "There's also the possibility of setting up a small arms range and qualifying all hands." I switched my eyes to Kramer. Fine was sorry he'd come, and Joyce wouldn't take the initiative; Kramer was my problem. "I see you have your Mark 9, Major," I said, holding out my hand. "May I see it?" I smiled pleasantly.

I hoped I had hit him quickly and smoothly enough, before he had had time to adjust to the situation. Even for a hard operator like Kramer, it took mental preparation to openly defy his Commander, particularly in casual conversation. But possession of the weapon was more than casual....

I looked at him, smiling, my hand held out. He wasn't ready; he pulled the pistol from its case, handed it to me.

I flipped the chamber open, glanced at the charge indicator, checked the action. "Nice weapon," I said. I laid it on the open bar at my right.

Joyce opened his mouth to speak. I cut in in the same firm snappy tone I use on the bridge. "Let me see yours, Lieutenant."

He flushed, looked at Kramer, then passed the pistol over without a word. I took it, turned it over thoughtfully, and then rose, holding it negligently by the grip.

"Now, if you gentlemen don't mind, I have a few things to attend to." I was not smiling. I looked at Kramer with expressionless eyes. "I think we'd better keep our little chat confidential for the present. I think I can promise you action in the near future, though."

They filed out, looking as foolish as three preachers caught in a raid on a brothel. I stood without moving until the door closed. Then I let my breath out. I sat down and finished off the Scotch in one drag.

"You were lucky, boy," I said aloud. "Three gutless wonders."

* * * *

I looked at the Mark 9's on the table. A blast from one of those would have burned all four of us in that enclosed room. I dumped them into a drawer and loaded my Browning 2mm. The trouble wasn't over yet, I knew. After this farce, Kramer would have to make another move to regain his prestige. I unlocked the door, and left it slightly ajar. Then I threw the main switch and stretched out on my bunk. I put the Browning needler on the little shelf near my right hand.

Perhaps I had made a mistake, I reflected, in eliminating formal discipline as far as possible in the shipboard routine. It had seemed the best course for a long cruise under the present conditions. But now I had a morale situation that could explode in mutiny at the first blunder on my part.

I knew that Kramer was the focal point of the trouble. He was my senior staff officer, and carried a great deal of weight in the Officer's Mess. As a medic, he knew most of the crew better than I. I thought I knew Kramer's driving motive, too. He had always been a great success with the women. When he had volunteered for the mission he had doubtless pictured himself as quite a romantic hero, off on a noble but hopeless quest. Now, after four years in deep space, he was beginning to realize that he was getting no younger, and that at best he would have spent a decade of his prime in monastic seclusion. He wanted to go back now, and salvage what he could.

It was incredible to me that this movement could have gathered followers, but I had to face the fact; my crew almost to a man had given up the search before it was well begun. I had heard the first rumors only a few weeks before, but the idea had spread through the crew like wildfire. Now, I couldn't afford drastic action, or risk forcing a blowup by arresting ringleaders. I had to baby the situation along with an easy hand and hope for good news from the Survey Section. A likely find now would save us.

There was still every reason to hope for success in our search. To date all had gone according to plan. We had followed the route of Omega as far as it had been charted, and then gone on, studying the stars ahead for evidence of planets. We had made our first finds early in the fourth year of the voyage. It had been a long tedious time since then of study and observation, eliminating one world after another as too massive, too cold, too close to a blazing primary, too small to hold an atmosphere. In all we had discovered twelve planets, of four suns. Only one had looked good enough for close observation. We had moved in to televideo range before realizing it was an all-sea world.

Now we had five new main-sequence suns ahead within six months' range. I hoped for a confirmation on a planet at any time. To turn back now to a world that had pinned its last hopes on our success was unthinkable, yet this was Kramer's plan, and that of his followers. They would not prevail while I lived. Still it was not my plan to be a party to our failure through martyrdom. I intended to stay alive and carry through to success. I dozed lightly and waited.

* * * *

I awoke when they tried the door. It had swung open a few inches at the touch of the one who had tried it, not expecting it to be unlatched. It stood ajar now, the pale light from the hall shining on the floor. No one entered. Kramer was still fumbling, unsure of himself. At every surprise with which I presented him, he was paralyzed, expecting a trap. Several minutes passed in tense silence; then the door swung wider.

"I'll be forced to kill the first man who enters this room," I said in a steady voice. I hadn't picked up the gun.

I heard urgent whispers in the hall. Then a hand reached in behind the shelter of the door and flipped the light switch. Nothing happened, since I had opened the main switch. It was only a small discomfiture, but it had the effect of interfering with their plan of action, such as it was. These men were being pushed along by Kramer, without a clearly thought out plan. They hardly knew how to go about defying lawful authority.

I called out, "I suggest you call this nonsense off now, and go back to your quarters, men. I don't know who is involved in this, yet. You can get away clean if you leave quietly, now, before you've made a serious mistake."

I hoped it would work. This little adventure, abortive though it was, might serve to let off steam. The men would have something to talk about for a few precious days. I picked up the needler and waited. If the bluff failed, I would have to kill someone.

Distantly I heard a metallic clatter. Moments later a tremor rattled the objects on the shelf, followed a few seconds later by a heavy shuddering. Papers slid from my desk, fluttered across the floor. The whiskey bottle toppled, rolled to the far wall. I felt dizzy, as my bunk seemed to tilt under me. I reached for the intercom key and flipped it.

"Taylor," I said, "this is the Captain. What's the report?"

There was a momentary delay before the answer came. "Captain, we've taken a meteor strike aft, apparently a metallic body. It must have hit us a tremendous wallop because it's set up a rotation. I've called out Damage Control."

"Good work, Taylor," I said. I keyed for Stores; the object must have hit about there. "This is the Captain," I said. "Any damage there?"

I got a hum of background noise, then a too-close transmission. "Uh, Cap'n, we got a hole in the aft bulkhead here. I slapped a seat pad over it. Man, that coulda killed somebody."

* * * *

I flipped off the intercom and started aft at a run. My visitors had evaporated. In the passage men stood, milled, called questions. I keyed my mike as I ran. "Taylor, order all hands to emergency stations."

It was difficult running, since the floors had assumed an apparent tilt. Loose gear was rolling and sliding along underfoot, propelled forward by centrifugal force. Aft of Stores, I heard the whistle of escaping air and high pressure gasses from ruptured lines. Vapor clouds fogged the air. I called for floodlights for the whole sector.

Clay appeared out of the fog with his damage control crew. "Sir," he said, "it's punctured inner and outer shells in two places, and fragments have riddled the whole sector. There are at least three men dead, and two hurt."

"Taylor," I called, "let's have another damage control crew back here on the triple. Get the medics back here, too." Clay and his men put on masks and moved off. I borrowed one from a man standing by and followed. The large exit puncture was in the forward cargo lock. The room was sealed off, limiting the air loss.

"Clay," I said, "pass this up for the moment and get that entry puncture sealed. I'll put the extra crew in suits to handle this."

* * * *

I moved back into clear air and called for reports from all sections. The worst of the damage was in the auxiliary power control room, where communication and power lines were slashed and the panel cut up. The danger of serious damage to essential equipment had been very close, but we had been lucky. This was the first instance I had heard of encountering an object at hyper light speed.

It was astonishing how this threat to our safety cleared the air. The men went about their duties more cheerfully than they had for months, and Kramer was conspicuous by his subdued air. The emergency had reestablished at least for the time the normal discipline; the men still relied on the Captain in trouble.

Damage control crews worked steadily for the next seventy-two hours, replacing wiring, welding, and testing. Power Section jockeyed endlessly, correcting air motions. Meanwhile, I checked almost hourly with Survey Section, hoping for good news to consolidate the improved morale situation.

It was on Sunday morning, just after dawn relief that Lt. Taylor came up to the bridge looking sick.

"Sir," he said, "we took more damage than we knew with that meteor strike." He stopped and swallowed hard.

"What have you got, Lieutenant?" I said.

"We missed a piece. It must have gone off on a tangent through stores into the cooler. Clipped the coolant line, and let warm air in. All the fresh frozen stuff is contaminated and rotten." He gagged. "I got a whiff of it, sir. Excuse me." He rushed away.

This was calamity.

We didn't carry much in the way of fresh natural food; but what we had was vital. It was a bulky, delicate cargo to handle, but the chemists hadn't yet come up with synthetics to fill all the dietary needs of man. We could get by fine for a long time on vitamin tablets and concentrates; but there were nutritional elements that you couldn't get that way. Hydroponics didn't help; we had to have a few ounces of fresh meat and vegetables grown in sunlight every week, or start to die within months.

* * * *

I knew that Kramer wouldn't let this chance pass. As Medical Officer he would be well within his rights in calling to my attention the fact that our health would soon begin to suffer. I felt sure he would do so as loudly and publicly as possible at the first opportunity.

My best move was to beat him to the punch by making a general announcement, giving the facts in the best possible light. That might take some of the sting out of anything Kramer said later.

I gave it to them, short and to the point. "Men, we've just suffered a serious loss. All the fresh frozen stores are gone. That doesn't mean we'll be going on short rations; there are plenty of concentrates and vitamins aboard. But it does mean we're going to be suffering from deficiencies in our diet.

"We didn't come out here on a pleasure cruise; we're on a mission that leaves no room for failure. This is just one more fact for us to face. Now let's get on with the job."

I walked into the wardroom, drew a cup of near-coffee, and sat down. The screen showed a beach with booming surf. The sound track picked up the crash and hiss of the breakers. Considering the red plague that now covered the scene, I thought it was a poor choice. I dialed for a high view of rolling farmland.

Mannion sat at a table across the room with Kirschenbaum. They were hunched over their cups, not talking. I wondered where they stood. Mannion, Communications Officer, was neurotic, but an old Armed Force man. Discipline meant a lot to him. Kirschenbaum, Power Chief, was a joker, with cold eyes, and smarter than he seemed. The question was whether he was smart enough to idealize the stupidity of retreat now.

Kramer walked in, not wasting any time. He saw me and came over. He stopped a few feet from the table, and said loudly, "Captain, I'd like to know your plans, now that the possibility of continuing is out."

I sipped my near-coffee and looked at the rolling farmland. I didn't answer him. If I could get him mad, I could take him at his game.

Kramer turned red. He didn't like being ignored. The two at the other table were watching.

"Captain," Kramer said loudly. "As Medical Officer I have to know what measures you're taking to protect the health of the men."

This was a little better. He was on the defensive now; explaining why he had a right to question his Commander. I wanted him a little hotter though.

I looked up at him. "Kramer," I said in a clear, not too loud voice, "you're on watch. I don't want to find you hanging around the wardroom making light chit-chat until you're properly relieved from duty." I went back to my near-coffee and the farmland. A river was in view now, and beyond it distant mountains.

Kramer was furious. "Joyce has relieved me, Captain," he said, controlling his voice with an effort. "I felt I'd better take this matter up with you as soon as possible, since it affects the health of every man aboard." He was trying to keep cool, in command of himself.

"I haven't authorized any changes in the duty roster, Major," I said mildly. "Report to your post." I was riding the habit of discipline now, as far as it would carry me. I hoped that disobedience to a direct order, solidly based on regulations, was a little too big a jump for Kramer at the moment. Tomorrow it might be different. But it was essential that I break up the scene he was staging.

He wilted. "I'll see you at 1700 in the chart room, Kramer," I said as he turned away. Mannion and Kirschenbaum looked at each other, then finished their near-coffee hurriedly and left. I hoped their version of the incident would help deflate Kramer's standing among the malcontents.

I left the wardroom and took the lift up to the bridge and checked with Clay and his survey team.

"I think I've spotted a slight perturbation in Delta 3, Captain," Clay said. "I'm not sure, we're still pretty far out."

"All right, Clay," I said. "Stay with it."

Clay was one of my more dependable men, dedicated to his work. Unfortunately, he was no man of action. He would have little influence in a show-down.

* * * *

I was at the Schmidt when I heard the lift open. I turned; Kramer, Fine, Taylor, and a half a dozen enlisted crew chiefs crowded out, bunched together. They were all wearing needlers. At least they'd learned that much, I thought.

Kramer moved forward. "We feel that the question of the men's welfare has to be dealt with right away, Captain," he said smoothly.

I looked at him coldly, glanced at the rest of his crew. I said nothing.

"What we're faced with is pretty grim, even if we turn back now. I can't be responsible for the results if there's any delay," Kramer said. He spoke in an arrogant tone. I looked them over, let the silence build.

"You're in charge of this menagerie?" I said, looking at Kramer. "If so, you've got thirty seconds to send them back to their kennels. We'll go into the matter of unauthorized personnel on the bridge later. As for you, Major, you can consider yourself under arrest in quarters. Now *Move*."

Kramer was ready to stare me down, but Fine gave me a break by tugging at his sleeve. Kramer shook him loose, snarling. At that the crew chiefs faded back into the lift. Fine and Taylor hesitated, then joined them. Kramer started to shout after them, then got hold of himself. The lift moved down.

Kramer thought about going for his needler. I looked at him through narrowed eyes. He decided to rely on his mouth, as usual. He licked his lips. "All right, I'm under arrest," he said. "But as Medical Officer of this vessel it's my duty to remind you that you can't live without a certain minimum of fresh organic food. We've got to start back now." He was pale, but determined. He couldn't bear the thought of getting bald and toothless from dietary deficiency. The girls would never give him another look.

"We're going on, Kramer," I said. "As long as we have a man aboard still able to move. Teeth or no teeth."

"Deficiency disease is no joke, Captain," Kramer said. "You can get all the symptoms of leprosy, cancer and syphilis just by skipping a few necessary elements in your diet. And we're missing most of them."

"Giving me your opinions is one thing, Kramer," I said. "Mutiny is another."

Clay stood beside the main screen, wide-eyed. I couldn't send Kramer down under his guard. "Let's go, Kramer," I said. "I'm locking you up myself."

We rode down in the lift. The men who had been with Kramer stood awkwardly, silent as we stepped out into the passage. I spotted two chronic trouble-makers among them. I thought I might as well call them now as later. "Williams and Nagle," I said, "this officer is under arrest. Escort him to his quarters and lock him in." As they stepped forward hesitantly, Kramer said, "Keep your filthy hooks off me." He started down the passage.

* * * *

If I could get Kramer put away before anybody else started trouble, I might be able to bluff it through. I followed him and his two sheepish guards down past the power section, and the mess. I hoped there would be no crowd there to see their hero Kramer under guard.

I was out of luck. Apparently word had gone out of Kramer's arrest, and the corridor was clogged with men. They stood unmoving as we approached. Kramer stopped.

"Clear this passage, you men," I said.

Slowly they began to move back, giving ground reluctantly.

Suddenly Kramer shouted. "That's right, you whiners and complainers, clear the way so the Captain can take me back to the missile deck and shoot me. You just want to talk about home; you haven't got the guts to do anything about it."

The moving mass halted, milled. Someone shouted, "Who's he think he is, anyway."

Kramer whirled toward me. "He thinks he's the man who's going to let you all rot alive, to save his record."

"Williams, Nagle," I said loudly, "clear this passage."

* * * *

Williams started half-heartedly to shove at the men nearest him. A fist flashed out and snapped his head back. That was a mistake; Williams pulled his needler, and fired a ricochet down the passage.

"'Bout twelve a you yellow-bellies git outa my way," he yelled. "I'm comin' through."

Nagle moved close to Williams, and shouted something to him. The noise drowned it. Kramer swung back to me, frantic to regain his sway over the mob.

"Once I'm out of the way, there'll be a general purge," he roared. The hubbub faded, as men turned to hear him.

"You're all marked men. He's gone mad. He won't let one of you live." Kramer had their eyes now. "Take him now," he shouted, and seized my arm to begin the action.

He'd rushed it a little. I hit him across the face with the back of my hand. No one jumped to his assistance. I drew my 2mm. "If you ever lay a hand on your Commanding Officer again, I'll burn you where you stand, Kramer."

Then a voice came from behind me. "You're not killing anybody without a trial, Captain." Joyce stood there with two of the crew chiefs, needler in hand. Fine and Taylor were not in sight.

I pushed Kramer out of my way and walked up to Joyce.

"Hand me that weapon, Junior, butt first," I said. I looked him in the eye with all the glare I had. He stepped back a pace.

"Why don't you jump him," he called to the crowd.

The wall annunciator hummed and spoke.

"Captain Greylorn, please report to the bridge. Unidentified body on main scope."

Every man stopped in his tracks, listening. The annunciator continued. "Looks like it's decelerating, Captain."

I holstered my pistol, pushed past Joyce, and trotted for the lift. The mob behind me broke up, talking, as men under long habit ran for action stations.

Clay was operating calmly under pressure. He sat at the main screen, and studied the blip, making tiny crayon marks.

"She's too far out for a reliable scanner track, Captain," he said, "but I'm pretty sure she's braking."

If that were true, this might be the break we'd been living for. Only manned or controlled bodies decelerated in deep space.

"How did you spot it, Clay?" I asked. Picking up a tiny mass like this was a delicate job, even when you knew its coordinates.

"Just happened to catch my eye, Captain," he said. "I always make a general check every watch of the whole forward quadrant. I noticed a blip where I didn't remember seeing one before."

"You have quite an eye, Clay," I said. "How about getting this object in the beam."

"We're trying now, Captain," he said. "That's a mighty small field, though."

Joyce called from the radar board, "I think I'm getting an echo at 15,000, sir. It's pretty weak."

Miller, quiet and meticulous, delicately tuned the beam control. "Give me your fix, Joyce," he said. "I can't find it."

Joyce called out his figures, in seconds of arc to three places.

"You're right on it, Joyce," Miller called a minute later. "I got it. Now pray it don't get away when I boost it."

Clay stepped over behind Miller. "Take it a few mags at a time," he said calmly.

I watched Miller's screen. A tiny point near the center of the screen swelled to a spec, and jumped nearly off the screen to the left. Miller centered it again, and switched to a higher power. This time it jumped less, and resolved into two tiny dots.

* * * *

Step by step the magnification was increased as ring after ring of the lens antenna was thrown into play. Each time the centering operation was more delicate. The image grew until it filled a quarter of the screen. We stared at it in fascination.

It showed up in stark silhouette, in the electronic "light" of the radar scope. Two perfect discs, joined by a fine filament. As we watched, their relative positions slowly shifted, one moving across, half occluding the other.

As the image drifted, Miller worked with infinite care at his console to hold it on center, in sharp focus.

"Wish you'd give me an orbit on this thing, Joyce," he said, "so I could lock onto it."

"It ain't got no orbit, man," Joyce said. "I'm trackin' it, but I don't understand it. That rock is on a closing curve with us, and slowin' down fast."

"What's the velocity, Joyce?" I asked.

"Averagin' about 1,000 relative, Captain, but slowin' fast."

"All right, we'll hold our course," I said.

I keyed for a general announcement.

"This is the Captain," I said. "General Quarters. Man action stations and prepare for possible contact within one hour."

"Missile Section. Arm No. 1 Battery and stand by."

Then I added, "We don't know what we've got here, but it's not a natural body. Could be anything from a torpedo on up."

I went back to the Beam screen. The image was clear, but without detail. The two discs slowly drew apart, then closed again.

"I'd guess that movement is due to rotation of two spheres around a common center," Clay said.

"I agree with you," I said. "Try to get me a reading on the mass of the object."

I wondered whether Kramer had been locked up as I had ordered, but at this moment it seemed unimportant. If this was, as I hoped, a contact with our colony, all our troubles were over.

The object (I hesitated to call it a ship) approached steadily, still decelerating. Now Clay picked it up on the televideo, as it paralleled our course forty-five hundred miles out.

"Captain, it's my guess the body will match speeds with us at about 200 miles, at his present rate of deceleration," Clay said.

"Hold everything you've got on him, and watch closely for anything that might be a missile," I said.

* * * *

Clay worked steadily over his chart table. Finally he turned to me. "Captain, I get a figure of over a hundred million tons mass; and calibrating the scope images gives us a length of nearly two miles."

I let that sink in. I had a strong and very empty feeling that this ship, if ship it were, was not an envoy from any human colony.

The annunciator hummed and spoke. "Captain, I'm getting a very short wave transmission from a point out on the starboard bow. Does that sound like your torpedo?" It was Mannion.

"That's it, Mannion," I said. "Can you make anything of it?"

"No, sir," he answered. "I'm taping it, so I can go to work on it."

Mannion was our language and code man. I hoped he was good.

"What does it sound like," I asked. "Tune me in."

After a moment a high hum came from the speaker. Through it I could hear harsh chopping consonants, a whining intonation. I doubted that Mannion would be able to make anything of that gargle.

Our Bogie closed steadily. At four hundred twenty-five miles he reversed relative directions, and began matching our speed, moving closer to our course. There was no doubt he planned to parallel us.

I made a brief announcement to all hands describing the status of the action. Clay worked over his televideo, trying to clear the image. I watched as the blob on the screen swelled and flickered. Suddenly it flashed into clear stark definition. Against a background of sparkling black, the twin spheres gleamed faintly in reflected starlight.

There were no visible surface features; the iodine-colored forms and their connecting shaft had an ancient and alien look.

We held our course steadily, watching the stranger maneuver. Even at this distance it looked huge.

"Captain," Clay said, "I've been making a few rough calculations. The two spheres are about 800 yards in diameter, and at the rate the structure is rotating it's pulling about six gravities."

That settled the question of human origin of the ship. No human crew would choose to work under six gee's.

Now, paralleling us at just over two hundred miles, the giant ship spun along, at rest relative to us. It was visible now through the direct observation panel, without magnification.

* * * *

I left Clay in charge on the bridge, and I went down to the Com Section.

Joyce sat at his board, reading instruments and keying controls. So he was back on the job. Mannion sat, head bent, monitoring his recorder. The room was filled with the keening staccato of the alien transmission.

"Getting anything on video?" I asked. Joyce shook his head. "Nothing, Captain. I've checked the whole spectrum, and this is all I get. It's coming in on about a dozen different frequencies; no FM."

"Any progress, Mannion?" I said.

He took off his headset. "It's the same thing, repeated over and over, just a short phrase. I'd have better luck if they'd vary it a little."

"Try sending," I said.

Joyce tuned the clatter down to a faint clicking, and switched his transmitter on. "You're on, Captain," he said.

"This is Captain Greylorn, UNACV Galahad; kindly identify yourself." I repeated this slowly, half a dozen times. It occurred to me that this was the first known time in history a human being had addressed a non-human intelligence. The last was a guess, but I couldn't interpret our guest's purposeful maneuverings as other than intelligent.

I checked with the bridge; no change. Suddenly the clatter stopped, leaving only the carrier hum.

"Can't you tune that whine out, Joyce?" I asked.

"No, sir," he replied. "That's a very noisy transmission. Sounds like maybe their equipment is on the blink."

We listened to the hum, waiting. Then the clatter began again.

"This is different," Mannion said. "It's longer."

I went back to the bridge, and waited for the next move from the stranger, or for word from Mannion. Every half hour I transmitted a call identifying us, followed by a sample of our language. I gave them English, Russian, and Standard Interlingua. I didn't know why, but somehow I had a faint hope they might understand some of it.

I stayed on the bridge when the watch changed. I had some food sent up, and slept a few hours on the OD's bunk.

Fine replaced Kramer on his watch when it rolled around. Apparently Kramer was out of circulation. At this point I did not feel inclined to pursue the point.

We had been at General Quarters for twenty-one hours when the wall annunciator hummed.

"Captain, this is Mannion. I've busted it...."

"I'll be right there," I said, and left at a run.

Mannion was writing as I entered ComSection. He stopped his recorder and offered me a sheet. "This is what I've got so far, Captain," he said.

I read: INVADER; THE MANCJI PRESENCE OPENS COMMUNICATIONS.

"That's a highly inflected version of early Interlingua, Captain," Mannion said. "After I taped it, I compensated it to take out the rise-and-fall tone, and then filtered out the static. There were a few sound substitutions to figure out, but I finally caught on. It still doesn't make much sense, but that's what it says."

"I wonder what we're invading," I said. "And what is the 'Mancji Presence'?"

"They just repeat that over and over," Mannion said. "They don't answer our call."

"Try translating into old Interlingua, adding their sound changes, and then feeding their own rise-and-fall routine to it," I said. "Maybe that will get a response."

I waited while Mannion worked out the message, then taped it on top of their whining tone pattern. "Put plenty of horse-power behind it," I said. "If their receivers are as shaky as their transmitter, they might not be hearing us."

We sent for five minutes, then tuned them back in and waited. There was a long silence from their side, then they came back with a long spluttering sing-song.

Mannion worked over it for several minutes. .ldThey must have understood us, here's what I get," he said:

THAT WHICH SWIMS IN THE MANCJI SEA; WE ARE AWARE THAT YOU HAVE THIS TRADE TONGUE. YOU RANGE FAR. IT IS OUR WHIM TO INDULGE YOU; WE ARE AMUSED THAT YOU PRESUME HERE; WE ACKNOWLEDGE YOUR INSOLENT DEMANDS.

"It looks like we're in somebody's back yard," I said. "They acknowledge our insolent demands, but they don't answer them." I thought a moment. "Send this," I said. "We'll out-strut them:"

THE MIGHTY WARSHIP GALAHAD REJECTS YOUR JURISDICTION.

TELL US THE NATURE OF YOUR DISTRESS AND WE MAY CHOOSE TO OFFER AID.

Mannion raised an eyebrow. "That ought to rock them," he said.

"They were eager to talk to us," I said. "That means they want something, in my opinion. And all the big talk sounds like a bluff of our own is our best line."

"Why do you want to antagonize them, Captain?" Joyce asked. "That ship is over a thousand times the size of this can."

"Joyce, I suggest you let me forget you're around," I said.

* * * *

The Mancji whine was added to my message, and it went out. Moments later this came back:

MANCJI HONOR DICTATES YOUR SAFE-CONDUCT; TALK IS WEARYING; WE FIND IT CONVENIENT TO SOLICIT A TRANSFER OF ELECTROSTATIC FORCE.

"What the devil does that mean?" I said. "Tell them to loosen up and explain themselves."

Mannion wrote out a straight query, and sent it. Again we waited for a reply.

It came, in a long windy paragraph stating that the Mancji found electro-static baths amusing, and that "crystallization" had drained their tanks. They wanted a flow of electrons from us to replenish their supply.

"This sounds like simple electric current they're talking about, Captain," Mannion said. "They want a battery charge."

"They seem to have power to burn," I said. "Why don't they generate their own juice? Ask them; and find out where they learned Interlingua."

Mannion sent again; the reply was slow in coming back. Finally we got it:

THE MANCJI DO NOT EMPLOY MASSIVE GENERATION-PIECE WHERE ACCUMULATOR-PIECE IS SUFFICIENT. THIS SIMPLE TRADE SPEECH IS OF OLD KNOWLEDGE. WE SELECT IT FROM SYMBOLS WE ARE PLEASED TO SENSE EMPATTERNED ON YOUR HULL.

That made some sort of sense, but I was intrigued by the reference to Interlingua as a trade language. I wanted to know where they had learned it. I couldn't help the hope I started building on the idea that this giant knew our colony, in spite of the fact that they were using an antique version of the language, predating Omega by several centuries.

I sent another query, but the reply was abrupt and told nothing except that Interlingua was of "old knowledge."

Then Mannion entered a long technical exchange, getting the details of the kind of electric power they wanted.

"We can give them what they want, no sweat, Captain," he said after half an hour's talk. "They want DC; 100 volt, 50 amp will do."

"Ask them to describe themselves," I directed. I was beginning to get an idea.

Mannion sent, got his reply. "They're molluscoid, Captain," he said. He looked shocked. "They weigh about two tons each."

"Ask them what they eat," I said.

I turned to Joyce as Mannion worked over the message. "Get Kramer up here, on the double," I said.

* * * *

Kramer came in five minutes later, looking drawn and rumpled. He stared at me sullenly.

"I'm releasing you from arrest temporarily on your own parole, Major," I said. "I want you to study the reply to our last transmission, and tell me what you can about it."

"Why me?" Kramer said. "I don't know what's going on." I didn't answer him.

There was a long tense half hour wait before Mannion copied out the reply that came in a stuttering nasal. He handed it to me.

As I had hoped, the message, after a preliminary recital of the indifference of the Mancji to biological processes of ingestion, recited a list of standard biochemical symbols.

"Can we eat this stuff?" I asked Kramer, handing him the sheet.

He studied it, and some of his accustomed swagger began to return. "I don't know what the flowery phrases are all about, but the symbols refer to common proteins, lipins, carbohydrates, vitamins, and biomins," he said. "What is this, a game?"

"All right, Mannion," I said. I was trying to hold back the excitement. "Ask them if they have fresh sources of these substances aboard."

The reply was quick; they did.

"Tell them we will exchange electric power for a supply of these foods. Tell them we want samples of half a dozen of the natural substances."

Again Mannion coded and sent, received and translated, sent again.

"They agree, Captain," he said at last. "They want us to fire a power lead out about a mile; they'll come in close and shoot us a specimen case with a flare on it. Then we can each check the other's merchandise."

"All right," I said. "We can use a ground-service cable; rig a pilot light on it, and kick it out, as soon as they get in close."

"We'll have to splice a couple of extra lengths to it," Mannion said.

"Go to it, Mannion," I said. "And send two of your men out to make the pick-up." This wasn't a communications job, but I wanted a reliable man handling it.

I returned to the bridge and keyed for Bourdon, directed him to arm two of his penetration missiles, lock them onto the stranger, and switch over to my control. With the firing key in my hand, I stood at the televideo screen and watched for any signs of treachery. The ship moved in, came to rest filling the screen.

Mannion's men reported out. I saw the red dot of our power lead move away, then a yellow point glowed on the side of the vast iodine-colored wall looming across the screen.

Nothing else emerged from the alien ship. The red pilot drifted across the face of the sphere. Mannion reported six thousand feet of cable out before the pilot disappeared abruptly.

"Captain," Mannion reported, "they're drawing power."

"O.K.," I said. "Let them have a sample, then shut down."

I waited, watching carefully, until Mannion reported the cannister inside.

"Kramer," I said. "Run me a fast check on the samples in that container."

Kramer was recovering his swagger. "You'll have to be a little more specific," he said. "Just what kind of analysis do you have in mind? Do you want a full…."

"I just want to know one thing, Kramer," I said. "Can we assimilate these substances, yes or no. If you don't feel like co-operating, I'll have you lashed to your bunk, and injected with them. You claim you're a medical officer; let's see you act like one." I turned my back to him.

Mannion called. "They say the juice we fed them was 'amusing,' Captain. I guess that means it's O.K."

"I'll let you know in a few minutes how their samples pan out," I said.

* * * *

Kramer took half an hour before reporting back. "I ran a simple check such as I normally use in a routine mess inspection," he began. He couldn't help trying to take the center of the stage to go into his Wise Doctor and Helpless Patient routine.

"Yes or no," I said.

"Yes, we can assimilate most of it," he said angrily. "There were six samples. Two were gelatinous substances, non-nutritive. Three were vegetable-like, bulky and fibrous, one with a high iodine content; the other was a very normal meaty specimen."

"Which should we take?" I said. "Remember your teeth when you answer."

"The high protein, the meaty one," he said. "Marked '6'."

I keyed for Mannion. "Tell them that in return for 1,000 KWH we require 3,000 kilos of sample six," I said.

Mannion reported back. "They agreed in a hurry, Captain. They seem to feel pretty good about the deal. They want to chat, now that they've got a bargain. I'm still taping a long tirade."

"Good," I said. "Better get ready to send about six men with an auxiliary pusher to bring home the bacon. You can start feeding them the juice again."

I turned to Kramer. He was staring at the video image. "Report yourself back to arrest in quarters, Kramer," I said. "I'll take your services today into account at your court-martial."

Kramer looked up, with a nasty grin. "I don't know what kind of talking oysters you're trafficking with, but I'd laugh like hell if they vaporized your precious tub as soon as they're through with you." He walked out.

Mannion called in again from ComSection. "Here's their last, Captain," he said. "They say we're lucky they had a good supply of this protein aboard. It's one of their most amusing foods. It's a creature they discovered in the wild state and it's very rare. The wild ones have died out, and only their domesticated herds exist."

"O.K., we're lucky," I said. "It better be good or we'll step up the amperage and burn their batteries for them."

"Here's more," Mannion said. "They say it will take a few hours to prepare the cargo. They want us to be amused."

I didn't like the delay, but it would take us about 10 hours to deliver the juice to them at the trickle rate they wanted. Since the sample was O.K., I was assuming the rest would be too. We settled down to wait.

I left Clay in charge on the bridge and made a tour of the ship. The meeting with the alien had apparently driven the mood of mutiny into the background. The men were quiet and busy. I went to my cabin and slept for a few hours.

* * * *

I was awakened by a call from Clay telling me that the alien had released his cargo for us. Mannion's crew was out making the pick-up. Before they had maneuvered the bulky cylinder to the cargo hatch, the alien released our power lead.

I called Kramer and told him to meet the incoming crew and open and inspect the cargo. If it was the same as the sample, I thought, we had made a terrific trade. Discipline would recover if the men felt we still had our luck.

Then Mannion called again. "Captain," he said excitedly, "I think there may be trouble coming. Will you come down, sir?"

"I'll go to the bridge, Mannion," I said. "Keep talking."

I tuned my speaker down low and listened to Mannion as I ran for the lift.

"They tell us to watch for a little display of Mancji power. They ran out some kind of antenna. I'm getting a loud static at the top of my short wave receptivity."

I ran the lift up and as I stepped onto the bridge I said, "Clay, stand by to fire."

As soon as the pick-up crew was reported in, I keyed course corrections to curve us off sharply from the alien. I didn't know what he had, but I liked the idea of putting space between us. My P-Missiles were still armed and locked.

Mannion called, "Captain, they say our fright is amusing, and quite justified."

I watched the televideo screen for the first sign of an attack. Suddenly the entire screen went white, then blanked. Miller, who had been at the scanner searching over the alien ship at close range, reeled out of his seat, clutching at his eyes. "My God, I'm blinded," he shouted.

Mannion called, "Captain, my receivers blew. I think every tube in the shack exploded!"

I jumped to the direct viewer. The alien hung there, turning away from us in a leisurely curve. There was no sign of whatever had blown us off the air. I held my key, but didn't press it. I told Clay to take Miller down to Medic. He was moaning and in severe pain.

Kramer reported in from the cargo deck. The cannister was inside now, coating up with frost. I told him to wait, then sent Chilcote, my demolition man, in to open it. Maybe it was booby-trapped. I stood by at the DVP and waited for other signs of Mancjo power to hit us. The general feeling was tense.

Apparently they were satisfied with one blast of whatever it was; they were dwindling away with no further signs of life.

After half an hour of tense alertness, I ordered the missiles disarmed.

I keyed for General. "Men, this is the Captain," I said. "It looks as though our first contact with an alien race has been successfully completed. He is now at a distance of three hundred and moving off fast. Our screens are blown, but there's no real damage. And we have a supply of fresh food aboard; now let's get back to business. That colony can't be far off."

That may have been rushing it some, but if the food supply we'd gotten was a dud, we were finished anyway.

We watched the direct-view screen till the ship was lost; then followed on radar.

"It's moving right along, Captain," Joyce said, "accelerating at about two gee's."

"Good riddance," Clay said. "I don't like dealing with armed maniacs."

"They were screwballs all right," I said, "but they couldn't have happened along at a better time. I only wish we had been in a position to squeeze a few answers out of them."

"Yes, sir," Clay said. "Now that the whole thing's over, I'm beginning to think of a lot of questions myself."

The annunciator hummed. I heard what sounded like hoarse breathing. I glanced at the indicator light. It was the cargo deck mike that was open.

I keyed. "If you have a report, Chilcote, go ahead," I said.

Suddenly someone was shouting into the mike, incoherently. I caught words, cursing. Then Chilcote's voice, "Captain," he said. "Captain, please come quick." There was a loud clatter, noise, then only the hum of the mike.

"Take over, Clay," I said, and started back to the cargo deck at a dead run.

* * * *

Men crowded the corridor, asking questions, milling. I forced my way through, found Kramer surrounded by men, shouting.

"Break this up," I shouted. "Kramer, what's your report?"

Chilcote walked past me, pale as chalk. I pushed through to Kramer.

"Get hold of yourself, and make your report, Kramer," I said. "What started this riot?"

Kramer stopped shouting, and stood looking at me, panting. The crowded men fell silent.

"I gave you a job to do, Major," I said; "opening a cargo can. Now you take it from there."

"Yeah, Captain," he said. "We got it open. No wires, no traps. We hauled the load out of the can on to the floor. It was one big frozen mass, wrapped up in some kind of netting. Then we pulled the covering off."

"All right, go ahead," I said.

"That load of fresh meat your star-born pals gave us consists of about six families of human beings; men, women, and children." Kramer was talking for the crowd now, shouting. "Those last should be pretty tender when you ration out our ounce a week, Captain."

The men milled, wide-eyed, open-mouthed, as I thrust through to the cargo lock. The door stood ajar and wisps of white vapor curled out into the passage.

I stepped through the door. It was bitter cold in the lock. Near the outer hatch the bulky cannister, rimed with white frost, lay in a pool of melting ice. Before it lay the half shrouded bulk that it had contained. I walked closer.

They were frozen together into one solid mass. Kramer was right. They were as human as I. Human corpses, stripped, packed together, frozen. I pulled back the lightly frosted covering, and studied the glazed white bodies.

Kramer called suddenly from the door. "You found your colonists, Captain. Now that your curiosity is satisfied, we can go back where we belong. Out here man is a tame variety of cattle. We're lucky they didn't know we were the same variety, or we'd be in their food lockers now ourselves. Now let's get started back. The men won't take 'no' for an answer."

I leaned closer, studying the corpses. "Come here, Kramer," I called. "I want to show you something."

"I've seen all there is to see in there," Kramer said. "We don't want to waste time; we want to change course now, right away."

* * * *

I walked back to the door, and as Kramer stepped back to let me precede him out the door, I hit him in the mouth with all my strength. His head snapped back against the frosted wall. Then he fell out into the passage.

I stepped over him. "Pick this up and put it in the brig," I said. The men in the corridor fell back, muttering. As they hauled Kramer upright I stepped through them and kept going, not running but wasting no time, toward the bridge. One wrong move on my part now and all their misery and fear would break loose in a riot the first act of which would be to tear me limb from limb.

I travelled ahead of the shock. Kramer had provided the diversion I had needed. Now I heard the sound of gathering violence growing behind me.

I was none too quick. A needler flashed at the end of the corridor just as the lift door closed. I heard the tiny projectile ricochet off the lift shaft.

I rode up, stepped onto the bridge and locked the lift. I keyed for Bourdon, and to my relief got a quick response. The panic hadn't penetrated to Missile Section yet.

"Bourdon, arm all batteries and lock onto that Mancji ship," I ordered. "On the triple."

I turned to Clay. "I'll take over, Clay," I said. "Alter course to intercept our late companion at two and one-half gee's."

Clay looked startled, but said only, "Aye, sir."

I keyed for a general announcement. "This is the Captain," I said. "Action station, all hands in loose acceleration harness. We're going after Big Brother. You're in action against the enemy now, and from this point on I'm remembering. You men have been having a big time letting off steam; that's over now. All sections report."

One by one the sections reported in, all but Med. and Admin. Well, I could spare them for the present. The pressure was building now, as we blasted around in a hairpin curve, our acceleration picking up fast.

I ordered Joyce to lock his radar on target, and switch over to autopilot control. Then I called Power Section.

"I'm taking over all power control from the bridge," I said. "All personnel out of the power chamber and control chamber."

The men were still under control, but that might not last long. I had to have the entire disposition of the ship's power, control, and armament under my personal direction for a few hours at least.

Missile Section reported all missiles armed and locked on target. I acknowledged and ordered the section evacuated. Then I turned to Clay and Joyce. Both were plenty nervous now; they didn't know what was brewing.

"Lieutenant Clay," I said. "Report to your quarters; Joyce, you too. I want to congratulate both of you on a soldierly performance these last few hours."

They left without protest. I was aware that they didn't want to be too closely identified with the Captain when things broke loose.

* * * *

I keyed for a video check of the interior of the lift as it started back up. It was empty. I locked it up.

Now we were steady on course, and had reached our full two and a half gees. I could hardly stand under that acceleration, but I had one more job to do before I could take a break.

Feet dragging, I unlocked the lift and rode it down. I was braced for violence as I opened the lift door, but I was lucky. There was no one in the corridor. I could hear shouts in the distance. I dragged myself along to Power Section and pushed inside. A quick check of control settings showed everything as I had ordered it. Back in the passage, I slammed the leaded vault door to and threw in the combination lock. Now only I could open it without blasting.

* * * *

Control Section was next. It, too, was empty, all in order. I locked it, and started across to Missiles. Two men appeared at the end of the passage, having as hard a time as I was. I entered the cross corridor just in time to escape a volley of needler shots. The mutiny was in the open now, for sure.

I kept going, hearing more shouting. I was sure the men I had seen were heading for Power and Control. They'd get a surprise. I hoped I could beat them to the draw at Missiles, too.

As I came out in B corridor, twenty feet from Missiles, I saw that I had cut it a bit fine. Three men, crawling, were frantically striving against the multi-gee field to reach the door before me. Their faces were running with sweat, purple with exertion.

I had a slight lead; it was too late to make a check inside before locking up. The best I could hope for was to lock the door before they reached it.

I drew my Browning and started for the door. They saw me and one reached for his needler.

"Don't try it," I called. I concentrated on the door, reached it, swung it closed, and as I threw in the lock a needler cracked. I whirled and fired. The man in the rear had stopped and aimed as the other two came on. He folded. The other two kept coming.

I was tired. I wanted a rest. "You're too late," I said. "No one but the Captain goes in there now." I stopped talking, panting. I had to rest. The two came on. I wondered why they struggled so desperately after they were beaten. My thinking was slowing down.

I suddenly realized they might be holding me for the crowd to arrive. I shuffled backwards towards the cross corridor. I barely made it. Two men on a shuttle cart whirled around the corner a hundred feet aft. I lurched into my shelter in a hail of needler fire. One of the tiny slugs stung through my calf and ricocheted down the passage.

I called to the two I had raced; "Tell your boys if they ever want to open that door, just see the Captain."

I hesitated, considering whether or not to make a general statement.

"What the hell," I decided. "They all know there's a mutiny now. It won't hurt to get in a little life-insurance."

I keyed my mike. "This is the Captain," I said. "This ship is now in a state of mutiny. I call on all loyal members of the Armed Forces to resist the mutineers actively, and to support their Commander. Your ship is in action against an armed enemy. I assure you this mutiny will fail, and those who took part in it will be treated as traitors to their Service, their homes, and their own families who now rely on them.

"We are accelerating at two and one-half gravities, locked on a collision course with the Mancji ship. The mutineers cannot enter the Bridge, Power, Control, or Missiles Sections since only I have the combination. Thus they're doomed to failure.

"I am now returning to the Bridge to direct the attack and destruction of the enemy. If I fail to reach the Bridge, we will collide with the enemy in less than three hours, and our batteries will blow."

Now my problem was to make good my remark about returning to the Bridge. The shuttle had not followed me, presumably fearing ambush. I took advantage of their hesitation to cross back to corridor A at my best speed. I paused once to send a hail of needles ricocheting down the corridor behind me, and I heard a yelp from around the corner. Those needles had a fantastic velocity, and bounced around a long time before stopping.

At the corridor, I lay down on the floor for a rest and risked a quick look. A group of three men were bunched around the Control Section door, packing smashite in the hairline crack around it. That wouldn't do them any good, but it did occupy their attention.

I faded back into the cross passage, and keyed the mike. I had to give them a chance.

"This is the Captain," I said. "All personnel not at their action stations are warned for the last time to report there immediately. Any man found away from his post from this point on is in open mutiny and can expect the death penalty. This is the last warning."

The men in the corridor had heard, but a glance showed they paid no attention to what they considered an idle threat. They didn't know how near I was.

I drew my needler, set it for continuous fire, pushed into the corridor, aimed, and fired. I shot to kill. All three sprawled away from the door, riddled, as the metal walls rang with the cloud of needles.

I looked both ways, then rose, with effort, and went to the bodies. I recognized them as members of Kirschenbaum's Power Section crew. I keyed again as I moved on toward the lift at the end of the corridor, glancing back as I went.

"Corley, Mac Williams, and Reardon have been shot for mutiny in the face of the enemy," I said. "Let's hope they're the last to insist on my enforcing the death penalty."

* * * *

Behind me, at the far end of the corridor, men appeared again. I flattened myself in a doorway, sprayed needles toward them, and hoped for the best. I heard the singing of a swarm past me, but felt no hits. The mutineers offered a bigger target, and I thought I saw someone fall. As they all moved back out of sight, I made another break for the lift.

I was grateful they hadn't had time to organize. I kept an eye to the rear, and sent a hail of needles back every time a man showed himself. They ducked out to fire every few seconds, but not very effectively. I had an advantage over them; I was fighting for the success of the mission and for my life, with no one to look to for help; they were each one of a mob, none eager to be a target, each willing to let the other man take the risk.

I was getting pretty tired. I was grateful for the extra stamina and wind that daily calisthenics in a high-gee field had given me; without that I would have collapsed before now; but I was almost ready to drop. I had my eyes fixed on the lift door; each step, inch by inch, was an almost unbearable effort. With only a few feet to go, my knees gave; I went down on all fours. Another batch of needles sang around me, and vivid pain seared my left arm. It helped. The pain cleared my head, spurred me. I rose and stumbled against the door.

Now the combination. I fought a numbing desire to faint as I pressed the lock control; three, five, two, five…

I twisted around as I heard a sound. The shuttle was coming toward me, men lying flat on it, protected by the bumper plate. I leaned against the lift door, and loosed a stream of needles against the side of the corridor, banking them toward the shuttle. Two men rolled off the shuttle in a spatter of blood. Another screamed, and a hand waved above the bumper. I needled it.

* * * *

I wondered how many were on the shuttle. It kept coming. The closer it came, the more effective my bank shots were. I wondered why it failed to return my fire. Then a hand rose in an arc and a choke bomb dropped in a short curve to the floor. It rolled to my feet, just starting to spew. I kicked it back. The shuttle stopped, backed away from the bomb. A jet of brown gas was playing from it now. I aimed my needler, and sent it spinning back farther. Then I turned to my lock.

Now a clank of metal against metal sounded behind me; from the side passage a figure in radiation armor moved out. The suit was self-powered and needle proof. I sent a concentrated blast at the head, as the figure awkwardly tottered toward me, ungainly in the multi-gee field. The needles hit, snapped the head back. The suited figure hesitated, arms spread, stepped back and fell with a thunderous crash. I had managed to knock him off balance, maybe stun him.

I struggled to remember where I was in the code sequence; I went on, keyed the rest. I pushed; nothing. I must have lost count. I started again.

I heard the armored man coming on again. The needler trick wouldn't work twice. I kept working. I had almost completed the sequence when I felt the powered grip of the suited man on my arm. I twisted, jammed the needler against his hand, and fired. The arm flew back, and even through the suit I heard his wrist snap. My own hand was numb from the recoil. The other arm of the suit swept down and struck my wounded arm. I staggered away from the door, dazed with the pain.

I side-stepped in time to miss another ponderous blow. Under two and a half gees, the man in the suit was having a hard time, even with power assisted controls. I felt that I was fighting a machine instead of a man.

As he stepped toward me again, I aimed at his foot. A concentrated stream of needles hit, like a metallic fire hose, knocked the foot aside, toppled the man again. I staggered back to my door.

But now I realized I couldn't risk opening it; even if I got in, I couldn't keep my suited assailant from crowding in with me. Already he was up, lurching toward me. I had to draw him away from the door.

The shuttle sat unmoving. The mob kept its distance. I wondered why no one was shooting; I guessed they had realized that if I were killed there would be no way to enter the vital control areas of the ship; they had to take me alive.

* * * *

I made it past the clumsy armored man and started down the corridor toward the shuttle. I moved as slowly as I could while still eluding him. He lumbered after me. I reached the shuttle; a glance showed no one alive there. Two men lay across it. I pulled myself onto it and threw in the forward lever. The shuttle rolled smoothly past the armored man, striking him a glancing blow that sent him down again. Those falls, in the multi-gee field, were bone crushing. He didn't get up.

I reached the door again, rolled off the shuttle, and reached for the combination. I wished now I'd used a shorter one. I started again; heard a noise behind me. As I turned, a heavy weight crushed me against the door.

I was held rigid, my chest against the combination key. The pressure was cracking my ribs and still it increased. I twisted my head, gasping. The shuttle held me pinned to the door. The man I had assumed out of action was alive enough to hold the lever down with savage strength. I tried to shout, to remind him that without me to open the doors, they were powerless to save the ship. I couldn't speak. I tasted blood in my mouth, and tried to breathe. I couldn't. I passed out.

CHAPTER 2

I emerged into consciousness to find the pressure gone, but a red haze of pain remained. I lay on my back and saw men sitting on the floor around me.

A blow from somewhere made my head ring. I tried to sit up. I couldn't make it. Then Kramer was beside me, slipping a needle into my arm. He looked pretty bad himself. His face was bandaged heavily, and one eye was purple. He spoke in a muffled voice through stiff jaws. His tone was deliberate.

"This will keep you conscious enough to answer a few questions," he said. "Now you're going to give me the combinations to the locks so we can call off this suicide run; then maybe I'll doctor you up."

I didn't answer.

"The time for clamming up is over, you stupid braggard," Kramer said. He raised his fist and drove a hard punch into my chest. I guess it was his shot that kept me conscious. I couldn't breathe for a while, until Kramer gave me a few whiffs of oxygen. I wondered if he was fool enough to think I might give up my ship.

After a while my head cleared a little. I tried to say something. I got out a couple of croaks, and then found my voice.

"Kramer," I said.

He leaned over me. "I'm listening," he said.

"Take me to the lift. Leave me there alone. That's your only chance." It seemed to me like a long speech, but nothing happened. Kramer went away, came back. He showed me a large scalpel from his medical kit. "I'm going to start operating on your face. I'll make you into a museum freak. Maybe if you start talking soon enough I'll change my mind."

I could see the watch on his wrist. My mind worked very slowly. I had trouble getting any air into my lungs. We would intercept in one hour and ten minutes.

It seemed simple to me. I had to get back to the Bridge before we hit. I tried again. "We only have an hour," I said.

Kramer lost control. He jabbed the knife at my face, screeching through gritted teeth. I jerked my head aside far enough that the scalpel grated along my cheekbone instead of slashing my mouth. I hardly felt it.

"We're not dying because you were a fool," Kramer yelled. "I've taken over; I've relieved you as unfit for command. Now open up this ship or I'll slice you to ribbons." He held the scalpel under my nose in a fist trembling with fury. The chrome plated blade had a thin film of pink on it.

I got my voice going again. "I'm going to destroy the Mancji ship," I said. "Take me to the lift and leave me there." I tried to add a few words, but had to stop and work on breathing again for a while. Kramer disappeared.

I realized I was not fully in command of my senses. I was clamped in a padded claw. I wanted to roll over. I tried hard, and made it. I could hear Kramer talking, others answering, but it seemed too great an effort to listen to the words.

I was lying on my face now, head almost against the wall. There was a black line in front of me, a door. My head cleared a bit. It must have been Kramer's shot working on me. I turned my head and saw Kramer standing now with half a dozen others, all talking at once. Apparently Kramer's display of uncontrolled temper had the others worried. They wanted me alive. Kramer didn't like anyone criticizing him. The argument was pretty violent. There was scuffling—and shouts.

I saw that I lay about twenty feet from the lift; too far. The door before me, if I remembered the ship's layout, was a utility room, small and containing nothing but a waste disposal hopper. But it did have a bolt on the inside, like every other room on the ship.

I didn't stop to think about it; I started trying to get up. If I'd thought I would have known that at the first move from me all seven of them would land on me at once. I concentrated on getting my hands under me, to push up. I heard a shout, and turning my head, saw Kramer swinging at someone. I went on with my project.

Hands under my chest, I raised myself a little, and got a knee up. I felt broken rib ends grating, but felt no pain, just the padded claw. Then I was weaving on all fours. I looked up, spotted the latch on the door, and put everything I had into lunging at it. My finger hit it, the door swung in, and I fell on my face; but I was half in. Another lunge and I was past the door, kicking it shut as I lay on the floor, reaching for the lock control. Just as I flipped it with an extended finger, someone hit the door from outside, a second too late.

It was dark, and I lay on my back on the floor, and felt strange short-circuited stabs of what would have been agonizing pain running through my chest and arm. I had a few minutes to rest now, before they blasted the door open.

I hated to lose like this, not because we were beaten, but because we were giving up. My poor world, no longer fair and green, had found the strength to send us out as her last hope. But somewhere out here in the loneliness and distance we had lost our courage. Success was at our fingertips, if we could have found it; instead, in panic and madness, we were destroying ourselves.

* * * *

My mind wandered; I imagined myself on the Bridge, half-believed I was there. I was resting on the OD bunk, and Clay was standing beside me. A long time seemed to pass…. Then I remembered I was on the floor, bleeding internally, in a tiny room that would soon lose its door. But there was someone standing beside me.

I didn't feel too disappointed at being beaten; I hadn't hoped for much more than a breather, anyway. I wondered why this fellow had abandoned his action station to hide there. The door was still shut. He must have been there all along, but I hadn't seen him when I came in. He stood over me, wearing greasy overalls, and grinned down at me. He raised his hand. I was getting pretty indifferent to blows; I couldn't feel them.

The hand went up, the man straightened and held a fairly snappy salute. "Sir," he said. "Space'n first class Thomas."

I didn't feel like laughing or cheering or anything else; I just took it as it came.

"At ease, Thomas," I managed to say. "Why aren't you at your duty station?" I went spinning off somewhere after that oration.

Thomas was squatting beside me now. "Cap'n, you're hurt, ain't you? I was wonderin' why you was down here layin down in my 'Sposal station."

"A scratch," I said. I thought about it for a while. Thomas was doing something about my chest. This was Thomas' disposal station. Thomas owned it. I wondered if a fellow could make a living with such a small place way out here, with just an occasional tourist coming by. I wondered why I didn't send one of them for help; I needed help for some reason....

"Cap'n, I been overhaulin' my converter units, I jist come in. How long you been in here, Cap'n?" Thomas was worried about something.

I tried hard to think. I hadn't been here very long; just a few minutes. I had come here to rest.... Then suddenly I was thinking clearly again.

* * * *

Whatever Thomas was, he was apparently on my side, or at least neutral. He didn't seem to be aware of the mutiny. I realized that he had bound my chest tightly with strips of shirt; it felt better.

"What are you doing in here, Thomas?" I asked. "Don't you know we're in action against a hostile ship?"

Thomas looked surprised. "This here's my action station, Cap'n," he said. "I'm a Waste Recovery Technician, First Class, I keep the recovery system operatin'."

"You just stay in here?" I asked.

"No, sir," Thomas said. "I check through the whole system. We got three main disposal points and lots a little ones, an' I have to keep everything operatin'. Otherwise this ship would be in a bad way, Cap'n."

"How did you get in here?" I asked. I looked around the small room. There was only one door, and the gray bulk of the converter unit which broke down wastes into their component elements for re-use nearly filled the tiny space.

"I come in through the duct, Cap'n," Thomas said. "I check the ducts every day. You know, Cap'n," he said shaking his head, "they's some bad laid-out ductin' in this here system. If I didn't keep after it, you'd be gettin' clogged ducts all the time. So I jist go through the system and keep her clear."

From somewhere, hope began again. "Where do these ducts lead?" I asked. I wondered how the man could ignore the mutiny going on around him.

"Well, sir, one leads to the mess; that's the big one. One leads to the wardroom, and the other one leads up to the Bridge."

My God, I thought, the Bridge.

"How big are they?" I asked. "Could I get through them?"

"Oh, sure, Cap'n," Thomas said. "You can get through 'em easy. But are you sure you feel like inspectin' with them busted ribs?"

I was beginning to realize that Thomas was not precisely a genius. "I can make it," I said.

"Cap'n," Thomas said diffidently, "it ain't none a my business, but don't you think maybe I better get the doctor for ya?"

"Thomas," I said, "maybe you don't know; there's a mutiny under way aboard this ship. The doctor is leading it. I want to get to the Bridge in the worst way. Let's get started."

Thomas looked very shocked. "Cap'n, you mean you was hurt by somebody? I mean you didn't have a fall or nothin', you was beat up?" He stared at me with an expression of incredulous horror.

"That's about the size of it," I said. I managed to sit up. Thomas jumped forward and helped me to my feet. Then I saw that he was crying.

"You can count on me, Cap'n," he said. "Jist lemme know who done it, an' I'll feed 'em into my converter."

I stood leaning against the wall, waiting for my head to stop spinning. Breathing was difficult, but if I kept it shallow, I could manage. Thomas was opening a panel on the side of the converter unit.

"It's O.K. to go in Cap'n," he said. "She ain't operatin'."

The pull of the two and a half gees seemed to bother him very little. I could barely stand under it, holding on. Thomas saw my wavering step and jumped to help me. He boosted me into the chamber of the converter and pointed out an opening near the top, about twelve by twenty-four inches.

"That there one is to the Bridge, Cap'n," he said. "If you'll start in there, sir, I'll follow up."

* * * *

I thrust head and shoulders into the opening. Inside it was smooth metal, with no handholds. I clawed at it trying to get farther in. The pain stabbed at my chest.

"Cap'n, they're workin' on the door," Thomas said. "They already been at it for a little while. We better get goin'."

"You'd better give me a push, Thomas," I said. My voice echoed hollowly down the duct.

Thomas crowded into the chamber behind me then, lifting my legs and pushing. I eased into the duct. The pain was not so bad now.

"Cap'n, you gotta use a special kinda crawl to get through these here ducts," Thomas said. "You grip your hands together out in front of ya, and then bend your elbows. When your elbows jam against the side of the duct, you pull forward."

I tried it; it was slow, but it worked.

"Cap'n," Thomas said behind me. "We got about seven minutes now to get up there. I set the control on the converter to start up in ten minutes. I think we can make it O.K., and ain't nobody else comin' this way with the converter goin'. I locked the control panel so they can't shut her down."

That news spurred me on. With the converter in operation, the first step in the cycle was the evacuation of the ducts to a near-perfect vacuum. When that happened, we would die instantly with ruptured lungs; then our dead bodies would be sucked into the chamber and broken down into useful raw materials. I hurried.

I tried to orient myself. The duct paralleled the corridor. It would continue in that direction for about fifteen feet, and would then turn upward, since the Bridge was some fifteen feet above this level. I hitched along, and felt the duct begin to trend upward.

"You'll have to get on your back here, Cap'n," Thomas said. "She widens out on the turn."

I managed to twist over. Thomas was helping me by pushing at my feet. As I reached a near-vertical position, I felt a metal rod under my hand. That was a relief; I had been expecting to have to go up the last stretch the way a mountain climber does a rock chimney, back against one wall and feet against the other.

I hauled at the rod, and found another with my other hand. Below, Thomas boosted me. I groped up and got another, then another. The remaining slight slant of the duct helped. Finally my feet were on the rods. I clung, panting. The heat in the duct was terrific. Then I went on up. That was some shot Kramer had given me.

* * * *

Above I could see the end of the duct faintly in the light coming up through the open chamber door from the utility room. I remembered the location of the disposal slot on the Bridge now; it had been installed in the small apartment containing a bunk and a tiny galley for the use of the Duty Officer during long watches on the Bridge.

I reached the top of the duct and pushed against the slot cover. It swung out easily. I could see the end of the chart table, and beyond, the dead radar screen. I reached through and heaved myself partly out. I nearly fainted at the stab from my ribs as my weight went on my chest. My head sang. The light from below suddenly went out. I heard a muffled clank; then a hum began, echoing up the duct.

"She's closed and started cyclin' the air out, Cap'n," Thomas said calmly. "We got about half a minute."

I clamped my teeth together and heaved again. Below me Thomas waited quietly. He couldn't help me now. I got my hands flat against the bulkhead and thrust. The air was whistling around my face. Papers began to swirl off the chart table. I twisted my body frantically, kicking loose from the grip of the slot, fighting the sucking pull of air. I fell to the floor inside the room, the slot cover slamming behind me. I staggered to my feet. I pried at the cover, but I couldn't open it against the vacuum. Then it budged, and Thomas' hand came through. The metal edge cut into it, blood started, but the cover was held open half an inch. I reached the chart table, almost falling over my leaden feet, seized a short permal T-square, and levered the cover up. Once started, it went up easily. Thomas face appeared, drawn and pale, eyes closed against the dust being whirled into his face. He got his arms through, heaved himself a little higher. I seized his arm and pulled. He scrambled through.

I knocked the T-square out of the way and the cover snapped down. Then I slid to the floor, not exactly out, but needing a break pretty bad. Thomas brought bedding from the OD bunk and made me comfortable on the floor.

"Thomas," I said, "when I think of what the security inspectors who approved the plans for this arrangement are going to say when I call this little back door to their attention, it almost makes it worth the trouble."

"Yes, sir," Thomas said. He sprawled on the deck and looked around the Bridge, staring at the unfamiliar screens, indicator dials, controls.

* * * *

From where I lay, I could see the direct vision screen. I wasn't sure, but I thought the small bright object in the center of it might be our target. Thomas looked at the dead radar screen, then said, "Cap'n, that there radarscope out of action?"

"It sure is, Thomas," I said. "Our unknown friends blew the works before they left us." I was surprised that he recognized a radarscope.

"Mind if I take a look at it, Cap'n?" he said.

"Go ahead," I replied. I tried to explain the situation to Thomas. The elapsed time since we had started our pursuit was two hours and ten minutes; I wanted to close to no more than a twenty mile gap before launching my missiles; and I had better alert my interceptor missiles in case the Mancji hit first.

Thomas had the cover off the radar panel and was probing around. He pulled a blackened card out of the interior of the panel.

"Looks like they overloaded the fuse," Thomas said. "Got any spares, Cap'n?"

"Right beside you in the cabinet," I said. "How do you know your way around a radar set, Thomas?"

Thomas grinned. "I useta be a radar technician third before I got inta waste disposal," he said. "I had to change specialities to sign on for this cruise."

I had an idea there'd be an opening for Thomas a little higher up when this was over.

I asked him to take a look at the televideo, too. I was beginning to realize that Thomas was not really simple; he was merely uncomplicated.

"Tubes blowed here, Cap'n," he reported. "Like as if you was to set her up to high mag right near a sun; she was overloaded. I can fix her easy if we got the spares."

I didn't take time to try to figure that one out. I could feel the dizziness coming on again.

"Thomas," I called, "let me know when we're at twenty miles from target." I wanted to tell him more, but I could feel consciousness draining away. "Then…" I managed, "first aid kit…shot…."

I could still hear Thomas. I was flying away, whirling, but I could hear his voice. "Cap'n, I could fire your missiles now, if you was to want me to," he was saying. I struggled to speak. "No. Wait." I hoped he heard me.

* * * *

I floated a long time in a strange state between coma and consciousness. The stuff Kramer had given me was potent. It kept my mind fairly clear even when my senses were out of action. I thought about the situation aboard my ship.

I wondered what Kramer and his men were planning now, how they felt about having let me slip through their fingers. The only thing they could try now was blasting their way into the Bridge. They'd never make it. The designers of these ships were not unaware of the hazards of space life; the Bridge was an unassailable fortress. They couldn't possibly get to it.

I guessed that Kramer was having a pretty rough time of it now. He had convinced the men that we were rushing headlong to sure destruction at the hands of the all-powerful Mancji, and that their Captain was a fool. Now he was trapped with them in the panic he had helped to create. I thought that in all probability they had torn him apart.

I wavered in and out of consciousness. It was just as well; I needed the rest. Then I heard Thomas calling me. "We're closin' now, Cap'n," he said. "Wake up, Cap'n, only twenty-three miles now."

"Okay," I said. My body had been preparing itself for this, now it was ready again. I felt the needle in my arm. That helped, too.

"Hand me the intercom, Thomas," I said. He placed the mike in my hand. I keyed for a general announcement.

"This is the Captain," I said. I tried to keep my voice as steady as possible. "We are now at a distance of twenty-one miles from the enemy. Stand by for missile launching and possible evasive action. Damage control crews on the alert." I paused for breath.

"Now we're going to take out the Mancji ship, men," I said. "All two miles of it."

I dropped the mike and groped for the firing key. Thomas handed it to me.

"Cap'n," he said, bending over me. "I notice you got the selector set for your chemical warheads. You wouldn't want me to set up pluto heads for ya, would ya, Cap'n?"

"No, thanks, Thomas," I said. "Chemical is what I want. Stand by to observe." I pressed the firing key.

Thomas was at the radarscope. "Missiles away, Cap'n. Trackin' O.K. Looks like they'll take out the left half a that dumbbell."

I found the mike again. "Missiles homing on target," I said. "Strike in thirty-five seconds. You'll be interested to know we're employing chemical warheads. So far there is no sign of offense or defense from the enemy." I figured the news would shock a few mutineers. David wasn't even using his slingshot on Goliath. He was going after him bare-handed. I wanted to scare some kind of response out of them. I needed a few clues as to what was going on below.

I got it. Joyce's voice came from the wall annunciator. "Captain, this is Lt. Joyce reporting." He sounded scared all the way through, and desperate. "Sir, the mutiny has been successfully suppressed by the loyal members of the crew. Major Kramer is under arrest. We're prepared to go on with the search for the Omega Colony. But Sir…" he paused, gulping. "We ask you to change course now before launching any effective attack. We still have a chance. Maybe they won't bother with us when those firecrackers go off…"

* * * *

I watched the direct vision screen. Zero second closed in. And on the screen the face of the left hand disk of the Mancji ship was lit momentarily by a brilliant spark of yellow, then another. A discoloration showed dimly against the dark metallic surface. It spread, and a faint vapor formed over it. Now tiny specs could be seen moving away from the ship. The disk elongated, with infinite leisure, widening.

"What's happenin'? Cap'n?" Thomas asked. He was staring at the scope in fascination. "They launchin' scouts, or what?"

"Take a look here, Thomas," I said. "The ship is breaking up."

The disk was an impossibly long ellipse now, surrounded by a vast array of smaller bodies, fragments and contents of the ship. Now the stricken globe moved completely free of its companion. It rotated, presenting a crescent toward us, then wheeled farther as it receded from its twin, showing its elongation. The sphere had split wide open. Now the shattered half itself separated into two halves, and these in turn crumbled, strewing debris in a widening spiral.

"My God, Cap'n," Thomas said in awe. "That's the greatest display I ever seen. And all it took to set her off was 200 kilos a PBL. Now that's somethin'."

I keyed the mike again. "This is the Captain," I said. "I want ten four-man patrols ready to go out in fifteen minutes. The enemy ship has been put out of action and is now in a derelict condition. I want only one thing from her; one live prisoner. All Section chiefs report to me on the Bridge on the triple."

"Thomas," I said, "go down in the lift and open up for the Chiefs. Here's the release key for the combination; you know how to operate it?"

"Sure, Cap'n; but are you sure you want to let them boys in here after the way they jumped you an' all?"

I opened my mouth to answer, but he beat me to it. "Fergit I asked ya that, Cap'n, pleasir. You ain't been wrong yet."

"It's O.K., Thomas," I said. "There won't be any more trouble."

* * * *

EPILOGUE

On the eve of the twentieth anniversary of Reunion Day, a throng of well-heeled celebrants filled the dining room and overflowed onto the terraces of the Star Tower Dining Room, from whose 5,700 foot height above the beaches, the Florida Keys, a hundred miles to the south, were visible on clear days.

The *Era* reporter stood beside the vast glass entry way surveying the crowd, searching for celebrities from whom he might elicit bits of color to spice the day's transmission.

At the far side of the room, surrounded by chattering admirers, stood the Ambassador from the New Terran Federation; a portly, graying, jolly ex-Naval officer. A minor actress passed at close range, looking the other way. A cabinet member stood at the bar talking earnestly to a ball player, ignoring a group of hopeful reporters and fans.

The *Era* stringer, an experienced hand, passed over the hard pressed VIP's near the center of the room and started a face-by-face check of the less gregarious diners seated at obscure tables along the sides of the room.

He was in luck; the straight-backed gray-haired figure in the dark civilian suit, sitting alone at a tiny table in an alcove, caught his eye. He moved closer, straining for a clear glimpse through the crowd. Then he was sure. He had the biggest possible catch of the day in his sights; Admiral of Fleets Frederick Greylorn.

The reporter hesitated; he was well aware of the Admiral's reputation for near-absolute silence on the subject of his already legendary cruise, the fabulous voyage of the *Galahad*. He couldn't just barge in on the Admiral and demand answers, as was usual with publicity-hungry politicians and show people. He could score the biggest story of the century today; but he had to hit him right.

You couldn't hope to snow a man like the Admiral; he wasn't somebody you could push around. You could sense the solid iron of him from here.

Nobody else had noticed the solitary diner. The *Era* man drifted closer, moving unhurriedly, thinking furiously. It was no good trying some tricky approach; his best bet was the straight-from-the-shoulder bit. No point in hesitating. He stopped beside the table.

The Admiral was looking out across the Gulf. He turned and glanced up at the reporter.

The news man looked him squarely in the eye. "I'm a reporter, Admiral," he said. "Will you talk to me?"

The Admiral nodded to the seat across from him. "Sit down," he said. He glanced around the room.

The reporter caught the look. "I'll keep it light, sir," he said. "I don't want company either." That was being frank.

* * * *

"You want the answers to some questions, don't you?" the Admiral said.

"Why, yes, sir," the reporter said. He started to inconspicuously key his pocket recorder, but caught himself. "May I record your remarks, Admiral?" he said. Frankness all the way.

"Go ahead," said the Admiral.

"Now, Admiral," the reporter began, "the Terran public has of course…"

"Never mind the patter, son," the Admiral said mildly. "I know what the questions are. I've read all the memoirs of the crew. They've been coming out at the rate of about two a year for some time now. I had my own reasons for not wanting to add anything to my official statement."

The Admiral poured wine into his glass. "Excuse me," he said. "Will you join me?" He signalled the waiter.

"Another wine glass, please," he said. He looked at the golden wine in the glass, held it up to the light. "You know, the Florida wines are as good as any in the world," he said. "That's not to say the California and Ohio wines aren't good. But this Flora Pinellas is a genuine original, not an imitation Rhine; and it compares favorably with the best of the old vintages, particularly the '87."

The glass arrived and the waiter poured. The reporter had the wit to remain silent.

* * * *

"The first question is usually, how did I know I could take the Mancji ship. After all, it was big, vast. It loomed over us like a mountain. The Mancji themselves weighed almost two tons each; they liked six gee gravity. They blasted our communication off the air, just for practice. They talked big, too. We were invaders in their territory. They were amused by us. So where did I get the notion that our attack would be anything more than a joke to them? That's the big question." The Admiral shook his head.

"The answer is quite simple. In the first place, they were pulling six gees by using a primitive dumbbell configuration. The only reason for that type of layout, as students of early space vessel design can tell you, is to simplify setting up a gee field effect using centrifugal force. So they obviously had no gravity field generators.

"Then their transmission was crude. All they had was simple old-fashioned short-range radio, and even that was noisy and erratic. And their reception was as bad. We had to use a kilowatt before they could pick it up at 200 miles. We didn't know then it was all organically generated; that they had no equipment."

The Admiral sipped his wine, frowning at the recollection. "I was pretty sure they were bluffing when I changed course and started after them. I had to hold our acceleration down to two and a half gees because I had to be able to move around the ship. And at that acceleration we gained on them. They couldn't beat us. And it wasn't because they couldn't take high gees; they liked six for comfort, you remember. No, they just didn't have the power."

* * * *

The Admiral looked out the window.

"Add to that the fact that they apparently couldn't generate ordinary electric current. I admit that none of this was conclusive, but after all, if I was wrong we were sunk anyway. When Thomas told me the nature of the damage to our radar and communications systems, that was another hint. Their big display of Mancji power was just a blast of radiation right across the communication spectrum; it burned tubes and blew fuses; nothing else. We were back in operation an hour after our attack.

"The evidence was there to see, but there's something about giant size that gets people rattled. Size alone doesn't mean a thing. It's rather like the bluff the Soviets ran on the rest of the world for a couple of decades back in the war era, just because they sprawled across half the globe. They were a giant, though it was mostly frozen desert. When the showdown came they didn't have it. They were a pushover.

"All right, the next question is why did I choose H. E. instead of going in with everything I had? That's easy, too. What I wanted was information, not revenge. I still had the heavy stuff in reserve and ready to go if I needed it, but first I had to try to take them alive. Vaporizing them wouldn't have helped our position. And I was lucky; it worked.

"The, ah, confusion below evaporated as soon as the Section chiefs got a look at the screens and realized that we had actually knocked out the Mancji. We matched speeds with the wreckage and the patrols went out to look for a piece of ship with a survivor in it. If we'd had no luck we would have tackled the other half of the ship, which was still intact and moving off fast. But we got quite a shock when we found the nature of the wreckage." The Admiral grinned.

"Of course today everybody knows all about the Mancji hive intelligence, and their evolutionary history. But we were pretty startled to find that the only wreckage consisted of the Mancji themselves, each two-ton slug in his own hard chitin shell. Of course, a lot of the cells were ruptured by the explosions, but most of them had simply disassociated from the hive mass as it broke up. So there was no ship; just a cluster of cells like a giant bee hive, and mixed up among the slugs, the damnedest collection of loot you can imagine. The odds and ends they'd stolen and tucked away in the hive during a couple hundred years of camp-following.

"The patrols brought a couple of cells alongside, and Mannion went out to try to establish contact. Sure enough, he got a very faint transmission, on the same bands as before. The cells were talking to each other in their own language. They ignored Mannion even though his transmission must have blanketed everything within several hundred miles. We eventually brought one of them into the cargo lock and started trying different wave-lengths on it. Then Kramer had the idea of planting a couple of electrodes and shooting a little juice to it. Of course, it loved the DC, but as soon as we tried AC, it gave up. So we had a long talk with it and found out everything we needed to know.

* * * *

"It was a four-week run to the nearest outpost planet of the New Terran Federation, and they took me on to New Terra aboard one of their fast liaison vessels. The rest you know. We, the home planet, were as lost to the New Terrans as they were to us. They greeted us as though we were their own ancestors come back to visit them.

"Most of my crew, for personal reasons, were released from duty there, and settled down to stay.

"The clean-up job here on Earth was a minor operation to their Navy. As I recall, the trip back was made in a little over five months, and the Red Tide was killed within four weeks of the day the task force arrived. I don't think they wasted a motion. One explosive charge per cell, of just sufficient size to disrupt the nucleus. When the critical number of cells had been killed, the rest died overnight.

"It was quite a different Earth that emerged from under the plague, though. You know it had taken over all of the land area except North America and a strip of Western Europe, and all of the sea it wanted. It was particularly concentrated over what had been the jungle areas of South America, Africa, and Asia. You must realize that in the days before the Tide, those areas were almost completely uninhabitable. You have no idea what the term Jungle really implied. When the Tide died, it disintegrated into its component molecules; and the result was that all those vast fertile Jungle lands were now beautifully levelled and completely cleared areas covered with up to twenty feet of the richest topsoil imaginable. That was what made it possible for old Terra to become what she is today; the Federation's truck farm, and the sole source of those genuine original Terran foods that all the rest of the worlds pay such fabulous prices for.

"Strange how quickly we forget. Few people today remember how we loathed and feared the Tide when we were fighting it. Now it's dismissed as a blessing in disguise."

The Admiral paused. "Well," he said, "I think that answers the questions and gives you a bit of homespun philosophy to go with it."

* * * *

"Admiral," said the reporter, "you've given the public some facts it's waited a long time to hear. Coming from you, sir, this is the greatest story that could have come out of this Reunion Day celebration. But there is one question more, if I may ask it. Can you tell me, Admiral, just how it was that you rejected what seemed to be prima facie proof of the story the Mancji told; that they were the lords of creation out there, and that humanity was nothing but a tame food animal to them?"

The Admiral sighed. "I guess it's a good question," he said. "But there was nothing supernatural about my figuring that one. I didn't suspect the full truth, of course. It never occurred to me that we were the victims of the now well-known but still inexplicable sense of humor of the Mancji, or that they were nothing but scavengers around the edges of the Federation. The original Omega ship had met them and seen right through them.

* * * *

"Well, when this hive spotted us coming in, they knew enough about New Terra to realize at once that we were strangers, coming from outside the area. It appealed to their sense of humor to have the gall to strut right out in front of us and try to put over a swindle. What a laugh for the oyster kingdom if they could sell Terrans on the idea that they were the master race. It never occurred to them that we might be anything but Terrans; Terrans who didn't know the Mancji. And they were canny enough to use an old form of Interlingua; somewhere they'd met men before.

"Then we needed food. They knew what we ate, and that was where they went too far. They had, among the flotsam in their hive, a few human bodies they had picked up from some wreck they'd come across in their travels. They had them stashed away like everything else they could lay a pseudopod on. So they stacked them the way they'd seen Terran frozen foods shipped in the past, and sent them over. Another of their little jokes.

"I suppose if you're already overwrought and eager to quit, and you've been badly scared by the size of an alien ship, it's pretty understandable that the sight of human bodies, along with the story that they're just a convenient food supply, might seem pretty convincing. But I was already pretty dubious about the genuineness of our pals, and when I saw those bodies it was pretty plain that we were hot on the trail of Omega Colony. There was no other place humans could have come from out there. We had to find out the location from the Mancji."

"But, Admiral," said the reporter, "true enough they were humans, and presumably had some connection with the colony, but they were naked corpses stacked like cordwood. The Mancji had stated that these were slaves, or rather domesticated animals; they wouldn't have done you any good."

"Well, you see, I didn't believe that," the Admiral said. "Because it was an obvious lie. I tried to show some of the officers, but I'm afraid they weren't being too rational just then.

"I went into the locker and examined those bodies; if Kramer had looked closely, he would have seen what I did. These were no tame animals. They were civilized men."

"How could you be sure, Admiral? They had no clothing, no identifying marks, nothing. Why didn't you believe they were cattle?"

"Because," said the Admiral, "all the men had nice neat haircuts."

IT COULD BE ANYTHING

"S he'll be pulling out in a minute, Brett," Mr. Phillips said. He tucked his railroader's watch back in his vest pocket. "You better get aboard—if you're still set on going."

"It was reading all them books done it," Aunt Haicey said. "Thick books, and no pictures in them. I knew it'd make trouble." She plucked at the faded hand-embroidered shawl over her thin shoulders, a tiny bird-like woman with bright anxious eyes.

"Don't worry about me," Brett said. "I'll be back."

"The place'll be yours when I'm gone," Aunt Haicey said. "Lord knows it won't be long."

"Why don't you change your mind and stay on, boy?" Mr. Phillips said, blinking up at the young man. "If I talk to Mr. J.D., I think he can find a job for you at the plant."

"So many young people leave Casperton," Aunt Haicey said. "They never come back."

Mr. Phillips clicked his teeth. "They write, at first," he said. "Then they gradually lose touch."

"All your people are here, Brett," Aunt Haicey said. "Haven't you been happy here?"

"Why can't you young folks be content with Casperton?" Mr. Phillips said. "There's everything you need here."

"It's that Pretty-Lee done it," Aunt Haicey said. "If it wasn't for that girl—"

A clatter ran down the line of cars. Brett kissed Aunt Haicey's dry cheek, shook Mr. Phillips' hand, and swung aboard. His suitcase was on one of the seats. He put it up above in the rack, and sat down, turned to wave back at the two old people.

It was a summer morning. Brett leaned back and watched the country slide by. It was nice country, Brett thought; mostly in corn, some cattle, and away in the distance the hazy blue hills. Now he would see what was on the other side of them: the cities, the mountains, and the ocean. Up until now all he knew about anything outside of Casperton was what he'd read or seen pictures of. As far as he was concerned, chopping wood and milking cows back in Casperton, they might as well not have existed. They were just words and pictures printed on paper. But he didn't want to just read about them. He wanted to see for himself.

Pretty-Lee hadn't come to see him off. She was probably still mad about yesterday. She had been sitting at the counter at the Club Rexall, drinking a soda and reading a movie magazine with a big picture of an impossibly pretty face on the cover—the kind you never see just walking down the street. He had taken the next stool and ordered a coke.

"Why don't you read something good, instead of that pap?" he asked her.

"Something good? You mean something dry, I guess. And don't call it…that word. It doesn't sound polite."

"What does it say? That somebody named Doll Starr is fed up with glamor and longs for a simple home in the country and lots of kids? Then why doesn't she move to Casperton?"

"You wouldn't understand," said Pretty-Lee.

He took the magazine, leafed through it. "Look at this: all about people who give parties that cost thousands of dollars, and fly all over the world having affairs with each other and committing suicide and getting divorced. It's like reading about Martians."

"I still like to read about the stars. There's nothing wrong with it."

"Reading all that junk just makes you dissatisfied. You want to do your hair up crazy like the pictures in the magazines and wear weird-looking clothes—"

Pretty-Lee bent her straw double. She stood up and took her shopping bag. "I'm very glad to know you think my clothes are weird—"

"You're taking everything I say personally. Look." He showed her a full-color advertisement on the back cover of the magazine. "Look at this. Here's a man supposed to be cooking steaks on some kind of back-yard grill. He looks like a movie star; he's dressed up like he was going to get married; there's not a wrinkle anywhere. There's not a spot on that apron. There isn't even a grease spot on the frying pan. The lawn is as smooth as a billiard table. There's his son; he looks just like his pop, except that he's not grey at the temples. Did you ever really see a man that handsome, or hair that was just silver over the ears and the rest glossy black? The daughter looks like a movie starlet, and her mom is exactly the same, except that she has that grey streak in front to match her husband. You can see the car in the drive; the treads of the tires must have just been scrubbed; they're not even dusty. There's not a pebble out of place; all the flowers are in full bloom; no dead ones. No leaves on the lawn; no dry twigs showing on the trees. That other house in the background looks like a palace, and the man with the rake, looking over the fence: he looks like this one's twin brother, and he's out raking leaves in brand new clothes—"

Pretty-Lee grabbed her magazine. "You just seem to hate everything that's nicer than this messy town—"

"I don't think it's nicer. I like you; your hair isn't always perfectly smooth, and you've got a mended place on your dress, and you feel human, you smell human—"

"Oh!" Pretty-Lee turned and flounced out of the drug store.

* * * *

Brett shifted in the dusty plush seat and looked around. There were a few other people in the car. An old man was reading a newspaper; two old ladies whispered together. There was a woman of about thirty with a mean-looking kid; and some others. They didn't look like magazine pictures, any of them. He tried to picture them doing the things you read in newspapers: the old ladies putting poison in somebody's tea; the old man giving orders to start a war. He thought about babies in houses in cities, and airplanes flying over, and bombs falling down: huge explosive bombs. Blam! Buildings fall in, pieces of glass and stone fly through the air. The babies are blown up along with everything else—

But the kind of people he knew couldn't do anything like that. They liked to loaf and eat and talk and drink beer and buy a new tractor or refrigerator and go fishing. And if they ever got mad and hit somebody—afterwards they were embarrassed and wanted to shake hands....

The train slowed, came to a shuddery stop. Through the window he saw a cardboardy-looking building with the words BAXTER'S JUNCTION painted across it. There were a few faded posters on a bulletin board. An old man was sitting on a bench, waiting. The two old ladies got off and a boy in blue jeans got on. The train started up. Brett folded his jacket and tucked it under his head and tried to doze off....

* * * *

Brett awoke, yawned, sat up. The train was slowing. He remembered you couldn't use the toilets while the train was stopped. He got up and went to the end of the car. The door was jammed. He got it open and went inside and closed the door behind him. The train was going slower, clack-clack... clack-clack...clack; clack...cuh-lack...

He washed his hands, then pulled at the door. It was stuck. He pulled harder. The handle was too small; it was hard to get hold of. The train came to a halt. Brett braced himself and strained against the door. It didn't budge.

He looked out the grimy window. The sun was getting lower. It was about three-thirty, he guessed. He couldn't see anything but some dry-looking fields.

Outside in the corridor there were footsteps. He started to call, but then didn't. It would be too embarrassing, pounding on the door and yelling, "Let me out! I'm stuck in the toilet..."

He tried to rattle the door. It didn't rattle. Somebody was dragging something heavy past the door. Mail bags, maybe. He'd better yell. But dammit, the door couldn't be all that hard to open. He studied the latch. All he had to do was turn it. He got a good grip and twisted. Nothing.

He heard the mail bag bump-bump, and then another one. To heck with it; he'd yell. He'd wait until he heard the footsteps pass the door again and then he'd make some noise.

Brett waited. It was quiet now. He rapped on the door anyway. No answer. Maybe there was nobody left in the car. In a minute the train would start up and he'd be stuck here until the next stop. He banged on the door. "Hey! The door is stuck!"

It sounded foolish. He listened. It was very quiet. He pounded again. The car creaked once. He put his ear to the door. He couldn't hear anything. He turned back to the window. There was no one in sight. He put his cheek flat against it, looked along the car. He saw only dry fields.

He turned around and gave the door a good kick. If he damaged it, it was too bad; the railroad shouldn't have defective locks on the doors. If they tried to make him pay for it, he'd tell them they were lucky he didn't sue the railroad...

* * * *

He braced himself against the opposite wall, drew his foot back, and kicked hard at the lock. Something broke. He pulled the door open.

He was looking out the open door and through the window beyond. There was no platform, just the same dry fields he could see on the other side. He came out and went along to his seat. The car was empty now.

He looked out the window. Why had the train stopped here? Maybe there was some kind of trouble with the engine. It had been sitting here for ten minutes or so now. Brett got up and went along to the door, stepped down onto the iron step. Leaning out, he could see the train stretching along ahead, one car, two cars—

There was no engine.

Maybe he was turned around. He looked the other way. There were three cars. No engine there either. He must be on some kind of siding...

Brett stepped back inside, and pushed through into the next car. It was empty. He walked along the length of it, into the next car. It was empty too. He went back through the two cars and his own car and on, all the way to the end of the train. All the cars were empty. He stood on the platform at the end of the last car, and looked back along the rails. They ran straight, through the dry fields, right to the horizon. He stepped down to the ground, went along the cindery bed to the front of the train, stepping on the ends of the wooden ties. The coupling stood open. The tall, dusty coach stood silently on its iron wheels, waiting. Ahead the tracks went on—

And stopped.

He walked along the ties, following the iron rails, shiny on top, and brown with rust on the sides. A hundred feet from the train they ended. The cinders went on another ten feet and petered out. Beyond, the fields closed in. Brett looked up at the sun. It was lower now in the west, its light getting yellow and late-afternoonish. He turned and looked back at the train. The cars stood high and prim, empty, silent. He walked back, climbed in, got his bag down from the rack, pulled on his jacket. He jumped down to the cinders, followed them to where they ended. He hesitated a moment, then pushed between the knee-high stalks. Eastward across the field he could see what looked like a smudge on the far horizon.

He walked until dark, then made himself a nest in the dead stalks, and went to sleep.

* * * *

He lay on his back, looking up at pink dawn clouds. Around him, dry stalks rustled in a faint stir of air. He felt crumbly earth under his fingers. He sat up, reached out and broke off a stalk. It crumbled into fragile chips. He wondered what it was. It wasn't any crop he'd ever seen before.

He stood, looked around. The field went on and on, dead flat. A locust came whirring toward him, plumped to earth at his feet. He picked it up. Long elbowed legs groped at his fingers aimlessly. He tossed the insect in the air. It fluttered away. To the east the smudge was clearer now; it seemed to be a grey wall, far away. A city? He picked up his bag and started on.

He was getting hungry. He hadn't eaten since the previous morning. He was thirsty too. The city couldn't be more than three hours' walk. He tramped along, the dry plants crackling under his feet, little puffs of dust rising from the dry ground. He thought about the rails, running across the empty fields, ending…

He had heard the locomotive groaning up ahead as the train slowed. And there had been feet in the corridor. Where had they gone?

He thought of the train, Casperton, Aunt Haicey, Mr. Phillips. They seemed very far away, something remembered from long ago. Up above the sun was hot. That was real. The rest seemed unimportant. Ahead there was a city. He would walk until he came to it. He tried to think of other things: television, crowds of people, money: the tattered paper and the worn silver—

Only the sun and the dusty plain and the dead plants were real now. He could see them, feel them. And the suitcase. It was heavy; he shifted hands, kept going.

There was something white on the ground ahead, a small shiny surface protruding from the earth. Brett dropped the suitcase, went down on one knee, dug into the dry soil, pulled out a china teacup, the handle missing.

Caked dirt crumbled away under his thumb, leaving the surface clean. He looked at the bottom of the cup. It was unmarked. Why just one teacup, he wondered, here in the middle of nowhere? He dropped it, took up his suitcase, and went on.

* * * *

After that he watched the ground more closely. He found a shoe; it was badly weathered, but the sole was good. It was a high-topped work shoe, size 10½-C. Who had dropped it here? He thought of other lone shoes he had seen, lying at the roadside or in alleys. How did they get there…?

Half an hour later he detoured around the rusted front fender of an old-fashioned car. He looked around for the rest of the car but saw nothing. The wall was closer now; perhaps five miles more.

A scrap of white paper fluttered across the field in a stir of air. He saw another, more, blowing along in the fitful gusts. He ran a few steps, caught one, smoothed it out.

BUY NOW—PAY LATER!

He picked up another.

PREPARE TO MEET GOD

A third said:

WIN WITH WILLKIE

* * * *

The wall loomed above him, smooth and grey. Dust was caked on his skin and clothes, and as he walked he brushed at himself absently. The suitcase dragged at his arm, thumped against his shin. He was very hungry and thirsty. He sniffed the air, instinctively searching for the odors of food. He had been following the wall for a long time, searching for an opening. It curved away from him, rising vertically from the level earth. Its surface was porous, unadorned, too smooth to climb. It was, Brett estimated, twenty feet high. If there were anything to make a ladder from—

Ahead he saw a wide gate, flanked by grey columns. He came up to it, put the suitcase down, and wiped at his forehead with his handkerchief. Through the opening in the wall a paved street was visible, and the facades of buildings. Those on the street before him were low, not more than one or two stories, but behind them taller towers reared up. There were no people in sight; no sounds stirred the hot noon-time air. Brett picked up his bag and passed through the gate.

For the next hour he walked empty pavements, listening to the echoes of his footsteps against brownstone fronts, empty shop windows, curtained glass doors, and here and there a vacant lot, weed-grown and desolate. He paused at cross streets, looked down long vacant ways. Now and then a distant sound came to him: the lonely honk of a horn, a faintly tolling bell, a clatter of hooves.

He came to a narrow alley that cut like a dark canyon between blank walls. He stood at its mouth, listening to a distant murmur, like a crowd at a funeral. He turned down the narrow way.

It went straight for a few yards, then twisted. As he followed its turnings the crowd noise gradually grew louder. He could make out individual voices now, an occasional word above the hubbub. He started to hurry, eager to find someone to talk to.

Abruptly the voices—hundreds of voices, he thought—rose in a roar, a long-drawn Yaaayyyyy…! Brett thought of a stadium crowd as the home team trotted onto the field. He could hear a band now, a shrilling of brass, the clatter and thump of percussion instruments. Now he could see the mouth of the alley ahead, a sunny street hung with bunting, the backs of people, and over their heads the rhythmic bobbing of a passing procession, tall shakos and guidons in almost-even rows. Two tall poles with a streamer between them swung into view. He caught a glimpse of tall red letters:

… For Our Side!

* * * *

He moved closer, edged up behind the grey-backed crowd. A phalanx of yellow-tuniced men approached, walking stiffly, fez tassels swinging. A small boy darted out into the street, loped along at their side. The music screeched and wheezed. Brett tapped the man before him.

"What's it all about…?"

He couldn't hear his own voice. The man ignored him. Brett moved along behind the crowd, looking for a vantage point or a thinning in the ranks. There seemed to be fewer people ahead. He came to the end of the crowd, moved on a few yards, stood at the curb. The yellow-jackets had passed now, and a group of round-thighed girls in satin blouses and black boots and white fur caps glided into view, silent, expressionless. As they reached a point fifty feet from Brett, they broke abruptly into a strutting prance, knees high, hips flirting, tossing shining batons high, catching them, twirling them, and up again…

Brett craned his neck, looking for TV cameras. The crowd lining the opposite side of the street stood in solid ranks, drably clad, eyes following the procession, mouths working. A fat man in a rumpled suit and a panama hat squeezed to the front, stood picking his teeth. Somehow, he seemed out of place among the others. Behind the spectators, the store fronts looked normal, dowdy brick and mismatched glass and oxidizing aluminum, dusty windows and cluttered displays of cardboard, a faded sign that read TO-DAY ONLY—PRICES SLASHED. To Brett's left the sidewalk stretched, empty. To his right the crowd was packed close, the shout rising and falling. Now a rank of blue-suited policemen followed the majorettes, swinging along silently. Behind them, over them, a piece of paper blew along the street. Brett turned to the man on his right.

"Pardon me. Can you tell me the name of this town?"

The man ignored him. Brett tapped the man's shoulder. "Hey! What town is this?"

The man took off his hat, whirled it overhead, then threw it up. It sailed away over the crowd, lost. Brett wondered briefly how people who threw their hats ever recovered them. But then, nobody he knew would throw his hat…

"You mind telling me the name of this place?" Brett said, as he took the man's arm, pulled. The man rotated toward Brett, leaning heavily against him. Brett stepped back. The man fell, lay stiffly, his arms moving, his eyes and mouth open.

"Ahhhhh," he said. "Whum-whum-whum. Awww, jawww…"

Brett stooped quickly. "I'm sorry," he cried. He looked around. "Help! This man…"

Nobody was watching. The next man, a few feet away, stood close against his neighbor, hatless, his jaw moving.

"This man's sick," said Brett, tugging at the man's arm. "He fell."

The man's eyes moved reluctantly to Brett. "None of my business," he muttered.

"Won't anybody give me a hand?"

"Probably a drunk."

Behind Brett a voice called in a penetrating whisper: "Quick! You! Get into the alley…!"

He turned. A gaunt man of about thirty with sparse reddish hair, perspiration glistening on his upper lip, stood at the mouth of a narrow way like the one Brett had come through. He wore a grimy pale yellow shirt with a wide-flaring collar, limp and sweat-stained, dark green knee-breeches, soft leather boots, scuffed and dirty, with limp tops that drooped over his ankles. He gestured, drew back into the alley. "In here."

Brett went toward him. "This man…"

"Come on, you fool!" The man took Brett's arm, pulled him deeper into the dark passage. Brett resisted. "Wait a minute. That fellow…" He tried to point.

"Don't you know yet?" The red-head spoke with a strange accent. "Golems…You got to get out of sight before the—"

* * * *

The man froze, flattened himself against the wall. Automatically Brett moved to a place beside him. The man's head was twisted toward the alley mouth. The tendons in his weathered neck stood out. He had a three-day stubble of beard. Brett could smell him, standing this close. He edged away. "What—"

"Don't make a sound! Don't move, you idiot!" His voice was a thin hiss.

Brett followed the other's eyes toward the sunny street. The fallen man lay on the pavement, moving feebly, eyes open. Something moved up to him, a translucent brownish shape, like muddy water. It hovered for a moment, then dropped on the man like a breaking wave, flowed around him. The body shifted, rotating stiffly, then tilted upright. The sun struck through the fluid shape that flowed down now, amber highlights twinkling, to form itself into the crested wave, flow away.

"What the hell…!"

"Come on!" The red-head turned, trotted silently toward the shadowy bend under the high grey walls. He looked back, beckoned impatiently, passed out of sight around the turn—

Brett came up behind him, saw a wide avenue, tall trees with chartreuse springtime leaves, a wrought-iron fence, and beyond it, rolling green lawns. There were no people in sight.

"Wait a minute! What is this place?!"

His companion turned red-rimmed eyes on Brett. "How long have you been here?" he asked. "How did you get in?"

"I came through a gate. Just about an hour ago."

"I knew you were a man as soon as I saw you talking to the golem," said the red-head. "I've been here two months; maybe more. We've got to get out of sight. You want food? There's a place…" He jerked his thumb. "Come on. Time to talk later."

* * * *

Brett followed him. They turned down a side street, pushed through the door of a dingy cafe. It banged behind them. There were tables, stools at a bar, a dusty juke box. They took seats at a table. The red-head groped under the table, pulled off a shoe, hammered it against the wall. He cocked his head, listening. The silence was absolute. He hammered again. There was a clash of crockery from beyond the kitchen door. "Now don't say anything," the red-head said. He eyed the door behind the counter expectantly. It flew open. A girl with red cheeks and untidy hair, dressed in a green waitress' uniform appeared, swept up to the table, pad and pencil in hand.

"Coffee and a ham sandwich," said the red-head. Brett said nothing. The girl glanced at him briefly, jotted hastily, whisked away.

"I saw them here the first day," the red-head said. "It was a piece of luck. I saw how the Gels started it up. They were big ones—not like the tidiers-up. As soon as they were finished, I came in and tried the same thing. It worked. I used the golem's lines—"

"I don't know what you're talking about," Brett said. "I'm going to ask that girl—"

"Don't say anything to her; it might spoil everything. The whole sequence might collapse; or it might call the Gels. I'm not sure. You can have the food when it comes back with it."

"Why do you say 'when "it" comes back'?"

"Ah." He looked at Brett strangely. "I'll show you."

Brett could smell food now. His mouth watered. He hadn't eaten for twenty-four hours.

"Care, that's the thing," the red-head said. "Move quiet, and stay out of sight, and you can live like a County Duke. Food's the hardest, but here—"

The red-cheeked girl reappeared, a tray balanced on one arm, a heavy cup and saucer in the other hand. She clattered them down on the table.

"Took you long enough," the red-head said. The girl sniffed, opened her mouth to speak—and the red-head darted out a stiff finger, jabbed her under the ribs. She stood, mouth open, frozen.

Brett half rose. "He's crazy, miss," he said. "Please accept—"

"Don't waste your breath." Brett's host was looking at him triumphantly. "Why do I call it 'it'?" He stood up, reached out and undid the top buttons of the green uniform. The waitress stood, leaning slightly forward, unmoving. The blouse fell open, exposing round white breasts—unadorned, blind.

"A doll," said the red-head. "A puppet; a golem."

* * * *

Brett stared at her, the damp curls at her temple, the tip of her tongue behind her teeth, the tiny red veins in her round cheeks, and the white skin curving...

"That's a quick way to tell 'em," said the red-head. "The teat is smooth." He rebuttoned the uniform, then jabbed again at the girl's ribs. She straightened, patted her hair.

"No doubt a gentleman like you is used to better," she said carelessly. She went away.

"I'm Awalawon Dhuva," the red-head said.

"My name's Brett Hale." Brett took a bite of the sandwich.

"Those clothes," Dhuva said. "And you have a strange way of talking. What county are you from?"

"Jefferson."

"Never heard of it. I'm from Wavly. What brought you here?"

"I was on a train. The tracks came to an end out in the middle of nowhere. I walked...and here I am. What is this place?"

"Don't know." Dhuva shook his head. "I knew they were lying about the Fire River, though. Never did believe all that stuff. Religious hokum, to keep the masses quiet. Don't know what to believe now. Take the roof. They say a hundred kharfads up; but how do we know? Maybe it's a thousand—or only ten. By Grat, I'd like to go up in a balloon, see for myself."

"What are you talking about?" Brett said. "Go where in a balloon? See what?"

"Oh, I've seen one at the Tourney. Big hot-air bag, with a basket under it. Tied down with a rope. But if you cut the rope...! But you can bet the priests will never let that happen, no, sir." Dhuva looked at Brett speculatively. "What about your county: Fession, or whatever you called it. How high do they tell you it is there?"

"You mean the sky? Well, the air ends after a few miles and space just goes on—millions of miles—"

Dhuva slapped the table and laughed. "The people in Fesseron must be some yokels! Just goes on up; now who'd swallow that tale?" He chuckled.

"Only a child thinks the sky is some kind of tent," said Brett. "Haven't you ever heard of the Solar System, the other planets?"

"What are those?"

"Other worlds. They all circle around the sun, like the Earth."

"Other worlds, eh? Sailing around up under the roof? Funny; I never saw them." Dhuva snickered. "Wake up, Brett. Forget all those stories. Just believe what you see."

"What about that brown thing?"

"The Gels? They run this place. Look out for them, Brett. Stay alert. Don't let them see you."

* * * *

"What do they do?"

"I don't know—and I don't want to find out. This is a great place— I like it here. I have all I want to eat, plenty of nice rooms for sleeping. There's the parades and the scenes. It's a good life—as long as you keep out of sight."

"How do you get out of here?" Brett asked, finishing his coffee.

"Don't know how to get out; over the wall, I suppose. I don't plan to leave though. I left home in a hurry. The Duke—never mind. I'm not going back."

"Are all the people here...golems?" Brett said. "Aren't there any more real people?"

"You're the first I've seen. I spotted you as soon as I saw you. A live man moves different than a golem. You see golems doing things like knitting their brows, starting back in alarm, looking askance, and standing arms akimbo. And they have things like pursed lips and knowing glances and mirthless laughter. You know: all the things you read about, that real people never do. But now that you're here, I've got somebody to talk to. I did get lonesome, I admit. I'll show you where I stay and we'll fix you up with a bed."

"I won't be around that long."

"What can you get outside that you can't get here? There's everything you need here in the city. We can have a great time."

"You sound like my Aunt Haicey," Brett said. "She said I had everything I needed back in Casperton. How does she know what I need? How do you know? How do I know myself? I can tell you I need more than food and a place to sleep—"

"What more?"

"Everything. Things to think about and something worth doing. Why, even in the movies—"

"What's a movie?"

"You know, a play, on film. A moving picture."

"A picture that moves?"

"That's right."

"This is something the priests told you about?" Dhuva seemed to be holding in his mirth.

"Everybody's seen movies."

Dhuva burst out laughing. "Those priests," he said. "They're the same everywhere, I see. The stories they tell, and people believe them. What else?"

"Priests have nothing to do with it."

Dhuva composed his features. "What do they tell you about Grat, and the Wheel?"

"Grat? What's that?"

"The Over-Being. The Four-eyed One." Dhuva made a sign, caught himself. "Just habit," he said. "I don't believe that rubbish. Never did."

"I suppose you're talking about God," Brett said.

"I don't know about God. Tell me about it."

"He's the creator of the world. He's…well, superhuman. He knows everything that happens, and when you die, if you've led a good life, you meet God in Heaven."

"Where's that?"

"It's…" Brett waved a hand vaguely, "up above."

"But you said there was just emptiness up above," Dhuva recalled. "And some other worlds whirling around, like islands adrift in the sea."

"Well—"

"Never mind," Dhuva held up his hands. "Our priests are liars too. All that balderdash about the Wheel and the River of Fire. It's just as bad as your Hivvel or whatever you called it. And our Grat and your Mud, or Gog: they're the same—" Dhuva's head went up. "What's that?"

"I didn't hear anything."

* * * *

Dhuva got to his feet, turned to the door. Brett rose. A towering brown shape, glassy and transparent, hung in the door, its surface rippling. Dhuva whirled, leaped past Brett, dived for the rear door. Brett stood frozen. The shape flowed—swift as quicksilver—caught Dhuva in mid-stride, engulfed him. For an instant Brett saw the thin figure, legs kicking, upended within the muddy form of the Gel. Then the turbid wave swept across to the door, sloshed it aside, disappeared. Dhuva was gone.

Brett stood rooted, staring at the doorway. A bar of sunlight fell across the dusty floor. A brown mouse ran along the baseboard. It was very quiet. Brett went to the door through which the Gel had disappeared, hesitated a moment, then thrust it open.

He was looking down into a great dark pit, acres in extent, its sides riddled with holes, the amputated ends of water and sewage lines and power cables dangling. Far below light glistened from the surface of a black pool. A few feet away the waitress stood unmoving in the dark on a narrow strip of linoleum. At her feet the chasm yawned. The edge of the floor was ragged, as though it had been gnawed away by rats. There was no sign of Dhuva.

Brett stepped back into the dining room, let the door swing shut. He took a deep breath, picked up a paper napkin from a table and wiped his forehead, dropped the napkin on the floor and went out into the street, his suitcase forgotten now. At the corner he turned, walked along past silent shop windows crowded with home permanents, sun glasses, fingernail polish, suntan lotion, paper cartons, streamers, plastic toys, vari-colored garments of synthetic fiber, home remedies, beauty aids, popular music, greeting cards…

At the next corner he stopped, looking down the silent streets. Nothing moved. Brett went to a window in a grey concrete wall, pulled himself up to peer through the dusty pane, saw a room filled with tailor's forms, garment racks, a bicycle, bundled back issues of magazines without covers.

He went along to a door. It was solid, painted shut. The next door looked easier. He wrenched at the tarnished brass nob, then stepped back and kicked the door. With a hollow sound the door fell inward, taking with it the jamb. Brett stood staring at the gaping opening. A fragment of masonry dropped with a dry clink. Brett stepped through the breach in the grey facade. The black pool at the bottom of the pit winked a flicker of light back at him in the deep gloom.

* * * *

Around him, the high walls of the block of buildings loomed in silhouette; the squares of the windows were ranks of luminous blue against the dark. Dust motes danced in shafts of sunlight. Far above, the roof was dimly visible, a spidery tangle of trusswork. And below was the abyss.

At Brett's feet the stump of a heavy brass rail projected an inch from the floor. It was long enough, Brett thought, to give firm anchor to a rope. Somewhere below, Dhuva—a stranger who had befriended him—lay in the grip of the Gels. He would do what he could—but he needed equipment— and help. First he would find a store with rope, guns, knives. He would—

The broken edge of masonry where the door had been caught his eye. The shell of the wall, exposed where the door frame had torn away, was wafer-thin. Brett reached up, broke off a piece. The outer face—the side that showed on the street—was smooth, solid-looking. The back was porous, nibbled. Brett stepped outside, examined the wall. He kicked at the grey surface. A great piece of wall, six feet high, broke into fragments, fell on the sidewalk with a crash, driving out a puff of dust. Another section fell. One piece of it skidded away, clattered down into the depths. Brett heard a distant splash. He looked at the great jagged opening in the wall—like a jigsaw picture with a piece missing. He turned and started off at a trot, his mouth dry, his pulse thumping painfully in his chest.

Two blocks from the hollow building, Brett slowed to a walk, his footsteps echoing in the empty street. He looked into each store window as he passed. There were artificial legs, bottles of colored water, immense dolls, wigs, glass eyes—but no rope. Brett tried to think. What kind of store would handle rope? A marine supply company, maybe. But where would he find one?

Perhaps it would be easiest to look in a telephone book. Ahead he saw a sign lettered HOTEL. Brett went up to the revolving door, pushed inside. He was in a dim, marble-panelled lobby, with double doors leading into a beige-carpeted bar on his right, the brass-painted cage of an elevator directly before him, flanked by tall urns of sand and an ascending staircase. On the left was a dark mahogany-finished reception desk. Behind the desk a man stood silently, waiting. Brett felt a wild surge of relief.

"Those things, those Gels!" he called, starting across the room. "My friend—"

He broke off. The clerk stood, staring over Brett's shoulder, holding a pen poised over a book. Brett reached out, took the pen. The man's finger curled stiffly around nothing. A golem.

Brett turned away, went into the bar. Vacant stools were ranged before a dark mirror. At the tables empty glasses stood before empty chairs. Brett started as he heard the revolving door thump-thump. Suddenly soft light bathed the lobby behind him. Somewhere a piano tinkled *More Than You Know*. With a distant clatter of closing doors the elevator came to life.

Brett hugged a shadowed corner, saw a fat man in a limp seersucker suit cross to the reception desk. He had a red face, a bald scalp blotched with large brown freckles. The clerk inclined his head blandly.

"Ah, yes, sir, a nice double with bath…" Brett heard the unctuous voice of the clerk as he offered the pen. The fat man took it, scrawled something in the register. "… at fourteen dollars," the clerk murmured. He smiled, dinged the bell. A boy in tight green tunic and trousers and a pillbox cap with a chin strap pushed through a door beside the desk, took the key, led the way to the elevator. The fat man entered. Through the openwork of the shaft Brett watched as the elevator car rose, greasy cables trembling and swaying. He started back across the lobby—and stopped dead.

A wet brown shape had appeared in the entrance. It flowed across the rug to the bellhop. Face blank, the golem turned back to its door. Above, Brett heard the elevator stop. Doors clashed. The clerk stood poised behind the desk. The Gel hovered, then flowed away. The piano was silent now. The lights burned, a soft glow, then winked out. Brett thought about the fat man. He had seen him before…

He went up the stairs. In the second floor corridor Brett felt his way along in near-darkness, guided by the dim light coming through transoms. He tried a door. It opened. He stepped into a large bedroom with a double bed, an easy chair, a chest of drawers. He crossed the room, looked out across an alley. Twenty feet away white curtains hung at windows in a brick wall. There was nothing behind the windows.

There were sounds in the corridor. Brett dropped to the floor behind the bed.

"All right, you two," a drunken voice bellowed. "And may all your troubles be little ones." There was laughter, squeals, a dry clash of beads flung against the door. A key grated. The door swung wide. Lights blazed in the hall, silhouetting the figures of a man in black jacket and trousers, a woman in a white bridal dress and veil, flowers in her hand.

"Take care, Mel!"

"… do anything I wouldn't do!"

"… kiss the bride, now!"

The couple backed into the room, pushed the door shut, stood against it. Brett crouched behind the bed, not breathing, waiting. The couple stood at the door, in the dark, heads down…

Brett stood, rounded the foot of the bed, approached the two unmoving figures. The girl looked young, sleek, perfect-featured, with soft dark hair. Her eyes were half-open; Brett caught a glint of light reflected from the eyeball. The man was bronzed, broad-shouldered, his hair wavy and blond. His lips were parted, showing even white teeth. The two stood, not breathing, sightless eyes fixed on nothing.

Brett took the bouquet from the woman's hand. The flowers seemed real—except that they had no perfume. He dropped them on the floor, pulled at the male golem to clear the door. The figure pivoted, toppled, hit with a heavy thump. Brett raised the woman in his arms and propped her against the bed. Back at the door he listened. All was quiet now. He started to open the door, then hesitated. He went back to the bed, undid the tiny pearl buttons down the front of the bridal gown, pulled it open. The breasts were rounded, smooth, an unbroken creamy white...

In the hall, he started toward the stair. A tall Gel rippled into view ahead, its shape flowing and wavering, now billowing out, then rising up. The shifting form undulated toward Brett. He made a move to run, then remembered Dhuva, stood motionless. The Gel wobbled past him, slumped suddenly, flowed under a door. Brett let out a breath. Never mind the fat man. There were too many Gels here. He started back along the corridor.

Soft music came from double doors which stood open on a landing. Brett went to them, risked a look inside. Graceful couples moved sedately on a polished floor, diners sat at tables, black-clad waiters moving among them. At the far side of the room, near a dusty rubber plant, sat the fat man, studying a menu. As Brett watched he shook out a napkin, ran it around inside his collar, then mopped his face.

Never disturb a scene, Dhuva had said. But perhaps he could blend with it. Brett brushed at his suit, straightened his tie, stepped into the room. A waiter approached, eyed him dubiously. Brett got out his wallet, took out a five-dollar bill.

"A quiet table in the corner," he said. He glanced back. There were no Gels in sight. He followed the waiter to a table near the fat man.

* * * *

Seated, he looked around. He wanted to talk to the fat man, but he couldn't afford to attract attention. He would watch, and wait his chance.

At the nearby tables men with well-pressed suits, clean collars, and carefully shaved faces murmured to sleekly gowned women who fingered wine glasses, smiled archly. He caught fragments of conversation:

"My dear, have you heard..."

"... in the low eighties..."

"… quite impossible. One must…"

"… for this time of year."

The waiter returned with a shallow bowl of milky soup. Brett looked at the array of spoons, forks, knives, glanced sideways at the diners at the next table. It was important to follow the correct ritual. He put his napkin in his lap, careful to shake out all the folds. He looked at the spoons again, picked a large one, glanced at the waiter. So far so good…

"Wine, sir?"

Brett indicated the neighboring couple. "The same as they're having." The waiter turned away, returned holding a wine bottle, label toward Brett. He looked at it, nodded. The waiter busied himself with the cork, removing it with many flourishes, setting a glass before Brett, pouring half an inch of wine. He waited expectantly.

Brett picked up the glass, tasted it. It tasted like wine. He nodded. The waiter poured. Brett wondered what would have happened if he had made a face and spurned it. But it would be too risky to try. No one ever did it.

Couples danced, resumed their seats; others rose and took the floor. A string ensemble in a distant corner played restrained tunes that seemed to speak of the gentle faded melancholy of decorous tea dances on long-forgotten afternoons. Brett glanced toward the fat man. He was eating soup noisily, his napkin tied under his chin.

The waiter was back with a plate. "Lovely day, sir," he said.

"Great," Brett agreed.

The waiter placed a covered platter on the table, removed the cover, stood with carving knife and fork poised.

"A bit of the crispy, sir?"

Brett nodded. He eyed the waiter surreptitiously. He looked real. Some golems seemed realer than others; or perhaps it merely depended on the parts they were playing. The man who had fallen at the parade had been only a sort of extra, a crowd member. The waiter, on the other hand, was able to converse. Perhaps it would be possible to learn something from him…

"What's…uh…how do you spell the name of this town?" Brett asked.

"I was never much of a one for spelling, sir," the waiter said.

"Try it."

"Gravy, sir?"

"Sure. Try to spell the name."

"Perhaps I'd better call the headwaiter, sir," the golem said stiffly.

From the corner of an eye Brett caught a flicker of motion. He whirled, saw nothing. Had it been a Gel?

"Never mind," he said. The waiter served potatoes, peas, refilled the wine glass, moved off silently. The question had been a little too unortho-dox, Brett decided. Perhaps if he led up to the subject more obliquely…

* * * *

When the waiter returned Brett said, "Nice day."

"Very nice, sir."

"Better than yesterday."

"Yes indeed, sir."

"I wonder what tomorrow'll be like."

"Perhaps we'll have a bit of rain, sir."

Brett nodded toward the dance floor. "Nice orchestra."

"They're very popular, sir."

"From here in town?"

"I wouldn't know as to that, sir."

"Lived here long yourself?"

"Oh, yes, sir." The waiter's expression showed disapproval. "Would there be anything else, sir?"

"I'm a newcomer here," Brett said. "I wonder if you could tell me—"

"Excuse me, sir." The waiter was gone. Brett poked at the mashed potatoes. Quizzing golems was hopeless. He would have to find out for himself. He turned to look at the fat man. As Brett watched he took a large handkerchief from a pocket, blew his nose loudly. No one turned to look. The orchestra played softly. The couples danced. Now was as good a time as any...

Brett rose, crossed to the other's table. The man looked up.

"Mind if I sit down?" Brett said. "I'd like to talk to you."

The fat man blinked, motioned to a chair. Brett sat down, leaned across the table. "Maybe I'm wrong," he said quietly, "but I think you're real."

The fat man blinked again. "What's that?" he snapped. He had a high petulant voice.

"You're not like the rest of them. I think I can talk to you. I think you're another outsider."

The fat man looked down at his rumpled suit. "I...ah...was caught a little short today. Didn't have time to change. I'm a busy man. And what business is it of yours?" He clamped his jaw shut, eyed Brett warily.

"I'm a stranger here," Brett said. "I want to find out what's going on in this place—"

"Buy an amusement guide. Lists all the shows—"

"I don't mean that. I mean these dummies all over the place, and the Gels—"

"What dummies? Jells? Jello? You don't like Jello?"

"I love Jello. I don't—"

"Just ask the waiter. He'll bring you your Jello. Any flavor you like. Now if you'll excuse me..."

"I'm talking about the brown things; they look like muddy water. They come around if you interfere with a scene."

The fat man looked nervous. "Please. Go away."

"If I make a disturbance, the Gels will come. Is that what you're afraid of?"

"Now, now. Be calm. No need for you to get excited."

"I won't make a scene," Brett said. "Just talk to me. How long have you been here?"

"I dislike scenes. I dislike them intensely."

"When did you come here?"

"Just ten minutes ago. I just sat down. I haven't had my dinner yet. Please, young man. Go back to your table." The fat man watched Brett warily. Sweat glistened on his bald head.

"I mean this town. How long have you been here? Where did you come from?"

"Why, I was born here. Where did I come from? What sort of question is that? Just consider that the stork brought me."

"You were born here?"

"Certainly."

"What's the name of the town?"

* * * *

"Are you trying to make a fool of me?" The fat man was getting angry. His voice was rising.

"Shhh," Brett cautioned. "You'll attract the Gels."

"Blast the Jilts, whatever that is!" the fat man snapped. "Now, get along with you. I'll call the manager."

"Don't you know?" Brett said, staring at the fat man. "They're all dummies; golems, they're called. They're not real."

"Who're not real?"

"All these imitation people at the tables and on the dance floor. Surely you realize—"

"I realize you're in need of medical attention." The fat man pushed back his chair and got to his feet. "You keep the table," he said. "I'll dine elsewhere."

"Wait!" Brett got up, seized the fat man's arm.

"Take your hands off me—" The fat man went toward the door. Brett followed. At the cashier's desk Brett turned suddenly, saw a fluid brown shape flicker—

"Look!" He pulled at the fat man's arm—

"Look at what?" The Gel was gone.

"It was there: a Gel."

The fat man flung down a bill, hurried away. Brett fumbled out a ten, waited for change. "Wait!" he called. He heard the fat man's feet receding down the stairs.

"Hurry," he said to the cashier. The woman sat glassy-eyed, staring at nothing. The music died. The lights flickered, went off. In the gloom Brett saw a fluid shape rise up—

He ran, pounding down the stairs. The fat man was just rounding the corner. Brett opened his mouth to call—and went rigid, as a translucent shape of mud shot from the door, rose up to tower before him. Brett stood, mouth half open, eyes staring, leaning forward with hands outflung. The Gel loomed, its surface flickering—waiting. Brett caught an acrid odor of geraniums.

A minute passed. Brett's cheek itched. He fought a desire to blink, to swallow—to turn and run. The high sun beat down on the silent street, the still window displays.

Then the Gel broke form, slumped, flashed away. Brett tottered back against the wall, let his breath out in a harsh sigh.

Across the street he saw a window with a display of camping equipment, portable stoves, boots, rifles. He crossed the street, tried the door. It was locked. He looked up and down the street. There was no one in sight. He kicked in the glass beside the latch, reached through and turned the knob. Inside he looked over the shelves, selected a heavy coil of nylon rope, a sheath knife, a canteen. He examined a Winchester repeating rifle with a telescopic sight, then put it back and strapped on a .22 revolver. He emptied two boxes of long rifle cartridges into his pocket, then loaded the pistol. He coiled the rope over his shoulder and went back out into the empty street.

* * * *

The fat man was standing in front of a shop in the next block, picking at a blemish on his chin and eyeing the window display. He looked up with a frown, started away as Brett came up.

"Wait a minute," Brett called. "Didn't you see the Gel? the one that cornered me back there?"

The fat man looked back suspiciously, kept going.

"Wait!" Brett caught his arm. "I know you're real. I've seen you belch and sweat and scratch. You're the only one I can call on—and I need help. My friend is trapped—"

The fat man pulled away, his face flushed an even deeper red. "I'm warning you, you maniac: get away from me...!"

Brett stepped close, rammed the fat man hard in the ribs. He sank to his knees, gasping. The panama hat rolled away. Brett grabbed his arm, steadied him.

"Sorry," he said. "I had to be sure. You're real, all right. We've got to rescue my friend, Dhuva—"

The fat man leaned against the glass, rolling terrified eyes, rubbing his stomach. "I'll call the police!" he gasped.

"What police?" Brett waved an arm. "Look. Not a car in sight. Did you ever see the street that empty before?"

"Wednesday afternoon," the fat man gasped.

"Come with me. I want to show you. It's all hollow. There's nothing behind these walls—"

"Why doesn't somebody come along?" the fat man moaned.

"The masonry is only a quarter-inch thick," Brett said. "Come on; I'll show you."

"I don't like it," said the fat man. His face was pale and moist. "You're mad. What's wrong? It's so quiet..."

"We've got to try to save him. The Gel took him down into this pit—"

"Let me go," the man whined. "I'm afraid. Can't you just let me lead my life in peace?"

"Don't you understand? The Gel took a man. They may be after you next."

"There's no one after me! I'm a business man...a respectable citizen. I mind my own business, give to charity, go to church. All I want is to be left alone!"

* * * *

Brett dropped his hands from the fat man's arms, stood looking at him: the blotched face, pale now, the damp forehead, the quivering jowls. The fat man stooped for his hat, slapped it against his leg, clamped it on his head.

"I think I understand now," said Brett. "This is your place, this imitation city. Everything's faked to fit your needs—like in the hotel. Wherever you go, the scene unrolls in front of you. You never see the Gels, never discover the secret of the golems—because you conform. You never do the unexpected."

"That's right. I'm law-abiding. I'm respectable. I don't pry. I don't nose into other people's business. Why should I? Just let me alone..."

"Sure," Brett said. "Even if I dragged you down there and showed you, you wouldn't believe it. But you're not in the scene now. I've taken you out of it—"

Suddenly the fat man turned and ran a few yards, then looked back to see whether Brett was pursuing him. He shook a round fist.

"I've seen your kind before," he shouted. "Troublemakers."

Brett took a step toward him. The fat man yelped and ran another fifty feet, his coat tails bobbing. He looked back, stopped, a fat figure alone in the empty sunny street.

"You haven't seen the last of me!" he shouted. "We know how to deal with your kind." He tugged at his vest, went off along the sidewalk. Brett watched him go, then started back toward the hollow building.

* * * *

The jagged fragments of masonry Brett had knocked from the wall lay as he had left them. He stepped through the opening, peered down into the murky pit, trying to judge its depth. A hundred feet at least. Perhaps a hundred and fifty.

He unslung the rope from his shoulder, tied one end to the brass stump, threw the coil down the precipitous side. It fell away into darkness, hung swaying. It was impossible to tell whether the end reached any solid footing below. He couldn't waste any more time looking for help. He would have to try it alone.

There was a scrape of shoe leather on the pavement outside. He turned, stepped out into the white sunlight. The fat man rounded the corner, recoiled as he saw Brett. He flung out a pudgy forefinger, his protruding eyes wide in his blotchy red face.

"There he is! I told you he came this way!" Two uniformed policemen came into view. One eyed the gun at Brett's side, put a hand on his own.

"Better take that off, sir."

"Look!" Brett said to the fat man. He stooped, picked up a crust of masonry. "Look at this—just a shell—"

"He's blasted a hole right in that building, officer!" the fat man shrilled. "He's dangerous."

The cop ignored the gaping hole in the wall. "You'll have to come along with me, sir. This gentleman registered a complaint…"

Brett stood staring into the cop's eyes. They were pale blue eyes, looking steadily back at him from a bland face. Could the cop be real? Or would he be able to push him over, as he had other golems?

"The fellow's not right in the head," the fat man was saying to the cop. "You should have heard his crazy talk. A troublemaker. His kind have got to be locked up!"

The cop nodded. "Can't have anyone causing trouble."

"Only a young fellow," said the fat man. He mopped at his forehead with a large handkerchief. "Tragic. But I'm sure that you men know how to handle him."

"Better give me the gun, sir." The cop held out a hand. Brett moved suddenly, rammed stiff fingers into the cop's ribs. He stiffened, toppled, lay rigid, staring up at nothing.

"You…you killed him," the fat man gasped, backing. The second cop tugged at his gun. Brett leaped at him, sent him down with a blow to the ribs. He turned to face the fat man.

"I didn't kill them! I just turned them off. They're not real, they're just golems."

"A killer! And right in the city, in broad daylight."

"You've got to help me!" Brett cried. "This whole scene: don't you see? It has the air of something improvised in a hurry, to deal with the unexpected factor; that's me. The Gels know something's wrong, but they can't quite figure out what. When you called the cops the Gels obliged—"

* * * *

Startlingly the fat man burst into tears. He fell to his knees.

"Don't kill me…oh, don't kill me…"

"Nobody's going to kill you, you fool!" Brett snapped. "Look! I want to show you!" He seized the fat man's lapel, dragged him to his feet and across the sidewalk, through the opening. The fat man stopped dead, stumbled back—

"What's this? What kind of place is this?" He scrambled for the opening.

"It's what I've been trying to tell you. This city you live in—it's a hollow shell. There's nothing inside. None of it's real. Only you…and me. There was another man: Dhuva. I was in a cafe with him. A Gel came. He tried to run. It caught him. Now he's…down there."

"I'm not alone," the fat man babbled. "I have my friends, my clubs, my business associates. I'm insured. Lately I've been thinking a lot about Jesus—"

He broke off, whirled, and jumped for the doorway. Brett leaped after him, caught his coat. It ripped. The fat man stumbled over one of the cop-golems, went to hands and knees. Brett stood over him.

"Get up, damn it!" he snapped. "I need help and you're going to help me!" He hauled the fat man to his feet. "All you have to do is stand by the rope. Dhuva may be unconscious when I find him. You'll have to help me haul him up. If anybody comes along, any Gels, I mean—give me a signal. A whistle…like this—" Brett demonstrated. "And if I get in trouble, do what you can. Here…" Brett started to offer the fat man the gun, then handed him the hunting knife. "If anybody interferes, this may not do any good, but it's something. I'm going down now."

The fat man watched as Brett gripped the rope, let himself over the edge. Brett looked up at the glistening face, the damp strands of hair across the freckled scalp. Brett had no assurance that the man would stay at his post, but he had done what he could.

"Remember," said Brett. "It's a real man they've got, like you and me...not a golem. We owe it to him." The fat man's hands trembled. He watched Brett, licked his lips. Brett started down.

* * * *

The descent was easy. The rough face of the excavation gave footholds. The end of a decaying timber projected; below it was the stump of a crumbling concrete pipe two feet in diameter. Brett was ten feet below the rim of floor now. Above, the broad figure of the fat man was visible in silhouette against the jagged opening in the wall.

Now the cliff shelved back; the rope hung free. Brett eased past the cut end of a rusted water pipe, went down hand over hand. If there were nothing at the bottom to give him footing, it would be a long climb back...

Twenty feet below he could see the still black water, pockmarked with expanding rings where bits of debris dislodged by his passage peppered the surface.

There was a rhythmic vibration in the rope. Brett felt it through his hands, a fine sawing sensation...

He was falling, gripping the limp rope...

He slammed on his back in three feet of oily water. The coils of rope collapsed around him with a sustained splashing. He got to his feet, groped for the end of the rope. The glossy nylon strands had been cleanly cut.

* * * *

For half an hour Brett waded in waist-deep water along a wall of damp clay that rose sheer above him. Far above, bars of dim sunlight crossed the upper reaches of the cavern. He had seen no sign of Dhuva...or the Gels.

He encountered a sodden timber that projected above the surface of the pool, clung to it to rest. Bits of flotsam—a plastic pistol, bridge tallies, a golf bag—floated in the black water. A tunnel extended through the clay wall ahead; beyond, Brett could see a second great cavern rising. He pictured the city, silent and empty above, and the honey-combed earth beneath. He moved on.

An hour later Brett had traversed the second cavern. Now he clung to an outthrust spur of granite directly beneath the point at which Dhuva had disappeared. Far above he could see the green-clad waitress standing stiffly on her ledge. He was tired. Walking in water, his feet floundering in soft mud, was exhausting. He was no closer to escape, or to finding Dhuva, than he had been when the fat man cut the rope. He had been a fool to leave the man alone, with a knife...but he had had no choice.

He would have to find another way out. Endlessly wading at the bottom of the pit was useless. He would have to climb. One spot was as good as another. He stepped back and scanned the wall of clay looming over him.

Twenty feet up, water dripped from the broken end of a four-inch water main. Brett uncoiled the rope from his shoulder, tied a loop in the end, whirled it and cast upward. It missed, fell back with a splash. He gathered it in, tried again. On the third try it caught. He tested it, then started up. His hands were slippery with mud and water. He twined the rope around his legs, inched higher. The slender cable was smooth as glass. He slipped back two feet, then inched upward, slipped again, painfully climbed, slipped, climbed.

After the first ten feet he found toe-holds in the muddy wall. He worked his way up, his hands aching and raw. A projecting tangle of power cable gave a secure purchase for a foot. He rested. Nearby, an opening two feet in diameter gaped in the clay: a tunnel. It might be possible to swing sideways across the face of the clay and reach the opening. It was worth a try. His stiff, clay-slimed hands would pull him no higher.

He gripped the rope, kicked off sideways, hooked a foot in the tunnel mouth, half jumped, half fell into the mouth of the tunnel. He clung to the rope, shook it loose from the pipe above, coiled it and looped it over his shoulder. On hands and knees he started into the narrow passage.

* * * *

The tunnel curved left, then right, dipped, then angled up. Brett crawled steadily, the smooth stiff clay yielding and cold against his hands and sodden knees. Another smaller tunnel joined from the left. Another angled in from above. The tunnel widened to three feet, then four. Brett got to his feet, walked in a crouch. Here and there, barely visible in the near-darkness, objects lay imbedded in the mud: a silver-plated spoon, its handle bent; the rusted engine of an electric train; a portable radio, green with corrosion from burst batteries.

At a distance, Brett estimated, of a hundred yards from the pit, the tunnel opened into a vast cave, green-lit from tiny discs of frosted glass set in the ceiling far above. A row of discolored concrete piles, the foundations of the building above, protruded against the near wall, their surfaces nibbled and pitted. Between Brett and the concrete columns the floor was littered with pale sticks and stones, gleaming dully in the gloom.

Brett started across the floor. One of the sticks snapped underfoot. He kicked a melon-sized stone. It rolled lightly, came to rest with hollow eyes staring toward him. A human skull.

* * * *

The floor of the cave covered an area the size of a city block. It was blanketed with human bones, with here and there a small cat skeleton or the fanged snout-bones of a dog. There was a constant rustling of rats that played among the rib cages, sat atop crania, scuttled behind shin-bones.

Brett picked his way, stepping over imitation pearl necklaces, zircon rings, plastic buttons, hearing aids, lipsticks, compacts, corset stays, prosthetic devices, rubber heels, wrist watches, lapel watches, pocket watches with corroded brass chains.

Ahead Brett saw a patch of color: a blur of pale yellow. He hurried, stumbling over bone heaps, crunching eyeglasses underfoot. He reached the still figure where it lay slackly, face down. Gingerly he squatted, turned it on its back. It was Dhuva.

Brett slapped the cold wrists, rubbed the clammy hands. Dhuva stirred, moaned weakly. Brett pulled him to a sitting position. "Wake up!" he whispered. "Wake up!"

Dhuva's eyelids fluttered. He blinked dully at Brett.

"The Gels may turn up any minute," Brett hissed. "We have to get away from here. Can you walk?"

"I saw it," said Dhuva faintly. "But it moved so fast…"

"You're safe here for the moment," Brett said. "There are none of them around. But they may be back. We've got to find a way out!"

Dhuva started up, staring around. "Where am I?" he said hoarsely. Brett seized his arm, steadied him on his feet.

"We're in a hollowed-out cave," he said. "The whole city is undermined with them. They're connected by tunnels. We have to find one leading back to the surface."

Dhuva gazed around at the acres of bones. "It left me here for dead."

"Or to die," said Brett.

"Look at them," Dhuva breathed. "Hundreds ... thousands ..."

"The whole population, it looks like. The Gels must have whisked them down here one by one."

"But why?"

"For interfering with the scenes. But that doesn't matter now. What matters is getting out. Come on. I see tunnels on the other side."

They crossed the broad floor, around them the white bones, the rustle of rats. They reached the far side of the cave, picked a six-foot tunnel which trended upward, a trickle of water seeping out of the dark mouth. They started up the slope.

"WE have to have a weapon against the Gels," said Brett.

"Why? I don't want to fight them." Dhuva's voice was thin, frightened. "I want to get away from here ... even back to Wavly. I'd rather face the Duke."

"This was a real town, once," said Brett. "The Gels have taken it over, hollowed out the build-ings, mined the earth under it, killed off the people, and put imitation people in their place. And no-body ever knew. I met a man who's lived here all his life. He doesn't know. But we know ... and we have to do something about it."

"It's not our business. I've had enough. I want to get away."

"The Gels must stay down below, somewhere in that maze of tunnels. For some reason they try to keep up appearances ... but only for the people who belong here. They play out scenes for the fat man, wherever he goes. And he never goes anywhere he isn't expected to."

"We'll get over the wall somehow," said Dhuva. "We may starve, crossing the dry fields, but that's better than this."

They emerged from the tunnel into a coal bin, crossed to a sagging door, found themselves in a boiler room. Stairs led up to sunlight. In the street, in the shadow of tall buildings, a boxy sedan was parked at the curb. Brett went to it, tried the door. It opened. Keys dangled from the ignition switch. He slid into the dusty seat. Behind him there was a hoarse scream. Brett looked up. Through the streaked windshield he saw a mighty Gel rear up before Dhuva, who crouched back against the blackened brick front of the building.

"Don't move, Dhuva!" Brett shouted. Dhuva stood frozen, flattened against the wall. The Gel towered, its surface rippling.

Brett eased from the seat. He stood on the pavement, fifteen feet from the Gel. The rank Gel odor came in waves from the creature. Beyond it he could see Dhuva's white terrified face.

Silently Brett turned the latch of the old-fashioned auto hood, raised it. The copper fuel line curved down from the firewall to a glass sediment cup. The knurled retaining screw turned easily; the cup dropped into Brett's hand. Gasoline ran down in an amber stream. Brett pulled off his damp coat, wadded it, jammed it under the flow. Over his shoulder he saw Dhuva, still rigid—and the Gel, hovering, uncertain.

The coat was saturated with gasoline now. Brett fumbled a match box from his pocket. Wet. He threw the sodden container aside. The battery caught his eye, clamped in a rusted frame under the hood. He jerked the pistol from its holster, used it to short the terminals. Tiny blue sparks jumped. He jammed the coat near, rasped the gun against the soft lead poles. With a whoosh! the coat caught; yellow flames leaped, soot-rimmed. Brett snatched at a sleeve, whirled the coat high. The great Gel, attracted by the sudden motion, rushed at him. He flung the blazing garment over the monster, leaped aside.

The creature went mad. It slumped, lashed itself against the pavement. The burning coat was thrown clear. The Gel threw itself across the pavement, into the gutter, sending a splatter of filthy water over Brett. From the corner of his eye, Brett saw Dhuva seize the burning coat, hurl it into the pooled gasoline in the gutter. Fire leaped twenty feet high; in its center the great Gel bucked and writhed. The ancient car shuddered as the frantic monster struck it. Black smoke boiled up; an unbe-lievable stench came to Brett's nostrils. He backed, coughing. Flames roared around the front of the car. Paint blistered and burned. A tire burst. In a final frenzy, the Gel whipped clear, lay, a great blackened shape of melting rubber, twitching, then still.

"They've tunneled under everything," Brett said. "They've cut through power lines and water lines, concrete, steel, earth; they've left the shell, shored up with spidery-looking trusswork. Some-how they've kept water and power flowing to wherever they needed it—"

"I don't care about your theories," Dhuva said; "I only want to get away."

"It's bound to work, Dhuva. I need your help."

"No."

"Then I'll have to try alone." He turned away.

"Wait," Dhuva called. He came up to Brett. "I owe you a life; you saved mine. I can't let you down now. But if this doesn't work ... or if you can't find what you want—"

"Then we'll go."

Together they turned down a side street, walking rapidly. At the next corner Brett pointed.

"There's one!" They crossed to the service station at a run. Brett tried the door. Locked. He kicked at it, splintered the wood around the lock. He glanced around inside. "No good," he called. "Try the next building. I'll check the one behind."

He crossed the wide drive, battered in a door, looked in at a floor covered with wood shavings. It ended ten feet from the door. Brett went to the edge, looked down. Diagonally, forty feet away, the underground fifty-thousand-gallon storage tank which supplied the gasoline pumps of the station perched, isolated, on a column of striated clay, ribbed with chitinous Gel buttresses. The trun-cated feed lines ended six feet from the tank. From Brett's position, it was impossible to say wheth-er the ends were plugged.

Across the dark cavern a square of light appeared. Dhuva stood in a doorway looking toward Brett.

"Over here, Dhuva!" Brett uncoiled his rope, arranged a slip-noose. He measured the distance with his eye, tossed the loop. It slapped the top of the tank, caught on a massive fitting. He smashed the glass from a window, tied the end of the rope to the center post. Dhuva arrived, watched as Brett went to the edge, hooked his legs over the rope, and started across to the tank.

It was an easy crossing. Brett's feet clanged against the tank. He strad-dled the six-foot cylinder, worked his way to the end, then clambered down to the two two-inch feed lines. He tested their resilience, then lay flat, eased out on them. There were plugs of hard waxy material in the cut ends of the pipes. Brett poked at them with the pistol. Chunks loosened and fell. He worked for fifteen minutes before the first trickle came. Two minutes later, two thick streams of gasoline were pouring down into the darkness.

* * * *

Brett and Dhuva piled sticks, scraps of paper, shavings, and lumps of coal around a core of gaso-line-soaked rags. Directly above the heaped tinder a taut rope stretched from the window post to a child's wagon, the steel bed of which contained a second heap of combustibles. The wagon hung half over the ragged edge of the floor.

"It should take about fifteen minutes for the fire to burn through the rope," Brett said. "Then the wagon will fall and dump the hot coals in the gasoline. By then it will have spread all over the sur-face and flowed down side tunnels into other parts of the cavern system."

"But it may not get them all."

"It will get some of them. It's the best we can do right now. You get the fire going in the wagon; I'll start this one up."

Dhuva sniffed the air. "That fluid," he said. "We know it in Wavly as phlogistoneum. The wealthy use it for cooking."

"We'll use it to cook Gels." Brett struck a match. The fire leaped up, smoking. Dhuva watched, struck his match awkwardly, started his blaze. They stood for a moment watching. The nylon curled and blackened, melting in the heat.

"We'd better get moving," Brett said. "It doesn't look as though it will last fifteen minutes."

They stepped out into the street. Behind them wisps of smoke curled from the door. Dhuva seized Brett's arm. "Look!"

Half a block away the fat man in the panama hat strode toward them at the head of a group of men in grey flannel. "That's him!" the fat man shouted, "the one I told you about. I knew the scoundrel would be back!" He slowed, eyeing Brett and Dhuva warily.

"You'd better get away from here, fast!" Brett called. "There'll be an explosion in a few minutes—"

"Smoke!" the fat man yelped. "Fire! They've set fire to the city! There it is! pouring out of the window ... and the door!" He started forward. Brett yanked the pistol from the holster, thumbed back the hammer.

"Stop right there!" he barked. "For your own good I'm telling you to run. I don't care about that crowd of golems you've collected, but I'd hate to see a real human get hurt—even a cowardly one like you."

"These are honest citizens," the fat man gasped, standing, staring at the gun. "You won't get away with this. We all know you. You'll be dealt with ..."

"We're going now. And you're going too."

"You can't kill us all," the fat man said. He licked his lips. "We won't let you destroy our city."

AS the fat man turned to exhort his followers Brett fired, once twice, three times. Three golems fell on their faces. The fat man whirled.

"Devil!" he shrieked. "A killer is abroad!" He charged, mouth open. Brett ducked aside, tripped the fat man. He fell heavily, slamming his face against the pavement. The golems surged forward. Brett and Dhuva slammed punches to the sternum, took clumsy blows on the shoulder, back, chest. Golems fell. Brett ducked a wild swing, toppled his attacker, turned to see Dhuva deal with the last of the dummies. The fat man sat in the street, dabbing at his bleeding nose, the panama still in place.

"Get up," Brett commanded. "There's no time left."

"You've killed them. Killed them all ..." The fat man got to his feet, then turned suddenly and plunged for the door from which a cloud of smoke poured. Brett hauled him back. He and Dhuva started off, dragging the struggling man between them. They had gone a block when their prisoner, with a sudden frantic jerk, freed himself, set off at a run for the fire.

"Let him go!" Dhuva cried. "It's too late to go back!"

The fat man leaped fallen golems, wrestled with the door, disappeared into the smoke. Brett and Dhuva sprinted for the corner. As they rounded it a tremendous blast shook the street. The pave-ment before them quivered, opened in a wide crack. A ten-foot section dropped from view. They skirted the gaping hole, dashed for safety as the facades along the street cracked, fell in clouds of dust. The street trembled under a second explosion. Cracks opened, dust rising in puffs from the long wavering lines. Masonry collapsed around them. They put their heads down and ran.

Winded, Brett and Dhuva walked through the empty streets of the city. Behind them, smoke blackened the sky. Embers floated down around them. The odor of burning Gel was carried on the wind. The late sun shone on the blank pavement. A lone golem in a tasseled fez, left over from the morning's parade, leaned stiffly against a lamp post, eyes blank. Empty cars sat in driveways. TV antennae stood forlornly against the sunset.

"That place looks lived-in," said Brett, indicating an open apartment window with a curtain bil-lowing above a potted geranium. "I'll take a look."

He came back shaking his head. "They were all in the TV room. They looked so natural at first; I mean, they didn't look up or anything when I walked in. I turned the set off. The electricity is still working anyway. Wonder how long it will last?"

They turned down a residential street. Underfoot the pavement trembled at a distant blast. They skirted a crack, kept going. Occasional golems stood in awkward poses or lay across sidewalks. One, clad in black, tilted awkwardly in a gothic entry of fretted stone work. "I guess there won't be any church this Sunday," said Brett.

He halted before a brown brick apartment house. An untended hose welled on a patch of sickly lawn. Brett went to the door, stood listening, then went in. Across the room the still figure of a woman sat in a rocker. A curl stirred on her smooth forehead. A flicker of expression seemed to cross the lined face. Brett started forward. "Don't be afraid. You can come with us—"

He stopped. A flapping window-shade cast restless shadows on the still golem features on which dust was already settling. Brett turned away, shaking his head.

"All of them," he said. "It's as though they were snipped out of paper. When the Gels died their dummies died with them."

"Why?" said Dhuva. "What does it all mean?"

"Mean?" said Brett. He shook his head, started off again along the street. "It doesn't mean any-thing. It's just the way things are."

* * * *

Brett sat in a deserted Cadillac, tuning the radio.

"...anybody hear me?" said a plaintive voice from the speaker. "This is Ab Gullorian, at the Twin Spires. Looks like I'm the only one left alive. Can anybody hear me?"

Brett tuned. "... been asking the wrong questions ... looking for the Final Fact. Now these are strange matters, brothers. But if a flower blooms, what man shall ask why? What lore do we seek in a symphony...?"

He twisted the knob again. "... Kansas City. Not more than half a dozen of us. And the dead! Piled all over the place. But it's a funny thing: Doc Potter started to do an autopsy—"

Brett turned the knob. "... CQ, CQ, CQ. This is Hollip Quate, calling CQ, CQ. There's been a disaster here at Port Wanderlust. We need—"

"Take Jesus into your hearts," another station urged.

"... to base," the radio said faintly, with much crackling. "Lunar Observatory to base. Come in, Lunar Control. This is Commander McVee of the Lunar Detachment, sole survivor—"

"... hello, Hollip Quate? Hollip Quate? This is Kansas City calling. Say, where did you say you were calling from...?"

"It looks as though both of us had a lot of mistaken ideas about the world outside," said Brett. "Most of these stations sound as though they might as well be coming from Mars."

"I don't understand where the voices come from," Dhuva said. "But all the places they name are strange to me ... except the Twin Spires."

"I've heard of Kansas City," Brett said, "but none of the other ones."

The ground trembled. A low rumble rolled. "Another one," Brett said. He switched off the ra-dio, tried the starter. It groaned, turned over. The engine caught, sputtered, then ran smoothly.

"Get in, Dhuva. We might as well ride. Which way do we go to get out of this place?"

"The wall lies in that direction," said Dhuva. "But I don't know about a gate."

"We'll worry about that when we get to it," said Brett. "This whole place is going to collapse be-fore long. We really started something. I suppose other underground storage tanks caught—and gas lines, too."

A building ahead cracked, fell in a heap of pulverized plaster. The car bucked as a blast sent a ripple down the street. A manhole cover popped up, clattered a few feet, dropped from sight. Brett swerved, gunned the car. It leaped over rubble, roared along the littered pavement. Brett looked in the rear-view mirror. A block behind them the street ended. Smoke and dust rose from the immense pit.

"We just missed it that time!" he called. "How far to the wall?"

"Not far! Turn here ..."

Brett rounded the corner with a shrieking of tires. Ahead the grey wall rose up, blank, feature-less.

"This is a dead end!" Brett shouted.

"We'd better get out and run for it—"

"No time! I'm going to ram the wall! Maybe I can knock a hole in it."

Dhuva crouched; teeth gritted. Brett held the accelerator to the floor, roared straight toward the wall. The heavy car shot across the last few yards, struck—

And burst through a curtain of canvas into a field of dry stalks.

Brett steered the car in a wide curve to halt and look back. A blackened panama hat floated down, settled among the stalks. Smoke poured up in a dense cloud from behind the canvas wall. A fetid stench pervaded the air.

"That finishes that, I guess," Brett said.

"I don't know. Look there."

Brett turned. Far across the dry field columns of smoke rose from the ground.

"The whole thing's undermined," Brett said. "How far does it go?"

"No telling. But we'd better be off. Perhaps we can get beyond the edge of it. Not that it mat-ters. We're all that's left ..."

"You sound like the fat man," Brett said. "But why should we be so surprised to find out the truth? After all, we never saw it before. All we knew—or thought we knew—was what they told us. The moon, the other side of the world, a distant city ... or even the next town. How do we really know what's there ... unless we go and see for ourselves? Does a goldfish in his bowl know what the ocean is like?"

"Where did they come from, those Gels? How much of the world have they undermined? What about Wavly? Is it a golem country too? The Duke ... and all the people I knew?"

"I don't know, Dhuva. I've been wondering about the people in Casperton. Like Doc Welch. I used to see him in the street with his little black bag.

I always thought it was full of pills and scal-pels; but maybe it really had zebra's tails and toad's eyes in it. Maybe he's really a magician on his way to cast spells against demons. Maybe the people I used to see hurrying to catch the bus every morning weren't really going to the office. Maybe they go down into caves and chip away at the foundations of things. Maybe they go up on rooftops and put on rainbow-colored robes and fly away. I used to pass by a bank in Casperton: a big grey stone building with little curtains over the bottom half of the windows. I never go in there. I don't have any-thing to do in a bank. I've always thought it was full of bankers, banking ... Now I don't know. It could be anything ..."

"That's why I'm afraid," Dhuva said. "It could be anything."

"Things aren't really any different than they were," said Brett, "... ex-cept that now we know." He turned the big car out across the field toward Casperton.

"I don't know what we'll find when we get back. Aunt Haicey, Pretty-Lee ... But there's only one way to find out."

The moon rose as the car bumped westward, raising a trail of dust against the luminous sky of evening.

A BAD DAY FOR VERMIN

Originally published in Galaxy Science Fiction, *February 1964.*

Judge Carter Gates of the Third Circuit Court finished his chicken salad on whole wheat, thoughtfully crumpled the waxed paper bag and turned to drop it in the waste basket behind his chair—and sat transfixed.

Through his second-floor office window, he saw a forty-foot flower-petal shape of pale turquoise settling gently between the well-tended petunia beds on the courthouse lawn. On the upper, or stem end of the vessel, a translucent pink panel popped up and a slender, graceful form not unlike a large violet caterpillar undulated into view.

Judge Gates whirled to the telephone. Half an hour later, he put it to the officials gathered with him in a tight group on the lawn.

"Boys, this thing is intelligent; any fool can see that. It's putting together what my boy assures me is some kind of talking machine, and any minute now it's going to start communicating. It's been twenty minutes since I notified Washington on this thing. It won't be long before somebody back there decides this is top secret and slaps a freeze on us here that will make the Manhattan Project look like a publicity campaign. Now, I say this is the biggest thing that ever happened to Plum County—but if we don't aim to be put right out of the picture, we'd better move fast."

"What you got in mind, Jedge?"

"I propose we hold an open hearing right here in the courthouse, the minute that thing gets its gear to working. We'll put it on the air—Tom Clembers from the radio station's already stringing wires, I see. Too bad we've got no TV equipment, but Jody Hurd has a movie camera. We'll put Willow Grove on the map bigger'n Cape Canaveral ever was."

"We're with you on that, Carter!"

Ten minutes after the melodious voice of the Fianna's translator had requested escort to the village headman, the visitor was looking over the crowded courtroom with an expression reminiscent of a St. Bernard puppy hoping for a romp. The rustle of feet and throat-clearing subsided and the speaker began:

"People of the Green World, happy the cycle—"

Heads turned at the clump of feet coming down the side aisle; a heavy-torsoed man of middle age, bald, wearing a khaki shirt and trousers and rimless glasses and with a dark leather holster slapping his hip at each step, cleared the end of the front row of seats, planted himself, feet apart, yanked a heavy nickel-plated .44 revolver from the holster, took aim and fired five shots into the body of the Fianna at a range of ten feet.

The violet form whipped convulsively, writhed from the bench to the floor with a sound like a wet fire hose being dropped, uttered a gasping twitter, and lay still. The gunman turned, dropped the pistol, threw up his hands, and called:

"Sheriff Hoskins, I'm puttin' myself in yer pertective custody."

* * * *

There was a moment of stunned silence; then a rush of spectators for the alien. The sheriff's three-hundred-and-nine-pound bulk bellied through the shouting mob to take up a stand before the khaki-clad man.

"I always knew you was a mean one, Cecil Stump," he said, unlimbering handcuffs, "ever since I seen you makin' up them ground-glass baits for Joe Potter's dog. But I never thought I'd see you turn to cold-blooded murder." He waved at the bystanders. "Clear a path through here; I'm takin' my prisoner over to the jail."

"Jest a dad-blamed minute, Sheriff." Stump's face was pale, his glasses were gone and one khaki shoulder strap dangled—but what was almost a grin twisted one meaty cheek. He hid his hands behind his back, leaned away from the cuffs. "I don't like that word 'prisoner'. I ast you fer pertection. And better look out who you go throwin' that word 'murder' off at, too. I ain't murdered nobody."

The sheriff blinked, turned to roar, "How's the victim, Doc?"

A small gray head rose from bending over the limp form of the Fianna. "Deader'n a mackerel, Sheriff."

"I guess that's it. Let's go, Cecil."

"What's the charge?"

"First degree murder."

"Who'd I murder?"

"Why, you killed this here…this stranger."

"That ain't no stranger. That's a varmint. Murder's got to do with killin' humerns, way I understand it. You goin' to tell me that thing's humern?"

Ten people shouted at once:

"—human as I am!"

"—intelligent being!"

"—tell me you can simply kill—"

"—must be some kind of law—"

The sheriff raised his hands, his jowls drawn down in a scowl. "What about it, Judge Gates? Any law against Cecil Stump killing the…uh…?"

The judge thrust out his lower lip. "Well, let's see," he began. "Technically—"

"Good Lord!" someone blurted. "You mean the laws on murder don't define what constitutes—I mean, what—"

"What a humern is?" Stump snorted. "Whatever it says, it sure-bob don't include no purple worms. That's a varmint, pure and simple. Ain't no different killin' it than any other critter."

"Then, by God, we'll get him for malicious damage," a man called. "Or hunting without a license—out of season!"

"—carrying concealed weapons!"

Stump went for his hip pocket, fumbled out a fat, shapeless wallet, extracted a thumbed rectangle of folded paper, offered it.

"I'm a licensed exterminator. Got a permit to carry the gun, too. I ain't broken no law." He grinned openly now. "Jest doin' my job, Sheriff. And at no charge to the county."

* * * *

A smaller man with bristly red hair flared his nostrils at Stump. "You blood-thirsty idiot!" He raised a fist and shook it. "We'll be a national disgrace—worse than Little Rock! Lynching's too good for you!"

"Hold on there, Weinstein," the sheriff cut in. "Let's not go gettin' no lynch talk started."

"Lynch, is it!" Cecil Stump bellowed, his face suddenly red. "Why, I done a favor for every man here! Now you listen to me! What is that thing over there?" He jerked a blunt thumb toward the judicial bench. "It's some kind of critter from Mars or someplace—you know that as well as me! And what's it here for? It ain't for the good of the likes of you and me, I can tell you that. It's them or us. And this time, by God, we got in the first lick!"

"Why you…you…hate-monger!"

"Now, hold on right there. I'm as liberal-minded as the next feller. Hell, I like a nigger—and I can't hardly tell a Jew from a white man. But when it comes to takin' in a damned purple worm and callin' it humern—that's where I draw the line."

Sheriff Hoskins pushed between Stump and the surging front rank of the crowd. "Stay back there! I want you to disperse, peaceably, and let the law handle this."

"I reckon I'll push off now, Sheriff," Stump hitched up his belt. "I figgered you might have to calm 'em down right at first, but now they've had a chance to think it over and see I ain't broken no law, ain't none of these law-abiding folks going to do anything illegal—like tryin' to get rough with a licensed exterminator just doin' his job." He stooped, retrieved his gun.

"Here, I'll take that," Sheriff Hoskins said. "You can consider your gun license canceled—and your exterminatin' license, too."

Stump grinned again, handed the revolver over.

"Sure. I'm cooperative, Sheriff. Anything you say. Send it around to my place when you're done with it." He pushed his way through the crowd to the corridor door.

"The rest of you stay put!" a portly man with a head of bushy white hair pushed his way through to the bench. "I'm calling an emergency Town Meeting to order here and now!"

* * * *

He banged the gavel on the scarred bench top, glanced down at the body of the dead alien, now covered by a flag.

"Gentlemen, we've got to take fast action. If the wire services get hold of this before we've gone on record, Willow Grove'll be a blighted area."

"Look here, Willard," Judge Gates called, rising. "This—this mob isn't competent to take legal action."

"Never mind what's legal, Judge. Sure, this calls for Federal legislation—maybe a Constitutional amendment—but in the meantime, we're going to redefine what constitutes a person within the incorporated limits of Willow Grove!"

"That's the least we can do," a thin-faced woman snapped, glaring at Judge Gates. "Do you think we're going to set here and condone this outrage?"

"Nonsense!" Gates shouted. "I don't like what happened any better than you do—but a person—well, a person's got two arms and two legs and—"

"Shape's got nothing to do with it," the chairman cut in. "Bears walk on two legs! Dave Zawocky lost his in the war. Monkeys have hands."

"Any intelligent creature—" the woman started.

"Nope, that won't do, either; my unfortunate cousin's boy Melvin was born an imbecile, poor lad. Now, folks, there's no time to waste. We'll find it very difficult to formulate a satisfactory definition based on considerations such as these. However, I think we can resolve the question in terms that will form a basis for future legislation on the question. It's going to make some big changes in things. Hunters aren't going to like it—and the meat industry will be affected. But if, as it appears, we're entering into an era of contact with…ah…creatures from other worlds, we've got to get our house in order."

"You tell 'em, Senator!" someone yelled.

"We better leave this for Congress to figger out!" another voice insisted.

"We got to do something…."

The senator held up his hands. "Quiet, everybody. There'll be reporters here in a matter of minutes. Maybe our ordinance won't hold water. But it'll start 'em thinking—and it'll make a lots better copy for Willow Grove than the killing."

"What you got in mind, Senator?"

"Just this:" the Senator said solemnly. "A person is...*any harmless creature*...."

Feet shuffled. Someone coughed.

"What about a man who commits a violent act, then?" Judge Gates demanded. "What's he, eh?"

"That's obvious, gentlemen," the senator said flatly. "He's vermin."

* * * *

On the courthouse steps Cecil Stump stood, hands in hip pockets, talking to a reporter from the big-town paper in Mattoon, surrounded by a crowd of late-comers who had missed the excitement inside. He described the accuracy of his five shots, the sound they had made hitting the big blue snake, and the ludicrous spectacle the latter had presented in its death agony. He winked at a foxy man in overalls picking his nose at the edge of the crowd.

"Guess it'll be a while 'fore any more damned reptiles move in here like they owned the place," he concluded.

The courthouse doors banged wide; excited citizens poured forth, veering aside from Cecil Stump. The crowd around him thinned, broke up as its members collared those emerging with the hot news. The reporter picked a target.

"Perhaps you'd care to give me a few details of the action taken by the...ah...Special Committee, sir?"

Senator Custis pursed his lips. "A session of the Town Council was called," he said. "We've defined what a person is in this town—"

Stump, standing ten feet away, snorted. "Can't touch me with no *ex post factory* law."

"—and also what can be classified as vermin," Custis went on.

Stump closed his mouth with a snap.

"Here, that s'posed to be some kind of slam at me, Custis? By God, come election time...."

Above, the door opened again. A tall man in a leather jacket stepped out, stood looking down. The crowd pressed back. Senator Custis and the reporter moved aside. The newcomer came down the steps slowly. He carried Cecil Stump's nickel-plated .44 in his hand.

Standing alone now, Stump watched him.

"Here," he said. His voice carried a sudden note of strain. "Who're you?"

The man reached the foot of the steps, raised the revolver and cocked it with a thumb.

"I'm the new exterminator," he said.

END AS A HERO

Originally published in **Galaxy Science Fiction**, *June 1963.*

I

In the dream I was swimming in a river of white fire and the dream went on and on. And then I was awake—and the fire was still there, fiercely burning at me.

I tried to move to get away from the flames, and then the real pain hit me. I tried to go back to sleep and the relative comfort of the river of fire, but it was no go. For better or worse, I was alive and conscious.

I opened my eyes and took a look around. I was on the floor next to an unpadded acceleration couch—the kind the Terrestrial Space Arm installs in seldom-used lifeboats. There were three more couches, but no one in them. I tried to sit up. It wasn't easy but, by applying a lot more will-power than should be required of a sick man, I made it. I took a look at my left arm. Baked. The hand was only medium rare, but the forearm was black, with deep red showing at the bottom of the cracks where the crisped upper layers had burst....

There was a first-aid cabinet across the compartment from me. I tried my right leg, felt broken bone-ends grate with a sensation that transcended pain. I heaved with the other leg, scrabbled with the charred arm. The crawl to the cabinet dwarfed Hillary's trek up Everest, but I reached it after a couple of years, and found the microswitch on the floor that activated the thing, and then I was fading out again....

* * * *

I came out of it clear-headed but weak. My right leg was numb, but reasonably comfortable, clamped tight in a walking brace. I put up a hand and felt a shaved skull, with sutures. It must have been a fracture. The left arm—well, it was still there, wrapped to the shoulder and held out stiffly by a power truss that would keep the scar tissue from pulling up and crippling me. The steady pressure as the truss contracted wasn't anything to do a sense-tape on for replaying at leisure moments, but at least the cabinet hadn't amputated. I wasn't complaining.

As far as I knew, I was the first recorded survivor of contact with the Gool—if I survived.

I was still a long way from home, and I hadn't yet checked on the condition of the lifeboat. I glanced toward the entry port. It was dogged shut. I could see black marks where my burned hand had been at work.

I fumbled my way into a couch and tried to think. In my condition—with a broken leg and third-degree burns, plus a fractured skull—I shouldn't have been able to fall out of bed, much less make the trip from *Belshazzar's* CCC to the boat; and how had I managed to dog that port shut? In an emergency a man was capable of great exertions. But running on a broken femur, handling heavy levers with charred fingers and thinking with a cracked head were overdoing it. Still, I was here—and it was time to get a call through to TSA headquarters.

I flipped the switch and gave the emergency call-letters Col. Ausar Kayle of Aerospace Intelligence had assigned to me a few weeks before. It was almost five minutes before the "acknowledge" came through from the Ganymede relay station, another ten minutes before Kayle's face swam into view. Even through the blur of the screen I could see the haggard look.

"Granthan!" he burst out. "Where are the others? What happened out there?" I turned him down to a mutter.

"Hold on," I said. "I'll tell you. Recorders going?" I didn't wait for an answer—not with a fifteen-minute transmission lag. I plowed on:

"*Belshazzar* was sabotaged. So was *Gilgamesh*—I think. I got out. I lost a little skin, but the aid cabinet has the case in hand. Tell the Med people the drinks are on me."

I finished talking and flopped back, waiting for Kayle's reply. On the screen, his flickering image gazed back impatiently, looking as hostile as a swing-shift ward nurse. It would be half an hour before I would get his reaction to my report. I dozed off—and awoke with a start. Kayle was talking.

"—your report. I won't mince words. They're wondering at your role in the disaster. How does it happen that you alone survived?"

"How the hell do I know?" I yelled—or croaked. But Kayle's voice was droning on:

"… you Psychodynamics people have been telling me the Gool may have some kind of long-range telehypnotic ability that might make it possible for them to subvert a loyal man without his knowledge. You've told me yourself that you blacked out during the attack—and came to on the lifeboat, with no recollection of how you got there.

"This is war, Granthan. War against a vicious enemy who strike without warning and without mercy. You were sent out to investigate the possibility of—what's that term you use?—hyper-cortical invasion. You know better than most the risk I'd be running if you were allowed to pass the patrol line.

"I'm sorry, Granthan. I can't let you land on Earth. I can't accept the risk."

"What do I do now?" I stormed. "Go into orbit and eat pills and hope you think of something? I need a doctor!"

Presently Kayle replied. "Yes," he said. "You'll have to enter a parking orbit. Perhaps there will be developments soon which will make it possible to…ah…restudy the situation." He didn't meet my eye. I knew what he was thinking. He'd spare me the mental anguish of knowing what was coming. I couldn't really blame him; he was doing what he thought was the right thing. And I'd have to go along and pretend—right up until the warheads struck—that I didn't know I'd been condemned to death.

II

I tried to gather my wits and think my way through the situation. I was alone and injured, aboard a lifeboat that would be the focus of a converging flight of missiles as soon as I approached within battery range of Earth. I had gotten clear of the Gool, but I wouldn't survive my next meeting with my own kind. They couldn't take the chance that I was acting under Gool orders.

I wasn't, of course. I was still the same Peter Granthan, psychodynamicist, who had started out with Dayan's fleet six weeks earlier. The thoughts I was having weren't brilliant, but they were mine, all mine….

But how could I be sure of that?

Maybe there was something in Kayle's suspicion. If the Gool were as skillful as we thought, they would have left no overt indications of their tampering—not at a conscious level.

But this was where psychodynamics training came in. I had been reacting like any scared casualty, aching to get home and lick his wounds. But I wasn't just any casualty. I had been trained in the subtleties of the mind— and I had been prepared for just such an attack.

Now was the time to make use of that training. It had given me one resource. I could unlock the memories of my subconscious—and see again what had happened.

I lay back, cleared my mind of extraneous thoughts, and concentrated on the trigger word that would key an auto-hypnotic sequence….

Sense impressions faded. I was alone in the nebulous emptiness of a first-level trance. I keyed a second word, slipped below the misty surface into a dreamworld of vague phantasmagoric figures milling in their limbo of sub-conceptualization. I penetrated deeper, broke through into the vividly hallucinatory third level, where images of mirror-bright immediacy clamored for attention. And deeper….

* * * *

The immense orderly confusion of the basic memory level lay before me. Abstracted from it, aloof and observant, the monitoring personality-fraction scanned the pattern, searching the polydimensional continuum for evidence of an alien intrusion.

And found it.

As the eye instantaneously detects a flicker of motion amid an infinity of static detail, so my inner eye perceived the subtle traces of the probing Gool mind, like a whispered touch deftly rearranging my buried motivations.

I focused selectively, tuned to the recorded gestalt.

"*It is a contact, Effulgent One!*"

"*Softly, now! Nurture the spark well. It but trembles at the threshold....*"

"*It is elusive, Master! It wriggles like a gorm-worm in the eating trough!*"

A part of my mind watched as the memory unreeled. I listened to the voices—yet not voices, merely the shape of concepts, indescribably intricate. I saw how the decoy pseudo-personality which I had concretized for the purpose in a hundred training sessions had fought against the intruding stimuli—then yielded under the relentless thrust of the alien probe. I watched as the Gool operator took over the motor centers, caused me to crawl through the choking smoke of the devastated control compartment toward the escape hatch. Fire leaped up, blocking the way. I went on, felt ghostly flames whipping at me—and then the hatch was open and I pulled myself through, forcing the broken leg. My blackened hand fumbled at the locking wheel. Then the blast as the lifeboat leaped clear of the disintegrating dreadnought—and the world-ending impact as I fell.

At a level far below the conscious, the embattled pseudo-personality lashed out again—fighting the invader.

"*Almost it eluded me then, Effulgent Lord. Link with this lowly one!*"

"*Impossible! Do you forget all my teachings? Cling, though you expend the last filament of your life-force!*"

Free from all distraction, at a level where comprehension and retention are instantaneous and total, my monitoring basic personality fraction followed the skillful Gool mind as it engraved its commands deep in my subconscious. Then the touch withdrew, erasing the scars of its passage, to leave me unaware of its tampering—at a conscious level.

Watching the Gool mind, I learned.

The insinuating probe—a concept regarding which psychodynamicists had theorized—was no more than a pattern in emptiness....

But a pattern which I could duplicate, now that I had seen what had been done to me.

Hesitantly, I felt for the immaterial fabric of the continuum, warping and manipulating it, copying the Gool probe. Like planes of paper-thin crystal, the polyfinite aspects of reality shifted into focus, aligning themselves.

Abruptly, a channel lay open. As easily as I would stretch out my hand to pluck a moth from a night-flower, I reached across the unimaginable void—and sensed a pit blacker than the bottom floor of hell, and a glistening dark shape.

There was a soundless shriek. *"Effulgence! It reached out—touched me!"*

* * * *

Using the technique I had grasped from the Gool itself, I struck, stifling the outcry, invaded the fetid blackness and grappled the obscene gelatinous immensity of the Gool spy as it spasmed in a frenzy of xenophobia—a ton of liver writhing at the bottom of a dark well.

I clamped down control. The Gool mind folded in on itself, gibbering. Not pausing to rest, I followed up, probed along my channel of contact, tracing patterns, scanning the flaccid Gool mind....

I saw a world of yellow seas lapping at endless shores of mud. There was a fuming pit, where liquid sulphur bubbled up from some inner source, filling an immense natural basin. The Gool clustered at its rim, feeding, each monstrous shape heaving against its neighbors for a more favorable position.

I probed farther, saw the great cables of living nervous tissue that linked each eating organ with the brain-mass far underground. I traced the passages through which tendrils ran out to immense caverns where smaller creatures labored over strange devices. These, my host's memory told me, were the young of the Gool. Here they built the fleets that would transport the spawn to the new worlds the Prime Overlord had discovered, worlds where food was free for the taking. Not sulphur alone, but potassium, calcium, iron and all the metals—riches beyond belief in endless profusion. No longer would the Gool tribe cluster—those who remained of a once-great race—at a single feeding trough. They would spread out across a galaxy—and beyond.

But not if I could help it.

The Gool had evolved a plan—but they'd had a stroke of bad luck.

In the past, they had managed to control a man here and there, among the fleets, far from home, but only at a superficial level. Enough, perhaps, to wreck a ship, but not the complete control needed to send a man back to Earth under Gool compulsion, to carry out complex sabotage.

Then they had found me, alone, a sole survivor, free from the clutter of the other mind-fields. It had been their misfortune to pick a psychodynamicist. Instead of gaining a patient slave, they had opened the fortress door to an unseen spy. Now that I was there, I would see what I could steal.

A timeless time passed. I wandered among patterns of white light and white sound, plumbed the deepest recesses of hidden Gool thoughts, fared along strange ways examining the shapes and colors of the concepts of an alien mind.

I paused at last, scanning a multi-ordinal structure of pattern within pattern; the diagrammed circuits of a strange machine.

I followed through its logic-sequence; and, like a bomb-burst, its meaning exploded in my mind.

From the vile nest deep under the dark surface of the Gool world in its lonely trans-Plutonian orbit, I had plucked the ultimate secret of their kind.

Matter across space.

* * * *

"You've got to listen to me, Kayle," I shouted. "I know you think I'm a Gool robot. But what I have is too big to let you blow it up without a fight. Matter transmission! You know what that can mean to us. The concept is too complex to try to describe in words. You'll have to take my word for it. I can build it, though, using standard components, plus an infinite-area antenna and a moebius-wound coil—and a few other things...."

I harangued Kayle for a while, and then sweated out his answer. I was getting close now. If he couldn't see the beauty of my proposal, my screens would start to register the radiation of warheads any time now.

Kayle came back—and his answer boiled down to "no."

I tried to reason with him. I reminded him how I had readied myself for the trip with sessions on the encephaloscope, setting up the cross-networks of conditioned defensive responses, the shunt circuits to the decoy pseudo-personality, leaving my volitional ego free. I talked about subliminal hypnotics and the resilience quotient of the ego-complex.

I might have saved my breath.

"I don't understand that psychodynamics jargon, Granthan," he snapped. "It smacks of mysticism. But I understand what the Gool have done to you well enough. I'm sorry."

I leaned back and chewed the inside of my lip and thought unkind thoughts about Colonel Ausar Kayle. Then I settled down to solve the problem at hand.

I keyed the chart file, flashed pages from the standard index on the reference screen, checking radar coverages, beacon ranges, monitor stations, controller fields. It looked as though a radar-negative boat the size of mine might possibly get through the defensive net with a daring pilot, and as a condemned spy, I could afford to be daring.

And I had a few ideas.

III

The shrilling of the proximity alarm blasted through the silence. For a wild moment I thought Kayle had beaten me to the punch; then I realized it was the routine DEW line patrol contact.

"Z four-oh-two, I am reading your IFF. Decelerate at 1.8 gee preparatory to picking up approach orbit...."

The screen went on droning out instructions. I fed them into the autopilot, at the same time running over my approach plan. The scout was moving in closer. I licked dry lips. It was time to try.

I closed my eyes, reached out—as the Gool mind had reached out to me—and felt the touch of a Signals Officer's mind, forty thousand miles distant, aboard the patrol vessel. There was a brief flurry of struggle; then I dictated my instructions. The Signals Officer punched keys, spoke into his microphone:

"As you were, Z four-oh-two. Continue on present course. At Oh-nineteen seconds, pick up planetary for re-entry and let-down."

I blanked out the man's recollection of what had happened, caught his belated puzzlement as I broke contact. But I was clear of the DEW line now, rapidly approaching atmosphere.

"Z four-oh-two," the speaker crackled. "This is planetary control. I am picking you up on channel forty-three, for re-entry and let-down."

There was a long pause. Then:

"Z four-oh-two, countermand DEW Line clearance! Repeat, clearance countermanded! Emergency course change to standard hyperbolic code ninety-eight. Do not attempt re-entry. Repeat: do not attempt re-entry!"

It hadn't taken Kayle long to see that I'd gotten past the outer line of defense. A few more minutes' grace would have helped. I'd play it dumb, and hope for a little luck.

"Planetary, Z four-oh-two here. Say, I'm afraid I missed part of that, fellows. I'm a little banged up—I guess I switched frequencies on you. What was that after 'pick up channel forty-three'...?"

"Four-oh-two, sheer off there! You're not cleared for re-entry!"

"Hey, you birds are mixed up," I protested. "I'm cleared all the way. I checked in with DEW—"

It was time to disappear. I blanked off all transmission, hit the controls, following my evasive pattern. And again I reached out—

A radar man at a site in the Pacific, fifteen thousand miles away, rose from his chair, crossed the darkened room and threw a switch. The radar screens blanked off....

For an hour I rode the long orbit down, fending off attack after attack. Then I was clear, skimming the surface of the ocean a few miles southeast of Key West. The boat hit hard. I felt the floor rise up, over, buffeting me against the restraining harness.

I hauled at the release lever, felt a long moment of giddy disorientation as the escape capsule separated from the sinking lifeboat deep under the surface. Then my escape capsule was bobbing on the water.

I would have to risk calling Kayle now—but by voluntarily giving my position away, I should convince him I was still on our side—and I was badly in need of a pick-up. I flipped the sending key.

"This is Z four-oh-two," I said. "I have an urgent report for Colonel Kayle of Aerospace Intelligence."

Kayle's face appeared. "Don't fight it, Granthan," he croaked. "You penetrated the planetary defenses—God knows how. I—"

"Later," I snapped. "How about calling off your dogs now? And send somebody out here to pick me up, before I add sea-sickness to my other complaints."

"We have you pinpointed," Kayle cut in. "It's no use fighting it, Granthan."

* * * *

I felt cold sweat pop out on my forehead. "You've got to listen, Kayle," I shouted. "I suppose you've got missiles on the way already. Call them back! I have information that can win the war—"

"I'm sorry, Granthan," Kayle said. "It's too late—even if I could take the chance you were right."

A different face appeared on the screen.

"Mr. Granthan, I am General Titus. On behalf of your country, and in the name of the President—who has been apprised of this tragic situation—it is my privilege to inform you that you will be awarded the Congressional Medal of Honor—posthumously—for your heroic effort. Although you failed, and have in fact been forced, against your will, to carry out the schemes of the inhuman enemy, this in no way detracts from your gallant attempt. Mr. Granthan, I salute you."

The general's arm went up in a rigid gesture.

"Stow that, you pompous idiot!" I barked. "I'm no spy!"

Kayle was back, blanking out the startled face of the general.

"Goodbye, Granthan. Try to understand...."

I flipped the switch, sat gripping the couch, my stomach rising with each heave of the floating escape capsule. I had perhaps five minutes. The missiles would be from Canaveral.

I closed my eyes, forced myself to relax, reached out....

I sensed the distant shore, the hot buzz of human minds at work in the cities. I followed the coastline, found the Missile Base, flicked through the cluster of minds.

"—*missile on course; do right, baby. That's it, right in the slot.*"

I fingered my way through the man's mind and found the control centers. He turned stiffly from the plotting board, tottered to a panel to slam his hand against the destruct button.

Men fell on him, dragged him back. "—*fool, why did you blow it?*"

I dropped the contact, found another, who leaped to the panel, detonated the remainder of the flight of six missiles. Then I withdrew. I would have a few minutes' stay of execution now.

I was ten miles from shore. The capsule had its own power plant. I started it up, switched on the external viewer. I saw dark sea, the glint of star-light on the choppy surface, in the distance a glow on the horizon that would be Key West. I plugged the course into the pilot, then leaned back and felt outward with my mind for the next attacker.

IV

It was dark in the trainyard. I moved along the tracks in a stumbling walk. Just a few more minutes, I was telling myself. *A few more minutes and you can lie down...rest....*

The shadowed bulk of a box car loomed up, its open door a blacker square. I leaned against the sill, breathing hard, then reached inside for a grip with my good hand.

Gravel scrunched nearby. The beam of a flashlight lanced out, slipped along the weathered car, caught me. There was a startled exclamation. I ducked back, closed my eyes, felt out for his mind. There was a confused murmur of thought, a random intrusion of impressions from the city all around. It was hard, too hard. I had to sleep—

I heard the snick of a revolver being cocked, and dropped flat as a gout of flame stabbed toward me, the imperative Bam! echoing between the cars. I caught the clear thought:

"God-awful looking, shaved head, arm stuck out; him all right—"

I reached out to his mind and struck at random. The light fell, went out, and I heard the unconscious body slam to the ground like a poled steer.

It was easy—if I could only stay awake.

I gritted my teeth, pulled myself into the car, crawled to a dark corner behind a crate and slumped down. I tried to evoke a personality fraction to set as a guard, a part of my mind to stay awake and warn me of danger. It was too much trouble. I relaxed and let it all slide down into darkness.

* * * *

The car swayed, click-clack, click-clack. I opened my eyes, saw yellow sunlight in a bar across the litter on the floor. The power truss creaked, pulling at my arm. My broken leg was throbbing its indignation at the treatment it had received—walking brace and all—and the burned arm was yelling aloud for more of that nice dope that had been keeping it from realizing how bad it was. All things considered, I felt like a badly embalmed mummy—except that I was hungry. I had been a fool not to fill my pockets when I left the escape capsule in the shallows off Key Largo, but things had been happening too fast.

I had barely made it to the fishing boat, whose owner I had coerced into rendezvousing with me before shells started dropping around us. If the gunners on the cruiser ten miles away had had any luck, they would have finished me—and the hapless fisherman—right then. We rode out a couple of near misses, before I put the cruiser's gunnery crew off the air.

At a fishing camp on the beach, I found a car—with driver. He dropped me at the railyard, and drove off under the impression he was in town for groceries. He'd never believe he'd seen me.

Now I'd had my sleep. I had to start getting ready for the next act of the farce.

I pressed the release on the power truss, gingerly unclamped it, then rigged a sling from a strip of shirt tail. I tied the arm to my side as inconspicuously as possible. I didn't disturb the bandages.

I needed new clothes—or at least different ones—and something to cover my shaved skull. I couldn't stay hidden forever. The yard cop had recognized me at a glance.

I lay back, waiting for the train to slow for a town. I wasn't unduly worried—at the moment. The watchman probably hadn't convinced anyone he'd actually seen me. Maybe he hadn't been too sure himself.

The click-clack slowed and the train shuddered to a stop. I crept to the door, peered through the crack. There were sunny fields, a few low buildings in the distance, the corner of a platform. I closed my eyes and let my awareness stretch out.

"—lousy job. What's the use? Little witch in the lunch room…up in the hills, squirrel hunting, bottle of whiskey…."

I settled into control gently, trying not to alarm the man. I saw through his eyes the dusty box car, the rust on the tracks, the listless weeds growing among cinders, and the weathered boards of the platform. I turned him, and saw the dingy glass of the telegraph window, a sagging screen door with a chipped enameled cola sign.

I walked the man to the door, and through it. Behind a linoleum-topped counter, a coarse-skinned teen-age girl with heavy breasts and wet patches under her arms looked up without interest as the door banged.

My host went on to the counter, gestured toward the waxed-paper-wrapped sandwiches under a glass cover. "I'll take 'em all. And candy bars, and cigarettes. And give me a big glass of water."

"Better git out there and look after yer train," the girl said carelessly. "When'd you git so all-fired hungry all of a sudden?"

"Put it in a bag. Quick."

"Look who's getting bossy—"

My host rounded the counter, picked up a used paper bag, began stuffing food in it. The girl stared at him, then pushed him back. "You git back around that counter!"

She filled the bag, took a pencil from behind her ear.

"That'll be one eighty-five. Cash."

My host took two dog-eared bills from his shirt pocket, dropped them on the counter and waited while the girl filled a glass. He picked it up and started out.

"Hey! Where you goin' with my glass?"

The trainman crossed the platform, headed for the boxcar. He slid the loose door back a few inches against the slack latch, pushed the bag inside, placed the glass of water beside it, then pulled off his grimy railroader's cap and pushed it through the opening. He turned. The girl watched from the platform. A rattle passed down the line and the train started up with a lurch. The man walked back toward the girl. I heard him say: "Friend o' mine in there—just passin' through."

I was discovering that it wasn't necessary to hold tight control over every move of a subject. Once given the impulse to act, he would rationalize his behavior, fill in the details—and never know that the original idea hadn't been his own.

I drank the water first, ate a sandwich, then lit a cigarette and lay back. So far so good. The crates in the car were marked "U. S. Naval Aerospace Station, Bayou Le Cochon". With any luck I'd reach New Orleans in another twelve hours. The first step of my plan included a raid on the Delta National Labs; but that was tomorrow. That could wait.

* * * *

It was a little before dawn when I crawled out of the car at a siding in the swampy country a few miles out of New Orleans. I wasn't feeling good, but I had a stake in staying on my feet. I still had a few miles in me. I had my supplies—a few candy bars and some cigarettes—stuffed in the pockets of the tattered issue coverall. Otherwise, I was unencumbered. Unless you wanted to count the walking brace on my right leg and the sling binding my arm.

I picked my way across mushy ground to a pot-holed black-top road, started limping toward a few car lights visible half a mile away. It was already hot. The swamp air was like warmed-over subway fumes. Through the drugs, I could feel my pulse throbbing in my various wounds. I reached out and touched the driver's mind; he was thinking about shrimps, a fish-hook wound on his left thumb and a girl with black hair. "Want a lift?" he called.

I thanked him and got in. He gave me a glance and I pinched off his budding twinge of curiosity. It was almost an effort now not to follow his thoughts. It was as though my mind, having learned the trick of communications with others, instinctively reached out toward them.

An hour later he dropped me on a street corner in a shabby marketing district of the city and drove off. I hoped he made out all right with the dark-haired girl. I spotted a used-clothing store and headed for it.

Twenty minutes later I was back on the sidewalk, dressed in a pinkish-gray suit that had been cut a long time ago by a Latin tailor—maybe to settle a grudge. The shirt that went with it was an unsuccessful violet. The black string tie lent a dubious air of distinction. I'd swapped the railroader's cap for a tarnished beret. The man who had supplied the outfit was still asleep. I figured I'd done him a favor by taking it. I couldn't hope to pass for a fisherman—I wasn't the type. Maybe I'd get by as a coffee-house derelict.

I walked past fly-covered fish stalls, racks of faded garments, grimy vegetables in bins, enough paint-flaked wrought iron to cage a herd of brontosauri, and fetched up at a cab stand. I picked a fat driver with a wart.

"How much to the Delta National Laboratories?"

He rolled an eye toward me, shifted his toothpick.

"What ya wanna go out there for? Nothing out there."

"I'm a tourist," I said. "They told me before I left home not to miss it."

He grunted, reached back and opened the door. I got in. He flipped his flag down, started up with a clash of gears and pulled out without looking.

"How far is it?" I asked him.

"It ain't far. Mile, mile and a quarter."

"Pretty big place, I guess."

He didn't answer.

We went through a warehousing district, swung left along the water-front, bumped over railroad tracks, and pulled up at a nine-foot cyclone fence with a locked gate.

"A buck ten," my driver said.

I looked out at the fence, a barren field, a distant group of low buildings. "What's this?"

"This is the place you ast for. That'll be a buck ten, mister."

I touched his mind, planted a couple of false impressions and withdrew. He blinked, then started up, drove around the field, pulled up at an open gate with a blue-uniformed guard. He looked back at me.

"You want I should drive in, sir?"

"I'll get out here."

He jumped out, opened my door, helped me out with a hand under my good elbow. "I'll get your change, sir," he said, reaching for his hip.

"Keep it."

"Thank YOU." He hesitated. "Maybe I oughta stick around. You know."

"I'll be all right."

"I hope so," he said. "A man like you—you and me—" he winked. "After all, we ain't both wearing berets fer nothing."

"True," I said. "Consider your tip doubled. Now drive away into the sunrise and forget you ever saw me."

* * * *

He got into the car, beaming, and left. I turned and sized up the Delta Labs.

There was nothing fancy about the place; it consisted of low brick and steel buildings, mud, a fence and a guard who was looking at me.

I sauntered over. "I'm from Iowa City," I said. "Now, the rest of the group didn't come—said they'd rather rest one day. But I like to see it all. After all, I paid—"

"Just a minute," the guard said, holding up a palm. "You must be lost, fella. This here ain't no tourist attraction. You can't come in here."

"This is the cameo works?" I said anxiously.

He shook his head. "Too bad you let your cab go. It's an hour yet till the bus comes."

A dun-painted staff car came into view, slowed and swung wide to turn in. I fingered the driver's mind. The car swerved, braked to a halt. A portly man in the back seat leaned forward, frowning. I touched him. He relaxed. The driver leaned across and opened the door. I went around and got in. The guard was watching, open-mouthed.

I gave him a two-finger salute, and the car pulled through the gate.

"Stop in front of the electronics section," I said. The car pulled up. I got out, went up the steps and pushed through the double glass doors. The car sat for a moment, then moved slowly off. The passenger would be wondering why the driver had stopped—but the driver wouldn't remember.

I was inside the building now; that was a start. I didn't like robbery in broad daylight, but it was a lot easier this way. I wasn't equal to climbing any walls or breaking down any locked doors—not until I'd had a transfusion, a skin graft and about three months' vacation on a warm beach somewhere.

A man in a white smock emerged from a door. He started past me, spun—

"I'm here about the garbage," I said. "Damn fools *will* put the cans in with the edible. Are you the one called?"

"How's that?"

"I ain't got all the morning!" I shrilled. "You scientist fellers are all alike. Which way is the watchamacallit—equipment lab?"

"Right along there." He pointed. I didn't bother to thank him. It wouldn't have been in character.

A thin man with a brush mustache eyed me sharply as I pushed through the door. I looked at him, nodding absently. "Carry on with your work," I said. "The audit will be carried out in such a way as to disturb you as little as possible. Just show me your voucher file, if you please."

He sighed and waved toward a filing cabinet. I went to it and pulled a drawer open, glancing about the room. Full shelves were visible through an inner door.

Twenty minutes later I left the building, carrying a sheet metal carton containing the electronic components I needed to build a matter transmitter—except for the parts I'd have to fabricate myself from raw materials. The load was heavy—too heavy for me to carry very far. I parked it at the door and waited until a pick-up truck came along.

It pulled over. The driver climbed out and came up the walk to me. "Are you—uh…?" He scratched his head.

"Right." I waved at my loot. "Put it in the back." He obliged. Together we rolled toward the gate. The guard held up his hand, came forward to check the truck. He looked surprised when he saw me.

"Just who are you, fella?" he said.

I didn't like tampering with people any more than I had to. It was a lot like stealing from a blind man: easy, but nothing to feel proud of. I gave him a light touch—just the suggestion that what I would say would be full of deep meaning.

"You know—the regular Wednesday shipment," I said darkly. "Keep it quiet. We're all relying on you."

"Sure thing," he said, stepping back. We gunned through the gate. I glanced back to see him looking after the truck, thinking about the Wednesday shipment on a Friday. He decided it was logical, nodded his head and forgot the whole thing.

* * * *

V

I'd been riding high for a couple of hours, enjoying the success of the tricks I'd stolen from the Gool. Now I suddenly felt like something the student morticians had been practicing on. I guided my driver through a second-rate residential section, looking for an M.D. shingle on a front lawn.

The one I found didn't inspire much confidence—you could hardly see it for the weeds—but I didn't want to make a big splash. I had to have an assist from my driver to make it to the front door. He got me inside, parked my box beside me and went off to finish his rounds, under the impression that it had been a dull morning.

The doctor was a seedy, seventyish G.P. with a gross tremor of the hands that a good belt of Scotch would have helped. He looked at me as though I'd interrupted something that was either more fun or paid better than anything I was likely to come up with.

"I need my dressing changed, Doc," I said. "And maybe a shot to keep me going."

"I'm not a dope peddler," he snapped. "You've got the wrong place."

"Just a little medication—whatever's usual. It's a burn."

"Who told you to come here?"

I looked at him meaningfully. "The word gets around."

He glared at me, gnashed his plates, then gestured toward a black-varnished door. "Go right in there."

He gaped at my arm when the bandages were off. I took a quick glance and wished I hadn't.

"How did you do this?"

"Smoking in bed," I said. "Have you got…something that…."

He caught me before I hit the floor, got me into a chair. Then he had that Scotch he'd been wanting, gave me a shot as an after-thought, and looked at me narrowly.

"I suppose you fell out of that same bed and broke your leg," he said.

"Right. Hell of a dangerous bed."

"I'll be right back." He turned to the door. "Don't go away. I'll just… get some gauze."

"Better stay here, Doc. There's plenty of gauze right on that table."

"See here—"

"Skip it, doc. I know all about you."

"What?"

"I said *all* about you."

He set to work then; a guilty conscience is a tough argument to answer.

He plastered my arm with something and rewrapped it, then looked the leg over and made a couple of adjustments to the brace. He clucked over the stitches in my scalp, dabbed something on them that hurt like hell, then shoved an old-fashioned stickpin needle into my good arm.

"That's all I can do for you," he said. He handed me a bottle of pills. "Here are some tablets to take in an emergency. Now get out."

"Call me a cab, Doc."

* * * *

I listened while he called, then lit a cigarette and watched through the curtains. The doc stood by, worrying his upper plate and eyeing me. So far

I hadn't had to tinker with his mind, but it would be a good idea to check. I felt my way delicately.

—oh God, why did I... long time ago... Mary ever knew... go to Arizona, start again, too old.... I saw the nest of fears that gnawed at him, the frustration and the faint flicker of hope but not quite dead. I touched his mind, wiped away scars....

"Here's your car," he said. He opened the door, looking at me. I started past him.

"Are you sure you're all right?" he said.

"Sure, Pop. And don't worry. Everything's going to be okay."

The driver put my boxes on the back seat. I got in beside him and told him to take me to a men's clothing store. He waited while I changed my hand-me-downs for an off-the-hook suit, new shirt and underwear and a replacement beret. It was the only kind of hat that didn't hurt. My issue shoes were still good, but I traded them in on a new pair, added a light raincoat, and threw in a sturdy suitcase for good measure. The clerk said something about money and I dropped an idea into his mind, paused long enough to add a memory of a fabulous night with a redhead. He hardly noticed me leaving.

I tried not to feel like a shop-lifter. After all, it's not every day a man gets a chance to swap drygoods for dreams.

In the cab, I transferred my belongings to the new suitcase, then told the driver to pull up at an anonymous-looking hotel. A four-star admiral with frayed cuffs helped me inside with my luggage. The hackie headed for the bay to get rid of the box under the impression I was a heavy tipper.

I had a meal in my room, a hot bath, and treated myself to a three hour nap. I woke up feeling as though those student embalmers might graduate after all.

I thumbed through the phone book and dialed a number.

"I want a Cadillac or Lincoln," I said. "A new one—not the one you rent for funerals—and a driver who won't mind missing a couple nights' sleep. And put a bed pillow and a blanket in the car."

I went down to the coffee room then for a light meal. I had just finished a cigarette when the car arrived—a dark blue heavyweight with a high polish and a low silhouette.

"We're going to Denver," I told the driver. "We'll make one stop tomorrow—I have a little shopping to do. I figure about twenty hours. Take a break every hundred miles, and hold it under seventy."

He nodded. I got in the back and sank down in the smell of expensive upholstery.

"I'll cross town and pick up U.S. 84 at—"

"I leave the details to you," I said. He pulled out into the traffic and I got the pillow settled under me and closed my eyes. I'd need all the rest

I could get on this trip. I'd heard that compared with the Denver Records Center, Fort Knox was a cinch. I'd find out for sure when I got there.

* * * *

The plan I had in mind wasn't the best I could have concocted under more leisurely circumstances. But with every cop in the country under orders to shoot me on sight, I had to move fast. My scheme had the virtue of unlikeliness. Once I was safe in the Central Vault—supposed to be the only H-bomb-proof structure ever built—I'd put through a phone call to the outside, telling them to watch a certain spot; say the big desk in the President's office. Then I'd assemble my matter transmitter and drop some little item right in front of the assembled big shots. They'd have to admit I had something. And this time they'd have to start considering the possibility that I wasn't working for the enemy.

It had been a smooth trip, and I'd caught up on my sleep. Now it was five A.M. and we were into the foothills, half an hour out of Denver. I ran over my lines, planning the trickiest part of the job ahead—the initial approach. I'd listened to a couple of news broadcasts. The FBI was still promising an arrest within hours. I learned that I was lying up, or maybe dead, in the vicinity of Key West, and that the situation was under control. That was fine with me. Nobody would expect me to pop up in Denver, still operating under my own power—and wearing a new suit at that.

The Records Center was north of the city, dug into mountainside. I steered my chauffeur around the downtown section, out a street lined with dark hamburger joints and unlit gas stations to where a side road branched off. We pulled up. From here on, things might get dangerous—if I was wrong about how easy it was all going to be. I brushed across the driver's mind. He set the brake and got out.

"Don't know how I came to run out of gas, Mr. Brown," he said apologetically. "We just passed a station but it was closed. I guess I'll just have to hike back into town. I sure am sorry; I never did that before."

I told him it was okay, watched as he strode off into the pre-dawn gloom, then got into the front seat and started up. The gate of the Reservation surrounding the Record Center was only a mile away now. I drove slowly, feeling ahead for opposition. There didn't seem to be any. Things were quiet as a poker player with a pat hand. My timing was good.

* * * *

I stopped in front of the gate, under a floodlight and the watchful eye of an M.P. with a shiny black tommygun held at the ready. He didn't seem surprised to see me. I rolled down the window as he came over to the car.

"I have an appointment inside, Corporal," I said. I touched his mind. "The password is 'hot-point'."

He nodded, stepped back, and motioned me in. I hesitated. This was almost too easy. I reached out again....

"... *middle of the night... password... nice car... I wish...*"

I pulled through the gate and headed for the big parking lot, picking a spot in front of a ramp that led down to a tall steel door. There was no one in sight. I got out, dragging my suitcase. It was heavier now, with the wire and magnets I'd added. I crossed the drive, went up to the doors. The silence was eerie.

I swept the area, searching for minds, found nothing. The shielding, I decided, blanked out everything.

There was a personnel door set in the big panel, with a massive combination lock. I leaned my head against the door and felt for the mechanism, turning the dial right, left, right....

The lock opened. I stepped inside, alert.

Silence, darkness. I reached out, sensed walls, slabs of steel, concrete, intricate mechanisms, tunnels deep in the ground....

But no personnel. That was surprising—but I wouldn't waste time questioning my good luck. I followed a corridor, opened another door, massive as a vault, passed more halls, more doors. My footsteps made muffled echoes. I passed a final door and came into the heart of the Records Center.

There were lights in the chamber around the grim, featureless periphery of the Central Vault. I set the valise on the floor, sat on it and lit a cigarette. So far, so good. The Records Center, I saw, had been over-rated. Even without my special knowledge, a clever locksmith could have come this far—or almost. But the Big Vault was another matter. The great integrating lock that secured it would yield only to a complex command from the computer set in the wall opposite the vault door. I smoked my cigarette and, with eyes closed, studied the vault.

I finished the cigarette, stepped on it, went to the console, began pressing keys, tapping out the necessary formulations. Half an hour later I finished. There was a whine from a servo motor; a crimson light flashed. I turned and saw the valve cycle open, showing a bright-lit tunnel within.

* * * *

I dragged my bag inside, threw the lever that closed the entry behind me. A green light went on. I walked along the narrow passage, lined with gray metal shelves stacked with gray steel tape drums, descended steps, came into a larger chamber fitted out with bunks, a tiny galley, toilet facilities, shelves stocked with food. There was a radio, a telephone and a second telephone, bright red. That would be the hot-line to Washington. This was the sanctum sanctorum, where the last survivors could wait out the final holocaust—indefinitely.

I opened the door of a steel cabinet. Radiation suits, tools, instruments. Another held bedding. I found a tape-player, tapes—even a shelf of books. I found a first aid kit and gratefully gave myself a hypo-spray jolt of neurite. My pains receded.

I went on to the next room; there were wash tubs, a garbage disposal unit, a drier. There was everything here I needed to keep me alive and even comfortable until I could convince someone up above that I shouldn't be shot on sight.

A heavy door barred the way to the room beyond. I turned a wheel, swung the door back, saw more walls lined with filing cabinets, a blank facade of gray steel; and in the center of the room, alone on a squat table—a yellow plastic case that any Sunday Supplement reader would have recognized.

It was a Master Tape, the Utter Top Secret Programming document that would direct the terrestrial defense in case of a Gool invasion.

It was almost shocking to see it lying there—unprotected except for the flimsy case. The information it contained in micro-micro dot form could put my world in the palm of the enemy's hand.

The room with the tool kit would be the best place to work, I decided. I brought the suitcase containing the electronic gear back from the outer door where I'd left it, opened it and arranged its contents on the table. According to the Gool these simple components were all I needed. The trick was in knowing how to put them together.

There was work ahead of me now. There were the coils to wind, the intricate antenna arrays to lay out; but before I started, I'd take time to call Kayle—or whoever I could get at the other end of the hot-line. They'd be a little startled when I turned up at the heart of the defenses they were trying to shield.

I picked up the receiver and a voice spoke:

"Well, Granthan. So you finally made it."

VI

"Here are your instructions," Kayle was saying. "Open the vault door. Come out—stripped—and go to the center of the parking lot. Stand there with your hands over your head. A single helicopter manned by a volunteer will approach and drop a gas canister. It won't be lethal, I promise you that. Once you're unconscious, I'll personally see to it that you're transported to the Institute in safety. Every effort will then be made to overcome the Gool conditioning. If we're successful, you'll be awakened. If not...."

He let the sentence hang. It didn't need to be finished. I understood what he meant.

I was listening. I was still not too worried. Here I was safe against anything until the food ran out—and that wouldn't be for months.

"You're bluffing, Kayle," I said. "You're trying to put the best face on something that you can't control. If you'd—"

"You were careless at Delta Labs, Granthan. There were too many people with odd blanks in their memories and too many unusual occurrences, all on the same day. You tipped your hand. Once we knew what we were up against, it was simply a matter of following you at an adequate distance. We have certain shielding materials, as you know. We tried them all. There's a new one that's quite effective.

"But as I was saying, we've kept you under constant surveillance. When we saw which way you were heading, we just stayed out of sight and let you trap yourself."

"You're lying. Why would you want me here?"

"That's very simple," Kayle said harshly. "It's the finest trap ever built by man—and you're safely in it."

"Safely is right. I have everything I need here. And that brings me to my reason for being here—in case you're curious. I'm going to build a matter transmitter. And to prove my good faith, I'll transmit the Master Tape to you. I'll show you that I could have stolen the damned thing if I'd wanted to."

"Indeed? Tell me, Granthan, do you really think we'd be fools enough to leave the Master Tape behind when we evacuated the area?"

"I don't know about that—but it's here."

"Sorry," Kayle said. "You're deluding yourself." His voice was suddenly softer, some of the triumph gone from it. "Don't bother struggling, Granthan. The finest brains in the country have combined to place you where you are. You haven't a chance, except to do as I say. Make it easy on yourself. I have no wish to extend your ordeal."

"You can't touch me, Kayle. This vault is proof against a hell-bomb, and it's stocked for a siege...."

"That's right," Kayle said. His voice sounded tired. "It's proof against a hell-bomb. But what if the hell-bomb's in the vault with you?"

* * * *

I felt like a demolition man, working to defuse a block-buster, who's suddenly heard a loud click! from the detonator. I dropped the phone, stared around the room. I saw nothing that could be a bomb. I ran to the next room, the one beyond. Nothing. I went back to the phone, grabbed it up.

"You ought to know better than to bluff now, Kayle!" I yelled. "I wouldn't leave this spot now for half a dozen hypothetical hell-bombs!"

"In the center room," Kayle said. "Lift the cover over the floor drain. You'll find it there. You know what they look like. Don't tamper with its mechanism; it's internally trapped. You'll have to take my word for it we didn't bother installing a dummy."

I dropped the phone, hurried to the spot Kayle had described. The bomb casing was there—a dull gray ovoid, with a lifting eye set in the top. It didn't look dangerous. It just lay quietly, waiting....

Back at the telephone, I had trouble finding my voice. "How long?" I croaked.

"It was triggered when you entered the vault," Kayle said. "There's a time mechanism. It's irreversible; you can't force anyone to cancel it. And it's no use your hiding in the outer passages.

"The whole center will be destroyed in the blast. Even it can't stand against a bomb buried in its heart. But we'll gladly sacrifice the center to eliminate you."

"How long!"

"I suggest you come out quickly, so that a crew can enter the vault to disarm the bomb."

"*How long!*"

"When you're ready to emerge, call me." The line went dead.

I put the phone back in its cradle carefully, like a rare and valuable egg.

I tried to think. I'd been charging full speed ahead ever since I had decided on my scheme of action while I was still riding the surf off the Florida coast, and I'd stuck to it. Now it had hatched in my face—and the thing that had crawled out wasn't the downy little chick of success. It had teeth and claws and was eyeing me like a basilisk....

But I still had unplayed aces—if there was time.

I had meant to use the matter transmitter to stage a dramatic proof that I wasn't the tool of the enemy. The demonstration would be more dramatic than I'd planned. The bomb would fit the machine as easily as the tape. The wheels would be surprised when their firecracker went off—right on schedule—in the middle of the Mojave Desert.

I set to work, my heart pounding. If I could bring this off—if I had time—if the transmitter worked as advertised....

The stolen knowledge flowed smoothly, effortlessly. It was as though I had been assembling matter transmitters for years, knew every step by heart. First the moebius windings; yard after yard of heavy copper around a core of carbon; then the power supply, the first and second stage amplimitters....

How long? In the sump in the next room, the bomb lay quietly ticking. How long...?

* * * *

The main assembly was ready now. I laid out cables, tying my apparatus in to the atomic power-source buried under the vault. The demand, for one short instant, would tax even those mighty engines. I fixed hooks at the proper points in the room, wove soft aluminum wire in the correct pattern. I was almost finished now. How long? I made the last connections, cleared away the litter. The matter transmitter stood on the table, complete. At any instant, the bomb would reduce it—and the secret of its construction—to incandescent gas—unless I transmitted the bomb out of range first. I turned toward the laundry room—and the telephone rang.

I hesitated, then crossed the room and snatched it up.

"Listen to me," Kayle said grimly. "Give me straight, fast answers. You said the Master Tape was there, in the vault with you. Now tell me: What does it look like?"

"What?"

"The…ah…dummy tape. What is its appearance?"

"It's a roughly square plastic container, bright yellow, about a foot thick. What about it?"

Kayle's voice sounded strained. "I've made inquiries. No one here seems to know the exact present location of the Master Tape. Each department says that they were under the impression that another handled the matter. I'm unable to learn who, precisely, removed the Tape from the vault. Now you say there is a yellow plastic container—"

"I know what the Master Tape looks like," I said. "This is either it or a hell of a good copy."

"Granthan," Kayle said. There was a note of desperation in his voice now. "There have been some blunders made. I knew you were under the influence of the Gool. It didn't occur to me that I might be too. Why did I make it possible for you to successfully penetrate to the Central Vault? There were a hundred simpler ways in which I could have dealt with the problem. We're in trouble, Granthan, serious trouble. The tape you have there is genuine. We've all played into the enemy's hands."

"You're wasting valuable time, Kayle," I snapped. "When does the bomb go up?"

"Granthan, there's little time left. Bring the Master Tape and leave the vault—"

"No dice, Kayle. I'm staying until I finish the transmitter, then—"

"Granthan! If there's anything to your mad idea of such a machine, destroy it! Quickly! Don't you see the Gool would only have given you the secret in order to enable you to steal the tape!"

I cut him off. In the sudden silence, I heard a distant sound—or had I sensed a thought? I strained outward….

"…volunteered… damn fool… thing on my head is heavy… better work….

"… now… okay… valve, gas… kills in a split second… then get out…."

I stabbed out, pushed through the obscuring veil of masonry, sensed a man in the computer room, dressed in gray coveralls, a grotesque shield over his head and shoulders. He reached for a red-painted valve—

I struck at his mind, felt him stagger back, fall. I fumbled in his brain, stimulated the sleep center. He sank deep into unconsciousness. I leaned against the table, weak with the reaction. Kayle had almost tricked me that time.

* * * *

I reached out again, swept the area with desperate urgency. Far away, I sensed the hazy clutter of many minds, out of range. There was nothing more. The poisonous gas had been the only threat—except the bomb itself. But I had to move fast, before my time ran out, to transmit the bomb to a desert area....

I paused, stood frozen in mid-move. A desert. What desert?

The transmitter operated in accordance with as rigid a set of laws as did the planets swinging in their orbits; strange laws, but laws of nature none the less. No receiver was required. The destination of the mass under transmission was determined by the operator, holding in his mind the five-dimensional conceptualization of the target, guiding the action of the machine.

And I had no target.

I could no more direct the bomb to a desert without a five-fold grasp of its multi-ordinal spatial, temporal, and entropic co-ordinates than I could fire a rifle at a target in the dark.

I was like a man with a grenade in his hand, pin pulled—and locked in a cell.

I swept the exocosm again, desperately. And caught a thin, live line. I traced it; it cut through the mountain, dived deep underground, crossed the boundless plain....

Never branching, it bored on, turning upward now—and ending.

I rested, gathering strength, then probed, straining....

There was a room, men. I recognized Kayle, gray-faced, haggard. A tall man in braided blue stood near him. Others stood silently by, tension on every face. Maps covered the wall behind them.

I was looking into the War Room at the Pentagon in Washington. The line I had traced was the telephonic hot-line, the top-security link between the Record Center and the command level. It was a heavy cable, well protected and always open. It would free me from the trap. With Gool-tutored skill I scanned the room, memorized its co-ordinates. Then I withdrew.

Like a swimmer coming up from a long dive, I fought my way back to the level of immediate awareness. I sagged into a chair, blinking at the drab walls, the complexity of the transmitter. I must move fast now, place the bomb in the transmitter's field, direct it at the target. With an effort I got to my feet, went to the sump, lifted the cover. I grasped the lifting eye, strained—and the bomb came up, out onto the floor. I dragged it to the transmitter….

And only then realized what I'd been about to do.

My target.

The War Room—the nerve-center of Earth's defenses. And I had been ready to dump the hell bomb there. In my frenzy to be rid of it I would have played into the hands of the Gool.

VII

I went to the phone.

"Kayle! I guess you've got a recorder on the line. I'll give you the details of the transmitter circuits. It's complicated, but fifteen minutes ought to—"

"No time," Kayle cut in. "I'm sorry about everything, Granthan. If you've finished the machine, it's a tragedy for humanity—if it works. I can only ask you to try—when the Gool command comes—not to give them what they want. I'll tell you, now, Granthan. The bomb blows in—" there was a pause—"two minutes and twenty-one seconds. Try to hold them off. If you can stand against them for that long at least—"

I slammed the phone down, cold sweat popping out across my face. Two minutes…too late for anything. The men in the War Room would never know how close I had come to beating the Gool—and them.

But I could still save the Master Tape. I wrestled the yellow plastic case that housed the tape onto the table, into the machine.

And the world vanished in a blaze of darkness, a clamor of silence.

NOW, MASTERS! NOW! LINK UP! LINK UP!

Like a bad dream coming back in daylight, I felt the obscene presence of massed Gool minds, attenuated by distance but terrible in their power, probing, thrusting. I fought back, struggling against paralysis, trying to gather my strength, use what I had learned….

SEE, MASTERS, HOW IT WOULD ELUDE US. BLANK IT OFF, TOGETHER NOW….

The paths closed before me. My mind writhed, twisted, darted here and there—and met only the impenetrable shield of the Gool defenses.

IT TIRES, MASTERS. WORK SWIFTLY NOW. LET US IMPRESS ON THE SUBJECT THE CO-ORDINATES OF THE BRAIN PIT. The conceptualization drifted into my mind. *HERE, MAN. TRANSMIT THE TAPE HERE!*

As from a distance, the monitor personality fraction watched the struggle. Kayle had been right. The Gool had waited—and now their moment had come. Even my last impulse of defiance—to place the tape in the machine—had been at the Gool command. They had looked into my mind. They understand psychology as no human analyst ever could; and they had led me in the most effective way possible, by letting me believe I was the master. They had made use of my human ingenuity to carry out their wishes—and Kayle had made it easy for them by evacuating a twenty-mile radius around me, leaving the field clear for the Gool.

HERE—The Gool voice rang like a bell in my mind: *TRANSMIT THE TAPE HERE!*

Even as I fought against the impulse to comply, I felt my arm twitch toward the machine.

THROW THE SWITCH! the voice thundered.

I struggled, willed my arm to stay at my side. Only a minute longer, I thought. Only a minute more, and the bomb would save me....

LINK UP, MASTERS!

I WILL NOT LINK. YOU PLOT TO FEED AT MY EXPENSE.

NO! BY THE MOTHER WORM, I PLEDGE MY GROOVE AT THE EATING TROUGH. FOR US THE MAN WILL GUT THE GREAT VAULT OF HIS NEST WORLD!

ALREADY YOU BLOAT AT OUR EXPENSE!

FOOL!! WOULD YOU BICKER NOW? LINK UP!

* * * *

The Gool raged—and I grasped for an elusive thought and held it. The bomb, only a few feet away. The waiting machine. And the Gool had given me the co-ordinates of their cavern....

With infinite sluggishness, I moved.

LINK UP, MASTERS: THEN ALL WILL FEED....

IT IS A TRICK. I WILL NOT LINK.

I found the bomb, fumbled for a grip.

DISASTER, MASTERS! NOW IS THE PRIZE LOST TO US, UNLESS YOU JOIN WITH ME!

My breath choked off in my throat; a hideous pain coiled outward from my chest. But it was unimportant. Only the bomb mattered. I tottered, groping. There was the table; the transmitter....

I lifted the bomb, felt the half-healed skin of my burned arm crackle as I strained....

I thrust the case containing the Master Tape out of the field of the transmitter, then pushed, half-rolled the bomb into position. I groped for the switch, found it. I tried to draw breath, felt only a surge of agony. Blackness was closing in....

The co-ordinates....

From the whirling fog of pain and darkness, I brought the target concept of the Gool cavern into view, clarified it, held it....

MASTERS! HOLD THE MAN! DISASTER!

Then I felt the Gool, their suspicions yielding to the panic in the mind of the Prime Overlord, link their power against me. I stood paralyzed, felt my identity dissolving like water pouring from a smashed pot. I tried to remember—but it was too faint, too far away.

Then from somewhere a voice seemed to cut in, the calm voice of an emergency reserve personality fraction. "You are under attack. Activate the reserve plan. Level Five. Use Level Five. Act now. Use Level Five...."

Through the miasma of Gool pressure, I felt the hairs stiffen on the back of my neck. All around me the Gool voices raged, a swelling symphony of discord. But they were nothing. Level Five....

There was no turning back. The compulsions were there, acting even as I drew in a breath to howl my terror—

Level Five. Down past the shapes of dreams, the intense faces of hallucination; Level Three; Level Four and the silent ranked memories.... And deeper still—

Into a region of looming gibbering horror, of shadowy moving shapes of evil, of dreaded presences that lurked at the edge of vision....

Down amid the clamor of voiceless fears, the mounting hungers, the reaching claws of all that man had feared since the first tailless primate screamed out his terror in a tree-top: the fear of falling, the fear of heights.

Down to Level Five. Nightmare level.

* * * *

I groped outward, found the plane of contact—and hurled the weight of man's ancient fears at the waiting Gool—and in their black confining caves deep in the rock of a far world, they felt the roaring tide of fear—fear of the dark, and of living burial. The horrors in man's secret mind confronted the horrors of the Gool Brain Pit. And I felt them break, retreat in blind panic from me—

All but one. The Prime Overlord reeled back with the rest, but his was a mind of terrible power. I sensed for a moment his bloated immense form, the seething gnawing hungers, insatiable, never to be appeased. Then he rallied—but he was alone now.

LINK UP, MASTERS! THE PRIZE IS LOST. KILL THE MAN! KILL THE MAN!

I felt a knife at my heart. It fluttered—and stopped. And in that instant, I broke past his control, threw the switch. There was the sharp crack of imploding air. Then I was floating down, ever down, and all sensation was far away.

MASTERS! KILL TH

The pain cut off in an instant of profound silence and utter dark.

Then sound roared in my ears, and I felt the harsh grate of the floor against my face as I fell, and then I knew nothing more.

* * * *

"I hope," General Titus was saying, "that you'll accept the decoration now, Mr. Granthan. It will be the first time in history that a civilian has been accorded this honor—and you deserve it."

I was lying in a clean white bed, propped up by big soft pillows, with a couple of good-looking nurses hovering a few feet away. I was in a mood to tolerate even Titus.

"Thanks, General," I said. "I suggest you give the medal to the volunteer who came in to gas me. He knew what he was going up against; I didn't."

"It's over, now, Granthan," Kayle said. He attempted to beam, settled for a frosty smile. "You surely understand—"

"Understanding," I said. "That's all we need to turn this planet—and a lot of other ones—into the kind of worlds the human mind needs to expand into."

"You're tired, Granthan," Kayle said. "You get some rest. In a few weeks you'll be back on the job, as good as new."

"That's where the key is," I said. "In our minds; there's so much there, and we haven't even scratched the surface. To the mind nothing is impossible. Matter is an illusion, space and time are just convenient fictions—"

"I'll leave the medal here, Mr. Granthan. When you feel equal to it, we'll make the official presentation. Television...."

He faded off as I closed my eyes and thought about things that had been clamoring for attention ever since I'd met the Gool, but hadn't had time to explore. My arm....

I felt my way along it—from inside—tracing the area of damage, watching as the bodily defenses worked away, toiling to renew, replace. It was a slow, mindless process. But if I helped a little....

It was easy. The pattern was there. I felt the tissues renew themselves, the skin regenerate.

The bone was more difficult. I searched out the necessary minerals, diverted blood; the broken ends knit....

The nurse was bending over me, a bowl of soup in her hand.

* * * *

"You've been asleep for a long time, sir," she said, smiling. "How about some nice chicken broth now?"

I ate the soup and asked for more. A doctor came and peeled back my bandages, did a double-take, and rushed away. I looked. The skin was new and pink, like a baby's—but it was all there. I flexed my right leg; there was no twinge of pain.

I listened for a while as the doctors gabbled, clucked, probed and made pronouncements. Then I closed my eyes again. I thought about the matter transmitter. The government was sitting on it, of course. A military secret of the greatest importance, Titus called it. Maybe someday the public would hear about it; in the meantime—

"How about letting me out of here?" I said suddenly. A pop-eyed doctor with a fringe of gray hair blinked at me, went back to fingering my arm. Kayle hove into view.

"I want out," I said. "I'm recovered, right? So now just give me my clothes."

"Now, now, just relax, Granthan. You know it's not as simple as that. There are a lot of matters we must go over."

"The war's over," I said. "You admitted that. I want out."

"Sorry." Kayle shook his head. "That's out of the question."

"Doc," I said. "Am I well?"

"Yes," he said. "Amazing case. You're as fit as you'll ever be; I've never—"

"I'm afraid you'll have to resign yourself to being here for a while longer, Granthan," Kayle said. "After all, we can't—"

"Can't let the secret of matter transmission run around loose, hey? So until you figure out the angles, I'm a prisoner, right?"

"I'd hardly call it that, Granthan. Still…."

I closed my eyes. The matter transmitter—a strange device. A field, not distorting space, but accentuating certain characteristics of a matter field in space-time, subtly shifting relationships….

Just as the mind could compare unrelated data, draw from them new concepts, new parallels….

The circuits of the matter transmitter…and the patterns of the mind….

The exocosm and the endocosm, like the skin and the orange, everywhere in contact….

Somewhere there was a beach of white sand, and dunes with graceful sea-oats that leaned in a gentle wind. There was blue water to the far horizon, and a blue sky, and nowhere were there any generals with medals and television cameras, or flint-eyed bureaucrats with long schemes….

And with this gentle folding…thus….

And a pressure here…aso….

I opened my eyes, raised myself on one elbow—and saw the sea. The sun was hot on my body, but not too hot, and the sand was white as sugar. Far away, a seagull tilted, circling.

A wave rolled in, washed my foot in cool water.

I lay on my back, and looked up at white clouds in a blue sky, and smiled—then laughed aloud.

Distantly the seagull's cry echoed my laughter.

DOORSTEP

Originally published in **Galaxy Magazine**, *February 1961.*

Steadying his elbow on the kitchen table serving as desk, Brigadier General Straut leveled his binoculars and stared out through the second-floor window of the farmhouse at the bulky object lying canted at the edge of the wood lot. He watched the figures moving over and around the gray mass, then flipped the lever on the field telephone at his elbow.

"How are your boys doing, Major?"

"General, since that box this morning—"

"I know all about the box, Bill. So does Washington by now. What have you got that's new?"

"Sir, I haven't got anything to report yet. I have four crews on it, and she still looks impervious as hell."

"Still getting the sounds from inside?"

"Intermittently, General."

"I'm giving you one more hour, Major. I want that thing cracked."

The general dropped the phone back on its cradle and peeled the cellophane from a cigar absently. He had moved fast, he reflected, after the State Police notified him at nine forty-one last night. He had his men on the spot, the area evacuated of civilians, and a preliminary report on its way to Washington by midnight. At two thirty-six, they had discovered the four-inch cube lying on the ground fifteen feet from the huge object—missile, capsule, bomb—whatever it was. But now—several hours later—nothing new.

The field phone jangled. Straut grabbed it up.

"General, we've discovered a thin spot up on the top side. All we can tell so far is that the wall thickness falls off there...."

"All right. Keep after it, Bill."

This was more like it. If Brigadier General Straut could have this thing wrapped up by the time Washington awoke to the fact that it was something big—well, he'd been waiting a long time for that second star. This was his chance, and he would damn well make the most of it.

* * * *

He looked across the field at the thing. It was half in and half out of the woods, flat-sided, round-ended, featureless. Maybe he should go over and give it a closer look personally. He might spot something the others were missing. It might blow them all to kingdom come any second; but what the hell, he had earned his star on sheer guts in Normandy. He still had 'em.

He keyed the phone. "I'm coming down, Bill," he told the Major. On impulse, he strapped a pistol belt on. Not much use against a house-sized bomb, but the heft of it felt good.

The thing looked bigger than ever as the jeep approached it, bumping across the muck of the freshly plowed field. From here he could see a faint line running around, just below the juncture of side and top. Major Greer hadn't mentioned that. The line was quite obvious; in fact, it was more of a crack.

With a sound like a baseball smacking the catcher's glove, the crack opened, the upper half tilted, men sliding—then impossibly it stood open, vibrating, like the roof of a house suddenly lifted. The driver gunned the jeep. There were cries, and a ragged shrilling that set Straut's teeth on edge. The men were running back now, two of them dragging a third.

Major Greer emerged from behind the object, looked about, ran toward General Straut shouting. "... a man dead. It snapped; we weren't expecting it...."

Straut jumped out beside the men, who had stopped now and were looking back. The underside of the gaping lid was an iridescent black. The shrill noise sounded thinly across the field. Greer arrived, panting.

"What happened?" Straut snapped.

"I was...checking over that thin spot, General. The first thing I knew it was...coming up under me. I fell; Tate was at the other side. He held on and it snapped him loose, against a tree. His skull—"

"What the devil's that racket?"

"That's the sound we were getting from inside before, General. There's something in there, alive—"

"All right, pull yourself together, Major. We're not unprepared. Bring your half-tracks into position. The tanks will be here soon."

Straut glanced at the men standing about. He would show them what leadership meant.

"You men keep back," he said. He puffed his cigar calmly as he walked toward the looming object. The noise stopped suddenly; that was a relief. There was a faint and curious odor in the air, something like chlorine...or seaweed...or iodine.

There were no marks in the ground surrounding the thing. It had apparently dropped straight in to its present position. It was heavy, too—the soft soil was displaced in a mound a foot high all along the side.

Behind him, Straut heard a yell. He whirled. The men were pointing; the jeep started up, churned toward him, wheels spinning. He looked up. Over the edge of the gray wall, six feet above his head, a great reddish limb, like the claw of a crab, moved, groping.

Straut yanked the .45 from its holster, jacked the action and fired. Soft matter spattered, and the claw jerked back. The screeching started up again angrily, then was drowned in the engine roar as the jeep slid to a stop.

Straut stooped, grabbed up a leaf to which a quivering lump adhered, jumped into the vehicle as it leaped forward; then a shock and they were going into a spin and....

* * * *

"Lucky it was soft ground," somebody said. And somebody else asked, "What about the driver?"

Silence. Straut opened his eyes. "What...about...."

A stranger was looking down at him, an ordinary-looking fellow of about thirty-five.

"Easy, now, General Straut. You've had a bad spill. Everything is all right. I'm Professor Lieberman, from the University."

"The driver," Straut said with an effort.

"He was killed when the jeep went over."

"Went...over?"

"The creature lashed out with a member resembling a scorpion's stinger. It struck the jeep and flipped it. You were thrown clear. The driver jumped and the jeep rolled on him."

Straut pushed himself up.

"Where's Greer?"

"I'm right here, sir." Major Greer stepped up, stood attentively.

"Those tanks here yet?"

"No, sir. I had a call from General Margrave; there's some sort of hold-up. Something about not destroying scientific material. I did get the mortars over from the base."

Straut got to his feet. The stranger took his arm. "You ought to lie down, General—"

"Who the hell is going to make me? Greer, get those mortars in place, spaced between your tracks."

The telephone rang. Straut seized it. "General Straut."

"General Margrave here, Straut. I'm glad you're back on your feet. There'll be some scientists from the State University coming over. Cooperate with them. You're going to have to hold things together at least until I can get another man in there to—"

"Another man? General Margrave, I'm not incapacitated. The situation is under complete control—"

"It is, is it? I understand you've got still another casualty. What's happened to your defensive capabilities?"

"That was an accident, sir. The jeep—"

"We'll review that matter at a later date. What I'm calling about is more important right now. The code men have made some headway on that box of yours. It's putting out a sort of transmission."

"What kind, sir?"

"Half the message—it's only twenty seconds long, repeated—is in English. It's a fragment of a recording from a daytime radio program; one of the network men here identified it. The rest is gibberish. They're still working over it."

"What—"

"Bryant tells me he thinks there may be some sort of correspondence between the two parts of the message. I wouldn't know, myself. In my opinion, it's a threat of some sort."

"I agree, General. An ultimatum."

"Right. Keep your men back at a safe distance from now on. I want no more casualties."

* * * *

Straut cursed his luck as he hung up the phone. Margrave was ready to relieve him, after he had exercised every precaution. He had to do something fast, before this opportunity for promotion slipped out of his hands.

He looked at Major Greer. "I'm neutralizing this thing once and for all. There'll be no more men killed."

Lieberman stood up. "General! I must protest any attack against this—"

Straut whirled. "I'm handling this, Professor. I don't know who let you in here or why—but I'll make the decisions. I'm stopping this man-killer before it comes out of its nest, maybe gets into that village beyond the woods. There are four thousand civilians there. It's my job to protect them." He jerked his head at Greer, strode out of the room.

Lieberman followed, pleading. "The creature has shown no signs of aggressiveness, General Straut—"

"With two men dead?"

"You should have kept them back—"

"Oh, it was my fault, was it?" Straut stared at Lieberman with cold fury. This civilian pushed his way in here, then had the infernal gall to accuse him, Brigadier General Straut, of causing the death of his own men. If he had the fellow in uniform for five minutes....

"You're not well, General. That fall—"

"Keep out of my way, Professor," Straut said. He turned and went on down the stairs. The present foul-up could ruin his career; and now this egghead interference....

With Greer at his side, Straut moved out to the edge of the field.

"All right, Major. Open up with your .50 calibers."

Greer called a command and a staccato rattle started up. The smell of cordite and the blue haze of gunsmoke—this was more like it. He was in command here.

Lieberman came up to Straut. "General, I appeal to you in the name of science. Hold off a little longer; at least until we learn what the message is about."

"Get back from the firing line, Professor." Straut turned his back on the civilian, raised the glasses to observe the effect of the recoilless rifle. There was a tremendous smack of displaced air, and a thunderous boom as the explosive shell struck. Straut saw the gray shape jump, the raised lid waver. Dust rose from about it. There was no other effect.

"Keep firing, Greer," Straut snapped, almost with a feeling of triumph. The thing was impervious to artillery; now who was going to say it was no threat?

"How about the mortars, sir?" Greer said. "We can drop a few rounds right inside it."

"All right, try that before the lid drops."

And what we'll try next, I don't know, he thought.

* * * *

The mortar fired with a muffled thud. Straut watched tensely. Five seconds later, the object erupted in a gout of pale pink debris. The lid rocked, pinkish fluid running down its opalescent surface. A second burst, and a third. A great fragment of the menacing claw hung from the branch of a tree a hundred feet from the ship.

Straut grabbed up the phone. "Cease fire!"

Lieberman stared in horror at the carnage.

The telephone rang. Straut picked it up.

"General Straut," he said. His voice was firm. He had put an end to the threat.

"Straut, we've broken the message," General Margrave said excitedly. "It's the damnedest thing I ever...."

Straut wanted to interrupt, announce his victory, but Margrave was droning on.

"... strange sort of reasoning, but there was a certain analogy. In any event, I'm assured the translation is accurate. Here's how it reads in English...."

Straut listened. Then he carefully placed the receiver back on the hook.

Lieberman stared at him.

"What did it say?"

Straut cleared his throat. He turned and looked at Lieberman for a long moment before answering.

"It said, 'Please take good care of my little girl.'"

A TRACE OF MEMORY

Originally published in 1963.

PROLOGUE

He awoke and lay for a moment looking up at a low ceiling, dimly visible in a faint red glow, feeling the hard mat under his back. He turned his head, saw a wall and a panel on which a red indicator light glared.

He swung his legs over the side of the narrow couch and sat up. The room was small, grey-painted, unadorned. Pain throbbed in his forearm. He shook back the loose sleeve of the strange purple garment, saw a pattern of tiny punctures in the skin. He recognized the mark of a feeding Hunter.... Who would have dared?

A dark shape on the floor caught his eye. He slid from the couch, knelt by the still body of a man in a purple tunic stained black with blood. Gently he rolled the body onto its back.

Ammaerln!

He seized the limp wrist. There was a faint pulse. He rose—and saw a second body and, near the door, two more. Quickly he went to each....

All three were dead, hideously slashed. Only Ammaerln still breathed, faintly.

He went to the door, shouted into the darkness. The ranged shelves of a library gave back a brief echo. He turned back to the grey-walled room, noticed a recording monitor against a wall. He fitted the neurodes to the dying man's temples. But for this gesture of recording Ammaerln's life's memories, there was nothing he could do. He must get him to a therapist— and quickly.

He crossed the library, found a great echoing hall beyond. This was not the Sapphire Palace beside the Shallow Sea. The lines were unmistakeable: he was aboard a ship, a far-voyager. Why? How? He stood uncertain. The silence was absolute.

He crossed the Great Hall and entered the observation lounge. Here lay another dead man, by his uniform a member of the crew. He touched a knob and the great screens glowed blue. A giant crescent swam into focus, locked; soft blue against the black of space. Beyond it a smaller companion hung, gray-blotched, airless. What worlds were these?

* * * *

An hour later he had ranged the vast ship from end to end. In all, seven corpses, cruelly slashed, peopled the silent vessel. In the control sector the communicator lights glowed, but to his call there was no answer from the strange world below.

He turned to the recording room. Ammaerln still breathed weakly. The memory recording had been completed; all that the dying man remembered of his long life was imprinted now in the silver cylinder. It remained only to color-code the trace.

His eyes was caught by a small cylinder projecting from the aperture at the side of the high couch where he had awakened his own memory-trace! So he himself had undergone the Change. He took the color-banded cylinder, thrust it into a pocket—then whirled at a sound. A nest of Hunters, swarming globes of pale light, clustered at the door. Then they were on him. They pressed close, humming in their eagerness. Without the proper weapon he was helpless.

He caught up the limp body of Ammaerln. With the Hunters trailing in a luminous stream he ran with his burden to the shuttle-boat bay.

Three shuttles lay in their cradles. He groped to a switch, his head swimming with the sulphurous reek of the Hunters; light flooded the bay, driving them back. He entered the lifeboat, placed the dying man on a cushioned couch.

It had been long since he had manned the controls of a ship, but he had not forgotten.

* * * *

Ammaerln was dead when the lifeboat reached the planetary surface. The vessel settled gently and the lock cycled. He looked out at a vista of ragged forest.

This was no civilized world. Only the landing ring and the clearing around it showed the presence of man.

There was a hollow in the earth by a square marker block at the eastern perimeter of the clearing. He hoisted the body of Ammaerln to his back and moved heavily down the access ladder. Working bare-handed, he deepened the hollow, placed the body in it, scraped earth over it. Then he rose and turned back toward the shuttle boat.

Forty feet away, a dozen men, squat, bearded, wrapped in the shaggy hides of beasts, stood between him and the access ladder. The tallest among them shouted, raised a bronze sword threateningly. Behind these, others clustered at the ladder. Motionless he watched as one scrambled up, reached the top, disappeared into the boat. In a moment the savage reappeared at the opening and hurled down handfuls of small bright objects. Shouting, others clambered up to share the loot. The first man again vanished within the boat. Before the foremost of the others had gained the entry, the port closed, shutting off a terrified cry from within.

Men dropped from the ladder as it swung up. The boat rose slowly, angling toward the west, dwindling. The savages shrank back, awed.

The man watched until the tiny blue light was lost against the sky.

CHAPTER I

The ad read: *Soldier of fortune seeks companion in arms to share unusual adventure. Foster, Box 19, Mayport.*

I crumpled the newspaper and tossed it in the general direction of the wire basket beside the park bench, pushed back a slightly frayed cuff, and took a look at my bare wrist. It was just habit; the watch was in a hock shop in Tupelo, Mississippi. It didn't matter. I didn't have to know what time it was.

Across the park most of the store windows were dark along the side street. There were no people in sight; they were all home now, having dinner. As I watched, the lights blinked off in the drug store with the bottles of colored water in the window; the left the candy and cigar emporium at the end of the line. I fidgeted on the hard bench and felt for a cigarette I didn't have. I wished the old boy back of the counter would call it a day and go home. As soon as it was dark enough, I was going to rob his store.

* * * *

I wasn't a full-time stick-up artist. Maybe that's why that nervous feeling was playing around under my rib cage. There was really nothing to it. The wooden door with the hardware counter lock that would open almost as easily without a key as with one; the sardine-can metal box with the day's receipts in it. I'd be on my way to the depot with fare to Miami in my pocket ten minutes after I cracked the door. I'd learned a lot harder tricks than petty larceny back when I had a big future ahead with Army Intelligence. That was a long time ago, and I'd had a lot of breaks since then—none good.

I got up and took another turn around the park. It was a warm evening, and the mosquitoes were out. I caught a whiff of frying hamburger from the Elite Cafe down the street. It reminded me that I hadn't eaten lately. There were lights on at the Commercial Hotel and one in the ticket office at the station. The local police force was still sitting on a stool at the Rexall talking to the counter girl. I could see the .38 revolver hanging down in a worn leather holster at his hip. All of a sudden, I was in a hurry to get it over with.

I took another look at the lights. All the stores were dark now. There was nothing to wait for. I crossed the street, sauntered past the cigar store. There were dusty boxes of stogies in the window and piles of homemade fudge stacked on plates with paper doilies under them. Behind them, the interior of the store looked grim and dead. I looked around, then turned down the side street toward the back door—

A black sedan eased around the corner and pulled in to the curb. A face leaned over to look at me through lenses like the bottoms of tabasco bottles. The hot evening air stirred, and I felt my damp shirt cold against my back.

"Looking for anything in particular, Mister?" the cop said.

I just looked at him.

"Passing through town, are you?" he asked.

For some reason I shook my head.

"I've got a job here," I said. "I'm going to work—for Mr. Foster."

"What Mr. Foster?" The cop's voice was wheezy, but relentless; a voice used to asking questions.

I remembered the ad—something about an adventure; Foster, Box 19. The cop was still staring at me.

"Box nineteen," I said.

He looked me over some more, then reached across and opened the door. "Better come on down to the station house with me, Mister," he said.

* * * *

At Police Headquarters, the cop motioned me to a chair, sat down behind a desk, and pulled a phone to him. He dialed slowly, then swiveled his back to me to talk. Insects danced around the bare light bulb. There was an odor of leather and unwashed bedding. I sat and listened to a radio in the distance wailing a sad song.

It was half an hour before I heard a car pull up outside. The man who came through the door was wearing a light suit that was neither new nor freshly pressed, but had that look of perfect fit and taste that only the most expensive tailoring can achieve. He moved in a relaxed way, but gave an impression of power held in reserve. At first glance I thought he was in his middle thirties, but when he looked my way I saw the fine lines around the blue eyes. I got to my feet. He came over to me.

"I'm Foster," he said, and held out his hand. I shook it.

"My name is Legion," I said.

The desk sergeant spoke up. "This fellow says he come here to Mayport to see you, Mr. Foster."

Foster looked at me steadily. "That's right, Sergeant. This gentleman is considering a proposition I've made."

"Well, I didn't know, Mr. Foster," the cop said.

"I quite understand, Sergeant," Foster said. "We all feel better, knowing you're on the job."

"Well, you know," the cop said.

"We may as well be on our way then," Foster said. "If you're ready, Mr. Legion."

"Sure, I'm ready," I said. Mr. Foster said goodnight to the cop and we went out. On the pavement in front of the building I stopped.

"Thanks, Mr. Foster," I said. "I'll comb myself out of your hair now."

Foster had his hand on the door of a deceptively modest-looking cabriolet. I could smell the solid leather upholstery from where I stood.

"Why not come along to my place, Legion," he said. "We might at least discuss my proposition."

I shook my head. "I'm not the man for the job, Mr. Foster," I said. "If you'd like to advance me a couple of bucks, I'll get myself a bite to eat and fade right out of your life."

"What makes you so sure you're not interested?"

"Your ad said something about adventure. I've had my adventures. Now I'm just looking for a hole to crawl into."

"I don't believe you, Legion." Foster smiled at me, a slow, calm smile. "I think your adventures have hardly begun."

I thought about it. If I went along, I'd at least get a meal—and maybe even a bed for the night. It was better than curling up under a tree.

"Well," I said, "a remark like that demands time for an explanation." I got into the car and sank back in a seat that seemed to fit me the way Foster's jacket fit him.

"I hope you won't mind if I drive fast," Foster said. "I want to be home before dark." We started up and wheeled away from the curb like a torpedo sliding out of the launching tube.

* * * *

I got out of the car in the drive at Foster's house, and looked around at the wide clipped lawn, the flower beds that were vivid even by moonlight, the line of tall poplars and the big white house.

"I wish I hadn't come," I said. "This kind of place reminds me of all the things I haven't gotten out of life."

"Your life's still ahead of you," Foster said. He opened the slab of mahogany that was the front door, and I followed him inside. At the end of a short hall he flipped a switch that flooded the room before us with soft light. I stared at an expanse of pale grey carpet about the size of a tennis court, on which rested glowing Danish teak furniture upholstered in rich colors. The walls were a rough-textured grey; here and there were expensively framed abstractions. The air was cool with the heavy coolness of air conditioning.

Foster crossed to a bar that looked modest in the setting, in spite of being bigger than those in most of the places I'd seen lately.

"Would you care for a drink?" he said.

I looked down at my limp, stained suit and grimy cuffs.

"Look, Mr. Foster," I said. "I just realized something. If you've got a stable, I'll go sleep in it—"

Foster laughed. "Come on; I'll show you the bath."

* * * *

I came downstairs, clean, showered, and wearing a set of Foster's clothes. I found him sitting, sipping a drink and listening to music.

"The *Liebestodt*," I said. "A little gloomy, isn't it?"

"I read something else into it," Foster said. "Sit down and have a bite to eat and a drink."

I sat in one of the big soft chairs and tried not to let my hand shake as I reached for one of the sandwiches piled on the coffee table.

"Tell me something, Mr. Legion," Foster said. "Why did you come here, mention my name—if you didn't intend to see me?"

I shook my head. "It just worked out that way."

"Tell me something about yourself," Foster said.

"It's not much of a story."

"Still, I'd like to hear it."

"Well, I was born, grew up, went to school——"

"What school?"

"University of Illinois."

"What was your major?"

"Music."

Foster looked at me, frowning slightly.

"It's the truth," I said. "I wanted to be a conductor. The army had other ideas. I was in my last year when the draft got me. They discovered I had what they considered an aptitude for intelligence work. I didn't mind it. I had a pretty good time for a couple of years."

"Go on," Foster said. Well, I'd had a bath and a good meal. I owed him something. If he wanted to hear my troubles, why not tell him?

"I was putting on a demonstration. A defective timer set off a charge of H-E fifty seconds early on a one-minute setting. A student was killed; I got off easy with a busted eardrum and a pound or two of gravel imbedded in my back. When I got out of the hospital, the army felt real bad about letting me go—but they did. My terminal leave pay gave me a big weekend in San Francisco and set me up in business as a private investigator.

"I had enough left over after the bankruptcy proceedings a few months later to get me to Las Vegas. I lost what was left and took a job with a casino operator named Gonino.

"I stayed with Gonino for nearly a year. Then one night a visiting bank clerk lost his head and shot him eight times with a .22 target pistol. I left town the same night.

"After that I sold used cars for a couple of months in Memphis; then I made like a life guard at Daytona; baited hooks on a thirty-foot tuna boat out of Key West; all the odd jobs with low pay and no future. I spent a couple of years in Cuba; all I got out of that was two bullet scars on the left leg, and a prominent position on a CIA blacklist.

"After that things got tough. A man in my trade can't really hope to succeed in a big way without the little blue card in the plastic cover to back his play. I was headed south for the winter, and I picked Mayport to run out of money."

I stood up. "I sure enjoyed the bath, Mr. Foster, and the meal, too—I'd like real well to get into that bed upstairs and have a night's sleep just to make it complete; but I'm not interested in the job." I turned away and started across the room.

"Legion," Foster said. I turned. A beer bottle was hanging in the air in front of my face. I put a hand up fast and the bottle slapped my palm.

"Not bad set of reflexes for a man whose adventures are all behind him," Foster said.

I tossed the bottle aside. "If I'd missed, that would have knocked my teeth out," I said angrily.

"You didn't miss—even though you're weaving a little from the beer. And a man who can feel a pint or so of beer isn't an alcoholic—so you're clean on that score."

"I didn't say I was ready for the rummy ward," I said. "I'm just not interested in your proposition—whatever it is."

"Legion," Foster said, "maybe you have the idea I put that ad in the paper last week on a whim. The fact is, I've been running it—in one form or another—for over eight years."

I looked at him and waited.

"Not only locally—I've run it in the big-city papers, and in some of the national weekly and monthly publications. All together, I've had perhaps fifty responses."

Foster smiled wryly. "About three quarters of them were from women who thought I wanted a playmate. Several more were from men with the same idea. The few others were hopelessly unsuitable."

"That's surprising," I said. "I'd have thought you'd have brought half the nuts in the country out of the woodwork by now."

Foster looked at me, not smiling. I realized suddenly that behind the urbane façade there was a hint of tension, a trace of worry in the level blue eyes.

"I'd like very much to interest you in what I have to say, Legion. I think you lack only one thing—confidence in yourself."

I laughed shortly. "What are the qualifications you think I have? I'm a jack of no trades——"

"Legion, you're a man of considerable intelligence and more than a little culture; you've travelled widely and know how to handle yourself in difficult situations—or you wouldn't have survived. I'm sure your training includes techniques of entry and fact-gathering not known to the average man; and perhaps most important, although you're an honest man, you're capable of breaking the law—when necessary."

"So that's it," I said.

"No, I'm not forming a mob, Legion. As I said in the ad—this is an unusual adventure. It may—probably will—involve infringing various statutes and regulations of one sort or another. After you know the full story I'll leave you to judge whether it's justifiable."

If Foster was trying to arouse my curiosity, he was succeeding. He was dead serious about whatever it was he was planning. It sounded like something no one with good sense would want to get involved in—but on the other hand, Foster didn't look like the sort of man to do anything foolish....

"Why don't you tell me what this is all about?" I said. "Why would a man with all this—" I waved a hand at the luxurious room—"want to pick a hobo like me out of the gutter and talk him into taking a job?"

"Your ego has taken a severe beating, Legion—that's obvious. I think you're afraid that I'll expect too much of you—or that I'll be shocked by some disclosure you may make. Perhaps if you'd forget yourself and your problems for the moment, we could reach an understanding——"

"Yeah," I said. "Just forget my problems...."

"Chiefly money problems, of course. Most of the problems of this society involve the abstraction of values that money represents."

"Okay," I said. "I've got my problems, you've got yours. Let's leave it at that."

"You feel that because I have material comfort, my problems must of necessity be trivial ones," Foster said. "Tell me, Mr. Legion: have you ever known a man who suffered from amnesia?"

* * * *

Foster crossed the room to a small writing desk, took something from a drawer, then looked at me.

"I'd like you to examine this," he said.

I went over and took the object from his hand. It was a small book, with a cover of drab-colored plastic, unornamented except for an embossed design of two concentric rings. I opened the cover. The pages were as thin as tissue, but opaque, and covered with extremely fine writing in strange foreign characters. The last dozen pages were in English. I had to hold the book close to my eyes to read the minute script:

January 19, 1710. Having come nigh to calamity with the near loſs of the key, I will henceforth keep this journal in the English tongue....

"If this is an explanation of something, it's too subtle for me," I said.

"Legion, how old would you say I am?"

"That's a hard one," I said. "When I first saw you I would have said the late thirties, maybe. Now, frankly, you look closer to fifty."

"I can show you proof," Foster said, "that I spent the better part of a year in a military hospital in France. I awakened in a ward, bandaged to the eyes, and with no memories whatever of my life before that day. According to the records made at the time, I appeared to be about thirty years of age."

"Well," I said, "amnesia's not so unusual among war casualties, and you seem to have done pretty well since."

Foster shook his head impatiently. "There's nothing difficult about acquiring material wealth in this society, though the effort kept me well occupied for a number of years—and diverted my thoughts from the question of my past life. The time came, however, when I had the leisure to pursue the matter. The clues I had were meagre enough; the notebook I've shown you was found near me, and I had a ring on my finger." Foster held out his hand. On the middle finger was a massive signet, engraved with the same design of concentric circles I had seen on the cover of the notebook.

"I was badly burned; my clothing was charred. Oddly enough, the notebook was quite unharmed, though it was found among burned debris. It's made of very tough stuff."

"What did you find out?"

"In a word—nothing. No military unit claimed me. I spoke English, from which it was deduced that I was English or American——"

"They couldn't tell which, from your accent?"

"Apparently not; it appears I spoke a sort of hybrid dialect."

"Maybe you're lucky. I'd be happy to forget my first thirty years."

"I spent a considerable sum of money in my attempts to discover my past," Foster went on. "And several years of time. In the end I gave it up. And it wasn't until then that I found the first faint inkling."

"So you did find something," I said.

"Nothing I hadn't had all along. The notebook."

"I'd have thought you would have read that before you did anything else," I said. "Don't tell me you put it in the bureau drawer and forgot it."

"I read it, of course—what I could read of it. Only a relatively small section is in English. The rest is a cipher. And what I read seemed meaningless—quite unrelated to me. You've glanced through it; it's no more than a journal, irregularly kept, and so cryptic as to be little better than a code itself. And of course the dates; they range from the early eighteenth century through the early twentieth."

"A sort of family record, maybe," I said. "Carried on generation after generation. Didn't it mention any names, or places?"

"Look at it again, Legion," Foster said. "See if you notice anything odd—other than what we've already discussed."

I thumbed through the book again. It was no more than an inch thick, but it was heavy—surprisingly heavy. There were a lot of pages—I shuffled through hundreds of closely written sheets, and yet the book was less than half used. I read bits here and there:

"May 4, 1746. The Voyage was not a Succeſs. I must forsake this avenue of Enquiry...."

"October 23, 1790. Builded the weſt Barrier a cubit higher. Now the fires burn every night. Is there no limit to their infernal perſiſtence?"

"January 19, 1831. I have great hopes for the Philadelphia enterprise. My greatest foe is impatience. All preparations for the Change are made, yet I confeſs I am uneasy...."

"There are plenty of oddities," I said. "Aside from the entries themselves. This is supposed to be old—but the quality of the paper and binding beats anything I've seen. And that handwriting is pretty fancy for a quill pen——"

"There's a stylus clipped to the spine of the book," Foster said. "It was written with that."

I looked, pulled out a slim pen, then looked at Foster. "Speaking of odd," I said. "A genuine antique early colonial ball-point pen doesn't turn up every day——"

"Suspend your judgement until you've seen it all," Foster said.

"And two hundred years on one refill—that's not bad." I riffled through the pages, then I tossed the book onto the table. "Who's kidding who, Foster?" I said.

"The book was described in detail in the official record, of which I have copies. They mention the paper and binding, the stylus, even quote some of the entries. The authorities worked over it pretty closely, trying to identify me. They reached the same conclusion as you—that it was the work of a crackpot; but they saw the same book you're looking at now."

"So what? So it was faked up some time during the war—what does that prove? I'm ready to concede it's forty years old——"

"You don't understand, Legion," Foster said. "I told you I woke up in a military hospital in France. But it was an AEF hospital and the year was 1918."

CHAPTER II

I glanced sideways at Foster. He didn't look like a nut....

"All I've got to say is," I said, "you're a hell of a spry-looking ninety."

"You find my appearance strangely youthful. What would be your re-action if I told you that I've aged greatly in the past few months? That a year ago I could have passed as no older than thirty without the slightest difficulty——"

"I don't think I'd believe you," I said. "And I'm sorry, Mr. Foster; but I don't believe the bit about the 1918 hospital either. How can I? It's——"

"I know. Fantastic. But let's go back a moment to the book itself. Look closely at the paper; it's been examined by experts. They're baffled by it. Attempts to analyze it chemically failed—they were unable to take a sam-ple. It's impervious to solvents——"

"They couldn't get a sample?" I said. "Why not just tear off the corner of one of the sheets?"

"Try it," Foster said.

I picked up the book and plucked at the edge of one of the blank sheets, then pinched harder and pulled. The paper held. I got a better grip and pulled again. It was like fine, tough leather, except that it didn't even stretch.

"It's tough, all right," I said. I took out my pocket knife and opened it and worked on the edge of the paper. Nothing. I went over to the bureau and put the paper flat against the top and sawed at it, putting my weight on the knife. I raised the knife and brought it down hard. I didn't so much as mark the sheet. I put the knife away.

"That's some paper, Mr. Foster," I said.

"Try to tear the binding," Foster said. "Put a match to it. Shoot at it if you like. Nothing will make an impression on that material. Now, you're a logical man, Legion. Is there something here outside ordinary experience or is there not?"

I sat down, feeling for a cigarette. I still didn't have.

"What does it prove?" I said.

"Only that the book is not a simple fraud. You're facing something which can't be dismissed as fancy. The book exists. That is our basic point of departure."

"Where do we go from there?"

"There is a second factor to be considered," Foster went on. "At some time in the past I seem to have made an enemy. Someone, or something, is systematically hunting me."

I tried a laugh, but it felt out of place. "Why not sit still and let it catch up with you? Maybe it could tell you what the whole thing is about."

Foster shook his head. "It started almost thirty years ago," he said. "I was driving south from Albany, New York, at night. It was a long straight stretch of road, no houses. I noticed lights following me. Not headlights—something that bobbed along, off in the fields along the road. But they kept pace, gradually moving alongside. Then they closed in ahead, keeping out of range of my headlights. I stopped the car. I wasn't seriously alarmed, just curious. I wanted a better look, so I switched on my spotlight and played it on the lights. They disappeared as the light touched them. After half a dozen were gone, the rest began closing in. I kept picking them off. There was a sound, too, a sort of high-pitched humming. I caught a whiff of sulphur then, and suddenly I was afraid—deathly afraid. I caught the last one in the beam no more than ten feet from the car. I can't describe the horror of the moment——"

"It sounds pretty weird," I said. "But what was there to be afraid of? It must have been some kind of heat lightning."

"There is always the pat explanation," Foster said. "But no explanation can rationalize the instinctive dread I felt. I started up the car and drove on—right through the night and the next day. I sensed that I must put distance between myself and whatever it was I had met. I bought a home in California and tried to put the incident out of my mind—with limited success. Then it happened again."

"The same thing? Lights?"

"It was more sophisticated the next time. It started with interference—static—on my radio. Then it affected the wiring in the house. All the lights began to glow weakly, even though they were switched off. I could feel it—feel it in my bones—moving closer, hemming me in. I tried the car; it wouldn't start. Fortunately, I kept a few horses at that time. I mounted and rode into town—and at a fair gallop, you may be sure. I saw the lights, but outdistanced them. I caught a train and kept going."

"I don't see——"

"It happened again; four times in all. I thought perhaps I had succeeded in eluding it at last. I was mistaken. I have had definite indications that my time here is drawing to a close. I would have been gone before now, but there were certain arrangements to be made."

"Look," I said. "This is all wrong. You need a psychiatrist, not an ex-tough guy. Delusions of persecution——"

"It seemed obvious that the explanation was to be found somewhere in my past life," Foster went on. "I turned to the notebook, my only link. I copied it out, including the encrypted portion. I had photostatic enlargements made of the initial section—the part written in unfamiliar characters. None of the experts who have examined the script have been able to identify it.

"I necessarily, therefore, concentrated my attention on the last section—the only part written in English. I was immediately struck by a curious fact I had ignored before. The writer made references to an Enemy, a mysterious 'they', against which defensive measures had to be taken."

"Maybe that's where you got the idea," I said. "When you first read the book——"

"The writer of the log," Foster said, "was dogged by the same nemesis that now follows me."

"It doesn't make any sense," I said.

"For the moment," Foster said, "stop looking for logic in the situation. Look for a pattern instead."

"There's a pattern, all right," I said.

"The next thing that struck me," Foster went on, "was a reference to a loss of memory—a second point of some familiarity to me. The writer expresses frustration at the inability to remember certain facts which would have been useful to him in his pursuit."

"What kind of pursuit?"

"Some sort of scientific project, as nearly as I can gather. The journal bristles with tantalizing references to matters that are never explained."

"And you think the man that wrote it had amnesia?"

"Not exactly amnesia, perhaps," Foster said. "But there were things he was unable to remember."

"If that's amnesia, we've all got it," I said. "Nobody's got a perfect memory."

"But these were matters of importance; not the kinds of thing that simply slip one's mind."

"I can see how you'd want to believe the book had something to do with your past, Mr. Foster," I said. "It must be a hard thing, not knowing your own life story. But you're on the wrong track. Maybe the book is a story you started to write—in code, so nobody would accidentally read the stuff and kid you about it."

"Legion, what was it you planned to do when you got to Miami?"

The question caught me a little off-guard. "Well, I don't know," I hedged. "I wanted to get south, where it's warm. I used to know a few people——"

"In other words, nothing," Foster said. "Legion, I'll pay you well to stay with me and see this thing through."

I shook my head. "Not me, Mr. Foster. The whole thing sounds—well, the kindest word I can think of is 'nutty.'"

"Legion," Foster said, "do you really believe I'm insane?"

"Let's just say this all seems a little screwy to me, Mr. Foster."

"I'm not asking you just to work for me," Foster said. "I'm asking for your help."

"You might as well look for your fortune in tea leaves," I said, irritated. "There's nothing in what you've told me."

"There's more, Legion. Much more. I've recently made an important discovery. When I know you're with me, I'll tell you. You know enough now to accept the fact that this isn't entirely a figment of my imagination."

"I don't know anything," I said. "So far it's all talk."

"If you're concerned about payment——"

"No, damn it," I barked. "Where are the papers you keep talking about? I ought to have my head examined for sitting here humoring you. I've got troubles enough——" I stopped talking and rubbed my hands over my scalp. "I'm sorry, Mr. Foster," I said. "I guess what's really griping me is that you've got everything I think I want—and you're not content with it. It bothers me to see you off chasing fairies. If a man with his health and plenty of money can't enjoy life, what the hell is there for anybody?"

Foster looked at me thoughtfully. "Legion, if you could have anything in life you wanted, what would you ask for?"

"Anything? I've wanted a lot of different things. Once I wanted to be a hero. Later, I wanted to be smart, know all the answers. Then I had the idea that a chance to do an honest job, one that needed doing, was the big thing. I never found that job. I never got smart either, or figured out how to tell a hero from a coward, without a program."

"In other words," Foster said, "you were looking for an abstraction to believe in—in this case, Justice. But you won't find justice in nature. It's a thing that only man expects or acknowledges."

"There are some good things in life; I'd like to get a piece of them."

"Don't lose your capacity for dreaming, in the process."

"Dreams?" I said. "Oh, I've got those. I want an island somewhere in the sun, where I can spend my time fishing and watching the sea."

"You're speaking cynically—but you're still attempting to concretize an abstraction," Foster said. "But no matter—materialism is simply another form of idealism."

I looked at Foster. "But I know I'll never have those things—or that Justice you were talking about, either. Once you really know you'll never make it...."

"Perhaps unattainability is an essential element of any dream," Foster said. "But hold onto your dream, whatever it is—don't ever give it up."

"So much for philosophy," I said. "Where is it getting us?"

"You'd like to see the papers," Foster said. He fished a key ring from an inner pocket. "If you don't mind going out to the car," he said, "and perhaps getting your hands dirty, there's a strong-box welded to the frame. I keep photostats of everything there, along with my passport, emergency funds and so on. I've learned to be ready to travel on very short notice. Lift the floorboards; you'll see the box."

"It's not all that urgent," I said. "I'll take a look in the morning—after I've caught up on some sleep. But don't get the wrong idea—it's just my knot-headed curiosity."

"Very well," Foster said. He lay back, sighed. "I'm tired, Legion," he said. "My mind is tired."

"Yeah," I said, "so is mine—not to mention other portions of my anatomy."

"Get some sleep," Foster said. "We'll talk again in the morning."

* * * *

I pushed back the light blanket and slid out of bed. Underfoot, the rug was as thick and soft as a working girl's mink. I went across to the closet and pushed the button that made the door slide aside. My old clothes were still lying on the floor where I had left them, but I had the clean ones Foster had lent me. He wouldn't mind if I borrowed them for a while longer—it would be cheaper for him in the long run. Foster was as looney as a six-day bike racer, but there was no point in my waiting around to tell him so.

The borrowed outfit didn't include a coat. I thought of putting my old jacket on but it was warm outside and a grey pin-stripe with grease spots wouldn't help the picture any. I transferred my personal belongings from the grimy clothes on the floor, and eased the door open.

Downstairs, the curtains were drawn in the living room. I could vaguely make out the outline of the bar. It wouldn't hurt to take along a bite to eat. I groped my way behind the bar, felt along the shelves, found a stack of small cans that rattled softly. Nuts, probably. I reached to put a can on the bar and it clattered against something I couldn't see. I swore silently, felt over the obstruction. It was bulky, with the cold smoothness of metal, and there were small projections with sharp corners. It felt for all the world like——

I leaned over it and squinted. With the faint gleam of moonlight from a chink in the heavy curtains falling just so, I could almost make out the shape; I crouched a little lower, and caught the glint of light along the perforated jacket of a .30 calibre machine gun. My eye followed the barrel, made out the darker square of the entrance hall, and the tiny reflection of light off the polished brass doorknob at the far end.

I stepped back, flattened against the wall, with a hollow feeling inside. If I had tried to walk through that door....

Foster was crazy enough for two ordinary nuts. My eyes flicked around the room. I had to get out quickly before he jumped out and said *Boo!* and I died of heart failure. The windows, maybe. I came around the end of the bar, got down and crawled under the barrel of the gun and over to the heavy drapes, pushing them aside. Pale light glowed beyond the glass. Not the soft light of the moon, but a milky, churning glow that reminded me of the phosphorescence of sea water….

I dropped the curtain, ducked back under the gun into the hall, and pushed through a swinging door into the kitchen. There was a faint glow from the luminous handle of the refrigerator. I yanked it open, spilling light on the floor, and looked around. Plenty of gleaming white fixtures—but no door out. There was a window, almost obscured by leaves. I eased it open and almost broke my fist on a wrought-iron trellis.

Back in the hall, I tried two more doors, both locked. A third opened, and I found myself looking down the cellar stairs. They were steep and dark as cellar stairs always seem to be, but they might be the way out. I felt for a light switch, flipped it on. A weak illumination showed me a patch of damp-looking floor at the foot of the steps. It still wasn't inviting, but I went down.

There was an oil furnace in the center of the room, with dusty duct-work spidering out across the ceiling; some heavy packing cases of rough wood were stacked along one wall, and at the far side of the room, there was a boarded-up coal bin—but no cellar door.

I turned to go back up. Then I heard a sound and froze. Somewhere a cockroach scuttled briefly. Then I heard the sound again, a faint grinding of stone against stone. I peered through the cob-webbed shadows, my mouth suddenly dry. There was nothing.

The thing for me to do was to get up the stairs fast, batter the iron trellis out of the kitchen window, and run like hell. The trouble was, I had to move to do it, and the sound of my own steps was so loud it was paralyzing. Compared to this, the shock of stumbling over the gun was just a mild kick, like finding a whistle in your Cracker-jacks. Ordinarily I didn't believe in things that went bump in the night, but this time I was hearing the bumps myself, and all I could think about was Edgar Allen Poe and his cheery tales about people who got themselves buried before they were thoroughly dead.

There was another sound, then a sharp snap, and I saw light spring up from a crack that opened across the floor in the shadowy corner. That was enough for me. I jumped for the stairs, took them three at a time, and banged through the kitchen door. I grabbed up a chair, swung it around and slammed it against the trellis. It bounced back and cracked me across the mouth. I dropped it, tasting blood. Maybe that was what I needed. The panic faded before a stronger emotion—anger. I turned and barged along the dark hall to the living room—and lights suddenly went on. I whirled and saw Foster standing in the hall doorway, fully dressed.

"OK, Foster!" I yelled. "Just show me the way out of here."

Foster held my eyes, his face tense. "Calm yourself, Mr. Legion," he said softly. "What's happened here?"

"Get over there to that gun," I snapped, nodding toward the .30 calibre on the bar. "Disarm it, and then get the front door open. I'm leaving."

Foster's eyes flicked over the clothes I was wearing.

"So I see," he said. He looked me in the face again. "What is it that's frightened you, Legion?"

"Don't act so innocent," I said. "Or am I supposed to get the idea the brownies set up that booby trap while you were asleep?"

His eyes went to the gun and his expression tightened. "It's mine," he said. "It's an automatic arrangement. Something's activated it—and without sounding my alarm. You haven't been outside, have you?"

"How could I——"

"This is important, Legion," Foster rapped. "It would take more than the sight of a machine gun to panic you. What have you seen?"

"I was looking for a back door," I said. "I went down to the cellar. I didn't like it down there so I came back up."

"What did you see in the cellar?" Foster's face looked strained, colorless.

"It looked like…" I hesitated. "There was a crack in the floor, noises, lights…."

"The floor," Foster said. "Certainly. That's the weak point." He seemed to be talking to himself.

I jerked a thumb over my shoulder. "Something funny going on outside your windows, too."

Foster looked toward the heavy hangings. "Listen carefully, Legion," he said. "We are in grave danger—both of us. It's fortunate you arose when you did. This house, as you must have guessed by now, is something of a fortress. At this moment, it is under attack. The walls are protected by some rather formidable defenses. I can't say as much for the cellar floor; it's merely three feet of ferro-concrete. We'll have to go now—very swiftly, and very quietly."

"OK—show me," I said. Foster turned and went back along the hall to one of the locked doors where he pressed something. The door opened and I followed him inside a small room. He crossed to a blank wall, pressed against it. A panel slid aside—and Foster jumped back.

"God's wounds!" he gasped. He threw himself at the wall and the panel closed. I stood stock still; from somewhere there was a smell like sulphur.

"What the hell goes on?" I said. My voice cracked, as it always does when I'm scared.

"That odor," Foster said. "Quickly—the other way!"

I stepped back and Foster pushed past me and ran along the hall, with me at his heels. I didn't look back to see what was at my own heels. Foster took the stairs three at a time, pulled up short on the landing. He went to his knees, shoved back an Isfahan rug as supple as sable, and gripped a steel ring set in the floor. He looked at me, his face white.

"Invoke thy gods," he said hoarsely, and heaved at the ring. A section of floor swung up, showing the first step of a flight leading down into a black hole. Foster didn't hesitate; he dropped his feet in, scrambled down. I followed. The stairs went down about ten feet, ending on a stone floor. There was the sound of a latch turning, and we stepped out into a larger room. I saw moonlight through a row of high windows, and smelled the fragrance of fresh night air.

"We're in the garage," Foster whispered. "Go around to the other side of the car and get in—quietly." I touched the smooth flank of the rakish cabriolet, felt my way around it, and eased the door open. I slipped into the seat and closed the door gently. Beside me, Foster touched a button and a green light glowed on the dash.

"Ready?" he said.

"Sure."

The starter whined half a turn and the engine caught. Without waiting, Foster gunned it, let in the clutch. The car leaped for the closed doors, and I ducked, and then saw the doors snap aside as the low-slung car roared out into the night. We took the first turn in the drive at forty, and rounded onto the highway at sixty, tires screaming. I took a look back and caught a glimpse of the house, its stately façade white in the moonlight—and then we were out of sight over a rise.

"What's it all about?" I called over the rush of air. The needle touched ninety, kept going.

"Later," Foster barked. I didn't feel like arguing. I watched in the mirror for a few minutes, wondering where all the cops were tonight. Then I settled down in the padded seat and watched the speedometer eat up the miles.

CHAPTER III

It was nearly four-thirty and a tentative grey streak showed through the palm fronds to the east before I broke the silence.

"By the way," I said. "What was the routine with the steel shutters, and the bullet-proof glass in the kitchen, and the handy home-model machine gun covering the front door? Mice bad around the place, are they?"

"Those things were necessary—and more."

"Now that the short hairs along my spine have relaxed," I said, "the whole thing looks pretty silly. We've run far enough now to be able to stop and turn around and stick our tongues out."

"Not yet—not for a long while yet."

"Why don't we just go back home," I went on, "and——"

"No!" Foster said sharply. "I want your word on that, Legion. No matter what—don't ever go near that house again."

"It'll be daylight soon," I said. "We'll feel pretty asinine about this little trip after the sun comes up, but don't worry, I won't tell anybody——"

"We've got to keep moving," Foster said. "At the next town, I'll telephone for seats on a flight out of Miami."

"Hold on," I said. "You're raving. What about your house? We didn't even stick around long enough to make sure the TV was turned off. And what about passports, and money, and luggage? And what makes you think I'm going with you?"

"I've kept myself in readiness for this emergency," Foster said. "There are disposition instructions for the house on file with a legal firm in Jacksonville. There is nothing to connect me with my former life, once I've changed my name and disappeared. As for the rest—we can buy luggage in the morning. My passport is in the car; perhaps we'd better go first to Puerto Rico, until we can arrange for one for you."

"Look," I said. "I got spooked in the dark, that's all. Why not just admit we made fools of ourselves?"

Foster shook his head. "The inherent inertia of the human mind," he said. "How it fights to resist new ideas."

"The kind of new ideas you're talking about could get both of us locked up in the chuckle ward," I said.

"Legion," Foster said, "I think you'd better write down what I'm going to tell you. It's important—vitally important. I won't waste time with preliminaries. The notebook I showed you—it's in my jacket. You must read the English portion of it. Afterwards, what I'm about to say may make more sense."

"I hope you don't feel your last will and testament coming on, Mr. Foster," I said. "Not before you tell me what that was we were both so eager to get away from."

"I'll be frank with you," Foster said flatly. "I don't know."

* * * *

Foster wheeled into the dark drive of a silent service station, eased to a stop, set the brake and slumped back in the seat.

"Do you mind driving for a while, Legion?" he said. "I'm not feeling very well."

"Sure I'll drive," I said. I opened the door and got out and went around to his side. Foster sat limply, eyes closed, his face drawn and strained. He looked older than he had last night—years older. The night's experiences hadn't taken anything off my age, either.

Foster opened his eyes, looked at me blankly. He seemed to gather himself with an effort. "I'm sorry," he said. "I'm not myself."

He moved over and I got in the driver's seat. "If you're sick," I said, "we'd better find a doctor."

"No, it's all right," he said blurrily. "Just keep going...."

"We're a hundred and fifty miles from Mayport now," I said.

Foster turned to me, started to say something—and slumped in a dead faint. I grabbed for his pulse; it was strong and steady. I rolled up an eyelid and a dilated pupil stared sightlessly. He was all right—I hoped. But the thing to do was get him in bed and call a doctor. We were at the edge of a small town. I let the brake off and drove slowly into town, swung around a corner and pulled up in front of the sagging marquee of a run-down hotel. Foster stirred as I cut the engine.

"Foster," I said. "I'm going to get you into a bed. Can you walk?" He groaned softly and opened his eyes. They were glassy. I got out and got him to the sidewalk. He was still half out. I walked him into the dingy lobby and over to a reception counter where a dim bulb burned. I dinged the bell. It was a minute before an old man shuffled out from where he'd been sleeping. He yawned, eyed me suspiciously, looked at Foster.

"We don't want no drunks here," he said. "Respectable house."

"My friend is sick," I said. "Give me a double with bath. And call a doctor."

"What's he got?" the old man said. "Ain't contagious, is it?"

"That's what I want a doctor to tell me."

"I can't get the doc 'fore in the morning. And we got no private bathrooms."

I signed the register. We rode the open-cage elevator to the fourth floor, went along a gloomy hall to a door painted a peeling brown. It didn't look inviting; the room inside wasn't much better. There was a lot of flowered wallpaper and an old-fashioned wash-stand and two wide beds. I stretched Foster out on one. He lay relaxed, a serene expression on his face—the kind undertakers try for but never quite seem to manage. I sat down on the other bed and pulled off my shoes. It was my turn to have a tired mind. I lay on the bed and let it sink down like a grey stone into still water.

* * * *

I awoke from a dream in which I had just discovered the answer to the riddle of life. I tried to hold onto it, but it slipped away; it always does.

Grey daylight was filtering through the dusty windows. Foster lay slackly on the broad sagging bed, a ceiling lamp with a faded fringed shade casting a sickly yellow light over him. It didn't make things any cheerier; I flipped it off.

Foster was lying on his back, arms spread wide, breathing heavily. Maybe it was only exhaustion, and he didn't need a doctor after all. He'd probably wake up in a little while, raring to go.

As for me, I was feeling hungry again. I'd have to have a buck or so for sandwiches. I went over to the bed and called Foster's name. He didn't move. If he was sleeping that soundly, maybe I wouldn't bother him....

I eased his wallet out of his coat pocket, took it to the window and checked it. It was fat. I took a ten, put the wallet on the table. I remembered Foster had said something about money in the car. I had the keys in my pocket. I got my shoes on and let myself out quietly. Foster hadn't moved.

Down on the street I waited for a couple of yokels who were looking over Foster's car to move on, then slid into the seat, leaned over, and got the floor boards up. The strong-box was set into the channel of the frame. I scraped the road dirt off the lock and opened it with a key from Foster's key ring, took out the contents. There was a bundle of stiffish papers, a passport, some maps—marked up—and a wad of currency that made my mouth go dry. I riffled through it: fifty grand if it was a buck.

I stuffed the papers, money, and passport back in the box and locked it, and climbed out onto the sidewalk. A few doors down the street there was a dirty window lettered MAE'S EAT. I went in, ordered hamburgers and coffee to go, and sat at the counter with Foster's keys in front of me, thinking about the car that went with them. The passport only needed a little work on the picture to get me wherever I wanted to go, and the money would buy me my choice of islands. Foster would have a nice long nap, and then take a train home. With his dough, he'd hardly miss what I took.

The counterman put a paper bag in front of me and I paid him and went out. I stood by the car, jingling the keys on my palm and thinking. I could be in Miami in an hour, and I knew where to go for the passport job. Foster was a nice guy and I liked him—but I'd never have a break like this again. I reached for the car door and a voice said, "Paper, mister?"

I jumped and looked around. A dirty-faced kid was looking at me. "Sure," I said. I gave him a single and took the paper, flipped it open. A Mayport dateline caught my eye:

POLICE RAID HIDEOUT

A surprise raid by local police led to the discovery here today of a secret gangland fortress. Chief Chesters of the Mayport Police stated that the raid came as an aftermath of the arrival in the city yesterday of a notorious northern gang member. A number of firearms, including army-type machine guns, were seized in the raid on a house 9 miles from Mayport on the Fernandina road. The raid was said by Chief Chesters to be the culmination of a lengthy investigation.

C.R. Foster, 50, owner of the property, is missing and feared dead. Police are seeking the ex-convict who visited the house last night. It is feared that Foster may have been the victim of a gangland murder.

I banged through the door to the darkened room and stopped short. In the gloom I could see Foster sitting on the edge of the bed, looking my way.

"Look at this," I yelped, flapping the paper in his face. "Now the cops are dragging the state for me—and on a murder rap at that! Get on the phone and get this thing straightened out—if you can. You and your little green men! The cops think they've stumbled on Al Capone's arsenal. You'll have fun explaining that one...."

Foster looked at me interestedly. He smiled.

"What's funny about it, Foster?" I yelled. "Your dough may buy you out, but what about me?"

"Forgive me for asking," Foster said pleasantly, "But—who are you?"

* * * *

There are times when I'm slow on the uptake, but this wasn't one of them. The implications of what Foster had said hit me hard enough to make my knees go weak.

"Oh, no, Mr. Foster," I said. "You can't lose your memory again—not right now, not with the police looking for me. You're my alibi; you're the one that has to explain all the business about the guns and the ad in the paper. I just came to see about a job, remember?"

My voice was getting a little shrill. Foster sat looking at me, wearing an expression between a frown and a smile, like a credit manager turning down an application.

He shook his head slightly. "My name is not Foster."

"Look," I said. "Your name was Foster yesterday—that's all I care about. You're the one that owns the house the cops are all upset about. And you're the corpse I'm supposed to have knocked off. You've got to go to the cops with me—right now—and tell them I'm just an innocent bystander."

I went to the window and raised the shades to let some light into the room, turned back to Foster.

"I'll explain to the cops about you thinking the little men were after you—" I stopped talking and stared at Foster. For a wild moment I thought I'd made a mistake—that I'd wandered into the wrong room. I knew Foster's face, all right; the light was bright enough now to see clearly; but the man I was talking to couldn't have been a day over twenty years old.

* * * *

I went close to him, staring hard. There were the same cool blue eyes, but the lines around them were gone. The black hair grew lower and thicker than I remembered it, and the skin was clear.

I sat down hard on my bed. "*Mama mia*," I said.

"*¿Que es la dificultad?*" Foster said.

"Shut up," I moaned. "I'm confused enough in one language." I was trying hard to think but I couldn't seem to get started. A few minutes earlier I'd had the world by the tail—just before it turned around and bit me. Cold sweat popped out on my forehead when I thought about how close I had come to driving off in Foster's car; every cop in the state would be looking for it by now—and if they found me in it, the jury wouldn't be out ten minutes reaching a verdict of guilty.

Then another thought hit me—the kind that brings you bolt upright with your teeth clenched and your heart hammering. It wouldn't be long before the local hick cops would notice the car out front. They'd come in after me, and I'd tell them it belonged to Foster. They'd take a look at him and say, "nuts, the bird we want is fifty years old, and where did you hide the body?"

I got up and started pacing. Foster had already told me there was nothing to connect him with his house in Mayport; the locals there had seen enough of him to know he was pushing middle age, at least. I could kick and scream and tell them this twenty-year-old kid was Foster, but I'd never make it stick. There was no way to prove my story; they'd figure Foster was dead and that I'd killed him—and anybody who thinks you need a *corpus* to prove murder better read his Perry Mason again.

I glanced out of the window and did a double take. Two cops were standing by Foster's car. One of them went around to the back and got out a pad and took down the license number, then said something over his shoulder and started across the street. The second cop planted himself by the car, his eye on the front of the hotel.

I whirled on Foster. "Get your shoes on," I croaked. "Let's get the hell out of here."

We went down the stairs quietly and found a back door opening on an alley. Nobody saw us go.

* * * *

An hour later, I sagged in a grimy coach seat and studied Foster, sitting across from me—a middle-aged nut with the face of a young kid and a mind like a blank slate. I had no choice but to drag him with me; my only chance was to stick close and hope he got back enough of his memory to get me off the hook.

It was time for me to be figuring my next move. I thought about the fifty thousand dollars I had left behind in the car, and groaned. Foster looked concerned.

"Are you in pain?" he said.

"And how I'm in pain," I said. "Before I met you I was a homeless bum, broke and hungry. Now I can add a couple more items: the cops are after me, and I've got a mental case to nursemaid."

"What law have you broken?" Foster said.

"None," I barked. "As a crook, I'm a washout. I've planned three larcenies in the last twelve hours, and flunked out on all of them. And now I'm wanted for murder."

"Whom did you kill?" Foster inquired courteously.

I leaned across so I could snarl in his face: "You!" Then, "Get this through your head, Foster. The only crime I'm guilty of is stupidity. I listened to your crazy story; because of you I'm in a mess I'll never get straightened out." I leaned back. "And then there's the question of old men that take a nap and wake up in their late teens; we'll go into that later, after I've had my nervous breakdown."

"I'm sorry if I've been the cause of difficulty," Foster said. "I wish that I could recall the things you've spoken of. Is there anything I can do to assist you now?"

"And you were the one who wanted help," I said. "There is one thing; let me have the money you've got on you; we'll need it."

Foster got out his wallet—after I told him where it was—and handed it to me. I looked through it; there was nothing in it with a photo or fingerprints. When Foster said he had arranged matters so that he could disappear without a trace, he hadn't been kidding.

"We'll go to Miami," I said. "I know a place in the Cuban section where we can lie low, cheap. Maybe if we wait a while, you'll start remembering things."

"Yes," Foster said. "That would be pleasant."

"You haven't forgotten how to talk, at least," I said. "I wonder what else you can do. Do you remember how you made all that money?"

"I can remember nothing of your economic system," Foster said. He looked around. "This is a very primitive world, in many respects," he said. "It should not be difficult to amass wealth here."

"I never had much luck at it," I said. "I haven't even been able to amass the price of a meal."

"Food is exchanged for money?" Foster asked.

"Everything is exchanged for money," I said. "Including most of the human virtues."

"This is a strange world," Foster said. "It will take me a long while to become accustomed to it."

"Yeah, me, too," I said. "Maybe things would be better on Mars."

Foster nodded. "Perhaps," he said. "Perhaps we should go there."

I groaned, then caught myself. "No, I'm not in pain," I said. "But don't take me so literally, Foster."

We rode along in silence for a while.

"Say, Foster," I said. "Have you still got that notebook of yours?"

Foster tried several pockets, came up with the book. He looked at it, turned it over, frowning.

"You remember it?" I said, watching him.

He shook his head slowly, then ran his finger around the circles embossed on the cover.

"This pattern," he said. "It signifies...."

"Go on, Foster," I said. "Signifies what?"

"I'm sorry," he said. "I don't remember."

I took the book and sat looking at it. I didn't really see it, though. I was seeing my future. When Foster didn't turn up, they'd naturally assume he was dead. I'd been with him just before his disappearance. It wasn't hard to see why they'd want to talk to me—and my having vanished too wouldn't help any. My picture would blossom out in post offices all over the country; and even if they didn't catch me right away, the murder charge would always be there, hanging over me.

It wouldn't do any good to turn myself in and tell them the whole story; they wouldn't believe me, and I wouldn't blame them. I didn't really believe it myself, and I'd lived through it. But then, maybe I was just imagining that Foster looked younger. After all, a good night's rest——

I looked at Foster, and almost groaned again. Twenty was stretching it; eighteen was more like it. I was willing to swear he'd never shaved in his life.

"Foster," I said. "It's got to be in this book; who you are, where you came from——It's the only hope I've got."

"I suggest we read it, then," Foster said.

"A bright idea," I said. "Why didn't I think of that?" I thumbed through the book to the section in English and read for an hour. Starting with the entry dated January 19, 1710, the writer had scribbled a few lines every few months. He seemed to be some kind of pioneer in the Virginia Colony. He complained about prices, and the Indians, and the ignorance of the other settlers and every now and then threw in a remark about the Enemy. He often took long trips, and when he got home, he complained about those, too.

"It's a funny thing, Foster," I said. "This is supposed to have been written over a period of a couple of hundred years, but it's all in the same hand. That's kind of odd, isn't it?"

"Why should a man's handwriting change?" Foster said.

"Well, it might get a little shaky there toward the last, don't you agree?"

"Why is that?"

"I'll spell it out, Foster," I said. "Most people don't live that long. A hundred years is stretching it, to say nothing of two."

"This must be a very violent world, then," Foster said.

"Skip it," I said. "You talk like you're just visiting. By the way; do you remember how to write?"

Foster looked thoughtful. "Yes," he said. "I can write."

I handed him the book and the stylus. "Try it," I said. Foster opened to a blank page, wrote, and handed the book back to me.

"Always and always and always," I read.

I looked at Foster. "What does that mean?" I looked at the words again, then quickly flipped to the pages written in English. I was no expert on penmanship, but this came up and cracked me right in the eye.

The book was written in Foster's hand.

* * * *

"It doesn't make sense," I was saying for the fortieth time. Foster nodded sympathetic agreement.

"Why would you write out this junk yourself, and then spend all that time and money trying to have it deciphered? You said experts worked over it and couldn't break it. But," I went on, "you must have known you wrote it; you knew your own handwriting. But on the other hand, you had amnesia before; you had the idea you might have told something about yourself in the book...."

I sighed, leaned back and tossed the book over to Foster. "Here, you read a while," I said. "I'm arguing with myself and I can't tell who's winning."

Foster looked the book over carefully.

"This is odd," he said.

"What's odd?"

"The book is made of khaff. It is a permanent material—and yet it shows damage."

I sat perfectly still and waited.

"Here on the back cover," Foster said. "A scuffed area. Since this is khaff, it cannot be an actual scar. It must have been placed there."

I grabbed the book and looked. There was a faint mark across the back cover, as though the book had been scraped on something sharp. I remembered how much luck I had had with a knife. The mark had been put here, disguised as a casual nick in the finish. It had to mean something.

"How do you know what the material is?" I asked.

Foster looked surprised. "In the same way that I know the window is of glass," he said. "I simply know."

"Speaking of glass," I said. "Wait till I get my hands on a microscope. Then maybe we'll begin to get some answers."

CHAPTER IV

The two-hundred pound señorita with the wart on her upper lip put a pot of black Cuban coffee and a pitcher of salted milk down beside the two chipped cups, leered at me in a way that might have been appealing thirty years before, and waddled back to the kitchen. I poured a cup, gulped half of it, and shuddered. In the street outside the cafe a guitar cried *Estrellita*.

"Okay, Foster," I said. "Here's what I've got: The first half of the book is in pot-hooks—I can't read that. But this middle section: the part coded in regular letters—it's actually encrypted English. It's a sort of résumé of what happened." I picked up the sheets of paper on which I had transcribed my deciphering of the coded section of the book, using the key that had been micro-engraved in the fake scratch on the back cover.

I read:

> For the first time, I am afraid. My attempt to construct the communicator called down the Hunters upon me. I made such a shield as I could contrive, and sought their nesting place.
>
> I came there and it was in that place that I knew of old, and it was no hive, but a pit in the ground, built by men of the Two Worlds. And I would have come into it, but the Hunters swarmed in their multitudes. I fought them and killed many, but at last I fled away. I came to the western shore, and there I hired bold sailors and a poor craft, and set forth.
>
> In forty-nine days we came to shore in this wilderness, and there were men as from the dawn of time, and I fought them, and when they had learned fear, I lived among them in peace, and the Hunters have not found this place. Now it may be that my saga ends here, but I will do what I am able.
>
> The Change may soon come upon me; I must prepare for the stranger who will come after me. All that he must know is in these pages. And say I to him:
>
> Have patience, for the time of this race draws close. Venture not again on the Eastern continent, but wait, for soon the Northern sailors must come in numbers into this wilderness. Seek out their cleverest metal-workers, and when it may be, devise a shield, and only then return to the pit of the Hunters. It lies in the plain, 50/10,000 parts of the girth of this(?) to the west of the Great Chalk Face, and 1470 parts north from the median line, as I reckon. The stones mark it well with the sign of the Two Worlds.

I looked across at Foster. "It goes on then with a blow-by-blow account of dealings with aborigines. He was trying to get them civilized in a hurry. They figured he was a god and he set them to work building roads and cutting stone and learning mathematics and so on. He was doing all he could to set things up so this stranger who was to follow him would know the score, and carry on the good work."

Foster's eyes were on my face. "What is the nature of the Change he speaks of?"

"He never says—but I suppose he's talking about death," I said. "I don't know where the stranger is supposed to come from."

"Listen to me, Legion," Foster said. There was a hint of the old anxious look in his eyes. "I think I know what the Change was. I think he knew he would forget——"

"You've got amnesia on the brain, old buddy," I said.

"——and the stranger is—himself. A man without a memory."

I sat frowning at Foster. "Yeah, maybe," I said. "Go on."

"And he says that all that the stranger needs to know is there—in the book."

"Not in the part I decoded," I said. "He describes how they're coming along with the road-building job, and how the new mine panned out—but there's nothing about what the Hunters are, or what had gone on before he tangled with them the first time."

"It must be there, Legion; but in the first section, the part written in alien symbols."

"Maybe," I said. "But why the hell didn't he give us a key to that part?"

"I think he assumed that the stranger—himself—would remember the old writing," Foster said. "How could he know that it would be forgotten with the rest?"

"Your guess is as good as any," I said. "Maybe better; you know how it feels to lose your memory."

"But we've learned a few things," Foster said. "The pit of the Hunters—we have the location."

"If you call this 'ten thousand parts to the west of chalk face' a location," I said.

"We know more than that," Foster said. "He mentions a plain; and it must lie on a continent to the east——"

"If you assume that he sailed from Europe to America, then the continent to the east would be Europe," I said. "But maybe he went from Africa to South America, or——"

"The mention of Northern sailors—that suggests the Vikings——"

"You seem to know a little history, Foster," I said. "You've got a lot of odd facts tucked away."

"We need maps," Foster said. "We'll look for a plain near the sea——"

"Not necessarily."

"——and with a formation called a chalk face to the east."

"What's this 'median line' business?" I said. "And the bit about ten thousand parts of something?"

"I don't know. But we must have maps."

"I bought some this afternoon," I said. "I also got a dime-store globe. I figured we might need them. Let's get out of this and back to the room, where we can spread out. I know it's a grim prospect, but...." I got to my feet, dropped some coins on the oilcloth-covered table, and led the way out.

It was a short half block to the flea trap we called home. We kept out of it as much as we could, holding our long daily conferences across the street at the Novedades. The roaches scurried as we passed up the dark stairway to our not much brighter room. I crossed to the bureau and opened a drawer.

"The globe," Foster said, taking it in his hands. "I wonder if perhaps he meant a ten-thousandth part of the circumference of the earth?"

"What would he know about——"

"Disregard the anachronistic aspect of it," Foster said. "The man who wrote the book knew many things. We'll have to start with some assumptions. Let's make the obvious ones: that we're looking for a plain on the west coast of Europe, lying——" He pulled a chair up to the scabrous table and riffled through to one of my scribbled sheets: "50/10,000s of the circumference of the earth—that would be about 125 miles—west of a chalk formation, and 3675 miles north of a median line...."

"Maybe," I said, "he means the Equator."

"Certainly. Why not? That would mean our plain lies on a line through——" he studied the small globe "——Warsaw, and south of Amsterdam."

"But this part about a rock outcropping," I said. "How do we find out if there's any conspicuous chalk formation around there?"

"We can consult a geology text. There may be a library in this neighborhood."

"The only chalk deposits I ever heard about," I said, "are the White cliffs of Dover."

"White cliffs...."

We both reached for the globe at once.

"One hundred twenty-five miles west of the chalk cliffs," said Foster. He ran a finger over the globe. "North of London, but south of Birmingham. That puts us reasonably near the sea——"

"Where's the atlas?" I said. I rummaged, came up with a cheap tourists' edition, flipped the pages.

"Here's England," I said. "Now we look for a plain."

Foster put a finger on the map. "Here," he said. "A large plain—called Salisbury."

"Large is right," I said. "It would take years to find a stone cairn on that. We're getting excited about nothing. We're looking for a hole in the ground, hundreds of years old—if this lousy notebook means anything—maybe marked with a few stones—in the middle of miles of plain. And it's all guesswork anyway...." I took the atlas, turned the page.

"I don't know what I expected to get out of decoding those pages," I said. "But I was hoping for more than this."

"I think we should try, Legion," Foster said. "We can go there, search over the ground. It would be costly, but not impossible. We can start by gathering capital——"

"Wait a minute, Foster," I said. I was staring at a larger-scale map showing southern England. Suddenly my heart was thudding. I put a finger on a tiny dot in the center of Salisbury Plain.

"Six, two and even," I said. "There's your Pit of the Hunters...."

Foster leaned over, read the fine print.

"Stonehenge."

* * * *

I read from the encyclopedia page:

—this great stone structure, lying on the Plain of Salisbury, Wiltshire, England, is pre-eminent among megalithic monuments of the ancient world. Within a circular ditch 300' in diameter, stones up to 22' in height are arranged in concentric circles. The central altar stone, over 16' long, is approached from the northeast by a broad roadway called the Avenue—

"It is not an altar," said Foster.

"How do you know?"

"Because——" Foster frowned. "I know, that's all."

"The journal said the stones were arranged in the sign of the Two Worlds," I said. "That means the concentric circles, I suppose; the same thing that's stamped on the cover of the notebook."

"And the ring," Foster said.

"Let me read the rest: *A great sarsen stone stands upright in the Avenue; the axis through the two stones, when erected, pointed directly to the rising of the sun on Midsummer Day. Calculations based on this observation indicate a date of approximately 1600 B.C.*"

Foster took the book and I sat on the window sill and looked out at a big Florida moon over the ragged line of roofs with a skinny royal palm sticking up in silhouette. It didn't look much like the postcard views of Miami. I lit a cigarette and thought about a man who long ago had crossed the North Atlantic in a dragon boat to be a god among the Indians. I wondered where he came from, and what it was he was looking for, and what kept him going in spite of the hell that showed in the spare lines of the journal he kept. If, I reminded myself, he had ever existed....

Foster was poring over the book. "Look," I said. "Let's get back to earth. We have things to think about, plans to make. The fairy tales can wait until later."

"What do you suggest?" Foster said. "That we forget the things you've told me, and the things we've read here, discard the journal, and abandon the attempt to find the answers?"

"No," I said. "I'm no sorehead. Sure, there's some things here that somebody ought to look into—some day. But right now what I want is the cops off my neck. And I've been thinking. I'll dictate a letter; you write it—your lawyers know your handwriting. Tell them you were on the thin edge of a nervous breakdown—that's why all the artillery around your house—and you made up your mind suddenly to get away from it all. Tell them you don't want to be bothered, that's why you're travelling incognito, and that the northern mobster that came to see you was just stupid, not a killer. That ought to at least cool off the cops——"

Foster looked thoughtful. "That's an excellent suggestion," he said. "Then we need merely to arrange for passage to England, and proceed with the investigation."

"You don't get the idea," I said. "You can arrange things by mail so we get our hands on that dough of yours——"

"Any such attempt would merely bring the police down on us," Foster said. "You've already pointed out the unwisdom of attempting to pass myself off as—myself."

"There ought to be a way…." I said.

"We have only one avenue of inquiry," Foster said. "We have no choice but to explore it. We'll take passage on a ship to England——"

"What'll we use for money—and papers? It would cost hundreds. Unless——" I added, "——we worked our way. But that's no good. We'd still need passports—plus union cards and seamen's tickets."

"Your friend," Foster said. "The one who prepares passports. Can't he produce the other papers as well?"

"Yeah," I said. "I guess so. But it will cost us."

"I'm sure we can find a way to pay," Foster said. "Will you see him—early in the morning?"

I looked around the blowsy room. Hot night air stirred a geranium wilting in a tin can on the window sill. An odor of bad cooking and worse plumbing floated up from the street.

"At least," I said, "it would mean getting out of here."

CHAPTER V

It was almost sundown when Foster and I pushed through the door to the saloon bar at the Ancient Sinner and found a corner table. I watched

Foster spread out his maps and papers. Behind us there was a murmur of conversation and the thump of darts against a board.

"When are you going to give up and admit we're wasting our time?" I said. "Two weeks of tramping over the same ground, and we end up in the same place."

"We've hardly begun our investigation," Foster said mildly.

"You keep saying that," I said. "But if there ever was anything in that rock-pile, it's long gone. The archaeologists have been digging over the site for years, and they haven't come up with anything."

"They don't know what to look for," Foster said. "They were searching for indications of religious significance, human sacrifice—that sort of thing."

"We don't know what we're looking for either," I said. "Unless you think maybe we'll meet the Hunters hiding under a loose stone."

"You say that sardonically," Foster said. "But I don't consider it impossible."

"I know," I said. "You've convinced yourself that the Hunters were after us back at Mayport when we ran off like a pair of idiots."

"From what you've told me of the circumstances—" Foster began.

"I know; you don't consider it impossible. That's the trouble with you; you don't consider anything impossible. It would make life a lot easier for me if you'd let me rule out a few items—like leprechauns who hang out at Stonehenge."

Foster looked at me, half-smiling. It had only been a few weeks since he woke up from a nap looking like a senior class president who hadn't made up his mind whether to be a preacher or a movie star, but he had already lost that mild, innocent air. He learned fast, and day by day I had seen his old personality reemerge and—in spite of my attempts to hold onto the ascendency—dominate our partnership.

"It's a failing of your culture," Foster said, "that hypothesis becomes dogma almost overnight. You're too close to your Neolithic, when the blind acceptance of tribal lore had survival value. Having learned to evoke the fire god from sticks, by rote, you tend to extend the principle to all 'established facts.'"

"Here's an established fact for you," I said. "We've got fifteen pounds left—that's about forty dollars. It's time we figure out where to go from here, before somebody starts checking up on those phoney papers of ours."

Foster shook his head. "I'm not satisfied that we've exhausted the possibilities here. I've been studying the geometric relationships between the various structures; I have some ideas I want to check. I think it might be a good idea to go out at night, when we can work without the usual crowd of tourists observing every move."

I groaned. "My dogs are killing me," I said. "Let's hope you'll come up with something better—or at least different."

"We'll have a bite to eat here, and wait until dark to start out," Foster said.

The publican brought us plates of cold meat and potato salad. I worked on a thin but durable slice of ham and thought about all the people, somewhere, who were sitting down now to gracious meals in the glitter of crystal and silver. I'd had too many greasy French fries in too many cheap dives the last few years. I could feel them all now, burning in my stomach. I was getting farther from my island all the time—And it was nobody's fault but mine.

"The Ancient Sinner," I said. "That's me."

Foster looked up. "Curious names these old pubs have," he said. "I suppose in some cases the origins are lost in antiquity."

"Why don't they think up something cheery," I said. "Like 'The Paradise Bar and Grill' or 'The Happy Hour Cafe'. Did you notice the sign hanging outside?"

"No."

"A picture of a skeleton. He's holding one hand up like a Yankee evangelist prophesying doom. You can see it through the window there."

Foster turned and looked out at the weathered sign creaking in the evening wind. He looked at it for a long time. When he turned back, there was a strange look around his eyes.

"What's the matter—?" I started.

Foster ignored me, waved to the proprietor, a short fat country man. He came over to the table, wiping his hands on his apron.

"A very interesting old building," Foster said. "We've been admiring it. When was it built?"

"Well, sir," the publican said, "This here house is a many a hundred year old. It were built by the monks, they say, from the monastery what used to stand nearby here. It were tore down by the King's men, Henry, that was, what time he drove the papists out."

"That would be Henry the Eighth, I suppose?"

"Aye, it would that. And this house is all that were spared, it being the brewing-house, as the king said were a worthwhile institution, and he laid on a tithe, that two kegs of stout was to be laid by for the king's use each brewing time."

"Very interesting," Foster said. "Is the custom still continued?"

The publican shook his head. "It were ended in my granfer's time, it being that the Queen were a teetotaller."

"How did it acquire the curious name—'The Ancient Sinner?'"

"The tale is," the publican said, "that one day a lay brother of the order were digging about yonder on the plain by the great stones, in search of the

Druid's treasure, albeit the Abbot had forbid him to go nigh the heathen ground, and he come on the bones of a man, and being of a kindly turn, he had the thought to give them Christian burial. Now, knowing the Abbott would nae permit it, he set to work to dig a grave by moonlight in holy ground, under the monastery walls. But the Abbott, being wakeful, were abroad and come on the brother a-digging, and when he asked the why of it, the lay brother having visions of penances to burden him for many a day, he ups and tells the Abbott it were a ale cellar he were about digging, and the Abbott, not being without wisdom, clapped him on the back, and went on his way. And so it was the ale-house got built, and blessed by the Abbott, and with it the bones that was laid away under the floor beneath the ale-casks."

"So the ancient sinner is buried under the floor?"

"Aye, so the tale goes, though I've not dug for him meself. But the house has been knowed by the name these four hundred years."

"Where was it you said the lay brother was digging?"

"On the plain, yonder, by the Druid's stones, what they call Stonehenge," the publican said. He picked up the empty glasses. "What about another, gentlemen?"

"Certainly," Foster said. He sat quietly across from me, his features composed—but I could see there was tension under the surface calm.

"What's this all about?" I asked softly. "When did you get so interested in local history?"

"Later," Foster murmured. "Keep looking bored."

"That'll be easy," I said. The publican came back and placed heavy glass mugs before us.

"You were telling us about the lay brother's finding the bones," Foster said. "You say they were buried in Stonehenge?"

The publican cleared his throat, glanced sideways at Foster.

"The gentlemen wouldna be from the University now, I suppose?" he said.

"Let's just say," Foster said easily, smiling, "that we have a great interest in these bits of lore—an interest supported by modest funds, of course."

The publican made a show of wiping at the rings on the table top.

"A costly business, I wager," he said. "Digging about in odd places and all. Now, knowing where to dig; that's important, I'll be bound."

"Very important," Foster said. "Worth five pounds, easily."

"'Twere my granfer told me of the spot; took me out by moonlight, he did, and showed me where his granfer had showed him. Told me it were a fine great secret, the likes of which a simple man could well take pride in."

"And an additional five pounds as a token of my personal esteem," Foster said.

The publican eyed me. "Well, a secret as was handed down father to son...."

"And, of course, my associate wishes to express his esteem, too," Foster said. "Another five pounds worth."

"That's all the esteem the budget will bear, Mr. Foster," I said. I got out the fifteen pounds and passed the money across to him. "I hope you haven't forgotten those people back home who wanted to talk to us," I said. "They'll be getting in touch with us any time now, I'll bet."

Foster rolled up the bills and held them in his hand. "That's true, Mr. Legion," he said. "Perhaps we shouldn't take the time...."

"But being it's for the advancement of science," the publican said, "I'm willing to make the sacrifice."

"We'll want to go out tonight," Foster said. "We have a very tight schedule."

The landlord dickered with Foster for another five minutes before he agreed to guide us to the spot where the skeleton had been found.

When he left, I began. "Now tell me."

"Look at the signboard again," Foster said. I looked. The skull smiled, holding up a hand.

"I see it," I said. "But it doesn't explain why you handed over our last buck——"

"Look at the hand. Look at the ring on the finger."

I looked again. A heavy ring was painted on the bony index finger, with a pattern of concentric circles.

It was a duplicate of the one on Foster's finger.

* * * *

The publican pulled the battered Morris Minor to the side of the highway and set the brake.

"This is as close as we best take the machine," he said. We got out, looked across the rolling plain where the megaliths of Stonehenge loomed against the last glow of sunset.

The publican rummaged in the boot, produced a ragged blanket and two long four-cell flashlights, gave one to Foster and the other to me. "Do nae use the electric torches until I tell ye," he said, "lest the whole county see there's folks abroad here." We watched as he draped the blanket over a barbed wire fence, clambered over, and started across the barren field. Foster and I followed, not talking.

The plain was deserted. A few lonely lights showed on a distant slope. It was a dark night with no moon. I could hardly see the ground ahead. A car moved along a distant road, its headlights bobbing.

We moved past the outer ring of stones, skirting fallen slabs twenty feet long.

"We'll break our necks," I said. "Let's have one of the flashlights."

"Not yet," Foster whispered.

Our guide paused; we came up to him.

"It were a mortal long time since I were last hereabouts," he said. "I best take me bearings off the Friar's Heel...."

"What's that?"

"Yon great stone, standing alone in the Avenue." We squinted; it was barely visible as a dark shape against the sky.

"The bones were buried there?" Foster asked.

"Nay, all by theirself, they was. Now it were twenty paces, granfer said, him bein fifteen stone and long in the leg...." The publican muttered to himself, pacing off distances.

"What's to keep him from just pointing to a spot after a while," I said to Foster, "and saying 'This is it'?"

"We'll wait and see," Foster said.

"They were a hollow, as it were, in the earth," the publican said, "with a bit of stone by it. I reckon it were fifty paces from here—" he pointed, "—yonder."

"I don't see anything," I said.

"Let's take a closer look." Foster started off and I followed, the publican trailing behind. I made out a dim shape, with a deep depression in the earth before it.

"This could be the spot," Foster said. "Old graves often sink—" Suddenly he grabbed my arm. "Look...!"

The surface of the ground before us seemed to tremble, then heave. Foster snapped on his flashlight. The earth at the bottom of the hollow rose, cracked open. A boiling mass of luminescence churned, and a globe of light separated itself, rose, bumbling along the face of the weathered stone.

"Saints preserve us," the publican said in a choked voice. Foster and I stood, rooted to the spot, watching. The lone globe rose higher—and abruptly shot straight toward us. Foster threw up an arm and ducked. The ball of light veered, struck him a glancing blow, darted off a few yards, hovered. In an instant, the air was alive with the spheres, boiling up from the ground, and hurtling toward us, buzzing like a hive of yellow-jackets. Foster's flashlight lanced out toward the swarm.

"Use your light, Legion!" he shouted hoarsely. I was still standing, frozen. The globes rushed straight at Foster, ignoring me. Behind me, I heard the publican turn and run. I fumbled with the flashlight switch, snapped it on, swung the beam of white light on Foster. The globe at his head vanished as the light touched it. More globes swarmed to Foster—and popped like soap bubbles in the flashlight's glare—but more swarmed to take their places. Foster reeled, fighting at them. He swung the light—and I heard it smash against the stone behind him. In the instant darkness, the globes clustered thick around his head.

"Foster," I yelled, "run!"

He got no more than five yards before he staggered, went to his knees. "Cover," he croaked. He fell on his face. I rushed the mass of darting globes, took up a stance straddling his body. A sulphurous reek hung around me. I coughed, concentrated on beaming the lights around Foster's head. No more were rising from the crack in the earth now. A suffocating cloud pressed around both of us, but it was Foster they went for. I thought of the slab; if I could get my back to it, I might have a chance. I stooped, got a grip on Foster's coat, and started back, dragging him. The lights boiled around me. I swept the beam of light and kept going until my back slammed against the stone. I crouched against it. Now they could only come from the front.

I glanced at the cleft the lights had come from. It looked big enough to get Foster into. That would give him some protection. I tumbled him over the edge, then flattened my back against the slab and settled down to fight in earnest.

I worked in a pattern, sweeping vertically, then horizontally. The globes ignored me, drove toward the cleft, fighting to get at Foster, and I swept them away as they came. The cloud around me was smaller now, the attack less ravenous. I picked out individual globes, snuffed them out. The hum became ragged, faltered. Then there were only a few globes around me, milling wildly, disorganized. The last half dozen fled, bumbling away across the plain.

I slumped against the rock, sweat running down into my eyes, my lungs burning with the sulphur.

"Foster," I gasped. "Are you all right?"

He didn't answer. I flashed the light onto the cleft. It showed me damp clay, a few pebbles.

Foster was gone.

CHAPTER VI

I scrambled to the edge of the pit and played the light around inside. It shelved back at one side, and a dark mouth showed, sloping down into the earth—the hiding place from which the globes had swarmed.

Foster was wedged in the opening. I scrambled down beside him, tugged him back to the level ground. He was still breathing; that was something.

I wondered if the pub owner would come back, now that the lights were gone—or if he'd tell someone what had happened, bring out a search party.

Somehow, I doubted it. He didn't seem like the type to ask for trouble with the ghosts of ancient sinners.

Foster groaned and opened his eyes. "Where are…they?" he muttered.

"Take it easy, Foster," I said. "You're OK now."

"Legion," Foster said. He tried to sit up. "The Hunters…."

"OK, call 'em Hunters if you want to. I haven't got a better name for them. I worked them over with the flashlights. They're gone."

"That means…."

"Let's not worry about what it means. Let's just get out of here."

"The Hunters—they burst out of the ground—from a cleft in the earth."

"That's right. You were halfway into the hole. I guess that's where they were hiding."

"The Pit of the Hunters," Foster said.

"If you say so," I said. "Lucky you didn't go down it."

"Legion, give me the flashlight."

"I feel something coming on that I'm not going to like," I said. I handed him the light and he flashed it into the tunnel mouth. I saw a polished roof of black glass arching four feet over the rubble-strewn bottom of the shaft. A stone, dislodged by my movement, clattered away down the 30 slope.

"Hell, that tunnel's man-made," I said, peering into it. "And I don't mean neolithic man."

"Legion, we'll have to see what's down there," Foster said.

"We could come back later, with ropes and big insurance policies," I said.

"But we won't," said Foster. "We've found what we were looking for——"

"Sure," I said, "and it serves us right. Are you sure you feel good enough to make like Alice and the White Rabbit?"

"I'm sure. Let's go."

Foster thrust his legs into the opening, slid over the edge and disappeared. I followed him. I eased down a few feet, glanced back for a last look at the night sky, then lost my grip and slid. I hit bottom hard enough to knock the wind out of me. I got to my hands and knees on a level, gravel-strewn floor.

"What is this place?" I dug the flashlight out of the rubble, flashed it around. We were in a low-ceilinged room ten yards square. I saw smooth walls, the dark bulks of massive shapes that made me think of sarcophagi in Egyptian burial vaults—except that these threw back highlights from dials and levers.

"For a couple of guys who get shy in the company of cops," I said, "we've a talent for doing the wrong thing. This is some kind of Top Secret military installation."

"Impossible," Foster replied. "This couldn't be a modern structure, at the bottom of a rubble-filled shaft——"

"Let's get out of here fast," I said. "We've probably set off an alarm already."

As if in answer, a low chime cut across our talk. Pearly light sprang up on a square panel. I got to my feet, moved over to stare at it. Foster came to my side.

"What do you make of it?" he said.

"I'm no expert on stone-age relics," I said. "But if that's not a radar screen, I'll eat it."

I sat down in the single chair before the dusty control console, and watched a red blip creep across the screen. Foster stood behind me.

"We owe a debt to that ancient sinner," he said. "Who would have dreamed he'd lead us here?"

"Ancient sinner?" I said. "This place is as modern as next year's juke box."

"Look at the symbols on the machines," Foster said. "They're identical with those in the first section of the journal."

"All pot-hooks look alike to me," I said. "It's this screen that's got me worried. If I've got it doped out correctly, that blip is either a mighty slow airplane—or it's at one hell of an altitude."

"Modern aircraft operate at great heights," Foster said.

"Not at this height," I said. "Give me a few more minutes to study these scales...."

"There are a number of controls here," Foster said, "obviously intended to activate mechanisms—"

"Don't touch 'em," I said. "Unless you want to start World War III."

"I hardly think the results would be so drastic," Foster replied. "Surely this installation has a simple purpose—unconnected with modern wars—but very possibly connected with the mystery of the journal—and of my own past."

"The less we know about this, the better," I said. "At least, if we don't mess with anything, we can always claim we just stepped in here to get out of the rain——"

"You're forgetting the Hunters," said Foster.

"Some new anti-personnel gimmick."

"They came out of this shaft, Legion. It was opened by the pressure of the Hunters bursting out."

"Why did they pick that precise moment—just as we arrived?" I asked.

"I think they were aroused," said Foster. "I think they sensed the presence of their ancient foe."

I swung around to look at him.

"I see the way your thoughts are running," I said. "You're their Ancient Foe, now, huh? Just let me get this straight: that means that umpteen hundred years ago, you personally had a fight with the Hunters—here at Stonehenge. You killed a batch of them and ran. You hired some kind of Viking ship and crossed the Atlantic. Later on, you lost your memory, and started being a guy named Foster. A few weeks ago you lost it again. Is that the picture?"

"More or less."

"And now we're a couple of hundred feet under Stonehenge—after a brush with a crowd of luminous stinkbombs—and you're telling me you'll be nine hundred on your next birthday."

"Remember the entry in the journal, Legion? 'I came to the place of the Hunters, and it was a place I knew of old, and there was no hive, but a Pit built by men of the Two Worlds....'"

"Okay," I said. "So you're pushing a thousand."

I glanced at the screen, got out a scrap of paper, and scribbled a rapid calculation. "Here's another big number for you. That object on the screen is at an altitude—give or take a few percent—of thirty thousand miles."

I tossed the pencil aside, swung around to frown at Foster. "What are we mixed up in, Foster? Not that I really want to know. I'm ready to go to a nice clean jail now, and pay my debt to society—"

"Calm down, Legion," Foster said. "You're raving."

"OK," I said, turning back to the screen. "You're the boss. Do what you like. It's just my reflexes wanting to run. I've got no place to run to. At least with you I've always got the wild hope that maybe you're not completely nuts, and that somehow——"

I sat upright, eyes on the screen. "Look at this, Foster," I snapped. A pattern of dots flashed across the screen, faded, flashed again....

"Some kind of IFF," I said. "A recognition signal. I wonder what we're supposed to do now."

Foster watched the screen, saying nothing.

"I don't like that thing blinking at us," I said. "It makes me feel conspicuous." I looked at the big red button beside the screen. "Maybe if I pushed that...." Without waiting to think it over, I jabbed at it.

A yellow light blinked on the control panel. On the screen, the pattern of dots vanished. The red blip separated, a smaller blip moving off at right angles to the main mass.

"I'm not sure you should have done that," Foster said.

"There *is* room for doubt," I said in a strained voice. "It looks like I've launched a bomb from the ship overhead."

* * * *

The climb back up the tunnel took three hours, and every foot of the way I was listening to a refrain in my head: This may be it; this may be it; this may be....

I crawled out of the tunnel mouth and lay on my back, breathing hard. Foster groped his way out beside me.

"We'll have to get to the highway," I said, untying the ten-foot rope of ripped garments that had linked us during the climb. "There's a telephone at the pub; we'll notify the authorities...." I glanced up.

"Hold it!" I grabbed Foster's arm and pointed overhead. "What's that?"

Foster looked up. A brilliant point of blue light, brighter than a star, grew perceptibly as we watched.

"Maybe we won't get to notify anybody after all," I said. "I think that's our bomb—coming home to roost."

"That's illogical," Foster said. "The installation would hardly be arranged merely to destroy itself in so complex a manner."

"Let's get out of here," I yelled.

"It's approaching us very rapidly," Foster said. "The distance we could run in the next few minutes would be trivial by comparison with the killing radius of a modern bomb. We'll be safer sheltered in the cleft than on the open."

"We could slide down the tunnel," I said.

"And be buried?"

"You're right; I'd rather fry on the surface."

We crouched, watching the blue glare directly overhead, growing larger, brighter. I could see Foster's face by its light now.

"That's no bomb," Foster said. "It's not falling; it's coming down slowly...like a——"

"Like a slowly falling bomb," I said. "And it's coming right down on top of us. Goodbye, Foster. I can't claim it's been fun knowing you, but it's been different. We'll feel the heat at any second now. I hope it's fast."

The glaring disc was the size of the full moon now, unbearably bright. It lit the plain like a pale blue sun. There was no sound. As it dropped lower, the disc foreshortened and I could see a dark shape above it, dimly lit by the glare thrown back from the ground.

"The thing is the size of a ferry boat," I said.

"It's going to miss us," Foster said. "It will come to ground several hundred feet to the east of us."

We watched the slender shape float down with dreamlike slowness, now five hundred feet above, now three hundred, then hovering just above the giant stones.

"It's coming down smack on top of Stonehenge," I yelled.

We watched as the vessel settled into place dead center on the ancient ring of stones. For a moment they were vividly silhouetted against the flood of blue radiance; then abruptly, the glare faded and died.

"Foster," I said. "Do you think it's barely possible——"

A slit of yellow light appeared on the side of the hull, then it widened to a square. A ladder extended itself, dropping down to touch the ground.

"If somebody with tentacles starts down that ladder," I said, in an unnaturally shrill voice, "I'm getting out of here."

"No one will emerge," Foster said quietly. "I think we'll find, Legion, that this ship of space is at our disposal."

* * * *

"I'm not going aboard that thing," I said for the fifth time. "I'm not sure of much in this world, but I'm sure of that."

"Legion," Foster said, "This is no twentieth century military vessel. It obviously homed on the transmitter in the underground station, which appears to be directly under the old monument—which is several thousand years old——"

"And I'm supposed to believe the ship has been orbiting the earth for the last few thousand years, waiting for someone to push the red button? You call that logical?"

"Given permanent materials, such as those the notebook is made of, it's not impossible—or even difficult."

"We got out of the tunnel alive. Let's settle for that."

"We're on the verge of solving a mystery that goes back through the centuries," said Foster, "a mystery that I've pursued, if I understand the journal, through many lifetimes——"

"One thing about losing your memory: you don't have any fixed ideas to get in the way of your theories."

Foster smiled grimly. "The trail has brought us here. We must follow it—wherever it leads."

I lay on the ground, staring up at the unbelievable shape across the field, the beckoning square of light. "This ship—or whatever it is," I said; "it drops down out of nowhere and opens its doors. And you want to walk right into the cosy interior."

"Listen!" Foster cut in.

I heard a low rumbling then, a sound that rolled ominously, like distant guns.

"More ships—" I started.

"Jet aircraft," Foster said. "From the bases in East Anglia probably. Of course, they'll have tracked our ship in—"

"That's all for me," I yelled, getting to my feet. "The secret's out—"

"Get down, Legion," Foster shouted. The engines were a blanketing roar now.

"What for? They——"

Two long lines of fire traced themselves across the sky, curving down—

I hit the dirt behind the stone in the same instant the rockets struck. The shock wave slammed at the earth like a monster thunderclap, and I saw the tunnel mouth collapse. I twisted, saw the red interior of the jet tailpipe as the fighter hurtled past, rolling into a climbing turn.

"They're crazy," I yelled. "Firing on——"

A second barrage blasted across my indignation. I hugged the muck and waited while nine salvoes shook the earth. Then the rumble died, reluctantly. The air reeked of high explosives.

"We'd have been dead now if we'd tried the tunnel," I gasped spitting dirt. "It caved at the first rocket. And if the ship was what you thought, Foster, they've destroyed something——"

The sentence died unnoticed. The dust was settling and through it the shape of the ship reared up, unchanged except that the square of light was gone. As I watched, the door opened again and the ladder ran out once more, invitingly.

"They'll try next time with nukes," I said. "That may be too much for the ship's defenses—and it will sure be too much for us——"

"Listen," Foster cut in. A deeper rumble was building in the distance.

"To the ship!" Foster called. He was up and running, and I hesitated just long enough to think about trying for the highway and being caught in the open—and then I was running, too. Ahead, Foster stumbled crossing the ground that had been ripped up by the rocket bursts, made it to the ladder, and went up it fast. The growl of the approaching bombers grew, a snarl of deadly hatred. I leaped a still-smoking stone fragment, took the ladder in two jumps, plunged into the yellow-lit interior. Behind me, the door smacked shut.

I was standing in a luxuriously fitted circular room. There was a pedestal in the center of the floor, from which a polished bar projected. The bones of a man lay beside it. While I stared, Foster sprang forward, seized the bar, and pulled. It slid back easily. The lights flickered and I had a moment of vertigo. Nothing else happened.

"Try it the other way," I yelled. "The bombs will fall any second—" I went for it, hand outstretched. Foster thrust in front of me. "Look!"

I stared at the glowing panel he was pointing to—a duplicate of the one in the underground chamber. It showed a curved white line, with a red point ascending from it.

"We're clear," Foster said. "We've made a successful take-off."

"But we can't be moving—there's no acceleration. There must be soundproofing—that's why we can't hear the bombers—"

"No soundproofing would help if we were at ground zero," Foster said. "This ship is the product of an advanced science. We've left the bombers far behind."

"Where are we going? Who's steering this thing?"

"It steers itself, I would judge," Foster said. "I don't know where we're going, but we're well on the way."

I looked at him in amazement. "You like this, don't you, Foster? You're having the time of your life."

"I can't deny that I'm delighted at this turn of events," Foster said. "Don't you see? This vessel is a launch, or lifeboat, under automatic control. And it's taking us to the mother ship."

"Okay, Foster," I said. I looked at the skeleton on the floor behind him. "But I hope we have better luck than the last passenger."

CHAPTER VII

It was two hours later, and Foster and I stood silent before a ten-foot screen that had glowed into life when I touched a silver button beside it. It showed us a vast emptiness of bottomless black, set thick with corruscating points of polychrome brilliance that hurt to look at. And against that backdrop: a ship, vast beyond imagining, blotting out half the titanic vista with its bulk——

But dead.

Even from the distance of miles, I could sense it. The great black torpedo shape, dull moonlight glinting along the unbelievable length of its sleek flank, drifted: a derelict. I wondered for how many centuries it had waited here—and for what?

"I feel," said Foster, "somehow—I'm coming home." I tried to say something, croaked, cleared my throat.

"If this is your jitney," I said, "I hope they didn't leave the meter ticking on you. We're broke."

"We're closing rapidly," said Foster. "Another ten minutes, I'd guess...."

"How do we go about heaving to, alongside? You didn't come across a book of instructions, did you?"

"I think I can predict that the approach will be automatic."

"This is your big moment, isn't it?" I said. "I've got to hand it to you, pal; you've won out by pluck, just like the Rover Boys."

The ship appeared to move smoothly closer, looming over us, fine golden lines of decorative filigree work visible now against the black. A tiny square of pale light appeared, grew into a huge bay door that swallowed us.

The screen went dark, there was a gentle jar, then motionlessness. The port opened, silently.

"We've arrived," Foster said. "Shall we step out and have a look?"

"I wouldn't think of going back without one," I said. I followed him out and stopped dead, gaping. I had expected an empty hold, bare metal walls. Instead, I found a vaulted cavern, shadowed, mysterious, rich with a thousand colors. There was a hint of strange perfume in the air, and I heard low music that muttered among stalagmite-like buttresses. There were pools, playing fountains, waterfalls, dim vistas stretching away, lit by slanting rays of muted sunlight.

"What kind of place is it?" I asked. "It's like a fairyland, or a dream."

"It's not an earthly scheme of decoration," Foster said, "but I find it strangely pleasing."

"Hey, look over there," I yelped suddenly, pointing. An empty-eyed skull stared past me from the shadows at the base of a column.

Foster went over to the skull, stood looking down at it. "There was a disaster here," he said. "That much is plain."

"It's creepy," I said. "Let's go back; I forgot to get film for my Brownie."

"The long-dead pose no threat," said Foster. He was kneeling, looking at the white bones. He picked up something, stared at it. "Look, Legion."

I went over. Foster held up a ring.

"We're onto something hot, pal," I said. "It's the twin to yours."

"I wonder…who he was."

I shook my head. "If we knew that—and who killed him—or what—"

"Let's go on. The answers must be here somewhere." Foster moved off toward a corridor that reminded me of a sunny avenue lined with chestnut trees—though there were no trees, and no sun. I followed, gaping.

For hours we wandered, looking, touching, not saying much but saturated in wonder, like kids in a toy factory. We came across another skeleton, lying among towering engines. Finally we paused in a giant storeroom stacked high with supplies.

"Have you stopped to think, Foster," I said, fingering a length of rose-violet cloth as thin as woven spider webs. "This boat's a treasure-house of salable items. Talk about the wealth of the Indies—"

"I seek only one thing here, my friend," Foster said; "my past."

"Sure," I said. "But just in case you don't find it, you might consider the business angle. We can set up a regular shuttle run, hauling stuff down—"

"You earthmen," sighed Foster. "For you every new experience is immediately assessed in terms of its merchandising possibilities. Well, I leave that to you."

"Okay, okay," I said. "You go on ahead and scout around down that way, if you want—where the technical-looking stuff is. I want to browse around here for a while."

"As you wish."

"We'll meet at this end of the big hall we passed back there. Okay?"

Foster nodded and went on. I turned to a bin filled with what looked like unset emeralds the size of walnuts. I picked up a handful, juggled them lovingly.

"Anyone for marbles?" I murmured to myself.

Hours later, I came along a corridor that was like a path through a garden that was a forest, crossed a ballroom like a meadow floored in fine-grained rust-red wood and shaded by giant ferns, and went under an arch into the hall where Foster sat at a long table cut from yellow marble. A light the color of sunrise gleamed through tall pseudo-windows.

I dumped an armfull of books on the table. "Look at these," I said. "All made from the same stuff as the journal. And the pictures...."

I flipped open one of the books, a heavy folio-sized volume, to a double-page spread in color showing a group of bearded Arabs in dingy white djellabas staring toward the camera, a flock of thin goats in the background. It looked like the kind of picture the National Geographic runs, except that the quality of the color and detail was equal to the best color transparencies.

"I can't read the print," I said, "but I'm a whiz at looking at pictures. Most of the books showed scenes like I hope I never see in the flesh, but I found a few that were made on earth—God knows how long ago."

"Travel books, perhaps," Foster said.

"Travel books that you could sell to any university on earth for their next year's budget," I said, shuffling pages. "Take a look at this one."

Foster looked across at the panoramic shot of a procession of shaven-headed men in white sarongs, carrying a miniature golden boat on their shoulders, descending a long flight of white stone steps leading from a colonnade of heroic human figures with folded arms and painted faces. In the background, brick-red cliffs loomed up, baked in desert heat.

"That's the temple of Hat-Shepsut in its prime," I said. "Which makes this print close to four thousand years old. Here's another I recognize." I turned to a smaller, aerial view, showing a gigantic pyramid, its polished stone facing chipped in places and with a few panels missing from the lower levels, revealing the cruder structure of massive blocks beneath.

"That's one of the major pyramids, maybe Khufu's," I said. "It was already a couple thousand years old, and falling into disrepair. And look at this——" I opened another volume, showed Foster a vivid photograph of a great shaggy elephant with a pinkish trunk upraised between wide-curving yellow tusks.

"A mastodon," I said. "And there's a woolly rhino, and an ugly-looking critter that must be a sabre-tooth. This book is *old....*"

"A lifetime of rummaging wouldn't exhaust the treasures aboard this ship," said Foster.

"How about bones? Did you find any more?"

Foster nodded. "There was a disaster of some sort. Perhaps disease. None of the bones was broken."

"I can't figure the one in the lifeboat," I said. "Why was he wearing a necklace of bear's teeth?" I sat down across from Foster. "We've got plenty of mysteries to solve, all right, but there are some other items we'd better talk about. For instance: where's the kitchen? I'm getting hungry."

Foster handed me a black rod from among several that lay on the table. "I think this may be important," he said.

"What is it, a chop stick?"

"Touch it to your head, above the ear."

"What does it do—give you a massage?"

I pressed it to my temple....

I was in a grey-walled room, facing a towering surface of ribbed metal. I reached out, placed my hands over the proper perforations. The housings opened. For apparent malfunction in the quaternary field amplifiers, I knew, auto-inspection circuit override was necessary before activation——

I blinked, looked around at the yellow table, and piled books, the rod in my hand.

"I was in some kind of powerhouse," I said. "There was something wrong with—with...."

"The quaternary field amplifiers," Foster said.

"I seemed to be right there," I said. "I understood exactly what it was all about."

"These are technical manuals," Foster said. "They'll tell us everything we need to know about the ship."

"I was thinking about what I was getting ready to do," I said, "the way you do when you're starting into a job; I was trouble-shooting the quaternary whatzits—and I knew how...!"

Foster got to his feet and moved toward the doorway. "We'll have to start at one end of the library and work our way through," he said. "It will take us a while, but we'll get the facts we need. Then we can plan."

* * * *

Foster picked a handful of briefing rods from the racks in the comfortably furnished library and started in. The first thing we needed was a clue as to where to look for food and beds, or for operating instructions for the ship itself. I hoped we might find the equivalent of a library card-catalog; then we could put our hands on what we wanted in a hurry.

I went to the far end of the first rack and spotted a short row of red rods that stood out vividly among the black ones. I took one out, thought it over, decided it was unlikely that it was any more dangerous than the others, and put it against my temple....

As the bells rang, I applied neuro-vascular tension, suppressed cortical areas upsilon-zeta and iota, and stood by for——

I jerked the rod from my head, my ears still ringing with the shrill alarm. The effect of the rods was like reality itself, but intensified, all attention focused single-mindedly on the experience at hand. I thought of the entertainment potentialities of the idea. You could kill a tiger, ride an airplane down in flames, face the heavyweight champion——I wondered about the stronger sensations, like pain and fear. Would they seem as real as the impulse to check the whatchamacallits or tighten up your cortical thingamajigs?

I tried another rod.

At the sound of the apex-tone, I racked instruments, walked, not ran, to the nearest transfer-channel——

Another:

Having assumed duty as Alert Officer, I reported first to coordination Control via short-line, and confirmed rapport—

These were routine SOP's covering simple situations aboard ship. I skipped a few, tried again:

Needing a xivometer, I keyed instruction-complex One, followed with the code—

Three rods further along, I got this:

The situation falling outside my area of primary conditioning, I reported in corpo to Technical Briefing, Level Nine, Section Four, Sub-section Twelve, Preliminary. I recalled that it was now necessary to supply my activity code...my activity code...my activity code... (A sensation of disorientation grew; confused images flickered like vague background-noise; then a clear voice cut across the confusion:)

You have suffered partial personality-fade. Do not be alarmed. Select a general background orientation rod from the nearest emergency rack. Its location is....

I was moving along the stacks, to pause in front of a niche where a U-shaped plastic strip was clamped to the wall. I removed it, fitted it to my head—(Then:) I was moving along the stacks, to pause in front of a niche—

I was leaning against the wall, my head humming. The red stick lay on the floor at my feet. That last bit had been potent: something about a general background briefing—

"Hey, Foster!" I called, "I think I've got something...." He appeared from the stacks.

* * * *

"As I see it," I said, "this background briefing should tell us all we need to know about the ship; then we can plan our next move more intelligently. We'll know what we're doing." I took the thing from the wall, just as I had seemed to do in the phantom scene the red rod had projected for me.

"These things make me dizzy," I said, handing it to Foster. "Anyway you're the logical one to try it."

He took the plastic shape, went to the reclining seat at the near end of the library hall, and settled himself. "I have an idea this one will hit harder than the others," he said.

He fitted the clamp to his head and...instantly his eyes glazed; he slumped back, limp.

"Foster!" I yelled. I jumped forward, started to pull the plastic piece from his head, then hesitated. Maybe Foster's abrupt reaction was standard procedure—but I didn't like it much.

I went on reasoning with myself. After all, this was what the red rod had indicated as normal procedure in a given emergency. Foster was merely having his faded personality touched up. And his full-blown, three-dimensional personality was what we needed to give us the answers to a lot of the questions we'd been asking. Though the ship and everything in it had lain unused and silent for forgotten millenia, still the library should be good. The librarian was gone from his post for forgotten centuries, and Foster was lying unconscious, and I was thirty thousand miles from home—but I shouldn't let trifles like that worry me....

I got up and prowled the room. There wasn't much to look at except stacks and more stacks. The knowledge stored here was fantastic, both in magnitude and character. If I ever get home with a load of these rods....

I strolled through a door leading to another room. It was small, functional, dimly lit. The middle of the room was occupied by a large and elaborate divan with a cap-shaped fitting at one end. Other curious accoutrements were ranked along the walls. There wasn't much in them to thrill me. But bone-wise I had hit the jackpot.

Two skeletons lay near the door, in the final slump of death. Another lay beside the fancy couch. There was a long-bladed dagger beside it.

I squatted beside the two near the door and examined them closely. As far as I could tell, they were as human as I was. I wondered what kind of men they had been, what kind of world they had come from, that could build a ship like this and stock it as it was stocked.

The dagger that lay near the other bones was interesting: it seemed to be made of a transparent orange metal, and its hilt was stamped in a repeated pattern of the Two Worlds motif. It was the first clue as to what had taken place among these men when they last lived: not a complete clue, but a start.

I took a closer look at an apparatus like a dentist's chair parked against the wall. There were spidery-looking metal arms mounted above it, and a series of colored glass lenses. A row of dull silver cylinders was racked against the wall. Another projected from a socket at the side of the machine. I took it out and looked at it. It was a plain pewter-colored plastic, heavy and smooth. I felt pretty sure it was a close cousin to the chopsticks stored in the library. I wondered what brand of information was recorded in it as I dropped it in my pocket.

I lit a cigarette and went out to where Foster lay. He was still in the same position as when I had left him. I sat down on the floor beside the couch to wait.

* * * *

It was an hour before he stirred, heaved a sigh, and opened his eyes. He reached up, pulled off the plastic headpiece, dropped it on the floor.

"Are you okay?" I said. "Brother, I've been sweating...."

Foster looked at me, his eyes traveling up to my uncombed hair and down to my scuffed shoes. His eyes narrowed in a faint frown. Then he said something—in a language that seemed to be all Z's and Q's.

"Don't spring any surprises on me, Foster," I said hoarsely. "Talk American."

A look of surprise crossed his face. He stared into my eyes again, then glanced around the room.

"This is a ship's library," he said.

I heaved a sigh of relief. "You gave me a scare, Foster. I thought for a second your memory was wandering again."

Foster was watching my face as I spoke. "What was it all about?" I said. "What have you found out?"

"I know you," said Foster slowly. "Your name is Legion."

I nodded. I could feel myself getting tense again. "Sure, you know me. Just take it easy pal. This is no time to lose your marbles." I put a hand on his shoulder. "You remember, we were—"

He shook my hand off. "That is not the custom in Vallon," he said coldly.

"Vallon?" I echoed. "What kind of routine is this, Foster? We were friends when we walked into this room an hour ago. We were hot on the trail of something, and I'm human enough to want to know how it turned out."

"Where are the others?"

"There's a couple of 'others' in the next room," I snapped. "But they've lost a lot of weight. I can find you several more, in the same condition. Outside of them there's only me——"

Foster looked at me as if I wasn't there. "I remember Vallon," he said. He put a hand to his head. "But I remember, too, a barbaric world, brutal and primitive. You were there. We traveled in a crude rail-car, and then in a barge that wallowed in the sea. There were narrow, ugly rooms, evil odors, harsh noises."

"That's not a very flattering portrait of God's country," I said, "but I'm afraid I recognize it."

"The people were the worst," Foster said. "Misshapen, diseased, with swollen abdomens and wasted skin and withered limbs."

"Some of the boys don't get out enough," I said.

"The Hunters! We fled from them, Legion, you and I. And I remember a landing-ring...." He paused. "Strange, it had lost its cap-stones and fallen into ruin."

"Us natives call it Stonehenge."

"The Hunters burst out of the earth. We fought them. But why should the Hunters seek me?"

"I was hoping you'd tell me," I said. "Do you know where this ship came from? And why?"

"This is a ship of the Two Worlds," he replied. "But I know nothing of how it came to be here."

"How about all that stuff in the journal? Maybe now you—"

"The journal!" Foster broke in. "Where is it?"

"In your coat pocket, I guess."

Foster felt through his jacket awkwardly, brought out the journal. He opened it.

I moved around to look over his shoulder. He had the book open to the first section, the part written in the curious alien characters that nobody had been able to decipher.

And he was reading it.

* * * *

We sat at the library table of deep green, heavy, polished wood, the journal open at its center. For hours I had waited while Foster read. Now at last he leaned back in his chair, ran a hand through the youthful black hair, and sighed.

"My name," he said, "was Qulqlan. And this," he laid his hand upon the book, "is my story. This is one part of the past I was seeking. And I remember none of it...."

"Tell me what the journal says," I asked. "Read it to me."

Foster picked it up, riffled the pages. "It seems that I awoke once before, in a small room aboard this vessel. I was lying on a memo-couch, by which circumstance I knew that I had suffered a Change—"

"You mean you'd lost your memory?"

"And regained it—on the couch. My memory-trace had been re-impressed on my mind. I awoke knowing my identity, but not how I came to be aboard this vessel. The journal says that my last memory was of a building beside the Shallow Sea."

"Where's that?"

"On a far world—called Vallon."

"Yeah? And what next?"

"I looked around me and saw four men lying on the floor, slashed and bloody. One was alive. I gave him what emergency treatment I could, then searched the ship. I found three more men, dead; none living. Then the Hunters attacked, swarming to me—"

"Our friends the fire-balls?"

"Yes; they would have sucked the life from me—and I had no shield of light. I fled to the lifeboat, carrying the wounded man. I descended to the planet below: your earth. The man died there. He had been my friend, a man named Ammaerln. I buried him in a shallow depression in the earth and marked the place with a stone."

"The ancient sinner," I said.

"Yes…I suppose it was his bones the lay brother found."

"And we found out last night that the depression was the result of dirt sifting into the ventilator shaft. But I guess you didn't know anything about the underground installation, way back then. Doesn't the journal say anything…?"

"No there is no mention made of it here." Foster shook his head. "How curious to read of the affairs of this stranger—and know he is myself."

"How about the Hunters? How did they get to earth?"

"They are insubstantial creatures," said Foster, "yet they can endure the vacuum of space. I can only surmise that they followed the lifeboat down."

"They were tailing you?"

"Yes; but I have no idea why they pursued me. They're harmless creatures in the natural state, used to seek out the rare fugitive from justice on Vallon. They can be attuned to the individual; thereafter, they follow him and mark him out for capture."

"Kind of like bloodhounds," I said. "Say, what were you: a big-time racketeer on Vallon?"

"The journal is frustratingly silent as to my Vallonian career," said Foster. "But this whole matter of the unexplained inter-galactic voyage and the evidences of violence aboard the ship make me wonder whether I, and perhaps others of my companions, were being exiled for crimes done in the Two Worlds."

"Wow! So they sicced the Hunters on you!" I said. "But why did they hang around at Stonehenge all this time?"

"There was a trickle of power feeding the screens," said Foster. "They need a source of electrical energy to live; until a hundred years ago it was the only one on the planet."

"How did they get down into the shaft without opening it up?"

"Given time, they pass easily through porous substances. But, of course, last night, when I came on them after their long fast, they simply burst through in their haste."

"Okay. What happened next—after you buried the man?"

"The journal tells that I was set upon by natives, men who wore the hides of animals. One of their number entered the ship. He must have moved the drive lever. It lifted, leaving me marooned."

"So those were his bones we found in the boat," I mused, "the ones with the bear's-tooth necklace. I wonder why he didn't come into the ship."

"Undoubtedly he did. But remember the skeleton we found just inside the landing port? That must have been a fairly fresh and rather gory corpse at the time the savage stepped aboard. It probably seemed to him all too clear an indication of what lay in store for himself if he ventured further. In his terror he must have retreated to the boat to wait, and there starved to death.

"He was stranded in your world, and you were stranded in his."

"Yes," said Foster. "And then, it seems, I lived among the brute-men and came to be their king. I waited there by the landing ring through many years in the hope of rescue. Because I did not age as the natives did, I was worshipped as a god. I would have built a signalling device, but there were no pure metals, nothing I could use. I tried to teach them, but it was a work of centuries."

"I should think you could have set up a school, trained the smartest ones," I said.

"There was no lack of intelligent minds," Foster said. "It is plain that the savages were of the blood of the Two Worlds. This earth must have been seeded long ago by some ancient castaways."

"But how could you go on living—for hundreds of years? Are your people supermen that live forever?"

"The natural span of a human life is very great. Among your people, there is a wasting disease from which you all die young."

"That's no disease," I said. "You just naturally get old and die."

"The human mind is a magnificent instrument," Foster said, "not meant to wither quickly."

"I'll have to chew that one over," I said. "Why didn't you catch this disease?"

"All Vallonians are innoculated against it."

"I'd like a shot of that," I said. "But let's get back to you."

Foster turned the pages of the journal. "I ruled many peoples, under many names," he said. "I traveled in many lands, seeking for skilled metal-workers, glass-blowers, wise men. But always I returned to the landing-ring."

"It must have been tough," I said, "exiled on a strange world, living out your life in a wilderness, century after century...."

"My life was not without interest," Foster said. "I watched my savage people put aside their animal hides and learn the ways of civilization. I taught them how to build, and keep herds, and till the land. I built a great city, and I tried—foolishly—to teach their noble caste the code of chivalry of the Two Worlds. But although they sat at a round table like the great Ring-board at Okk-Hamiloth, they never really understood. And then they grew too wise, and wondered at their king, who never aged. I left them, and tried again to build a long-signaller. The Hunters sensed it, and swarmed to me. I drove them off with fires, and then I grew curious, and followed them back to their nest——"

"I know," I said. "'—and it was a place you knew of old: no hive but a Pit built by men.'"

"They overwhelmed me; I barely escaped with my life. Starvation had made the Hunters vicious. They would have drained my body of its life-energy."

"And if you'd known the transmitter was there—but you didn't. So you put an ocean between you and them."

"They found me even there. Each time I destroyed many of them, and fled. But always a few lived to breed and seek me out again."

"But your signaller—didn't it work?"

"No. It was a hopeless attempt. Only a highly developed technology could supply the raw materials. I could only teach what I knew, encourage the development of the sciences, and wait. And then I began to forget."

"Why?"

"A mind grows weary," Foster said. "It is the price of longevity. It must renew itself. Shock and privation hasten the Change. I had held it off for many centuries. Now I felt it coming on me.

"At home, on Vallon, a man would record his memory at such a time, store it electronically in a recording device, and, after the Change, use the memory-trace to restore, in his renewed body, his old recollections in toto. But, marooned as I was, my memories, once lost, were gone forever.

"I did what I could; I prepared a safe place, and wrote messages that I would find when I awoke——"

"When you woke up in the hotel, you were young again, overnight. How could it happen?"

"When the mind renews itself, erasing the scars of the years, the body, too, regenerates. The skin forgets its wrinkles, and the muscles their fatigue. They become again as they once were."

"When I first met you," I said, "you told me about waking up back in 1918, with no memory."

"Yours is a harsh world, Legion. I must have forgotten many times. Somewhere, some time, I lost the vital link, forgot my quest. When the Hunters came again, I fled, not understanding."

"You had a machine gun set up in the house at Mayport. What good was that against the Hunters?"

"None, I suppose," Foster replied. "But I didn't know. I only knew that I was—pursued."

"And by then you could have made a signaller," I said. "But you'd forgotten how—or even that you needed one."

"But in the end I found it—with your help, Legion. But still there is a mystery: What came to pass aboard this ship all those centuries ago? Why was I here? And what killed the others?"

"Look," I said. "Here's a theory: there was a mutiny, while you were in the machine having your memory fixed. You woke up and it was all over—and the crew was dead."

"That hypothesis will serve," said Foster. "But one day I must learn the truth of this matter."

"What I can't figure out is why somebody from Vallon didn't come after this ship. It was right here in orbit."

"Consider the immensity of space, Legion. This is one tiny world, among the stars."

"But there was a station here, fitted out for handling your ships. That sounds like it was a regular port of call. And the books with the pictures: they prove your people have been here off and on for thousands of years. Why would they stop coming?"

"There are such beacons on a thousand worlds," said Foster. "Think of it as a buoy marking a reef, a trailblaze in the wilderness. Ages could pass before a wanderer chanced this way again. The fact that the ventilator shaft at Stonehenge was choked with the debris of centuries when I first landed there shows how seldom this world was visited."

I thought about it. Bit by bit Foster was putting together the jig-saw pieces of his past. But he still had a long way to go before he had the big picture, frame and all. I had an idea:

"Say, you said you were in the memory machine. You woke up there—and you'd just had your memory restored. Why not do the same thing again, now? That is, if your brain can take another pounding this soon."

"Yes," he said. He stood up abruptly. "There's just a chance. Come!"

I followed him out of the library into the room with the bones. He moved over to look down at them curiously.

"Quite a fracas," I said. "Three of 'em."

"This would be the room where I awakened," said Foster. "These are the men I saw dead."

"They're still dead," I said. "But what about the machine?"

Foster walked across to the fancy couch, leaned down beside it, then shook his head. "No," he said. "Of course it wouldn't be here...."

"What?"

"My memory-trace: the one that was used to restore my memory—that other time."

Suddenly I recalled the cylinder I had pocketed hours before. With a surprising flutter at my heart I held it up, like a kid in a classroom who knows he's got the right answer. "This it?"

Foster glanced at it briefly. "No, that's an empty—like those you see filed over there." He pointed to the rack of pewter-colored cylinders on the opposite wall. "They would be used for emergency recordings. Regular multi-life memory-traces would be key-coded with a pattern of colored lines."

"It figures," I said. "That would have been too easy. We have to do everything the hard way." I looked around. "It's a big bureau to look for a collar button under, but I guess we can try."

"It doesn't matter, really. When I return to Vallon, I'll recover my past. There are vaults where every citizen's trace is stored."

"But you had yours here with you."

"It could only have been a copy. The master trace is never removed from Okk-Hamiloth."

"I guess you'll be eager to get back there," I said. "That'll be quite a moment for you, getting back home after all these years. Speaking of years: were you able to figure out how long you were marooned down on earth?"

"I lost all record of dates long ago," said Foster. "I can only estimate the time."

"About how long?" I persisted.

"Since I descended from this ship, Legion," he said, "three thousand years have passed."

* * * *

"I hate to see the team split up," I said. "You know, I was kind of getting used to being an apprentice nut. I'm going to miss you, Foster."

"Come with me to Vallon, Legion," he said.

We were standing in the observation lounge, looking out at the bright-lit surface of the earth thirty thousand miles away. Beyond it, the dead-white disk of the moon hung like a cardboard cutout.

"Thanks anyway, buddy," I said. "I'd like to see those other worlds of yours but in the end I might regret it. It's no good giving an Eskimo a television set. I'd just sit around on Vallon pining for home: beat-up people, stinks, and all."

"You could return here some day."

"From what I understand about traveling in a ship like this," I said, "a couple of hundred years would pass before I got back, even if it only seemed like a few weeks en route. I want to live out my life here—with the kind of people I know, in the world I grew up in. It has its faults, but it's home."

"Then there is nothing I can do, Legion," Foster said, "to reward your loyalty and express my gratitude."

"Well, ah," I said. "There is a little something. Let me take the lifeboat, and stock it with a few goodies from the library, and some of those marbles from the storeroom, and a couple of the smaller mechanical gadgets. I think I know how to merchandise them in a way that'll leave the economy on an even keel—and incidentally set me up for life. As you said, I'm a material-ist."

"As you wish," Foster said. "Take whatever you desire."

"One thing I'll have to do when I get back," I said, "is open the tunnel at Stonehenge enough to sneak a thermite bomb down it—if they haven't already found the beacon station."

"As I judge the temper of the local people," Foster said, "the secret is safe for at least three generations."

"I'll bring the boat down in a blind spot where radar won't pick it up," I said. "Our timing was good; in another few years, it wouldn't have been possible."

"And this ship would soon have been discovered," Foster said. "In spite of radar-negative screens."

I looked at the great smooth sphere hanging, haloed, against utter black. The Pacific Ocean threw back a brilliant image of the sun.

"I think I see an island down there that will fill the bill perfectly," I said. "And if it doesn't, there are a million more to choose from."

"You've changed, Legion," Foster said. "You sound like a man with a fair share of *joie de vivre*."

"I used to think I was a guy who never got the breaks," I said. "There's something about standing here looking at the world that makes that kind of thinking sound pretty dumb. There's everything down there a man needs to make his own breaks—even without a stock of trade goods."

"Every world has its rules of life," Foster said. "Some more complex than others. To face your own reality—that's the challenge."

"Me against the universe," I said. "With those odds, even a loser can look good." I turned to Foster. "We're in a ten-hour orbit," I said. "We'd better get moving. I want to put the boat down in southern South America. I know a place there where I can off-load without answering too many questions."

"You have several hours before the most favorable launch time," Foster said. "There's no hurry."

"Maybe not," I said. "But I've got a lot to do—" I took a last look toward the majestic planet beyond the viewscreen, "—and I'm eager to get started."

CHAPTER VIII

I sat on the terrace watching the sun go down into the sea and thinking about Foster, somewhere out there beyond the purple palaces on the far horizon, in the ship that had waited for him for three thousand years, heading home at last. It was strange to reflect that for him, traveling near the speed of light, only a few days had passed, while three years went by for me—three fast years that I had made good use of.

The toughest part had been the first few months, after I put the lifeboat down in a cañon in the desert country south of a little town called Itzenca, in Peru. I waited by the boat for a week, to be sure the vigilantes weren't going to show up, full of helpful suggestions and embarassing questions; then I hiked to town, carrying a pack with a few carefully selected items to start my new career. It took me two weeks to work, lie, barter, and plead my way to the seaport town of Callao and another week to line up passage home as a deck hand on a banana scow. I disappeared over the side at Tampa, and made it to Miami without attracting attention. As far as I could tell, the cops had already lost interest in me.

My old friend, the heavyweight señorita, wasn't overjoyed to see me, but she put me up, and I started in on my plan to turn my souvenirs into money.

The items I had brought with me from the lifeboat were a pocketful of little gray dominoes that were actually movie film, and a small projector to go with them. I didn't offer them for sale, direct. I made arrangements with an old acquaintance in the business of making pictures with low costume budgets for private showings; I set up the apparatus and projected my films, and he copied them in 35 mm. I told him that I'd smuggled them in from East Germany. He didn't think much of the Krauts, but he admitted you had to hand it to them technically; the special effects were absolutely top-notch. His favorite was one I called the Mammoth Hunt.

I had twelve pictures altogether; with a little judicious cutting and a dubbed-in commentary, they made up into fast-moving twenty-minute short subjects. He got in touch with a friend in the distribution end in New York, and after a little cagy fencing over contract terms, we agreed on a deal that paid a hundred thousand for the twelve, with an option on another dozen at the same price.

Within a week after the pictures hit the neighborhood theatres around Bayonne, New Jersey, in a cautious tryout, I had offers up to half a million for my next consignment, no questions asked. I left my pal Mickey to handle the details on a percentage basis, and headed back for Itzenca.

The lifeboat was just as I'd left it; it would have been all right for another fifty years, as far as the danger of anybody stumbling over it was concerned. I explained to the crew I brought out with me that it was a fake rocket ship, a prop I was using for a film I was making, I let them wander all over it and get their curiosity out of their systems. The concensus was that it wouldn't fool anybody; no tail fins, no ray guns, and the instrument panel was a joke; but they figured that it was my money, so they went to work setting up a system of camouflage nets (part of the plot, I told them) and off-loading my cargo.

A year after my homecoming, I had my island—a square mile of perfect climate, fifteen miles off the Peruvian coast—and a house that was tailored to my every whim by a mind-reading architect who made a fortune on the job—and earned it. The uppermost floor—almost a tower—was a strong-room, and it was there that I had stored my stock in trade. I had sold off the best of the hundred or so films I had picked out before leaving Foster, but there were plenty of other items. The projector itself was the big prize. The self-contained power unit converted nuclear energy to light with 99 percent efficiency. It scanned the "films", one molecular layer at a time, and projected a continuous picture—no sixteen-frames-a-second flicker here. The color and sound were absolutely life-like—with the result that I'd had a few complaints from my distributor that the Technicolor was kind of washed-out.

The principles involved in the projector were new, and—in theory, at least—way over the heads of our local physicists. But the practical application was nothing much. I figured that, with the right contacts in scientific circles to help me introduce the system, I had a billion-dollar industry up my sleeve. I had already fed a few little gimmicks into the market; a tough paper, suitable for shirts and underwear; a chemical that bleached teeth white as the driven snow; an all-color pigment for artists. With the knowledge I had absorbed from all the briefing rods I had studied, I had the techniques of a hundred new industries at my fingertips—and I hadn't exhausted the possibilities yet.

I spent most of a year roaming the world, discovering all the things that a free hand with a dollar bill could do for a man. The next year I put in fixing up the island, buying paintings and rugs and silver for the house, and a concert grand piano. After the first big thrill of economic freedom had worn off, I still enjoyed my music.

For six months I had a full-time physical instructor giving me a twenty-four-hour-a-day routine of diet, sleep, and all the precision body-building my metabolism could stand. At the end of the course I was twice the man I'd ever been, the instructor was a physical wreck, and I was looking around for a new hobby.

Now, after three years, it was beginning to get me: boredom, the disease of the idle rich, that I had sworn would never touch me. But thinking about wealth and having it on your hands are two different things, and I was beginning to remember almost with nostalgia the tough old times when every day was an adventure, full of cops and missed meals and a thousand unappeased desires.

Not that I was really suffering. I was relaxed in a comfortable chair, after a day of surf fishing and a modest dinner of Chateaubriand. I was smoking a skinny cigar rolled by an expert from the world's finest leaf, and listening to the best music a thousand-dollar hi-fi could produce. And the view, though free, was worth a million dollars a minute. After a while I would stroll down to the boathouse, start up the Rolls-powered launch, and tool over to the mainland, transfer to my Caddie convertible, and drive into town where a tall brunette from Stockholm was waiting for me to take her to the movies. My steady gal was a hard-working secretary for an electronics firm.

I finished up my stogie and leaned forward to drop it in a big silver ashtray, when something caught my eye out across the red-painted water. I sat squinting at it, then went inside and came out with a pair of 7x50 binoculars. I focused them and studied the dark speck that stood out clearly now against the gaudy sky. It was a heavy-looking power boat, heading dead toward my island.

I watched it come closer, swing off toward the hundred-foot concrete jetty I had built below the sea-wall, and ease alongside in a murmur of powerful engines. They died, and the boat sat in a sudden silence dwarfing the pier. I studied the bluish-grey hull, the inconspicuous flag aft. Two heavy deck guns were mounted on the foredeck, and there were four torpedoes slung in launching cradles. The hardware didn't make half as much impression on me as the ranks of helmeted men drawn up on deck.

I sat and watched. The men shuffled off onto the pier, formed up into two squads. I counted; forty-eight men, and a couple of officers. There was the faint sound of orders being barked, and the column stepped off, moving along the paved road that swung between the transplanted royal palms and hibiscus, right up to the wide drive that curved off to the house. They halted, did a left face, and stood at parade rest. The two officers, wearing class A's, and a tubby civilian with a brief case came up the drive, trying to look as casual as possible under the circumstances. They paused at the foot of the broad flight of Tennessee marble steps leading up to my perch.

The leading officer, a brigadier general, no less, looked up at me.

"May we come up, sir?" he said.

I looked across at the silent ranks waiting at the foot of the drive.

"If the boys want a drink of water, Sarge," I said, "tell 'em to come on over."

"I am General Smale," the B.G. said. "This is Colonel Sanchez of the Peruvian Army—" he indicated the other military type "—and Mr. Pruffy of the American Embassy at Lima."

"Howdy, Mr. Pruffy," I said. "Howdy, Mr. Sanchez. Howdy—"

"This…ah…call is official in nature, Mr. Legion," the general said. "It's a matter of great importance, involving the security of your country."

"OK, General," I said. "Come on up. What's happened? You boys haven't started another war, have you?"

They filed up onto the terrace, hesitated, then shook hands, and sat down gingerly in the chairs. Pruffy held his briefcase in his lap.

"Put your sandwiches on the table, if you like, Mr. Pruffy," I said. He blinked, gripped the briefcase tighter. I offered my hand-tooled cigars around; Pruffy looked startled, Smale shook his head, and Sanchez took three.

"I'm here," the general said, "to ask you a few questions, Mr. Legion. Mr. Pruffy represents the Department of State in the matter, and Colonel Sanchez—"

"Don't tell me," I said. "He represents the Peruvian government, which is why I don't ask you what an armed American force is doing wandering around on Peruvian soil."

"Here," Pruffy put in. "I hardly think—"

"I believe you," I said. "What's it all about, Smale?"

"I'll come directly to the point," he said. "For some time, the investigative and security agencies of the US government have been building a file on what for lack of a better name has been called 'The Martians.'" Smale coughed apologetically.

"A little over three years ago," he went on, "an unidentified flying object—"

"You interested in flying saucers, General?" I said.

"By no means," he snapped. "The object appeared on a number of radar screens, descending from extreme altitude. It came to earth at…" he hesitated.

"Don't tell me you came all the way out here to tell me you can't tell me," I said.

"—A site in England," Smale said. "American aircraft were dispatched to investigate the object. Before they could make identification, it rose again, accelerated at tremendous speed, and was lost at an altitude of several hundred miles."

"I thought we had better radar than that," I said. "The satellite program—"

"No such specialized equipment was available," Smale said. "An intensive investigation turned up the fact that two strangers—possibly Americans—had visited the site only a few hours before the—ah—visitation."

I nodded. I was thinking about the close call I'd had when I went back to see about lobbing a bomb down the shaft to obliterate the beacon station. There were plainclothes men all over the place, like old maids at a movie star's funeral. It was just as well; they never found it. The rocket blasts had collapsed the tunnel, and apparently the whole underground installation was made of non-metallic substances that didn't show up in detecting equipment. I had an idea metal was passé where Foster came from.

"Some months later," Smale went on, "a series of rather curious short films went on exhibition in the United States. They showed scenes representing conditions on other planets, as well as ancient and prehistoric incidents here on earth. They were prefaced with explanations that they merely represented the opinions of science as to what was likely to be found on distant worlds. They attracted wide interest, and with few exceptions, scientists praised their verisimilitude."

"I admire a clever fake," I said. "With a topical subject like space travel——"

"One item which was commented on as a surprising inaccuracy, in view of the technical excellence of the other films," Smale said, "was the view of our planet from space, showing the earth against the backdrop of stars. A study of the constellations by astronomers quickly indicated a 'date' approximately 7000 B.C. for the scene. Oddly, the north polar cap was shown centered on Hudson's Bay. No south polar cap was in evidence. The continent of Antarctica appeared to be at a latitude of some 30 degrees, entirely free of ice."

I looked at him and waited.

"Now, studies made since that time indicate that nine thousand years ago, the North Pole was indeed centered on Hudson's Bay," Smale said. "And Antarctica was in fact ice-free."

"That idea's been around a long time," I said. "There was a theory——"

"Then there was the matter of the views of Mars," the general went on. "The aerial shots of the 'canals' were regarded as very cleverly done." He turned to Pruffy, who opened his briefcase and handed a couple of photos across.

"This is a scene taken from the film," Smale said. It was an 8x10 color shot, showing a row of mounds drifted with pinkish dust, against a blue-black horizon.

Smale placed another photo beside the first. "This one," he said, "was taken by automatic cameras in the successful Mars probe of last year."

I looked. The second shot was fuzzy, and the color was shifted badly toward the blue, but there was no mistaking the scene. The mounds were drifted a little deeper, and the angle was different, but they were the same mounds.

"In the meantime," Smale bored on relentlessly, "a number of novel products appeared on the market. Chemists and physicists alike were dumfounded at the theoretical base implied by the techniques involved. One of the products—a type of pigment—embodied a completely new concept in crystallography."

"Progress," I said. "Why, when I was a boy——"

"It was an extremely tortuous trail we followed," Smale said. "But we found that all these curious observations making up the 'Martians' file had, in the end, only one factor in common. And that factor, Mr. Legion, was you."

CHAPTER IX

It was a few minutes after sunrise, and Smale and I were back on the terrace toying with the remains of ham steaks and honeydew.

"That's one advantage of being in jail in your own house—the food's good," I commented.

"I can understand your feelings," Smale said. "Frankly, I didn't relish this assignment. But it's clear that there are matters here which require explanation. It was my hope that you'd see fit to cooperate voluntarily."

"Take your army and sail off into the sunrise, General," I said. "Then maybe I'll be in a position to do something voluntary."

"Your patriotism alone——"

"My patriotism keeps telling me that where I come from, a citizen has certain legal rights," I said.

"This is a matter that transcends legal technicalities," Smale said. "I'll tell you quite frankly, the presence of the task force here only received *ex post facto* approval by the Peruvian government. They were faced with the *fait accompli*. I mention this only to indicate just how strongly the government feels in this matter."

"Seeing you hit the beach with a platoon of infantry was enough of a hint for me," I said. "You're lucky I didn't wipe you out with my disintegrator rays."

Smale choked on a bite of melon.

"Just kidding," I said. "But I haven't given you any trouble. Why the reinforcements?"

Small stared at me. "What reinforcements?"

I pointed with a fork. He turned, gazed out to sea. A conning tower was breaking the surface, leaving a white wake behind. It rose higher, water streaming off the deck. A hatch popped open, and men poured out, lining up. Smale got to his feet, his napkin falling to the floor.

"Sergeant!" he yelled. I sat, open-mouthed, as Smale jumped to the stair, went down it three steps at a time. I heard him bellowing, the shouts of men and the clatter of rifles being unstacked, feet pounding. I went to the marble banister and looked down. Pruffy was out on the lawn in purple pajamas, yelping questions. Colonel Sanchez was pulling at Smale's arm, also yelling. The Marines were forming up on the lawn.

"Let's watch those petunias, Sergeant," I yelled.

"Keep out of this, Legion," Smale shouted.

"Why should I be the only one not yelling," I yelled. "After all, I own the place."

Smale bounded back up the stairs. "You're my prime responsibility, Legion," he barked. "I'm getting you to a point of maximum security. Where's the cellar?"

"I keep it downstairs," I said. "What's this all about? Interservice rivalry? You afraid the sailors are going to steal the glory?"

"That's a nuclear-powered sub," Smale barked. "Gagarin class; it belongs to the Soviet Navy."

* * * *

I stood there with my mouth open, looking at Smale without seeing him, and trying hard to think fast. I hadn't been too startled when the Marines showed up; I had gone over the legal aspects of my situation months before, with a platoon of high-priced legal talent; I knew that sooner or later somebody would come around to hit me for tax evasion, draft dodging, or overtime parking; but I was in the clear. The government might resent my knowing a lot of things it didn't, but no one could ever prove I'd swiped them from Uncle Sam. In the end, they'd have to let me go—and my account in a Swiss bank would last me, even if they managed to suppress any new developments from my fabulous lab. In a way, I was glad the showdown had come.

But I'd forgotten about the Russians. Naturally, they'd be interested, and their spies were at least as good as the intrepid agents of the US Secret

Service. I should have realized that sooner or later, they'd pay a call—and the legal niceties wouldn't slow them down. They'd slap me into a brain laundry, and sweat every last secret out of me as casually as I'd squeeze a lemon.

The sub was fully surfaced now, and I was looking down the barrels of half a dozen five-inch rifles, any one of which could blast Smale's navy out of the water with one salvo. There were a couple of hundred men, I estimated, putting landing boats over the side and spilling into them. Down on the lawn, the sergeant was snapping orders, and the men were double-timing off to positions that must have been spotted in advance. It looked like the Russians weren't entirely unexpected. This was a game the big boys were playing, and I was just a pawn, caught in the middle. My rosy picture of me confounding the bureaucrats was fading fast. My island was about to become a battlefield, and whichever way it turned out, I'd be the loser. I had one slim possibility; to get lost in the shuffle.

Smale grabbed my arm. "Don't stand there, man!" he snapped. "Which way—"

"Sorry, General," I said, and slammed a hard right to his stomach. He folded, but still managed to lunge for me. I gave him a left to the jaw, and he dropped. I jumped over him, plunged through the French doors, and took the spiral glass stairway four at a time, whirled, and slammed the strong-room door behind me. The armored walls would stand anything short of a direct hit with a good-sized artillery shell, and the boys down below were unlikely to use any heavy stuff for fear of damaging the goods they'd been sent out to collect. I was safe for a little while.

Now I had to do some fast, accurate thinking. I couldn't carry much with me—when and if I made it off the island. A few briefing rods, maybe; what was left of the movies. But I had already audited most of the rods; I knew them as well as I know my tax bracket. One listen to a rod gave you a fast picture of the subject; two or three repeats engraved it on your brain. The only reason a man couldn't know everything was that too much, too fast, would overload the mind—and amnesia wiped the slate clean.

I didn't have time to use any more rods, and I couldn't carry anything. But just to walk off and leave it all....

I rummaged through odds and ends, stuffing small items into my pock-ets. I came across a dull silvery cylinder, three inches long, striped in black and gold—a memory-trace. It reminded me of something....

That was an idea. I still had the U-shaped plastic headpiece that Fos-ter had used to acquire a background knowledge of his old home. I had tried it once—for a moment. It had given me a headache in two seconds flat, just pressed against my temple. It had been lying here ever since. But maybe now was the time to try it again. Half the items I had here in my strong-room were mysteries, like the silver cylinder in my hand, but I knew exactly what the plastic headband could give me. It contained all anyone needed to know about Vallon and the Two Worlds, and all the marvels they possessed.

I glanced out the armor-glass window. Smale's Marines were trotting across the lawn; the Russians were fanning out along the water's edge. It looked like business all right. Still, it would take them a while to get warmed up—and more time still to decide to blast me out of my fort. It had taken an hour or so for Foster to soak up the briefing; maybe I wouldn't be much longer at it.

I tossed the cylinder aside, tried a couple of drawers, found the inconspicuous strip of plastic that encompassed a whole civilization. I carried it across to a chair, settled myself, then hesitated. This thing had been designed for an alien brain, not mine. Suppose it burnt out my wiring, left me here gibbering, for Smale or the Ruskis to work over?

But the alternative was to leave my island virtually empty-handed, settle for what I might in time manage to salvage from my account—if I could devise a way of withdrawing money without calling down the Gestapo....

No, I wouldn't go back to poverty without a struggle. What I could carry in my head would give me independence—even immunity from the greed of nations. I could barter my knowledge for my freedom.

There were plenty of things wrong with this picture, but it was the best I could do on short notice. Gingerly I fitted the U-shaped band to my head. There was a feeling of pressure, then a sensation like warm water rising about me. Panic tried to rise, faded. A voice seemed to reassure me. I was among friends, I was safe, all was well....

CHAPTER X

I lay in the dark, the memory of towers and trumpets and fountains of fire in my mind. I put up my hand, felt a coarse garment. Had I but dreamed...? I stirred. Light blazed in a widening band above my face. Through narrowed eyes I saw a room, a mean chamber, dusty, littered with ill-assorted rubbish. In a wall there was a window. I went to it, stared out upon a green sward, a path that curved downward to a white strand. It was a strange scene, and yet——

A wave of vertigo swept over me, faded. I blinked, tried to remember.

I reached up, felt something clamped over my head. I pulled it off and it fell to the floor with a faint clatter: a broad-spectrum briefing device, of the type used to indoctrinate unidentified citizens who had undergone a Change unprepared....

Suddenly, like water pouring down a drain, the picture in my mind faded, left me standing in my old familiar junk room, with a humming in my head and a throb in my temples. I had been about to try the briefing gimmick, and had wondered if it would work. It had—with a vengeance. For a minute there I had stumbled around the room like a stranger, yearning for dear old Vallon. I could remember the feeling—but it was gone now. I was just me, in trouble as usual.

There were a lot of tantalizing ideas floating around in my mind, right at the edge of consciousness. Later I'd have to sit down and go over them carefully. Right now, I had my hands full. Two armies had me cornered, and all the guns belonged to the opposition. That part was okay; I didn't want to fight anybody. All I wanted out of this situation was me.

A rattle of gunfire outside brought me to the window in a jump. It was the same view as a few moments before, but it made more sense now. There was the still smoking wreckage of the PT boat, sunk in ten feet of water a few yards from the end of the jetty. Somebody must have tried to make a run for it. The Russian sub was nowhere in sight; probably it had landed the men and backed out of danger from any unexpected quarter. Two or three corpses lay in view, down by the water's edge. From where I stood I couldn't say whether they were good guys or villains.

There were more shots, coming from somewhere off to the left. It looked like the boys were fighting it out old style: hand to hand, with small arms. It figured; after all, what they wanted was me and all my clever ideas intact, not a smoking ruin.

I don't know whether it was my romantic streak or my cynical one that had made me drive the architect nuts putting secret passages in the walls of my chateau and tunnels under the lawn, but I was glad now I had them. There was a narrow door in the west wall of the strong-room that gave onto a tight spiral stair. From there I could take my choice: the boathouse, the edge of the woods behind the house, or the beach a hundred yards north of the jetty. All I had to do was——

The house trembled a split second ahead of a terrific blast that slammed me to the floor. I felt blood start from my nose. Head ringing, I scrambled to my feet, groped through the dust to my escape hatch. Somebody outside was getting impatient. It wouldn't do to have my fancy getaway route fall in before I had used it. I felt another shell hit the house: mortars, I guessed, or rockets. I must have slept through the preliminaries and wakened just in time for the main bout.

My fingers were on the sensitive pressure areas that worked the concealed door. I took a last glance around the room, where the dust was just settling from the last blast. My eyes fell on a plain pewter-colored cylinder lying where I had tossed it an hour before—but now I knew what it was. In one jump I was across the room and had grabbed it up. I remembered finding it aboard the lifeboat when I tidied up; it had lain concealed among the bones of the man with the bear-tooth necklace. He must have come across it, admired its pretty colors, and tucked it away in his fur pants. And now I, with my Vallonian memories banked in my mind, could appreciate just how precious an object it was. It was Foster's memory. It would be only a copy, undoubtedly; still, I couldn't leave it behind.

A blast heavier than the last one rocked the house; a big chunk of plaster fell. It was way past time to go. Snorting and coughing from the dust, I got back to the emergency door, went through it, and started down.

At the bottom I paused to think it over, and the earth jumped again. I fell back, saw the roof of the beach tunnel collapse. That left the woods and the boathouse. I didn't have much time to decide; the tunnels might go any second. Apparently my architect had economized on the tunnel shorings. But then, he hadn't figured on any major wars happening in the front yard.

The fight was going on, as near as I could judge, to the south of the house and behind it. Probably the woods were full of skirmishers, taking advantage of the cover. The best bet was the boathouse, direct. I'd have preferred to wait until dark, but the idea didn't seem practical under the circumstances. I took a deep breath and started into the tunnel. With a little luck I'd find my boat intact. I would have to pull out under the noses of the combatants, but maybe the element of surprise would give me a few hundred yards' start. I had enough horses to beat anything afloat to the mainland—if I could make a clean break.

The tunnel was dark but that didn't bother me. It ran dead straight to the boathouse. I came to the wooden slat door and stood for a moment, listening; everything was quiet. I eased it open and stepped on to the ramp inside the building. In the gloom polished mahogany and chrome-work threw back muted highlights. I circled, slipped the mooring rope, and was about to step into the cockpit when I heard the bolt of a rifle smack home. I whirled, threw myself flat. The deafening *bam!* of a .30 calibre fired at close quarters laid a pattern of fine ripples on the black water. I rolled, hit with a splash that drowned a second shot, and dove deep. Three strokes took me under the door, out into the green gloom of open water. I hugged the yellowish sand of the bottom, angled off to the right, and kept going.

I had to get out of my jacket, and somehow I managed it, almost without losing a stroke. And there went all the goodies I'd stashed away in the pockets, down to the bottom of the drink. I still had Foster's memory-trace; it was in my slacks and there wasn't time to get out of them nor to kick off my tennis shoes. Ten strokes, fifteen, twenty. I knew my limit: twenty-five good strokes on a full load of air; but I had dived in a hurry….

Twenty-five…and another…and one more. And up above a man was waiting, rifle aimed, for my head to break the surface.

Thirty strokes, and here I come, ready or not. I rolled on my back, got my face above the surface. I got half a gulp of fresh air before the shot slapped spray into my face and echoed off across the water. I sank like a stone, kicked off, and made another twenty-five yards before I had to come up. The rifleman was faster this time. The bullet crossed my shoulder like a hot iron, and I was under water again. My kick-work was weak now; the strength was draining from my arms fast. I had to have air—but I could almost feel the solid smack of a steel-jacketed bullet against my skull. I had to keep going. My chest was on fire and there was a whirling blackness all around me. I felt consciousness fading, but maybe just one more stroke....

* * * *

As from a distance I observed the clumsy efforts of the swimmer, watched the flounderings of the poor, untrained creature....

It was apparent that an override of the autonomic system was required. With dispatch I activated cortical area omicron, re-routed the blood supply, drew an emergency oxygen source from stored fats, diverting the necessary energy to break the molecular bonds.

Now, with the body drawing on internal sources, ample for six hundred seconds at maximum demand, I stimulated areas upsilon and mu. I channeled full survival-level energy to the muscle complexes involved, increased power output to full skeletal tolerance, eliminated waste motion.

The body drove through the water with the fluid grace of a sea-denizen....

* * * *

I floated on my back, breathing in great surges of cool air and blinking at the crimson sky. I had been under water, a few yards from shore, drowning. Then there was an awareness, like a voice, telling me what to do. From out of the mass of Vallionan knowledge I had acquired, I had drawn what I needed. And now I was here, half a mile from the beach, winded but intact. But there was no time now to wonder at miracles....

I raised my head and glanced toward the house. A column of smoke rose from a gaping cavity where the bedroom windows used to be. A man jumped up, darted across the lawn, fell. I heard a shot a few seconds later, floating lazily across the still sunset water. There was no visible activity at the water's edge; the rifleman was gone. He probably thought he'd finished me, especially if he had noticed blood in the water.

I thought about sharks. I hadn't heard of any in this neighborhood, but a little blood was just the thing to bait them in. I twisted, got a look at the throbbing burn across my left shoulder where the rifleman's bullet had grazed; it was nothing much, just a skin gouge. It didn't seem to be bleeding. If it had been, there wasn't much I could do about it. It was no time for worrying. I had to keep my mind on the problem of getting to the mainland. It was a fifteen-mile swim, but if the boys on shore could keep each other occupied, I ought to be able to make it. I thought again about pulling off my pants and shoes but decided against it; I'd be in awkward shape without them—if I made it.

I felt beat: as though I hadn't eaten all day—which wasn't too strange, because I hadn't. Well, at least I wouldn't get stomach cramps while circling the island. From there I'd strike out for shore. And the first thing I would do when I got out of this would be to order the biggest, rarest steak in South America.

I took a last look toward the house. I could see fire inside it now. I guessed each side was rationalizing the destruction as denial to the enemy. It had been a nice place and I'd miss it. Some day somebody was going to pay for it.

CHAPTER XI

I sat at the kitchen table in Margareta's Lima apartment and gnawed the last few shreds off the stripped T-bone, while my girl poured me another cup of coffee.

"Now tell me about it," she said. "Why did they burn your house? And how did you succeed in getting here?"

"They got so interested in the fight, they lost their heads," I said. "That's the only explanation I can think of. I thought I'd be as safe as a two-dollar watch at a pickpockets' convention: I figured they'd go to some pains to avoid damaging me. I guessed wrong."

"But your own people...."

"Maybe they were right: they couldn't afford to let the Ruskis get me. Funny—if they'd just thought to write me a letter and ask for my co-operation...."

"But how did you get covered with mud? And the blood stains on your back?"

"I had a nice long swim: five hours' worth. Then another hour getting through a mangrove swamp. Lucky I had a moon. Then a three-hour hike... and here I am."

"I hope you're feeling better now that you've had something to eat. You looked terrible."

"Another block and I wouldn't have made it. I felt sucked dry. The scratch on my back is nothing, but maybe the shock... I don't know."

"Lie down now and sleep," said Margareta. "What do you want me to do?"

"Get me some clothes," I said. "A grey suit, white shirt, black tie and shoes. And go to my bank and draw some money, save five thousand. Oh yeah, see if there's anything in the papers. If you see anybody hanging around the lobby when you come back, don't come up; give me a call and I'll meet you."

She stood up. "This is really awful," she said. "Can't your embassy——"

"Didn't I mention it? A Mr. Pruffy, of the Embassy, came along to hold Smale's hand…not to mention a Colonel Sanchez. I wouldn't be surprised if the local cops weren't in the act by now…unless they all think I'm dead. That impression won't last long after you show up with a nice fresh check on my account and spend part of it on a man's suit. I'll get some sleep and light out as soon as you get back."

"Where will you go?"

"I'll get to the airport and play it by ear. I don't think they've alerted everybody. It was a hush-hush deal, until it went sour; now they're still picking up the pieces."

"The bank won't be open for hours yet," said Margareta. "Go to sleep and don't worry. I'll take care of everything."

I made it to the bedroom and slid out on the big wide bed, and consciousness slipped away like a silk curtain falling.

* * * *

I knew I wasn't alone as soon as I opened my eyes. I hadn't heard anything, but I could feel someone in the room. I sat up slowly, looked around.

He was sitting in the embroidered chair by the window: an ordinary-looking fellow in a tan tropical suit, with an unlighted cigarette in his mouth and no particular expression on his face.

"Go ahead, light up," I said. "Don't mind me."

"Thanks," he said, in a thin voice. He took a lighter from an inner pocket, flipped it, held it to the cigarette.

I stood up. There was a blur of motion from my visitor, and the lighter was gone and a short-nosed revolver was in its place.

"You've got the wrong scoop, mister," I said. "I don't bite."

"I'd rather you wouldn't move suddenly, Mr. Legion," he said. He coughed, his eyes on mine. "My nerves aren't what they used to be." The gun was still on me.

"Which side are you working for?" I said. "And can I put my shoes on, or are you afraid I'll pull a gat out of my sock?"

He rested the pistol on his knee. "Get completely dressed, Mr. Legion."

"Sorry," I said. "No can do. No clothes."

He frowned slightly. "My jacket will be a little small for you," he said. "But I think you can manage."

I was sitting on the bed again. "I'm going to get out a cigarette," I said. "Try not to shoot me." I reached for a package on the table, lit up. His eyes stayed on mine.

"How come you didn't figure I was dead?" I asked, blowing smoke at him.

"We checked the house," he said. "No body."

"Why, you incompetent asses. You were supposed to think I drowned."

"That possibility was considered. But we made the routine checks anyway."

"Nice of you to let me sleep it out. How long have you been here?"

"Only a few minutes," he said. He glanced at his watch. "We'll have to be going in another fifteen."

"What do you want with me?" I said. "You blew up everything you were interested in."

"The Department wants to ask you a few questions."

"Look, I'm just a dumb guy," I whined. "I don't know nothing about all that stuff. I was just the guy that peddled it, see?"

He took a drag on his cigarette, squinted at me through the smoke. "You ran up an A average in college," he said, "including English."

"You boys really do your homework." I looked at the pistol. "I wonder if you'd really shoot me," I mused.

"I'll try to make the position clear," he said. "Just to avoid any unfortunate misunderstanding. My instructions are to bring you in, alive—if possible. If it appears that you may evade arrest…or fall into the wrong hands, I'll be forced to use the gun."

I pulled my shoes on, thinking it over. My best chance to make a break was now, while there was only one watchdog. But I had a feeling he was telling the truth about shooting me. I had already seen the boys in action at the house.

He got up. "Let's step into the living room, Mr. Legion." I moved past him through the door. In the living room the clock on the mantel said eleven. I'd been asleep for five or six hours. Margareta ought to be getting back any minute….

"Put this on," he said. I took the light jacket, wedged myself into it, looked at my reflection in the big rectangular mirror that occupied most of a wall above the low divan.

"It's not the real me," I said. "I usually—"

The telephone rang.

I looked at my watchdog. He shook his head. We stood and listened to it ring. After a while it stopped.

"We'd better be going now," he said. "Walk ahead of me, please. We'll take the elevator to the basement and leave by the service entrance—"

He stopped talking, eyes on the door. There was the rattle of a key. The gun came up.

"Hold it," I snapped. "It's the girl who owns the apartment." I moved to face him, my back to the door.

"That was foolish of you, Legion," he said. "Don't move again."

I watched the door in the big mirror on the opposite wall. The knob turned, the door swung in…and a thin brown man in white shirt and white pants slipped into the room. As he pushed the door back he transferred a small automatic to his left hand. My keeper threw a lever on the revolver that was aimed at my belt buckle.

"Stand absolutely still, Legion," he said. "If you have a chance, that's it." He moved aside slightly, looked past me to the newcomer. I watched in the mirror as the man in white behind me swiveled to keep both of us covered.

"This is a fail-safe weapon," said my first owner to the new man. "I think you know about them. We leaked the information to you. I'm holding the trigger back; if my hand relaxes, it fires, so I'd be a little careful about shooting, if I were you."

The thin man swallowed, a black leather bow tie bobbing against his Adam's apple. He didn't say anything. He was having to make some tough decisions. His instructions would be the same as my other friend's: to bring me in alive, if possible.

"Who does this bird represent?" I asked my man. I noticed my voice was pitched half an octave higher than usual.

"He's a Soviet agent."

I looked in the mirror at the man again. "Nuts," I said. "He looks like a waiter in a chili joint. He probably came up to take our order."

"You talk too much when you're nervous," said my keeper between his teeth. He held the gun on me steadily. I watched his trigger finger to see if it looked like relaxing.

"I'd say it's a stalemate," I said. "Let's take it once more from the top. Both of you go out and—"

"Shut up, Legion." My man licked his lips, glanced at my face. "I'm sorry. It looks as though—"

"You don't want to shoot me," I blurted out loudly. In the mirror I had seen the door, which was standing ajar, ease open an inch, two inches. "You'll spoil this nice coat…." I kept on talking: "And anyway it would be a big mistake, because everybody knows Russian agents are stubby men with wide cheekbones and tight hats—"

Silently Margareta slipped into the room, took two quick steps, and slammed a heavy handbag down on the slicked-back pompadour that went with the Adam's apple. The man in white stumbled and fired a round into the rug. The automatic dropped from his hand, and my pal in tan stepped to him and hit him hard on the back of the head with his pistol. He whirled toward me, hissed "Play it smart" just loud enough for me to hear, then turned to Margareta. He slipped the gun into his pocket, but I knew he could get it out again in a hurry.

"Very nicely done, Miss," he said. "I'll have this person removed from your apartment. Mr. Legion and I were just going."

Margareta looked at me. I thought over two or three remarks but none of them seemed to fit. I didn't intend to see her get hurt—or involved. Apparently my FBI type was willing to leave her out of it, if I went quietly. On the other hand, this was my last chance to get out of the net before it closed for good. My keeper was watching, waiting for me to try something, tip Margareta off....

"It's okay, honey," I said. "This is Mr. Smith...of our Embassy. We're old friends." I stepped past her, headed for the door. My hand was on the knob when I heard a solid thunk behind me. I whirled in time to clip the FBI on the jaw as he fell forward. Margareta looked at me, wide-eyed.

"That handbag packs a wallop," I said. "Nice work, Maggie." I knelt, pulled off the fellow's belt, and cinched his hands behind his back with it. Margareta got the idea, did the same for the other man, who was beginning to groan now.

"Who are these men?" she said. "What——"

"I'll tell you all about it later. Right now, I have to get to some people I know, get this story on the wires, out in the open. State'll be a little shy about gunning me down or locking me up without trial, if I give the show enough publicity."

I reached in my pocket, handed her the black-and-gold-marked cylinder. "Just to be on the safe side," I said, "mail this to me: John Jones—at Itzenca, general delivery."

"All right," said Margareta. "And I have your things." She stepped into the hall, came back with a shopping bag and a suit carton. She took a wad of bills from her handbag and handed it to me.

I went to her and put my arms around her. "Listen, honey: as soon as I leave, go to the bank and draw fifty grand. Get out of the country. They haven't got anything on you except that you beaned a couple of intruders in your apartment, but it'll be better if you disappear. Leave an address care of Poste Restante, Basel, Switzerland. I'll get in touch when I can."

She put up an argument but I made my point. Twenty minutes later I was pushing through the big glass doors onto the sidewalk, clean-shaven, dressed to the teeth, with five grand on one hip and a .32 on the other. I'd had a good meal and a fair sleep, and against me the secret services of two or three countries didn't have a chance.

I got as far as the corner before they nailed me.

CHAPTER XII

"You have a great deal to lose," General Smale was saying, "and nothing to gain by your stubbornness. You're a young man, vigorous and, I'm sure, intelligent. You have a fortune of some million and a quarter dollars, which I assure you you'll be permitted to keep. As against that prospect, so long as you refuse to cooperate, we must regard you as no better than a traitorous criminal—and deal with you accordingly."

"What have you been feeding me?" I said. "My mouth tastes like somebody's old gym shoes and my arm's purple to the elbow. Don't you know it's illegal to administer drugs without a license?"

"The nation's security is at stake," snapped Smale.

"The funny thing is, it must not have worked, or you wouldn't be begging me to tell all. I thought that scopolamine or whatever you're using was the real goods."

"We've gotten nothing but gibberish," Smale said, "most of it in an incomprehensible language. Who the devil are you, Legion? Where do you come from?"

"You know everything," I said. "You told me yourself. I'm a guy named Legion, from Mount Sterling, Illinois, population one thousand eight hundred and ninety-two."

"I'm a humane man, Legion. But if necessary I'll beat it out of you."

"You?" I smiled, curling a lip. "You mean you'll call in a herd of plug-uglies: real crooks, to do the dirty work. My only crime is knowing something you politicians want, and you're willing to lie, cheat, steal, torture, and kill to get it. You know that and so do I; let's not kid each other. I know your measure as a man, Mr. General."

Smale had gone white. "I'm in a position to inflict agonies on you, you insolent rotter," he grated. "I've refrained from doing so. You might add that to your analysis of my character. I'm a soldier; I know my duty. I'm prepared to give my life; if need be, my honor. I'm even prepared to forego your good opinion—so long as I obtain for my government the information you're withholding."

"Turn me loose; then ask me in a nice way. As far as I know, I haven't got anything of military significance to tell you, but if I were treated as a free citizen I might be inclined to let you be the judge of that."

"Tell us now; then you'll go free."

"Sure," I said. "I invented a combination rocket ship and time machine. I traveled around the solar system and made a few short trips back into history. In my spare time I invented other gadgets. I'm planning to take out patents, so naturally I don't intend to spill any secrets. Can I go now?"

Smale got to his feet. "Until we can safely move you, you'll remain in this room. You're on the sixty-third floor of the Yordano Building. The windows are of unbreakable glass, in case you contemplate a particularly untidy suicide. Your person has been stripped of all potentially dangerous items, though I suppose you could still swallow your tongue and suffocate. The door is of heavy construction, and securely locked."

"I forgot to tell you," I said. "I mailed a letter to a friend, telling him all about you. The sheriff will be here with a posse any minute now, to spring me——"

"You mailed no letter," Smale said. "Unfortunately, we don't feel it would be advisable to allow any furniture to remain here which you might be foolish enough to dismantle for use as a weapon. It's rather a drab room to spend your future in, but until you decide to cooperate this will be your world."

I didn't say anything. I sat on the floor and watched him leave. I caught a glimpse of two uniformed men outside the door. No doubt they'd take turns looking through the peephole. I'd have solitude without privacy. I wondered if Margareta had managed to mail the cylinder.

I stretched out on the floor, which was padded with a nice thick rug, presumably so that I wouldn't beat my brains out against it just to spite them. I was way behind on my sleep: being interrogated while unconscious wasn't a very restful procedure. I wasn't too worried. In spite of what Smale said, they couldn't keep me here forever. Maybe Margareta had gotten clear and told the story to some newsmen; this kind of thing couldn't stay hidden forever. Or could it?

I thought about what Smale had said about my talking gibberish under the narcotics. That was an odd one....

Quite suddenly I got it. By means of the drugs they must have tapped a level where the Vallonian background briefing was stored: they'd been firing questions at a set of memories that didn't speak English. I grinned, then laughed out loud. Luck was still in the saddle with me.

* * * *

The glass was in double panels, set in aluminum frames and sealed with a plastic strip. The space between the two panels of glass was evacuated of air, creating an insulating barrier against the heat of the sun. I ran a finger over the aluminum. It was dural: good tough stuff. If I had something to pry with, I might possibly lever the metal away from the glass far enough to take a crack at the edge, the weak point of armor-glass...if I had something to hit it with.

Smale had done a good job of stripping the room—and me. I had my shirt and pants and shoes, but no tie or belt. I still had my wallet—empty, a pack of cigarettes with two wilted weeds in it, and a box of matches. Smale had missed a bet: I might set fire to my hair and burn to the ground. I might also stuff a sock down my throat and strangle, or hang myself with a shoe lace—but I wasn't going to.

I looked at the window some more. The door was too tough to tackle, and the heavies outside were probably hoping for an excuse to work me over. They wouldn't expect me to go after the glass; after all, I was still sixty-three stories up. What would I do if I did make it to the window sill? But we could worry about that later, after I had smelled the fresh air.

My forefinger found an irregularity in the smooth metal: a short groove. I looked closer, saw a screw head set flush with the aluminum surface. Maybe if the frame was bolted together——

No such luck; the screw I had found was the only one. What was it for? Maybe if I removed it I'd find out. But I'd wait until dark to try it. Smale hadn't left a light fixture in the room. After sundown I'd be able to work unobserved.

A couple of hours went by and no one came to disturb my solitude, not even to feed me. Maybe they planned to starve me out; or maybe they weren't used to being jailers and had forgotten the animals had to be fed.

I had a short scrap of metal I'd worked loose from my wallet. It was mild steel, flimsy stuff, only about an inch long, but I was hoping the screw might not be set too tight. Aluminum threads strip pretty easily, so it probably wasn't cinched up too hard.

There was no point in theorizing. It was dark now; I'd give it a try. I went to the window, fitted the edge of metal into the slotted screw-head, and twisted. It turned, just like that. I backed it off ten turns, twenty; it was a thick bolt with fine threads. It came free and air whooshed into the hole. The screw apparently sealed the panel after the air was evacuated.

I thought it over. If I could fill the space between the panels with water and let it freeze…quite a trick in the tropics. I might as well plan to fill it with gin and set it on fire.

I was going in circles. Every idea I had started with 'if'. I needed something I could manage with the materials at hand: cloth, a box of matches, a few bits of paper.

I got out a cigarette, lit up, and while the match was burning examined the hole from which I'd removed the plug. It was about three-sixteenths of an inch in diameter and an inch deep, and there was a hole near the bottom communicating with the air space between the glass panels. It was an old-fashioned method of manufacture but it seemed to have worked all right: the air was pumped out and the hole sealed with the screw. It had at any rate the advantage of being easy to service if the panel leaked. Now, with some way of pumping air *in*, I could blow out the panels.…

There was no pump on the premises but I did have some chemicals: the match heads. They were old style too, like a lot of things in Peru: the strike-once-and-throw-away kind.

I sat on the floor and started to work, chipping the heads off the match-sticks, collecting the dry, purplish material on a scrap of paper. Thirty-eight matches gave me a respectable sample. I packed it together, rolled it in the paper, and crimped the ends. Then I tucked the makeshift firecracker into the hole the screw had come from.

Using the metal scrap I scraped at the threads of the screw, burring them. Then I started it in the hole, half a dozen turns, until it came up against the match heads.

The shoes Margareta had bought me were the latest thing in Lima styles, with thin soles, pointed toes, and built-up leather heels: Bad on the feet, but just the thing to pound with. I thought about trying to work loose a piece of rug to shield my face, but decided against it. I'd have to stand aside and take my chances.

I took the shoe by the toe and hefted it: the flexible sole gave it a good action, like a well-made sap. There were still a couple of 'if's' in the equation, but a healthy crack on the screw ought to drive it against the packed match-heads hard enough to detonate them, and the expanding gasses from the explosion ought to exert enough pressure against the glass panels to break them. I'd know in a second.

I flattened myself against the wall, brought the shoe up, and laid it on the screw-head with everything I had....

There was a deafening boom, a blast of hot air, and a chemical stink, then a gust of cool night wind—and I was on the sill, my back to the street six hundred feet below, my fingers groping for a hold on the ledge above the window. I found a grip, pulled up, reached higher, got my feet on the muntin strip, paused to rest for three seconds, reached again....

I pulled my feet above the window level and heard shouts in the room below:

"—fool killed himself!"

"Get a light in here!"

I clung, breathing deep, and murmured thanks to the architect who had stressed a strong horizontal element in his façade and arranged the strip windows in bays set twelve inches from the face of the structure. Now, if the boys below would keep their eyes on the street long enough for me to get on the roof—

I looked up, to get an idea how far I'd have to go—and gripped the ledge convulsively as the whole building leaned out, tilting me back....

Cold sweat ran into my eyes. I squeezed the stone until my knuckles creaked, and held on. I laid my cheek against the rough plaster, listening to my heart thump. Adrenalin and high hopes had gotten me this far... and now it had all drained out and left me, a frail ground-loving animal, flattened against the cruel face of a tower, like a fly on a ceiling, with nothing between me and the unyielding concrete below but the feeble grip of fingers and toes. I started to yell for help, and the words stuck in my dry throat. I breathed in shallow gasps, feeling my muscles tightening, until I hung, rigid as a board, afraid even to roll my eyeballs for fear of dislodging myself. I closed my eyes, felt my hands going numb, and tried again to yell: only a thin croak emerged.

A minute earlier I had had only one worry: that they'd look up and see me. Now my worst fear was that they wouldn't.

This was the end. I'd been close before, but not like this. My fingers could take the strain for maybe another minute, maybe even two; then I'd let go, and the wind would whip at me for a few timeless seconds, before I hit….

I had had a lot of big ideas but in the cosmic scheme I was a gnat on a windshield. I thought I'd learned something, was a jump ahead of most guys, and could play the meaningless game with a certain flair. But my fancy philosophies were words written in smoke when they came up against the raw power of blind instinct. My conscious mind had an I.Q. of 148, but the idiot subconscious that had frozen me here hadn't learned anything since the first ape that had owned it rode out a storm in a tree-top and lived to be my ancestor…. I heard a sound and it was me, whimpering. I was a poor weakling, out of his element, bleating for mercy.

Down inside of me something didn't like the picture. A small defiance flickered, found a foothold, burned brighter. I would die…but that would solve a lot of problems. And if I had to die, at least I could die trying.

My mind moved in to take over from my body. It was the body that was wasting my last strength on a precarious illusion of safety, numbing my senses, paralyzing me. It was a tyranny I wouldn't accept. I needed a cool head and a steady hand and an unimpaired sense of balance; and if the imbecile body wouldn't cooperate the mind would take it by the scruff of the neck and force it. I'd been feeding this hulk for thirty-odd years; now it would do what I told it. First: loosen the grip—

Yes! If it killed me: bend those fingers! Sure, I might fall—all the way—and splatter when I hit, but did this lousy slab of meat expect to live forever? I had news for it: time was short, any way you figured.

I was standing a little looser now, my hands resting flat, my legs taking the load. I had a good wide ledge to stand on: nearly a foot, and in a minute I was going to reach up and get a new hold and lift one foot at a time…and if I slipped, at least I'd have done it my way.

I let go, and the building leaned out, and to hell with it….

I felt for the next ledge, gripped it, pulled up, found a toe-hold.

Sure, I was dead. It was a long way to the top, and there was a fancy cornice I'd never get over, but when the moment came and I started the long ride down I'd thumb my nose at the old hag, Instinct, who hadn't been as tough as she thought she was….

* * * *

I was under the cornice now, hanging on for a breather, and listening to the hooting and hollering from the window far below. A couple of heads had popped out and taken a look, but it was dark up where I was and all the attention was centered down where the crowd had gathered and lights were playing, looking for a mess. Pretty soon now they'd begin to get the drift—so I'd better be going.

I looked up at the overhang...and felt the old urge to clutch and hang on. So I leaned outward a little further, just to show me who was boss. It was a long reach, and I'd have to risk it all on one lunge because, if I missed, there wasn't any net, and my fingers knew it. I heard my nails rasp on the plaster. I grated my teeth together and unhooked one hand: it was like a claw carved from wood. I took a half-breath, bent my knees slightly; they were as responsive as a couple of bumper-jacks bolted on to the hip. Tough; but it was now or never....

I let go with both hands and stretched, leaning back....

My wooden hands bumped the edge, scrabbled, hooked on, as my legs swung free, and I was hanging like an old-time sailor strung up by the thumbs. A wind off the roof whipped at my face and now I was a tissue-paper doll, fluttering in the breeze.

I had to pull now, pull hard, heave myself up and over the edge, but I was tired, too tired. My crepe paper arms with the wooden hands seemed to belong to someone else, someone who'd been dead a long time....

But the someone was me: death was an old story, one that I wrote myself. This was something that had happened before, long ago, and the palindrome of life was finished where it started, and a dark curtain was falling....

Then from the darkness a voice was speaking in a strange language: a confusion of strange thought symbols, but through them an ever more insistent call:

... dilate the secondary vascular complex, shunt full conductivity to the upsilon neuro-channel. Now, stripping oxygen ions from fatty cell masses, pour in electro-chemical energy to the sinews....

With a smooth surge of power I pulled myself up, fell forward, rolled onto my back, and lay on the flat roof, the beautiful flat roof, still warm from the day's sun.

I was here, looking at the stars, safe; and later on when I had more time I'd stop to think about it. But now I had to move, before they had time to organize themselves, cordon off the building, and start a floor-by-floor search.

Staggering from the exertion of the long climb I got to my feet, went to the shed housing the entry to the service stair. The door was locked. I didn't waste any time kicking at it; I got a leg up and stood on the doorknob. Two jumps and it snapped off. I pushed the stub of the shaft through and tickled the back edge of the locking tongue, eased it out. The door opened.

A short flight of steps led down to a storeroom. There were dusty boards, dried-up paint cans, odd tools. I picked up a five-foot length of two-by-four and a hammer with one claw missing, and stepped out into the hall. The street was a long way down and I didn't feel like wasting time with stairs. I found the elevator, pushed the button, stood in front of it whistling. A fat man in a drab suit came along, looked at me distastefully, thought about telling me that workmen used the freight elevator, then changed his mind and said nothing.

The elevator arrived. I stepped in jauntily. The fat man followed me, pushed the button for the foyer. I smiled and nodded, went on whistling.

We stopped and the doors opened. I waited for the fat man to leave, then glanced out, tightening my grip on the hammer, and followed. I could see the lights in the street out front and in the distance there was the wail of a siren, but nobody in the lobby looked my way. I headed across toward the side exit, dumped the board at the door, tucked the hammer in the waist band of my pants, and stepped out onto the pavement. There were a lot of people hurrying past but this was Lima: they didn't waste a glance on a barefooted carpenter.

I moved off, not hurrying. There was a lot of rough country between me and Itzenca, the little town near which the life boat was hidden in a cañon, but I aimed to cover it in a week. Some time between now and tomorrow I'd have to figure out a way to equip myself with a few necessities, but I wasn't worried. A man who had successfully taken up human-fly work in middle life wouldn't have any trouble stealing a pair of boots.

Foster had shoved off for home three years ago, local time, although to him, aboard the ship, only a few weeks might have passed. My lifeboat was a midge compared to the mother ship he rode, but it had plenty of speed. Once aboard the lugger…and maybe I could put a little space between me and the big boys I was up against now.

I had used the best camouflage I knew of on the boat. The near-savage native bearers who had done my unloading and carried my Vallonian treasures across the desert to the nearest railhead were not the gossipy type. If General Smale's boys had heard about the boat, they hadn't mentioned it. And if they had: well, I'd solve that one when I got to it. There were still quite a few 'if's' in the equation, but my arithmetic was getting better all the time.

CHAPTER XIII

I took the precaution of sneaking up on the lifeboat in the dead of night, but I could have saved myself a crawl. Except for the fact that the camouflage nets had rotted away to shreds, the ship was just as I had left it, doors sealed. Why Smale's team hadn't found it, I didn't know; I'd think that one over when I was well away from Earth.

It had been a long tough trip from Lima to the cañon, but I had made it without interference. I had swapped my platinum finger ring for a beat-up .38 pistol, but I hadn't had to use it. In a shabby bar in one of the villages I passed through I had heard a battered radio sputtering news; there was no mention of the assault on the island, or of my escape. It seemed that all parties were willing to cover it up and pretend it hadn't happened.

I went into the post office at Itzenca and picked up the parcel Margareta had mailed me with Foster's memory-trace in it. While I was checking to see whether Uncle Sam's minions had intercepted the package and substituted a carrot, I felt something rubbing against my shin. I glanced down and saw a grey and white cat, reasonably clean and obviously hungry. I don't know whether I'd ploughed through a field of wild catnip the night before or if it was my way with a finger behind the furry ears, but Kitty followed me out of Itzenca and right into the bush. She kept pace with me, leading most of the time, as far as the space boat, and was the first one aboard.

I didn't waste time with formalities. I had once audited a briefing rod on the boat's operation—not that I had ever expected to use the information for a take-off. Once aboard, I hit the controls and cut a swathe through the atmosphere that must have sent fingers jumping for panic buttons from Washington to Moscow.

I didn't know how many weeks or months of unsullied leisure stretched ahead of me now. There would be time and to spare for exploring the boat, working out a daily routine, chewing over the details of both my memories, and laying plans for my arrival on Foster's world, Vallon. But first I wanted to catch a show that was making a one-night stand for me only: the awe-inspiring spectacle of the retreating earth.

I dropped into a seat opposite the screen and flipped into view the big luminous ball of wool that was my home planet. I'd been hoping to get a last look at my island, but I couldn't see it. The whole sphere was blanketed in cloud: a thin worn blanket in places but still intact. But the moon was a sight! An undipped Edam cheese with the markings of Roquefort. For a quarter of an hour I watched it grow until it filled my screen. It was too close for comfort. I dumped the tabby out of my lap and adjusted a dial. The dead world swept past, and I had a brief glimpse of burst bubbles of craters that became the eyes and mouth and pock marks of a face on a head that swung away from me in disdain and then the sibling planets dwindled and were gone forever.

The lifeboat was completely equipped, and I found comfortable quarters. An ample food supply was available by the touch of a panel on the table in the screen-room. That was a trick my predecessor with the dental jewelery hadn't discovered, I guessed. During the courses of my first journey earthward and on my visits to the boat for saleable playthings while she lay in dry-dock, I had discovered most of the available amenities aboard.

Now I luxuriated in a steaming bath of recycled water, sponged down with disposable towels packed in scented alcohol, fed the cat and myself, and lay down to sleep for about two weeks.

By the third week I was reasonably refreshed and rested. The scars from my recent brushes with what passed as the law were healed. I had gotten over regretting the toys I'd left behind on my island and the money in my banks in Lima and Switzerland, and even Margareta. I was headed for a new world; there was no point in dragging along old attachments.

The cat was a godsend, I began to realize. I named her Itzenca, after the village where she adopted me, and I talked to her by the hour. I always had felt that there was a subtle difference between talking to somebody else and talking to yourself. The latter gets a little tedious after the first few days but you can keep the other up indefinitely. So Itz got talked to plenty as we rode to the stars.

"Say, Itz," said I, "where would you like your sand box situated? Right there in front of the TV screen? There's not much traffic there, since we cleared the solar system. You'd have the place all to yourself."

No, said Itzenca by a flirt of her tail. And she walked over behind a crate that had never been unloaded on earth.

I pulled out a box of junk and slid the sand box in its place. Itzenca promptly lost interest and instead jumped up on the junk box which fell off the bench and scattered small objects of khaff and metal in all directions.

"Come back here, blast you," I said, "and help me pick up this stuff."

Itz bounded after a dull-gleaming silver object that was still rolling. I was there almost as quick as she was and grabbed up the cylinder. Suddenly the horsing around was over. This thing was somebody's memory.

I dropped onto a bench to examine it, my Vallonian-inspired pulse pounding. "Where the heck did this come from, cat?" I said.

Itz jumped up into my lap and nosed the cylinder. I was trying to hark back to those days three years before when I had loaded the lifeboat with all the loot it would carry, for the trip back to earth.

"Listen, Itz, we've got to do some tall remembering. Let's see: there was a whole rack of blanks in the memory-recharging section of the room where we found the three skeletons. Yeah, now I remember: I pulled this one out of the recorder set, which means it had been used, but not yet color-coded. I showed it to Foster when he was hunting his own trace. He didn't realize I'd pulled it out of the machine and he thought it was an empty. But I'll bet you somebody had his mind taped, and then left in a hurry, before the trace could be color-coded and filed.

"On the other hand, maybe it's a blank that had just been inserted when somebody broke up the play-house.... But wasn't there something Foster said...about when he woke up, way back when, with a pile of fresh corpses around him? He gave somebody emergency treatment and to a Vallonian that would include a complete memory-transcription.... Do you realize what I've got here in my hand, Itz?"

She looked up at me inquiringly.

"This is what's left of the guy that Foster buried: his pal, Ammaerln, I think he called him. What's inside this cylinder used to be tucked away in the skull of the ancient sinner. The guy's not so dead after all. I'll bet his family will pay plenty for this trace, and be grateful besides. That'll be an ace in the hole in case I get too hungry on Vallon."

I got up and crossed the apartment; Itz followed me out to my sleeping couch. I dropped the trace in a drawer beside Foster's own memory.

"Wonder how Foster's making out without his past, Itz? He claimed the one I've got here would only be a copy of the original stored at Okk-Hamiloth, but my briefing didn't say anything about copying memories. He must be somebody pretty important to rate that service."

Suddenly my eyes were riveted to the markings on Foster's trace lying in the drawer. "'Sblood! The royal colors!" I sat down on the bed with a lurch. "Itzenca, old gal, it looks like we'll be entering Vallonian society from the top. We've been consorting with a member of the Vallonian nobility!"

During the days that followed, I tried again and again to raise Foster on the communicator...without result. I wondered how I'd find him among the millions on the planet. My best bet would be to get settled down in the Vallonian environment, then start making a few inquiries.

I would play it casually: act the part of a Vallonian who had merely been travelling for a few hundred years—which wasn't unheard of—and play my cards close to my gravy stains until I learned what the score was. With my Vallonian briefing I ought to be able to carry it off. The Vallonians might not like illegal immigrants any better than they did back home, so I'd keep my interesting foreign background to myself.

I would need a new name. I thought over several possibilities and selected "Drgon". It was as good a Vallonian jawbreaker as any.

I canvassed the emergency wardrobe that was standard equipment on Far-Voyager lifeboats. There was everything from fur-lined parka-type suits for outings on worlds like Pluto to sheer silk one-man-air-conditioner balloon over-alls for stepping out on Venus. In amongst them was a selection of dresses reminiscent of ancient Greece. They had been the sharp style of Vallon when Foster left home. They looked comfortable. I picked one in a sober color, then got busy with the cutting and seaming unit to fit it to my frame. I didn't plan to attract unnecessary attention with ill-fitting garments when I crossed my first Vallonians.

Itzenca watched with interest. "What the heck am I going to do with you on Vallon?" I asked her. "The only cat on the planet. You may have to put up with an iggrfn for a boy friend," I said searching my Vallonian memory. "They're about the nearest thing to you in size and shape...but they're kind of objectionable, personality wise."

I finished off my new duds, then dug through the handicrafts gear and picked out a sheet of khaffite, a copper-like Vallonian alloy that was supposed to have almost the durability of khaff without being so hard to work. There were appropriate tools in the little workshop for shaping it and adding decoration.

"Don't worry," I said to Itz. "You won't go ashore shabbily clad either. You'll be a knockout in this item." I parked her on the workbench and sat down to my tools. I clipped out an inch-wide strip of the khaffite, shaped it in a circle, and fitted it with a slip-out catch. After a leisurely meal I spent what passed for an evening etching "ITZENCA" on the new collar with plenty of curlicues. Then I fitted it on her; she didn't seem to mind a bit.

"There. All set to wow those Vallonians like they've never been wowed." Itzenca purred.

We strolled into the observation lounge. Strange bright-hued star systems glowed far away. "We'll be stepping out with our memories any night now," I said.

* * * *

The proximity alarms were ringing. I watched the screen with its image of a great green world rimmed on one edge with glaring white from the distant giant sun, on the other flooded with a cool glow reflected from the blue outer planet. The trip was almost over and my confidence was beginning to fray around the edges. In a few minutes I would be stepping into an unknown world, all set to find my old pal Foster and see the sights. I didn't have a passport, but there was no reason to anticipate trouble. All I had to do was let my natural identity take a back seat and allow my Vallonian background to do the talking. And yet....

Now Vallon spread out below us, a misty grey-green landscape, bright under the glow of the immense moonlike sister world, Cinte. I had set the landing monitor for Okk-Hamiloth, the capital city of Vallon. That was where Foster would have headed, I guessed. Maybe I could pick up the trail there.

The city was directly below: a vast network of blue-lit avenues. I hadn't been contacted by Planetary Control. That was normal enough, however. A small vessel coming in on auto could handle itself.

A little apprehensively I ran over my lines a last time: I was Drgon, citizen of the Two Worlds, back from a longer-than-average season of far-voyaging and in need of briefing rods to bring me up to date on developments at home. I also required assignment of quarters. My tailoring was impeccable, my command of the language a little rusty from long non-use, and the only souvenirs I had to declare were a tattered native costume from my last port of call, a quaint weapon from the same, and a small animal I had taken a liking to.

* * * *

The landing ring was visible on the screen now, coming slowly up to meet us. There was a gentle shock and then absolute stillness. I watched the port cycle open; I went to it and looked out at the pale city stretching away to the hills. I took a breath of the fragrant night air spiced with a long-forgotten perfume, and the part of me that was now Vallonian ached with the inexpressible emotion of homecoming.

I started to buckle on my pistol and gather up a few belongings, then decided to wait until I'd met the welcoming committee. I whistled to Itzenca and we stepped out and down. We crossed the clipped green, luminous in the glow from the lights over the high-arched gate marking the path that curved up toward the bright-lit terraces above. There was no one in sight. Bright Cintelight showed me the gardens and walks and, when I reached the terraces, the avenues beyond…but no people. I stood by a low wall of polished marble and thought about it. It was about midnight, and the nights on Vallon lasted twenty-eight hours, but there should have been some activity here. This was a busy port: scheduled vessels, private yachts, official ships, all of them came and went from Okk-Hamiloth. But not tonight.

The cat and I walked across the terrace, passed through the open arch to a refreshment lounge. The low tables and cushioned couches stood empty under the rosy light from the ceiling panels. My slippered feet whispered on the polished floor.

I stood and listened: dead silence. There wasn't even the hum of a mosquito; all such insect pests had been killed off long ago. The lights glowed, the tables waited invitingly. How long had they waited?

I sat down at one of them and thought hard. I had made a lot of plans, but I hadn't counted on a deserted spaceport. How was I going to ask questions about Foster if there was no one to ask?

I got up and moved on through the empty lounge, past a wide arcade, out onto a terraced lawn. A row of tall poplar-like trees made a dark wall beyond a still pool, and behind them distant towers loomed, colored lights sparkled. A broad avenue swept in a wide curve between fountains, slanted away to the hills. A hundred yards from where I stood a small vehicle was parked at the curb; I headed for it.

It was an open two-seater, low-slung, cushioned, finished in violet inlays against bright chrome. I slid into the seat, looked over the controls, while Itzenca skipped to a place beside me. There was a simple lever arrangement: a steering tiller. It looked easy. I tried a few pulls and pushes; lights blinked on the panel, the car quivered, lifted a few inches, drifted slowly across the road. I moved the tiller, twiddled things; the car moved off toward the towers. I didn't like the controls; a wheel and a couple of foot pedals would have suited me better; but it beat walking.

* * * *

Two hours later we had cruised the city…and found nothing. It hadn't changed from what my extra memory recalled—except that all the people were gone. The parks and boulevards were trimmed, the fountains and pools sparkled, the lights glowed…but nothing moved. The automatic dust precipitators and air filters would run forever, keeping things clean and neat; but there was no one there to appreciate it. I pulled over, sat watching the play of colored lights on a waterfall, and considered. Maybe I'd find more of a clue inside one of the buildings. I left the car and picked one at random: a tall slab of pink crystal. Inside, I looked around at a great airy cavern full of rose-colored light and listened to the purring of the cat and my own breathing. There was nothing else to hear.

I picked a random corridor, went along it, passed through empty rooms. It was all in the old Vallonian style: walls paneled in jade, brocades hangings in iridescent colors, rugs like pools of fire. In one chamber I picked up a cloak of semi-velvet and put it over my shoulders; I was getting cold in my daytime street dress. Walking among the tangible ghosts of the long past didn't warm me up any. We climbed a wide spiral stair, passed from vacant room to vacant room. I thought of the people who had once used them. Where were they now?

I found a clarinet-like musical instrument and blew a few notes on it. It had a deep mellow tone that echoed along the deserted corridor. I thought it sounded a lot like I felt: sad and forgotten. I went out onto a lofty terrace overlooking gardens, leaned on a balustrade, and looked up at the brilliant disc of Cinte. It loomed enormous, its diameter four times that of the earthly moon.

"We've come a long way to find nothing," I said to Itzenca. She pushed her way along my leg and flexed her tail in a gesture meant to console. But it didn't help. After the long wait, the tension of expectation, I felt suddenly as empty as the silent halls of the building.

I sat on the balustrade and leaned back against the polished pink wall, took out the clarinet and blew some blue notes. That which once had been was no more; remembering it, I played the *Pavane for a Dead Princess*, and felt a forlorn nostalgia for a glory I had never known.…

I finished and looked up at a sound. Four tall men in grey cloaks and a glitter of steel came toward me from the shadows.

* * * *

I had dropped the clarinet and was on my feet. I tried to back up but the balustrade stopped me. The four spread out. The man in the lead fingered a wicked-looking short club and spoke to me—in gibberish. I blinked at him and tried to think of a snappy comeback.

He snapped his fingers and two of the others came up; they reached for my arms. I started to square off, fist cocked, then relaxed; after all, I was just a tourist, Drgon by name. Unfortunately, before I could get my fist back, the man with the club swung it and caught me across the forearm. I yelled, jumped back, found myself grappled by the others. My arm felt dead to the shoulder. I tried a kick and regretted that too; there was armor under the cloaks. The club wielder said something and pointed at the cat....

It was time I wised up. I relaxed, tried to coax my *alter ego* into the foreground. I listened to the rhythm of the language: it was Vallonian, badly warped by time, but I could understand it:

"——musician would be an Owner!" one of them said.

Laughter.

"Whose man are you, piper? What are your colors?"

I curled my tongue, tried to shape it around the sort of syllables I heard them uttering; it seemed to me a gross debasement of the Vallonian I knew. Still I managed an answer:

"I...am a...citizen...of Vallon."

"A dog of a masterless renegade?" The man with the club hefted it, glowered at me. "And what wretched dialect is that you speak?"

"I have...been long a-voyaging," I stuttered. "I ask...for briefing rods...and for a...dwelling place."

"A dwelling place you'll have," the man said. "In the men's shed at Rath-Gallion." He gestured, and handcuffs snapped on my wrists.

He turned and stalked away, and the others hustled me after him. Over my shoulder I got a glimpse of a cat's tail disappearing over the balustrade. Outside, a long grey air-car waited on the lawn. They dumped me in the back seat, climbed aboard. I got a last look at the spires of Okk-Hamiloth as we tilted, hurtled away across the low hills.

Somewhere in the shuffle I had lost my new cloak. I shivered. I listened to the talk, and what I heard didn't make me feel any better. The chain between my wrists kept up a faint jingling. I gathered I'd be hearing a lot of that kind of music from now on. I had had an idealistic notion of wanting to fit into this new world, find a place in its society. I'd found a place all right: a job with security.

I was a slave.

CHAPTER XIV

It was banquet night at Rath-Gallion, and I gulped my soup in the kitchen and ran over in my mind the latest batch of jingles I was expected to perform. I had only been on the Estate a few weeks, but I was already

Owner Gope's favorite piper. If I kept on at this rate, I would soon have a cell to myself in the slave pens.

Sime, the pastry cook, came over to me.

"Pipe us a merry tune, Drgon," he said, "and I'll reward you with a frosting pot."

"With pleasure, good Sime," I said. I finished off the soup and got out my clarinet. I had tried out half a dozen strange instruments, but I still liked this one best. "What's your pleasure?"

"One of the outland tunes you learned far-voyaging," called Cagu, the bodyguard.

I complied with the *Beer Barrel Polka*. They pounded the table and hallooed when I finished, and I got my goody pan. Sime stood watching me scrape at it.

"Why don't you claim the Chief Piper's place, Drgon?" Sime said. "You pipe rings around the lout. Then you'd have freeman status, and could sit among us in the kitchen almost as an equal."

I went after the last of the chocilla frosting, licked my fingers, and laid the pot aside.

"I'd gladly be the equal of such a pastry cook as yourself, good Sime," I said. "But what can a slave-piper do?"

Sime blinked at me. "You can challenge the Chief Piper," he said. "There's none can deny you're his master in all but name. Don't fear the outcome of the Trial; you'll triumph sure." He glanced around at the kitchen staff. "Is it not so, goodmen?"

"I'll warrant it," the soup-master said. "If you lose, I'll take your stripes for you."

"You're going too fast for me, goodmen," I said. "How can I claim another's place?"

Sime waved his arms. "You have far-voyaged long indeed, Piper Drgon. Know you naught of how the world wags these days? One would take you for a Cintean heretic."

"As I've said, goodmen: in my youth all men were free; and the High King ruled at Okk-Hamiloth——"

"'Tis ill to speak of these things," said Sime in a low tone. "Only Owners know their former lives…though I've heard it said that long ago no man was so mean but that he recorded his lives and kept them safe. How you came by yours, I ask not; but do not speak of it. Owner Gope is a jealous master. Though a most generous and worshipful lord," he added hastily, looking around.

"I won't speak of it then, good Sime," I said. "But I have been long away. Even the language has changed, so that I wrench my tongue in the speaking of it. Advise me, if you will."

Sime puffed out his cheeks, frowning at me. "I scarce know where to start," he said. "All things belong to the Owners…as is only right." He looked around for confirmation. The others nodded. "Men of low skill are likewise property; and 'tis well 'tis so; else would they starve as masterless strays…if the Greymen failed to find them first." He made a sign and spat. So did everybody else.

"Now men of good skill are freemen, each earning rewards as befits his ability. I am Chief Pastry Cook to the Lord Gope, with the perquisites of that station, therefore that none other equals my talents." He looked around truculently, saw no challengers. "And thus it is with us all."

"And if some varlet claims the place of any man here," put in Cagu, "then he gotta submit to the Trial."

"Then," said Sime, pulling at his apron agitatedly, "this upstart pastry cook must cook against me; and all in the Hall will judge; and he who prevails is the Chief Pastry Cook, and the other takes a dozen lashes for his impertinence."

"But fear not, Drgon," spoke Cagu. "A Chief Piper ain't but a five-stroke man. Only a tutor is lower down among freemen. And anyway, the good Soup-master had promised to take the lash for you."

There was a bellow from the door, and I grabbed my clarinet and scrambled after the page. Owner Gope didn't like to wait around for piper-slaves. I saw him looming up at his place, as I darted through to my assigned position within the huge circle of the viand-loaded table. The Chief Piper had just squeezed his bagpipe-like instrument and released a windy blast of discordant sound. He was a lean, squint-eyed creature, fond of ordering the slave-pipers about. He pranced in an intricate pattern, pumping away at his vari-colored bladders, until I winced at the screech of it. Owner Gope noticed him about the same time. He picked up a heavy brass mug and half-rose to peg it at the Chief Piper, who saw it just in time to duck. The mug hit a swollen air-bag; a yellow one with green tassels; it burst with a sour bleat.

"As sweet a note as has been played tonight," roared Owner Gope. "Begone, lest you call up the hill devils——"

His eye fell on me. "Here's Dugon, or Digen," he cried. "Now here's a true piper. Summon up a fair melody, Dgron, to clear the fumes of the last performer from the air before the wine sours."

I bowed low, wet my lips, and launched into the *One O'Clock Jump*. To judge from the roar that went up when I finished, they liked it. I followed with *Little Brown Jug* and *String of Pearls*. Gope pounded and the table quieted down.

"The rarest slave in all Rath-Gallion, I swear it," he bellowed. "Were he not a slave, I'd drink his health."

"By your leave, Owner?" I said.

Gope stared, then nodded indulgently. "Speak then, Dugong," he said.

"I claim the place of Chief Piper. I——"

Yells rang out; Gope grinned widely.

"So be it," he said. "Shall the vote be taken now, or must we submit to more of the vile bladderings ere we proclaim our good Dagron Chief Piper?"

"Proclaim him!" somebody shouted.

"There must be a Trial," another offered dubiously.

Gope slammed a huge hand against the table. "Bring Lylk, the Chief Piper, before me," he yelled. "He of the wretched air-skins."

The Piper reappeared, fingering his bladders nervously.

"The place of the Chief Piper is declared vacant," Gope said loudly. The piper pinched a pink bladder, which emitted a thin squeak.

"——since the former Chief Piper has been advanced in degree to a new office," continued Gope. A blue bladder moaned, lost amid yells and cheers.

"Let these air-bags be punctured," Gope cried. "I banish their rancid squeals forever from Rath-Gallion. Now, let all know: this former piper is now Chief Fool to this household. Let him wear the broken bladders as a sign of his office." There was a roar of laughter, glad cries, whistles. Volunteers leaped to rip the colored air-bags; they died in a final flurry of trills and flutters. A fool-slave tied the draggled instrument to the ex-piper's head.

I gave them *Mairzy Doats* and the former piper capered gingerly. Owner Gope roared with laughter. I followed with *The Dipsy Doodle* and the new fool, encouraged by success, leaped and grimaced, pirouetted, strutted, bladders bobbing; the crowd laughed until the tears flowed.

"A great day for Rath-Gallion," Gope shouted. "By the horns of the sea-god, I have gained a prince of pipers and a king of fools! I proclaim them to be ten-lash men, and both shall have places at table henceforth!"

The Fool and I followed up with three more numbers, then Gope let us squeeze into a space on a hard bench at the far side of the table. A table slave put loaded plates before us.

"Well done, good Drgon," he whispered. "Do not forget us slaves in your new honor."

"Don't worry," I said, sniffling the aroma of a big slab of roast beef. "I'll be sneaking down for a snack every night about Cinte-rise."

I looked around the barbarically decorated hall, seeing things in a new way. There's nothing like a little slavery to make a man appreciate even a modest portion of freedom. Everything I had thought I knew about Vallon had been wrong: the centuries that had passed had changed things—and not for the better. The old society that Foster knew was dead and buried. The old palaces and villas lay deserted, the spaceports unused. And the old system of memory-recording that Foster described was lost and forgotten.

I didn't know what kind of a cataclysm could have plunged the seat of a galactic empire back into feudal darkness—but it had happened.

So far I hadn't found a trace of Foster. My questions had gotten me nothing but blank stares. Maybe Foster hadn't made it; there could have been an accident in space. Or perhaps he was somewhere on the opposite side of the world. Vallon was a big planet and communications were poor. Maybe Foster was dead. I could live out a long life here and never find the answers.

I remembered my own disappointment at the breakdown of my illusions that night at Okk-Hamiloth. How much more heartbreaking must have been Foster's experience when and if he had arrived back here. And now we were both in the same boat: with our memories of the old Vallon and the dreary spectacle of the new providing plenty of food for bitterness.

And Foster's memory that I had been bringing him for a keepsake: what a laugh that was! Far from being a superfluous duplicate of a master trace to which he had expected easy access, my copy of the trace was now, with the vaults at Okk-Hamiloth sealed and forbidden, of the greatest possible importance to Foster—and there wasn't a machine left on the planet to play it on.

Well, I still meant to find Foster if it took me——

Owner Gope was humming loudly and tunelessly to himself. I knew the sign. I got ready to play again. Being Chief Piper probably wasn't going to be just one big bowl of cherries, but at least I wasn't a slave now. I had a long way to go, but I was making progress.

* * * *

Owner Gope and I got along well. He was a shrewd old duck and he liked having such an unusual piper on hand. He had heard from the Greymen, the free-lance police force, how I had landed at the deserted port. He warned me, in an oblique way, not to let word get out that I knew anything about old times in Vallon. The whole subject was tabu—especially the old capital city and the royal palaces themselves. Small wonder that my trespassing there had brought the Greymen down on me in doublequick time.

Gope took me with him everywhere he went: by air-car, ground-car, or formal river barge. There were still a lot of vehicles around, though few people seemed to know how to use them, simple as they were to operate. The air-cars were more useful, since they required no roads, but Gope preferred the ground cars. I think he liked the sensation of speed you got barrelling along a ninety or a hundred on one of the still-perfect roads that had originally been intended merely as scenic drives.

One afternoon several months after my promotion I dropped in at the kitchen. I was due to shove off with Owner Gope and his usual retinue for a visit to Bar-Ponderone, a big estate a hundred miles north of Rath-Gallion in the direction of Okk-Hamiloth. Sime and my other old cronies fixed me up with a healthy lunch, and warned me that it would be a rough trip; the stretch of road we'd be using was a favorite hang-out of road pirates.

"What I don't understand," I said, "is why Gope doesn't mount a couple of guns on the car and blast his way through the raiders. Every time he goes off the Estate he's taking his life in his hands."

The boys were shocked. "Even piratical renegades would never dream of taking a man's life, good Drgon," Sime said. "Every Owner, far and near, would band together to hunt such miscreants down. And their own fellows would abet the hunters! Nay, none is so low as to steal all a man's lives."

"The corsairs themselves know full well that in their next life they may be simple goodmen—even slaves," the Chief Wine-Pourer put in. "For you know, good Drgon, that when a member of a pirate band suffers the Change the others lead the newman to an Estate, that he may find his place...."

"How often do these Changes come along?" I asked.

"It varies greatly. Some men, of great strength and moral power, have been known to go on unchanged for three or four hundred years. But the ordinary man lives a life of eighty to one hundred years." Sime paused. "Or it may be less. A life of travail and strife can age one sooner than one of peace and retirement. Or unusual vicissitudes can shorten a life remarkably. A cousin of mine, who was marooned on the Great Stony Place in the southern half-world and who wandered for three weeks without more to eat or drink than a small bag of wine, underwent the Change after only fourteen years. When he was found his face was lined and his hair had greyed, in the way that presages the Change. And it was not long before he fell in a fit, as one does, and slept for a night and a day. When he awoke he was a newman: young and knowing nothing."

"Didn't you tell him who he was?"

"Nay!" Sime lowered his voice. "You are much favored of Owner Gope, good Drgon, and rightly. Still, there are matters a man talks not of——"

"A newman takes a name and sets out to learn whatever trade he can," put in the Carver of Roasts. "By his own skills he can rise...as you have risen, good Drgon."

"Don't you have memory machines—or briefing rods?" I persisted. "Little black sticks: you touch them to your head and——"

Sime made a motion in the air. "I have heard of these wands: a forbidden relic of the Black Arts——"

"Nuts," I said. "You don't believe in magic, do you, Sime? The rods are nothing but a scientific development by your own people. How you've managed to lose all knowledge of your own past——"

Sime raised his hands in distress. "Good Drgon, press us not in these matters. Such things are forbidden."

"Okay, boys. I guess I'm just nosy."

I went on out to the car and climbed in to wait for Owner Gope. Trying to learn anything about Vallon's history was about like questioning a village of Eskimos about the great trek over from Asia: they didn't know anything.

I had reached a few tentative conclusions on my own, however. My theory was that some sudden social cataclysm had broken down the system of personality reinforcement and memory recording that had given continuity to the culture. Vallonian society, based as it was on the techniques of memory preservation, had gradually disintegrated. Vallon was plunged into a feudal state resembling its ancient social pattern of fifty thousand years earlier, prior to the development of memory recording.

The people, huddled together on Estates for protection from real or imagined perils and shunning the old villas and cities as tabu—except for those included in Estates—knew nothing of space travel and ancient history. Like Sime, they had no wish even to speak of such matters.

I might have better luck with my detective work on a big Estate like Bar-Ponderone. I was looking forward to today's trip. I was cramped on Rath-Gallion. It was a small, poor Estate, covering only about twenty square miles, with half a dozen villages of farmers and craftsmen and the big house of Owner Gope. I had seen all of it—and it was a dead end.

Gope appeared, with Cagu and two other bodyguards, four dancing girls, and an extra-large gift hamper. They took their places and the driver started up and wheeled the heavy car out onto the highroad. I felt a pulse of excitement as we accelerated in the direction of Bar-Ponderone. Maybe at the big Estate I'd get news of Foster.

We were doing about fifty down a winding mountain road. I was in the front seat beside the driver, fiddling with my clarinet, and watching the road from the corner of my eye. I was wishing the driver's knuckles didn't show white on the speed control lever. He drove like a drunken spinster, fast but nervous. It wasn't entirely his fault: Gope insisted on plenty of speed. I was grateful for the auto steer mechanism; at least we couldn't drive over a cliff.

We rounded a curve, the wheels screeching from the driver's awkward, too-fast swing into the turn, and saw another car in the road a quarter of a mile ahead, not moving but parked—sideways. The driver hit the brakes.

Behind us Owner Gope yelled "Pirates! Don't slacken your pace, driver."

"But, but, Owner Gope——" the driver gasped.

"Ram the blackguards, if you must!" Gope shouted. "But don't stop!"

The girls in the back yelped in alarm. The flunkies set up a wail. The driver rolled his eyes, almost lost control, then gritted his teeth, reached out to switch off the anti-collision circuit and slam the speed control lever against the dash. I watched for two long heartbeats as we roared straight for the blockading car, then I slid over and grabbed for the controls. The driver held on, frozen. I reared back and clipped him on the jaw. He crumpled into his corner, mouth open and eyes screwed shut, as I hit the auto-steer override and worked the tiller. It was an awkward position for steering, but I preferred it to hammering in at ninety per.

The car ahead was still sitting tight, now a hundred yards away, now fifty. I cut hard to the right, toward the rising cliff face; the car backed to block me. At the last instant I whipped to the left, barreled past with half an inch to spare, rocketed along the ragged edge with the left wheel rolling on air, then whipped back into the center of the road.

"Well done!" yelled Cagu.

"But they'll give chase!" Gope shouted. "Assassins! Masterless swine!"

The driver had his eyes open now. "Crawl over me!" I barked. He mumbled and clambered past me and I slid into his seat, still clinging to the accelerator lever and putting up the speed. Another curve was coming up. I grabbed a quick look in the rear-viewer: the pirates were swinging around to follow us.

"Press on!" commanded Gope. "We're close to Bar-Ponderone; it's no more than five miles——"

"What kind of speed have they got?" I called back.

"They'll beat us easy," said Cagu cheerfully.

"What's the road like ahead?"

"A fair road, straight and true, now that we've descended the mountain," answered Gope.

We squealed through the turn and hit a straightaway. A curving road branched off ahead. "What's that?" I snapped.

"A winding trail," gasped the driver. "It comes on Bar-Ponderone, but by a longer way."

I gauged my speed, braked minutely, and cut hard. We howled up the steep slope, into a turn between hills.

Gope shouted, "What madness is this? Are you in league with the villains...?"

"We haven't got a chance on the straightaway," I called back. "Not in a straight speed contest." I whipped the tiller over, then back the other way, following the tight S-curves. We flashed past magnificent vistas of rugged peaks and rolling plains, but I didn't have time to admire the view. There were squeals from the odalisques in the rear seats, a gabble of excited talk. I caught a glimpse of our pursuers, just heading into the side road behind us.

"Any way they can head us off?" I yelled.

"Not unless they have confederates stationed ahead," said Gope, "but these pariahs work alone."

I worked the brake and speed levers, handled the tiller. We swung right, then left, higher and higher, then down a steep grade and up again. The pirate car rounded a turn, only a few hundred yards behind now. I scanned the road ahead, followed its winding course along the mountainside, through a tunnel, then out again to swing around the shoulder of the next peak.

"Pitch something out when we go through the tunnel!" I yelled. "Anything!"

"My cloak," cried Gope. "And the gift hamper."

One of the flunkies started to moan. The girls caught the fever, joined in with shrill lamentations.

"Silence!" roared Gope. "Lend a hand here, or by the sea-devil's beard you'll be jettisoned with the rest!"

We roared into the tunnel mouth. There was a blast of air as the rear deck cover opened. Gope and Cagu hefted the heavy gift hamper, tumbled it out, followed it with a cloak, a wine jug, assorted sandals, bracelets, fruit. Then we were back in the sunlight and I was fighting the curve. In the rear-viewer I saw the pirates burst from the tunnel mouth, Gope's black and yellow cloak spread over the canopy, smashed fruit spattered over it, the remains of the hamper dragging under the chassis. The car rocked and a corner of the cloak lifted, clearing the driver's view barely in time.

"Tough luck," I said. "We've got a long straight stretch ahead, and I'm fresh out of ideas...."

The other car gained. I held the speed bar against the dash but we were up against a faster car; it was a hundred yards behind us, then fifty, then pulling out to go alongside. I slowed imperceptibly, let him get his front wheels past us, then cut sharply. There was a clash of wheel fairings, and I fought the tiller as we rebounded from the heavier car. He crept forward, almost alongside again; shoulder to shoulder we raced at ninety-five down the steep grade....

I hit the brakes and cut hard to the left, slapped his right rear wheel, slid back. He braked too; that was a mistake. The heavy car lost traction, sliding. In slow motion, off-balanced in a skid, it rose on its nose, ploughing up a cloud of dust. The hamper whirled away, the cloak fluttered and was gone, then the pirate car seemed to float for an instant in air, before it dropped, wheels up, out of sight over the sheer cliff. We raced alone down the slope and out onto the wooded plain toward the towers of Bar-Ponderone.

A shout went up; Owner Gope leaned forward to pound my back. "By the nine eyes of the Hill Devil!" he bellowed, "masterfully executed! The prince of Pipers is a prince of Drivers too! This night you'll sit by my side at the ring-board at Bar-Ponderone in the rank of a hundred-lash Chief Driver, I swear it!"

"Compared with making a left turn off the Outer Drive at 5:15 on a Friday, that was nothing," I said. I held onto the tiller and tried breathing again. I'd been a fool to try to flip a heavier car—but it had worked. And now I'd gotten another promotion. I was doing okay.

"And let no man raise a charge of Assassination," Gope went on. "I'll not see so clever a Driver-Piper immured. I charge you all: say nothing of this! We'll consider that the rascals merely outdid themselves in their villainy."

That was the first I'd thought of that angle. To take a human life was still the one unthinkable crime in this world of immortals—because you took not just one, but all a man's lives. The punishment was walling up for life...but just one life. In my case one would be enough; I didn't have any spares. I had taken a bigger chance with Gope than I had with the pirates.

Life here was a series of gambles, but it looked like the chance-takers got ahead fast. My best bet was to stay on the make and calculate the odds when it was over.

* * * *

I spent the first day at Bar-Ponderone rubber-necking the tall buildings and keeping an eye open for Foster, on the off chance that I might pass him on the street. It was about as likely as running into an old high school chum from Perth Amboy among the body servants of the Shah of Afghanistan, but I kept looking.

By sunset I was no wiser than before. Dressed in the latest in Vallonian cape and ruffles, I was sitting with my buddy Cagu, Chief Bodyguard to Owner Gope, at a small table on the first terrace at the Palace of Merry-making, Bar-Ponderone's biggest community feasting hall. It looked like a Hollywood producer's idea of a twenty-first century night club, complete with nine dance floors on five levels, indoor pools, fountains, two thousand tables, musicians, girls, noise, colored lights, and food fit for an Owner. It was open to all fifty-lash goodmen of the Estate and to guests of equivalent rank. After the back-country life at Rath-Gallion it looked like the big time to me.

Cagu was a morose-looking old cuss, but good-hearted. His face was cut and scarred from a thousand encounters with other bodyguards and his nose had been broken so often that it was invisible in profile.

"Where do you manage to get in all the fights, Cagu?" I asked him. "I've known you for three months, and I haven't seen a blow struck in anger yet."

"Here." He grinned, showing me some broken front teeth. "Swell places, these big Estates, good Drgon; lotsa action."

"What do you do, get in street fights?"

"Nah. The boys show up down here, tank up, cruise around, you know."

"They start fights here in the dining room?"

"Sure. Good crowd here; lotsa laughs."

I picked up my drink, raised it to Cagu—and got it in my lap as somebody jostled my arm. I looked up. A battle-scarred thug stood over me.

"Who'sa punk, Cagu?" he said in a hoarse whisper. He probed at a back tooth with a silver pick, rolled his eyes from me to my partner.

Cagu stood up, and threw a punch to the other plug-ugly's paunch. He *oof!*ed, clinched, eyed me resentfully over Cagu's shoulder. Cagu pushed him away, held him at arm's length.

"Howsa boy, Mull?" he said. "Lay offa my sidekick; greatest little piper ina business, and a top driver too."

Mull rubbed his stomach, sat down beside me. "Ya losin' your punch, Cagu." He looked at me. "Sorry about that. I thought you was one of the guys." He signaled a passing waiter-slave. "Bring my friend a new suit. Make it snappy."

"Don't the customers kind of resent it when you birds stage a heavy-weight bout in the aisle?" I asked. "A drink in the lap is routine. It could happen in any joint in Manhattan. But a seven-course meal would be over-doing it."

"Nah; we move down inta the Spot." He waved a thumb in the general direction of somewhere else. He looked me over. "Where ya been, Piper? Your first time ina Palace?"

"Drgon's been travelling," said Cagu. "He's okay. Lemme tell ya the time these pirates pull one, see...."

Cagu and Mull swapped lies while I worked on my drinking. Although I hadn't learned anything on my day's looking around at Bar-Ponderone, it was still a better spot for snooping than Rath-Gallion. There were two major cities on the Estate and scores of villages. Somewhere among the population I might have better luck finding someone to talk history with... or someone who knew Foster.

"Hey!" growled Mull. "Look who's comin'."

I followed his gaze. Three thick-set thugs swaggered up to the table. One of them, a long-armed gorilla at least seven feet tall, reached out, took Cagu and Mull by the backs of their necks, and cracked their skulls together. I jumped up, ducked a hoof-like fist...and saw a beautiful burst of fireworks followed by soothing darkness.

* * * *

I fumbled in the dark with the lengths of cloth entangling my legs, sat up, cracked my head——

I groaned, freed a leg from the chair rungs, groped my way out from under the table. A Waiter-slave helped me up, dusted me off. The seven-foot lout lolling in a chair glanced my way, nodded.

"You shouldn't hang out with lugs like that Mull," he said. "Cagu told me you was just a piper, but the way you come outa that chair—" He shrugged, turned back to whatever he was watching.

I checked a few elbow and knee joints, worked my jaw, tried my neck: all okay.

"You the one that slugged me?" I asked.

"Huh? Yeah."

I stepped over to his chair, picked a spot, and cleared my throat. "Hey, you," I said. He turned, and I put everything I had behind a straight right to the point of the jaw. He went over, feet in the air, flipped a rail, and crashed down between two tables below. I leaned over the rail. A party of indignant Tally-clerks stared up at me.

"Sorry, folks," I said. "He slipped."

A shout went up from the floor some distance away. I looked. In a cleared circle two levels below a pair of heavy-shouldered men were slugging it out. One of them was Cagu. I watched, saw his opponent fall. Another man stepped in to take his place. I turned and made my way down to the ring-side.

Cagu exchanged haymakers with two more opponents before he folded and was hauled from the ring. I propped him up in a chair, fitted a drink into his fist, and watched the boys pound each other. It was easy to see why the scarred face was the sign of their craft; there was no defensive fighting whatever. They stood toe-to-toe and hit as hard as they could, until one collapsed. It wasn't fancy, but the fans loved it. Cagu came to after a while and filled me in on the fighters' backgrounds.

"So they're all top boys," he said. "But it ain't like in the old days when I was in my prime. I could've took any three of these bums. The only one maybe I woulda had a little trouble with is Torbu."

"Which one is he?"

"He ain't down there yet; he'll show to take on the last boys on their feet."

More gladiators pushed their way to the Spot, pulled off gaily-patterned cloaks and weskits, and waded in. Others folded, were dragged clear, revived to down another and shot cheer on the fray.

After an hour the waiting line had dwindled away to nothing. The two battlers on the Spot slugged, clinched, breathed hard, swung and missed; the crowd booed.

"Where's Torbu?" Cagu wondered.

"Maybe he didn't come tonight," I said.

"Sure, you met him; he knocked you under the table."

"Oh, him?"

"Where'd he go?"

"The last I saw he was asleep on the floor," I said.

"Hozzat?"

"I didn't much like him slugging me. I clobbered him one."

"Hey!" yelped Cagu. His face lit up. He got to his feet.

"Hold it," I said. "What's—?"

Cagu pushed his way through to the Spot, took aim, and floored the closest fighter, turned and laid out the other. He raised both hands above his head.

"Rath-Gallion gotta Champion," he bellowed. "Rath-Gallion takes on all comers." He turned, waved to me. "Our boy, Drgon, he—"

There was a bellow behind me, even louder than Cagu's. I turned, saw Torbu, his hair mussed, his face purple, pushing through the crowd.

"Jussa crummy minute," he yelled. "I'm the Champion around here—" He aimed a haymaker at Cagu; Cagu ducked.

"Our boy, Drgon, laid you out cold, right?" he shouted. "So now he's the champion."

"I wasn't set," bawled Torbu. "A lucky punch." He turned to the fans. "I'm tying my shoelace, see? And this guy—"

"Come on down, Drgon," Cagu called, waving to me again. "We'll show—" Torbu turned and slammed a roundhouse right to the side of Cagu's jaw; the old fighter hit the floor hard, skidded, lay still. I got to my feet. They pulled him to the nearest table, hoisted him into a chair. I made my way down to the little clearing in the crowd. A man bending over Cagu straightened, face white. I pushed him aside, grabbed the bodyguard's wrist. There was no pulse. Cagu was dead.

Torbu stood in the center of the Spot, mouth open. "What...?" he started. I pushed between two fans, went for him. He saw me, crouched, swung.

I ducked, uppercut him. He staggered back. I pressed him, threw lefts and rights to the body, ducked under his wild swings, then rocked his head left and right. He stood, knees together, eyes glazed, hands down. I measured him, right-crossed his jaw; he dropped like a log.

Panting, I looked across at Cagu. His scarred face, white as wax, was strangely altered now; it looked peaceful. Somebody helped Torbu to his feet, walked him to the ring-side. It had been a big evening. Now all I had to do was take the body home....

I went over to where Cagu was laid out on the floor. Shocked people stood staring. Torbu was beside the body. A tear ran down his nose, dripped on Cagu's face. Torbu wiped it away with a big scarred hand.

"I'm sorry, old friend," he said. "I didn't mean it."

I picked Cagu up and got him over my shoulder, and all the way to the far exit it was so quiet in the Palace of Merrymaking that I could hear my own heavy breathing and the tinkle of fountains and the squeak of my fancy yellow plastic shoes.

* * * *

In the bodyguards' quarters I laid Cagu out on a bunk, then faced the dozen scowling bruisers who stared down at the still body.

"Cagu was a good man," I said. "Now he's dead. He died like an animal…for nothing. That ended all his lives, didn't it, boys? How do you like it?"

Mull glowered at me. "You talk like we was to blame," he said. "Cagu was my compeer too."

"Whose pal was he a thousand years ago?" I snapped. "What was he—once? What were you? Vallon wasn't always like this. There was a time when every man was his own Owner—"

"Look, you ain't of the Brotherhood—" one thug started.

"So that's what you call it? But it's just another name for an old racket. A big shot sets himself up as dictator—"

"We got our Code," Mull said. "Our job is to stick up for the Owner…and that don't mean standing around listening to some japester callin' names."

"I'm not calling names," I snapped. "I'm talking rebellion. You boys have all the muscle and most of the guts in this organization. Why do you sit on your tails and let the boss live off the fat while you murder each other for the amusement of the patrons? I say let's pay him a call—right now. You had a birthright…once. But it's up to you to collect it…before some more of you go the way Cagu did."

There was an angry mutter. Torbu came in, face swollen. I backed up to a table, ready for trouble.

"Hold it, you birds," Torbu said. "What's goin' on?"

"This guy! He's talkin' revolt and treason," somebody said.

"He wants we should pull some rough stuff—on Owner Qohey hisself."

Torbu came up to me. "You're a stranger around Bar-Ponderone. Cagu said you was okay. You worked me over pretty good…and I got no hard feelin's; that's the breaks. But don't try to start no trouble here. We got our Code and our Brotherhood. We look out for each other; that's good enough for us. Owner Qohey ain't no worse than any other Owner…and by the Code, we'll stand by him!"

"Listen to me," I said. "I know the history of Vallon: I know what you were once and what you could be again. All you have to do is take over the power. I can lead you to the ship I came here in. There are briefing rods aboard, enough to show you—"

"That's enough," Torbu broke in. He made a cabalistic sign in the air. "We ain't gettin' mixed up in no tabu ghost-boats or takin' on no magicians and demons—"

"Hogwash! That tabu routine is just a gag to keep you away from the cities so you won't discover what you're missing—"

"I don't wanna hafta take you to the Greymen, Drgon," Torbu growled. "Leave it lay."

"These cities," I ploughed on. "They're standing there, empty, as perfect as the day they were built. And you live in these flea-bitten quarters, jammed inside the town walls, so the Greymen and renegades won't get you."

"You wanna run things here?" Mull put in. "Go see Qohey."

"Let's all go see Qohey!" I said.

"That's something you'll have to do alone," said Torbu. "You better move on, Drgon. I ain't turnin' you in; I know how you felt about Cagu gettin' killed and all—but don't push it too far."

I knew I was licked. They were as stubborn as a team of mules—and just about as smart.

Torbu motioned; I followed him outside.

"You wanna turn things upside-down, don't you? I know how it is; you ain't the first guy to get ideas. We can't help you. Sure, things ain't like they used to be here—and prob'ly they never were. But we got a legend: someday the Rthr will come back...and then the Good Time will come back too."

"What's the Rthr?" I said.

"Kinda like a big-shot Owner. There ain't no Rthr now. But a long time ago, back when our first lives started, there was a Rthr that was Owner of all Vallon, and everybody lived high, and had all their lives...." Torbu stopped, eyed me warily.

"Don't say nothing to nobody," he went on, "about what I been tellin' you. That's a secret of the Brotherhood. But it's kind of like a hope we got—that's what we're waitin' for, through all our lives. We got to do the best we can, and keep true to the Code and the Brotherhood...and someday the Rthr will come back...maybe."

"Okay," I said. "Dream on, big boy. And while you're treasuring your rosy dreams you'll get your brains kicked out, like Cagu." I turned away.

"Listen, Drgon. It's no good buckin' the system: it's too big for one guy...or even a bunch of guys...but—"

I looked up. "Yeah?"

"... if you gotta stick your neck out—see Owner Gope." Abruptly Torbu turned and pushed back through the door.

See Owner Gope, huh? Okay, what did I have to lose? I headed back along the corridor toward Owners' country.

* * * *

I stood in the middle of the deep-pile carpet in Gope's suite, trying to keep my temper hot enough to supply the gall I needed to bust in on an Owner in the middle of the night. He sat in his ceremonial chair and stared at me impassively.

"With your help or without it," I said, "I'm going to find the answers."

"Yes, good Drgon," he said, not bellowing for once. "I understand. But there are matters you know not of—"

"Just get me back into the spaceport, noble Gope. I have enough briefing rods aboard to prove my point—and a few other little items to boot."

"It's forbidden. Do you not understand—"

"I understand too much," I snapped.

He straightened, eyed me with a touch of the old ferocity. "Mind your tone, Drgon! I'm Owner—"

I broke in. "Do you remember Cagu? Maybe you remember him as a newman, young, handsome, like a god out of some old legend. You've seen him live his life. Was it a good life? Did the promise of youth ever get paid off?"

Gope closed his eyes. "Stop," he said. "This is bad, bad…."

"'And the deaths they died I have watched beside, and the lives they led were mine,'" I quoted. "Are you proud of them? And what about yourself? Don't you ever wonder what you might have been…back in the Good Time?"

"Who are you?" asked Gope, his eyes fixed on mine. "You speak Old Vallonian, you rake up the forbidden knowledge, and challenge the very Powers…." He got to his feet. "I could have you immured, Drgon. I could hand you to the Greymen, for a fate I shudder to name." He turned and walked the length of the room restlessly, then turned back to me and stopped.

"Matters stand ill with this fair world," he said. "Legend tells us that once men lived as the High Gods on Vallon. There was a mighty Owner, Rthr of all Vallon. It is whispered that he will come again—"

"Your legends are all true. You can take my word for that! But that doesn't mean some supernatural sugar daddy is going to come along and bail you out. And don't get the idea I think I'm the fabled answer to prayers. All I mean is that once upon a time Vallon was a good place to live and it could be again. Right now, it's like a land under an enchantment—and you sleeping beauties need waking up. Your cities and roads and ships are still here, intact. But nobody knows how to run them and you're all afraid to try. Who scared you off? Who started the rumors? What broke down the memory recording system? Why can't we all go to Okk-Hamiloth and use the Archives to give everybody back what he's lost—"

"These are dread words," said Gope.

"There must be somebody behind it. Or there was once. Who is he?"

Gope thought. "There is one man pre-eminent among us: the Great Owner, Owner of Owners: Ommodurad by name. Where he dwells I know not. This is a secret possessed only by his intimates."

"What does he look like? How do I get to see him?"

Gope shook his head. "I have seen him but once, closely cowled. He is a tall man, and silent. 'Tis said—" Gope lowered his voice, "—by his black arts he possesses all his lives. An aura of dread hangs about him—"

"Never mind that jazz," I said. "He's a man, like other men. Stick a knife between his ribs and you put an end to him, aura and all."

"I do not like this talk of death. Let the doer of evil deeds be immured; it is sufficient."

"First let's find him. How can I get close to him?"

"There are those Owners who are his confidants," said Gope, "his trusted agents. It is through them that we small Owners learn of his will."

"Can we enlist one of them?"

"Never. They are bound to him by ties of darkness, spells and incantations."

"I'm a fast man with a pair of loaded dice myself. It's all done with mirrors. Let's stick to the point, noble Gope. How can I work into a spot with one of these big shots?"

"Nothing easier. A Driver and Piper of such skills as your own can claim what place he chooses."

"How about bodyguarding? Suppose I could take a heavy named Torbu; would that set me in better with a new Owner?"

"Such is no place for a man of your abilities, good Drgon," Gope exclaimed. "True, 'tis a place most close to an Owner, but there is much danger in it. The challenge to a bodyguard involves the most bloody hand-to-hand combat, second only to the rigors of a challenge to an Owner himself."

"What's that?" I snapped. "Challenge an Owner?"

"Be calm, good Drgon," said Gope, staring at me incredulously. "No common man with his wits about him will challenge an Owner."

"But I could if I wanted to?"

"In sooth…if you have tired of life—of all your lives; 'tis as good a way to end them as another. But you must know, good Drgon: an Owner is a warrior trained in the skills of battle. None less than another such may hope to prevail."

I smacked my fist into my palm. "I should have thought of this sooner! The cooks cook for their places, the pipers pipe…and the best man wins. It figures that the Owners would use the same system. But what's the procedure, noble Gope? How do you get your chance to prove who can own the best?"

"It is a contest with naked steel. It is the measure and glory of an Owner that he alone stands ready to prove his quality against the peril of death itself." Gope drew himself up with pride.

"What about the bodyguards?" I asked. "They fight—"

"With their hands, good Drgon. And they lack skill with those. A death such as you described tonight—that is a rare and sorry accident."

"It showed up this whole grubby farce in its true colors. A civilization like that of Vallon—reduced to this."

"Still, it is sweet to live—by whatever rules——"

"I don't believe that...and neither do you. What Owner can I challenge? How do I go about it?"

"Give up this course, good Drgon—"

"Where's the nearest buddy of the Big Owner?"

Gope threw up his hands. "Here, at Bar-Ponderone. Owner Qohey. But—"

"And how do I call his bluff?"

Gope put a hand on my shoulder. "It is no bluff, good Drgon. It is long now since last Owner Qohey stood to his blade to protect his place, but you may be sure he has lost none of his skill. Thus it was he won his way to Bar-Ponderone, while lesser knights, such as myself, contented themselves with meaner fiefs."

"I'm not bluffing either, noble Gope," I said, stretching a point. "I was no harness-maker in the Good Time."

"It is your death—"

"Tell me how I offer the challenge...or I'll twist his nose in the main banqueting salon tomorrow night."

Gope sat down heavily, raised his hand, and let them fall. "If I tell you not, another will. But I will not soon find another Piper of your worth."

CHAPTER XV

Gaudy hangings of purple cut the light of the sun to a rich gloom in the enormous, high-vaulted Audience Hall. A rustling murmur was audible in the room as uneasy courtiers and suppliants fidgeted, waiting for the appearance of the Owner.

It had been two months since Gope had explained to me how a formal challenge to an Owner was conducted, and, as he pointed out, this was the only kind of challenge that would help. If I waylaid the man and cut him down, even in a fair fight, his bodyguards would repay the favor before I could establish the claim that I was their legitimate new boss.

I had spent three hours every day in the armory at Rath-Gallion, trading buffets with Gope and a couple of the bodyguards. The thirty-pound slab of edged steel had felt right at home in my hand that first day—for about a minute. I had the borrowed knowledge to give me all the technique I needed, but the muscle power for putting the knowledge into practice was another matter. After five minutes I was slumped against the wall, gulping air, while Gope whistled his sticker around my head and talked.

"You laid on like no piper, good Drgon. Yet have you much to learn in the matter of endurance."

—And he was at me again. I spent the afternoon back-pedaling and making wild two-handed swings and finally fell down—pooped. I couldn't have moved if Gope had had at me with a hot poker.

Gope and the others laughed til they cried, then hauled me away to my room and let me sleep. They rolled me out the next morning to go at it again.

As Gope said, there was no time to waste...and after two months of it I felt ready for anything. Gope had warned me that Owner Qohey was a big fellow, but that didn't bother me. The bigger they came, the bigger the target....

There was a murmur in a different key in the Audience Hall and tall gilt doors opened at the far side of the room. A couple of liveried flunkies scampered into view, then a seven-foot man-eater stalked into the hall, made his way to the dias, turned to face the crowd....

He was enormous: his neck was as thick as my thigh, his features chipped out of granite, the grey variety. He threw back his brilliant purple cloak from his shoulders and reached out an arm like an oak root for the ceremonial sword one of the flunkies was struggling with. He took the sword with its sheath, sat down, and stood it between his feet, his arms folded on top.

"Who has a grievance?" he spoke. The voice reverberated like the old Wurlitzer at the Rialto back home.

This was my cue. There he was, just asking for it. All I had to do was speak up. Owner Qohey would gladly oblige me. The fact that next to him Primo Carnera would look dainty shouldn't slow me down.

I cleared my throat with a thin squeak, and edged forward, not very far.

"I have one little item—" I started.

Nobody was listening. Up front a big fellow in a black toga was pushing through the crowd. Everybody turned to stare at him: there was a craning of necks. The crowd drew back from the dias leaving an opening. The man in black stepped into the clear, flung back the flapping garment from his right arm, and whipped out a long polished length of razor-edged iron. It was beginning to look like somebody had beaten me to the punch.

The newcomer stood there in front of Qohey with the naked blade making all the threat that was needed. Qohey stared at him for a long moment, then stood, gestured to a flunky. The flunky turned, cleared his throat.

"The place of Bar-Ponderone has been claimed!" he recited in a shrill voice. "Let the issue be joined!" He skittered out of the way and Qohey rose, threw aside his purple cloak and cowl, and stepped down. I pushed forward to get a better look.

The challenger in black tossed his loose garment aside, stood facing Qohey in a skin-tight jerkin and hose; heavy moccasins of soft leather were laced up the calf. He was magnificently muscled but Qohey towered over him like a tree, with a build that would have taken the Mr. Muscle Beach title any time he cared to try for it.

I didn't know whether to be glad or sad that the initiative had been taken out from under me. If the man in black won, I wondered would I then be able to step in in turn and take him on? He was a lot smaller than Qohey but there was always the chance....

Qohey unsheathed his fancy iron and whirled it like it was a lady's putter. I felt sorry for the smaller man, who was just standing, watching him. He really didn't have a chance.

I had got through to the fore rank by now. The challenger turned and I saw his face. I stopped dead, while fire bells clanged in my head.

The man in black was Foster.

* * * *

In dead silence Qohey and Foster squared off, touched their sword points to the floor in some kind of salute...and Qohey's slicer whipped up in a vicious cut. Foster leaned aside, just far enough, then countered with a flick that made Qohey jump back. I let out a long breath and tried swallowing. Foster was like a terrier up against a bull, but it didn't seem to bother him—only me. I had come light years to find him, just in time to see him get his head lopped off.

Qohey's blade flashed, cutting at Foster's head. Foster hardly moved. Almost effortlessly, it seemed, he interposed his heavy weapon between the attacking steel and himself. *Clash, clang!* Qohey hacked and chopped... and Foster played with him. Then Foster's arm flashed out and there was blood on Qohey's wrist. A gasp went up from the crowd. Now Foster took a step forward, struck...and faltered! In an instant Qohey was on him and the two men were locked, chest to chest. For a moment Foster held, then Qohey's weight told, and Foster reeled back. He tried to bring up the sword, seemed to struggle, then Qohey lashed out again. Foster twisted, took the blow awkwardly just above the hand guard, stumbled...and fell.

Qohey leaped to him, raised the sword—

I hauled mine half way out of its sheath and pushed forward.

"Let the man be put away from my sight," rumbled Qohey. He lowered his immense sword, turned, pushed aside a flunky who had bustled up with a wad of bandages. As he strode from the room a swarm of bodyguards fanned out between the crowd and Foster. I could see him clumsily struggling to rise, then I was shoved back, still craning for a glimpse. There was something wrong here; Foster had acted like a man suddenly half-paralyzed. Had Qohey doped him in some way?

The cordon stopped pushing, turned their backs to the crowd. I tugged at the arm of the man beside me.

"Did you see anything strange there?" I started.

He pulled free. "Strange? Yea, the mercy of our Lord Qohey! Instead of meting out death on the spot, our Owner was generous—"

"I mean about the fight." I grabbed his arm again to keep him from moving off.

"That the impudent rascal would dare to claim the place of Owner at Bar-Ponderone: there's wonder enough for any man," he snapped. "Unhand me, fellow!"

I unhanded him and tried to collect my wits. What now? I tapped a bodyguard on the shoulder. He whirled, club in hand.

"What's to be the fate of the man?" I asked.

"Like the Boss said: they're gonna immure the bum for his pains."

"You mean wall him up?"

"Yeah. Just a peep hole to pass chow in every day…so's he don't starve, see?" The bodyguard chuckled.

"How long—?"

"He'll last; don't worry. After the Change, Owner Qohey's got a new-man—"

"Shut up," another bruiser said.

The crowd was slowly thinning. The bodyguards were relaxing, standing in pairs, talking. Two servants moved about where the fight had taken place, making mystical motions in the air above the floor. I edged forward, watching them. They seemed to be plucking imaginary flowers. Strange….

I moved even farther forward to take a closer look, then saw a tiny glint…. A servant hurried across, made gestures. I pushed him aside, groped…and my fingers encountered a delicate filament of wire. I pulled it in, swept up more. The servants had stopped and stood watching me, muttering. The whole area of the combat was covered with the invisible wires, looping up in coils two feet high.

No wonder Foster had stumbled, had trouble raising his sword. He had been netted, encased in a mesh of incredibly fine tough wire…and in the dim light even the crowd twenty feet away hadn't seen it. Owner Qohey was a good man with the chopper but he didn't rely on that alone to hold onto his job.

I put my hand on my sword hilt, chewed my lower lip. I had found Foster…but it wouldn't do me—or Vallon—much good. He was on his way to the dungeons, to be walled up until the next Change. And it would be three months before I could legally make another try for Qohey's place. After seeing him in action I was glad I hadn't tried today. He wouldn't have needed any net to handle me.

I would have to spend the next three months working on my swordplay, and hope Foster could hold out. Maybe I could sneak a message—

A heavy blow on the back sent me spinning. Four bodyguards moved to ring me in, clubs in hand. They were strangers to me, but across the room I saw Torbu looming, looking my way....

"I saw him; he started to pull that fancy sword," said one of the guards.

"He was asking me questions—"

"Unbuckle it and drop it," another ordered me. "Don't try anything!"

"What's this all about?" I said. "I have a right to wear a Ceremonial Sword at an Audience—"

"Move in, boys!" The four men stepped toward me, the clubs came up. I warded off a smashing blow with my left arm, took a blinding crack across the face, felt myself going down—another blow, and another: killing ones....

Then I was aware of being dragged, endlessly, of voices barking sharp questions, of pain.... After a long time it was dark, and silent, and I slept.

* * * *

I groaned and the sound was dead, muffled. I put out a hand and touched stone on my right. My left elbow touched stone. I made an instinctive move to sit up and smacked my head against more stone. My new room was confining. Gingerly I felt my face...and winced at the touch. The bridge of my nose felt different: it was lower than it used to be, in spite of the swelling. I lay back and traced the pattern of pain. There was the nose—smashed flat—with secondary aches around the eyes. They'd be beautiful shiners, if I could see them. Now the left arm: it was curled close to my side and when I moved it I saw why: it wasn't broken, but the shoulder wasn't right, and there was a deep bruise above the elbow. My knees and shin, as far as I could reach, were caked with dried blood. That figured: I remembered being dragged.

I tried deep-breathing; my chest seemed to be okay. My hands worked. My teeth were in place. Maybe I wasn't as sick as I felt.

But where the hell was I? The floor was hard, cold. I needed a big soft bed and a little soft nurse and a hot meal and a cold drink....

Foster! I cracked my head again and flopped back, groaned some more. It still sounded pretty dead.

I swallowed, licked my lips, felt a nice split that ran well into the bristles. I had attended the Audience clean-shaven. Quite a few hours must have passed since then. They had taken Foster away to immure him, somebody said. Then the guards had tapped me, worked me over....

Immured! I got a third crack on the head. Suddenly it was hard to breathe. I was walled up, sealed away from the light, buried under the foundations of the giant towers of Bar-Ponderone. I felt their crushing weight....

I forced myself to relax, breathe deep. Being immured wasn't the same as being buried alive—not exactly. This was the method these latter-day Vallonians had figured out to end a man's life effectively…without ending all his lives. They figured to keep me neatly packaged here until my next Change, thus acquiring another healthy newman for the kitchen or the stables. They didn't know the only Change that would happen to me was death.

They'd have to feed me; that meant a hole. I ran my fingers along the rough stone, found an eight-inch square opening on the left wall, just under the ceiling. I reached through it, felt nothing but the solidness of its thick sides. How thick the wall was I had no way of determining.

I was feeling dizzy. I lay back and tried to think….

* * * *

I was awake again. There had been a sound. I moved, and felt something hit my chest.

I groped for it; it was a small loaf of hard bread. I heard the sound again and a second object thumped against me.

"Hey!" I yelled, "listen to me! I'll die in here. I'm not like the rest of you; I won't go through a Change. I'll rot here till I die…!"

I listened. The silence was absolute.

"Answer me!" I screamed. "You're making a mistake…!"

I gave up when my throat got raw. The people who dropped the bread through the little holes to the prisoners had heard a lot of yelling in their time. They didn't listen any more. I felt for the other item that had been pushed in to me. It was a water bottle made of tough plastic. I fumbled the cap off, took a swallow. It wasn't good. I tried the bread; it was tough, tasteless. I lay and chewed, and wondered what I was supposed to do about toilet facilities; it was an interesting problem. I could see it was going to be a great life, while it lasted. I laughed: a weak snort of despair.

As a world-saver I was a bust. I hadn't even been able to get around to bailing out my pal Foster after Qohey had booby-trapped him. I wondered where he was now. Sealed up in the next cubby-hole probably. But he hadn't answered my yells.

Yeah, mine had been a great idea, but it hadn't worked out. I had come a long, long way and now I was going to die in this reeking hole. I had a sudden vision of steaks uneaten, and life unlived. I would have been good for another few decades anyway—

And then I had another thought: if I never had them was it going to be because I hadn't tried? Abruptly I was planning. I would keep calm and use my head. I wouldn't wear myself out with screams and struggles. I'd figure the angles, use everything I had to make the best try I could.

First, to explore the tomb-like cell. It hurt to move, but that didn't matter. I felt over the walls, estimating size. My chamber was three feet wide, two feet high, and seven feet long. The walls were relatively smooth, except for a few mortar joints. The stones were big: eighteen inches or so by a couple of feet. I scratched at the mortar; it was rock hard.

I wondered how they'd gotten me in. Some of the stones must be newly placed...or else there was a door. I couldn't feel anything as far as my hands would reach. Maybe at the other end....

I tried to twist around: no go. The people who had built the cage knew just how to dimension it to keep the occupant oriented the way they wanted him. He was supposed to just lie quietly and wait for the bread and water to fall through the hole above his chest.

That was reason enough to change positions. If they wanted me to stay put I'd at least have the pleasure of defying the rules. And there just might be a reason why they didn't want me moving around.

I turned on my side, pulled my legs up, hugged them to my chest, worked my way down...and jammed. My skinned knees and shins didn't help any. I inched them higher, wincing at the pain, then braced my hands against the floor and roof and forced my torso toward my feet....

Still no go. The rough stone was shredding my back. I moved my knees apart; that eased the pressure a little. I made another inch.

I rested, tried to get some air. It wasn't easy: my chest was crushed between my thighs and the stone wall at my back. I breathed shallowly, wondering whether I should go back or try to push on. I tried to move my legs; they didn't like the idea. I might as well go on. It would be no fun either way and if I waited I'd stiffen up, while inactivity and no food and loss of blood would weaken me further every moment. I wouldn't do better next time—not even as well. This was the time. Now.

I set myself, pushed again. I didn't move. I pushed harder, scraping my palms raw against the stone. I was stuck—good. I went limp suddenly. Then I panicked, in the grip of claustrophobia. I snarled, rammed my hands hard against the floor and wall, and heaved—and felt my lacerated back slip along the stone, sliding on a lubricating film of blood. I pushed again, my back curved, doubled; my knees were forced up beside my ears. I couldn't breathe at all now and my spine was breaking. It didn't matter. I might as well break it, rip off all the hide, bleed to death; I had nothing to lose. I shoved again, felt the back of my head grate; my neck bent, creaking...then I was through, stretching out to flop on my back, gasping, my head where my feet had been. Score one for our side.

* * * *

It took a long time to get my breath back and sort out my various abrasions. My back was worst then my legs and hands. There was a messy spot on the back of my head and sharp pains shot down my spine, and I was getting tired of breathing through my mouth instead of my smashed nose. Other than that I'd never felt better in my life. I had plenty of room to relax in, I could breathe. All I had to do was rest, and after a while they'd drop some more nice bread and water in to me....

I shook myself awake. There was something about the absolute darkness and silence that made my mind want to curl up and sleep, but there was no time for that. If there had been a stone freshly set in mortar to seal the chamber after I had been stuffed inside, this was the time to find it—before it set too hard. I ran my hands over the wall, found the joints. The mortar was dry and hard in the first; in the next...under my fingernail soft mortar crumbled away. I traced the joint; it ran around a twelve-by-eighteen-inch stone. I raised myself on my elbows, settled down to scratching at it.

Half an hour later I had ten bloody tips and a half-inch groove dug out around the stone. It was slow work and I couldn't go much farther without a tool of some sort. I felt for the water bottle, took off the cap, tried to crush it. It wouldn't crush. There was nothing else in the cell.

Maybe the stone would move, mortar and all, if I shoved hard enough. I set my feet against the end wall, my hands against the block, and strained until the blood roared in my ears. No use. It was planted as solid as a mother-in-law in the spare bedroom.

I was lying there, just thinking about it, when I became aware of something. It wasn't a noise, exactly. It was more like a fourth-dimensional sound heard inside the brain...or the memory of one.

But my next sensation was perfectly real. I felt four little feet walking gravely up my belly toward my chin.

It was my cat, Itzenca.

CHAPTER XVI

For a while I toyed with the idea of just chalking it up as a miracle. Then I decided it would be a nice problem in probabilities. It had been seven months since we had parted company on the pink terrace at Okk-Hamiloth. Where would I have gone if I had been a cat? And how could I have found me—my old pal from earth?

Itzenca exhaled a snuffle in my ear.

"Come to think of it, the stink is pretty strong, isn't it? I guess there's nobody on Vallon with quite the same heady fragrance. And what with the close quarters here, the concentration of sweat, blood, and you-name-it must be pretty penetrating."

Itz didn't seem to care. She marched around my head and back again, now and then laid a tentative paw on my nose or chin, and kept up a steady rumbling purr. The feeling of affection I had for that cat right then was close to being one of my life's grand passions. My hands roamed over her scrawny frame, fingered again the khaffite collar I had whiled away an hour in fashioning for her aboard the lifeboat—

My head hit the stone wall with a crack I didn't even notice. In ten seconds I had released the collar clasp, pulled the collar from Itzenca's neck, thumbed the stiff khaffite out into a blade about ten inches long, and was scraping at the mortar beyond my head at fever heat.

* * * *

They had fed me three times by the time the groove was nine inches deep on all sides of the block; and the mortar had hardened. But I was nearly through, I figured. I took a rest, then made another try at loosening the block. I thrust the blade into the slot, levered gently at the stone. If it was only supported on one edge now, as it would be if it were a little less than a foot thick, it should be about ready to go. I couldn't tell.

I put down my scraper, got into position, and pushed. I wasn't as strong as I had been; there wasn't much force in the push. Again I rested and again I tried. Maybe there was only a thin crust of mortar still holding; maybe one more ounce of pressure would do it. I took a deep breath, strained…and felt the block shift minutely.

Now! I heaved again, teeth gritted, drew back my feet, and thrust hard. The stone slid out with a grating sound, dropped half an inch. I paused to listen: all quiet. I shoved again, and the stone dropped with a heavy thud to the floor outside. With no loss of time I pushed through behind it, felt a breath of cooler air, got my shoulders free, pulled my legs through…and stood, for the first time in how many days….

I had already figured my next move. As soon as Itzenca had stepped out I reached back in, groped for the water bottle, the dry crusts I had been saving, and the wad of bread paste I had made up. I reached a second time for a handful of the powdered mortar I had produced, then lifted the stone. I settled it in place, using the hard bread as supports, then packed the open joint with gummy bread. I dusted it over with dry mortar, then carefully swept up the debris—as well as I could in the total darkness. The bread-and-water man would have a light and he was due in half an hour or so—as closely as I had been able to estimate the time of his regular round. I didn't want him to see anything out of the ordinary. I was counting on finding Foster filed away somewhere in the stacks, and I'd need time to try to release him.

I moved along the corridor, counting my steps, one hand full of bread-crumbs and stone dust, the other feeling the wall. There were narrow side branches every few feet: the access ways to the feeding holes. Forty-one paces from my slot I came to a wooden door. It wasn't locked, but I didn't open it. I wasn't ready to use it yet.

I went back, passed my hole, continued nine paces to a blank wall. Then I tried the side branches. They were all seven-foot stubs, dead ends; each had the eight-inch holes on either side. I called Foster's name softly at each hole…but there was no answer. I heard no signs of life, no yells or heavy breathing. Was I the only one here? That wasn't what I had figured on. Foster had to be in one of these delightful bedrooms. I had come across the universe to see him and I wasn't going to leave Bar-Ponderone without him.

It was time to get ready for the bread man. I had a choice of trying to get back into my hole and replacing the block, or of hiding in one of the side branches. I thought it over for a couple of microseconds and decided against getting back in my tomb. If there were as many vacancies here as I guessed, I'd be safe in any one of the side passages but my own.

I groped my way into a convenient hidey-hole, Itzenca at my heels. With half a year's experience at dodging humans behind her, she could be trusted not to show at the crucial moment, I figured. I had just jettisoned my handful of trash in the backmost corner of the passage when there was a soft grating sound from the door. I flattened myself against the wall. I'd know in a second or two how observant the keeper was.

A light splashed on the floor; it must have been dim but seemed to my eyes like the blaze of noon. Soft footsteps sounded. I held my breath. A man in bodyguard's trappings, basket in hand, moved past the entry of the branch where I stood, went on. I breathed again. Now all I had to do was keep an eye on the feeder, watch where he stopped. I stepped to the corridor, risked a glance, saw him entering a branch far down the corridor. As he disappeared I made it three branches farther along, ducked out of sight.

I heard him coming back. I flattened myself. He went by me, opened the door. It closed behind him and the darkness and silence settled down once more. I stood where I was, feeling like a guy who's just showed up for a party…on the wrong day.

The bread man had stopped at one cell only—mine. Foster wasn't here.

* * * *

It was a long wait for the next feeding but I put the time to use. First I had a good nap; I hadn't been getting my rest while I scratched my way out of my nest. I woke up feeling better and started thinking about the next move. The bodyguard who brought the food was the first item: I had had to get a set of clothes somewhere and he'd be the easiest source to tap. If my mental clock was right it was about time—

The door creaked, and I did a fast fade down a side branch. The guard shuffled into view; now was the time. I moved out—quietly, I thought, and he whirled, dropped the load and bottle, and fumbled at his club hilt. I didn't have a club to slow me down. I went at him, threw a beautiful right, square to the mouth. He went over backwards, with me on top. I heard his head hit with a sound like a length of rubber hose slapping a grapefruit. He didn't move.

I pulled the clothes off him, struggled into them. They didn't fit too well and they probably smelled gamey to anybody who hadn't spent a week where I had, but details like those didn't count anymore. I tore his sash into strips and tied him. He wasn't dead—quite, but I had reason to know that any yelling he did was unlikely to attract much attention. I hoped he'd enjoy the rest and quiet until the next feeding time. By then I expected to be long gone. I lifted the door open and stepped out into a dimly-lit corridor.

With Itzenca abreast of me I moved along in absolute stillness, passed a side corridor, came to a heavy door: locked. We retraced our steps, went down the side hall, found a flight of worn steps, followed them up two flights, and emerged in a dark room. A line of light showed around a door. I went to it, peered through the crack. Two men in stained kitchen-slave tunics fussed over a boiling cauldron. I pushed through the door.

The two looked up, startled. I rounded a littered table, grabbed up a heavy soup ladle, and skulled the nearest cook just as he opened up to yell. The other one, a big fellow, went for a cleaver. I caught him in two jumps, laid him out cold beside his pal.

I found an apron, ripped it up, and tied and gagged the two slaves, then hauled them into a storeroom. I was stacking Vallonians away like a squirrel storing nuts.

I came back into the kitchen. It was silent now. The room reeked of sour soup. A stack of unpleasantly familiar loaves stood by the oven. I gave them a kick that collapsed the pile as I passed to pick up a knife. I hacked tough slices from a cold haunch of Vallonian mutton, threw one to Itzenca across the table, and sat and gnawed the meat while I tried to think through my plans.

Owner Qohey was a big man to tackle but he was the one with the answers. If I could make my way to his apartment and if I wasn't stopped before I'd forced the truth out of him, then I might get to Foster and tell him that if he had the memory playback machine I had the memory, if it hadn't been filched from the bottom of a knapsack aboard a lifeboat parked at Okk-Hamiloth.

Four 'if's' and a 'might'—but it was something to shoot at. My first move would be to locate Qohey's quarters, somewhere here in the Palace, and get inside. My bodyguard's outfit was as good a disguise as any for the attempt.

I finished off my share of the meat and got to my feet. I'd have to find a place to clean myself up, shave—

The rear door banged open and two bodyguards came through it, talking loudly, laughing.

"Hey, cook! Set out meat for—"

The heavy in the lead stopped short, gaping at me. I gaped back. It was Torbu.

"Drgon! How did you…?" He trailed off.

The other bodyguard came past him, looked me over. "You're no Brother of the Guard—" he started.

I reached for the cleaver the kitchen-slave had left on the table, backed against a tall wall cupboard. The bodyguard unlimbered his club.

"Hold it, Blon," said Torbu. "Drgon's okay." He looked at me. "I kind of figured you for done for, Drgon. The boys worked you over pretty good."

"Yeah," I returned, "and thanks for your help in stopping it."

"This is the miscreant we immured!" Blon burst out. "Take him!"

Torbu shifted. "Hold it a minute," he said. He looked uncomfortable.

"Listen, you two!" I said. "You claim to believe in the system around here. You think it's a great life, all fair play and no holds barred and plenty of goodies for the winner. I know, it was tough about Cagu, but that's life, isn't it? But what about the business I saw in that Audience Hall? You guys try not to think about that angle, is that it?"

"The noble Owner's gotta right—" Blon started.

"I didn't like the caper with the wires, Blon," said Torbu. "You didn't either; neither did most of the boys—"

"And I don't remember getting much of a show myself," I said. "There are a couple of your buddies I plan to look up when I have some free time—"

"I didn't lay a hand on you, Drgon," said Torbu. "I didn't want no part of that."

"It was the Owner's orders," said Blon. "What was I gonna go, tell him——"

"Never mind," I said. "I'll tell him myself. That's all I want: just a short interview with the Owner—minus the wire nets."

"Wow…" drawled Torbu, "yeah, that'd be a bout." He turned to Blon. "This guy's got a punch, Blon. He don't look so hot but he could swap buffets with the Fire Drgon he's named after. If he's that good with a long blade—"

"Just lend me one," I said, "and show me the way to his apartment."

"The noble Owner'll cut this clown to ribbons in two minutes flat," said Blon.

"Let's get the boys."

"How could we explain it afterwards to the noble Owner?" said Blon. "He ain't gonna think much of guys he thought was immured nice and safe turnin' up in his bedchamber…armed."

"We're Brothers of the Guard," said Torbu. "We ain't got much but we got our Code. It don't say nothing about wires. If we don't back up our oath to the Brotherhood we ain't no better than slaves." He turned to me. "Come on, Drgon. We'll take you to the Guardroom so you can clean up and put on a good blade. If you're gonna lose all your lives at once, you wanna do it right."

* * * *

Torbu watched as the boys belted and strapped me into a guardsman's fighting outfit. I had made him uneasy, maybe even started him thinking. If I could last—just those 'two minutes flat'—before Owner Qohey killed me, then he'd collect his bet, I'd be out of his hair, and he could go back to being Torbu, a plain tough guy with a Code he could still believe in. And if I won....

I felt better in the clean trappings of tough leather and steel. Torbu led the way and fifteen bodyguards followed, like a herd of trolls. There were few palace servants out at this hour; those who saw us gaped from a safe distance and went on about their business. We crossed the empty Audience Hall, climbed a wide staircase, went along a spacious corridor hung with rich brocades and carpeted in deep-pile silk, with soft lights glowing around ornate doors.

We stopped before a great double door. Two guards in dress purple sauntered over to see what it was all about. Torbu clued them in. They hesitated, looked us over....

"We're goin' in, rookie," said Torbu. "Open up." They did.

I pushed past Torbu into a room whose splendor made Gope's state apartment look like a four-dollar motel. Bright Cintelight streamed through tall windows, showed me a wide bed and somebody in it. I went to it, grabbed the bedclothes, and hauled them off onto the floor. Owner Qohey sat up slowly—seven feet of muscle. He looked at me, glanced past me to the foremost of my escort....

He was out of the bed like a tiger, coming straight for me. There was no time to fumble with the sword. I went to meet him, threw all my weight into a right haymaker and felt it connect. I plunged past, whirled.

Qohey was staggering...but still on his feet. I had hit him with everything I had, nearly broken my fist...and he was still standing. I couldn't let him rest. I was after him, slammed a hard punch to the kidneys, caught him across the jaw as he turned, drove a left and right into his stomach——

A girder fell from the top of the Golden Gate Bridge and shattered every bone in my body. There was a booming like heavy surf, and I was floating in it, dead. Then I was in Hell, being prodded by red-hot tridents.... I blinked my eyes. The roaring was fading now. I saw Qohey, leaning against the foot of the bed, breathing heavily. I had to get him.

I got my feet under me, stood up. My chest was caved in and my left arm belonged to somebody else. Okay; I still had my right. I made it over to Qohey, maneuvered into position. He didn't look at me; he seemed to be having trouble breathing; those gut punches had gotten to him. I picked a spot just behind the right ear, reared back, and threw a trip-hammer punch with my shoulder and legs behind it. I felt the jaw go. Qohey jumped the foot-board and piled onto the floor like a hundred-car freight hitting an open switch. I sat down on the edge of the bed and sucked in air and tried to ignore the whirling lights that were closing in.

After awhile I noticed Torbu standing in front of me with the cat under one arm. Both of them were grinning at me. "Any orders, Owner Drgon?"

I found my voice. "Wake him up and prop him in a chair. I want to talk to him."

Ex-Owner Qohey didn't much like the idea but after Torbu and a couple of other strong-arm lads had explained the situation to him in sign language he decided to cooperate.

"Get off his head, Mull," Torbu said. "And untwist that rope, Blon. Owner Drgon wants him in a conversational mood. You guys are gonna make him feel self-conscious."

I had been feeling over my ribs, trying to count how many were broken and how many just bent. Qohey's punch was a lot like the kick of a two-ton ostrich. He was looking at me now, eyes wild.

"Qohey, I want to ask you a few questions. If I don't like the answers, I'll see if I can't find quarters for you in the basement annex. I just left a cozy room there myself. There's no view to speak of but it's peaceful."

Qohey grunted something. He was having trouble talking around his broken jaw.

"The fellow in black," I said, "the one who claimed your place as Owner. You netted him and had your bully boys haul him off somewhere. I want to know where."

Qohey grunted again.

"Hit him, Torbu," I said. "It will help his enunciation." Torbu kicked the former Owner in the shin. Qohey jumped and glowered at him.

"Call off your dogs," he mumbled. "You'll not find the upstart you seek here."

"Why not?"

"I sent him away."

"Where?"

"To that place from which you and your turncoat crew will never fetch him back."

"Be more specific."

Qohey spat.

"Torbu didn't much like that crack about turncoats," I said. "He's eager to show you how little. I advise you to talk fast and plain, before you lose a whole raft of lives."

"Even these swine would never dare—" I took out the needle-pointed knife I was wearing as part of my get-up. I put the point against Qohey's throat and pushed gently until a trickle of crimson ran down the thick neck.

"Talk," I said quietly, "or I'll cut your throat myself."

Qohey had shrunk back as far as he could in the heavy chair.

"Seek him then, assassin," he sneered. "Seek him in the dungeons of the Owner of Owners."

"Keep talking," I prompted.

"The Great Owner commanded that the slave be brought to him…at the Palace of Sapphires by the Shallow Sea."

"Has this Owners' Owner got a name? How'd he hear about him?"

"Lord Ommodurad," Qohey's voice grated out. He was watching Torbu's foot. "There was that about the person of the stranger that led me to inform him."

"When did he go?"

"Yesterday."

"You know this Sapphire Palace, Torbu?"

"Sure," he answered. "But the place is tabu; it's crawlin' with demons and warlocks. The word is, there's a curse on the—"

"Then I'll go in alone," I said. I put the knife away. "But first I've got a call to make at the spaceport at Okk-Hamiloth."

"Sure, Owner Drgon. The port's easy. Some say it's kind of haunted too but that's just a gag; the Greymen hang out there."

"We can take care of the Greymen," I said. "Get fifty of your best men together and line up some air-cars. I want the outfit ready to move out in half an hour."

"What about this chiseler?" asked Torbu.

"Seal him up until I get back. If I don't make it, I know he'll understand."

CHAPTER XVII

It was not quite dawn when my task force settled down on the smooth landing pad beside the lifeboat that had brought me to Vallon. It stood as I had left it seven earth-months before: the port open, the access ladder extended, the interior lights lit. There weren't any spooks aboard but they had kept visitors away as effectively as if there had been. Even the Greymen didn't mess with ghost-boats. Somebody had done a thorough job of indoctrination on Vallon.

"You ain't gonna go inside that accursed vessel, are you, Owner Drgon?" asked Torbu, making his cabalistic sign in the air. "It's manned by gobblins—"

"That's just propaganda. Where my cat can go, I can go. Look."

Itzenca scampered up the ladder, and had disappeared inside the boat by the time I took the first rung. The guards gawked from below as I stepped into the softly lit lounge. The black-and-gold cylinder that was Foster's memory lay in the bag I had packed and left behind, months before; with it was the other, plain one: Ammaerln's memory. Somewhere in Okk-Hamiloth must be the machine that would give these meaning. Together Foster and I would find it.

I found the .38 automatic lying where I had left it. I picked up the worn belt, strapped it around me. My Vallonian career to date suggested it would be a bright idea to bring it along. The Vallonians had never developed any personal armament to equal it. In a society of immortals knives were considered lethal enough for all ordinary purposes.

"Come on, cat," I said. "There's nothing more here we need."

Back on the ramp I beckoned my platoon leaders over.

"I'm going to the Sapphire Palace," I said. "Anybody that doesn't want to go can check out now. Pass the word."

Torbu stood silent for a long moment, staring straight ahead.

"I don't like it much, Owner," he said. "But I'll go. And so will the rest of 'em."

"There'll be no backing out, once we shove off," I said. "And by the way—" I jacked a round into the chamber of the pistol, raised it, and fired the shot into the air. They all jumped. "If you ever hear that sound, come a-running."

The men nodded, turned to their cars. I picked up the cat and piled into the lead vehicle next to Torbu.

"It's a half-hour run," he said. "We might run into a little Greyman action on the way. We can handle 'em."

We lifted, swung to the east, barrelled along at low altitude.

"What do we do when we get there, boss?" said Torbu.

"We play it by ear. Let's see how far we can get on pure gall before Ommodurad drops the hanky."

* * * *

The palace lay below us, rearing blue towers to the twilit sky like a royal residence in the Munchkin country. Beyond it, sunset colors reflected from the silky surface of the Shallow Sea. The timeless stones and still waters looked much as they had when Foster set out to lose his identity on earth, three thousand years before. But its magnificence was lost on these people. The hulking crew around me never paused to wonder about the marvels wrought by their immortal ancestors—themselves. Stolidly, they lived their feudal lives in dismal contrast with the monuments all about them.

I turned to my cohort of hoodlums. "You boys claim it's the demons and warlocks that keep the whole of Vallon at arm's length from this place. In that case there's no protocol for a new Owner's reception at the Blue Palace. A guy with a little luck and even less of a memory than usual could skip the goblins and play it good-natured but dumb: show up at the Palace grounds, out of common politeness to the Top Dog, to pay his respects. Anything wrong with that?"

"What if they rush us first…before we got time to go into the act?" said somebody in the mob.

"That's where the luck comes in," I said. "Anybody else?"

Torbu looked around at his henchmen. There was some shrugging of shoulders, a few grunts. He looked at me. "You do the figurin', Owner," he said. "The boys will back your play."

We were dropping toward the wide lawns now and still no opposition showed itself. Then the towering blue spires were looming over us, and we saw men forming up behind the blue-stained steel gates of the Great Pavilion.

"A reception committee," I said. "Hold tight, fellas. Don't start anything. The further in we get peaceably, the less that leaves to do the hard way."

The cars settled down gently, well-grouped, and Torbu and I climbed out. As quickly as the other boats disgorged their men, ranks were closed, and we moved off toward the gates. Itzenca, as mascot, brought up the rear. Still no excitement, no rush by the Palace guards. Had too many centuries of calm made them lackadaisical, or did Ommodurad use a brand of visitor-repellent we couldn't see from here?

We made it to the gate…and it opened.

"In we go," I said, "but be ready…."

The uniformed men inside the compound, obviously chosen for their beef content, kept their distance, looked at us questioningly. We pulled up on a broad blue-paved drive and waited for the next move. About now somebody should stride up to us and offer the key to the city—or something. But there seemed to be a hitch. It was understandable. After all there hadn't been any callers dropping cards here for about 2900 years.

It was a long five minutes before a hard case in a beetle-backed carapace of armor and a puffy pink cape bustled down the palace steps and came up to us.

"Who comes in force to the Sapphire Palace?" he demanded, glancing past me at my team-mates.

"I'm Owner Drgon, fellow," I barked. "These are my honor guard. What provincial welcome is this, from the Great Owner to a loyal liege-man?"

That punctured his pomposity a little. He apologized—in a half-hearted way—mumbled something about arrangements, and beckoned over a couple of side-men. One of them came over and spoke to Torbu, who looked my way, hand on dagger hilt.

"What's this?" I said. "Where I go, my men go."

"There is the matter of caste," said my pink-caped greeter. "Packs of retainers are not ushered *en masse* into the presence of Lord Ommodurad, Owner of Owners."

I thought that one over and failed to come up with a plausible loophole.

"Okay, Torbu," I said. "Keep the boys together and behave yourselves. I'll see you in an hour. Oh, and see that Itzenca gets made comfy."

The beetle man snapped a few orders, then waved me toward the palace with the slightest bow I ever saw. A six-man guard kept me company up the steps and into the Great Pavilion.

I guess I expected the usual velvet-draped audience chamber or barbarically splendid Hall, complete with pipers, fools, and ceremonial guards. What I got was an office, about sixteen by eighteen, blue-carpeted and tasteful…but bare-looking. I stopped in front of a block of blue-veined grey marble with a couple of quill pens in a crystal holder and, underneath, leg room for a behemoth, who was sitting behind the desk.

He got to his feet with all the ponderous mass of Nero Wolfe but a lot more agility and grace. "You wish?" he rumbled.

"I'm Owner Drgon, ah…Great Owner," I said. I'd planned to give my host the friendly-but-dumb routine. I was going to find the second part of the act easy. There was something about Ommodurad that made me feel like a mouse who'd just changed his mind about the cheese. Qohey had been big, but this guy could crush skulls as most men pinch peanut hulls, and in his eyes was the kind of remote look that came of three millenia of not even having to mention the power he asserted.

"You ignore superstition," observed the Big Owner. He didn't waste many words, it seemed. Gope had said he was the silent type. It wasn't a bad lead; I decided to follow it.

"Don't believe in 'em," I said.

"To your business then," he continued. "Why?"

"Just been chosen Owner at Bar-Ponderone," I said. "Felt it was only fitting that I come and do obeisance before Your Grace."

"That expression is not used."

"Oh." This fellow had a disconcerting way of not getting sucked in. "Lord Ommodurad?"

He nodded just perceptibly, then turned to the foremost of the herd who had brought me in. "Quarters for the guest and his retinue." His eyes had already withdrawn, like the head of a Galapagos turtle into its enormous shell, in contemplation of eternal verities. I piped up again.

"Ah, pardon me…." The piercing stare of Ommodurad's eyes was on me again. "There was a friend of mine—," I gulped, "swell guy, but impulsive. It seems he challenged the former Owner of Bar-Ponderone…."

Ommodurad did no more than twitch an eye-brow but suddenly the air was electric. His stare didn't waver by a millimeter but the lazy slouch of the six guards had altered to sprung steel. They hadn't moved but I felt them now all around me and not a foot away. I had a sinking feeling that I'd gone too far.

"—so I thought maybe I'd crave Your Excellency's help, if possible, to locate my pal," I finished weakly. For an interminable minute the Owner of Owners bored into me with his eyes. Then he raised a finger a quarter of an inch. The guards relaxed.

"Quarters for the guest and his retinue," repeated Ommodurad. He withdrew then…without moving. I was dismissed.

I went quietly, attended by my hulking escort.

I tried hard not to let my expression show any excitement, but I was feeling plenty.

Ommodurad was close-mouthed for a reason. I was willing to bet that he had his memories of the Good Time intact.

Instead of the debased modern dialect that I'd heard everywhere since my arrival, Ommodurad spoke flawless Old Vallonian.

* * * *

It was 27 o'clock and the Palace of Sapphires was silent. I was alone in the ornate bed chamber the Great Owner had assigned me. It was a nice room but I wouldn't learn anything staying in it. Nobody had said I was confined to quarters. I'd do a little scouting and see what I could pick up, if anything. I slung on the holster and .38 and slid out of the darkened chamber into the scarcely lighter corridor beyond. I saw a guard at the far end; he ignored me. I headed in the opposite direction.

None of the rooms was locked. There was no arsenal at the Palace and no archives that lesser folk than the Great Owner could use with profit. Everything was easy of access. I guessed that Ommodurad rightly counted on indifference to keep snoopers away. Here and there guards eyed me as I passed along but they said nothing.

I saw again by Cintelight the office where Ommodurad had received me, and near it an ostentatious hall with black onyx floor and ceiling, gold hangings, and ceremonial ring-board. But the center of attraction was the familiar motif of the concentric circles of the Two Worlds, sketched in beaten gold across the broad wall of black marble behind the throne. Here the idea had been elaborated on. Outward from both the inner and outer circles flamed the waving lines of a sunburst. At dead center, a boss, like a sword hilt in form, chased in black and gold, erupted a foot from the wall. It was the first time I'd seen the symbol since I'd arrived on Vallon. I found it strangely exciting—like a footprint in the sand.

I went on, toured the laundry and inspected pantries large and small and caught a whiff of stables. The palace was asleep; few of its occupants noticed me, and those who did hung back, silent. It looked as if the Great Owner had given orders to let me roam freely. Somehow I didn't find that comforting.

Then I came into a purple-vaulted hall and saw a squad of guards, the same six who'd kept me such close company earlier in the day. They were drawn up at parade rest, three on each side of a massive ivory door. Somebody lived in safety and splendor on the other side.

Six sets of hard eyes turned my way. It was too late to duck back out of sight. I trotted up to the first of the row of guards. "Say, fella," I stage-whispered, "where's the ah—you know."

"Every bed chamber is equipped," he said gruffly, raising his sword and fingering its tip lovingly.

"Yeah? I never noticed." I moved off, looking chastened. If they thought I was a kewpie, so much the better. I was a mouse in cat country here and I wasn't ready to fake a *meow*—not yet.

On the ground floor I found Torbu and his cohort quartered in a barrack-room off the main entry hall.

"We're still in enemy territory," I reminded Torbu. "I want every man ready."

"No fear, boss," said Torbu. "All my bullies got an eye on the door and a hand on a knife-hilt."

"Have you seen or heard anything useful?"

"Naw. These local dullards fall dumb at the first query."

"Keep your ears cocked. I want at least two men awake and on the alert all night."

"You bet, noble Drgon."

I judged distances carefully as I went back up the two flights to my own room. Inside I dropped into a brocaded easy chair and tried to add up what I'd seen.

First: Ommodurad's apartment, as nearly as I could judge, was directly over my own, two floors up. That was a break—or maybe I was where I was for easier surveillance. I'd skip that angle, I decided. It tended to discourage me and I needed all the enthusiasm I could generate.

Second: I wasn't going to learn anything useful trotting around corridors. Ommodurad wasn't the kind to leave traces of skullduggery lying around where the guests would see them.

And third: I should have known better than to hit this fortress with two squads and a .38 in the first place. Foster was here; Qohey had said so and the Great Owner's reaction to my mention of him confirmed it. What was it about Foster, anyway, that made him so interesting to these Top People? I'd have to ask him that one when I found him. But to do that I'd have to leave the beaten track.

I went to the wide double window and looked up. A cloud swept from the great three-quarters face of Cinte, blue in the southern sky, and I could see an elaborately carved façade ranging up past a row of windows above my own to a railed balcony bathed in a pale light from the apartment within. If my calculations were correct that would be Ommodurad's digs. The front door was guarded like an octogenarian's harem but the back way looked like a breeze.

I pulled my head back in and thought about it. It was risky…but it had that element of the unexpected that just might let me get away with it. Tomorrow the Owner of Owners might have thought it through and switched me to another room…or to a cell in the basement. Then too, wall-scaling didn't occur to these Vallonians as readily as it did to a short-timer from earth. They had too much to lose to risk it on a chancey climb.

Too much thinking is never a good idea when your pulse is telling you it's time for action. I rolled a heavy armoire fairly soundlessly over the deep-pile carpet and lodged it against the door. That might slow down a casual caller. I slipped the magazine out of the automatic, fitted nine greasy brass cartridges into it, slammed it home, dropped the pistol back in the holster. It had a comforting weight. I buttoned the strap over it and went back to the window.

The clouds were back across Cinte's floodlight; that would help. I stepped out. The deep carving gave me easy handholds and I made it to the next windowsill without even working up a light sweat. Compared with my last climb, back in Lima, this was a cinch.

I rested a moment, then clambered around the dark window—just in case there was an insomniac on the other side of the glass—and went on up. I reached the balcony, had a hairy moment as I groped outward for a hold on the smooth floor-tiling above…and then I was pulling up and over the ornamental iron work.

The balcony was narrow, about twenty feet long, giving on half a dozen tall glass doors. Three showed light behind heavy draperies, three were dark. I moved close, tried to see something past the edge of the draperies. No go. I put an ear to the glass, thought maybe I heard a sound, like a distant volcano. That would be Ommodurad's bass rumble. The bear was in his cave.

I went along to the dark doors and on impulse tried a handle. It turned and the door swung in soundlessly. I felt my pulse pick up a double-time beat. I stood peering past the edge of the door into the ink-black interior. It didn't look inviting. In fact it looked repellent. Even a country boy like me could see that to step into the dragon's den without even a Zippo to spot the footstools with would be the act of a nitwit.

I swallowed hard, got a firm grip on my pistol, and went in.

A soft fold of drapery brushed my face and I had the pistol out and my back to the wall with a speed that would have made Earp faint with envy. My adrenals gave a couple of wild jumps and my nervous system followed with a variety of sensations, none pleasant.

It took me a minute to get my Adam's apple swallowed again and remind myself that I was a rough tough son-of-a-gun from the planet earth who had parlayed one short life into more trouble than most Vallonians managed in half of eternity, and I was on my way to get my pal Foster out of a tight spot, hand him back his memory, and set the Two Worlds back on the rails they had fallen off of about six hundred years before Alexander started looking around for his first rumble.

I stopped before I got so confident I charged into the next room and challenged Ommodurad to wrestle, two falls out of three. I could hear his voice better now, muttering beyond the partition. If I could make out what he was saying....

I edged along the wall, found a heavy door, closed and locked. No help there. I felt my way further, found another door. Delicately I tried the handle, eased it open a crack.

A closet, half filled with racked garments. But I could hear more clearly now. Maybe it was a double closet with communicating doors both to the room I was in and to the next one where the Great Owner was still rambling on. Apparently something had overcome his aversion to talking. There were pauses that must have been filled in by the replies of somebody else who didn't have the vocal timbre Ommodurad did.

I felt my way through the hanging clothing, felt over the closet walls. I was out of luck: there was no other door. I put an ear to the wall. I could catch an occasional word:

"... ring...Okk-Hamiloth...vaults...."

It sounded like something I'd like to hear more about. How could I get closer? On impulse I reached up, touched a low ceiling...and felt a ridge like the trim around an access panel to a crawl space.

I crossed my fingers, stood on tip-toe to push at the panel. Nothing moved. I felt around in the dark, encountered a low shelf covered with shoes. I investigated; it was movable. I eased it aside a foot or two, piled the shoes on the floor, and stepped up.

The panel was two feet long on a side, with no discernible hinges or catch. I pushed some more, then gritted my teeth and heaved. There was a startlingly loud *crack!* and the panel lifted. I blinked away the dust that settled in my eyes, reached to feel around within the opening, touched nothing but rough floor boards.

This would be an excellent time, I reflected, to back out of here, get a few hours' sleep, and tomorrow bid Ommodurad a hearty farewell. Then in a few months, after I had had time to organize my new Estate and align a few supporting Owners I could come back in force.

I cocked my head, listening. Ommodurad had stopped talking and another voice said something. Then there was a heavy thump, the clump of feet, and a metallic sound. After a moment the Great Owner's voice came again…and the other voice answered.

I stretched, grabbed the edge of the opening, and pulled myself up. I leaned forward, got a leg up, and rolled silently onto the rough floor. Feeling my way, I crawled, felt a wall rising, followed it, turned a corner…. The voices were louder, quite suddenly. I saw why: there was a ventilating register ahead, gridded light gleaming through it. I crept along to the opening, lay flat, peered through it and saw three men.

Ommodurad was standing with his back to me, a giant figure swathed to the eyes in purple robes. Beside him a lean redhead with a leg that had been broken and badly set stood round-shouldered, teeth bared in an eager grimace, clutching a rod of office. The third man was Foster.

* * * *

Foster stood, legs braced apart as though to withstand an earthquake, hands manacled before him. He looked steadily at the redhead, like a man marking a tree for cutting.

"I know nothing of these crimes," he said.

Ommodurad turned, swept out of sight. The redhead motioned. Foster turned away, moving stiffly, passed from my view. I heard a door open and close. I lay where I was and tried to sort out half a dozen conflicting impulses that clamored for attention. A few were easy: it wouldn't help matters to yell "Stop, thief!" or to fall through the register and chase after Foster with loud cries of joy. It wouldn't be much better to scramble out, dash downstairs, and turn out my bodyguards to raid Ommodurad's apartment.

What might do some good was to gather more information. It had been bad luck that I had arrived at my peephole a few minutes too late to hear what the interview had been all about. But I might still make use of my advantage.

I felt over the register, found fasteners at the corners. They lifted easily and the metal grating tilted back into my hands. I laid it aside, poked my head out. The room was empty, as far as I could see. It was time to take a few chances. I reversed my position, let my legs through the opening, and dropped softly to the floor. I reached back up and managed to prop the grating in position—just in case.

It was a fancy chamber, hung in purple and furnished for a king. I poked through the pigeonholes of a secretary, opened a few cupboards, peered under the bed. It looked like I wasn't going to find any useful clues lying around loose.

I went to the glass doors to the balcony, unlocked one and left it ajar—in case I wanted to leave in a hurry. There was another door across the room. I went over and tried it: locked.

That gave me something definite to look for: a key. I rummaged some more in the secretary, then tried the drawer in a small table beside a broad couch and came up with a nice little steel key that looked like maybe....

I tried it. It was. Luck was still coming my way. I pushed open the door, saw a dark room beyond. I felt for a light switch, flicked it on, pushed the door shut behind me.

The room looked like the popular idea of a necromancer's study. The windowless walls were lined with shelves packed closely with books. The high black-draped ceiling hung like a hovering bat above the ramparted floor of bare, dark-polished wood. Narrow tables choked with books and instruments stood along a side of the chamber and at the far end I saw a deep-cushioned couch with a heavy dome-shaped apparatus like a beauty shop hair-dryer mounted at one end. I recognized it: it was a memory reinforcing machine, the first I had seen on Vallon.

I crossed the room and examined it. The last one I had seen—on the Far-Voyager in the room near the library—had been a stark utility model. This was a deluxe job, with soft upholstery and bright metal fittings and more dials and idiot lights than a late model Detroit status symbol. This solved one of the problems that had been hovering around the edge of my mind. I had fetched Foster's memory back to him, but without a machine to use it in it was just a tantalizing souvenir. Now all I had to do was sneak him away from Ommodurad, make it back here....

All of a sudden I felt tired, vulnerable, helpless, and all alone. I had been taking wild chances, setting my head more and more brazenly into the kind of iron noose the Big Owner would arrange for his enemies...and without the ghost of a plan, without even an idea of what was going on. What was Ommodurad's interest in Foster? Why did he hide away here, keeping the rest of Vallon away with rumors of magic and spells? What connection did he have with the disaster that had befallen the Two Worlds—now reduced to One, and a poor one at that.

And why was I, a plain Joe named Legion, mixed up in it right to the eyebrows, when I could be sitting safe at home in a clean federal pen?

The answer to that last one wasn't too hard to recite: I had had a pal once, a smooth character named Foster, who had pulled me back from the ragged edge just when I was about to make a bigger mistake than usual. He had been a gentleman in the best sense of the word, and he had treated me like one. Together we had shared a strange adventure that had made me rich and had showed me that it was never too late to straighten your back and take on whatever the Fates handed out.

I had come running his way when trouble got too thick back home. And I'd found him in a worse spot that I was in. He had come back, after the most agonizing exile a man had ever suffered, to find his world fallen back into savagery, and his memory still eluding him. Now he was in chains, without friends and without hope…but still not broken, still standing on his own two feet.…

But he was wrong on one point: he had one little hope. Not much: just a hard-luck guy with a penchant for bad decisions, but I was here and I was free. I had my pistol on my hip and a neat back way into the Owner's bedroom, and if I played it right and watched my timing and had maybe just a little luck, say about the amount it took to hit the Irish Sweepstakes, I might bring it off yet.

Right now it was time to return to my crawl-space. Ommodurad might come back and talk some more, tip me off to a vulnerable spot in the armor of his fortress. I went to the door, flicked off the light, turned the handle… and went rigid.

Ommodurad was back. He pulled off the purple cloak, tossed it aside, strode to a wall bar. I clung to the crack of the door, not daring to move even to close it.

"But my lord," the voice of the redhead said, "I know he remembers—"

"Not so," Ommodurad's voice rumbled. "On the morrow I strip his mind to the bare clean jelly.…"

"Let me, dread lord. With my steel I'll have the truth from him."

"Such a one as he your steel has never known!" the bass voice snarled.

"Great Owner, I crave but one hour…tomorrow, in the Ceremonial Chamber. I shall environ him with the emblems of the past—"

"Enough!" Ommodurad's fist slammed against the bar, made glasses jump. "On such starveling lackwits as you a mighty empire hangs. It is a crime before the Gods and on his head I lay it." The Owner tossed off a glass, jerked his head at the cowering man. "Still, I grant thy boon. Now begone, babbler of folly."

The redhead ducked, grinning, disappeared. Ommodurad muttered to himself, strode up and down the room, stood staring out into the night. He noticed the open balcony door, pulled it shut with a curse. I held my breath but no general check of doors followed.

The big man threw off his clothes then. He clambered up on the wide couch, touched a switch somewhere, and the room was dark. Within five minutes I heard the heavy breathing of deep sleep.

I had found out one thing anyway: tomorrow was Foster's last day. One way or another Ommodurad and the redhead between them would destroy him. That didn't leave much time. But since the project was already hopeless it didn't make much difference.

I had a choice of moves now: I could tip-toe across to the register and try to wiggle through it without waking up the brontosaurus on the bed... or I could try for the balcony door a foot from where he slept...or I could stay put and wait him out. The last idea had the virtue of requiring no immediate daring adventures. I could just curl up on the floor, or, better still, on the padded couch....

A weird idea was taking shape in my mind like a genie rising from a bottle. I felt in my pocket, pulled out the two small cylinders that represented two men's memories of hundreds of years of living. One belonged to Foster, the one with the black and golden bands; but the other was the property of a stranger who had died three thousand years ago, out in space....

This cylinder, barely three inches long, held all the memories of a man who had been Foster's confidant when he was Qulqlan, a man who knew what had happened aboard the ship, what the purpose of the expedition had been, and what conditions they had left behind on Vallon.

I needed that knowledge. I needed any knowledge I could get, to add a feather-weight to my side of the balance when the showdown came. The cylinder would tell me plenty, including, possibly, the reason for Ommodurad's interest in Foster.

It was simple to use. I merely placed the cylinder in the receptacle in the side of the machine, took my place, lowered the helmet into position... and in an hour or so I would awaken with another man's memories stored in my brain, to use as I saw fit.

It would be a crime to waste the opportunity. The machine I had found here was probably the only one still in existence on Vallon. I had blundered my way into the one room in the palace that could help me in what I had to do; I had been lucky; I couldn't waste that luck.

I went across to the soft-cushioned chair, spotted the recess in its side, and thrust the plain cylinder into it; it seated with a click.

I sat on the couch, lay back, reached up to pull the headpiece down into position against my skull....

There was an instant of pain—like a pre-frontal lobotomy performed without anesthetic.

Then blackness.

CHAPTER XVIII

I stood beside the royal couch where Qulqlan the Rthr lay and I saw that this was the hour for which I had waited long, for the Change was on him....

The time-scale stood at the third hour of the Death watch; all aboard slept save myself alone. I must move swiftly and at the Dawn watch show them the deed well done.

I shook the sleeping man; him who had once been the Rthr—king no more, by the law of the Change. He wakened slowly, looked about him, with the clear eyes of the newborn.

"Rise," I commanded. And the king obeyed.

"Follow me," I said. He made to question me, after the manner of those newly awakened from their Change. I bade him be silent. Like a lamb he came and I led him through shadowed ways to the cage of the Hunters. They rose, keen in their hunger, to my coming, as I had trained them.

I took the arm of Qulqlan and thrust it into the cage. The Hunters clustered, taking the mark of their prey. He watched, innocent eyes wide.

"That which you feel is pain, mindless one," I spoke. "It is a thing of which you will learn much in the time before you." Then they had done, and I set the time catch.

In my chambers I cloaked the innocent in a plain purple robe and afterward led him to the cradle where the lifeboat lay....

And by virtue of the curse of the Gods which is upon me one was there before me. I waited not, but moved as the haik strikes and took him fair in the back with my dagger. I dragged the body into hiding behind the flared foot of a column. But no sooner was he hidden well away than others came from the shadows, summoned by some device I know not of. They asked of the Rthr wherefore he walked by night, robed in the colors of Ammaerln of Bros-Ilyond. And I knew black despair, that my grand design foundered thus in the shallows of their zeal.

Yet I spoke forth, with a great show of anger, that I, Ammaerln, vizier and companion to the Rthr, did but walk and speak in confidence with my liege lord.

But they persisted, Gholad foremost among them. And then one saw the hidden corse and in an instant they ringed me in:

Then did I draw the long blade and hold it at the throat of Qulqlan. "Press me not; or your king will surely die," I said. And they feared me and shrank back.

"Do you dream that I, Ammaerln, wisest of the wise, have come here for the love of Far-Voyaging?" I raged. "Long have I plotted against this hour, to lure the king a-voyaging in this his princely yacht, his faithful vizier at his side, that the Change might come to him far from his court. Then would the ancient wrong be redressed.

"There are those men born to rule, as the dream-tree seeks the sun—and such a one am I! Long has this one, now mindless, denied to me my destiny. But behold: I, with a stroke, shall set things aright.

"Below us lies a green world, peopled by savages. Not one am I to take blood vengeance on a man newborn from the Change. Instead I shall set him free to take up his life there below. May the Fates lead him again to royal state if that be their will—"

But there were naught but fools among them and they drew steel. I cried out to them that all, all should share!

But they heeded me not but rushed upon me. Then did I turn to Qulqlan and drive the long blade at his throat, but Gholad threw himself before him and fell in his place. Then they pressed me and I did strike out against three who hemmed me close, and though they took many wounds they persisted in their madness, one leaping in to strike and another at my back, so that I whirled and slashed at shadows who danced away.

In the end I hunted them down in those corners whither they had dragged themselves and each did I put to the sword. And I turned at last to find the Rthr gone and some few with them, and madness took me that I had been gulled like a tinker by common men.

In the chamber of the memory couch would I find them. There they would seek to give back to the mindless one that memory of past glories which I had schemed so long to deny him. Almost I wept to see such cunning wasted. Terrible in my wrath I came upon them there. There were but two and, though they stood shoulder to shoulder in the entry way, their poor dirks were no match for my long blade. I struck them dead and went to the couch, to lay my hand on the cylinder marked with the vile gold and black of Qulqlan, that I might destroy it and with it the Rthr, forever—

And I heard a sound and whirled about. A hideous figure staggered to me from the gloom and for an instant I saw the flash of steel in the bloody hand of the accursed Gholad whom I had left for dead. Then I knew cold agony between my ribs....

* * * *

Gholad lay slumped against the wall, his face greenish above the blood-soaked tunic. When he spoke air whistled through his slashed throat.

"Have done, traitor who once was honored of the king," he whispered. "Have you no pity for him who once ruled in justice and splendor at High Okk-Hamiloth?"

"Had you not robbed me of my destiny, murderous dog," I croaked, "that splendor would have been mine."

"You came upon him helpless," gasped Gholad. "Make some amends now for your shame. Let the Rthr have his mind, which is more precious than his life."

"I but rest to gather strength. Soon will I rise and turn him from the couch. Then will I die content."

"Once you were his friend," Gholad whispered. "By his side you fought, when both of you were young. Remember that...and have pity. To leave him here, in this ship of death, mindless and alone...."

"I have loosed the Hunters!" I shrieked in triumph. "With them will the Rthr share this tomb until the end of time!"

Then I searched within me and found a last terrible strength and I rose up...and even as my hand reached out to pluck away the mind trace of the king I felt the bloody fingers of Gholad on my ankle, and then my strength was gone. And I was falling headlong into that dark well of death from which there is no returning....

* * * *

I woke up and lay for a long time in the dark without moving, trying to remember the fragments of a strange dream of violence and death. I could still taste the lingering dregs of some bitter emotion. But I had more important things to think about than dreams. For just a moment I couldn't remember what it was I had to do; then with a start I remembered where I was. I had lain down on the couch and pulled the headpiece into place—

It hadn't worked.

I thought hard, tried to tap a new reservoir of memories, drew a blank. Maybe my earth-mind was too alien for the Vallonian memory-trace to affect. It was another good idea that hadn't worked out. But at least I had had a good rest. Now it was time to get moving. First—to see if Ommodurad was still asleep. I started to sit up—

Nothing happened.

I had a moment of vertigo, as my inner ear tried to accommodate to having stayed in the same place after automatically adjusting to my intention of rising. I lay perfectly still and tried to think it through.

I had tried to move...and hadn't so much as twitched a muscle. I was paralyzed...or tied up...or maybe, if I was lucky, imagining things. I could try it again and next time—

I was afraid to try. Suppose I tried and nothing happened—again? It was better to lie here and tell myself it was all a mistake. Maybe I should go back to sleep and wake up later and try it again....

This was ridiculous. All I had to do was sit up. I—

Nothing. I lay in the dark and tried to will an arm to move, my head to turn. It was as though I had no arm, no head—just a mind—alone in the dark. I strained to sense the ropes that held me down: still nothing. No ropes, no arms, no body. There was no pressure against me from the couch, no vagrant itch or cramp, no physical sensation. I was a disembodied brain, lying nestled in a great bed of pitchblack cotton wool.

Then, abruptly, I was aware of myself—not the gross mechanism of bone and muscle, but the neuro-electric field generated within a brain alive with flashing currents and a lightning interplay of molecular forces. A sense of orientation grew. I occupied a block of cells…here in the left hemisphere. The mass of neural tissue loomed over me, gigantic. And "I"… "I" was reduced to the elemental ego, who possessed as a material appurtenance "my" arms and legs, "my" body, "my" brain…. Relieved of outside stimuli, I was able now to conceptualize myself as I actually was: an insubstantial state existing in an immaterial continuum, created by the action of neural currents within the cerebrum, as a magnetic field is created in space by the flow of electricity.

And I knew what had happened. I had opened my mind to invasion by alien memories. The other mind had seized upon the sensory centers and driven me to this dark corner. I was a fugitive within my own skull.

For a timeless time I lay stunned, immured now as the massive stones of Bar-Ponderone had never confined me. My basic self-awareness still survived, out was shunted aside, cut off from any contact with the body itself.

With shadowy fingers of imagination I clawed at the walls surrounding me, fought for a glimpse of light, for a way out.

And found none.

* * * *

Then, at last, I began again to think.

I must analyze my awareness of my surroundings, seek out channels through which impulses from sensory nerves flowed, and tap them.

I tried cautiously; an extension of my self-concept reached out with ultimate delicacy. There were the ranked infinities of cells, there the rushing torrents of gross fluid, there the taut cables of the interconnecting web, and there—

Barrier! Blank and impregnable, the wall reared up. My questing tendril of self-stuff raced over the surface like an ant over a melon, and found no tiniest fissure. It loomed alien, inscrutable: the invader who had stolen my brain.

I withdrew. To dissipate my force was senseless. I must select a point of attack, hurl against it all the power of my surviving identity…before it too dwindled away and the abstraction that was Legion vanished forevermore.

The last of the phantom emotions that had clung—for how long?—to the incorporeal mind field had faded now, leaving me with no more than an intellectual determination to reassert myself. Dimly I recognized this sign of my waning sense of identity but there was no surge of instinctive fear. Instead I coolly assessed my resources—and almost at once stumbled into an unused channel, here within my own self-field. For a moment I recoiled from the outré configuration of the stored patterns…and then I remembered.

I had been in the water, struggling, while the Red soldier waited, rifle aimed. And then: a flood of data, flowing with cold, impersonal precision. And I had deftly marshalled the forces of my body to survive.

And once more: as I hung by numbed fingers under the cornice of the Yordano Building, the cold voice had spoken.

And I had forgotten. The miracle had been pushed back, rejected by the conscious mind. But now I knew: this was the knowledge that I had received from the background briefing device that I had used in my island strong-room before I fled. This was the survival data known to all Old Vallonians of the days of the Two Worlds. It had lain here, unused, the secrets of superhuman strength and endurance…buried by the imbecile of censorself's aversion to the alien.

But the ego alone remained now, stripped of the burden of neurosis, freed from subconscious pressures. The levels of the mind were laid bare, and I saw close at hand the regions where dreams were born, the barren sources of instinctive fear-patterns, the linkages to blinding emotions; and all lay now under my overt control.

Without further hesitation I tapped the stored Vallonian knowledge, encompassed it, made it mine. Then again I approached the barrier, spread out across it, probed in vain—

"… *vile primitive….*"

The thought thundered out with crushing force. I recoiled, then renewed my attack, alert now. I knew what to do.

I sought and found a line of synaptic weakness, burrowed at it—

"… *intolerable…vestigial…erasure….*"

I struck instantly, slipped past the shield, laid firm hold on an optic receptor bank. The alien mind threw itself against me, but too late. I held secure and the assault faded, withdrew. Cautiously I extended my interpretive receptivity. There was a pattern of pulses, oscillations in the lambda/mu range. I tuned, focussed—

Abruptly I was seeing. For a moment my fragile equilibrium tottered, as I strove to integrate the flow of external stimuli into my bodiless self-concept. Then a balance was struck: I held my ground and stared through the one eye I had recaptured from the usurper.

And I reeled again!

Bright daylight blazed in the chamber of Ommodurad. The scene shifted as the body moved about, crossing the room, turning…. I had assumed that the body still lay in the dark but instead, it walked, without my knowledge, propelled by a stranger.

The field of vision flashed across the couch. Ommodurad was gone.

I sensed that the entire left lobe, disoriented by the loss of the eye, had slipped now to secondary awareness, its defenses weakened. I retreated momentarily from my optic outpost, laid a temporary traumatic block across the access nerves to keep the intruder from reasserting possession, and concentrated my force in an attack on the auricular channels. It was an easy rout. Instantly my eye coordinated its impressions with those coming in along the aural nerves…and heard my voice mouth a curse.

The body was standing beside a bare wall with a hand laid upon it. In the wall a recess partly obscured by a sliding panel stood empty.

The body turned, strode to a doorway, emerged into a gloomy violet-shadowed corridor. The glance flicked from the face of one guard to another. They stared in open-mouthed surprise, brought weapons up.

"You dare to bar the path to the Lord Ammaerln?" My voice slashed at the men. "Stand aside, as you value your lives."

And the body pushed past them, striding off along the corridor. It passed through a great archway, descended a flight of marble stairs, came along a hall I had seen on my tour of the Palace of Sapphires and into the Onyx Chamber with the great golden sunburst that covered the high black wall.

In the Great Owner's chair at the ring-board Ommodurad sat scowling at the lame courtier whose red hair was hidden now under a black cowl. Between them Foster stood, the heavy manacles dragging at his wrists. Ommodurad turned; his face paled, then flushed darkly. He rose, teeth bared.

The gaze of my eye fixed on Foster. Foster stared back, a look of incredulity growing on his face.

"My Lord Rthr," I heard my voice say. The eye swept down and fixed on the manacles. The body drew back a step, as if in horror.

"You overreach yourself, Ommodurad!" my voice cried harshly.

Ommodurad stepped toward me, his immense arm raised.

"Lay not a hand on me, dog of a usurper!" my voice roared out. "By the Gods, would you take me for common clay?"

And, unbelievably, Ommodurad paused, stared in my face.

"I know you as the upstart Drgon, petty Owner," he rumbled. "But I know I see another there behind your pale eyes."

"Foul was the crime that brought me to this pass," my voice said. "But…know that your master, Ammaerln, stands before you, in the body of a primitive!"

"Ammaerln…!" Ommodurad jerked as though he had been struck.

My body turned, dismissing him. The eye rested on Foster.

"My liege," my voice said unctuously. "I swear the dog dies for this treason——"

"It is a mindless one, intruder," Ommodurad broke in. "Seek no favor with the Rthr for he that was Rthr is no more. You deal with me now."

My body whirled on Ommodurad. "Give a thought to your tone, lest your ambitions prove your death!"

Ommodurad put a hand to his dagger. "Ammaerln of Bros-Ilyond you may be, or a changeling from dark regions I know not of. But know that this day I hold all power in Vallon."

"And what of this one who was once Qulqlan? What consort do you hold with him you say is mindless?" I saw my hand sweep out in a contemptuous gesture at Foster.

"An end to patience!" the Great Owner roared. "Shall I stand in my inner citadel and give account of myself to a madman?" He started toward my body.

"Does the fool, Ommodurad, forget the power of the great Ammaerln?" my voice said softly. And the towering figure hesitated once more, searching my face. "The Rthr's hour is past...and yours, bungler and fool," my voice went on. "Your months—or is it years?—of self-delusion are ended." My voice rose in a bellow: "Know that I...Ammaerln, the great... have returned to rule at High Okk-Hamiloth."

"Months?" rumbled Ommodurad. "Indeed, I believe the tales of the Greymen are true and that an evil spirit has returned to haunt me. You speak of months?" He threw back his head, laughed a choked throaty laugh that was half sob.

"Know, demon, or madman, or ancient prince of evil: for thirty centuries have I brooded alone, sealed from an empire by a single key!"

I felt the shock rack through and through the invader mind. This was the opportunity I had hoped for. Quick as thought I moved, slashed at the wavering shield, and was past it——

I grappled onto the foul mind-matrix, scanned its symbolisms: a miasma of twisted concepts like great webs, asquirm with bristling nodes like crouching spiders—and through it all a yammering torrent of deformed thought-shapes.

In my eagerness I was careless. The invader mind, recovering, struck back. Too late I felt it slip into my awareness, flick over the stored information. I leaped to protect one fact...and lost my gains. With only a single tenuous line of rapport with the alien mind still open, I clung, shaken—but hugging precious patterns of stolen data. My raid had been no more than an irritation to the other mind...but I had fetched away a mass of information. I interpreted it, integrated it, matched it to known patterns. A complex structure of relationships evolved, growing into a new awareness.

Upon the mind-picture of Foster's face was now super-imposed another: that of Qulqlan, Rthr of all Vallon, ruler of the Two Worlds!

And other pictures, snatched from the intruder mind, were present now in the earth-consciousness of me, Legion.

The Vaults, deep in the rock under the fabled city of Okk-Hamiloth, where the mind-trace of every citizen was stored, sealed by the Rthr and keyed to his mind alone.

Ammaerln, urging the king to embark on a Far-Voyage, stressing the burden of government, tempting him to bring with him the royal mind-trace; Qulqlan's acquiescence and Ammaerln's secret joy at the advancement of his scheme; the coming of the Change for the Rthr, aboard ship, far out in space—and the vizier's bold stroke; and then the fools who found him at the lifeboat…and the loss of all, all….

There my own memories took up the tale: the awakening of Foster, unsuspecting, and his recording of the mind of the dying Ammaerln; the flight from the Hunters; the memory-trace of the king that lay for three millenia among neolithic bones until I, a primitive, plucked it from its place; and the pocket of a coarse fibre garment where the cylinder lay now—on the hip of the body I inhabited but as inaccessible to me as if it had been a million miles away.

But there was a second memory-trace—Ammaerln's. I had crossed a galaxy to come to Foster, and with me, locked in an unmarked pewter cylinder, I had brought Foster's ancient nemesis.

I had given it life, and a body.

Foster, once Rthr, had survived against all logic and had come back, back from the dead: the last hope of a golden age….

To meet his fate at my hands.

* * * *

"Three thousand years," I heard my voice saying. "Three thousand years have the men of Vallon lived mindless, with the glory that was Vallon locked away in a vault without a key."

"I, alone," said Ommodurad, "have borne the curse of knowledge. Long ago, in the days of the Rthr, I took my mind-trace from the vaults in anticipation of the day of days when he should fall. Little joy has it brought me."

"And now," my voice said, "you think to force this mind—that is no mind—to unseal the vault?"

"I know it for a hopeless task," Ommodurad said. "At first I thought—since he speaks the tongue of old Vallon—that he dissembled. But he knows nothing. This is but the dry husk of the Rthr…and I sicken of the sight. I would fain kill him now and let the long farce end."

"Not so!" my voice cut in. "Once I decreed exile to the mindless one. So be it!"

The face of Ommodurad twisted in its rage. "Your witless chatterings too! I tire of them."

"Wait!" my voice snarled. "Would you put aside the key?"

There was a silence as Ommodurad stared at my face. I saw my hand rise into view. Gripped in it was Foster's memory-trace.

"The Two Worlds lie in my hand," my voice spoke. "Observe well the black and golden bands of the royal memory-trace. Who holds this key is all-powerful. As for the mindless body yonder, let it be destroyed."

Ommodurad locked eyes with mine. Then, "Let the deed be done," he said.

The redhead drew a long stiletto from under his cloak, smiling. I could wait no longer....

Along the link I had kept through the intruder's barrier I poured the last of the stored energy of my mind. I felt the enemy recoil, then strike back with crushing force. But I was past the shield.

As the invader reached out to encircle me I shattered my unified forward impulse into myriad nervous streamlets that flowed on, under, over and around the opposing force; I spread myself through and through the inner all-mass, drawing new power from the trunk sources.

I caught a vicious blast of pure wrath that rocked me and then I grappled, shield to shield, with the alien. And he was stronger.

Like a corrosive fluid the massive personality-gestalt shredded my extended self-field. I drew back, slowly, reluctantly. I caught a shadowy impression of the body, standing rigid, eyes blank, and sensed a rumbling voice that spoke: "Quick! The intruder!"

Now! I struck for the right optic center, clamped down with a death grip.

The enemy mind went mad as the darkness closed in. I heard my voice scream and I saw in vivid pantomime the vision that threatened the invader: the redhead darting to me, the stiletto flashing——

And then the invading mind broke, swirled into chaos, and was gone....

I reeled, shocked and alone inside my skull. The brain loomed, dark and untenanted now. I began to move, crept along the major nerve paths, reoccupied the cortex——

Agony! I twisted, felt again with a massive return of sensation my arms, my legs, opened both eyes to see blurred figures moving. And in my chest a hideous pain....

I was sprawled on the floor, gasping. Sudden understanding came: the redhead had struck...and the other mind, in full rapport with the pain centers, had broken under the shock, left the stricken brain to me alone.

As through a red veil I saw the giant figure of Ommodurad loom, stoop over me, rise with the royal cylinder in his hand. And beyond, Foster, strained backward, the chain between his wrists garroting the redhead. Ommodurad turned, took a step, flicked the man from Foster's grasp and hurled him aside. He drew his dagger. Quick as a hunting cat Foster leaped, struck with the manacles...and the knife clattered across the floor. Ommodurad backed away with a curse, while the redhead seized the stiletto he had let fall and moved in. Foster turned to meet him, staggering, and raised heavy arms.

I fought to move, got my hand as far as my side, fumbled with the leather strap. The alien mind had stolen from my brain the knowledge of the cylinder but I had kept from it the fact of the pistol. I had my hand on its butt now. Painfully I drew it, dragged my arm up, struggled to raise the weapon, centered it on the back of the mop of red hair, free now of the cowl...and fired.

Ommodurad had found his dagger. He turned back from the corner where Foster had sent it spinning. Spattered with the blood of the redhead, Foster retreated until his back was at the wall: a haggard figure against the gaudy golden sunburst. The flames of beaten metal shimmered and flared before my dimming vision. The great gold circles of the Two Worlds seemed to revolve, while waves of darkness rolled over me.

But there was a thought: something I had found among the patterns in the intruder's mind. At the center of the sunburst rose a boss, in black and gold, erupting a foot from the wall, like a sword-hilt....

The thought came from far away. The sword of the Rthr, used once, in the dawn of a world, by a warrior king—but laid away now, locked in its sheath of stone, keyed to the mind-pattern of the Rthr, that none other might ever draw it to some ignoble end.

A sword, keyed to the basic mind-pattern of the king....

I drew a last breath, blinked back the darkness. Ommodurad stepped past me, knife in hand, toward the unarmed man.

"Foster," I croaked. "The sword...."

Foster's head came up. I had spoken in English; the syllables rang strangely in that outworld setting. Ommodurad ignored the unknown words.

"Draw...the sword...from the stone!... You're...Qulqlan...Rthr...of Vallon."

I saw him reach out, grasp the ornate hilt. Ommodurad, with a cry, leaped toward him—

The sword slid out smoothly, four feet of glittering steel. Ommodurad stopped, stared at the manacled hands gripping the hilt of the fabled blade. Slowly he sank to his knees, bent his neck.

"I yield, Qulqlan," he said. "I crave the mercy of the Rthr."

Behind me I heard thundering feet. Dimly I was aware of Torbu raising my head, of Foster leaning over me. They were saying something but I couldn't hear. My feet were cold, and the coldness crept higher.

I felt hands touch me and the cool smoothness of metal against my temples. I wanted to say something, tell Foster that I had found the answer, the one that had always eluded me before. I wanted to tell him that all lives are the same length when viewed from the foreshortened perspective of death, and that life, like music, requires no meaning but only a certain symmetry.

But it was too hard. I tried to cling to the thought, to carry it with me into the cold void toward which I moved, but it slipped away and there was only my self-awareness, alone in emptiness, and the winds that swept through eternity blew away the last shred of ego and I was one with darkness....

EPILOGUE

I awoke to a light like that of a morning when the world was young. Gossamer curtains fluttered at tall windows, through which I saw a squadron of trim white clouds riding in a high blue sky.

I turned my head, and Foster stood beside me, dressed in a short white tunic.

"That's a crazy set of threads, Foster," I said, "but on your build it looks good. But you've aged; you look twenty-five if you look a day."

Foster smiled. "Welcome to Vallon, my friend," he said in English. I noticed that he faltered a bit over the words, as if he hadn't used them for a long time.

"Vallon," I said. "Then it wasn't all a dream?"

"Regard it as a dream, Legion. Your life begins today."

"There was something," I said, "something I had to do. But it doesn't seem to matter. I feel relaxed inside...."

Someone came forward from behind Foster.

"Gope," I said. Then I hesitated. "You are Gope, aren't you?" I said in Vallonian.

He laughed. "I was known by that name once," he said, "but my true name is Gwanne."

My eyes fell on my legs. I saw that I was wearing a tunic like Foster's except that mine was pale blue.

"Who put the dress on me?" I asked. "And where's my pants?"

"This garment suits you better," said Gope. "Come. Look in the glass."

I got to my feet, stepped to a long mirror, glanced at the reflection. "It's not the real me, boys," I started——Then I stared, open-mouthed. A Hercules, black-haired and clean-limbed, stared back. I shut my mouth...and his mouth shut. I moved an arm and he did likewise. I whirled on Foster.

"What...how...who...?"

"The mortal body that was Legion died of its wounds," he said, "but the mind that was the man was recorded. We have waited many years to give that mind life again."

I turned back to the mirror, gaped. The young giant gaped back. "I remember," I said. "I remember...a knife in my guts...and a redheaded man...and the Great Owner, and...."

"For his crimes," told Gope, "he went to a place of exile until the Change should come on him. Long have we waited."

I looked again and now I saw two faces in the mirror and both of them were young. One was low down, just above my ankles, and it belonged to a cat I had known as Itzenca. The other, higher up, was that of a man I had known as Ommodurad. But this was a clear-eyed Ommodurad, just under twenty-one.

"Onto the blank slate we traced your mind," said Gope.

"He owed you a life, Legion," Foster said. "His own was forfeit."

"I guess I ought to kick and scream and demand my original ugly puss back," I said slowly, studying my reflection, "but the fact is, I like looking like Mr. Universe."

"Your earthly body was infected with the germs of old age," said Foster. "Now you can look forward to a great span of life."

"But come," said Gope. "All Vallon waits to honor you." He led the way to the tall window.

"Your place is by my side at the great ring-board," said Foster. "And afterwards: all of the Two Worlds lie before you."

I looked past the open window and saw a carpet of velvet green that curved over foothills to the rim of a forest. Down the long sward I saw a procession of bright knights and ladies come riding on animals, some black, some golden palomino, that looked for all the world like unicorns.

My eyes traveled upward to where the light of a great white sun flashed on blue towers. And somewhere trumpets sounded.

"It looks like a pretty fair offer," I said. "I'll take it."

www.ingramcontent.com/pod-product-compliance
Lightning Source LLC
Chambersburg PA
CBHW032252020726
47495CB00001B/78